I0611112

BORDERLAND PROVINCES

Authors: Matthew J. Finch, Greg A. Vaughan, and Bill Webb
Developer: Matthew J. Finch
Producer: Bill Webb
Editor: Jeff Harkness
5E Rules Conversion: James Redmon

Layout and Graphic Design: Charles A. Wright
Front Cover Art: Artem Shukaev
Interior Art: Patricia Smith, Jason Sholtis, Felipe Gaona, David Day, Peter Bergting, Richard Thomas
Cartography: Robert Altbauer, Ed Bourelle

Necromancer Games is not affiliated with Wizards of the Coast™.
We make no claim to or challenge to any trademarks held by Wizards of the Coast™.

NECROMANCER GAMES

5th Edition Rules, 1st Edition Feel

Table of Contents

Other Products from Frog God Games

You can find these product lines and more at our website, **froggodgames.com**, and on the shelves of many retail game stores. Superscripts indicate the available game systems: "PF" means the Pathfinder Roleplaying Game, "5e" means Fifth Edition, and "S&W" means *Swords & Wizardry*. If there is no superscript it means that it is not specific to a single rule system.

GENERAL RESOURCES

Swords & Wizardry Complete [S&W]
The Tome of Horrors Complete [PF, S&W]
Tome of Horrors 4 [PF, S&W]
Tome of Adventure Design
Monstrosities [S&W]
Bill Webb's Book of Dirty Tricks
Razor Coast: Fire as She Bears [PF]
Book of Lost Spells [5e]
Fifth Edition Foes [5e]
Book of Alchemy* [5e, PF, S&W]

THE LOST LANDS

Rappan Athuk [PF, S&W]
Rappan Athuk Expansions Vol. I [PF, S&W]
The Slumbering Tsar Saga [PF, S&W]
The Black Monastery [PF, S&W]
Cyclopean Deeps Vol. I [PF, S&W]
Cyclopean Deeps Vol. II [PF, S&W]
Razor Coast [PF, S&W]
Razor Coast: Heart of the Razor [PF, S&W]
Razor Coast: Freebooter's Guide to the Razor Coast [PF, S&W]
LL0: The Lost Lands Campaign Setting*
LL1: Stoneheart Valley [PF, S&W]
LL2: The Lost City of Barakus [PF, S&W]

LL3: Sword of Air [PF, S&W]
LL4: Cults of the Sundered Kingdoms [PF, S&W]
LL5: Borderland Provinces [5e, PF, S&W]
LL6: The Northlands Saga Complete [PF, S&W]
LL7: The Blight* [PF, S&W]
LL8: Bard's Gate Complete* [PF, S&W]
LL9: Adventures in the Borderland Provinces [5e, PF, S&W]

QUESTS OF DOOM

Quests of Doom (Vol. 1) [5e]
Quests of Doom (Vol. 2) [5e]
Quests of Doom (includes the 5e Vol. 1 and 2, but for PF and S&W only) [PF, S&W]
Quests of Doom 2 [5e]
Quests of Doom 3* [5e, S&W]
Quests of Doom 4* [5e, PF, S&W]

PERILOUS VISTAS

Dead Man's Chest (pdf only) [PF]
Dunes of Desolation [PF]
Fields of Blood [PF]
Mountains of Madness* [PF]

* (forthcoming from **Frog God Games**)

Preface

The Lost Lands is our massive project to publish the world setting behind all the **Necromancer Games** and **Frog God Games** adventures published from the year 2000 to the present day. It is a massive project spearheaded by Greg Vaughan, who has compiled all the information from all these modules, and connected the dots into a vast world map with extensive notes about how it all fits together. Greg is preparing the world book itself, for a planned release sometime in 2017.

There are a number of different ways to portray a world setting and bring it to life as a framework for adventures. Some of them work better for different types of gaming, and ultimately that's what everything comes down to: your group's actual gaming sessions. A world setting isn't something that exists for its own sake. Its purpose is to be a backdrop for fun games and adventures. Therefore, we decided in 2014 or so that the way we wanted to present the world shouldn't be in any sort of standard format, book after book. Rather, each of the Lost Lands books — at least for the next couple of years — will be structured to match various different types of campaigns and gaming. Form should follow function, as they say.

Greg, Bill and I discussed a few different ways in which the form of a book can reflect the needs of particular types of gaming. There is the mini-campaign (such as **The Lost City of Barakus** and **Stoneheart Valley**); there is the massive single-adventure (such as **Rappan Athuk** and **Sword of Air**); there is the adventure series/path (such as **Cults of the Sundered Kingdoms** and **The Northlands Saga Complete**). This book represents yet another of these approaches, which is a far-ranging sandbox designed for traveling between one specific objective to another, with scattered small adventures to serve as those objectives. This kind of campaign might be called "picaresque," or it might be analogized to the game *Traveller*, or the TV shows *Firefly* and *Star Trek*, and — to return to the fantasy analogy — to the wanderings of Elric, Conan, and Fafhrd and the Gray Mouser. It's for the sort of characters who say, "We're all done here. Let's go make trouble somewhere else. Who has the map?"

So I think of this book as a "dragonflight-level" of detail. It focuses on countries and towns, widely separated adventure hooks, patrons that might hire adventurers, political intrigue, influential villains, and large-scale dangers rather than detailed, room-by-room adventure locations. The format is tailored for Game Masters who run far-flung campaigns that might go anywhere, providing the right sort of information for pivoting and adapting to what the characters do as they travel. The book includes an introductory adventure called *Rogues in Remballo*, several one-session lairs and, as an additional resource, we're also writing a separate book of individual, scattered adventures set in the region.

I'm deeply indebted to Greg Vaughan, who shouldered the enormous task of integrating hundreds of adventures into a coherent, living campaign world and provided me with richly detailed notes for the outline of the Borderland Provinces.

I hope you enjoy it, and may your dice never fail you!

— Matt Finch
May 5, 2015

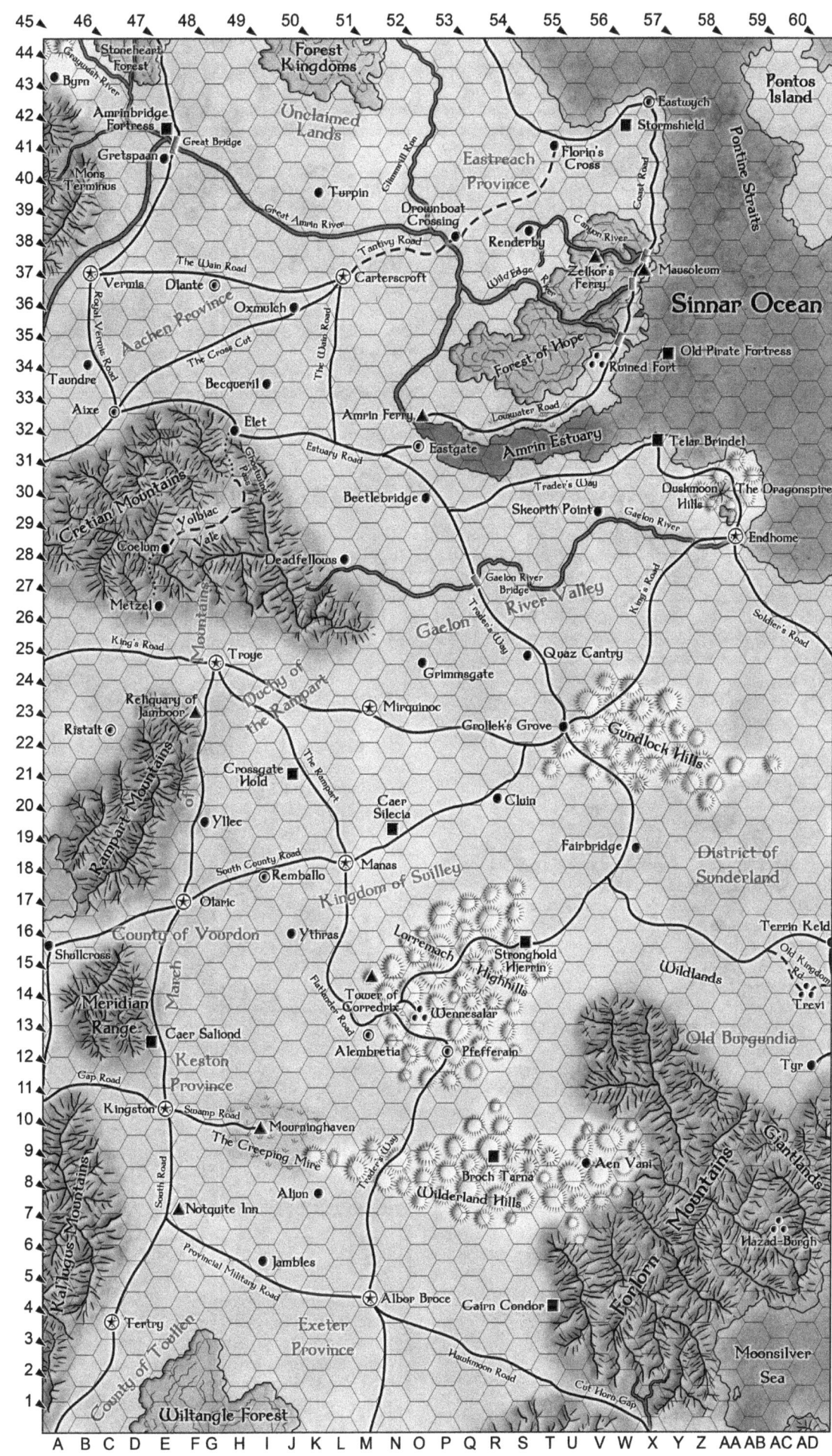

Introduction

The Lost Lands: Borderland Provinces describes the lands that make up roughly the western and northernmost portions of the Sinnar Coast region, including the areas where adventurers may find the great dungeons of Rappan Athuk. If you have always wanted to weave a Rappan Athuk campaign into the larger world around it, this is the book you've been requesting for a decade or more.

These are lands where the great tide of an empire is drawing back, leaving its old provinces to fend for themselves but still trying to hold its ancient grip upon them. Unlike the Sundered Kingdoms to the east, the Borderland Provinces are not plunged into chaos — at least, not yet.

It is an eternal truth that gaps left by the slow retreat of a decaying and decadent civilization are inevitably filled; either by young and vigorous new civilizations rising to offer new hopes and aspirations, or by a self-devouring maelstrom of war, pillage, plague, and barbarism. Such times are the knife-edges of history, where the deeds of heroes may shift the course of entire kingdoms. They are times of struggle and fear, times of desperation and wild hopes, times when legends are made.

And these times have arrived.

From the deep-infested halls of Rappan Athuk in the north, to the green depths of the Wiltangle Forest in the south, the imperial aspirations of the Kingdoms of Foere are crumbling, and their forces are in retreat. Unlike the Sundered Kingdoms farther to the east, where disaster and chaos reign unchecked, the lands bordering the March of Mountains have managed to cling tenaciously to social order. A new power is rising here, in the western Plains of Suilley, to supplant and replace the decaying power of the Foerdewaith, namely the Kingdom of Suilley. Three hundred or so years ago, the Foerdewaith Lord-Governor of Suilley declared himself an independent king, and his nobles, mostly Foerdewaith themselves, succeeded in pushing back the armies of their own former empire, essentially stealing an entire kingdom for themselves. As the power of the distant Foere continued to decay in the rest of the provinces, Suilley has stepped into the gap. Over the generations, the "Stolen Kingdom" has slowly been increasing the loyalty and trust of its own citizens, gaining the fealty of more petty nobles in the hinterlands, and expanding its reach beyond the original borders of the province. In the last century, as all imperial authority collapsed and the imperial armies disappeared, many of Suilley's neighboring provinces have thrown off all allegiance to the Kingdoms of Foere and sworn fealty to the King of Suilley instead, desperate to re-establish some kind of stability in their own lands. And so the present day dawns with the Kingdom of Suilley in sudden possession by default of a vast and disorganized patchwork of feudal realms. The kingdom has a relatively stable domain around the capital city of Manas but utterly lacks the resources to protect or govern all the realms now pleading to be pulled back from the edge of their own ruin by the hand of the Suilleyn King. To complicate the situation, not all of the Borderland Provinces are comfortable with the rise of the Kingdom of Suilley, and some view Suilley as no less a foreign overlord than the Foere. Nevertheless, Suilley is perhaps the best hope of the Borderland Provinces if they wish to avoid the grim fate of the Sundered Kingdoms. The situation is dire, but Suilley and its allies are prepared to fight to keep the lamp of civilization burning here.

The regions described in this book are geographically and culturally quite distinct from each other, all with their own different histories and heroes, all facing their own particular threats. They are united, however, by a single, historical watershed event: the slowly receding tide of the influence and protection of the Kingdoms of Foere.

This book includes a poster map of the area it describes, but a bigger poster-sized map of the entire Sinnar Coast Region exists, it was originally sold with the **The Lost Lands: The Lost City of Barakus** Kickstarter and is now also available separately from **Frog God Games** (while supplies last). If you plan on getting a copy of **The Lost Lands: Cults of the Sundered Kingdoms**, covering the lands east of the Borderland Provinces, you should definitely get your hands on one of the Sinnar Coast Region poster maps so you can have an overall picture of the areas described in both books.

Using the Book

Map Locations

The cities and towns on the map are not everything there is. The map is a scattering of a few important places — and also several unimportant places that figure in one of our adventure modules. With a scale of 50 miles per hex, there's a lot of unseen detail for you to add based on what your campaign needs, including forests, hills, and even entire cities. Don't be constrained by what you see in the map: It is deliberately crafted as a patchwork of random detail, not a comprehensive encyclopedia.

Organization

The book is organized country by country, with a chapter for each. Some geographical features like the March of Mountains have their own chapters, but, in general, forests and ranges of hills are described in the country's chapter. Roads may have descriptions in more than one chapter because risks and likely encounters change along the way. For example, the Trader's Way seems to appear everywhere as it wends its way across the map.

Encounter Tables

Since this part of the Lost Lands is designed to handle a lot of long-distance, travel-type adventures, we've provided lots of encounter tables for the main roads and a couple of iconic locations. The encounter categories are numbered in the encounter table, and detailed together in the back as an appendix. Since these are random encounters, there's no page-flipping between the main text of the book and the appendix — everything needed during the encounter is together in the appendix entry.

History of the Borderland Provinces

With the exception of the northern provinces of Aachen and Eastreach, the history of the Borderland Provinces is the history of the western Plains of Suilley, a fertile region well-watered by rivers unlike the more-arid eastern plains beyond the Trader's Way, scattered with hills and lakes. Numerous deep forests grow tall and dark in the deeper soil along the rivers, remnants of a much greater primeval forest that once stretched across the region, and wildlife abounds throughout the area.

The Use of Place Names

The following history makes use of many names of places and nations that did not actually exist at the time when the described events occurred. These names are merely used for your reference and would either have had a different name in ancient times or, in the case of modern nation-states, often no name at all as they were not particularly differentiated from any other stretch of the forest at that time.

Before the Hyperborean Age

At the dawning of the Hyperborean Age in the Borderland Provinces, before the arrival of Polemarch Oerson and his legions 109 years before the start of the Imperial Record, the areas now known as the Borderland Provinces were almost entirely covered by primordial forest, the eastern extent of the Great Akadonian Forest. The vast, primeval depths of the trees extended westward far beyond the March of Mountains all the way to the shores of the distant Crescent Sea. On the Borderland Provinces map, the forest extended eastward all the way to where the Trader's Way now runs from Eastgate to Albor Broce, and all the way south, off the map, to the Helwall.

Various neolithic human villages (the "Ancient Ones," as they are usually called) were scattered about through the great forest, but the forest's primary occupants were elves. The great forest housed many tribes of wood elves, but the vast majority of elvenkind in this area were "high elves," ruled by their own nobles and part of a loose confederation with the greater elven lords of the western forests beyond the Crescent Sea.

The Ancient Ones

A shamanic culture, as described in **Cults of the Sundered Kingdoms**, once occupied the eastern Plains of Sull (as that region was known in ancient times), and the original people of the western plains bore many resemblances to their eastern cousins. Being a forest people, the westerners were far less numerous, but their mark remains upon the land, for they left many stone cairns, henges, and rock-paintings that have survived the centuries and catastrophes that have swept through the lands they once inhabited. A majority of the inhabitants of the Western Plains of Suilley are, ultimately, descendants of these primitive peoples, and many of the ancient traditions are still practiced, especially in the hinterlands where few foreign invaders have ventured for long.

Coming of the Hyperboreans

The first great historical shift to take place in the western Plains of Sull came with the arrival of the Hyperboreans, who marched southward through the lands where Eastreach Province is now found. The vast legion, under the leadership of Polemarch Oerson, reached the Great Amrin River, conquering the tribes they encountered, and continued to move downriver along its banks, also at that time the edge of the Great Akadonian Forest. Crossing the Great Amrin, the legion followed the edge of the forest to the Gaelon River, and then began the process of conquering the plains to the east. As the pacification of the Ancient Ones in the plain continued, Oerson's conquered territory continued to edge southward across a short spur of the Gundlock Hills and then south to the Lorremach Highhills. Finally prepared to confront the elves of the forest, Oerson's forces began a systematic pattern of raiding and small-scale fortification, including the occupation of the small tribal town of Manas located in a deep notch in the forest where seasonal mud kept the forest from growing as a contiguous mass, breaking it into numerous small woods.

Unbeknownst to the Hyperboreans, news from the embattled elven nobles facing Oerson's raids had reached the greater elven lords beyond the March of Mountains, and a vast elven host had been gathered from far and wide to repel the attacking humans. This army arrived at the forest's eastern edge and hammered the Hyperborean army back northward in defeat. Oerson pulled his forces back along the same route he had followed into the region, a dramatic escape from annihilation known as Oerson's Perilous March.

The Hyperborean legion occupied itself in the west, making vast conquests in unthinkably rapid succession, including a now-legendary defeat of the elven high lords in the area of the Stoneheart Valley. Oerson eventually returned to the Borderland Provinces area and re-occupied the plains with no effective opposition remaining from the elves. Moving southward across the Wilderland Hills, the Hyperboreans encountered the Heldring barbarians of the Helcynngae Peninsula, and suffered their second major defeat. Unable to subdue the Heldrings, the Hyperboreans drew their borders back to the natural barrier of the Lorremach Highhills,

Extent of Great Akadonian Forest
at the dawn of the Hyperborean Age

building the fortress of Stronghold Hjerrin to secure the gap between the Lorremach and the Forlorn Mountains.

Somewhere in this history, one of the mysteries of ancient civilization emerges. The Hyperborean record indicates the fortification and settlement of areas once covered by the Great Akadonian Forest not long before. There exists no record as to whether the forests receded due to some sort of tree blight, or the activity of the Hyperboreans themselves; it may have been some combination of both. Certainly, trading posts and small fortifications were built in the Duchy of the Rampart, once firmly within the perimeter of the forest. There is ample evidence that the Hyperboreans cut massive road-trails through the forest, but such activity does not seem to explain any sort of general deforestation. By all record, the area of the great forest remained very heavily wooded, but the trees no longer formed an unbroken whole.

As the conquest of the Borderland Provinces region took hold, Hyperborean civilization did too, establishing the first great tide of civilization.

The Great Calamities

To varying degrees, the area of the Borderland Provinces has suffered through some catastrophic events that have shaped the region's history. These are the shifting of the planet's poles in 2491 I.R., the catastrophic wildfires from the destruction of Curgantium in 2496, and the Fiend Rains of 3439. The descent of darkness upon the seas of the Gulf of Akados in 1491 might also be included in the list, but for the most part the only effect on the Borderland Provinces region was actually positive: It allowed the little coastal town of Endhome to rise to a much stronger role in sea-trading.

The shifting of the poles in 2491 I.R. temporarily reduced rainfall in the area that now constitutes Suilley and the Gaelon River valley, making these regions particularly vulnerable to the wildfires that would spread from the destruction of Curgantium five years later. Unlike the plains to the east where famines were caused by the droughts, the Borderland Provinces benefitted from their nearby mountains and highlands, for snow continued to form on the mountains and run off with the thaw, feeding rivers that still ran true, even if narrower and slower than before.

However, the Borderlands did not fare so well when the windswept maelstrom of fire swept across the plains from the destruction of Curgantium in 2496 I.R. The parched grasses ignited like tinder, causing a wave of flames to reach from Curgantium all the way to the distant Matagost Peninsula. The fires, unlike the droughts, caused famines of incalculable damage, massively depopulating the entire region and culling arable land to a mere fraction of what had once been cultivated and tamed. This disaster set back civilization in many of the provinces by a hundred years or more, depending on how one measures the progress of a civilization. Learning survived in such places as Endhome, saved by the Gaelon River's firebreak; Vermis, which was located just beyond the reach of the fires; and Troye, blocked from the fires by the Cretian Mountains. Many remnants of the great continental forest that had once covered the area burned away, feeding the onrushing flames. From this point in history, although many great — even vast — forests still remained, the Borderland Provinces region could no longer be described as predominantly forested.

The much more recent Fiend Rains, beginning in 3439 I.R., bore another catastrophe to the Plains of Suilley. Vast rainfall lasting ten years caused flooding and famine, devastation of crops and arable land, and structural damage to recent and ancient structures alike. This time, the Duchy of the Rampart was not spared, and disaster also followed in the Kingdom of Suilley, the County of Vourdon, Keston Province, and worst of all in the County of Toullen, where a dithering leadership failed to respond to the crisis.

Lost Lands Timeline of the Borderland Provinces

Imperial Record (I.R.)	Erylle Cycle (E.C.)	Huun Chronicle (H.C.)	
Arrival of the Hyperborean Empire in the Borderland and Beyond			
−109	6376		Polemarch Oerson leads Hyperborean Legion out of Boros and into Akados
−102	6383		Wild elves drive Hyperboreans from forest; Legion advances along forest's edge passing through region that will become the Sundered Kingdoms
−92	6393		Elven high lords gather elven host; Oerson's Perilous March begins
−91	6394		Elves defeated by human and mountain dwarf alliance at Lake Crimmormere
−88	6397		Oerson's advance checked at Helcynngae Peninsula; Legion withdraws into hills between March of Mountains and Forlorn Mountains; Stronghold Hjerrin erected in Lorremach Highhills
−83	6402		Construction of Helwall begun, Legion breeds horses on plains east of Lorremach Highhills
−73	6412		Helwall completed, Heldring contained on peninsula; Exeter Province established, foundations laid for forts at Albor Broce and Sylvos
−69	6416		Town of Sessilbridge established
−28	6457		Death of Oerson
−17	6468		Monarchs of Boros send episcopi to Akados
−11	6474		Hyperborean Rebellion; Construction begins on Tower of Oerson
−2	6483		Tower of Oerson completed
1	6485		Battle of Hummaemidon; Birth of Imperial Record
128	6612		Hyperboreans colonize Insula Extremis, battle Heldring on Helcynngae Peninsula
212	6696		Hill dwarves of Irkaina teach ironworking to Hyperboreans
288	6772		Stratego Verin and his Legion destroyed by Heldring in Peninsular Campaign; Militias raised from Helwall to Apothasalos fearing Heldring attack; Coastal forts erected south of Matagost Range to guard against sea invasion, forts of Albor Broce and Sylvos expanded
687	7171		**Beginning of Pax Hyperborea**
1491	7975		The Great Darkness covers waters of Gulf of Akados region for three years; sea trade to the north ceases
1492	7976		Small port of Endhome becomes hub of trade on eastern coast, grows to be known as "Trading Capital of the Continent"
2491	8975		Poles of Boros shift; Goitre emerges, forming Tempest Meridians; Ice sheet begins forming over continent of Boros and World Roof
2496	8980	1	Tower of Oerson destroyed; Wildfires ravage Curgantium and spread across Akados, burning Plains of Suilley and Matagost Forest; Refugees flee across Dardanal Strait to Ramthion Island; Endhome spared devastation

Imperial Record (I.R.)	Erylle Cycle (E.C.)	Huun Chronicle (H.C.)	
2499	8983	4	Imperial Court relocated to Tircople; Western empire abandoned by Hyperboreans; Chaos descends among survivors of Suilley Plain and Matagost Peninsula End of the Hyperborean Age in the Provinces
2516	9000	21	Hyperboreans withdraw from Akados; Heldring cross the Helwall, forts of Sylvos and Albor Broce destroyed
2517	9001	22	Heldring longships land on Ramthion Island and subjugate the populace; Heldring land in Southvale but cannot breach walls of Penmorome; Heldring advance checked at Stronghold Hjerrin in the south and withdraw to Exeter Province
2521	9005	26	Unnamed local chieftain brings Heldring mercenaries to Insula Extremis; Heldring conquer all of Southvale but Penmorome
2527	9011	32	Most Heldring in Exeter Province withdraw to Helcynngae Peninsula to take part in invasion of Insula Extremis
2560	9044	65	Daan forms his Cataphracts in service to Hyperborea
2566	9050	71	Daan acclaimed as Polemarch of Insula Extremis
2576	9060	81	Daan defeats Heldring at Battle of Agedium
2581	9065	86	Daan's Legion marches on Tircople, passing through Plains of Suilley
2584	9068	89	Daan falls as he destroys the lich-queen Trystecce; Few warriors return home to Plains of Suilley
2585	9069	90	Daanites withdraw to Ynys Cyrmagh; Daanites name the rest of the world as Lloegyr—the Lost Lands
2632	9116	137	Last Hyperboreans quietly disappear from Tircople
2690	9174	195	Knights of Macobert formed, mounted upon destriers bred in eastern Suilley Rise of the Kingdom of Foere
2698	9182	203	King Macobert begins uniting Akados as Kingdom of Foere
2720	9204	225	Province of Aachen established extending to the Great Bridge
2744	9228	249	Macobert crowned Overking of the Hyperborean Monarchy of the Foerdewaith
2745	9229	250	Foerdewaith provinces of Suilley and Matagost established
2751	9235	256	Province of Burgundia established to maintain garrison forts at Salyos and Parthos; Construction begins on city of Trevi
2762	9246	267	Overking Macobert and his Knights march on sealed city of Penmorome; Province of Southvale created
2763	9247	268	Construction begins on imperial capital at Courghais
2765	9249	270	Death of Macobert; Son Magnusson succeeds to the throne; Issuance of Eastreach Decree; Provinces of Eastreach and Pontus Tinigal established
2768	9252	273	Overking Magnusson completes imperial capital at Courghais
2776	9260	281	Death of Magnusson I; Grandson Magnusson II succeeds to the Throne
2781	9265	286	Red Plague strikes Kingdoms of Foere; One quarter of the population of the central lands dies, including Magnusson II; Son Osbert I succeeds to the throne
2797	9281	302	Red Plague returns and strikes central Kingdoms of Foere again; Much of the kingdom's central territories are depopulated due to the high death toll; Plague claims Overking Osbert I, who is succeeded by his son, Osbert II
2801	9285	306	Heldring armies cross Helwall again and roam along the March of Mountains, burning settlements and slaughtering their inhabitants; Overking Osbert II gathers a small army and marches south from Courghais to meet the Heldring in battle
2802	9286	307	Mitra appears to Overking Osbert II in the Hearthglen and predicts victory over the Heldring; Osbert builds a shrine to the Sun Father; Osbert II defeats Heldring at Oescreheit Downs, Helcynngae Peninsula pacified; Exeter Province split into Exeter and Cereduin provinces; Trebes constructed on ruins of Sylvos; War hero and nephew of Osbert II, Claud Oberhammer, given rulership of Troye and named Duke of the Rampart, Battle-Duke, and Sword of the Foerdewaith; Tradition of Dukes of the Rampart as Battle-Duke begins
2803	9287	308	Construction begun on garrison town of Kingston; Keston Province established
2805	9289	310	Ramthion Island petitions for entry into Kingdom of Foere; Province of Ramthion created

THE LOST LANDS: BORDERLAND PROVINCES

Imperial Record (I.R.)	Erylle Cycle (E.C.)	Huun Chronicle (H.C.)	
2822	9306	327	County of Vourdon created
2843	9327	348	Twin royal heirs Kennet and Cale born to Overking Paulus
2856	9340	361	County of Toullen established
2858	9342	363	Cale abdicates claim to throne and given port of Reme
2970	9454	475	Huun besiege Tircople, overrun part of Crusader States; Overking Yurid gathers Crusader army at Pontus Tinigal and Tros Zoas to sail for Khemit, march overland to Tircople; In absence of forces on Crusade in the East, the vampire lord known as the Singed Man rises in the Duchy of Kear and conquers it, ruling as its Infernal Tyrant
2971	9455	476	Second Great Crusade breaks Siege of Tircople and drives Huun from Sacred Table
2977	9461	482	Battle-Duke Ormand of the Rampart charged with freeing Kear from the Singed Man, Foerdewaith army crushed by the Infernal Tyrant of Kear at Seilo Ford, Battle-Duke Ormand slain and rises as vampire spawn in the Singed Man's service
2983	9467	488	The vampire Ormand expands enslaved Realm of Kear from Eber to Tarry; Foere and Castorhage dispute political responsibility and neither raises further forces to try and dislodge the Infernal Tyrant
3030	9514	535	Founding of trade city of Bard's Gate at King's Bridge
3128	9612	633	Sir Varral the Blessed destroys the Singed Man and Duke Ormand, freeing Realm of Kear; Duchy of Kear reconstituted under Foerdewaith Crown with nephew of overking given title in Eber
3199	9683	704	Overking Oessum VIII calls for Fourth Great Crusade; Armies and fleet gather at Endhome to sail for Crusader Coast
3207	9691	712	Huun defeated at Battle of The Sickles; Overking Oessum slain; Graeltor crowned overking
3208	9692	713	Army of Light marches on temple-city of Tsar; Desolation of Tsar created
3213	9697	718	Foerdewaith Wars of Succession begin; Ramthion Island breaks from empire
3215	9699	720	Grand Admiral of Pontus Tinigal withdraws from Foere, declares himself Emperor of the Oceans Blue; Kingdom of Oceanus established on Pontos Island
3216	9700	721	Earl of Swordport mockingly declares himself Monarch of the Moonsilver Sea, assassinated by agents of Oceanus
3217	9701	722	Imperial fleet gathers at Highreach to attack Kingdom of Oceanus; Foerdewaith fleet defeated at Battle of Kapichi Point; City-state of Endhome declares neutrality, Foerdewaith garrison expelled
3218	9702	723	Foerdewaith army marches on Endhome; Army of Burgundia paid off by Oceanus and Endhome, surprises imperial army with flanking maneuver; Imperial army withdraws to Troye without bloodshed; Oceander army occupies Endhome
3221	9705	726	Imperial garrisons withdrawn from Salyos and Parthos; Kingdom of Burgundia declares its independence
3222	9706	727	Kingdom of Suilley declares independence; Eastern region of Suilley erupts in civil war; Foere attacks western Suilley
3223	9707	728	Foerdewaith army defeated by Suilley at Battle of Bullocks Bale
3226	9710	731	Matagost erupts into civil war; Suilley armies withdraw from Gundlock Hills drawing new eastern border at Trader's Way
3312	9796	817	Kingdom of Oceanus demands fealty from Burgundia, Southvale, and Ramthion Island; Invades Matagost Peninsula quickly ending civil war and bringing its factions to heel; Southvale surrenders; Ramthion refuses; Burgundia agrees to pay tribute to Pontus Tinigal to avoid invasion, calls to Foere for aid with promise of fealty; Suilley attacks troops sent by Foere to assist Burgundia; Foere withdraws beyond The Rampart and names region east of Suilley the District of Sunderland
3330	9814	835	Church of Mitra constructs Morninghaven Sanitorium in Hearthglen at Osbert's shrine
3333	9817	838	Burgundia and Oceanus reach peace agreement; Oceanus firmly controls Matagost, Southvale, and much of Sunderland
3336	9820	841	Keston Province and County of Toullen change their allegiance to Kingdom of Suilley
3337	9821	842	Oceander army marches from Matagost for Troye

Imperial Record (I.R.)	Erylle Cycle (E.C.)	Huun Chronicle (H.C.)	
3338	9822	843	Foerdewaith army defeats Oceanders soundly at Battle of the King's Road; Oceander forces withdraw back across Sunderland
3339	9823	844	Oceanus and Foere sign non-aggression treaty
3400	9884	905	Rappan Athuk: The Dungeon of Graves discovered in Forest of Hope
3423	9907	928	Merchants of Endhome establish Grollek's Grove as trading post between four nation-states: Endhome, Sunderland, Suilley, and Duchy of the Rampart
3436	9920	941	Captain Aldrin Shaw of Eastwych deserts from the navy of Foere, relocates to Swordport; Begins to gather small fleet of freebooters; Shaw's estate at Stormshield seized by governor of Eastwych
3439	9923	944	Unseasonal torrential rains begin to fall on the eastern slopes of the March of Mountains, the rains continue virtually nonstop causing extensive flooding, washout of roads, and undermining of city walls and building foundations; Duchy of the Rampart, Kingdom of Suilley, County of Vourdon, Keston Province, and County of Toullen are hardest hit
3442	9926	947	Captain Shaw's fleet driven from Swordport by earl's dragoons; Flees to Razor Sea
3443	9930	951	The rains have continued for four years; Casualties from flooding and mudslides have reached the tens of thousands, the destruction of property is on a massive scale, and trade on the South Road has virtually been brought to a halt, causing economic recession in the lands east of the mountains; The noted scholar and philosopher Oscobar of Vermis declares the rains to be the work of the forces of Darkness and calls them the Fiend Rains, he predicts they will continue for another 13 years; The strange blind mystic Lun of the Mountain calls the rain Ryna's Tears, but she gives no explanation why; Lun says the rains will end in 6 more years
3446	9930	951	Captain Shaw destroys small Foerdewaith colony on Razor Coast and founds Port Shaw
3449	9933	954	After 10 years, the Fiend Rains come to an end; The Borderland Provinces begin to dry out and dig themselves out of the mud; Drainage to the lowlands of the Hearthglen have become a spreading marsh that is eventually known as the Creeping Mire
3451	9935	956	Oceanus opens trade relations with Port Shaw
3455	9939	960	The Creeping Mire continues to grow and attracts dangerous inhabitants, making the road to Morninghaven Sanatorium perilous; Mitran pilgrims begin to disappear from the Swamp Road en route to Morninghaven
3466	9959	980	Unable to guarantee the safety of its pilgrims, the Church of Mitra sells Morninghaven Sanatorium to Baronet Wilbane Osterklieg, who turns it into a prison for the criminally insane
3486	9970	991	Keston Province assumes control of Morninghaven Sanatorium after arrest of Baronet Osterklieg
3506	9990	1011	Humanoid and barbaric human raiders descend from Wilderland Hills and burn village of Byrnum; Beginning of Wilderlands Clan War; County of Toullen sends small contingent of troops to assist Keston
3507	9991	1012	Kingdom of Suilley commits troops to assist beleaguered army of Keston Province against the Wilderlands clans; Exeter fortifies Albor Broce against incursions by the clans
3509	9993	1014	County of Vourdon and Exeter Province send assistance to Keston and Suilley troops; General Cormien wins Battle of Broch Tarna, breaking the strength of the hill clans and sending their margoyle masters fleeing back into the Forlorn Mountains
3515	9999	1020	King Ovar defeats Huun in Gulf of Akados and at Bard's Gate and pursues them into Irkainian Desert
3517	10,001	1022	Current year; Rumors of Ovar's return from Irkaina

Rise and Fall of Foere

The initial arrival of the authority of the Kingdoms of Foere in the Borderland Provinces, beginning circa 2720 I.R., brought a new degree of prosperity to the region, making trade and travel safer, and lessening the tyranny and over-taxation imposed by petty feudal lords. The advance of Foerdewaith domination was extremely rapid according to the historical annals of Foere, but considerably slower in actual reality. Provinces were declared before actually being conquered (as in the case of Eastreach Province), and provinces that were recorded as being fully incorporated into the Kingdoms were often controlled only in the largest towns, with Foerdewaith culture still a very long way from reaching the peasantry. All this being said, the scattered rural populace of the Borderland Provinces was desperate for order and peace; the laws and soldiery of Foere offered precisely this boon.

Upon the death of Overking Oessum VIII in the Fourth Great Crusade in 3207, and the loss of the Army of Light in the Forest of Hope three years later, the centuries of benefits brought by the Kingdoms of Foere began a slow process of collapse. For the most part, the initial stages of decline stemmed from distant events in the heart of Foere, rather than in the provinces themselves. The Foerdewaith Wars of Sucession most certainly laid the groundwork for the falling of the first domino outside the heartlands of Foere, the seccession of Ramthion Island in 3213. From this point onward, all the small cracks in the foundation of Foere's rule in the provinces began to widen. Issues that remained minor during times of prosperity, such as the inherent corruption in Eastreach Province's patchwork feudal system, and the treatment of provincial nobles as a lesser class by Foerdewaith nobility, flared into much larger problems when Foere's grip loosened, even so slightly. War and rebellion surged across the regions east of the provinces, in the area now known as the Sundered Kingdoms. Eventually, the contagion of unrest filtered westward, and the nobility of Suilley made their bid to be treated on an equal footing with the heartland kingdoms of Foere. The Overking's fateful, arrogant response to Suilley's gesture of crowning a new king toppled the most significant domino in the collapse of his provincial empire.

To Steal a Kingdom

In the year 3222 of the Imperial Record, the Province of Suilley crowned its Lord-Governor, Ghienvais Pas, as Ghienvais I, King of Suilley. Essentially the gesture was intended by the Suilleyn nobility to commence the formal process of being treated as equals of the nobility in Foere. They were no doubt influenced by the disorder in the provinces to the east, seeing an opportunity to improve their own status, but only a very few seem to have anticipated how badly the Overking, pressed on all sides, would consider the coronation as a threat to his own authority in a vital part of the empire.

Instead of considering the essentially loyalist nature of the Sulleyn coronation, the Overking declared all the nobles anathema, traitors who would be stripped of their lands and executed when captured. The shocked nobles of Suilley suddenly realized that they now had no choice if they wished to live other than to escape entirely from the Overking's rule. Perhaps matters might have gone differently if the Overking's army had subdued the province quickly, but the course of the short war reversed all expectations when the Foerdewaith army was crushed at the Battle of Bullock's Bale. With the great province of Suilley thrown into the status of an independent realm in the midst of war and rebellion on all sides, the shape of events in the provinces was utterly and irrevocably changed. A new player had been forced to join the game, and the new player, the King of Suilley, stood in a strategic position at the geographic center of the provinces.

Recent Years

The various locales in the Borderland Provinces have encountered different problems and opportunities from the slow erosion of Foerdewaith dominance. Some areas, Endhome in particular, have benefitted greatly.

Suilley is faced with the problems of becoming an imperial power far too quickly. Eastreach and Aachen are collapsing from within, for different reasons. Exeter Province is isolated and calcifying, and Keston Province has been shattered by slow military response to border threats. Toullen works to recover from the unchecked disaster of the Fiend Rains, supported only by the inadequate assistance Suilley can manage to scrape together. The situation is by no means irretrievable; given time and peace, the Borderland Provinces have a good chance of riding out the turbulence of Foere's retreating tide. On the other hand, any catastrophe, war, or powerful assault by the forces of evil could throw the provinces into a dark age reminiscent of the time following the great fires of Curgantium. The forces of good must be at their most vigilant when times like these arrive, for rest assured, the forces of evil are ready.

Peoples of the Borderland Provinces

Foerdewaith

The Foerdewaith are by far the most commonly found ethnicity in the Borderland Provinces, as in the Sundered Kingdoms to the east. These humans represent the many indigenous tribes that dwelt in the lands and were assimilated by the Hyperboreans when the Hyperboreans took over the region thousands of years ago. It was these tribes who were left behind when the Hyperboreans withdrew from Akados, and who later became part of the hegemony of Foere started by the first Foerdewaith overking, Macobert. Although the Foerdewaith were identified as a single people during the height of the Foerdewaith monarchy, this was only true as an ethnicity and a broadly shared cultural heritage from the Hyperboreans and the later rule of the overkings. Most Foerdewaith in the Borderland Provinces identify themselves as members of smaller regions, such as "Aachenlanders." The term Foerdewaith is now commonly used to refer to the inhabitants of the Kingdoms of Foere and those (mainly the nobility) who can trace ancestries leading back to the Kingdoms. These "Foerdewaith of Foere" consider the bloodline to be a sign of superiority.

Gaeleen

A people unique to the Gaelon Valley, these are riverfolk first and foremost. They ply the waters of the mighty Gaelon, selling their catch at the great trade-road bridges, in the markets of wealthy Endhome, or among the innumerable villages that line the shores up and down the river and its countless tributaries. They typically fish in large family groups from light, flat-bottomed skiffs, sometimes made from only woven reeds sealed with pitch for small families or lone fishermen, and are as comfortable with line and hook as they are with nets. Unlike the Foerdewaith fishermen who trawl the river with net-dragging fishing scows, they use their fishing nets in the old way, casting them into the waters and hauling them in by hand without benefit of block or tackle. The Foerdewaith fisherman often resent the smaller, more agile Gaeleen craft and their masters, and tend to look down on them as a people. The Gaeleen deny any relation to the peoples of the Kingdoms of Foere, instead claiming to have been born of the river itself and using their tendency to be skilled swimmers as alleged "proof" of the fact. Scholars scoff at this and surmise that the Gaeleen may be a remnant of a much earlier people called the Phoromyceans who once inhabited the region of Endhome and the Duskmoon Hills before disappearing from the historical record long ago. The Gaeleen are a smaller folk than the typical Foerdewaith, with skin tones that easily hold a tan from working on the waters under the sun all day long. Their hair ranges from dirty blonds to dark browns, with darker shades frequently being sun-bleached to a much lighter hue due to their chosen vocation, and eyes tend towards greens and blues. The Gaeleen are great story tellers and renowned singers, often claiming to "sing the fish into their nets" as they ply the waters of the Gaelon.

Vanigoths

The Vanigoths are a large but widely dispersed nation of human barbarians, predominantly found in the Wilderland Hills and the plains between the Lorremach Highlands and the Forlorn Mountains. They are probably mixed descendants of Heldring invaders and the pre-Hyperborean tribes of the Plains of Sull. The Vanigoths speak their own language, although most of them can communicate in a rudimentary Common. It is extremely rare for the disparate Vanigoth tribes to unite under a leader, although they have their own king in the fortress of Aen Vani, deep in the Wilderland Hills. The Vanigoths take battle-trophies from their victims, usually the head and some other trophy, often a hand or finger.

Dwarves

Dwarven clans of the Borderland Provinces are many and varied, generally living in the foothills of the great ranges of the March of Mountains. Most clans are hill dwarves that live in underground halls, operating separate mines that follow the ore. A single dwarven community might have two or three working mines. Additionally, most clans have small herds of sheep or goats that provide the dwarves with food that need not be brought in from the lowlands. Periodically, the dwarves load up a wagon with their forged blades, intricate jewelry, and other metalwork, and head down to the towns and villages of the lowlands to trade their work for gold and town-produced products. Cloth, beer, and leatherwork are all usually items the dwarven clans import, but some of them have craftsmen who inexplicably delight in making such things themselves. Some of the small dwarven caravans travel quite far to reach the markets they want, partly because their jewelry work is too expensive to find buyers in rural villages. Thus, wandering dwarven caravans are not a strikingly unusual sight anywhere in the Borderlands.

In addition to the foothill clans, there are a few large dwarven settlements, usually in the mountains themselves, with populations as large as many human towns. These communities are deep miners for the most part, and more isolated and insular than the foothill dwarves. They tend to trade their goods not with the human settlements, but with clans of the lower-lying dwarven communities. They are cordial but not very welcoming to non-dwarven visitors, for their redoubts hold secrets they prefer not to share.

The last group of dwarves in the provinces is possibly the most numerous, but also the most scattered; these are the clans and villages settled in the small hill formations scattered throughout the plains, and at the periphery of the Gaelon River Valley at the top of the watershed. As with the dwarves of the foothills, they are generally miners and herders at the same time.

The only dwarven culture that differs significantly from the other clans of the Borderland Provinces may be found in the Kal'Iugus mountain range, where there are significant numbers of mountain dwarves. These clans are extremely unfriendly to lowlanders, and there are rumors that they are even friends to the giants and barbarians of the northern reaches of that range.

Elves

There are a number of small elven communities across the Borderland Provinces region, living in the forests scattered through the hilly plains. The highest concentration of these communities is to be found in the forested parts of the Gaelon River Valley, often the river valleys of small tributaries that have supported forests for centuries without being occupied by humans. Although the elves generally keep to themselves, they usually have good relations with any nearby human settlements unless some past event has caused ill-will.

There are, however, isolated courts and shees where the elves are capricious and dangerous, well-attuned to the powers of the fey, and not friendly to outsiders. In general, nearby hamlets and villages are aware of the places where these elves live, and give them wide berth.

For the most part, the elves of the Borderland Provinces are high elves, dwelling in remnants of the primeval forest that once covered most of the continent, its borders roughly along the path of the Trader's Way. Because this region was once forested, the concentration of elves in the Borderland Provinces is higher than in the Sundered Kingdoms to the east, which were more predominantly plains-land even before the arrival of the Hyperboreans.

The elves here are not fond of the Hyperborean Empire, for their history with it is almost exclusively one of war and ruin. Unlike many humans, they do not view the relics or tales of Hyperborean antiquity with any reverence at all. This animosity does not extend to the Foerdewaith or to present-day humans, but a certain distaste for the Hyperborean gods might occasionally surface toward those who revere them.

Half-Elves

Half-elves are rarer in the Borderland Provinces than they are in the Sundered Kingdoms to the east, despite the fact that full-blooded elves are more common. Most likely the reason is that the elves of the Borderland Provinces tend to be a bit more isolated than the high elves of the Sundered Kingdoms region, living as they do in forest redoubts. Half-elves are not treated with suspicion by humans (for the most part), and they are generally assimilated into the community of the human parent rather than the elven one. Thus, while they are not particularly common, half-elves are merely considered a bit exotic, not monstrous, even in small villages.

Halflings

As with the rolling plains of the Sundered Kingdoms to the east, the hillier grasslands of the Borderland Provinces are well suited to halflings. Most halfling settlements are burrow-house communities in rural areas, within traveling distance of a town. Many of these particular towns have a family or two of halflings who make their living by taking care of visiting rurals, operating a halfling-sized inn, and buying the country goods for trade. Halflings are rare in ordinary towns that do not have a burrow-town in the vicinity, for, in general, halfings are not enthusiastic travelers and human-sized crowds can be a bit intimidating. Even small cities will often have one or two halfling families, for the same reasons as the human towns near halfling burrow-towns; despite the general homebody tendency of Borderlands halflings, there are always a few visitors in the city, whether they are wanderers or traders.

River Giants

There are few places in the Lost Lands where civilized folk are known to consort regularly with giantkind, and perhaps there are none where it occurs more frequently than the Gaelon River. There the river giants of the Windrush Clan have lived and fished in a great extended family for as long as anyone can remember. When Oerson first brought his Legion to the banks of the Gaelon, his journals relate how he was able to hire peaceful river giants to ferry his army across, and in the Perilous March some years later he credited the river giants with preventing the decimation of his Legion upon the river's south bank by the pursuing wild elves. The river giants of the Gaelon tend to be solitary or live in small family groups of no more than a handful and are known to keep giant specimens of otters or beavers as trained pets. They are peaceful, if somewhat shy of the smaller races, but will readily bring their great fishing hauls to riverside villages to sell and trade and never hesitate to scoop a foolish swimmer out of the water who has found himself literally out of his depth. The giants avoid larger human settlements and rarely carry passengers across the river, because they have learned that it angers the ferrymen among the "little folk" who lose the opportunity to gain those tolls. They seem to have a particular affinity for the Gaeleen and often laugh knowingly when those colorful fishermen speak of being "born of the river," though the giants never reveal any knowledge they may have on the subject, if any. River giants stand 10 feet tall and weigh around 900 pounds. Their skin tones have a brown or greenish tone, usually with a yellowish tinge like duckweed but sometimes deepening to an olive hue — especially when spending a great deal of time out in the sun — and their hair is almost always black or brown. The giants spend their lives upon the river, fishing and trading up and down its length on crude rafts and either live in rough shelters built upon these rafts or in simple huts upon rocky islands or sandbars where river forks converge.

Languages

Gaeling

The language of the Gaeleen river people, they claim this rhythmic tongue is the song of the winds and the currents. Though it has many borrowed words from Common and High Boros and even some Halfling, Gaeling is clearly a language unrelated to any others known in Akados. Believed to have descended from a much older language that predated the Hyperborean Empire and was largely lost even by the time Oerson's Legion first crossed over from the North, Gaeling is rarely beyond the valley of the Gaelon and has baffled scholars for years. It does not have its own written script, so those speakers of Gaeling who are literate use the script of the Common tongue to phonetically transcribe its sounds, leading to wild variations in spelling among speakers.

Gasquen

Gasquen was the language of the original tribe of Foere from whom Macobert descended. Unique in its linguistic etymology, its scope of use was originally limited to central Akados around the Star Sea. With the spread of the Foerdewaith empire, Gasquen was picked up in many places to identify with the new overking. But even Macobert himself realized that Gasquen was inadequate to communicate within his growing empire and set about establishing the Westerling military tongue as a vernacular to be used commonly among all his disparate peoples. Gasquen is now found only in isolated areas or noble courts that wish to strongly identify with Old Foere. In the Sundered Kingdoms, the Ramithi, who hate the Heldring influence on the Common tongue, speak Gasquen almost exclusively as a means of emphasizing their cultural identity in the face of generations of invasion of their island.

Vanigothic

The barbarian Vanigoths speak their own language, which is derived from an ancient mix of Old Suli and Helvaenic, but no longer sounds much like either one. It is possible to establish a very rudimentary understanding between a Heldring speaker and a Vanigothic speaker, but the Vanigoths generally speak enough of the Common tongue to make it a better means of communication.

Westerling (Common)

The common language of most of Akados, Westerling (as it is known outside of Akados) or Common (as it is more commonly known locally) is the language handed down to the civilizations of the continent by the Kingdom of Foere. The language of the overking's court as High Boros lost popularity among the aristocracy, and Westerling pervaded trade, diplomacy, and soldiering. It was from this last that it spread throughout the continent as Foerdewaith armies marched forth and the local auxiliary conscripts needed a means of communicating with their commanders. Related to Gasquen and High Boros with an unusually strong influence from the Heldring Helvaenic, Common began as something of a pidgin only to develop into a full language and the *lingua franca* of the West.

The "Naming" Appendices give the reader a bit more detail about how the Gasquen dialect has influenced the sound and feel of Westerling names in the Borderland Provinces. It is not a comprehensive guide, nor is it a rule. It is simply a tool for generating names with the proper "sound," if you want to go that route.

Technology Levels

One of the lines found in the information blocks for the various nation-states of the Borderland Provinces (and, indeed, for all of the forthcoming **Lost Lands** products) is "Technology Level." This line simply indicates the level of technological achievement that can be found throughout the land in question. There are always exceptions as some areas may be more erudite and others more savage, but this gives a general guideline of the types of weapons, armor, and equipment that can be found in the area. These levels can vary between even neighboring nations as one may be more insular and cut off from outside contact and ideas and another may be open to a great deal of trade bringing in new innovations from outside.

In general, characters should only be able to find equipment of the technology level listed and, in some circumstances, that of lower technology levels. For instance, just because the residents of a given nation have achieved a High Middle Ages technology level does not mean that they cannot find a wheeled conveyance just because that was invented during a Bronze Age technology level. Likewise, the short sword was developed in the Bronze Age and would still be available in later technology levels. Stone or bronze weapons and armor, however, would be unlikely to be found in a High Middle Ages technology level as few artisans in such a technology level have practiced that sort of crafting. As always, the GM must use his discretion to determine what might be available from a lower technology level.

It should be noted that the technology levels presented in **Lost Lands** products are not meant to represent real-world advancements in technology. There is, perhaps, a loose correlation in some of it, but it is instead intended to represent the developments of technology in the world of the **Lost Lands** specifically.

The technology levels most frequently found in the **Lost Lands** are as follows:

Stone Age

Materials: clay vessels, furs, hides, horn, stone tools and weapons, some copper, wood; **Armor:** hide armor; **Weapons:** dagger, javelin, shortbow, spear; **Warfare:** ambush, raiding bands, single combat; **Settlements:** rock shelters, semi-permanent camps; **Social Organization:**

tribes/bands; **Transportation:** paddled craft, trained animals; **General:** animal domestication, fire, horticulture, log rollers

Bronze Age

Materials: bronze tools and weapons, crude glass items, linen, papyrus, wool; **Armor:** breastplate, leather armor, padded armor; **Weapons:** composite shortbow, short sword; **Warfare:** organized armies, city walls (large city-states only); **Settlements:** capitals, cities, towns; **Social Organization:** city-states; **Transportation:** chariot, oars, sails, side rudder, wheel; **General:** agriculture, corbelled arch, hand loom, lever, oil lamp, plow, potter's wheel, pulley, sundial

Iron Age

Materials: cotton textiles, iron and steel tools and weapons, parchment; **Armor:** ring mail, scale mail, studded leather; **Weapons:** longbow, longsword; **Warfare:** cataphracts, catapults, hill forts; **Social Organization:** nations/empires; **General:** arch, dome, locks, loom, screw, water wheel

Dark Ages

Materials: cold iron, felt, porcelain, silk, silvered weapons; **Armor:** chain shirt, chainmail; **Warfare:** fortified towns (wooden stockades); **General:** horn window panes, hourglass, masterwork items

High Middle Ages

Materials: adamantine, mithral; **Armor:** half-plate armor; **Weapons:** composite longbow, greatsword, lance; **Warfare:** castles, cavalry; **Social Organization:** guilds; **Transportation:** stern rudder, stirrup; **General:** Gothic arch, lantern, spinning wheel, waterclock, windmill

Medieval

Materials: paper; **Armor:** full plate, tower shield; **Weapons:** bastard sword, crossbow, rapier, warbow; **Warfare:** gun powder, trebuchet; **Transportation:** astrolabe, compass; **General:** buttons, crude glass window panes, mechanical clock, mirror, power loom

Renaissance

Materials: finely ground glass; **Weapons:** firearms; **Warfare:** cannon; **Transportation:** caravels, coach lines, paddle-wheel boat; **General:** fine glass windows, glass lenses, printing press, rockets

Age of Sail

Materials: ship-borne cannon; **Social Organization:** colonial empires; **Transportation:** oceanic voyages, sextant; **General:** calculus, telescope

Industrial Revolution

General: clockworks, manufactures, steam power

Gender and Culture

The Borderland Provinces are relatively stable in terms of risks and politics, but this status is maintained by rough people who fight for a living and are generally quite good at it. The society is thus divided along the lines of those who fight, and those who are defended by them. This societal division is the primary one that supersedes all others in a world where battle training and experience are far more important than raw strength. Especially in the nobility, females are just as likely to be in the "those who fight" category as men. Rulership in the Borderland Provinces usually requires fighting prowess, so a noble's daughters generally receive the same training as their sons do; it's a simple matter of ensuring that the noble family can show a dangerous front to rebellious peasants and rival

noble houses alike. The more lance-carrying, plate-mailed riders in the family's line of battle, the better.

Among the peasantry and the middle classes in the cities, there might have been a bit more differentiation by gender except for the fact that everyone, to whatever extent they can manage, follows traditions established by the nobility. Over the centuries, this has led to a profound disregard for what you might think of as "traditional" gender roles, even among the non-fighting social orders. It still tends to be a distinction between those who are "tough" and dress more in clothes suitable for brawling (trousers, closely fitted sleeves, etc.) versus those who dress in whatever clothes might be traditional for their professions and cultures. The "tough" group is evenly divided between men and women, and so are the non-combatants. It is generally only among the "non-combatant" groups where one sees much difference between traditionally male and female clothing.

There is virtually no societal influence or expectation on the way spellcasters dress and act. It is never wise to annoy unknown spellcasters, and this lesson has been delivered enough times for society to catch on.

Religion
Shifting Tides

The predominant religious pantheon in the Borderland Provinces is the array of Hyperborean gods brought to the continent by the invaders 109 years before the beginning of the Imperial Record. Thyr, Solanus, Mithras, Jamboor, Telophus, Kamien, Yenomesh, Ceres, and Pan all have long-standing temples and dedicated followers throughout the region. After the end of the Hyperborean Age, the Foerdewaith invasion of the Borderland Provinces brought a second group of gods, including Archeillus, Quell, and Belon the Wise.

More recently, some of the popular gods of Bard's Gate have established followings, particularly in the northern part of the Borderlands. Sefagreth, a Hyperborean deity not previously well-known in the Borderland Provinces since Hyperborean times, has rapidly gained worshippers among the merchants and townsfolk. Most significant is the growth of the sun-cult of Mitra. In Foere and Bard's Gate, Mitra is becoming the predominant sun-god, supplanting the now rapidly-eroding Church of Solanus. Mitra is well known in the Borderland Provinces at this point, but Solanus is generally still considered the "real" goddess of the sun. However, the growing weakness of the Church in Reme and Bard's Gate is felt far away from these centers of civilization. The temples of Solanus in the Borderland Provinces are receiving fewer acolytes to train, less funding for buildings and good works, and less political support from the powers-that-be in the great trading cities.

The temples of Thyr and Muir are also in steady decline due to the rising power of the Mitran faith, although to different degrees. The worship of Muir has eroded to almost nothing in this area, although there are still many scattered small temples and shrines to the goddess of paladins. The temples of Thyr, on the other hand, are still very strong and well established. Their strength and influence are slowly decaying, but Thyr is still the most prominent and influential deity in the Borderlands.

Heresy!

Heretical faiths are a growing problem in the Borderland Provinces. Social unrest and political instability always create fertile ground for radical religious sentiments and bizarre theories, and some form of instability threatens almost all the Provinces. Moreover, the Church of Thyr is in decline, and the priesthood of Thyr has traditionally been the main force to seek out, investigate, judge, and destroy heresy in this part of the world.

See **Appendix H: Heresies** for more details about this dangerous threat.

In other parts of the world, the cult of Belon the Wise is beginning to replace the older faith of Jamboor, but most parts of the Borderland Provinces are conservative about such matters, and Jamboor remains the predominant god of knowledge across the area — with the sole exceptions of Eastgate and Endhome, trade cities that are more influenced by newfangled ideas from abroad.

Druidism

There is a certain antagonism between druidism and the god-centered religions of the Borderland Provinces, which dates back to the Hyperborean invasion of the Plains of Sull. Most of the resistance to the Hyperborean invasion, futile as it was, was organized by shamans and druids. As Oerson's forces rolled through the lands bordering on the Great Akadonian Forest, the hardiest of the defenders, many of them led by druids, retreated into the forests to continue fighting the invaders. As the forests continued to decline, and civilization to develop, these old druidic sects remained hostile to the influence of the Hyperboreans and their foreign gods. Over the course of centuries, the theological battle lines between druidism and traditional deity-worship stayed in place, with violence often breaking out between the two populations of worshippers. In the present day, the hostility is considerably less, and is mainly found in isolated communities. However, it is common to find clerics of the Hyperborean gods who disdain and distrust druids, and druids — particularly in the oldest of the druidic sects — who consider deity-centered worship to be sapping the strength of the world in favor of fat clerics and otherworldly gods.

Settlement Descriptions

Most of the information in a settlement's stat block is straightforward and self-explanatory, but a couple of the categories may need explanation.

Quick Summary

The first line of the settlement description is an instant picture of the community's size and general alignment. For example: LG small city. If the characters are just passing through, this line might be all you need.

Settlement Statistics

Type	Population	Purchase Limit
Thorp	Fewer than 50	500gp
Hamlet	50–100	1000gp
Village	101–1000	2000gp
Small town	1001–3000	4000gp
Large town	3001–6000	8000gp
Small city	6001–10,000	16,000gp
Large city	10,001–25,000	32,000gp
Metropolis	More than 25,000	64,000gp

Government

This is a quick guide to how the community is organized, usually fleshed out in the community's text description. Autocracy is a single leader such as an elected mayor, chosen by the community. A Council is also chosen by the community, but it is a group. An Overlord inherited, stole, or was appointed to rule (not chosen by the community, in other words). Magical means there is a magical component to the leader's rule, and Secret Syndicate means the so-called "ruler" is someone else's puppet. A settlement's government helps to establish its flavor and feel.

Population

Population shows the settlement's total adult population, including the elderly.

Notable NPCs

These people will most likely be described in the text, but if the characters are only in town to get healing at the local temple, you may want to know the high priest's name and level without reading through the whole description. It's not a complete list, especially for cities, but it is often helpful.

Maximum Clerical Spell Level

This line shows the highest level of clerical spell available in the community's temples. It is divided morally between Good, Neutral, and Evil. A temple of Good most certainly won't cast *raise dead* on anyone of Evil alignment, and will charge more to cast it on a person of Neutral alignment. Most Evil temples are secret, and this is noted in the entry. Characters of Evil alignment might have to ask around, very carefully, to find anyone at all, much less a high priest.

Purchase Limit

If you roll into a thorp of twenty peasants planning to sell the *staff of power* found in the depths of a nearby dungeon, you're going to be disappointed. Hard coinage is scarce in rural areas, and even towns can't raise the money to buy buckets of gems or powerful magical items. This line indicates the most that a settlement can spend on buying things from characters during a month.

Chapter One: Aachen Province

Aachen Province

(AWK-in or AH-khin)

Overview

Aachen Province remains loyal to the Kingdom of Foere, and is ruled by a Lord-Governor appointed by the Overking. It is a relatively peaceful province, but potential revolution is brewing among the nobility. Order in the province is beginning to decay as outside trade dwindles due to high taxes at the border, and the pressure of this decline is already affecting the farmers and peasantry.

General Information

Alignment: LN
Capital: Vermis (32,500)
Notable Settlements: Aixe (8600), Becqueril (172), Dlante (5329), Elet (1540), Gretspaan (1167), Taundre (467)
Ruler: Lord-Governor Theriven the Leopard (N male human **Ftr10**)
Government: feudalism (vassal of Foere)
Population: 2,238,000 (2,100,000 Foerdewaith; 105,000 halflings; 24,000 high elves; 9000 hill dwarves)
Humanoid: halfling (many), high elf (some), hill dwarf (few)
Monstrous: goblin, giant animal (bear, dragonfly, wolf, stag), bugbear, fey, ankheg, gnoll, ogre, basilisk, cockatrice, giant, manticore, peryton (near Cretian Mountains), tiger, undead, treant, wyvern (Cretian foothills), unicorn
Languages: Common, Halfling, Elvish, Dwarvish
Religion: Ceres, Freya, Thyr (declining), Mick O'Delving, Archeillus, Darach-Albith, Jamboor, Solanus (badly declining), Telophus, Belon the Wise, Kamien, Yenomesh.
Resources: grain, wool, cloth, manufactured goods, cotton, furs, gems (grade 1 and 2), silver
Technology Level: Medieval (cities), High Middle Ages (rural areas)

Borders and Lands

Aachen Province is found immediately to the west of Eastreach Province, in the Aachen Gap between the Mons Terminus range and the Cretian Mountains. Its boundaries are relatively well-established, with the exception of the rural boundaries with Eastreach Province. Starting clockwise from the Great Bridge, Aachen's border cuts southeast in a generally diagonal line, to just south of the Estuary Road's intersection with the Wain Road. It is this boundary that gets vague as it circles around farms and villages in the countryside. Thence, the line naturally follows the edge of the Cretian Mountains westward through the town of Elet and eventually to the city of Aixe. It is here that the boundary line crosses the Aachen Gap, and continues northwest to reach the southern extent of the Mons Terminus just north of the ruins of Curgantium. The western border is demarcated by the upper run of the Great Amrin River, hugging the edge of the Mons Terminus Range northward to the Great Bridge.

These boundaries correspond closely to the older concept of "the Aachenland," although the old Aachenland culture extends a bit farther south into Foere than the administrative boundaries of the province do.

History and People

The native Aachenlanders were absorbed into the Kingdoms of Foere when the province was established by King Macobert in the year 2720 I.R. At the time, the Aachenlanders were a loose affiliation of tribes having been previously united under the Hyperborean Empire, sharing a common language and trading among each other fairly peacefully. The original language of Aachen has entirely died out, first replaced by High Boros and then by the Common tongue, although it has left the Aachenlanders with a still-recognizable accent in their Westerling speech, and several idioms not found elsewhere, such as expressing "don't wait too long" by saying, "don't let fish eat you."

The entire region south of the city of Vermis was devastated by the vast wildfires spawned by the explosion of the Tower of Oerson in 2496, a wind-blown wave of flames that eventually spread all the way to the Matagost Peninsula, thousands of miles to the east. The city of Aixe was spared only due to its huge, lake-fed moat, and might still have starved to death in the ensuing famines if it were not sited directly upon a road leading to areas not affected by the fires. Untold thousands died from fire and famine in the rural areas of what would become the Province of Aachen; scholars estimate that the population of the area took 300 years to rebuild to its original numbers as they stood before the fires.

Trade and Commerce

As with the western region of Eastreach, Aachen is fairly well populated, with numerous farming towns and trading villages. A fairly extensive network of passable roads in the province allows even the smallest settlements access to large markets, so farms are generally large and prosperous in the Aachen heartlands. Moreover, Aachen's internal governance is much better organized than its rather corrupt northeastern neighbor Eastreach, with fewer so-called "tolls" being extorted from travelers by petty nobles and pocket fiefdoms. Many of the small towns in Aachen hold

great "fayres" during which peasants from the surrounding regions and traveling merchants from other towns congregate to buy and sell all manner of goods. Such fayres are often held three or four times per year.

Unlike its neighboring province of Eastreach, Aachen does not enjoy a lucrative financial relationship with Bard's Gate (for which the Lord-Governors have been more than a bit resentful in the past). For this reason, the Lords-Governor of Aachen charge fairly extortionate taxes on foreign caravans heading to and from Bard's Gate — which is in turn one of the many reasons Bard's Gate conducts so much traffic by riverboat through Eastreach, skirting Aachen entirely.

Loyalties and Diplomacy

Aachen is connected by high roads almost directly to the Overking's capital at Courghais, and remains loyal to the Kingdom of Foere. As such, the province is administered by a Lord-Governor on behalf of the Overking, currently by a somewhat frightening individual by the name of Theriven the Leopard.

Government

The Lord-Governorship is not a hereditary title, being an appointment granted in the Court of Courghais by the Overking. Thus far, no Lord-Governor has refused to surrender the office or establish a hereditary succession; most of them are, in any case, anxious to return to the civilized center of the Kingdoms of Foere once they have accumulated a modest fortune in the provinces.

As a general rule for understanding the government of Aachen:

• If it is a high road, a bridge, or a court of law, a Regional Governor is in charge of it.

• If it is a city, the mayor reports to the Lord-Governor and to no one else (although the Regional Governor still runs the court system).

• If it is a town, it either reports to the Lord-Governor as a city (a "free town"), or is governed by a noble as part of the feudal system, although the courts remain under the supervision of the Regional Governor.

• If it is a piece of land, a wagon-trail, or a village, a noble of some rank is in charge.

The province has seven major partitions ruled by Regional Governors who are appointed by the royal court in Foere in the same manner as the Lord-Governor, each of whom administers the roads, courts, and some of the towns across a wide region. Within the regional governorships, but reporting directly to the Lord-Governor, are well-defined feudal landgraves, each ruled by a noble lord bearing the title of "landsgraf," who administers the countryside (but not the courts or roads) over an area roughly 50 miles across. Local barons, in fealty to the landsgrafs, govern at the lowest level of the hierarchy. Most barons have the double responsibility of maintaining a court for the governor, while owing military and tithe duties to the landsgraf. These baronies can be of wildly varying sizes; many are little more than a small castle surrounded by a mile or so of dreary wilderness; others might encompass a small town and several miles of fertile farmland.

The seven Governorships of Aachen are: Aixe (containing 9 landgraves), Vermis (containing 13 landgraves), Gretspaan (containing 6 landgraves), Tremonde (containing 8 landgraves), Dlante (containing 4 landgraves), Sauv Lar (containing 7 landgraves), and Basivaine (containing 5 landgraves). At present, no landsgraf holds more than one landgrave, so there are 52 landsgrafs ruling the land of Aachen, in fealty to the office (but not specifically to the person) of the Lord-Governor.

Wilderness and Adventure

The relative stability of Aachen as a province should not be understood to suggest that the countryside is nothing but a placid expanse of fields and cheerful peasants, although many such places exist, especially in the heartlands. Many forests spread through the region, harboring beasts dire and strange, and there are countless areas in Aachen that have either never been tamed or that have been allowed to return to the wild. In particular, the lower reaches and foothills of the Cretians and the Mons Terminus mountain ranges are home to bandits and monsters alike. Settlements in these remote areas cling grimly to their existence in the face of these threats, receiving only sporadic, halfhearted support from those who boast of the province's stability.

The wilder parts of Aachen are home to tigers, which can be a threat to herding communities. The tigers of Aachen (often referred to as "leopards") are spotted rather than the striped varieties more commonly found in lands of the East, most likely a strain that has survived from the days when the land was covered with great forests.

Changing Times

Lord-Governor Theriven the Leopard is the veteran of several feudal wars, the younger son of a noble Foerdewaith family, born in Troye. Without any prospect of an inheritance, Theriven took service as a mercenary, and distinguished himself on the battlefield as a staunch supporter of Foere. He is a grim and unflinching man, intolerant of dissent and difficult to read. As a widely-traveled warrior, he is enough of a realist to see that even in the close province of Aachen the Kingdoms are no longer offering much support in return for the revenues they collect, and that the prosperity of "his" lands is slowly dwindling. He is unnervingly quiet on this subject, a complete cipher.

A vast number of the landsgrafs in Aachen resent the unequal bargain being given to them by the Royal Court, which is to pay high taxes in exchange for slight assistance. They hear of the power of the nobles in free Suilley, and look across the borders to see the riches of a predatory nobility in Eastreach Province; and they compare it to their own role as providers to a hungry, desperate, foreign empire. To most of them, the reason for the difference is obvious: It is the hand of Foere that keeps them weak. More and more they are talking behind closed doors, and training their men-at-arms in case the need arises to take one side or another in an armed resolution. So far, the situation cannot be described as a volatile one, for most of the landsgrafs consider themselves to be hereditary Foerdewaith, even if they are angered by their brethren nobles to the west.

A few nobles, predominantly barons but also a few landsgrafs, have begun to call their heritage "Fairdevaine" rather than "Foerdewaith," reflecting the local Aachenland dialect of the Westerling common speech. These are the nobles to watch the most closely, for if the nobility of Aachen begins to sever itself from the bloodlines of the Kingdom of Foere, rebellion is nigh. At the moment, though, most of the nobles perceive the situation as more of a family squabble among Foerdewaith lords in the same empire, not as a dispute between two different

nationalities. In short, lines are being drawn, but they are still faint. The pot simmers, but the heat remains low.

Aixe

(ECKS, or ah-YEEKS-uh)

The "Gateway to Foere," a well-known city of the Aachenlands

N small city
Government autocracy
Population 8600 (7650 humans; 570 hill dwarves; 380 halflings)
Notable NPCs
 Bertolde Kavre, Mayor-Palatine of Aixe, Baron of Tharhold and Kavredal (N male human **Ftr10**)
 Raoul Pollsgraf, Regional Governor of Aixe, Baron of Poll (LN male human **Ftr7**)
 Benidoc Justician, High Priest of Thyr (LG male human **Clr9** of Thyr)
 Umber Tome, High Priest of Belon the Wise (N male human **Clr9** of Belon)
 Aorundus the Arcane (N male human **Wiz11**)
 Octo of Peridor, Landsgraf (not resident) (N male human **Ftr6**)
Maximum Clerical Spell Level Good 5, Neutral 5, Evil 5 (hidden)
Purchase Maximum/Month 16,000gp

Appearance

The city of Aixe is a pleasant sight, its walls whitewashed and its towers fluttering with colorful banners, surrounded by a lake-fed moat 100ft across. Drawbridges lead over the moats to the city gates, each of which is crowned by a painted portcullis-and-key symbol. On the far side of the moat from the city, buildings are clustered near the drawbridges like small villages outside the city walls.

Aixe in General

The fortified city of Aixe describes itself as the "Gateway of Foere," and the rather self-important title has some basis in fact, for it is within the walls of Aixe that the high road from Foere branches into the province's three main highroads: the Cross Cut, the Estuary Road, and the Royal Vermis Road. Most of the province's trade with Foere passes through the gates of Aixe going one way or another.

As described, all four of the entrance gates have small "outer cities" on the far side of the drawbridges, where buildings have been built to avoid the crowding inside the walls. And within the walls, it is indeed crowded. Half-timber buildings press close against narrow, twisting streets, overshadowing them in many cases with built-out balconies. Caravans and travelers passing through the city must force their way through a pressing crowd of local wagons and citizens. To avoid crowding, many arriving caravans are admitted through the city in the early hours of the morning, beginning their journeys before dawn breaks and the city wakes to life.

The crossroad where the four high roads divide toward their respective city gates is a vast market fronted by the Court of the Governor of Aixe and the Hall of the Mayor-Palatine, as well as the city's Guildhall. The city guilds are not as powerful as they are in free cities, for they are ultimately subject to laws and decrees of the Lord-Governor in Vermis. Rather than having much political power in the city, they serve mainly to ensure that the city's products are of high quality, and that citizens are not cheated. However, there is a constant drumbeat from the guildmasters that Aixe should seek the status of a chartered city under its own government. The Overkings have thus far utterly forbidden the Lord-Governors from granting such a charter, so the efforts of the guilds have had little effect.

Government

As with the other major cities of Aachen, the area within the walls is ruled by a Mayor-Palatine who reports directly to the Lord-Governor, over the head of the Regional Governor. Just outside the wall, the situation is a bit complex. The surrounding roads (and the city's courts) are maintained by the Regional Governor of Aixe. However, the lands off the roads are part of the feudal system, held by the Landsgraf of Peridor. The Peridors maintain two "merchant camps" outside the city walls, wooden-walled palisades where caravans can assemble without trying to do so in the chaotic, crowded streets of the city.

History

Aixe is an old city dating back to the Hyperborean era, although it has long outgrown the small area originally enclosed by the Hyperborean walls (now torn down). Its prosperity from trade allowed it to build new walls over a century ago, but the city has again outgrown them and relies upon the open grounds beyond the city to provide needed space for new housing and for the assembly of caravans.

Originally, the Landsgraf of Peridor denied the city any taxes on the lucrative business of providing open space to caravans, but some years ago the Mayor-Palatine's guardsmen hauled the current Landsgraf's father from his residence in the city, declared him guilty within the hour, and summarily beheaded him in the city center, placing his head on a pike outside the merchant camp. The city then sent an apologetic letter to the Lord-Governor claiming that the entire affair had been a case of mistaken identity, they had thought the man was a pig thief named Boden. In order to prevent future cases of mistaken identity, the Peridors now pay the city a share of their profits.

Boden Bristleback, the actual pig thief, was never captured. He escaped the city, despite being grievously wounded, and fled to the Alder Zerin Forest, where his pursuers were attacked by a large pack of feral pigs. Routed by the porcine assault, the guardsmen were forced to retreat back to the city in disarray: empty-handed, wounded, and deeply embarrassed. The Mayor-Palatine died later in a mysterious hunting accident near the Peridor lands, and the Peridor family sent a large basket of overripe pomegranates to the city as a token of their respect.

As far as visitors are concerned, the city of Aixe is pleasantly friendly to foreigners. An entry toll is collected by the Governor's guards at the city gate, a small fee of 1sp per non-citizen entering the city, and since merchants absorb the city's transaction taxes, visitors who wish to sell gems or other treasure in the city can do so at good prices.

Nearby Adventures

A knight by the name of Jolien Vocard has been assigned by his baron to look into a small difficulty in one of the hamlets on the far reach of the baron's territory, a place twenty miles from Aixe, called Cledioun Par. Sir Jolien prefers not to leave the city at this time, being greatly enamored of a young lady who has several suitors. Rather than risk his chances with the lady, Sir Jolien wants to hire a few stalwart souls to look into the hamlet's problems on his behalf. He will pay an acceptable upfront sum of money unless the characters look disreputable, in which case he will pay half upfront and half upon their successful return. He has no idea what the hamlet's problem is, but he assumes it is something on the order of a rampaging bear or a few goblins.

Cledioun Par has a population of 20 peasants, all from two families that work together, the Cledis and the Pars. They have a square of six ramshackle stone buildings arranged to form a protective courtyard in the center. The leaders of the two families are Tourmic Par and Jen Cledi. When the characters arrive, Tourmic and Jen explain, with considerable embarrassment, that a pack of 6 hoar foxes has dug burrows in the nearby woods, and have been stealing chickens. One of the family members was badly wounded by the breath of one of the foxes, and they decided to send a petition to the baron for help.

The hoar foxes are in a nearby wood. Finding the burrow takes 1d6 hours, but it is more time-consuming than actually difficult. However, the characters face a second danger while they are searching through the woods, for some **cobra flowers** have taken root in the area as well. The characters have a 25% chance per hour spent searching, of encountering one of the cobra flowers before they find the hoar fox burrows.

The hoar fox burrows have five different exits, and unless the characters split up to guard different exits, the hoar foxes leave their lair to defend it from the outside while the characters gather around whichever burrow-exit they found. The foxes try to attack simultaneously and attempt to retreat from the woods entirely if they suffer losses. If the foxes retreat from the combat, they do not return to the woods, and the characters' mission is a success. If the characters manage to kill any of the foxes without damaging the pelts, these can be sold in Aixe for an extremely good price.

Cobra Flower: AC 11; **HP** 51 (6d10+18); **Spd** 5ft; **Melee** bite (+5, 10ft, 1d10+3 piercing plus 1d8 acid and grapple; **SA** grapple (bite hits automatically); **Immune** fright, exhaustion, psychic, stun, unconsciousness; **Vulnerable** necrotic; **Str** +3, **Dex** +1, **Con** +3 (+5), **Int** −5, **Wis** +1, **Cha** −1; **Senses** tremorsense 30ft; **AL** U; **CR** 2; **XP** 450. (*Fifth Edition Foes* 63)

Hoar Fox (6): AC 14; **HP** 26 (4d6+8); **Spd** 40ft; **Melee** bite (+5, 1d8+3 piercing); **SA** cold breath (recharge 5-6, 30ft, 2d8 cold, DC 13 Dex half); **Immune** cold; **Vulnerable** fire; **Str** +0, **Dex** +3, **Con** +2, **Int** −4, **Wis** +1, **Cha** +0; **Skills** Perception +3, Stealth +5; **Senses** darkvision 60ft; **Traits** winter hunter (in snow, tactical advantage on Perception and Stealth); **AL** U; **CR** 1; **XP** 200. (*Fifth Edition Foes* 145)

Amrinbridge Fortress

An outpost of Bard's Gate, guarding a bridge and collecting tolls

LN village/fortress
Government overlord (military commander)
Population 252 (192 humans, 41 half-elves, 12 hill dwarves, 7 high elves)
Notable NPCs
　Commander Borniss Weljerand (LN male human **Ftr8**
　Chaplain Morgana Mirley (LN female human **Clr4** of Vanitthu)
Maximum Clerical Spell Level Good —, Neutral 2, Evil —
Purchase Maximum/Month 2000gp

Appearance

The Great Bridge is a huge, fortified structure that spans the Great Amrin River. On the north side is a keep with an outer bailey, well-patrolled by soldiers wearing the livery of the city of Bard's Gate.

Description

Amrinbridge Fortress is located on the north side of the Amrin River at the Great Bridge, and maintains the gatehouse on the south side of the bridge as well. It is an outpost of the Bard's Gate military, and also contains the customs-house that charges taxes on traffic heading across the bridge. The fortress itself is a simple keep, with an outer bailey. A few civilians work in the keep, but virtually all the population is either Bard's Gate soldiery or Bard's Gate customs officials. There is no inn at the fortress, although anyone with official business here is given a room in the fortress itself.

The Keep houses a small garrison of Waymark cavalry (50) and an attachment of well-mounted couriers (20). The keep's garrison commander, Borniss Weljerand, is instructed to relay any important news or rumors by courier as quickly as possible to Bard's Gate. The officials of the customs-house are non-military; they collect taxes on traffic crossing the bridge in both directions, but northward travelers are charged an exorbitant toll, a punitive (and fairly lucrative) response to the high tariffs Aachen Province charges for travel along the Royal Vermis Road.

The high tolls charged for northward travel are a source of anger to the Aachenlander peasants living nearby, and they refer to Amrinbridge Fortress as "The Trollfort."

Becqueril
(BEK-er-il)

A baronial capital similar to hundreds of others

NG village
Government overlord
Population 172 (172 humans)
Notable NPCs
  Baron Jauntir of Becqueril (NG male human **Ftr9**)
  Goodman Clothiper, innkeeper of the Cat and Mouse (LG male human **Ftr2**)
  Friar Maulc (LN male human **Clr4** of Telophus)
Maximum Clerical Spell Level Good —, Neutral 2, Evil —
Purchase Maximum/Month 2000gp

Appearance

A small, stone keep atop a low hill overlooks a small village built directly below it. A fast-flowing stream runs nearby, past a wooden waterwheel mill, and a few more farmhouses and barns are visible across the fields. The houses of the village are mostly half-timber and plaster, with steeply sloped rooftops. One of these buildings is larger than the rest, and has a tavern sign hanging over the door.

Description

Becqueril is a village built around the ancestral castle of Baron Jauntir of Becqueril, whose domain extends approximately five miles in all directions from the castle. There are 15 knightly manor houses in the barony, and two other villages about the same size as Becqueril: the village of Oton and the village of Cthayr. The rest of the barony's population is scattered throughout the area in isolated hamlets.

Not Much to See

Overall, the village of Becqueril is a pleasant, rustic place, with a tavern, the Cat and Mouse, which rents three sleeping-rooms above the drinking hall. A water-driven mill, a smithy, and a leatherworker are the only real industry here, and visitors are a sensational break from the ordinary, everyday life of a rustic community.

Adventure

Jauntir's adult son and heir, Martin of Becqueril, has gone missing. The last time he was seen was in the Town of Elet, on his way to hunt with three of Jauntir's courtiers in the Ghostwind Pass south of the town. Jauntir is willing to pay a substantial reward to anyone who can find and return his son. For more information about Jauntir's missing heir, see *Perils of Ghostwind Pass* in **Quests of Doom Volume 2** by **Necromancer Games**.

Cretian Mountains

See **Chapter 7: March of Mountains**, *Cretian Mountains*

Cross Cut Road

A poorly constructed high road connecting Aachen and Eastreach Provinces

Appearance

This is certainly a road, but not a very good one. It is paved with stone, but with sections visible where the stones have buckled to form tilted surfaces and wide depressions in the road. It heads off into the countryside with no mile markers, and no significant verge between the trees and the road. Unlike most of the older high roads, the Cross Cut is not very straight; it follows terrain lines and forest edges, winding along the path of least resistance through the countryside.

A Bit of History

The Cross Cut Road began as little more than a long cart trail used by traders to get from Carterscroft in Eastreach Province to the city of Aixe without paying road taxes for use of the southern part of the Royal Vermis Road. The Cross Cut also allowed them to shave a tremendous number of miles off the journey, despite the roughness of the trail.

In the face of lost tax revenues, the Lord-Governor of Vermis eventually decreed the improvement of the trail into a decent road, to be maintained and taxed by the Regional Governors of Aixe, Tremond, and Sauv Lar. However, the people of Aachen soon discovered that when it came to the task of building a 300-mile road, they were not the equals of the ancient Hyperboreans, either in organization or expertise. The road has been a work in progress for almost two centuries, with a mix of dirt tracks interspersed with lengths of true, stone-paved road. At the point called "Glett's Error," two road engineers built to the edges of their adjoining survey maps, only to discover that one of the maps was off by a full four miles, necessitating a sudden 90-degree turn in the road, and a four-mile spur to connect the two sections.

Encounters

Encounter Chance: Make one encounter check in the morning, one in the afternoon, and one at night.
Risk Level: All encounters outside the city's one-hex radius are at the Medium-Risk level. Inside the one-hex radius around Aixe (and Carterscroft), there is an additional automatic encounter check in the surrounding hex and the city's hex. All encounters in the radius of these cities are at the Low-Risk level.

01–10	No Encounter
11–70	Mundane Encounter
71–00	Dangerous Encounter

Mundane Encounters: Cross Cut Road

1d100	Encounter
01–02	Annoyance (Encounter #3)
03–04	Baron and Retinue (Encounter #8)
05	Bears (Encounter #11)
06–12	Caravan (Provincial) (Encounter #15)

1d100	Encounter
13–14	Cleric (Encounter #19)
15	Druid (Encounter #31)
16–17	Elf (Encounter #34)
18–34	Farmer (Encounter #36)
35–42	Foot Patrol (Encounter #37)
43–52	Herder (Encounter #51)
53–57	Heretic (Encounter #52)
58	High Noble (Encounter #53)
59	Kenckoo Vagrant (Encounter #55)
60–64	Knight and Retinue (Encounter #56)
65–66	Leper (Encounter #60)
67–70	Minstrel (Encounter #65)
71–74	Mounted Patrol (Encounter #67)
75–76	Outlaw (Encounter #71)
77–79	Peasant (Encounter #74)
80–82	Penitent (Encounter #76)
83–85	Pilgrim (Encounter #78)
86–87	Prisoner (Encounter #79)
88–89	Small Trader (halfling) (Encounter #86)
90–93	Small Trader (human) (Encounter #85)
94–96	Stag (Encounter #87)
97	Wandering Refugee (Encounter #98)
98	Wild Horse or Pony (Encounter #103)
99–00	Wolf (Encounter #106)

Dangerous Encounters: Cross Cut Road

1d100	Encounter
01–04	Ankheg (Encounter #2)
05–06	Ant (Encounter #4)
07–21	Bandit (Encounter #7)
22	Basilisk (Encounter #9)
23	Blood Hawk (Encounter #12)
24–26	Bugbear (Encounter #13)
27	Bulette (Encounter #14)
28–29	Cockatrice (Encounter #21)
30–34	Dragon A (Encounter #27)
35–37	Giant, Hill (Encounter #41)
38–47	Gnoll (Encounter #43)
48–53	Goblins, Roaming (Encounter #45)
54–56	Lycanthrope (Encounter #59)
57–61	Manticore (Encounter #63)
62–66	Ogre (Encounter #69)
67–72	Owlbear (Encounter #72)
73–74	Robber Knight (Encounter #80)
75–77	Stirge (Encounter #88)
78	Tangtal (Encounter #89)
79–85	Tiger (Encounter #90)

1d100	Encounter
86–88	Troll (Encounter #92)
89–90	Unicorn (Encounter #93)
91	Undead A (Encounter #94)
92–93	Wasp, Giant (Encounter #99)
94–95	Weasel, Giant (Encounter #100)
96–00	Wyvern (Encounter #108)

Curgantium, Ruins of
(kur-GAN-tee-um)

Mysterious Hyperborean ruins, unfortunately located just off the edge of the map

The ruins of Curgantium are located just off the map of the Borderland Provinces, slightly to the southwest of Vermis. Once the great capital of the Hyperborean Empire, it is now a vast desolation of broken stone, overgrown with strange flowers and long grasses. The history of the ruins date back a thousand years to when the city was destroyed in the explosion of the Tower of Oerson, which housed the imperial throne. The inconceivable power of the blast and the subsequent conflagration utterly eradicated the city, giving rise to raging wildfires that devoured their way across the dry plains, killing countless more by flame and famine.

Although the ruins of Curgantium fall slightly beyond Aachen's borders, they are well known to all as a cursed place and are given a wide berth by all. Rivermen passing down the Great Amrin past the ancient stone wharves of the city spit and cross their fingers to ward off bad luck. Many swear that the river waters around Curgantium sometimes run red as blood or as black as night. No boat docks there even in the most inclement weather.

It is unknown to the world at large that the sewers beneath Curgantium are still intact, and serve as the headquarters for the continent-spanning master thieves' guild of vampires known as the Underguild. Such matters are given more detail in the adventure *Sewers of the Underguild* in the **Necromancer Games** publication **Quests of Doom Volume 1.**

Dlante
(deLANT)

A trade city with quaint customs regarding hats

N large town
Government overlord
Population 5329 (5223 humans; 106 halflings)
Notable NPCs
    Regional Governor Baroness Azile de Palaintre (N female human **noble**)
    Bishop Lantaster (N male human **Clr9** of Sefagreth)
    High Priestess Phalantis Rai (N female human **Clr9** of Zadastha)
    Father Loalde (LG male human **Clr7** of Thyr)
    Balyondis (N male human **Wiz12**)
Maximum Clerical Spell Level Good 4, Neutral 5, Evil 3 (hidden)
Purchase Maximum/Month 8,000gp

Appearance

After a few milestones along the road indicating distances to a place called Dlante, the town comes into view. Dlante is a town surrounded by white-painted stone walls, with five pointed towers, their conical roofs painted a bright red. Banners with a white diamond on a red background fly from the tower rooftops. In addition to the five towers, a large keep forms part of the town wall. Dlante is surrounded by a moat, and the gates can be reached only across a wide causeway over the moat. The causeway ends 10ft short of the gates; a stout wooden drawbridge spans the gap.

Governance

Dlante is the seat of the Governor of the Region of Dlante, which reaches to the border of Eastreach Province 50 miles to the East along the Wain Road. The Regional Governor is Azile de Palaintre, a noblewoman of Foere appointed to her post by the Overking's court in the city of Courghais. She is ill-tempered and rude to those of lower social status, but she has the redeeming quality of being less rapacious than any of the other regional governors in Aachen Province. Certainly she benefits greatly from local taxes and from her share of judicial bribery, but she keeps these sources of income to a modest sum rather than amassing whatever she can get. As a result, Dlante has managed to keep itself in good condition despite the slow decline of trade on the Wain Road. This section of the road is relatively well-patrolled, the milestones are maintained, and roadside inns are careful not to charge exorbitant prices to travelers. Dlante is well-regarded by the caravan merchants of Bard's Gate, and they always make stopovers here to re-provision and rest their horses.

The Dlanteans

The townsfolk of Dlante are universally heavyset, and the wealthiest of them have a definite tendency toward corpulence. By custom, the town citizens wear blue cylindrical hats with a very slight taper, essentially a fez without a tassel. The higher a citizen's social status, the taller the fez. Rich merchants strut around town in hats more than a foot tall, spangled with semiprecious stones and decorated with ostrich feathers, sometimes trimmed with blue-dyed fur. Ordinary laborers wear a modest fez decorated with a guild badge or a decorative copper button.

Visitors and Hats

Visitors to the city are cautioned at the gates not to wear blue hats, for this privilege is reserved to the citizens. However, the social status of visitors is also defined by the height of a fez-like hat and the splendidness of its decoration, as long as the hat is some color other than blue. It is quite a sight when a caravan from Bard's Gate arrives here, as everyone in the caravan, from cattle drovers to rich merchants, produces a red or green fez and dons it before proceeding through the city gates.

Regardless of a visitor's social status in the outside world, they find that the citizens of Dlante measure their guests by the hat. Those who wear tall, splendid hats are treated with respect; those in ordinary fezzes are treated cordially; and hatless individuals are treated as lowly peasants. Fortunately, a variety of fezzes is available to rent near the city gates, although all of them are fairly drab and short (and are not blue). The high-crowned, decorated fezzes of the upper classes are not rented, although they can be purchased in several haberdasheries throughout the city.

Interesting Places

Although Dlante is a small city, it offers temples to those who would worship, goods for those who would trade, and products for those who would buy.

Temple of Sefagreth

The god of cities and trade possesses the most significant of Dlante's temples. Priests assigned to the temple are not granted citizenship, so most of them wear medium-sized yellow fezzes with the god's holy symbol embroidered on the front. The temple is a circle of buildings around a small courtyard where the city's gem-traders and moneylenders congregate during the daytime hours to conduct business.

Temple of Zadastha

The temple of the goddess of love is Dlante's other major temple, although it is smaller than Sefagreth's fane. Virtually all of the priestesses are originally from Dlante, and visiting priestesses are granted honorary citizenship for the duration of their stay, so all of Zadasha's priestesses wear the blue fez of a citizen. The temple is a walled courtyard with three delicate towers. One tower is for the secret rites of the goddess, one is for the priests and priestesses, and the third contains a number of private trysting rooms where secret lovers can meet away from the prying eyes of other citizens (and sometimes, their actual spouses). All the citizens know that the temple has three tunnels leading to it from other nearby buildings that are used by the Zadasthan priestesses to smuggle couples into the temple unseen.

Unless the priestesses of Zadastha are particularly entranced by a tale of love, which does happen frequently, the rooms in the trysting tower are usually reserved for wealthier couples who can make substantial contributions to the temple.

Street of Sumptuaries

The Street of Sumptuaries is a broad avenue that runs from the gates to the city center. It is Dlante's main market, lined with booths, shops, carts, bales, and cargo. Most of the wares sold in the street are either foodstuffs or caravan cargo; more specialized goods are sold in the shops. Dlante produces excellent brandies and cordials, in addition to high-quality marionettes, beautifully tinted paper, and highly decorated cloth items from elaborate surcoats to fabulous (and very expensive) pavilion tents suitable for all strata of the nobility.

Mystery of the Secret Contraption

The Guild of Embroiderers is the city's most-prominent organization, and the art of embroidery is heavily regulated here. Many of the city's workers are employed by the guild in some capacity or other in the process, and good embroiderers are well paid. In addition to hand embroidery, there are two "contraptions" owned by the guild, large wooden machines that allow fast but slightly inaccurate embroidery of large surfaces of cloth. The "contraption embroidery" is generally sold to merchants traveling far from the city, and is considered a far inferior product to the hand embroidery prized by the guild and sold for much higher prices, usually by merchants on their way to Vermis or Bard's Gate. Recently, word came from Vermis that a large quantity of supposedly hand-embroidered cloth was actually contraption embroidery pawned off by some merchant in Dlante onto an unsuspecting buyer. The Guild of Embroiderers is in a quiet furor about this, suspecting that there might be an illicit embroidery contraption operating somewhere in the city walls. They might definitely engage a group of outsiders to track down the criminal operation, knowing that any citizen knowing of such a thing would have reported it. They offer a reward for finding the source of the illicit embroidery, and a large additional bonus if the contraption is recovered undamaged, for they would like to have a third one.

The secret embroidery contraption does indeed exist in the cellar of one of the city's cloth warehouses. The warehouse, and the secret operation, are run by a merchant named Giles Wallen. The contraption-embroidered cloth is smuggled out of the city by agents of the Wheelwrights Guild of Bard's Gate, and generally sold in Vermis without mentioning that the embroidery comes from Dlante; the Wheelwrights are usually careful to not leave a trail behind them. However, two cargoes of embroidery were accidentally switched while they were being loaded into caravans for departure, and the buyer of some handmade embroidery ended up with several bolts of the illicit contraption embroidery instead. The difference would not ordinarily have been spotted in the markets of Vermis except for the fact that the merchant advertised his wares as hand-embroidery from Dlante, which several of the Vermisian merchants could immediately spot as untrue. The merchant was hanged as a fraud, and the city of Vermis sent a strongly worded letter to the Guild of Embroiderers in Dlante about the episode.

If the characters investigate the situation, they might uncover or realize several things:

First, they might learn that one of the embroidering contraptions requires a source of power. At the guildhall, the two legal contraptions both run on wind power. If the characters comb through the city looking for windmills in the wrong places, they most likely find that Giles Wallen's warehouse has an inexplicable windmill built onto the top of it.

Secondly, they might inquire whether anyone who might have known how to build a contraption has disappeared recently. The answer is that no one has disappeared under suspicious circumstances. The only two guildsmen who have died recently drowned a year ago in a fishing accident in a lake to the south of the city near a hamlet called Surlywood. The peasants of Surlywood did indeed find the blue-hatted bodies of two skinny fishermen in the lake, and buried them, sending the hats back to the Embroiderers' Guild (based on the badges on the hats). The Guild agreed that the hats belonged to their missing guildmembers, and mourned the loss. The characters might exhume the bodies, or even take note that "skinny" is not an adjective ordinarily applied to guildsmen of Dlante. The only major citizen of Dlante who was away during that time, other than on a known caravan trip, was Giles Wallen.

Wallen enslaved the two Guildsmen, and still keeps them in his deep cellar with the contraption. He is assisted by three Vermisians, all of them hired by the Wheelwrights Guild, whom he passes off as "assistants." Each of them is a fighter of 5th level, so a fight in Wallen's cellar could turn dangerous.

Elet

(EL-et)

An ordinary, small, roadside town at the base of a strategic mountain pass into the Yolbiac Vale

N small town
Government overlord
Population 1540 (1434 humans; 73 hill dwarves; 33 halflings)
Notable NPCs
Mayor Alisce Elevard (LN female human **Wiz9**)
Montorioc Yeoman (LN male human **Clr6** of Telophus)
Faliara Wanderer (N female human **Clr6** of Pan)
Father Longbeard (grove outside town) (N male human **Drd8**)
Jorimander (N male human **Wiz9**)
Maximum Clerical Spell Level Good —, Neutral 4, Evil —
Purchase Maximum/Month 4000gp

Appearance

The Estuary Road winds through the foothills of the Cretian Mountains just to the south, and there is a bite to the wind as it blows off the peaks. According to a milestone cracked by repeated freezing and thawing, travelers are arriving at the town of Elet. It looks like a tumble of stones from a distance, but as they get closer, they see that the ruined appearance is just an illusion caused by the town's uneven, badly weathered wall, and the jumble of slate roofs visible within. Several wooden signs are posted at the battle-scarred city gates.

The signs read:

- Welcome to Elet!
- Beggars get one day, three meals, and a polite farewell
- Best Prices for travelers at the Knave-on-a-Cask
- Stay at the Dancing Dairymaid, no fleas
- Lycanthropes will be burned at the stake, no exceptions.
- Druids welcomed.

Description

Elet is a small, stone-walled town on the Estuary Road, roughly halfway between Aixe and Eastgate. It lies at the base of the Ghostwind Pass into the Yolbiac Vale, a dangerous crossing utterly impassable due to snow and terrifying winds during at least two months of the year. Trade with the strange valefolk on the far side of the mountain pass is sporadic at best, and most of Elet's wealth (such as it is) comes from travelers on the Estuary Road.

The town has a number of citizens who are of a local druidic faith, and the Ghostwind Pass contains three notable druidic holy sites: Olir Orphais, Ambioc Tor, and Cenaur Yltair. These are seldom visited by ordinary folk, even on pilgrimages, but Elet sees traveling druids from time to time on their way to the Pass to pay respect to one or another of these sites.

The town mayor is appointed by the Landsgraf, who lives in Castle Krevin, five miles from the town itself. The current Landsgraf is Karlat of Krevin (LN male human **Ftr9**).

History

The town is relatively insignificant other than for its strategic location at the base of the pass into the Yolbiac Vale; it is no larger than several other towns along the Estuary Road. It does have the unusual distinction of having been entirely legally female for a period of two months, five years in the past, as the result of an administrative dispute concerning magic. Mayor Alyn Elevard, a wizard of some note, magically transformed himself into a woman, ordering the alteration of all the town records to reflect her femininity and the new name of Alisce. When a small contingent of the town's merchants expressed their displeasure at the situation, the mayor responded by administratively ordering a change in all birth and tax registries of the town's entire male population into the female gender, throwing several wills and property deeds into ambiguity. Threatened by this legal siege, faced with the fact that most of the town's ordinary inhabitants treated the whole thing as a diverting sort of festival, and eyeing several new gallows being installed near the town gates, the protestors soon declared their effusive support for the mayor, her policies, and the transformation, accompanied by the payment of 100 bushels of grain to the mayor's personal accounts. Thus, after a brief two months of Elet's entirely-female legal status, the administrative records were returned to their normal state, the gallows were taken down, and events continued as normal, with Alisce's political power considerably strengthened by the brief confrontation. Everyone enjoys telling the story, but, after all, the town is close to the Yolbiac Vale. Stranger things have happened.

Accomodations

Elet has three inns, and the decline in trade has pushed them into fierce competition with each other. The Knave-on-a-Cask, the Dancing Dairymaid, and the Pork Pie all have bargain prices for rooms and food unless a large caravan is in town (10% chance).

More details about the Ghostwind Pass itself are available in *Perils of Ghostwind Pass*, an adventure in **Quests of Doom Volume 2** by **Necromancer Games**. If you do not have access to the book, the Ghostwind may be treated as an ordinary but brutal mountain pass.

Estuary Road
(Aachenland Portion)

The high road from Aixe to Eastgate, slowly decaying from lack of commerce

Appearance

This is a well-built stone road. It seems to be suffering a bit from neglect, for small trees and long grasses are beginning to take over the verge on either side of the thoroughfare, but not enough to allow bandits to leap out from heavy undergrowth.

General Description

The Estuary Road connects Aixe to Eastgate, passing through the town of Elet and several other small towns along the way. The road is guarded by patrols of the Governors of Aixe, Tremond, and Basivaine as it passes through their jurisdictions, but such patrols have been diminishing in size and frequency over the years. Several once-thriving fortified inns along the road now lie abandoned, so travelers should expect to sleep under the stars for a few nights of any journey between Aixe and Eastgate. Once the Estuary Road reaches the crossroad with the Wain Road and eastward, it enters the domains of Eastgate, and is much more reliably patrolled by the Waymark cavalry stationed in that city.

Encounters

Encounter Chance: Make one encounter check in the morning, one in the afternoon, and one at night.

Risk Level: All encounters outside a city's one-hex radius are at the Medium-Risk level. Inside the one-hex radius around Aixe, there is an additional automatic encounter check in the surrounding hex and the city's hex. All encounters in the radius of the city are at the Low-Risk level.

01–25	No Encounter
26–65	Mundane Encounter
66–00	Dangerous Encounter

Mundane Encounters: Estuary Road

1d100	Encounter
01–02	Annoyance (Encounter #3)
03–04	Baron and Retinue (Encounter #8)
05–07	Bear (Encounter #11)
08	Caravan (Bard's Gate) (Encounter #15)
09–12	Caravan (Provincial) (Encounter #16)
13–14	Cleric (Encounter #19)
15	Druid (Encounter #31)
16–18	Elf (Encounter #34)
19–30	Farmer (Encounter #36)
31–36	Foot Patrol (Encounter #37)
37–45	Herder (Encounter #51)
46–51	Heretic (Encounter #52)
52	High Noble (Encounter #53)
53–54	Kenckoo Vagrant (Encounter #55)

1d100	Encounter
55–59	Knight and Retinue (Encounter #56)
60–61	Leper (Encounter #60)
62–65	Minstrel (Encounter #65)
66–70	Mounted Patrol (Encounter #67)
71–74	Outlaw (Encounter #71)
75–77	Peasant (Encounter #74)
78–79	Penitent (Encounter #76)
80–81	Prisoner (Encounter #79)
82	Small Trader (dwarf) (Encounter #86)
83–85	Small Trader (human) (Encounter #85)
86–90	Stag (Encounter #87)
91–96	Wandering Refugee (Encounter #98)
97–00	Wolf (Encounter #106)

Dangerous Encounters: Estuary Road

1d100	Encounter
01	Ankheg (Encounter #2)
02–21	Bandit (Encounter #7)
22	Basilisk (Encounter #9)
23–27	Blood Hawk (Encounter #12)
28	Corpse Rook (Encounter #22)
29–33	Dragon A (Encounter #27)
34	Drake, Fire (Encounter #30)
35–36	Eagle, Giant (Encounter #33)
37	Ettin (Encounter #35)
38–40	Giant, Hill (Encounter #41)
41–42	Giant, Stone (Encounter #42)
43–47	Goblin Raider (Encounter #44) if near mountains, otherwise Goblin, Roaming (Encounter #45)
48–50	Griffon (Encounter #47) near Cretian Mountains only, otherwise Owlbears (Encounter #71)
51–55	Harpy (Encounter #50)
56–58	Korred (Encounter #58) near Cretian mountains only, otherwise Ankheg (Encounter #2)
59–60	Lycanthrope (Encounter #61)
61–65	Manticore (Encounter #63)
66–67	Ogre (Encounter #69)
68	Ogre Mage (Encounter #70)
69	Peryton (Encounter #77) near Cretian Mountains only, otherwise Tiger (Encounter #90)
70–73	Robber Knight (Encounter #80)
74–75	Roc (Encounter #81)
76	Satyr (Encounter #82) near Cretian Mountains only, otherwise Tiger (Encounter #90)
77–78	Stirge (Encounter #88)
79	Tiger (Encounter #90)
80–81	Troll (Encounter #92)

1d100	Encounter
82–83	Undead A (Encounter #94)
84–87	Vulchling (Encounter #97)
88–89	Wasp, Giant (Encounter #99)
90–91	Werewolf (Encounter #101) near Cretian Mountains only, otherwise Centaur (Encounter #17)
92–93	Witherstench (Encounter #104)
94–95	Wolverine, Giant (Encounter #105)
96	Wizard (Encounter #107)
97–00	Wyvern (Encounter #108)

Great Bridge

Ancient Hyperborean bridge over the Amrin River, with fortresses on each bank

Appearance

A bridge built on massive stone pillars crosses the wide Amrin River here. Fortresses stand on the north and south banks, and the two entrances to the bridge are like small castles themselves. The fortress on the south bank flies the flag of Aachen Province, while the bridge and the castle on the north bank both fly the banner of Bard's Gate.

History

The massive construction known as the Great Bridge was built by an early Hyperborean imperator to accommodate the movement of the Legions northward to battle the Huns, who were invading at that time through the passes in the Stoneheart Mountains. The bridge is made of stone, with 60ft castle towers flanking either end. It is 50ft wide, 370ft long, and rises to a height of 75ft above the river. Its massive supports are wide enough to easily allow barge traffic to pass beneath the 75ft height, and barge traffic is very frequent since it is the preferred method for merchants wishing to bring cargo south to Eastgate. The Great Bridge has been maintained by Bard's Gate since the rise of that city, and remains in excellent repair.

Two fortresses stand on the north and south banks of the bridge. To the north is Amrinbridge Fortress, an outpost of Bard's Gate. On the south bank stands the Gretspaan Citadel, Foere's most distant possession on the Royal Vermis Road, the far edge of the Overking's empire.

Amrinbridge Fortress and the Gretspaan Citadel are described separately.

Gretspaan Citadel

(GRET-spahn)

Ragged edge of the Foerdewaith empire

N small town
Government overlord
Population 1167 (926 humans; 102 halflings; 79 half-elves; 60 hill dwarves)
Notable NPCs
Lord Lucard Moutond, Citadel Commander (LN male human **Ftr8**)
Baron Auricard, Regional Governor of Gretspaan (N male human **noble**)
Battle-Chaplain Bajirad Lasalte (LN male human **Clr7** of Vanitthu)
Cassandre Velt (N female human **Clr6** of Belon the Wise
Ualmagond (LG male human **Wiz9**)
Maximum Clerical Spell Level Good —, Neutral 4, Evil —
Purchase Maximum/Month 4000gp

Appearance

This is a small town dominated by a large citadel-fortress located directly beside the Royal Vermis Road where it heads toward the Great Bridge, visible in the distance. The Citadel has a separate drum tower on the far side of the road, and a fortified bridge that arches across to link the citadel to this detached tower, allowing archers to fire down onto the road if need be. Both the citadel and the town walls are well-maintained, and the place bustles with the ordinary activities of a rural town. The flag of Aachen Province, a spotted yellow tiger on a green field, flies over both the citadel and the town.

A small green canopy is set up by the side of the road where it passes the town. Some clerks sit at a wooden table underneath the canopy's shade, accompanied by two bored-looking guardsmen wearing yellow and green surcoats with the spotted tiger.

Description

On the south bank of the Great Amrin River, just within the border of Aachen Province, stands the fortified citadel of Gretspaan, seat of the Regional Governor of Gretspaan. The citadel serves as a strong border fortress, and also quarters the various customs officials who collect their own tariffs on merchants entering the Province from Bard's Gate. These tariffs are extremely high, for the court of Courghais in Foere has authorized the Lord-Governor to charge a hefty surtax on Bard's Gate caravans, over and above the ordinary tariffs levied on citizens of Foere for the use of royal roads. The total population of Gretspaan, between soldiers, customs officials, and peasant staff, is approximately 1100.

Travelers are welcomed into the town, but are not permitted in the citadel unless they have business with the Regional Governor or the garrison. The temples of Belon and Vanitthu are located in the town, along with other small temples to Freya, Sefagreth, and Thyr.

Mons Terminus

See **Chapter 7: March of Mountains**, *Mons Terminus*

Nine Sisters

A monument of elven history

As Seen from the Road

The Nine Sisters are giant stone statues on a mountainside, visible from the road but difficult to reach. As one might expect from the name, there are nine of them, each depicting a female figure. The figures are elven, although this is not apparent from a distance since they are quite worn by many centuries of weathering. The statues are pre-Hyperborean, dating back to the time of the Great Akadian Forest when it lapped like a green tide against the mountains here.

This spot is considered a historical monument by the local high elves, although it is not a holy site or sacred ground.

Griffon Nest

A nest of **6 griffons** shelters mid-way up the cliff behind and above the statues, not visible even from the statues themselves. It is on a ledge backed up from the cliff edge, sheltered from weather by a stand of tall fir trees and the surrounding rock faces. The griffons do not attack elves unless they are attacked, but swoop down upon anyone else, even those accompanied by elves.

Griffon (6): AC 12; **HP** 59 (7d10+21); **Spd** 30ft, fly 80ft; **Melee** beak (+6, 1d8+4 piercing), claws (+6, 2d6+4 slashing); **SA** multiattack (beak, claws); **Str** +4, **Dex** +2, **Con** +3, **Int** −4, **Wis** +1, **Cha** −1; **Skills** Perception +5; **Senses** darkvision 60ft, keen sight; **AL** U; **CR** 2; **XP** 450.

Treasure: Hidden in the nests are 3 griffon eggs that could be sold or hatched by anyone who finds and takes them.

The Statues

Inspecting the statues reveals little of interest to treasure-seekers. The primary construction of the stonework is dwarven, but the detailed work is that of elves. The statues have deep foundations, and are all approximately 40ft tall. These are memorials to nine elven queens who ruled the area below when it was deeply forested, a dynasty that lasted three thousand years until the coming of the Hyperboreans. The area they ruled extended 50 miles or so in each direction from the statues (excluding the mountains), and there are no true records of their history other than these remaining monuments of eternal stone. Their names, which are not on the statues, appear in many elven songs from around this region, but their deeds are forgotten. The queens are, in order of age, Olsailalis, Peliwarin, Imildalis, Suwaline, Gyslaramil, Cymiscine, Berisailys, Wild Theral, and Vaissilune. Queen Vaissilune's statue is of a noticeably lower quality of stonework than the other eight statues, for it was carved immediately after the war with the Hyperboreans, when the elves were in disarray and had suffered grievous casualties. She is also the only queen depicted with a weapon in hand (a sword), and she bears a quiver of arrows on her back.

There is a 25% chance (each day) that a group of elves arrives at the Nine Sisters. These elves are members of a particular elven faction called the Galanduil, found mainly in the forests of southern Aachen.

The Galanduil Faction

The Galanduil are drawn from numerous high elven families in southern Aachen Province, although a few of them are scattered in the north as well. The Galanduil have been observing the slow dissolution of the human social order in the area, and they have concluded that in a century or so the human society of Aachen will collapse into chaos much like what is already happening in the Sundered Kingdoms to the east. The elves of the Galanduil faction are thus planning ahead to forge what they see as a more stable society than the one currently in place. They believe that humanity needs elven high lords with longer lives and a longer-term view than humans, an arrangement that would create a far better defense against the tide of war, monsters, and barbarity that periodically threatens human governments. They are not trying to take control at this time, which they believe would be premature; rather, they are waiting for the Lord-Governor of Aachen to fall, and the lands to collapse into chaos, before they step in to assume control over the ruins.

The Galanduil have no desire to hasten the fall of human order; they are convinced that it will be a terrible catastrophe for all concerned, including the elves. However, they consider it inevitable, to be staved off for as long as possible but ultimately something that requires planning for what happens during and after. Their plan focuses more on the elves than on the humans; they hope to re-create the old dynasty of the elven queens depicted in the huge statues. They have found an elf with a slight blood-connection to the queens, and are trying to get local elven communities and nobles to acknowledge the new queen. The Galanduil hope that if the broken elven monarchy of this area can be re-established, the queen will be able — when the collapse comes — to lead a better-organized assumption of control over the anarchy in the human realm.

Rather obviously, these elves hold humanity in low esteem. They will not care if the characters have killed the griffons here, but are suspicious of their motives for approaching the statues so closely. If the characters are mere fortune-seekers, the Galanduil lose interest in them. If, however, the characters are a heroic, civilization-protection sort of group, the Galaduil could certainly end up discussing their concerns about the fall of humanity, the need for staving off ruin, and even the solution of placing high elves at the top of the feudal hierarchies when everything falls apart.

As a further adventure hook, the Galanduil are fairly knowledgeable about trouble spots in the south of Aachen, and if the characters establish friendly relations with them, they can be a good source of general information.

Royal Vermis Road

A safe and well-traveled high road, falling into disrepair and greater danger than in times past

Appearance

This is a wide stone road, old but in relatively good condition. It is marked with milestones, presumably counting down the distance to the great city of Vermis, capital of Aachen Province.

Description

The Royal Vermis Road runs from Aixe to Vermis, and then north to the Great Bridge. By decree of the Overking in Courghais, any traffic other than from within a province of Foere, or from Foere itself, is subject to a surtax over and above the ordinary tolls that might be levied for the use of a road. The effect of the decree is simple, and can be boiled down to the simple order to "charge an increased tax on merchants from Bard's Gate."

What is little understood by the royal court, or by the appointed Foerdewaith authorities of the Aachenland, is that their surtax is one of the factors causing Aachen's decline. Once a source of revenue for the province, the merchants of Bard's Gate are now almost exclusively using the Great Amrin River for the trip south to Eastgate, circumventing Aachen entirely. Because upriver travel on the Great Amrin is only possible for lightly-laden barges, heavy cargo is indeed forced to make the return journey overland through Aachen's taxes, but the southbound half of Aachen's original revenue from trade has simply evaporated over the years as a result of the surtax. No one in power understands why the revenues are dwindling; after all, the tax is higher. Aachen's ruling class completely misunderstands how merchants think, and the result has been a gradual slide toward impoverishment of the entire province.

In consequence, the Royal Vermis Road is beginning to fall into disrepair, and patrols are becoming less frequent as time goes by. The road is not yet dangerous, especially for well-guarded caravans, but petty highway robbery is on the rise against ordinary travelers such as farmers, tinkers, minstrels, pilgrims, peddlers, and anyone else traveling in small, unarmed bands.

Encounters

Encounter Chance: Make one encounter check in the morning, one in the afternoon, and one at night.

Risk Level: All encounters outside a city's one-hex radius are at the Medium-Risk level. Inside the one-hex radius around Aixe, Vermis, and the Great Bridge, there is an additional automatic encounter check in the surrounding hex and the central hex. All encounters in the radius of the city are at the Low-Risk level.

01–02	No Encounter
03–65	Mundane Encounter
66–00	Dangerous Encounter

Mundane Encounters: Royal Vermis Road

1d100	Encounter
01–02	Annoyance (Encounter #3)
03–04	Baron and Retinue (Encounter #8)
05	Bear (Encounter #11)
06–10	Caravan (Bard's Gate) (Encounter #15)
11–16	Caravan (Provincial) (Encounter #16)

1d100	Encounter
17–18	Cleric (Encounter #19)
19–20	Elf (Encounter #34)
21–36	Farmer (Encounter #36)
37–43	Foot Patrol (Encounter #37)
44–54	Herder (Encounter #51)
55–58	Heretic (Encounter #52)
59–60	High Noble (Encounter #53)
61	Kenckoo Vagrant (Encounter #55)
62–66	Knight and Retinue (Encounter #56)
67	Leper (Encounter #60)
68	Military (Encounter #64)
69–72	Minstrel (Encounter #65)
73–78	Mounted Patrol (Encounter #67)
79	Noble of the Realm (Encounter #68)
80–82	Peasant (Encounter #74)
83–84	Penitent (Encounter #76)
85–87	Pilgrim (Encounter #78)
88–89	Prisoner (Encounter #79)
90–91	Small Trader (halfling) (Encounter #86)
92–96	Small Trader (human) (Encounter #85)
97	Stag (Encounter #87)
98	Wandering Refugee (Encounter #98)
99–00	Wolf (Encounter #106)

Dangerous Encounters: Royal Vermis Road

1d100	Encounter
01–04	Ankheg (Encounter #2)
05–19	Bandit (Encounter #7)
20–21	Bulette (Encounter #14)
22–25	Centaur (Encounter #17)
26	Cockatrice (Encounter #21)
27–30	Dragon A (Encounter #27)
31–32	Eagle, Giant (Encounter #33)
33	Ettin (Encounter #35)
34	Giant, Hill (Encounter #41)
35–48	Gnoll (Encounter #43)
49–54	Goblin, Roaming (Encounter #45)
55–58	Lycanthrope (Encounter #61)
59–64	Manticore (Encounter #63)
65–68	Ogre (Encounter #69)
69–73	Owlbear (Encounter #72)
74–75	Roc (Encounter #81)
76–79	Stirge (Encounter #88)
80–86	Tiger (Encounter #90)
87	Troll (Encounter #92)
88–89	Unicorn (Encounter #93)
90–92	Wasp, Giant (Encounter #99)

1d100	Encounter
93–94	Weasel, Giant (Encounter #100)
95–96	Wizard (Encounter #107)
98–00	Wyvern (Encounter #108)

Ruined Abbey of Telophus

One of many countless monster lairs

The Abbey

Along the Cross Cut Road stand the collapsed stone walls of an old abbey, destroyed at some point after the Eastreach Decree by forces unknown. The remains of the walls are no more than 4ft high, but they still show the abbey's original shape. They are overgrown with ivy, and grass and wild wheat grow tall between the broken flagstones of the old floor. A statue, worn smooth from its exposure to wind and rain, stands in the abbey's northwest corner. Clerics would be able to identify the statue as being the Telophus, the ancient Hyperborean god of farming and agriculture.

Inspecting the abbey floor results in finding several rectangular patches where the stone is of a different variety than the rest of the flagstones, and has weathered into a slightly different color. There are ten of these. Nine of them are the tombs of the abbots who supervised the place when it was a functioning place of worship and solitude. The tenth is a secret entrance to the abbey's cellar, and slides upward and to the side on now-rusted metal tracks that must once have been well-oiled and easy to use. Stairs lead down into a 40ft by 40ft chamber underneath the abbey floor.

Shadows in the Cellar

The cellar has become the home of **4 shadows** that rise through the cracked flagstones by night to feed upon animals, and sometimes on unwary travelers who make camp here or along the nearby road.

Shadow (4): AC 12; **HP** 16 (3d8+3); **Spd** 40ft; Melee touch (+4, 2d6+2 necrotic plus 1d4 Str drain); **SA** shadow stealth (hide as bonus); **Immune** exhaustion, fear, grapple, necrotic, paralysis, petrify, poison, prone, restraint; **Resist** acid, bludgeoning, piercing, and slashing from normal weapons, cold, fire, lightning, thunder; **Str** –2, **Dex** +2, **Con** +1, **Int** –2, **Wis** +0, **Cha** –1; **Skills** Stealth +4 (+6 dim light/darkness); **Senses** darkvision 60ft; **Traits** amorphous, sunlight weakness (tactical disadvantage on attack, checks, and saves); **AL** CE; **CR** 1/2; **XP** 100.

Treasure: The abbey kept its small stock of funds in this cellar in a large ironbound chest that can still be found in the corner. The chest is padlocked but is not trapped, and the key is actually looped over the padlock on a piece of string. Rust has rendered the lock almost completely unworkable, and ordinary lockpicks bend if they are used. The key is still strong enough to force the lock's inner workings and, of course, the padlock's bar can be broken fairly easily; it is also badly rusted.

The chest contains 500gp and 5 *potions of plant growth*, one of which has gone sour and smells different than the others. The sour potion acts in reverse, requiring any abnormal plant to make a saving throw or wither to death; normal plants simply die if they are exposed to the liquid. The other potions function normally if the entire potion is poured into a single plant or sprinkled around on several smaller plants. Finally, the chest contains a deed to the abbey itself, but it has been superseded by a later land grant and is worthless. Discovering this in a court of law would cost only 100gp, for the legal status is quite obvious to any attorney in Vermis.

Taundre
(TAWN-druh)

A small village with a big secret

CE village
Government secret syndicate
Population 467 (433 humans; 34 halflings)
Notable NPCs
Mayor Norman Gant (N male human **commoner**)
"Assistant Mayor" Moulain Fleece male (CN male human **Sor8**)
Tal Ramon (CE male human **Clr6** of Fraz-Urb'luu)
Maximum Clerical Spell Level Good –, Neutral —, Evil 4
Purchase Limit/Month 2000gp (but they claim 500gp)

Appearance

Taundre, as it is marked on milestones on the road, is an unremarkable village with sagging stone walls and a sleepy, countryside atmosphere. There is a small market fairground outside the walls, and a single guard lounging by the entrance gate.

Description

On the surface, Taundre apparently contains no temple or any other unusual feature to distinguish itself from dozens of other small country villages. The ordinary appearance is deliberate, for the village is actually the headquarters of perhaps the most far-flung criminal empire in the Borderland Provinces, a group called the Friendly Men. There is a temple in the village, but it is not advertised to visitors and is indeed kept hidden from most of the normal folk.

The Friendly Men

The Friendly Men are a powerful, widespread criminal empire with operations across most of the northern and central regions of the Borderland Provinces. Less influential and less powerful than the Wheelwrights of Bard's Gate, the Friendly Men avoid crossing paths with the Wheelwrights other than in Carterscroft and Eastgate, where a certain professional courtesy rules their interactions. Since the Friendly Men use Eastgate only as a way of getting various products onto ships, rather than as a source of revenue, there has been no territorial dispute between the two brotherhoods in that area.

The leaders of the Friendly Men do not live in Taundre itself, although a high-ranking agent of the society remains here at all times to ensure that communications remain open with the rest of the network. The Friendly Men have operations in Vermis and Aixe, as well as Troye, Manas, Alembretia, and Albor Broce. They are developing enterprises in Olaric and Kingston, but so far these efforts have been blocked by accidents, mistakes, and alert law enforcement.

Urban-based operations are mainly focused upon moving and trading goods, for the Friendly Men make a good business simply out of purchasing stolen goods, bringing them hundreds of miles to another city, and then selling them safely. However, the society also maintains protection rackets in large towns and cities, obtains and sells slaves ("indentured serfs"), and is starting to move its way into the usually-legal sale of opium and other such narcotics. Most of these operations are not directly conducted by members of the Friendly Men themselves, who tend to be financiers, traveling merchants, or masterminds. The connections can usually be traced from, as an example, an extortion racket to the Friendlyman behind the operation, since street criminals are prone to tell what they know when captured. However, the Friendly Men generally establish good connections with those in higher offices susceptible to bribery, and it is rare for the top Friendlyman in a city to end up in prison or swinging from a noose.

The current agent of the Friendly Men in Taundre is Moulain Fleece (CN human male sorcerer 8), whose three bodyguards are formidable fighters (6th level). Moulain is the village's assistant mayor. The actual mayor, Norman Gant, is a normal villager who handles the ordinary tasks of running a small, country village. Mayor Gant knows that Moulain and his strange visitors are quite unusual, and probably criminal, but their money maintains the town well, and they do not disturb the peace. Indeed, the one or two times that bandits have tried raiding the nearby countryside, Moulain sent one letter that apparently led to the slaughter of the bandits during the darkness of a single night, their bodies deposited in front of the city gates the following morning.

For an example of the activities of the Friendly Men, see the description of Luam Ghere in **Chapter 9: Suilley**, *Manas*.

Secret Temple of Fraz-Urb'luu

One of the "warehouses" in town is actually a temple, its existence suspected by the villagers but not questioned — in the past, citizens have disappeared shortly after asking too many questions. The temple does not proselytize, and for the most part it exists as a joint effort with the Friendly Men. The cleric of Fraz-Urb'luu is a woman named Marian Vientz (female human cleric of Fraz-Urb'luu 6), who spends most of her time running a small shop near the city gates, selling candy. The temple of Fraz-Urb'luu is the usual meeting place for members of the Friendly Men who do not wish to know each other's actual names or identities. They wear the traditional masks of Fraz-Urb'uu worshippers, and Marian ensures that the secrecy is properly maintained.

Vermis
(VIRM-iss, sometimes WIRM-us)

Resplendent Capital of Aachen Province

N metropolis
Government overlord
Population 32,500 (28,200 humans; 3000 halflings; 870 high elves; 385 hill dwarves; 45 other)
Notable NPCs
Mayor-Palatine Landour Sebat (LN male human **knight**)
High Overseer of the University of Vermis Quarathenes (NG male human **mage**)
Curator of the Twin-Temple of Thyr and Muir Jothiran Wise (LG male human **Clr12** of Thyr)
Reliquarian (high priestess) of Jamboor Parumina Yaz (N female human **Clr9** of Jamboor)
Esgryndior (CN male **adult black dragon**)
Maximum Clerical Spell Level Good 6, Neutral 5, Evil 5 (hidden)
Purchase Limit/Month 64,000gp

Appearance

Vermis is a great, sprawling metropolis with old Hyperborean-era walls encompassing two hills. Towers stand at intervals along the wall, flying the banners of Foere and the city's own flag of a black dragon on a yellow background. It is a river port with a busy harbor shielded by the city's hills, and three paved high roads enter the city at massive, well-guarded gates.

Description

The great city of Vermis is the capital of Aachen Province, and the seat of the Lord-Governor of all Aachen. As with the City of Aixe, the

city itself is governed by a Mayor-Palatine who reports directly to the Lord-Governor — the Regional Governor of Vermis only oversees the courts and the surrounding roads. The two hills visible from outside the city are the High Mercha (which is crowned by the white-walled College of Vermis) and the Groldhill, dominated by the grim citadel of Vermis Grold.

The River-Harbor

Vermis is a river-port city with a deep, hill-protected harbor in the Great Amrin River. The harbor is protected from river-pirates by an island-tower in the river that is known as the Harbor's Bite. Vast quantities of food and trade goods travel down to Vermis from the upriver farms and villages to feed the city's population. Trade goods find their way onto the city's riverboats, their great yellow sails proudly marked with the city's black dragon, boldly warning pirates not to incur the city's wrath.

College of Vermis

The College of Vermis, located at the top of the High Mercha hill, is a famed institute of classical studies, literature, medicine, alchemy, and philosophy. Virtually the only major topic not taught at the College is magic, which is considered by the school to be more of a craft than an intellectual discipline. As in most places, magic is taught under an apprenticeship system. The College is beginning to fall upon harder times as revenues from the Royal Vermis Road have declined over the years, and it is becoming less common for the noble families of the countryside to send their young adults to Vermis for advanced education.

Temples and Religion

Notable temples in Vermis include the Chapterhouse-Crypt of Jamboor below the High Mercha Hill; the aging stone cathedral of Solanus; the newly expanded temple of Mitra; the Twin-temple of Thyr and Muir; and the Great Mill-Temple of Ceres. The cathedral of Solanus holds the remains of the famous healer-seeress Joianthe of Nains (JOY-anth-ee) in an elaborate casket of silver studded with semi-precious stones, which pilgrims come to visit, praying for cures and healing. As the worship of Solanus continues to decline, fewer pilgrims arrive each year. The cathedral has already closed its academy of acolytes, and rented out most of the great temple's former outbuildings.

Esgryndior

The threat of reprisal borne on the black-dragon sails of Vermis's riverboats is no idle threat, for the city does indeed possess its own black dragon, a formidable beast named Esgryndior. The dragon lives in a cavern-hold beneath the Citadel of Vermis Grold, with an exit from the steepest cliff-face of the Groldhill. Esgryndior is not exactly tame, nor is he loyal to the city or the Lord-Governor, but he is deeply respectful of the power of the city's wizards and extraordinarily fond of being fed without needing to stir himself to find food. He revels in the admiration of the citizenry, and the awe of visiting peasants, and generally finds living in the city to be an excellent life for a dragon.

Esgryndior's presence in the city, and the fact that he deigns to follow orders from the Lord-Governor, keeps the area around the capital city almost entirely clear of major threats. Even other dragons that might think of attacking Esgryndior have enough intelligence not to tangle with the spellcasters and veteran fighters who would unquestionably come to the black dragon's aid. The safe harbor created by Esgryndior's presence extends only to a radius of 50 or 60 miles, however, for unless he is called upon to strike deep toward some other threat, the dragon chooses not to tire himself with long flights that feel like work instead of play.

Wain Road
(East-West Run)

A safe road, as roads go

The east-west run of the Wain Road extends from Vermis to Carterscroft in Eastreach Province, stone-paved for most of its length and well drained to avoid the deep mires of mud that plague ordinary dirt roads. It runs through territories that are relatively well-populated and peaceful. Although no form of long-distance travel is free from the risk of bandits or beasts, the Aachen portion of the Wain Road is certainly safer than most. Matters change slightly when the road crosses the border into Eastreach Province, suddenly developing a multitude of toll stations, some of which are unauthorized. In Aachen Province, however, the Governors of Vermis and Dlante are the only legal collectors of road-taxes, and they prevent such petty banditry with active patrols and summary executions.

Encounters

Encounter Chance: Make one encounter check in the morning, one in the afternoon, and one at night.

Risk Level: All encounters outside a city's one-hex radius are at the Medium-Risk level. Inside the one-hex radius around Vermis and Dlante, there is an additional automatic encounter check in the surrounding hex and the city's hex. All encounters in the radius of the cities are at the Low-Risk level.

01–05	No Encounter
06–69	Mundane Encounter
70–00	Dangerous Encounter

Mundane Encounters:
Wain Road (Aachen Province)

1d100	Encounter
01–02	Annoyance (Encounter #3)
03–04	Baron and Retinue (Encounter #8)
05	Bear (Encounter #11)
06–10	Caravan (Bard's Gate) (Encounter #15)

1d100	Encounter
11–15	Caravan (Aachen or Eastreach) (Encounter #16)
16–18	Cleric (Encounter #19)
19–20	Elf (Encounter #34)
21–36	Farmer (Encounter #36)
37–44	Foot Patrol (Encounter #37)
45–54	Herder (Encounter #51)
55–59	Heretic (Encounter #52)
60–61	High Noble (Encounter #53)
62–63	Kenckoo Vagrant (Encounter #55)
64–69	Knight and Retinue (Encounter #56)
70–71	Leper (Encounter #60)
72–75	Minstrel (Encounter #65)
76–80	Mounted Patrol (Encounter #67)
81–82	Outlaw (Encounter #71)
83–85	Peasant (Encounter #74)
86–87	Prisoner (Encounter #79)
88–89	Small Trader (halfling) (Encounter #86)
90–93	Small Trader (human) (Encounter #85)
94–95	Stag (Encounter #87)
96	Wandering Refugee (Encounter #98)
97–98	Wild Horse or Pony (Encounter #103)
99–00	Wolf (Encounter #106)

1d100	Encounter
92–94	Weasel, Giant (Encounter #100)
95	Witherstench (Encounter #104)
96–98	Wizard (Encounter #107)
99–00	Wyvern (Encounter #108)

Dangerous Encounters:
Wain Road (Aachen Province)

1d100	Encounter
01–04	Ankheg (Encounter #2)
05–25	Bandit (Encounter #7)
26–30	Bugbear (Encounter #13)
31–32	Bulette (Encounter #14)
33–36	Centaur (Encounter #17)
37–38	Cockatrice (Encounter #21)
39–42	Dragon A (Encounter #27)
43–44	Giant, Hill (Encounter #41)
45–52	Gnoll (Encounter #43)
53–58	Goblin, Roaming (Encounter #45)
59–60	Griffon (Encounter #47)
61–62	Lycanthrope (Encounter #61)
63–67	Manticore (Encounter #63)
68–70	Ogre (Encounter #69)
71	Ogre Mage (Encounter #70)
72–73	Owlbear (Encounter #72)
74–78	Robber Knight (Encounter #80)
79–82	Stirge (Encounter #88)
83–88	Tiger (Encounter #90)
89	Troll (Encounter #92)
90–91	Unicorn (Encounter #93)

Chapter Two: Amrin Estuary

Amrin Estuary

Overview

The Amrin Estuary is dominated politically and commercially by the city of Bard's Gate, far upriver on the Great Amrin. With the exception of the Estuary's north bank, the area is prosperous and relatively safe. Eastgate is the dominant city of the area, although it does not exert any meaningful political control over the country nobles; they dance sufficiently well to the tune of Eastgate's gold. The city patrols the main high roads, and the nobles are also organized into a League of Estuary Lords for mutual protection and benefit.

General Information

Alignment: CN
Capital: none (Bard's Gate controls both major cities)
Notable Settlements: Amrin Ferry (228), Eastgate (12,620), Telar Brindel (8,800)
Ruler: none
Government: semi-autonomy (suzerainty of Bard's Gate who controls the cities, the land is loosely governed by a League of Estuary Lords, all freeholders)
Population: 420,000 (378,000 Foerdewaith; 33,000 halflings; 6,300 half-elves; 2,700 high elves)
Humanoid: halfling (some), half-elf (few), high elf (few)
Monstrous: giant snake, goblin, boggard, green hag, ogre, cockatrice, catoblepas (coastal swamps); giant eel, giant gar, koalinth, kelpie, scrag, sea hag (estuary); crab swarm, sand snake, bugbear, giant crayfish, gremlin, sandling (shoreline)
Languages: Common, Halfling, Elvish
Religion: Freya (countryside), Dame Torren, Pekko, Thyr, Sefagreth (Eastgate), Vanitthu (Telar Brindel), Mick O'Delving, Tykee (shipboard), Quell
Resources: trade hub, fishing, foodstuffs, shipbuilding
Technology Level: Medieval (cities), High Middle Ages (rural)

Borders and Lands

The Amrin Estuary is a gulf at the mouth of the Great Amrin River, called an "estuary" only by common convention. As a political region rather than just a geographical feature, the "Estuary" includes the city of Eastgate, the waters of the estuary itself, and also the lands ranging south from the shoreline to the region of the Trader's Way where the higher land of the coastline begins to drop into the vast watershed of the Gaelon River and its tributaries. It is a territory that has been under the effective control of Bard's Gate for years, by means of the city's careful statecraft, shrewd alliances, and plentiful economic incentives. The northern bank of the Estuary is a part of Eastreach Province, and is thus not described here.

Trade and Commerce

All trade in the Amrin Estuary is dominated by the influence of Bard's Gate. The city of Eastgate is the avenue to the sea for Bard's Gate's extensive trade network, and the last leg of the Trader's Way runs along the south bank of the Estuary toward Telar Brindel and beyond that to Endhome. Except during the winter months, most of the Estuary's trade activity is by water through Eastgate, but during the cold winters the Trader's Way becomes the only reliable way for merchants to bridge the gap between Eastgate and Endhome, and their well-guarded caravans become a common sight on the road.

Loyalties and Diplomacy

The region's distance from Foere's centers of power, and its proximity to Pontos Island, has made it impractical for the Kingdom of Foere to exercise any meaningful power either in the waters of the Estuary or in the lands to the south since the collapse of the empire. Grinding their teeth, a succession of Foerdewaith kings have watched bitterly as Bard's Gate purchased more and more influence in this area over the years.

The estuary is Bard's Gate's main avenue of sea trade in the Gulf of Akados and beyond, so it is of vital interest to the city, and there is no question that Bard's Gate would respond militarily to any attempt to close its access to the Estuary.

Government

Other than in the cities of Eastgate and Telar Brindel, the countryside along the south bank of the Estuary has no centralized government. A number of feudal lords undertake the job of protecting their manors and freeholds, and serve as a barrier to keep southern brigands away from the Trader's Way. To this end, they are organized into a League of Estuary Lords, allowing for them to respond quickly in the case of incursions from the lands to the south. In return, Eastgate and Telar Brindel do not interfere in the affairs of these lords, or attempt to turn their lands into a further extension of the reach of Bard's Gate.

Wilderness and Adventure

The south bank of the Amrin Estuary is ordinarily a peaceful area protected by the League of Estuary Lords and potential reinforcements from the garrisons at Eastgate and Telar Brindel. However, it is always at risk to any nobles who form a weak link in the chain and, unlike feudal systems with a strict hierarchy, the nobles of the League of Estuary Lords are freeholders answerable to no one unless their failings are quite dramatic. Hence, there always seem to be minor problems breaking out that go unresolved by one baron or another. Monsters or bandits occasionally attack villages; strange diseases break out when a traveler on the Trader's Way brings along a strange disease from afar; and from time to time, there is a violent border dispute between some of the Estuary Lords themselves. This is a good proving ground for adventurers of lower level since it offers minor risks with numerous safe havens in riding distance.

Changing Times

Unlike most of the Borderland Provinces, the Amrin Estuary has remained almost untouched by the receding influence of Foere, and most changes have actually left the folk of the Estuary better off than before. The area is firmly within the influence of Bard's Gate, and Foere has been a traditional competitor with the great trading city. Eastgate's fortunes are on the rise with the decline of Foere (one example being the naval détente with Oceanus), and the increasing trade in this area has improved the lives not only of the Estuary Lords, but of the farmers, tradesfolk, and innkeepers along the length of the Trader's Way.

Amrin Ferry

A small ferryboat community serving the route to a dangerous, seldom-traveled high road

LN village
Government autocracy
Population 228 (203 humans [103 locals, 100 Waymark cavalry]; 25 halflings)
Notable NPCs
    Commander of the Amrin Ferry Garrison, Falzar Kennick (LN male human **Ftr7**)
    Bailiff (mayor) Winddrift Lowwater (LG female human **commoner**)
Maximum Clerical Spell Level Good —, Neutral —, Evil —
Purchase Maximum/Month 300gp (no merchants are here; they are all in Eastgate)

The Amrin Ferry is a fortified landing operated by Bard's Gate to protect river-barges that ferry local produce across the river to be sold in

Eastgate. Wagons filled with hay, firewood, and vegetables accompanied by Eastreacher peasants and the occasional cow make their way to the Ferry and thence to the city's hungry markets. Caravans almost never use the Lowwater Road; it is much safer for any Eastgate-Eastwych trade to sail along the coastline rather than traverse the neglected and dangerous road.

A small contingent of Waymark cavalry is stationed here and makes occasional patrols along the Lowwater Road.

Eastgate

A large city dominating the mouth of the Great Amrin River, avenue to the high seas for the merchants of Bard's Gate

N large city
Government overlord
Population 18,900 (3700 in winter) (15,350 humans; 1700 halflings; 800 half-elves; 620 hill dwarves; 430 high elves)
Notable NPCs
    Commissary Lurmis Vergen (LG male human **noble**)
    Sheriff of Eastgate, Sir Wallace of Nearside Manor (LN male human **Ftr5**)
    Chief Constable of Eastgate, Meliador Gane (CG male human **Wiz8**)
Maximum Clerical Spell Level Good 5, Neutral 5, Evil 5 (hidden)
Purchase Maximum/Month 32,000gp

Appearance

Eastgate is a large, walled city built at the mouth of the Great Amrin River. The flag of Bard's Gate flies atop the citadel along with the city's own banner, a gold ship on a field of deep blue.

Description

The city of Eastgate is Bard's Gate's avenue to the sea, and effectively a distant annex of Bard's Gate itself. It is a major market and clearinghouse for upriver and downriver traffic to and from Bard's Gate, being the place where outgoing cargo is taken from riverboat to ship, where goods from Telar Brindel are loaded onto riverboats or sold to intermediaries, and where ship cargos from distant ports are sold or consigned to merchants planning to make the extended journey to Bard's Gate.

Trade

The city is managed on behalf of Bard's Gate by an administrative Commissary appointed by the High Burgess of Bard's Gate, responsible for overseeing the logistics and scheduling of shipments on barges upriver, overland caravans, and the veritable fleet of coasters and galleons that trades here during the spring, summer, and autumn.

During these months, Eastgate's walls are packed with merchants, rivermen, ship captains, and traders of every conceivable kind of commodity. Bills of lading for goods held in warehouses are traded back and forth in shouted auctions, wagons piled high with vegetables creak their way in from the countryside to collide in vast entanglements in the streets, and the city's year-round citizens drive themselves to exhaustion looking after the needs of all these arrivals, making money hand-over-fist in the process.

"On the fourth day out from Carterscroft, great drifts of snow made the road impassable, and virtually the entire caravan packed themselves into a crofter's barn to weather the freezing storm overnight. With nary a finger's breadth of space between the cattle drovers, piled up to sleep in a great, snoring, farting carpet of humanity, it was as noisy and crowded as summer in Eastreach."

From *Tales of a Minstrel's Travels* by Gelwin Greenfiddler, published in the City of Bard's Gate by the Lyre Valley Press.

In the winter, when the river sometimes ices over and the tidal waters of the estuary become violent, the population drops to a fifth of its summertime high, deprived of most of its waterborne trade in both directions. The only mercantile activity in the winter city is the overland caravan trade going east and west.

Defenses

The city's main defensive garrison is a small force of cavalry of the Waymarch that can be reinforced, if necessary, by the second garrison at Amrin Ferry. A small volunteer militia drills outside the city gates once a week, and a permanent "Towerguard" of soldiers keeps watch from the towers of the city walls and guard the gates.

Law Enforcement

Sheriffs and constables handle actual law enforcement within the city, organized the same as their counterparts in Bard's Gate. The "Sheriff of Eastgate" is also considered an "Undersheriff of Bard's Gate," and the "Eastgate Chief of Constables" is technically a "Deputy Chief of Constables of Bard's Gate." Of course, these are fine distinctions when seen from the perspective of an accused criminal facing prison, but vital for arranging a banquet table by social rank. Preferably, adventurers will encounter Eastgate's justiciary officials in the latter context, but, regrettably, it is too often the former.

The Sheriffs are responsible for making arrests under warrant, and for maintaining jails and prisons, but they do not investigate crimes; essentially, they work as instruments of the courts rather than being ordinary police. The constables are a true police force; they make arrests in the course of their duties, and without a sheriff's warrant. The constables are responsible for the investigation of crimes, being the law-enforcement arm of the city's government rather than of the courts.

Crime in Eastgate has fallen rather significantly since the installation of Meliador Gane, a skilled master of the arts of divination, as the Chief of Constables. Chief Constable Gane is unorthodox in his methods, and enjoys the intellectual challenge of hunting down criminals. The constabulary holds him in a certain degree of awe, and so do many of the city's current prisoners.

The laws of Bard's Gate apply here as if Eastgate were merely a distant part of Bard's Gate itself, and most guilds of the larger city have representatives present, at least during the peak months when the river is navigable.

Estuary Road
(Eastgate Portion)

A safe road patrolled by Eastgate's cavalry

See entry under **Aachen Province** for a description of the Aachenland portion of the road, west of the crossroad with the Wain Road. The part of the road in Aachen Province is significantly more dangerous than this section.

The Estuary Road connects Eastgate to Aixe, and branches north to Carterscroft along the Wain Road. This part of the road sees far more traffic than the Aachenland portion farther west, for it is the last leg of the overland journey from Bard's Gate to Eastgate.

The Waymark cavalry stationed in Eastgate reliably patrols the road. A number of roadside inns are also found along the road's 200 miles within Eastgate's borders.

Encounters

Encounter Chance: Make one encounter check in the morning, one in the afternoon, and one at night.

Risk Level: All encounters on the Estuary Road are at the Medium-Risk level. Inside the one-hex radius around Eastgate, there is an additional automatic encounter check in the surrounding hex and the city's hex. All encounters in the radius of the city are at the Low-Risk level.

01–02	No Encounter
03–70	Mundane Encounter
71–00	Dangerous Encounter

Mundane Encounters: Estuary Road (Eastgate)

1d100	Encounter
01–02	Annoyance (Encounter #3)
03–04	Baron and Retinue (Encounter #8)
05	Bear (Encounter #11)
06–11	Caravan (Bard's Gate) (Encounter #15)
12–15	Caravan (Aachen or Eastreach) (Encounter #16)
16–17	Cleric (Encounter #19)
18–33	Farmer (Encounter #36)
34–40	Foot Patrol (Encounter #37)
41–50	Herder (Encounter #51)
51–55	Heretic (Encounter #52)
56–57	High Noble (Encounter #53)
58–59	Kenckoo Vagrant (Encounter #55)
60–65	Knight and Retinue (Encounter #56)
66–69	Minstrel (Encounter #65)
70–72	Mounted Patrol (Encounter #67)
73	Outlaw (Encounter #71)
74–81	Patrol of Waymark Cavalry (Encounter #73)
82–84	Peasant (Encounter #74)
85	Penitent (Encounter #76)
86–88	Pilgrim (Encounter #78)
89–90	Prisoner (Encounter #79)
91–93	Small Trader (dwarf or halfling) (Encounter #86)
94–98	Small Trader (human) (Encounter #85)
99–00	Stag (Encounter #87)

Dangerous Encounters: Estuary Road (Eastgate)

1d100	Encounter
01–02	Ankheg (Encounter #2)
03–10	Bandit (Encounter #7)
11	Basilisk (Encounter #9)
12–13	Bugbear (Encounter #13)
14–15	Bulette (Encounter #14)
16–17	Centaur (Encounter #17)
18–19	Cockatrice (Encounter #21)
20–23	Dragon A (Encounter #27)
24–27	Eagle, Giant (Encounter #33)
28–29	Ettin (Encounter #35)
30–32	Giant, Cloud (Encounter #40)
33–40	Gnoll (Encounter #43)
41–49	Goblin, Roaming (Encounter #45)
50–52	Hag (Encounter #48)
53–57	Lycanthrope (Encounter #61)
58–59	Manticore (Encounter #63)
60–61	Ogre Mage (Encounter #70)
62–66	Owlbear (Encounter #72)
67–74	Robber Knight (Encounter #80)
75	Roc (Encounter #81)
76–78	Stirge (Encounter #88)
79–80	Troll (Encounter #92)
81–82	Undead A (Encounter #94)
83–86	Vulchling (Encounter #97)
87–88	Wasp, Giant (Encounter #99)
89–92	Weasel, Giant (Encounter #100)
93–94	Witherstench (Encounter #104)
95–96	Wizard (Encounter #107)
97–00	Wyvern (Encounter #108)

Gillmonkey Lair

Problems in Tobersham

The small hamlet of Tobersham is located by the estuary, and makes its living by fishing. Unfortunately, a tribe of gillmonkeys, nasty little monkey-like sea creatures about the size of a halfling, has recently occupied the waters of a remote, rocky cove nearby. The gillmonkeys have taken to creeping around the hamlet by night, looking for food other than fish; they have already killed and eaten two of the hamlet's rat-catching cats. More frighteningly, they have begun scrabbling at the doors and shuttered windows of the buildings themselves, knowing that the villagers are inside but perhaps not yet brave enough to attack. The villagers have blocked their chimneys and reinforced the bars of their doors, but the increasing aggressiveness of the gillmonkeys is obviously leading toward a deadly conclusion.

No Help to be Found

Unfortunately, the local knight who holds the hamlet in fief cannot be located. Apparently he has run away with his mistress to parts unknown, leaving his wife, Dame Gwendil, to manage what was apparently a badly indebted estate. She has been in the city of Eastgate for the last week, attempting to borrow enough money to keep things afloat, but this has left the tenants without any means of protecting themselves. Only one of the manor's guards has remained with Gwendil, and he is with her in the city as a bodyguard. The baron who owns the fiefdom is unwilling to spend time solving the problems of a few peasants at the edge of the bankrupt manorial holdings of a missing knight. In consequence, the untrained peasants are left to their own devices in a situation that is becoming ever more alarming.

Hearing about the Situation

Unless the characters stumble onto Tobersham while traveling, they are far more likely to hear about the knight's disappearance and the manor's financial troubles than they are to hear about the troubles of a few peasants in a tiny coastal hamlet. They might encounter Dame Gwendil in the city of Eastgate, or if they make a stop anywhere on the Trader's Way along the south bank of the Estuary they might hear vague gossip about a rural knight who disappeared and left his wife in dire financial straits.

The Cove

Down the coast about a mile from Tobersham is a small cove surrounded by cliffs on all sides. The only way to reach it is by boat, or by a perilous climb down an 80ft rock wall. At the base of the cliff is a sea cave that is the lair of **10 gillmonkeys**. They are pets belonging to a **mermaid shaman** named **Illisishia** who plays with them in the sea cave during high tide, often bringing friends with her (an additional **1d4+1 merfolk warriors** who act as her personal guard). Illisishia cares little for the concerns of people who might be bothered by her pets on shore, but violence or bribes would work to gain her cooperation in moving them to another location. If the characters befriend her, she might help to point out the location and identity of a pirate ship that has secretly been operating in the waters of the estuary, giving characters the opportunity for a much more substantial (and rewarding) adventure.

Gillmonkey (10): AC 12; HP 7 (2d6); **Spd** 25ft, swim 30ft; **Melee** bite (+4, 1d6+2 piercing), claws (+4, 1d6+2 slashing); **SA** multiattack (bite, claws); **Str** –1, **Dex** +2 (+4), **Con** +0, **Int** +0, **Wis** +1, **Cha** –1; **Skills** Stealth +4; **Senses** darkvision 60ft, tremorsense 60ft (in water); **Traits** amphibious; **AL** CN; **CR** 1/4; **XP** 50. (**Fifth Edition Foes** 121)

Illisishia, Mermaid Shaman: AC 11 (16 with *barkskin*); HP 38 (7d8+7); **Spd** 10ft, swim 40ft; **Melee** trident (+2 or +4 with *shillelagh*, 1d6 or 1d8 with *shillelagh* or two-hands piercing; **SA** spells (+4, Wis, DC 12); **Str** +0, **Dex** +1, **Con** +1, **Int** +1, **Wis** +2, **Cha** 12 (+1); **Skills** Medicine +4, Nature +3, Perception +4; **Traits** amphibious; **AL** N; **CR** 2; **XP** 450.
  Spells (slots): 0 (at-will)—*druidcraft, resistance, shillelagh*; 1st (4)—*entangle, longstrider, speak with animals, thunderwave*; 2nd (3)—*animal messenger, barkskin*

Merfolk Warrior: AC 13; HP 22 (4d8+4); **Spd** 10ft, swim 40ft; **Melee** spear (+4, 1d6+2 or 1d8+2 two-hands piercing; **Str** +2, **Dex** +1, **Con** +1, **Int** –1, **Wis** +0, **Cha** –1; **Skills** Perception +2; **Traits** amphibious; **AL** N; **CR** 1/4; **XP** 50.

Telar Brindel
(TEL-are BRIN-del)

Sea port of the Bard's Gate navy, with good shipyards for mercantile vessels

LN small city
Government overlord
Population 8800 (7200 humans; 850 half-elves; 437 hill dwarves; 189 halflings; 73 high elves; 51 gnomes)
Notable NPCs
  Admiral of Telar Brindel, Sir Gowan Maulwin (LN male human **Ftr9**)
  High Priest Lorimar Greentide (CG male human **Clr8** of Quell)
  Cailin Quiet, High Priestess of Vanitthu (LN female human **Clr7** of Vanitthu)
  Forthilian the Sea-Mage (N male human **Wiz11**)
Maximum Clerical Spell Level Good 4, Neutral 4, Evil —
Purchase Maximum/Month 16,000gp

A major naval station for Foere after the secession of Pontus Tinigal and the maritime dominance achieved by Oceanus, Telar Brindel was largely left to its own devices, allowing it to fall under the influence of Bard's Gate. Repopulated and refurbished, Telar Brindel is a small garrison city that now exists for the most part to support the fleet of fighting ships maintained by Bard's Gate to protect its merchant vessels from pirates, sea beasts, and overzealous Oceander ships, as well as to protect the waters of the estuary from uninvited incursions.

Military Presence

As a military port, the city is well defended by a garrison of 500 Free Defenders along with the ships' complements for the vessels anchored in the harbor. Heavy catapults and ballistas protect the walls and harbor, in addition to two fire projectors designed by the Wizards' Guild of Bard's Gate and manned by a squad of its charter members. There are also 2 full companies of Waymark cavalry stationed here, though one is usually involved in patrolling the length of the Trader's Way toward Eastgate and Endhome. Finally, the high tower of the citadel holds stabling and quarters for three Griffon Riders who serve as scouts and messengers as needed.

Trade and Industry

A large portion of the city's population is engaged in the business of building and repairing ships, for Telar Brindel's shipbuilding facilities are better than those at Eastgate, where the harbor is devoted to trade. The shipwrights of Telar Brindel build warships for Bard's Gate's small navy, and generally have one or two merchant vessels under construction at any given time. Extensive repairs to a damaged ship may be obtained here, and the quality of work is excellent.

In addition to shipbuilding, Telar Brindel is a waypoint for merchants engaged in overland trade with Endhome, and of course also provides the basic manufacturing and markets of any small city serving the needs of the surrounding countryside.

Government

The city is governed by a council of elected burgesses, subject to the ultimate authority of the admiral in charge of the fleet and fortifications. Since the sea-fleet of Bard's Gate is almost entirely based in Telar Brindel, and the sailors drawn from the area of the Amrin Estuary, the admiral is generally a native or long-term resident of the city, or a noble from the nearby country who has advanced through the navy's ranks. The distant government of Bard's Gate has thus far been intelligent enough to realize that sending an admiral from a landlocked river-city to command a seagoing fleet is not a recipe for naval victories.

The current Admiral of Telar Brindel is Sir Gowan Maulwin, the second son of a knightly family whose landholdings are only four miles from the city, and which has a long tradition of sending younger sons (and sometimes daughters) to sea. There are a few other families with the same tradition, and they refer to themselves as the "Sea-knights." Admiral Maulwin is particularly fond of this term, and uses it whenever possible. He is a fair but somewhat inflexible person, willing to let the city run itself as it sees fit, but exerting iron control over his ships, sailors, marines, and fortifications. It is not unusual for him to hire mercenary marines to supplement the small "official" contingents of his warships, provided that he implicitly trusts the mercenaries. A reliable cleric in the group (particularly one of Thyr or Muir) is usually required for any party of mercenary marines to obtain such employment.

Letters of Marque

The admiral also has the authority to issue letters of marque, an official permission to hunt pirates without being accused of piracy oneself. Anyone leading a captured ship into the harbor of Telar Brindel should have one of these documents to present, or there will be an uncomfortable inquiry into the details of how (and why) the other ship was taken. A letter of marque also guarantees that any privateer ship recovering cargo owned by a merchant will not have to return it for a 50% salvage fee, but instead retain 90% of the rescued cargo's value.

Chapter Three: Eastreach Province

Eastreach Province

Overview

Eastreach Province is still loyal to the Kingdoms of Foere, and is governed by a Lord-Governor sent from the Overking's Court. The province has always suffered from fragmentation and decentralization in a complex feudal system, and the social order is now suffering very badly from corruption fueled by bribes from Bard's Gate. Internal travel is grinding almost to a halt due to "tolls" charged by petty barons, and as rural settlements become more isolated, the wilderness is beginning to creep back into civilized areas.

General Information

Alignment: N
Capital: Carterscroft (17,721)
Notable Settlements: Eastwych (26,204), Drownboat Crossing (4,287), Florin's Cross (526), Oxmulch (98), Renderby (2,640), Zelkor's Ferry (20+)
Ruler: Lord-Governor Meridiac of Courghais (N male human **Ftr10**)
Government: feudalism (vassal of Foere)
Population: 1,222,000 (1,110,000 Foerdewaith; 73,000 halflings; 15,300 high elves; 9,800 half-elves; 6,050 wood elves; 4,200 gnomes; 3,650 hill dwarves)
Humanoid: halfling (many), high elf (some), half-elf (few), wood elf (few), gnome (few), hill dwarf (few)
Monstrous: giant animal (bear, wolf and stag), kobold, bugbear, stirge, giant insect, worg, fey, giant spider, ratfolk, treant, trolls, undead, decapus, wyvern, green dragon (Forest of Hope); goblin, blood hawk, ogre, undead, ankheg, kenckoo, gnoll, green hag, fey, manticore, basilisk, copper dragon, bulette, (plains); giant snake, goblin, boggard, marsh jelly, hag, cockatrice, will-o'-wisp, black dragons (coastal swamps)
Languages: Common, Halfling, Elvish, Dwarvish, Gnomish
Religion: Sefagreth, Solanus (declining), Freya, Pekko, Kamien, Telophus, Mitra (rising), Archeillus, Tykee, Thyr, Darach-Albith
Resources: grain, foodstuffs, trade hub, livestock, fishing, salt, shipbuilding, timber
Technology Level: Medieval (Carterscroft, Eastwych), High Middle Ages, Dark Ages (some remote areas)

Borders and Lands

The official boundaries of Eastreach are defined as follows, beginning with Eastwych in the northeast.. From Eastwych, the border runs south along the Sinnar Coast and the north shore of the Amrin Estuary. From here, it runs north of the Amrin Ferry by some 50 miles, thence along the Estuary Road to the crossroad with the Wain Road. From here, all agree that the border extends somewhat diagonally northwest to the Great Bridge over the Amrin, but the exact line has never been properly established. From the Great Bridge, the boundary line follows the banks of the Great River Amrin downriver to the southeast, then travels north along the Glimmrill River almost to the coast, then eastward along the shoreline back to Eastwych. Bard's Gate controls the Amrin River Ferry, all of the waters of the Amrin Estuary, and the Estuary's entire south bank.

The lands north of the Great Amrin River, from the Glimmrill Run to the Great Bridge, is an unsettled wilderness all the way to the edge of the Stoneheart Forest, an expanse occupied by monsters, outlaws, and others who choose to live beyond the reach of established authority. Neither Bard's Gate nor Eastreach claim these lands, as they are dangerous and offer no measurable likelihood of tax revenues. From time to time, a Lord-Governor has offered minor patents of nobility for anyone willing to establish a freehold in the area beyond the Great Amrin. None of the resulting settlements has lasted more than a generation, and most came to a rather bad end.

The central and western lands of Eastreach are relatively populated and stable, with several farming and trading towns along the major roads. The northeast portion of Eastreach is likewise fairly well peopled, with the frequency of villages increasing as one draws nearer to Eastwych. By contrast, southeast Eastreach is but lightly populated, and in the Forest of Hope and along the coast of the Sinnar Ocean there are virtually no settlements at all.

History and People

In the year 2765, heralds at the Foerdewaith Court at Courghais issued the royal "Decree of Full Provincial Status to the lands of Eastreach, in Vassalage-Perpetual to the Overking in Foere." A hundred copies of the long document were painstakingly written to parchment, seals were affixed, and Foere had officially launched a privately funded invasion of the lands all the way from still-fledgling Aachen Province to the shores of the Sinnar Ocean. In essence, the so-called "Eastreach Decree" granted patents of nobility over lands not yet actually taken. Responsibility for "pacifying any unlawful resistance to the Overking's decree by subjects in such lands" was left to the knights and barons "upon taking possession of their lawful desmesnes in the Province." In other words, if a Foerdewaith noble, or even a mercenary leader, could carve out a piece of Eastreach, they owned it. However and unbeknownst to the Overking of Foere, the Decree of Eastreach was accompanied by a second, unwritten law: the Law of Unintended Consequences. The disorder and corruption of Eastreach Province clearly have their roots in the Decree.

In the same year as the Eastreach Decree, Foere also established Pontus Tinigal on Pontos Island, to form a base for the new Foerdewaith navy. This was a long-planned maneuver Macobert had organized years before, and already involved a decree that an Admiral of Foere and a Town Senate would govern the salt-producing town of Eastwych, thus ensuring that

the navy would have a supply port on the mainland. Annoying as it might have been for the citizens of Eastwych to learn they had been given away to a foreign navy, the town's special status as a naval possession spared it from the plunder and chaos the Eastreach Decree caused in the rest of the Province. Refugees from the countryside streamed into the town during the invasion, and the Admiral happily pressed them into service and shipped them off to Pontus Tinigal where they began reluctant careers as unpaid oarsmen on the poorly constructed galleys of the new Foerdewaith navy. It is to be noted that the shipbuilding skills of the Foerdewaith navy improved quickly over the years, but due to this incident, its popularity among the native Eastreachers took some time to repair.

Trade and Commerce

Eastreach Province, although it remains loyal to the Kingdoms of Foere, is on extremely good terms with the mercantile and political emissaries of Bard's Gate. Gold flows into the coffers of the Province (and of the Lord-Governor) to ensure that overland trade between Telar Brindel and Bard's Gate remains unmolested. The High Sheriff of Internal Revenue in Carterscroft oversees a force of sheriffs at the three main road-crossings into the Province, documenting the number of wagon-axles, people, and animals passing in and out, so the tax can be billed to Bard's Gate in the following year. Bard's Gate travelers are given a special token when they cross the border from Aachen on the Wain Road or the Cross Cut, and at the Estuary Road just north of the Eastgate crossroad. The same office operates taxing-posts along the internal roads to levy tolls upon anyone not holding one of the Bard's Gate tokens handed out at the borders. The position is a lucrative one, and an honest person has not held the post in centuries, as far as anyone can tell.

While actual troops from Bard's Gate are not allowed to travel the Eastreach roads (oddly military forces of the Duchy of the Waymarch under contract with Bard's Gate are a notable, if infrequent, exception due to long-held treaties between Foere and Reme), river traffic down the Amrin is neither stopped nor inspected by officials of the Province under the

general trade agreements in place. This allows Bard's Gate to move soldiers and cargo down the Great Amrin River between the Estuary and the Stoneheart River branch. In Eastgate, merchants and river captains pay Bard's Gate for access to the river, and these tolls are used, in part, to fund the payments made to Eastreach Province.

Along the eastern coast, the Coast Road and Lowwater Road are far worse maintained than the three great roads that intersect in Carterscroft. Although Eastreacher patrols ride the northern half of the coast, and Bard's Gate sends riders from Eastgate along Lowwater Road, these patrols are sporadic and unenergetic. The forces of Eastreach use the duty to train junior officers, and Bard's Gate uses it as punishment duty for disgraced officers, so the patrols are particularly ineffectual.

Loyalties and Diplomacy

Eastreach Province loosely maintains its status as a province of the Kingdoms of Foere, giving fealty to the throne in Courghais (the capital of Foere). As such, Eastreach marks the northeastern-most extent of the Foerdewaith realms.

Government

A Lord-Governor appointed in the Court of Courgais in Foere rules Eastreach on behalf of the Overking. Most governors serve for five years and then resign or are recalled to Foere. The position is a lucrative one, for the Lord-Governor takes a share of most of the province's rampant corruption. There are no Regional Governors below the rank of the Lord-Governor, as there are in Aachen. Rather, all of Eastreach Province's governance beneath the Lord-Governor is (theoretically, in any case) a feudal pyramid with the Overking of Foere at the top, dukes below the Overking, barons pledging fealty to the dukes, and knights, in turn, whose feudal obligations are due to the barons. The Lord-Governor's role is to be the voice and proxy of the distant Overking, which allows him to call upon the dukes in the same way as the Overking himself. A vast number of barons captured their lands independently, however, and thus do not report to any higher noble such as a duke. These highly-independent nobles must be called upon individually by the Lord-Governor, which is a monumental task for the central government. This highly unstable, volatile arrangement is a holdover from the original frontier land grants made to the nobles who led armies into the area, and the throne has never successfully reorganized it. In consequence, Eastreach is a patchwork of fiefdoms and freeholds, with only marginal interference by the greater nobles in the affairs of their vassals. The Lord-Governor maintains a Royal Court of Law only in the city of Carterscroft, although the courts hear appeals from the judgments of ducal and baronial courts that administer most of the criminal and civil cases of the province. As one might expect, the application of the laws varies wildly from one barony to another.

The system works poorly, is riddled with corruption and graft, and is the direct result of the original "Eastreach Decree" of 2765, which granted lands in Eastreach based on the vagaries of military conquest. When the dust of that conquest settled, it became apparent that the Eastreach Decree had created a province carved into an impossible number of fiefdoms with overlapping and disputed borders, no provision for maintaining a centralized government, and no means of changing the system. Another factor that tended to protect the new barons and lords of Eastreach was that the Eastreach Decree had assembled a particular *sort* of noble in the province. These were not parade-ground soldiers or tournament knights that had responded to the Overking's offer of lands that were not his to give. Rather, every siege-battered stone castle and fortified manor house in Eastreach now housed a complement of battle-hardened veterans: armed, trained, blooded, and considerably more loyal to their commanders than to the Overking. The Overking wisely decided that sweeping changes to the prerogatives of this particular group of nobles could wait a generation, and each Overking has made the same decision since.

As a province of the Kingdom of Foere, Eastreach is required by the Overking to maintain and shoulder most of the expenses of the Royal Navy of Foere, whose principal port on the eastern coast of Akados is the port city of Eastwych. The fleet prevents any maritime advances that might be made by the Empire of Oceanus onto the mainland. As a part of the agreements made between Eastreach Province and Bard's Gate, the city of Eastgate maintains a second fleet, funded and commanded by Bard's Gate, to patrol and defend the Amrin Estuary on Eastreach's behalf. Courghais does not care for this perceived violation of their sovereignty, but Eastreach makes sure that a significant portion of the Bard's Gate payments make it back to the Royal Treasury each year, keeping the Overking's Court appeased.

> *"Many point to the Eastreach Decree as the last and senile act of a dying king. I think quite the contrary. True, Foere filled the Province of Eastreach with scurrilous nobles, predatory knights, and fortune-seekers of all kinds, just at the same time Macobert was on his deathbed, leaving a legacy of troubles for his son Magnusson to deal with later on. On the other hand, the Eastreach Decree emptied central Foere of those same scurrilous nobles, predatory knights, and fortune-seekers, making it far easier for Magnusson to consolidate his power with all the troublemakers spending their energy and troops to take over a distant province. I believe Macobert's Eastreach Decree was shortsighted; no one believes it to have been in the best long-term interests of Foere. But I believe that Macobert was willing to sacrifice the well-being of a new province to ensure a safe transition of power for his son. In the long term, things in Eastreach probably worked out worse than Macobert envisioned, and Magnusson would most likely have consolidated his power even if he had faced the internal dissention his father feared. Nevertheless, though, I maintain that the Eastreach Decree was not the product of senility, but a well thought out gambit on Macobert's part to protect the succession, a gambit that simply had farther-reaching ramifications than anyone could have expected at the time."*
>
> — Bothwarc the Sage,
> Herald-Historian of Courghais, 3510 I.R.

Wilderness and Adventure

Eastreach Province is no longer as productive as it once was under the rule of Foere, and wilderness is beginning to encroach even upon areas once deemed completely safe. The eastern half of Eastreach Province was never particularly safe to begin with, and small communities in the east are actually finding themselves isolated from trade and protection, left to fend for themselves. This is particularly true in the belt of land between the Great Amrin River and the Forest of Hope, but the newfound phenomenon of the "widowed hamlet" is growing more common in the entire region from the central rivers all the way to the eastern seaboard. In addition to the obvious adventurers' destination of Rappan Athuk, the whole of eastern Eastreach offers plenty of scope for wandering adventurers to fight monsters, rescue villages, and even for higher-level characters to take a village under their wing as a freehold. New castles are needed, for the old ones lie neglected and crumbling as beasts prowl their walls; bandits are rife, and predatory tax collectors often arrive with armed soldiers to take even more than the bandits would. It is an area that cries for heroes, and finds none to answer the call.

Changing Times

Corruption and internal division are slowly eroding Eastreach Province, although the process is too gradual to be obvious. The flow of money from Bard's Gate pays the nobility well for their cooperation with Bard's Gate commerce, but little of the wealth makes its way into the lives of the common folk of the Province. The rich grow richer; the poor grow poorer. As more of the petty nobility try to get a place at the trough, they are creating more little borders within the realm, all of which charge tariffs on farmers and traders passing through. The result is a slow withering of overland journeys in the areas not served by the official high roads. As an example, trade down the Canyon River is on the increase, with merchants and traders becoming more willing to risk a long, dangerous circuit around the much-shorter but exorbitantly expensive overland trek through the country roads.

With the intense focus on money, the nobility is coming to see the peasantry as a resource, instead of perceiving themselves as guardians of the peasantry. More wilderness is encroaching upon the Province as the common folk lose their optimism and drive in the face of irresponsible feudal lords, who are far more interested in collecting taxes than in supporting the welfare of their tenants. Land is beginning to go fallow in some places, forests are no longer patrolled, and the risky business of smuggling is becoming more common than ordinary trade. To foreigners, the creeping rot in Eastreach is fairly apparent, but the solution is much less clear.

Amrin River

See *Great Amrin River* below.

Canyon River

Dangerous, rocky waters leading through dangerous, forested places to a dangerous road

The Canyon River rises from sources in a highland range of scattered hills, and flows down through several shallow canyons to the Forest of Hope, and thence to the Sinnar Ocean. Few of the upriver villages produce anything worth carrying down the dangerous stretch of forested river, since it leads nowhere other than the Coast Road and the ocean. However, the upriver hills produce just enough gems and furs to entice a few hardy merchants into making the keelboat trip downriver to Zelkor's Ferry, disembarking to the Coast Road, and then risking the overland journey either north to Eastwych or south to Eastgate. It is a circuitous route, much longer than the distances as the proverbial crow flies, but it

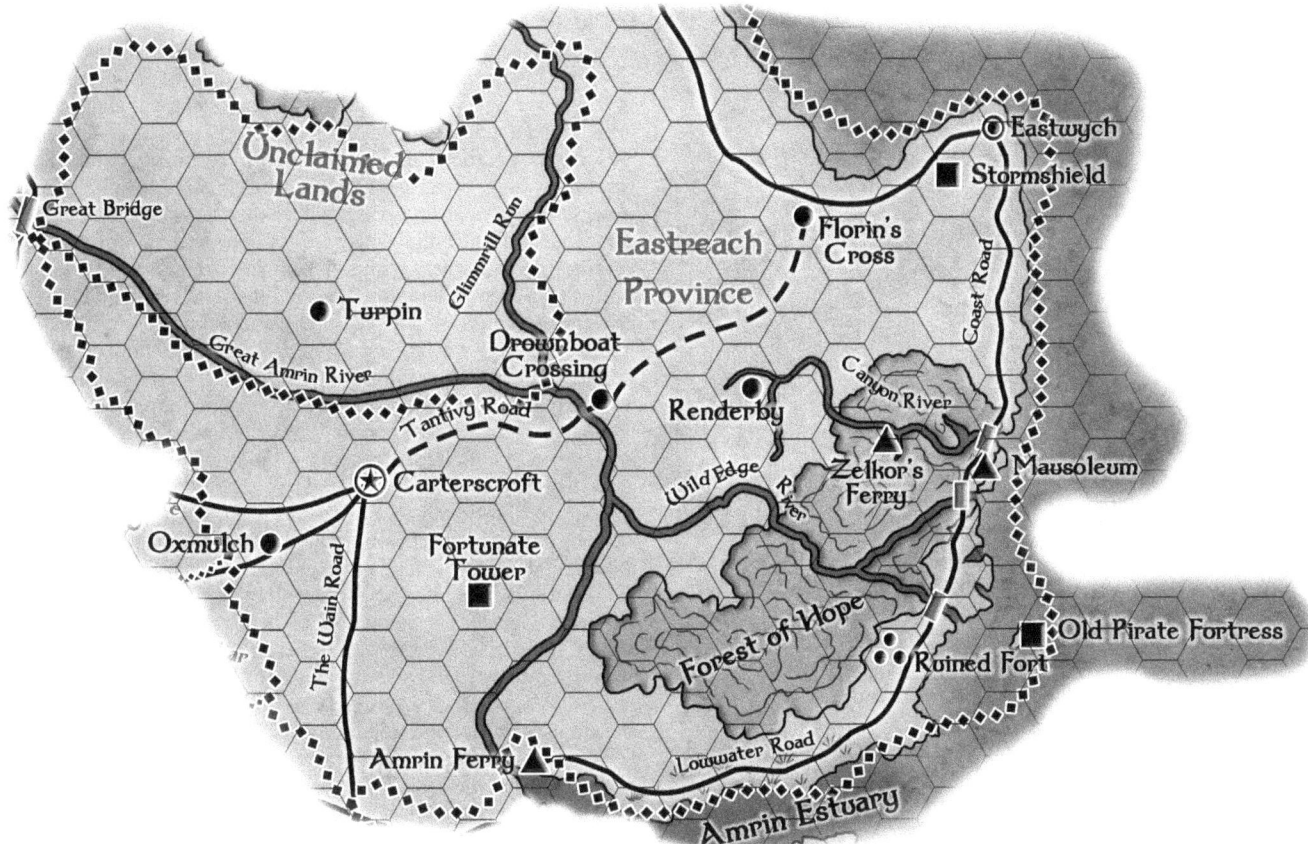

has the great benefit of avoiding taxes levied by every petty baron or sub-governor along the shorter but road-less land routes that could be taken to Carterscroft and Eastwych. Virtually all of these upriver traders are centered in the town of Renderby (population 2640), the only settlement of note in these highlands.

Carterscroft

Capital of Eastreach Province, a seething hive of corrupt officialdom

LN large city
Government overlord
Population 17,721 (14,130 humans; 2025 halflings; 1463 half-elves; 82 gnomes; 21 high elves)
Notable NPCs
Lord-Governor Hormengarde the Fat (N male human **Ftr9**)
Dalenus Whitebeard, High Priest of Thyr (LG male human **Clr13** of Thyr)
High Sheriff Sir Croaten Gui (LE male human **noble**)
Archbishop Sir Thomas Godwin (LN male human **Clr9** of Archeillus)
High Priest Wethinoc (N male human **Clr7** of Sefagreth)
Maximum Clerical Spell Level Good 6, Neutral 5, Evil 5 (hidden)
Purchase Maximum/Month 32,000gp

Appearance

Carterscroft is a large, walled city at the intersection of three main high-roads. A fourth major road, the Tantivy, leads from the city gates to the northeast, but it is an ordinary packed-dirt thoroughfare, not one of the stone-paved Hyperborean roads. The city towers fly the banner of Eastreach, a black flag showing a scroll and four coins below a purple crown.

Description

The city of Carterscroft is the capital of Eastreach. This is the headquarters of the provincial government's corruption, engineered by the merchants of the city of Bard's Gate for their own safe passage through the region.

History

Carterscroft emerged as a large trading town in the days of Hyperborea, a staging ground for traders and armies preparing to make the long journey between the core of the empire to the distant lands of the Isthmus of Irkaina, and even to distant Libynos beyond. The city is named for the massive fenced crofts that have always been set aside to form and organize caravans that often number a hundred or more travelers.

Government, Law Enforcement, and Bribes

A Mayor elected by the city's landowners governs the city of Carterscroft. While it is unusual for a Foerdewaith Provincial Capital to be self-governed, the law dates back to the original invasion of Eastreach by the Kingdoms of Foere. When the ragged but energetic invasion of Eastreach began in 2765 I.R., the Mayor of Carterscroft impounded all caravan cargoes inside the city walls, providing a large emergency store of food to withstand a siege. By the time the vanguard of the Foerdewaith invaders arrived at the city walls, they found a well-defended and well-provisioned stronghold facing them. For a while, the Foerdewaith barons and their forces contented themselves with seizing the lands around the city, but without a large army to invest the city, food supplies continued to be smuggled in, and it became clear that any siege would be prolonged and costly. Eventually, some of the more influential Foerdewaith nobles struck a deal with the city: In exchange for surrendering, Carterscroft would remain self-governed by its own citizenry, and only small numbers of Foerdewaith soldiers would be allowed in the city walls at any given time. The second part of the agreement was mutually forgotten once the province's Lord-Governor was installed in Carterscroft; even the worst of the invading barons would hardly pillage the Lord-Governor's own capital city. The first part of the agreement, entitling the city to elect its own mayor, has remained in place.

Any offense committed in the city walls, even treachery to the Crown, is tried by the city's Urban Courts. The Lord-Governor also has a Court of Justice in the city, adjudging all crimes and offenses committed outside Carterscroft from anywhere in the province. Because the Lord-Governor's Court of Justice is the highest in the land, it is actually considerably busier than the Urban Courts.

The Province of Eastreach is filled to bursting with tiny baronies owing their allegiance directly to the Overking instead of to a higher noble, due to the expansive "take-it-and-you-rule-it" provisions of the Eastreach Decree. Such barons are entitled to bring their grievances and squabbles directly to the Lord-Governor for resolution. If the Lord-Governor attempted to address all these petty issues directly, it would utterly paralyze the government of the Province, burying it in local disputes. Fortunately, the tool of bribery is available to the government, and offers a quick and convenient way to resolve otherwise-thorny legal questions.

The Urban and the Provincial court systems are eminently bribable, so wealthy individuals are unlikely to face any sort of energetic prosecution as long as enough silver crosses the right palms. This has drawn the ire of the priesthood of Thyr, as further described below.

Religion

Most of rural Eastreach Province worships the Hyperborean gods and goddesses rather than the divine patrons of invading Foere, or the fashionably newfangled deities whose worship is spreading from Bard's Gate. There is a developing split between the faiths of the peasantry and the patron gods revered by the nobility and merchants, and this split is reflected clearly here in the capital city. Archeillus, a god of nobility imported by the Foerdewaith invaders, has gained considerable traction among the nobility, and the worship of Sefagreth has begun to supplant the worship of Tykee among the merchants. The peasantry continues to worship Kamien, Freya, Solanus, and Telophus.

As a large city, Carterscroft is home to all sorts of small temples and shrines, including all of the above and others, but the predominant faiths are those of Archeillus, Tykee, and Sefagreth.

In recent years, the high priest of Thyr in Carterscroft has begun an active campaign to fight bribery and favoritism in the courts, issuing stern sermons and dire warnings. The government and wealthy citizens of the city have fought back actively against the high priest's campaign, cutting back or eliminating their donations to the temple, and even levying special taxes on Thyr's festival-days.

Institutions

The High Sheriff: Carterscroft is the seat of the High Sheriff of Internal Revenue, a lucrative posting appointed by the Lord-Governor to oversee payments from the merchants of Bard's Gate for safe passage through the Province. A significant portion of this money flows into the hands of the Lord-Governor and the High Sheriff, who take advantage of their short terms in office to amass personal fortunes before returning to Foere. The current High Sheriff is Sir Croaten Gui (prounounced "gwee"), a pleasant man who has hanged more than a hundred peasants for failure to pay taxes.

The Temple of Thyr

The temple has run into very hard times, even before High Priest Dalenus Whitebeard started his tirades against corruption in the city and oppression in the countryside. Unlike the rural peasantry, the city of Carterscroft and the noble classes are drifting away from the traditional Hyperborean gods such as Thyr, and turning toward newer, more fashionable deities such as Archeillus and Sefagreth.

The Temple of Archeillus

The worship of Archeillus, God of Rightful Rule and Protector of the Nobility, came to Eastreach along with the Foerdewaith invaders in 2765, never having been much worshipped outside central Foere. He is a god of legitimate rulership and bloodlines, especially worshipped by smaller lords, and defends the rights of the nobility to the letter of the law. At the outset of the Foerdewaith invasion of Eastreach, many of the Foerdewaith barons intending to seize lands in Eastreach consulted the priesthood of Archeillus. The question was whether their intention to seize Eastreach land under the Overking's decree was an unlawful overthrow of the Province's existing leadership, or the beneficial creation of a system of nobility in a chaotic land. After consulting the oracles and omens, the High Priest of Archeillus announced that the Overking's seizure of Eastreach was a valid extension of royal authority over an unruled land, and that as long as the invaders followed the Overking's instructions to the letter, they were authorized to dispossess the existing ruling class of Eastreach. Exalted by this divine support for their cause, many of the invading barons brought priests of Archeillus along with them on the assault to serve as counselors and chaplains.

Once the bloodbath in Eastreach ended, these priests of Archeillus were instrumental in drawing boundaries for the tangled patchwork of feudal rights in Eastreach, and ensuring that every petty noble received the greatest possible license for their tiny fiefdoms and estates under the Eastreach Decree. By doing so, they protected the rights of the lesser nobles, but played a large role in making Eastreach ungovernable by a centralized authority. This is a matter of no concern to the priesthood: Archeillus's inherent lawfulness is that of lineages, feudal rights, and continuity, not the compromises and generalities involved in the governance of nations. To the extent a country intrudes on the feudal rights of the petty nobility for any reason, the country is in the wrong — at least in the liturgy practiced among the lower gentry. This theology is the sword and shield of the petty nobles of Eastreach, hungry to gather a share of the trade money flowing through the Province.

The High Priest of Archeillus in Carterscroft is the tall, silver-haired Baron-Priest Oluard Mandrioc, a haughty and extremely aristocratic individual as one might expect. Oluard is not a cruel man, nor does he advocate tyrannical behavior by the nobles he advises; but he does not stand against tyranny either, so long as the authority behind it is valid. Many of his priests take a harder line against the peasantry, supporting harsh measures as a means of preventing rebellion or unrest. This priestly faction has gained a growing audience among petty nobles with cruel temperaments but impeccable family trees. Archeilleus is very popular among "robber barons" who charge taxes for everyone crossing their small borders, and who oppress their peasants to squeeze more money out of them.

The situation is made somewhat worse by an insignificant person in the Temple of Archeillus, a scribe by the name of Quillman Clark. Quillman is secretly an adherent of Fraz-Urb'luu, Demon-Prince of Deception. Quillman is responsible for making the final copies of letters sent from the temple to various petty barons, and he makes minor alterations. A letter telling a baron that he can take "only whatever taxes are legal" from his peasants might be changed, for example, to permit taking "whatever taxes are possible." With small changes to letters, the scribe is subtly changing the whole tenor of the temple's advice to the rural barons, a significant effect for such a minor, unassuming person.

Temples of Sefagreth and Tykee

The two predominant merchants' gods in Carterscroft, Sefagreth is a god of trade, and Tykee is a goddess of luck. Although Carterscroft is more of a stopping-point for the significant commerce traveling from Bard's Gate to Eastgate, many caravan-drivers and merchants in Carterscroft venerate these two deities enough to bring them up to a very prominent status in the city. Their temples are large, if not lavish, and the political influence of the temple of Sefagreth is measurable. The priesthood of Tykee does not play politics, but seems to do just fine without particular effort.

Coast Road, The

Seldom used, and infested with bandits and monstrous unpleasantries

The Coast Road runs north and south from Eastwych along the shores of the Sinnar Ocean, changing somewhere along the route into the Lowwater Road, which is patrolled by Bard's Gate rather than by Eastreach Province. Mention has already been made of the sporadic and ineffectual quality of these land patrols. For the entire length of the road, bridges over the various rivers that empty into the Sinnar Ocean are maintained by Eastreach Province.

One particular landmark of the Coast Road is the legendary Dungeon of Graves, known also as Rappan Athuk. For those who wish to engage in a more detailed and scholarly review of such unpleasant subjects, the section of road around the Dungeon of Graves is treated more thoroughly in **Rappan Athuk** and **Rappan Athuk: Expansions Volume I** by **Frog God Games**. Below Rappan Athuk lies an entrance to the Under Realms, deep tunnels that run countless miles beneath the earth. This underground realm is detailed in **Cyclopean Deeps: Volume 1 and Volume 2**, also available from **Frog God Games**.

Encounters

Encounter Chance: Make one encounter check in the morning, one in the afternoon, and one at night.

Risk Level: *The south portion of the road, starting at the Ruined Fort where the Lowwater Road changes into the Coast Road, and all the way northward alongside the Forest of Hope, is a High-Risk Area.* The northern half of the road, past the forest, is a Medium-Risk area. Inside the one-hex radius around Eastwych, there is an additional automatic encounter check in the surrounding hex and the city's hex. All encounters in the radius of the city are at the Low-Risk level.

01–30	No Encounter
31–55	Mundane Encounter
56–00	Dangerous Encounter

Mundane Encounters: Coast Road

1d100	Encounter
01–02	Baron and Retinue (Encounter #8)
03	Bear (Encounter #11)
04–08	Caravan (Eastreach) (Encounter #16)
09–10	Cleric (Encounter #19)
11	Druid (Encounter #31)
12–13	Elf (Encounter #34)
14–18	Farmer (Encounter #36)
19–28	Foot Patrol (Encounter #37)
29–36	Herder (Encounter #51)
37–42	Heretic (Encounter #52)
43–45	Kenckoo Vagrant (Encounter #55)
46–50	Knight and Retinue (Encounter #56)
51–55	Leper (Encounter #60)
56	Military (Encounter #64)
57–58	Minstrel (Encounter #65)
59–67	Mounted Patrol (Encounter #67)
68–72	Outlaw (Encounter #71)

1d100	Encounter
73–74	Peasant (Encounter #74)
75–78	Penitent (Encounter #76)
79	Pilgrim (Encounter #78)
80–82	Prisoner (Encounter #79)
83–86	Small Trader (human) (Encounter #85)
87–91	Stag (Encounter #87)
92	Wandering Refugee (Encounter #98)
93–95	Wild Horse or Pony (Encounter #103)
96–00	Wolf (Encounter #106)

Dangerous Encounters: Coast Road

1d100	Encounter
01	Ankheg (Encounter #2)
02–23	Bandit (Encounter #7)
24–25	Blood Hawk (Encounter #12)
26–27	Bugbear (Encounter #13)
28	Bulette (Encounter #14)
29–30	Demon (Encounter #24)
31–36	Dragon A (Encounter #27)
37–38	Eagle, Giant (Encounter #33)
39–40	Ettin (Encounter #35)
41–44	Ghoul (Encounter #39)
45–46	Giant, Hill (Encounter #41)
47–48	Gnoll (Encounter #43)
49–52	Goblin Raider (Encounter #44)
53–54	Goblin, Roaming (Encounter #45)
55–58	Harpy (Encounter #50)
59–60	Lycanthrope (Encounter #61)
61–65	Manticore (Encounter #63)
66–69	Ogre (Encounter #69)
70	Ogre Mage (Encounter #70)
71–74	Owlbear (Encounter #72)
75–78	Robber Knight (Encounter #80)
79–80	Shadow (Encounter #83)
81–82	Stirge (Encounter #88)
83	Tangtal (Encounter #89)
84–86	Troll (Encounter #92)
87–90	Undead A (Encounter #94)
91	Undead B (Encounter #95)
92–95	Vulchling (Encounter #97)
96	Wight (Encounter #102)
97–98	Wolverine, Giant (Encounter #105)
99–00	Wyvern (Encounter #108)

Forest of Hope

Horsefly Swamp

Dragonmarsh Lowlands

Rappan Athuk

Wild Edge River

Coast Road

Rappan Athuk
Wilderness Map (Players)

10 miles

Drownboat Crossing

Ferrying peasants from eastern to western Eastreach and back, for as long as anyone can remember

N large town
Government overlord
Population 4287 (3028 humans; 961 halflings; 230 half-elves; 68 high elves)
Notable NPCs
Baron Owen Foundofter (N male human **Ftr4**)
Sulliwyn Stormrush (N female human **Clr6** of Kamien)
The Reverend Qwain Main (CN male human **Clr4** of Moccavallo)
William Wildpiper (N male halfling **Brd2/Clr4** of Pan)
Drunken Dove Brownrobe (N male human **Wiz7**)
Maximum Clerical Spell Level Law —, Neutral 3, Evil 2 (hidden)
Purchase Maximum/Month 8000gp

Appearance

Dirt roads from the countryside converge for miles into one broad, unpaved track before entering the gates of Drownboat Crossing, the name marked on the few wooden signs along the roads. The town is at the edge of the Great Amrin River and flies a large banner over the gatehouse of a yellow boat with waves below it on a field of blue.

Description and Recent History

Drownboat Crossing is one of the few ferry-points across the Great Amrin upriver from the Amrin Ferry itself. Numerous cart tracks and dirt roads converge here, where farmers and merchants have crossed the ferry for generations. The town has four large boats that bring visitors across the wide river. On the far side of the river from Drownboat Crossing, there is a small dock and a building for the ferrymen-on-call on the far bank.

By use of well-placed bribes and a share of the revenue, the last Baron Foundofter managed to obtain a concession from the Lord-Governor to be the exclusive ferry-point for several miles of the Amrin's banks. Several traditional ferries were shut down, other than two that paid a large enough bribe to stay in operation.

It costs a silver noble (1sp) per person to be ferried across, and an additional noble if a wagon and draft animal are crossing as well. Despite what one would think from the town's name, the ferryboats are all sound and the passage is quite safe.

Lost Barge

If an adventure is sought in Drownboat Crossing, the characters may arrive to hear of a ferryboat that broke its moorings and floated downriver while still loaded with several bales of woolen cloth. The merchant whose cargo has been lost is incensed with the townspeople of the ferry, because they will not go searching for the unmoored barge until morning. The merchant offers a one-tenth share of any cloth recovered if the characters are willing to find and retrieve the boat. The merchant, whose name is Durton Mesley, fears (correctly) that several of the townsfolk or the peasants downriver would be happy to recover the cloth for themselves. Since the value of the cloth is approximately 1000gp, the one-tenth share is not trivial.

Eastwych
(EAST-wich)

Naval headquarters of the Kingdom of Foere

LN metropolis
Government council (city), overlord (naval base)
Population 26,204 (14,430 humans [Foerdewaith garrison and sailors]; 7232 humans; 2100 halflings; 1862 half-elves; 580 high elves)
Notable NPCs
Baron Teonj of Thovre, Grand Admiral of the Foerdewaith Fleet, (LN male human **Ftr11**)
Admiral Treston Artraguis, Commander of Eastwych Naval Base (LN male half-elf **Ftr8**)
High Priest John Augustinian (N male human **Clr12** of Quell)
High Priest Gesantu Sear (LG male human **Clr8** of Mitra)
Maximum Clerical Spell Level Good 4, Neutral 6, Evil 3 (hidden)
Purchase Maximum/Month 64,000gp

Appearance

This is a very heavily fortified seaport, with massive towers overlooking a deep harbor crowded with armed sailing galleons and long war-galleys, as well as merchant caravels and cogs. Trebuchets are mounted atop the larger towers, and the smaller towers bristle with mangonels and ballistas.

Description

Eastwych is a major port for the Kingdoms of Foere and principle headquarters of the Foerdewaith navy. The city is quite ancient, dating back to the pre-Hyperborean era as a major producer of salt. High-quality brine springs remain a major source of income to the present day.

In addition to the fleet, the Court of Courghais maintains a large garrison of Foerdewaith soldiers and marines here at the massive citadel to guard the port itself, patrol the nearby coastline, and serve as ships' companies for any naval venture that is ordered by the Overking. As a result, Eastwych has a complex system of laws and jurisdiction: The civilian Municipal Senate has its city court (called the Regular Court), the Citadel of Troops has a military court, and the Admiral of the Fleet has a third court dealing with matters maritime. By tradition, lawyers in Eastwych wear tall, square hats, dye their beards blue, and are adept at ensuring their clients cannot be legally prosecuted by any of the three courts. Those willing to pay the exorbitant fees can buy virtual immunity from the law, as long as they keep their transgressions to a moderate scope.

The post of Grand Admiral of the Foerdewaith Fleet is held, by tradition, by a noble of Eastreach Province, though the appointment can change at a moment's notice at the whims of Courghais and is subject to the orders of the Crown in all things concerning the fleet. The actual garrison and military personnel of Eastwych port and the Citadel of Troops, however, are commanded by an admiral assigned from Courghais itself and is never a local noble. While the Grand Admiral of the Fleet holds greater rank and command within the hierarchy, the admiral commanding the port in reality exercises more practical day-to-day power by design in order to prevent an loosening of the Overking's hold over his own fleet as happened 302 years before at the Imperial Port of Pontus Tinigal when Grand Admiral Maximilian d'Varago Pontos successfully named himself Emperor of Oceanus and stole the vast majority of Foere's naval power out from under the nose of Courghais with little real resistance.

Now the Royal Fleet's presence in Eastwych is vitally important since it prevents incursions by the Empire of Oceanus. Officially, the Foerdewaith marines quartered in the Citadel of Troops are ready at a moment's notice to invade and conquer the Island of Pontos and take back what was once the Overking's. In reality, of course, the garrison is by no means capable of such an ambitious enterprise, despite reports sent by the two Foerdewaith military commanders to their superiors in Courghais.

Estuary Road

Southern border of Eastreach Province, patrolled by Eastgate's (Bard's Gate's) cavalry

The Waymark cavalry, employed by the city of Bard's Gate but stationed in Eastgate, reliably patrol the road Moreover, a number of roadside inns provide safety and a modicum of comfort along the road's 200 miles within Eastgate's borders.

Encounters

Encounter Chance: Make one encounter check in the morning, one in the afternoon, and one at night.

Risk Level: All encounters on the Estuary Road are at the Medium-Risk level. Inside the one-hex radius around Eastgate, there is an additional automatic encounter check in the surrounding hex and the city's hex. All encounters in the radius of the city are at the Low-Risk level.

01–02	No Encounter
03–70	Mundane Encounter
71–00	Dangerous Encounter

Mundane Encounters: Estuary Road (Eastgate)

1d100	Encounter
01–02	Annoyance (Encounter #3)
03–04	Baron and Retinue (Encounter #8)
05	Bear (Encounter #11)
06–11	Caravan (Bard's Gate) (Encounter #15)
12–15	Caravan (Aachen or Eastreach) (Encounter #16)
16–17	Cleric (Encounter #19)
18–33	Farmer (Encounter #36)
34–40	Foot Patrol (Encounter #37)
41–50	Herder (Encounter #51)
51–55	Heretic (Encounter #52)
56–57	High Noble (Encounter #53)
58–59	Kenckoo Vagrant (Encounter #55)
60–65	Knight and Retinue (Encounter #56)
66–69	Minstrel (Encounter #65)
70–72	Mounted Patrol (Encounter #67)
73	Outlaw (Encounter #71)
74–81	Patrol of Waymark Cavalry (Encounter #73)
82–84	Peasant (Encounter #74)
85	Penitent (Encounter #76)
86–88	Pilgrim (Encounter #78)
89–90	Prisoner (Encounter #79)
91–93	Small Trader (dwarf or halfling) (Encounter #86)
94–98	Small Trader (human) (Encounter #85)
99–00	Stag (Encounter #87)

Dangerous Encounters: Estuary Road (Eastgate)

1d100	Encounter
01–02	Ankheg (Encounter #2)
03–10	Bandit (Encounter #7)
11	Basilisk (Encounter #9)
12–13	Bugbear (Encounter #13)
14–15	Bulette (Encounter #14)
16–17	Centaur (Encounter #17)
18–19	Cockatrice (Encounter #21)
20–23	Dragons A (Encounter #27)
24–27	Eagle, Giant (Encounter #33)
28–29	Ettin (Encounter #35)
30–32	Giant, Cloud (Encounter #40)
33–40	Gnoll (Encounter #43)
41–49	Goblin, Roaming (Encounter #45)
50–52	Hag (Encounter #48)
53–57	Lycanthrope (Encounter #61)
58–59	Manticore (Encounter #63)
60–61	Ogre Mage (Encounter #70)
62–66	Owlbear (Encounter #72)
67–74	Robber Knight (Encounter #80)
75	Roc (Encounter #81)
76–78	Stirge (Encounter #88)
79–80	Troll (Encounter #92)
81–82	Undead A (Encounter #94)
83–86	Vulchling (Encounter #97)
87–88	Wasp, Giant (Encounter #99)
89–92	Weasel, Giant (Encounter #100)
93–94	Witherstench (Encounter #104)
95–96	Wizard (Encounter #107)
97–00	Wyvern (Encounter #108)

Florin's Cross

A crossroad village

N village
Government overlord (bailiff appointed by the Lord-Governor)
Population 526 (480 humans; 31 hill dwarves; 11 half-elves; 4 gnomes)
Notable NPCs
  Bailiff, Lord Crothian Barne (N male human **Ftr8**)
  Innkeeper of the The Beard, Boskin Lewd (N male human **Ftr5**)
  Cedric Highborn (LN male human **Clr6** of Archeillus)
  Elispeth Tykeen (N female human **Clr4** of Tykee)
Maximum Clerical Spell Level Good —, Neutral 3, Evil —
Purchase Maximum/Month 2000gp

Appearance

This settlement is basically a stone castle with a village built beside it. A palisade of sharpened logs built as an extension of the castle's outer wall surrounds the village buildings. The castle flies the banner of Eastreach, a scroll and four coins under a purple crown. The stone-paved high road passes by the village gates, and a second road, made of packed dirt, enters the village gates directly from the south. A small river runs from the south near the dirt road past the settlement. The high road bridges the river just to the east of the village.

Description

Florin's Cross is a village located where the Tantivy Road reaches the Coast Road, standing by the side of the Scaramouche River where it runs north toward the sea. The settlement is an official possession of the Lord-Governor of the Province, and is run by the Bailiff of Florin's Cross, an appointed status currently held by Lord Crothian Barne, who no doubt paid well to get the posting. The bailiff and his family reside in the castle, which is called Florinfort and gives the village its name.

History

Florin's Cross is a relatively old settlement, but other than the castle it does not have a continuous history, having shrunken to a mere hamlet more than once during hard times. A stone wall once surrounded the village, but it was reduced to the foundations in the war following the Eastreach Decree and was never rebuilt. The settlement's stockade wall follows the original line of the stone foundations.

Buildings

The Beard Inn

Marked by a black, bushy beard painted on a hanging red sign, the Beard is the town's only inn, and by the evening it is usually filled by travelers looking for accommodations along the high road. The innkeeper, Boskin Lewd, is a massive individual who carries on the Lewd family's tradition of wearing a bushy beard decoratively tied with ribbons and tiny jingle bells. There is a large common room where the Beard serves food and drink along with the town's strong, dark ale. Most evenings, traveling minstrels are hired to play for the common room's company, if any are available; otherwise, the town's troupe of six mimes, the Tongue-Tied Fellows (LN male human **Mnk5**), entertain the patrons. The Tongue-Tied fellows are an interesting lot, all of them tremendously agile, with olive skin and startling yellow eyes. They are actually monks from the far-off Irkainian Desert, come to deliver a complex jade box to the Reliquary of Jamboor in the Duchy of the Rampart. However, a rival holy man who followed them across the sea cursed all of them with amnesia, and they have forgotten their original quest. They still keep the box safe in their house, certain that it is important but unable to remember its significance. In the meantime, they support themselves well by acting as mimes here and in the surrounding villages.

Florinfort

Florinfort is a stone keep with a small outer bailey where there is a forge, a dovecote, dog kennels, and stables. Only nobles, those on official business of the province, and personal guests of the bailiff are generally permitted access to the bailey, much less to the keep itself. Bailiff Crothian Barne has little to do with the town, treating the castle as his private home, as if it were not connected to a town at all. It is a requirement of his appointment that he holds a regular court of justice; but since he merely sells decisions to the highest bidder, not many people bother to use the court for settling disputes.

Crothian's garrison is a company of 10 archers and 15 footmen, all of whom remain in the keep, letting the townsfolk maintain their own militia and town watch. They accompany Lord Crothian when he makes his official monthly procession to accept taxes from the town, but otherwise their business is to guard the keep itself.

Secret Activities

Without much supervision by the bailiff, Florin's Cross has turned into a major smuggling operation, complete with innocent-looking forward scouts to spot tax-collectors and robber barons, wagons with false bottoms, and bribery arrangements with other peasants along the road who can store large cargoes in hidden chambers under barns, in copses of trees, and (in one case) a graveyard. They have started to get into the business of moving convicts, heretics, and outlaws away from the places where they can be recognized, and even hiding the crops of other villages to prevent the onerous taxation that has been growing over the years. Their most recent expansion is a hamlet on the coast by the mouth of the Scaramouche River, a place called Beaker Mooring, with 15 inhabitants, 2 fishing boats, and a dog. The smugglers of Florin's Cross have begun taking cargoes and fugitives north along the Scaramouche to Beaker Mooring, where the fisher-folk transport them along the coast faster and more safely than they can be brought along the Coast Road. All this activity is a matter of need, not greed. The demands of Eastreach's nobility have reached a fever pitch, where peasants are almost in danger of starving: Florin's Cross is keeping the area away from the brink of collapse. The townsfolk know that they are all risking execution by hanging, and since they have nothing to lose, the general spirit of rebellion is even starting to give rise to rumblings about eliminating some of the most tyrannical knights (and even barons) in the area.

Adventure

Characters who appear to disdain the nobility and the laws of the land might be recruited here for a couple of different plans. At the simplest level, they might be asked to guard a wagon of concealed fugitives down the river to Beaker Mooring, or along the Coast Road for 50 miles or so. They might even be asked to guard one of the fishing boats from Beaker Mooring if there is a particularly valuable fugitive to transport. Indeed, the town expects the arrival of just such a fugitive quite soon, the heir to a barony just seized by the Lord-Governor. The townsfolk are getting a very good commission on this "cargo," and want to ensure that the heir arrives safely in Eastwych, where he will be spirited away on a long trip to Bard's Gate.

Another idea being kicked around in Florin's Cross is something the townsfolk refer to as a "trailblaze," although they have not yet trusted anyone enough to try it out. This would be an ordinary journey through the patchwork of robber barons and rapacious knights of the countryside, but with the objective of killing illegal (and only illegal) tax collectors. The townsfolk consider that such a plan could open up a long corridor that would be usable for honest trade for quite some time. Interestingly, this particular plan is actually not against the law, since illegal tax collectors are technically bandits, even if the local nobles are the ones behind them. Characters might even get a bounty from the Church of Sefagreth.

Depending on the order in which things happen, there is another possible way the characters might get embroiled in the illegal activity at Florin's Cross. The Friendly Men are becoming aware that someone is conducting some very skillful smuggling operations in the area, and they want to get a piece of the action. If the characters are working with the Friendly Men (shame on them), they might get the assignment of ferreting out the source of the smuggling. For information on the Friendly Men, see **Chapter 1: Aachen Province, *Taundre***.

Forest of Hope

A dark forest with an utterly inappropriate name

The Forest of Hope was named for a local princess, rather than for any sort of hopefulness that might be offered by the sinister trees of this vast, forbidding forest. Most certainly the forest's original appellation is far more apt — the "Forest of Horrors." The name of Princess Hope's father, who named the forest in honor of his daughter, is lost to time; but he managed to immortalize his daughter in an unexpected and certainly unintended

This greed-formed mixture of matter and spirit is a rakshasa who styles himself as Lord Tyberis. Tyberis can ride the greed-winds in spirit form, and, thus far, he has restricted his activities to simple robbery of interesting-looking people. He has recently realized that true riches come from landholdings and peasant workers, so he is starting to take control of villages and hamlets by subverting the local knights using *charm* spells. So far, he has experimented only on the knights of three manor houses, waiting to see if anyone discovers the trick and traces it back to him. If the experiment works well, he will start accumulating the taxes from lands as far as he can successfully control the local nobility.

It is possible that characters might encounter Tyberis once he has already started to take control of more landholdings.

Lord Tyberus, Rakshasa: AC 17; **HP** 110 (13d8+52); **Spd** 40ft; **Melee** claw (+7, 2d6+2 slashing plus curse (no benefit of rest); **SA** innate spells (Cha+10, DC 18), multiattack (claw x2); **Immune** normal weapons; **Vulnerable** magic piercing weapons wielded by good; **Str** +2, **Dex** +3, **Con** +4, **Int** +1, **Wis** +3, **Cha** +5; **Skills** Deception +10, Insight +8; **Senses** darkvision 60ft; **Traits** limited magic immunity (6th or lower, tactical advantage on saves for other), spirit form; **AL** LE; **CR** 13; **XP** 10,000.

    Innate Spells: at will—*detect thoughts, disguise self, mage hand, minor illusion*; 3/day—*charm person, detect magic, invisibility, major image, suggestion*; 1/day—*dominate person, fly, plane shift, true seeing*. Equipment: robes, coronet of rubies (10,000gp), *ring of protection*, belt pouch containing 127gp and 2 sapphires (200gp each)

Glimmrill Run

(GLIM-rill)

Bordering on the Unclaimed Lands, essentially a frontier river

Description

This tributary of the Great Amrin River runs due south, forming the natural western border of Eastreach Province. On the far side of the river lies an unclaimed and ungoverned wilderness extending from the Province to the lands of Bard's Gate. The eastern bank is a patchwork of small baronies and fortified manorial estates with few roads joining them other than cart tracks, a feudal region that stretches north to the Forest Kingdoms (off map).

The Glimmrill Run has a serious problem with river pirates, far worse than the better-patrolled Great Amrin River. Trade on the Glimmrill Run is running less and less due to the fact that Eastreach Province is unwilling to deploy river patrols against the pirates. One or two towns along the river try to maintain a working river trade by arming their ships with mercenaries, but there is no longer any attempt to actually root out the pirates. As with the Great Amrin, the source of the pirates is a number of petty landholders along the river who provide safe harbors to the buccaneers in exchange for a share of the loot, often financing the purchasing and outfitting of the pirate vessels.

way. "Flirting with Princess Hope," given her association with the forest, is a widely used expression used to indicate that a person is about to do something not only stupid but also highly dangerous. Since this is exactly the province of many adventurers, they may hear it quite a lot.

The depths of the forest are choked with dens of giant spiders and other deadly predators such as trolls, stirges, and worgs. Outlaw bands take refuge in the tree-shadowed reaches, and each year ushers in a new hatching of young green dragons to plague the scattered settlements of the forest's western verge. Dragon season along the forest edge is a common testing-ground for young knights of Eastreach hoping to prove themselves, offering up battles with very small dragons whose size will necessarily be exaggerated in later retellings of the heroic tale.

Fortunate Tower

The lair of an ambitious and greedy rakshasa

Fortunate Tower looks like an ordinary tower on a hillside, but it is something quite different and much more disturbing, clear evidence of Eastreach's slide into corruption and venality. The hillside is a whirlwind, of sorts, where metaphysical winds of greed collect and concentrate themselves. The increasing rot of bribery, extortion, and greed for a hundred miles around has begun to form into tangible substance on this hillside. The tower was not there fifty years ago, and was never built by human hands. Its inhabitant, like the tower, formed from nowhere, the product of the greed-winds.

Great Amrin River (and tributary, Stoneheart River)

The river of rivers, celebrated in song and beloved by merchants

Description

The Great Amrin is one of the greatest river systems in all of Akados, magnificently wide and majestically slow flowing, although it conceals some treacherous currents and undertows that draw inexperienced river captains to their doom. The Great Amrin originates at the Star Sea and wends its way through Aachen Gap down to the Sinnar Ocean, joined by its great tributary, the Stoneheart River, north of the Great Bridge. The entire length of the river runs within the lands of the Kingdoms of Foere until it reaches Eastgate, but treaties with Bard's Gate allow the city unrestricted access to the Great Amrin for its shipping between the Stoneheart River fork and the Amrin Estuary. More about the river trade is described above under the Eastreach Province heading "Trade and Commerce."

The greatest problem with traveling on the Great Amrin River below the Stoneheart tributary is river piracy from the small fiefdoms along the northern bank. Fast-moving keelboats filled with pirates launch from the bank to pursue the slower-moving cargo barges, seeking to capture and loot them. When they succeed, the cargos are shared with whatever petty lord has been harboring them, and the pirates move on to another place of refuge under the protection of some other lord. From time to time, Bard's Gate makes reprisals against lords they believe to be harboring pirates, landing troops to burn down their manors and crops, but these counterattacks only slow down the activity of the pirates, without bringing it to a halt. From time to time, small parties of mercenary adventurers are paid to travel through the fiefdoms of the Great Amrin's north shore, and to "remove" the pirates they find. The problem is not particularly serious, but it does represent an occasional danger.

Lowwater Road, The

Tedious, dangerous, uncomfortably wet, and leads to even worse places

Description

The isolated Lowwater Road passes through the marshy ground along the northern edge of the Amrin Estuary, turning into the Coast Road along the way. It is in poor repair and sections are frequently lost under mud and marsh-water if the rains have been heavy. Despite the fact that Waymark cavalry out of Amrin Ferry patrol it occasionally, the road should be considered very dangerous. It is startlingly prone to disappearing travelers, and there are many legends and ghost stories to explain the disappearances. For all of these excellent reasons, the Lowwater Road is seldom used. At the beginning of any journey upon it, it is traditional to spit three times and dance several steps of a lively jig before specifically taking the first step upon the road.

Traveling north, the Lowwater Road leads to the Coast Road, which is no improvement whatsoever.

Encounters

Encounter Chance: Make one encounter check in the morning, one in the afternoon, and one at night.

Risk Level: All encounters along the Lowwater Road are at the Medium-Risk level, but as soon as it reaches the Ruined Fort and turns into the Coast Road, a High-risk area begins (see *Coast Road*).

01–30	No Encounter
31–55	Mundane Encounter
56–00	Dangerous Encounter

Mundane Encounters: Lowwater Road

1d100	Encounter
01–02	Baron and Retinue (Encounter #8)
03	Bear (Encounter #11)
04–08	Caravan (Eastreach) (Encounter #16)
09–10	Cleric (Encounter #19)
11	Druid (Encounter #31)
12–13	Elf (Encounter #34)
14–18	Farmer (Encounter #36)
19–28	Foot Patrol (Encounter #37)
29–37	Herder (Encounter #51)
38–42	Heretic (Encounter #52)
43–45	Kenckoo Vagrant (Encounter #55)
46–50	Knight and Retinue (Encounter #56)
51–55	Leper (Encounter #60)
56	Military (Encounter #64)
57–58	Minstrel (Encounter #65)
59–60	Mounted Patrol of a local baron (Encounter #67)
61–65	Outlaw (Encounter #71)
66–72	Patrol of Waymark Cavalry (Encounter #73)
73–74	Peasant (Encounter #74)
75–78	Penitent (Encounter #76)
79	Pilgrim (Encounter #78)
80–82	Prisoner (Encounter #79)
83–86	Small Trader (human) (Encounter #85)
87–91	Stag (Encounter #87)
92	Wandering Refugee (Encounter #98)
93–95	Wild Horse or Pony (Encounter #103)
96–00	Wolf (Encounter #106)

Dangerous Encounters: Lowwater Road

1d100	Encounter
01	Ankheg (Encounter #2)
02–23	Bandit (Encounter #7)
24–25	Blood Hawk (Encounter #12)
26–27	Bugbear (Encounter #13)
28	Bulette (Encounter #14)
29–30	Demon (Encounter #24)
31–36	Dragon A (Encounter #27)
37–38	Eagle, Giant (Encounter #33)
39–40	Ettin (Encounter #35)
41–44	Ghoul (Encounter #39)
45–46	Giant, Hill (Encounter #41)
47–48	Gnoll (Encounter #43)
49–52	Goblin Raider (Encounter #44)
53–54	Goblin, Roaming (Encounter #45)
55–58	Harpy (Encounter #50)
59–60	Lycanthrope (Encounter #61)
61–65	Manticore (Encounter #63)
66–69	Ogre (Encounter #69)
70	Ogre Mage (Encounter #70)
71–74	Owlbear (Encounter #72)
75–78	Robber Knight (Encounter #80)

1d100	Encounter
79–80	Shadow (Encounter #83)
81–82	Stirge (Encounter #88)
83	Tangtal (Encounter #89)
84–86	Troll (Encounter #92)
87–90	Undead A (Encounter #94)
91	Undead B (Encounter #95)
92–95	Vulchling (Encounter #97)
96	Wight (Encounter #102)
97–98	Wolverine, Giant (Encounter #105)
99–00	Wyvern (Encounter #108)

Mausoleum (Mausoleum of Rappan Athuk)

See *Rappan Athuk* below.

Old Pirate Fortress

An old pirate fortress

The old pirate fortress shown on the map is a relic of the differences of opinion between the Royal Navy of Foere and the Foerdewaith nobles who occupied the province after the Eastreach Decree of 2765. In the opinion of the particular noble who built this fort, his barony reached outward beyond the island shores and over the waters, authorizing him to engage in a bit of moderate piracy as one might reasonably expect. The Royal Navy out of Pontos Tinigal subscribed to a different opinion, and put an end to the baron's enterprising efforts, including putting an end to the baron himself.

For some generations following the baron's untimely demise, pirates continued to use the fortress as a base of operations. Eventually, though, the passing ships became faster and better armed, the Royal Navy continued their vigilance, and the fort fell into disuse.

Oxmulch

A hamlet with an unusually pungent product

N hamlet
Government overlord (the absentee baron appoints a hamlet reeve)
Population 98 (97 humans; 1 hill dwarf)
Notable NPCs
  Norman the Ox, Innkeeper of the White Ox (N male human **commoner**)
  Father Imbroglio (LG male human **Clr4** of Thyr)
  Clive, local drunk (CN male dwarf **Rog3**)
Maximum Clerical Spell Level Good 2, Neutral —, Evil —
Purchase Maximum/Month 1000gp

Appearance

A hamlet of fifteen buildings or so stands near the road, clustered together on a hill surrounded by fields and stone enclosures for the oxen that graze nearby. Judging by the number of enclosures, raising oxen must be the hamlet's main business, and there is certainly an omnipresent smell pervading the village to support that assertion.

Scents and Sensibility

The grasses around Oxmulch are extraordinarily nutritious for oxen, causing them to produce an extremely powerful fertilizer in large quantity. This manure is the hamlet's main product, brought by the cartload to surrounding farms where it is used in the fields most distant from habitation. Unfortunately, since the oxen are kept near Oxmulch, the hamlet has an extraordinarily ripe smell to it. The inhabitants are saturated with it, and anyone staying overnight here reeks of manure for at least 24 hours after leaving.

The Sign of the White Ox

Optimistically, perhaps, there is an inn located atop Oxmulch's hill, where the ordure smell is less pungent than in the lower fields. Because the hamlet is widely separated from other habitations (not surprisingly), many travelers on the Cross Cut Road are forced to either stay in the hamlet or travel through the night to reach another inn. The Sign of the White Ox offers comfortable beds, and the vegetables grown here in the manure-rich fields are enormous and tasty. The inn's food is absolutely delectable if one can ignore the occasional windborne whiff from the fields below the hill.

Rappan Athuk
(RAP-an AH-thuk, or ruh-PAN ah-THOOK)

Don't go down the well

The mausoleum of Rappan Athuk is only one of the many entrances to the great Dungeon of Graves, but it is the best known. Adventurers of all stripes make their way here to seek treasure and magic in the deep vaults below. Few return. It is perhaps worthy of note that even farther below the Dungeon of Graves one can find entrances to the Under Realms, the miles-long network of caverns that forms an entire and deadly subterranean world, populated by fell and eerie denizens of the lowest depths of the earth.

As noted earlier, far more detail about the Dungeon of Graves for those who wish to run adventures in the legendary dungeon are referred to **Rappan Athuk** by **Frog God Games**, and for those with players daring to explore into the Under Realms, one should most certainly obtain copies of the excellent **Cyclopean Deeps: Volume 1** and **Volume 2**, also published by **Frog God Games**.

50

Renderby

Bizarre rural highlanders with an odd economy

CN small town
Government autocracy
Population 2640 (2422 humans; 136 half-elves; 57 high elves; 25 halflings)
Notable NPCs
   Mayor Barth Lottenbandry (CN male human **commoner**)
   Gort Ramson, Proprietor of the Drunken Ram (CN male human **Ftr5**)
   Craile the Pious, "Priest" of Absolution Commerce (NE male human **Brd7**)
Maximum Clerical Spell Level Good —, Neutral —, Evil 4
Purchase Maximum/Month 4000gp

Renderby is the only significant town in the isolated highlands upriver from Zelkor's Ferry and the mouth of the Canyon River. By some strange twist of theology, the folk of the Renderby Hills are convinced that sins are transferred into whatever goods a person produces, and transferred to the eventual user or buyer. For this reason, merchants are a special class of individual, since their purchases absolve the seller's sins. Merchants dress in a distinctive orange coat in these highland regions to show their quasi-holy status, and purchase goods even from the worst sinners as long as the sinner offers a substantial discount on the price. From time to time, a village may even kidnap a merchant and force him to purchase their goods at lower than normal prices. Needless to say, the local merchants keep the place a well-guarded trade secret.

Most purchases in Renderby are made with chickens, which serve as a kind of substitute currency, since obviously chickens don't inherit the sins of the person who raised them. Visiting adventurers may be taken aback when the price of a round of beers in the Drunken Ram Tavern is "a quarter chicken." People keep records of partial-chicken transactions, and Mayor Lottenbandry has recently had some wooden "half-chicken" tokens made to facilitate partial-chicken transactions. Renderby is a strange place.

Ruined Fort

A ruined fort

The "Ruined Fort" to the south of the Mausoleum of Rappan Athuk is an old shell keep, once described as a "crumbling relic of a better time, hunched over the road like an old man beaten down by the rain." Its walls are scorched by dragonfire, and it is often occupied by the sorts of creatures one wishes to avoid. The fort once guarded the road and sea during the days before the Eastreach Decree of 2765, but it was put to siege during the Foerdewaith invasion and battered by catapults until the defenders yielded. The Lord-Governor has not seen fit to rebuild the fort, considering it a waste of "his" money to maintain a permanent garrison on such a seldom-used road.

Stoneheart River

The Stoneheart River is a tributary of the Great Amrin River. See *Great Amrin River*. It is found to the north of the Sinnar Coast Region map, and is thus not detailed here.

Stormshield

Unoccupied manor with legal entailments

Description

Stormshield is a private estate seized by the city of Eastwych in 3436 I.R. (81 years ago) after its owner, Captain Aldrin Shaw, deserted the

Royal Navy and absconded from Eastwych with a Foerdewaith cutter to Swordport in Hawkmoon. The unscrupulous Shaw went on to establish the town of Port Shaw on the Razor Coast. (See *Razor Coast* by **Frog God Games** for more information.) His estate was sold at auction decades later, and went through several owners, each going bankrupt in turn or coming to a bad end. It is currently unoccupied and is considered bad luck to own, though no one knows who currently owns it or where the documents of ownership can be found; the deed has not been updated with the Eastwych municipal clerk in more than a decade. More details about the deed to Stormshield may be found in *Sword of Air* by **Frog God Games**.

The Tantivy Road
(TAN-tiv-ee)

Nice, bucolic scenery. Nothing but peasants, porridge, and "tax collectors" for 450 miles… also, manticores.

Description

The Tantivy is a low-quality road of packed dirt and occasionally corduroy (earth-covered logs) where the path traverses marshy land. It is a long trail, for it is the only workable overland route from Carterscroft to the northern and eastern parts of the province. Unlike the high roads of Eastreach, the Tantivy is plagued by the same problems as most of rural Eastreach, namely barons who try to collect taxes from anyone entering their lands. Anyone using the Tantivy to cross long distances encounters numerous tax collectors, many of them little more than bandits.

Encounters

Encounter Chance: Make one encounter check in the morning, one in the afternoon, and one at night.

Risk Level: All encounters on the Tantivy Road are at the Medium-Risk level. Inside the one-hex radius around Carterscroft, there is an additional automatic encounter check in the surrounding hex and the city's hex. All encounters in the radius of the city are at the Low-Risk level.

01–10	No Encounter
11–70	Mundane Encounter
71–00	Dangerous Encounter

Mundane Encounters: Tantivy Road

1d100	Encounter
01–02	Annoyance (Encounter #3)
03–04	Baron and Retinue (Encounter #8)
05	Bear (Encounter #11)
06–12	Caravan (Eastreach) (Encounter #16)
13–14	Cleric (Encounter #19)
15–16	Druid (Encounter #31)
17–33	Farmer (Encounter #36)
34–42	Foot Patrol collecting taxes from travelers (Encounter #37)
43–51	Herder (Encounter #51)
52–57	Heretic (Encounter #52)
58	High Noble (Encounter #53)
59	Kenckoo Vagrant (Encounter #55)

1d100	Encounter
60–64	Knight and Retinue (Encounter #56)
65–66	Leper (Encounter #60)
67–70	Minstrel (Encounter #65)
71–74	Mounted Patrol (Encounter #67)
75–76	Outlaw (Encounter #71)
77–78	Peasant (Encounter #74)
79–81	Penitent (Encounter #76)
82	Pilgrim (Encounter #78)
83–87	Prisoner (Encounter #79)
88–89	Small Trader (halfling) (Encounter #86)
90–93	Small Trader (human) (Encounter #85)
94–95	Stag (Encounter #87)
96–98	Wandering Refugee (Encounter #98)
99–00	Wolf (Encounter #106)

Dangerous Encounters: Tantivy Road

1d100	Encounter
01–04	Ankheg (Encounter #2)
05–06	Ant (Encounter #4)
07–21	Bandit (Encounter #7)
22	Basilisk (Encounter #9)
23	Blood Hawk (Encounter #12)
24–26	Bugbear (Encounter #13)
27	Bulette (Encounter #14)
28–29	Cockatrice (Encounter #21)
30–34	Dragon A (Encounter #27)
35–37	Giant, Hill (Encounter #41)
38–47	Gnoll (Encounter #43)
48–53	Goblin, Roaming (Encounter #45)
54–56	Lycanthrope (Encounter #61)
57–61	Manticore (Encounter #63)
62–66	Ogre (Encounter #69)
67–72	Owlbear (Encounter #72)
73–74	Robber Knight (Encounter #80)
75–77	Stirge (Encounter #88)
78	Tangtal (Encounter #89)
79–85	Tiger (Encounter #90)
86–88	Troll (Encounter #92)
89–90	Unicorn (Encounter #93)
91	Undead A (Encounter #94)
92–93	Wasp, Giant (Encounter #99)
94–95	Weasel, Giant (Encounter #100)
96–00	Wyvern (Encounter #108)

Wain Road, The (North-South run)

A road that is no longer entirely safe, unless one travels with a Bard's Gate caravan

Appearance

The Wain Road is an old, Hyperborean road paved in stone and relatively straight.

Description

The north-south run of the Wain Road is entirely within Eastreach Province, and is the preferred route for Bard's Gate merchants making the overland trek to and from Eastgate (unless they are headed into central Foere itself). Under the special trade agreements negotiated with Bard's Gate, merchants of that city may travel the Wain Road free of tax, provided they carry one of the tokens assigned at Great Bridge or in Eastgate by sheriffs of the Lord-Governor. There are infrequent proverbial "pikes" along the road where locals pay a tax to continue along the road, also collected by the Lord-Governor's sheriffs. In addition to the legal pikes, locals and bandits occasionally set up their own toll-collecting stations, either claiming to be legitimate sheriffs or simply demanding a payment. The practice is more frequent on country roads, though, because the sheriffs are quick to hunt down anyone who poaches on the Lord-Governor's revenue from the high roads. Heads set up on actual pikes are seen occasionally where the sheriffs have meted out the Lord-Governor's justice to some deserving individuals.

See also the description of the east-west portion of the road, described in **Chapter 1: Aachen Province**, *Wain Road*.

Encounters

Encounter Chance: Make one encounter check in the morning, one in the afternoon, and one at night.

Risk Level: All encounters on the Wain Road are at the Medium-Risk level. Inside the one-hex radius around Carterscroft, there is an additional automatic encounter check in the surrounding hex and the city's hex. All encounters in the radius of the city are at the Low-Risk level.

01–05	No Encounter
06–64	Mundane Encounter
65–00	Dangerous Encounter

Mundane Encounters: Wain Road (Eastreach Province)

1d100	Encounter
01–02	Annoyance (Encounter #3)
03–04	Baron and Retinue (Encounter #8)
05	Bear (Encounter #11)
06–10	Caravan (Bard's Gate) (Encounter #15)
11–15	Caravan (Aachen or Eastreach) (Encounter #16)
16–18	Cleric (Encounter #19)
19–20	Elf (Encounter #34)
21–36	Farmer (Encounter #36)

1d100	Encounter
37–44	Foot Patrol (Encounter #37)
45–55	Herder (Encounter #51)
56–59	Heretic (Encounter #52)
60–61	High Noble (Encounter #53)
62–63	Kenckoo Vagrant (Encounter #55)
64–69	Knight and Retinue (Encounter #56)
70–71	Leper (Encounter #60)
72–75	Minstrel (Encounter #65)
76–80	Mounted Patrol (Encounter #67)
81–82	Outlaw (Encounter #71)
83–84	Peasant (Encounter #74)
85–87	Prisoner (Encounter #79)
88–89	Small Trader (halfling) (Encounter #86)
90–93	Small Trader (human) (Encounter #85)
94–95	Stags (Encounter #87)
96–98	Wandering Refugee (Encounter #98)
99–00	Wolf (Encounter #106)

Dangerous Encounters: Wain Road (Eastreach Province)

1d100	Encounter
01–04	Ankheg (Encounter #2)
05–25	Bandit (Encounter #7)
26–30	Bugbear (Encounter #13)
31–32	Bulette (Encounter #14)
33–36	Centaur (Encounter #17)
37–38	Cockatrice (Encounter #21)
39–42	Dragons A (Encounter #27)
43–44	Giant, Hill (Encounter #41)
45–52	Gnoll (Encounter #43)
53–58	Goblin, Roaming (Encounter #45)
59–60	Griffon (Encounter #47)
61–62	Lycanthrope (Encounter #61)
63–67	Manticore (Encounter #63)
68–70	Ogre (Encounter #69)
71–72	Owlbear (Encounter #72)
73–81	Robber Knight (Encounter #80)
82–85	Stirge (Encounter #88)
86–88	Tiger (Encounter #90)
89–90	Troll (Encounter #92)
91–94	Weasel, Giant (Encounter #100)
95	Witherstench (Encounter #104)
96–98	Wizard (Encounter #107)
99–00	Wyvern (Encounter #108)

Wild Edge River

Just don't go here

Description

The Wild Edge River is a bifurcation of the Great Amrin, where part of the Great Amrin's flow is broken away into a separate channel by a vast, triangular, stone pedestal. The smaller river created by the bifurcation cuts through the Forest of Hope, making a second fork in the middle of the forest. According to some accounts, the river is also split at its second division by the triangular base of a vast stone idol depicting an ancient, forgotten goddess. Hundreds of giant water snakes of a variety unseen elsewhere dwell in a catacomb of tunnels in the underwater stone foundations of the statue. The creatures make an eerie warbling cry by night, singing to the darkness. Understandably, no one ever comes to this place unless by accident.

The more massive triangular stone structure that cuts the flow of the Great Amrin at the upstream divide no longer appears to have a statue, and no giant, singing water snakes have ever been reported there. Both the stone structures are of pre-Hyperborean construction, and the stonework is superb. Curiously, centuries of flowing water have not eroded the stones themselves.

Zelkor's Ferry

(ZELL-cores)

A small ferry across the Canyon River, with a landing for riverboats, this little settlement is a common base camp for those foolish enough to explore the Mouth of Doom entrance to Rappan Athuk

N thorp
Government autocracy
Population 20+ (20+ humans)
Notable NPCs
  Gutmark, the ferryman (N male human **commoner**)
  Big Morgan, the blacksmith (LE male human **Ftr3**)
  Rasmus Pye, the trader (N male human **Wiz3**)
  Ulman Dark, the necromancer (NE male human **Wiz4**)
  Skorma, captain of the guard (N male human **Ftr4**)
  Odo Bristleback, the mayor-innkeeper (CN male human
    wereboar Bbn2)
Maximum Clerical Spell Level Good —, Neutral —, Evil —
Purchase Maximum/Month 500gp

Zelkor's Ferry is a tiny settlement near the mouth of the Canyon River. It is a common base of operations for adventurers en route to Rappan Athuk. An entrance to the Dungeon of Graves called the Mouth of Doom is found near the settlement, and this avenue into the great dungeons is widely considered to be less dangerous than the one at the Mausoleum (see *Rappan Athuk*, above). More detail about Zelkor's Ferry is contained in the Wilderness Section of ***Rappan Athuk*** by **Frog God Games**.

Chapter Four: Exeter Province

Exeter Province

(ECKS-eh-ter)

Overview

Exeter is a loyal province of the Kingdom of Foere, ruled by a Lord-Governor appointed by the Overking. It is cut off from the rest of the Kingdoms, and for the last ten years has been governed on the principle of defending the borders at all costs, without preemptive attacks against raiders, and without regard for the decline of law and order in the interior of the province. The population of the rural areas is under constant threat from roaming brigands and monsters of all kinds.

General Information

Alignment: LN
Capital: Albor Broce (14,830)
Notable Settlements: Cairn Condor (729), Jambles (2,721), Whitsun Measow (253)
Ruler: Lord-Governor Benevic of Lortsbar (LN male human **Ftr10**)
Government: feudalism (vassal of Foere)
Population: 1,326,560 (966,500 Foerdewaith; 206,000 Heldring; 62,000 halflings; 39,000 high elves; 26,560 half-orcs; 12,800 hill dwarves; 9,500 wood elves; 4,200 mountain dwarves)
Humanoid: halfling (some), high elf (some), half-orc (some), hill dwarf (some), wood elf (few), mountain dwarf (few)
Monstrous: wolf, goblin, giant animal, centaur, hobgoblin, orc, auroch, ogre-kin, ogre, corpse rook (plains); fey, ettercap, tangtal, wood giant, forest drake, lycanthrope, treant, corpse rook (Wiltangle forest); orc, ogre-kin, undead, quickwood, witherstench, ogre, harpy, half-ogre, vulchling, minotaur, troll (highlands); orc, rock troll, hill giant, peryton, ettin, gargoyle (Forlorn Mountains foothills)
Languages: Common, Helvaenic, Halfling, Elvish, Dwarvish
Religion: Ceres, Vanitthu, Freya, Frigg, Tykee, Odin, Hester, Mick O'Delving, Tyr, Mithras, Darach-Albith
Resources: foodstuffs, livestock, grain, trade hub, gems (grade 1), tobacco
Technology Level: High Middle Ages, Dark Ages (some isolated areas)

Borders and Lands

Exeter's capital is Albor Broce, which is built around the site of an ancient Hyperborean fortress. Its territory extends north to the Wilderland Hills, west to the intersection of the South Road and Provincial Military Road, south to the edges of the Wiltangle Forest, and east to Cut Horn Gap.

History and People

Exeter Province once extended all the way down to the Helwall, built 83 years before the Imperial Record began to chart the years, and in its early role as a military frontier, played a major role in battling the Heldring raiders at the dawn of the Hyperborean Empire. In 2802, after the Battle of Oescreheit Downs and the final defeat of the Heldring, the lands now governed as Cerediun province were divided away from the original, much larger Province of Exeter. The early history of the province is a long recitation of war and ruin: Heldring armies marching through the area to raid along the March of Mountains, Hyperborean and then Foerdewaith armies marching to bring them to battle, refugees, fire, and pillage. Ten years ago, Exeter Province was spared from the violence of the Wilderlands Clan War of 3506 that was fought almost exclusively in Keston Province and the Wilderland Hills of southern Suilley. This was an exception to the norm, however: Over the course of history, vast numbers of incursions into the regions between the March of Mountains and the Forlorn Mountains have pillaged their way through Exeter Province, skirting around castles and forts but ravaging the countryside unopposed by the province's much-weaker armies. Exeter Province has long held the uneasy position of serving as one of civilization's buffer zones.

As a result of this dismal and violent history, the province is not heavily settled.

Trade and Commerce

Exeter conducts and regulates overland trade with Hawkmoon to the east, which generates most of its revenue, and to some extent also trades with the Helcynngae Peninsula to the south (though this goes through Cerediun Province first, taking the most lucrative cut of tolls and taxes).

Loyalties and Diplomacy

Exeter maintains its loyalty to the Throne of Foere, though it has little contact with its liege state. The Overking's court sends a new Lord-Governor once every decade or so, and the former Lord-Governor assembles his retinue, guards, and profits for the journey home to Courghais. The Province has virtually stopped paying taxes to the

Court at Courghais after more than one large shipment of silver was annihilated by bandits while in transit. Small shipments of tax money are often sent, along with guards, with merchant caravans on their way to the County of Vourdon. The total of these sums, though, is a slight fraction of what the Overking could normally expect if the Province were not cut off from the rest of the Kingdoms.

In return, Exeter Province receives less help from the Royal Court in Courghais than it would ordinarily expect as a loyal province, even though it would send the taxes if it could.

Government

A Lord-Governor, residing in the capital of Albor Broce, administers Exeter Province on behalf of the Overking of Foere. The current Lord-Governor is Benevic of Lortsbar, a knight-commander who rose to fame in Foere after successfully holding off a massive assault upon a border castle under his command in the Duchy of Mains. Unfortunately, Lord Benevic's military expertise and attitudes are entirely defensive; on behalf of Exeter and Foere, he created a brilliant system of defenses and fortified the borders against attack, without focusing on the problems created by emptying the province's interior of troops.

Wilderness and Adventure

The wilderness is creeping in like nightfall. Troops no longer make regular patrols, and rural garrisons have been bled of their soldiers to man the forts and castles along the edge of the Wilderland Hills to the north. The population of Exeter Province has never been large, and settlements tend to be isolated, unguarded, and ripe for the plucking. Heroes are needed to stem the rising tide of chaos, and protect the lands of civilization! This area has the potential for all kinds of adventures, for there is wilderness in between almost every village and hamlet except along the high roads.

Changing Times

At present, the Lord-Governor keeps his troops carefully deployed in camps and small forts to watch for further incursions from the north in case of a repeat of the Wilderlands Clan War. A chain of signal fires has been arranged to warn the capital if battle is joined in the highlands. One unintended result of this caution is that the rest of the province is currently short on troops and patrols, with most of the soldiery concentrated along the northern border or walled up in Albor Broce. Ten years of this defensive strategy have caused burgeoning problems with beasts and monsters in the rural countryside, and unchecked banditry is on the rise.

Albor Broce

(AL-bor BRO-chee)

Excessively defended capital of Exeter Province

LN large city
Government overlord
Population 14,830 (11,222 humans; 2159 halflings; 830 high elves; 619 hill dwarves)
Notable NPCs
    Lord-Governor Benevic of Lortsbar (LN male human **Ftr10**)
    Sir Ghendric the Terrier, Commander of the Squires of the Ferret (LE male human **knight**)
    Sir Rohnic Ort, Minister of the Capital (LN male human **Ftr9**)
    Archbishop Suald Marchmain (LN male human **Clr9** of Vanitthu)
    High Priestess Lynn Fortuna (N female human **Clr8** of Tykee)
Maximum Clerical Spell Level Good —, Neutral 5, Evil 4 (hidden)
Purchase Maximum/Month 32,000gp

Albor Broce is the capital of Exeter Province, built 69 years before the beginning of the Imperial record. Built on the site of an early Hyperborean fort, the streets still run in the straight grid that the Hyperboreans laid out, though the city has long since outgrown the ditch that surrounded the fort. In some places in the city, the ditch and berm can still be discerned as a gentle, curving rise in the ground, and occasionally the citizens still find artifacts of old Hyperborea when digging for new wells or building foundations. The city is well-fortified with high stone walls, and Lord-Governor Benevic has personally supervised their repair and improvement. The Citadel of Broche, home and court of the Lord-Governor, is constantly abuzz with soldiers training at siege defense, and with the comings and goings of his force of counter-treason spies.

These spies are organized as the Squires of the Ferret, which does not grant its members the full status of knighthood (which the Lord-Governor awards only to those who are staunch warriors), but lends them approximately the same powers as a sheriff. The Provincial Order of the Squires of the Ferret is commanded by a knight by the name of Sir Ghendric the Terrier, who essentially functions as Lord Benevic's spymaster. Since the province actually contains only a very few subversive conspirators, the Terrier has to stretch a bit to justify his position, and has a long-standing practice of treating late tax payments as evidence of treasonous intent.

The troops stationed in Albor Broche are trained to perfection, although most are unbloodied in combat; they would be a formidable fighting force if challenged. They are efficient at keeping order in the city, and their informants are well paid; any sort of crime beyond petty thievery is extraordinarily rare within the city walls.

Unlike most cities in the Borderland Provinces, Albor Broche has no municipal government of its own; it is treated as part of the Lord-Governor's direct responsibility, and the Lord-Governor delegates most tasks to Sir Rohnic Ort, his "Minister of the Capital." Sir Ort is a capable administrator and an intelligent man. He is disturbed by the increasing lawlessness of the countryside beyond the capital, but he considers his role to be limited to the city and nothing but the city. Moreover, even if someone asked

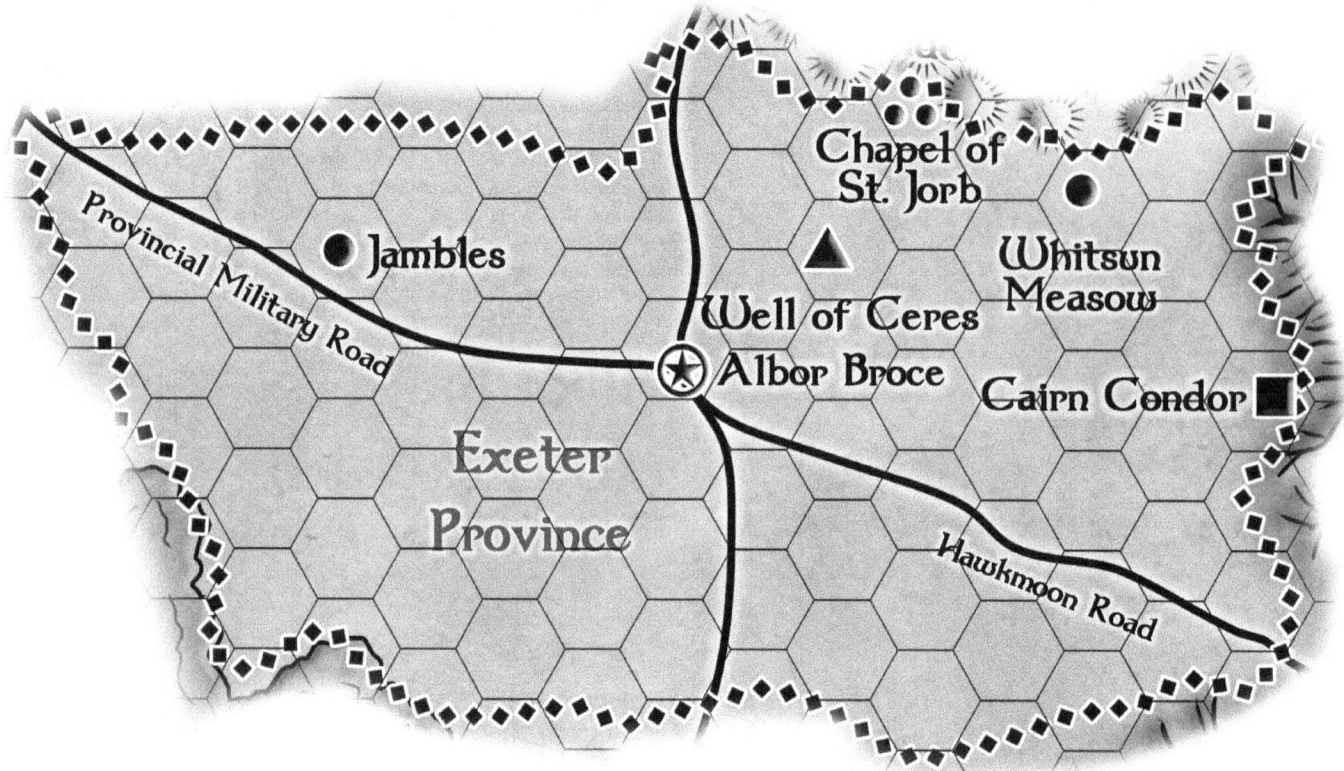

him for a solution to the problems in Exeter Province, he would have no answer. Sir Ort is trapped within the same defensive mentality as the Lord-Governor, unable to see that all the Province's resources for keeping order are deployed around the borders instead of balanced between the borders and the countryside. To be fair, Sir Ort has a weaker perspective than the Lord-Governor, since he is not privy to the Province's large-scale deployments. Sitting in the well-defended capital, he has no way of understanding that within 25 miles of his armories there are villages utterly undefended from even the threat of a few lightly-armed ruffians.

All traveling merchants passing through Albor Broche are required to bring their wagons to a large Customs House just inside the gate where the contents are tallied and then taxed at 2% of their value. The Lord-Governor's tax-assessors are not easily bribed, for they know they are watched carefully by the Squires of the Ferret, and accepting bribes is a capital crime.

Adventures

The Temple of Vanitthu and the Temple of Thyr are both offering rewards of 1000gp for the return, unharmed, of a heretic named Bantar Prayershield. Talking to the clerics reveals that he is said to be in a place called Whitsun Measow, presumably a small village somewhere in the Province, but no one knows where it is (this is not abnormal for small villages). See *Whitsun Measow*.

Cairn Condor

(cairn KON-dor)

Main border-stronghold of Exeter Province's eastern marches

Cairn Condor is a citadel built on the crest of a tall foothill at the base of the Forlorn Mountains. The fortress is manned by troops from the Lord-Governor's army, and is the base for all patrols along Exeter's 250-mile mountain frontier. Its walls are 40ft high, and the great keep rises to a height of 80ft. A huge farseeing lens called the "Condor's Eye" is mounted on the

keep's roof and allows the castle's defenders to see great distances along the mountain border and into many of the nearby mountain valleys where foes might be gathering. When weather permits, the lens is constantly manned, being rotated inch by inch to survey the landscape for enemies.

The long title of "Strategos of Cairn Condor and the Forlorn March" is held by Sir Pernanz Avor (NG male human **Ftr9**), who led Exeter Province's only attack into the Wilderland Hills during the Wilderlands Clan Wars, at the age of 31. Sir Pernanz is deeply concerned about the Lord-Governor's refusal to let border patrols pursue raiders back into their own territory, and considers the Forlorn March to be getting more vulnerable by the day; orcs, bandits, and other raiders confronted with Sir Pernanz's soldiers can simply retreat back into the mountains without fear of pursuit, ready to return another day. Many of his soldiers, frustrated at their enforced ineffectiveness and, hearing of unrest near their homes, have deserted to protect their loved ones instead of engaging in the futile border watch here.

Nevertheless, the fortress is well-garrisoned and receives supplies and payments regularly; the Lord-Governor does not stint his border defenses, he merely shackles them with rules. Sir Pernanz has begun siphoning some of the money to pay independent mercenaries who can attack the raiders in their holes and hideouts. Some of these mercenaries are even quartered in the fortress itself, eat with the troops, and train with them if they are not deployed.

The garrison of the fortress is 400 infantry, 200 cavalry, and 25 knights, together with 3 "counselor-mages" of 6th level.

Chapel of St. Jorb (Ruins) (JORB)

Ruined chapel, once a popular destination for pilgrimages, now rather dangerous

Introduction

The Ruined Chapel of St. Jorb is located just within the Wilderland Hills on a hilltop surrounded by ancient forestation. A single cart track once led here, but it is now overgrown with brush and recent tree growth, and cannot be found other than by an experienced woodsman or ranger. The general location of the chapel can be found in records of the Church of Mithras, and nearby villages can also direct travelers toward the site.

History

Since the time of St. Jorb, the chapel served not only as a religious site but also as a minor fortress defending against incursions from the hill clans and humanoids of the area. Volunteer soldiers of Mithras garrisoned the fortified chapel and mounted retaliatory raids against any reavers and brigands who attacked southward into the Province.

After St. Jorb's death, the chapel became a popular destination for pilgrimages, drawing Mithraic followers from as far away as Keston Province. Although Jorb's mace had been moved to Kingston as a holy relic, the statue of Mithras where Jorb prayed is considered a place of miracles. As with most temples of Mithras, the statue is found in a sanctified underground chamber. Unfortunately, during the Wilderlands Clan Wars ten years ago, the chapel was overwhelmed by a force of hill giants and ogres making their way toward the western reaches of the hills and into Keston. As mountain gargoyles plunged and swooped over the chapel, forcing the garrison to defend itself, the ground troops of the attackers lumbered from the tree line to reach the chapel, and slew the rest of the defenders in a desperate battle at the doors of the sanctum. In a wild celebration of their victory that lasted for days, the hill giants smashed down the outer wall of the fortification and reduced the sanctum to a pile of broken rock. Eventually the gargoyles brought their forces under control, and the horde moved on, leaving a desolated ruin in their wake.

A few pilgrims still occasionally make their way to the ruined chapel, where they have buried the dead and cleared away the entrance to the sanctified underground chamber where the statue still stands undamaged. In the last five years as the garrisons of Exeter Province retreated from the forts located in the hills themselves, pilgrimages have become more dangerous and less frequent. Not all such travelers have returned.

Current Situation

The buildings and walls of the chapel complex now lie completely in ruins, with grasses and sapling trees growing where the battle-chaplains and temple clerics of Mithras once walked. The place is now occupied by a gang of minotaurs who sleep in the chamber under the ruined sanctum, where the statue stands.

Chamber of the Statue

> A rectangular hole in the floor of the ruined chapel building reveals a flight of stone stairs leading down into the darkness. After making due preparations, you proceed down in your chosen marching order. At the bottom of the stairs, sixty feet below the surface, the stairway enters into a circular chamber eighty feet in diameter, with a domed ceiling that rises to a height of twenty feet at the apex. A marble statue stands against the northern wall across the chamber from you. It depicts a man holding the head of a bull in one hand and a sword in the other. In front of the statue there is wide bronze bowl four feet in diameter, and a large number of human skulls are arranged to either side of it.

Before the characters can investigate the room any further, they have to deal with the **5 minotaurs** that live here. One of them is always keeping an eye on the stairs, for this is a region where anything might come wandering around to investigate caves and other possible lairs.

Minotaur (5): **AC** 14; **HP** 76 (9d10+27); **Spd** 40ft; **Melee** greataxe (+6, 2d12+4 slashing) or gore (+6, 2d8+4

piercing); **SA** charge (move at least 10ft, hit with gore, take extra 2d8 piercing), reckless (gain tactical advantage but attack against also gain tactical advantage); **Str** +4, **Dex** +0, **Con** +3, **Int** –2, **Wis** +3, **Cha** –1; **Skills** Perception +7; **Senses** darkvision 60ft; **Traits** labyrinthine recall; **AL** CE; **CR** 3; **XP** 700.

> **Equipment:** loincloth, greataxe, belt pouch
> *Belt Pouch 1:* pair of human-bone dice, 87gp, 22cp
> *Belt Pouch 2:* five sticks of beef (yes, beef) jerky, 28gp, pearl (250gp)
> *Belt Pouch 3:* damaged ring of invisibility (roll percentile dice to see how much of a person becomes invisible or degree to which person fades entirely from sight, equal chance for either type of result)
> *Belt Pouch 4:* 80gp, 91sp, jade statue of Thyr, cracked (200gp)
> *Belt Pouch 5:* 54gp, 56sp, large set of iron toenail clippers, 2 opals (100gp each)

Once the minotaurs are dealt with, the characters can take a closer look at the temple. The minotaurs have left a quantity of filth and garbage scattered around, but they have not approached the statue or the skulls arrayed to either side of it. There are 25 skulls on each side of the statue, arranged in neat rows. These are the remains of the chapel's defenders, who died defending the sanctum. Earlier pilgrims placed them here as a memorial to their valorous martyrdom, always to reside with the god.

The Statue of Mithras

The statue does not convey any benefits or have any unusual qualities that would affect a group of adventurers. Anyone touching it experiences a rush of bravery and elation, but the feeling fades quickly and has no measurable effect other than to make clear that the statue is still a powerful relic of Mithras.

If, however, the characters are here with a major request (such as obtaining atonement for the heretic community of Whitsun Measow — see *Whitsun Measow*), the statue communicates with them through the voice and intercession of St. Jorb. They receive a sudden vision of many of the god's memories: vast Hyperborean armies on the march, sacrifices of bulls in underground temples such as this one, and high priests in battle armor standing before fields of slaughter. When the images fade, St. Jorb speaks through the mouth of the statue, and discusses what the characters want to achieve. Again, in order for the characters to gain this audience with the saint, their request must be selfless and fairly epic.

In the particular case of the Whitsun Measow heretics, which is the most likely reason for the characters to be here, the saint is willing to grant atonement to each heretic who touches the statue and recants all heresy. However, the boon is not granted without a price. Depending on the situation, the saint might ask either of the following tasks to be undertaken, or any other that might make sense:

1. The heretics must remain here, rebuild the chapel, and maintain the place as a site of pilgrimage. Since this would likely end in their slaughter at the hands of the beasts living in the Wilderland Hills, the rebuilt religious site would need one of Mithras' battle-chaplains to be stationed here as the new spiritual leader and defender of the reclaimed heretics. The characters would be charged with the task of going to Albor Broce to find such a cleric, and might end up needing to go all the way to Kingston if the Lord-Governor of Exeter refuses to grant permission for one of his own battle-chaplains to leave.

2. If one of the characters is a cleric of Mithras, the saint might actually grant the ruined chapel to the character as a personal stronghold to be held in the god's name. There would be no requirement that the heretics stay, but if a cleric is to establish a stronghold, it would make sense to invite the reformed heretics to stay at the stronghold as tenant farmers or herders.

Cut Horn Gap, Duchy of Dusquesne

The Cut Horn Gap is not properly considered a part of Exeter Province, for it comprises the small Duchy of Duquesne, currently under the rule of Duchess Shalindra. The origin of this duchy is unknown, and its political allegiances are unclear. Some scholars assume that the folk of the Duchy are descendants of the peoples that eventually moved to settle the Domain of Hawkmoon, or perhaps are a part of lost Parma. In any case, the duchess has made plain on many occasions that Dusquesne is not, nor ever was, a part of the Kingdoms of Foere. She has also refused every offer from the Kingdom of Suilley to join its ranks. Despite its rather enigmatic political status, the duchy remains the closest overland trading partner of the Domain of Hawkmoon, and the two domains are allied in mutual defense.

Hawkmoon Road

A relatively safe road between Albor Broce and the realms beyond the Cut Horn Gap

Appearance

Not one of the old, stone high roads built by the Hyperboreans, this flat hardpan trail is in poor condition, but still much better than a typical dirt road.

Description

The Hawkmoon Road connects the city of Albor Broce to the Duchy of Duquesne (due-KANE) in Cut Horn Gap. Long-patrols from Albor Broche ride the road to the border of that small duchy to ensure that its length in Exeter Province remains relatively safe, although this effort suffers from the fact that the few forts along the road are under orders to keep most of their garrisons behind walls in case of attacks from the mountains.

Encounters

Encounter Chance: Make one encounter check in the morning, one in the afternoon, and one at night.

Risk Level: All encounters on the Hawkmoon Road are at the Medium-Risk level. Inside the one-hex radius around Albor Broche, there is an additional automatic encounter check in the surrounding hex and the city's hex. All encounters in the radius of the city are at the Low-Risk level.

01–25	No Encounter
26–65	Mundane Encounter
66–00	Dangerous Encounter

Mundane Encounters: Hawkmoon Road

1d100	Encounter
01–02	Annoyance (Encounter #3)
03–04	Baron and Retinue (Encounter #8)
05–08	Bear (Encounter #11)
09–11	Caravan (Provincial) (Encounter #16)
12–13	Cleric (Encounter #19)
14	Druid (Encounter #31)
15–16	Elf (Encounter #34)
17–28	Farmer (Encounter #36)
29–30	Farmer, almost-empty wagons, skinny (Encounter #36)
31–35	Foot Patrol of the Ferrets, seeking outlaws (Encounter #37)
36	Foot Patrol, actually patrolling (Encounter #37)
37–44	Herder (Encounter #51)
45–48	Herder (Encounter #51) unless in Cut Horn Gap, in which case, Mountain Goats (Encounter #65)
49–51	Heretic (Encounter #52)
52–53	Kenckoo Vagrant (Encounter #55)
54–59	Knight and Retinue (Encounter #56)
60–61	Leper (Encounter #60)
62–64	Mounted Patrol (Encounter #67)
65–70	Outlaw, tax evasion (Encounter #71)
71–72	Peasant (Encounter #74)
73–74	Penitent (Encounter #76)
75–81	Prisoner, treason and/or tax evasion (Encounter #79)
82	Small Trader (dwarf) (Encounter #86)
83–85	Small Trader (halfling) (Encounter #85)
86–88	Stag (Encounter #87)
89–95	Wandering Refugee, home destroyed by monsters or bandits (Encounter #98)
96–00	Wolf (Encounter #106)

Dangerous Encounters: Hawkmoon Road

1d100	Encounter
01	Ankheg (Encounter #2)
02–21	Bandit (Encounter #7)
22	Basilisk (Encounter #9)
23–27	Blood Hawk (Encounter #12)
28	Corpse Rook (Encounter #22)
29–33	Dragons A (Encounter #27)
34	Drake, Fire (Encounter #30)
35–36	Eagle, Giant (Encounter #33)
37	Ettin (Encounter #35)
38–40	Giant, Hill (Encounter #41)
41–42	Giant, Stone (Encounter #42)
43–47	Goblin Raider (Encounter #44)
48–53	Griffon (Encounter #47) near Mountains only; otherwise, Owlbear (Encounter #72)
54–58	Harpy (Encounter #50)
59–60	Lycanthrope (Encounter #61)
61–65	Manticore (Encounter #63)
66–67	Ogre (Encounter #69)
68	Ogre Mage (Encounter #70)
69	Peryton (Encounter #77) near Mountains only; otherwise, Roaming Goblin (Encounter #45)

1d100	Encounter
70–74	Robber Knight (Encounter #80)
75–76	Roc (Encounter #81)
77–78	Stirge (Encounter #88)
79	Tiger (Encounter #90)
80–81	Troll (Encounter #92)
82–83	Undead A (Encounter #94)
84–87	Vulchling (Encounter #97)
88–89	Wasp, Giant (Encounter #99)
90–91	Werewolf (Encounter #101) near Mountains only; otherwise, Bugbear (Encounter #13)
92–93	Witherstench (Encounter #104)
94–95	Wolverine, Giant (Encounter #105)
96	Wizard (Encounter #107)
97–00	Wyvern (Encounter #108)

Jambles

(JAM-bulls)

Town with a large halfling population

LN small town
Government autocracy (elected mayor)
Population 2721 (2305 halflings; 396 humans; 20 high elves)
Notable NPCs
  Mayor Totho Bellfeather (LG male halfling **noble**)
  Lieutenant-Mayor Leanna Keene (NG female human **commoner**)
  Horkle Drumbeet, Squire of the Ferret (LE male halfling **Rog4**)
  Olivia Drinkfinder (NG female halfling **Clr6** of Pekko)
  Shannus Nobleheart (CG male halfling **Clr8** of Mick O'Delving)
  Parfandelia Hearthstone (CG female halfling **Clr9** of Mother Hubbard)
  Bodmic Badolat (LN male human **Clr6** of Telophus)
  Errilotzpen the Illuminate (N male human **Sor11**)
Maximum Clerical Spell Level Good 5, Neutral 4, Evil —
Purchase Maximum/Month 4000gp

Jambles is a small town walled with stone, located just by the Provincial Military Road about halfway between Albor Broce and the crossroad with the South Road. The area enclosed by the walls is unusually large for the town's population, and from the outside it looks like a small city. The town was originally a halfling village of burrow-houses and a few one-story structures, but its location on the road caused a slow influx of human traders and even a few elves. Now the area inside the walls is a strange mix of four-story human buildings alongside the burrow-houses and low-ceilinged buildings of the town's halfling population.

The town is benevolently governed by a halfling mayor, Totho Bellfeather, and a Lieutenant-Mayor, a human trader by the name of Leanna Keene. The town's charter calls for the halflings of the community to elect the mayor, and the humans to elect the Lieutenant-Mayor. This has maintained the overall halfling-culture feel that permeates Jambles.

Recently the town also became the regional headquarters of the Squires of the Ferret (see *Albor Broce*). The leader of the Lord-Governor's secret police here is a halfling by the name of Horkle Drumbeet. Horkle is a proud, greedy sort who enjoys his status as an officer of the Lord-Governor, and relishes the power it gives him over his fellow halflings and the big humans who otherwise make him a bit nervous.

Jambles has three inns for travelers to stay in during their visits. The first is the Highceiling, built for human dimensions. The second is the Windows, a burrow-hall with sleeping rooms along the length, each of which has a round window at ground level. Only the first two sleeping rooms along the hall are tall enough for humans to use comfortably; the rest of the rooms are sized for halflings and can also be used by dwarves. The town's third inn is the Badger's Head, with halfling-sized rooms on the ground floor and human-sized rooms on two upper floors.

The Highceiling and the Badger's Head are courtyards surrounded by a stable, a common room, and one or more buildings containing the rented rooms. The gates are locked by night, but a watchman opens them for guests entering or leaving during the night hours.

The town's main temple contains shrines to Pekko, the shared human, dwarven, gnome, and halfling god of ale and spirits; Mick O'Delving, patron deity of halflings; and the halfling hearth goddess Hester, known in Jambles by her more colloquial name of "Mother Hubbard". There is a human-run temple of Telophus (god of crops and seasons) as well. At one point, the town had a temple to the Hyperborean goddess Solanus, but the temple has closed and the building is now used for warehousing.

The main crops raised around Jambles are tobacco and barley, the fields dotted with burrow-halls of the more rural farming families who travel into the town only on market days. Low stone walls line the fields in a patchwork quilt, with enclosures for ponies. Most of these farms keep geese and dogs, and cannot be approached without creating an enormous racket of warning. Unlike the halflings of the town, the rural farmers are hostile and suspicious of "foreigners."

Unfortunately, the open and hospitable character of the town has begun to erode after a year of serving as a gathering place for the Ferrets. Squire Drumbeet supervises three agents who keep an eye out for traitors and tax-evaders. He also has the authority to order out the local sheriff's men to arrest anyone suspected of such crimes. Under increasing pressure from Ghendric the Terrier, head of the Squires in Albor Broce, to find criminals, Squire Drumbeet has had to become increasingly strict and inquisitive, to the point that even this pompous official is getting very uncomfortable with the questionable requirements being placed on him. So far he has not fallen into the trap of manufacturing crimes to generate revenue, but if he wishes to remain in his post he will most likely be forced into it soon.

The townsfolk know that Squire Drumbeet is always watching for minor infractions that can be classed as petty treason, and they are becoming steadily quieter and more careful in what they say.

The Notquite Inn

See **Chapter 6: Keston Province,** *The Notquite Inn*. The inn is located at the intersection of three borders, Keston, Exeter, and Toullen, and is not ruled by any of the three.

Provincial Military Road

Once a safe road, but no longer adequately patrolled

This ancient road was built in the days of war against the Heldring to connect the South Road with a direct route to the Helwall so that reinforcing armies were not faced with grueling overland travel across country. Despite the antiquity of its construction, the original paving stones remain in place, and the road is wide and level, making it easier to travel than many of the royal roads in the heartland of Foere.

Encounters

Encounter Chance: Make one encounter check in the morning, one in the afternoon, and one at night.

Risk Level: All encounters on the Provincial Military Road are at the Medium-Risk level. Inside the one-hex radius around Albor Broche, there is an additional automatic encounter check in the surrounding hex and the city's hex. All encounters in the radius of the city are at the Low-Risk level.

01–20	No Encounter
21–65	Mundane Encounter
66–00	Dangerous Encounter

Mundane Encounters: Provincial Military Road

1d100	Encounter
01–02	Annoyance (Encounter #3)
03–04	Baron and Retinue (Encounter #8)
05–06	Bear (Encounter #11)
07–11	Caravan (Provincial) (Encounter #16)
12–13	Cleric (Encounter #19)
14	Druid (Encounter #31)
15–16	Elf (Encounter #34)
17–31	Farmer (Encounter #36)
32–37	Foot Patrol (Encounter #37)
38–46	Herder (Encounter #51)
47–48	Heretic (Encounter #52)
49–50	High Noble (Encounter #53)
51	Kenckoo Vagrant (Encounter #55)
52–56	Knight and Retinue (Encounter #56)
57–58	Leper (Encounter #60)
59	Military (Encounter #64)
60–62	Minstrel (Encounter #65)
63–66	Mounted Patrol (Encounter #67)
67	Noble of the Realm (Encounter #68)
68–71	Outlaw (Encounter #71)
72–74	Peasant (Encounter #74)
75–77	Penitent (Encounter #76)
78–81	Prisoner (Encounter #79)
82	Small Trader (dwarf or halfling) (Encounter #86)
83–86	Small Trader (human) (Encounter #85)
87–88	Stag (Encounter #87)
89–93	Wandering Refugee (Encounter #98)
94	Wild Horse or Pony (Encounter #103)
95–00	Wolf (Encounter #106)

Dangerous Encounters: Provincial Military Road

1d100	Encounter
01	Ankheg (Encounter #2)
02–21	Bandit (Encounter #7)
22	Basilisk (Encounter #9)
23–27	Blood Hawk (Encounter #12)
28	Corpse Rook (Encounter #22)
29–33	Dragon A (Encounter #27)

1d100	Encounter
34	Drake, Fire (Encounter #30)
35–36	Eagle, Giant (Encounter #33)
37	Ettin (Encounter #35)
38–40	Giant, Hill (Encounter #41)
41–42	Giant, Stone (Encounter #42)
43–47	Goblin Raider (Encounter #44)
48–53	Griffon (Encounter #47)
54–58	Harpy (Encounter #50)
59–60	Lycanthrope (Encounter #61)
61–65	Manticore (Encounter #63)
66–67	Ogre (Encounter #69)
68–69	Ogre Mage (Encounter #70)
70–74	Robber Knight (Encounter #80)
75–76	Roc (Encounter #81)
77–78	Stirge (Encounter #88)
79	Tiger (Encounter #90)
80–81	Troll (Encounter #92)
82–83	Undead A (Encounter #94)
84–87	Vulchling (Encounter #97)
88–89	Wasp, Giant (Encounter #99)
90–91	Werewolf (Encounter #101)
92–93	Witherstench (Encounter #104)
94–95	Wolverine, Giant (Encounter #105)
96	Wizard (Encounter #107)
97–00	Wyvern (Encounter #108)

Trader's Way
(Exeter Province)

The seemingly endless Trader's Way continues southward through Exeter Province, a well-guarded stretch

Trader's Way is almost certainly the longest road in Akados, carrying trade from the Helwall far to the south in Cerediun Province all the way to Telar Brindel in the north. Through Exeter Province, the road is as well-patrolled as the Lord-Governor can manage, for it is the major artery for north-south trade running through the Province, and a vital factor in the prosperity of Exeter's capital city of Albor Broce. A certain degree of banditry is inevitable, of course, especially along such a long and often isolated thoroughfare. Indeed, certain villages seem to "lose" an unusual number of lone travelers, but the patrols have produced no proof of wrongdoing, and most of the missing wayfarers were, after all, foreigners from beyond Exeter's borders. The Lord-Governor's patrols do not range farther north than a great stone marker at the foot of the Wilderland Hills where the road begins to rise. The marker is deeply carved with a warning in the common Westerling tongue, warning travelers that they are passing beyond the Lord-Governor's "imperial" mandate.

Roughly halfway between Albor Broche and the edge of the Wilderland Hills, the Trader's Way becomes the boundary-line between Keston Province and Exeter Province. There is no particular sign of the border other than at the point where the road rises into the highlands. Two small castles there, one in the service of Exeter and one in the service of Keston Province, face each other across the road not more than a hundred yards apart (the Lord-Governor's stone warning-sign is also within sight of the two garrisons).

Encounters

Encounter Chance: Make one encounter check in the morning, one in the afternoon, and one at night.

Risk Level: All encounters on the Trader's Way within the borders of Exeter Province are at the Medium-Risk level, but *where they enter the Wilderland Hills into Suilley,* they become a High-Risk area (note also that the Lorremach Highhills to the north in Suilley are also a High-Risk area). Inside the one-hex radius around Albor Broche, there is an additional automatic encounter check in the surrounding hex and the city's hex. All encounters in the radius of the city are at the Low-Risk level.

01–20	No Encounter
21–65	Mundane Encounter
66–00	Dangerous Encounter

Mundane Encounters: Trader's Way (Exeter Province)

1d100	Encounter
01–02	Annoyance (Encounter #3)
03–04	Baron and Retinue (Encounter #8)
05–06	Bear (Encounter #11)
07–11	Caravan (Provincial) (Encounter #16)
12–13	Cleric (Encounter #19)
14	Druid (Encounter #31)
15–16	Elf (Encounter #34)
17–31	Farmer (Encounter #36)
32–37	Foot Patrol (Encounter #37)
38–45	Herder (Encounter #51)
46–48	Heretic (Encounter #52)
49–50	High Noble (Encounter #53)
51	Kenckoo Vagrant (Encounter #55)
52–56	Knight and Retinue (Encounter #56)
57–58	Lepers (Encounter #60)
59	Military (Encounter #64)
60–62	Minstrel (Encounter #65)
63–66	Mounted Patrol (Encounter #67)
67	Noble of the Realm (Encounter #68)
68–71	Outlaw (Encounter #71)
72–74	Peasant (Encounter #74)
75–77	Penitent (Encounter #76)
78–81	Prisoner (Encounter #79)
82	Small Trader (dwarf or halfling) (Encounter #86)
83–86	Small Trader (human) (Encounter #85)
87–88	Stag (Encounter #87)
89–93	Wandering Refugee (Encounter #98)
94	Wild Horse or Pony (Encounter #103)
95–00	Wolf (Encounter #106)

Dangerous Encounters: Trader's Way (Exeter Province)

1d100	Encounter
01	Ankheg (Encounter #2)
02–21	Bandit (Encounter #7)
22	Basilisk (Encounter #9)
23–27	Blood Hawk (Encounter #12)
28	Corpse Rook (Encounter #22)
29–33	Dragon A (Encounter #27)
34	Drake, Fire (Encounter #30)
35–36	Eagle, Giant (Encounter #33)
37	Ettin (Encounter #35)
38–40	Giant, Hill (Encounter #41)
41–42	Giant, Stone (Encounter #42)
43–47	Goblin Raider (Encounter #44)
48–53	Griffon (Encounter #47)
54–58	Harpy (Encounter #50)
59–60	Lycanthrope (Encounter #61)
61–65	Manticore (Encounter #63)
66–67	Ogre (Encounter #69)
68–69	Ogre Mage (Encounter #70)
70–74	Robber Knight (Encounter #80)
75–76	Roc (Encounter #81)
77–78	Stirge (Encounter #88)
79	Tiger (Encounter #90)
80–81	Troll (Encounter #92)
82–83	Undead A (Encounter #94)
84–87	Vulchling (Encounter #97)
88–89	Wasp, Giant (Encounter #99)
90–91	Werewolf (Encounter #101)
92–93	Witherstench (Encounter #104)
94–95	Wolverine, Giant (Encounter #105)
96	Wizard (Encounter #107)
97–00	Wyvern (Encounter #108)

Well of Ceres

(SAIR-ees)

Appearance

In the deep wilderness is a huge well, 20ft across, filled with water starting at a depth of 10ft. A 3ft wall surrounds it, carved with Hyperborean runes that praise the Goddess of Healing, Mercy, and Patience, "Protector of the Millstone."

Description

The Well of Ceres is isolated and unknown to the nearby peasantry, so it is likely to be encountered only if the characters are looking for it, either based on rumors or as a mission for the temples of Ceres.

The well-shaft descends 50ft below the waterline to an underground river where it opens into a circular chamber 100ft in diameter with its center directly under the well-shaft. The chamber is 20ft high from floor to ceiling, and the walls are graven with runes similar to those on the well's surface wall. Water fills the chamber.

There are three perils involved with exploring the Well, one in the surroundings aboveground, one halfway down the well shaft, and one at the bottom of the well itself in the underwater chamber.

Aboveground

The area around the well is closely wooded; although it is not truly a single forest, it is relatively close. The well is in a clearing, and is guarded by a **weakened clay golem**. The golem is curled up and covered in dirt and grass, appearing to be an ordinary hillock along with several others. If anyone disturbs the surface of the well water, the golem rises from its curled-up position and moves to defend the place it is charged to protect. This golem is old; its shaped armor is in the ancient Hyperborean style, as is its helmet. Its back, where it has been exposed to the weather for centuries, is pitted and eroded. Although the golem's magical characteristics and immunities are as strong as the day it was animated, the weather damage has weakened it.

Weakened Clay Golem: AC 14; **HP** 66 (7d10+28); **Spd** 20ft; **Melee** slam (+8, 2d10+5 bludgeoning plus hit point drain, DC 15 Con; **SA** haste (recharge 5-6, +2 AC bonus, tactical advantage of Dex saves, and bonus slam), multiattack (slam x2); **Immune** acid, charm, exhaustion, fear, non-adamantine normal weapons, paralysis, petrify, poison, psychic; **Str** +5, **Dex** –1, **Con** +4, **Int** –4, **Wis** –1, **Cha** –5; **Senses** darkvision 60ft; **Traits** acid absorption, berserk, immutable form, magic resistance, magic weapons; **AL** U; **CR** 7; **XP** 2900.

Halfway Down

At the halfway point down the well's 60ft shaft are two alcoves. They are not visible from the surface but can be dimly perceived once a character gets within 5ft vertical of them. Anyone descending all the way down to the level of the alcoves discovers an unpleasant surprise: **2 caryatid columns** are built into the alcove and attack intruders. Instead of using weapons, they try to grab and hold the first two characters within reach, and then just sink down the shaft into the circular chamber at the bottom. At this point, they attack normally, with the help of the denizens of the lower chamber.

Caryatid Column (2): AC 14; **HP** 30 (4d10+8); **Spd** 20ft; **Melee** longsword (+4, 1d10+2 slashing); **Immune** disease, exhaustion, fright, necrotic, paralysis, petrify, poison, psychic, stun, unconscious; **Resist** normal weapons; **Str** +2, **Dex** –1, **Con** +2, **Int** +0, **Wis** +0, **Cha** –5; **Senses** darkvision 60ft; **Traits** immunity to magic, shatter weapons; **AL** U; **CR** 1; **XP** 200. (*Fifth Edition Foes* 43)

The Lower Chamber

The lower chamber is infested with **swarm of piranha**, each 2ft long. They are a bright emerald green with irregular black stripes. These piranha attack any living creature that descends into the chamber.

Swarm of Piranha (20): AC 13; **HP** 28 (8d8–8); **Speed** 0ft, swim 40ft; **Melee** bites (+5, 4d6 piercing or 2d6 piercing at half or less hit points); **Str** +1, **Dex** +3, **Con** –1, **Int** –5, **Wis** –2, **Cha** –4; **Senses** darkvision 60ft; **Traits** blood frenzy (tactical advantage on attack against wounded), swarm (occupy creature's space), water breathing; **AL** U; **CR** 1; **XP** 200.

The Stone of Ceres

The reason why the temples of Ceres might send adventurers on a quest to the well is located against the northern wall of the circular lower chamber. It is an ordinary-looking millstone, but it is graven all over with runes and symbols of the goddess. The stone itself is not magical, but it is something of a focus for the goddess's attention, a relic hidden away during some long-forgotten war when a nearby temple was soon to be overcome in battle. The followers of Ceres hid the millstone in this underwater hiding-place, and returned to the temple where they were all slain, leaving the millstone's location lost to memory.

If the millstone can be returned to a major temple of Ceres, the goddess grants one *wish* to the rescuers, in addition to any reward that might be given by the priestesses themselves. The millstone could also factor into the battle with the heretics of Whitsun Measow. If it is recovered by the characters, it grants complete absolution to any of the Whitsun Measow heretics (assuming that they recant their heresy) when one of the heretics touches it, provided that the characters who rescued the millstone are present at the time. Using the millstone as a relic in this way does not keep the characters from getting their full reward if they return the millstone to a temple of Ceres. The millstone requires no additional sacrifice or quest in return for granting absolution to the heretics: Ceres is, after all, a goddess of mercy.

Whitsun Measow
(WIT-sun MEE-zo)

Wretched hive of scum and villainy

CE village
Government overlord
Population 253 (253 humans)
Notable NPCs
    Lum Yandly, "King Lum" (CE male human **bandit captain**)

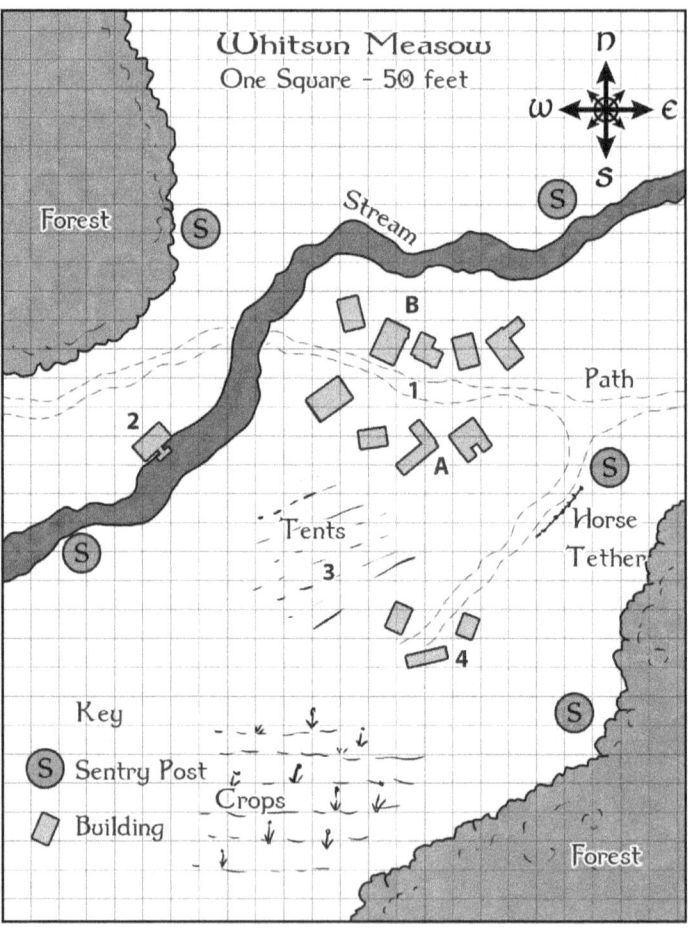

Bantar Prayershield, Canticalist Heretic CE male human
high priest of Mathrigaunt)
Sir Thrant (CE male human **knight**)
Maximum Clerical Spell Level Good —, Neutral —, Evil 4
Purchase Maximum/Month 2000gp

Appearance

This is an unwalled settlement with a few well-built houses at the center and a sea of huts, hovels, and tents surrounding them. Mounted sentries watch the approaches, and many of the people milling about look like they are armed. An unpleasant smell of unwashed people and open latrines wafts in the air.

History

Whitsun Measow was originally an ordinary village, but three years ago bandits took it over and converted it into a stronghold for outlaws and heretics. The "King" of Whitsun Measow is a bandit chief named Lum Yandly who accumulated a small army of 150 outlaws from dispossessed peasants, heretics, and ordinary bandits before deciding to set up a permanent base. The village is now host to all kinds of refugees from justice — many of these are people fleeing from false accusations of tax-evasion levied by the Squires of the Ferrets, but the core of King Lum's force is formed by heretics and brigands.

Heretics

Most of the heretics in Whitsun Measow are followers of the Canticalist Heresy led by Bantar Prayershield. Prayershield is, unknowingly, a cleric of the demon prince Mathrigaunt as a result of placing his faith in the *Discordian Hymnal*. He believes himself to still be a cleric of Thyr, his original vocation, but he actually has been receiving his spells from the demon prince for more than a year. According to Prayershield in the fiery sermons he makes to his flock, the traditional clergy of Thyr, Telophus, and Solanus are concealing the truth about the hymnal, which contains the original Hyperborean songs of praise for these gods. To hear Prayershield tell it, the priesthoods keep the "secret" hymns for themselves as a source of power they deny to ordinary worshippers. The heretic leader is utterly and obsessively dedicated to the task of returning the use of the so-called original hymns to the common folk to allow them to thrive in the blessings of the gods. In truth, of course, all the songs of praise being chanted by the heretics of Whitsun Measow in the morning and evening are actually strengthening the power of Mathrigaunt. Prayershield's alignment has shifted from LG to CE, but he is completely unaware of the corruption he harbors in his soul. He is still kindly and generous, caring deeply about the flock he is leading into ultimate perdition. If Prayershield is ever taken by the authorities, there is no question that he will burn at the stake.

In addition to Prayershield's Canticalist heretics, a few Inoculist heretics are mixed in with the crew of outlaws. They believe that they are granted immunity from disease in addition to knowing the secret hymns of the gods. They keep a low profile because, rather ironically, if Prayershield learned of their beliefs he would have *them* burned as heretics.

Bantar Prayershield's force of heretics is 50 strong. Five of them are **fanatics**, and the rest are armed in the same way as King Lum's regular bandits, though they are much cleaner and for the most part act as honest citizens (other than the constant attempts to proselytize visitors and give them copies of the "True Hymnal.")

Bandits

King Lum's bandit force is made up of 100 warriors, 10 of whom are **sergeants**.

Refugees

In addition to the fighting force assembled at Whitsun Measow, there are another 100 non-combatant refugees: the elderly, the children, and the injured. Some of these have been subjected to the rack by the Squires of the Ferret, and virtually all of them have lost their homes in one way or another. They fully support the violent rebellion they are embroiled in, and are willing to die here if it appears that the authorities are coming for them once again.

Map of Whitsun Measow

Sentry posts: Not counting the mill (**Area 2**) and the guards outside the village buildings, each area marked with a circled "S" is a post with 3 **bandit/heretic sentries**. At each of these, there is a 10% chance that the sentries are engaged in a theological discussion and are not alert.

Sentry (3): AC 12; HP 11 (2d8+2); **Spd** 30ft; **Melee** shortsword (+3, 1d6+1 slashing); **Ranged** light crossbow (+3, 80ft/320ft, 1d8+1 piercing); **Str** +0, **Dex** +1, **Con** +1, **Int** +0, **Wis** +0, **Cha** +0; **AL** CE; **CR** 1/8; **XP** 25
> **Equipment:** leather armor, shortsword, light crossbow, belt pouch with 1d10gp

1. Old Village

This is a cluster of nine buildings, all of them built of stone with thatched roofs. A guard stands watch at the door of each building.

The stone buildings at the center of the bandit camp were once the homes of farmers and are now the homes of the bandit leadership that rules Whitsun Measow. The buildings to the north of the cart trail belong to Bantar Prayershield's heretics, and the buildings to the south are used by King Lum's most loyal bandits. The **Building A** is King Lum's house, and the **Building B** is Bantar Prayershield's abode.

Each of the regular buildings serves as home to **10 bandits** or **heretics**, one of whom is a **sergeant** or **fanatic**. One of the 10 is always on watch outside the door, looking out for threats to Bantar or King Lum. They are not particularly alert, but they are definitely not asleep, for one never knows if one of the leaders might come strolling down the path, and Prayershield, at least, is a strict taskmaster.

Bantar and **King Lum** share their buildings with their bodyguards. Lum's bodyguard is an **ogre**, and Prayershield's bodyguard is a robber knight named **Sir Thrant** who narrowly escaped being burned as a heretic in the city of Albor Broce.

Defense of the Village Center:

King Lum, Bandit Captain: AC 15; HP 65 (10d8+20); **Spd** 30ft; **Melee** +1 scimitar (+6, 1d6+3 slashing), dagger (+5, 1d4+3 piercing); **Ranged** dagger (+5, 20ft/60ft, 1d4+3 piercing); **SA** multiattack (scimitar x2, dagger or ranged dagger x2), parry (reaction, +2 AC vs. single melee); **Str** +2 (+4), **Dex** +3 (+5), **Con** +2, **Int** +2, **Wis** +0 (+2), **Cha** +2; **Skills** Athletics +4, Deception +4; **AL** CE; **CR** 2; **XP** 450.
> **Equipment:** studded leather armor, +1 scimitar, 2 daggers, belt pouch containing 39gp, 107sp, 2 gold earrings (25gp each), and the key to his treasure chest, warhorse, saddle

Bantar Prayershield: AC 15; HP 58 (9d8+18); **Spd** 30ft; **Melee** flail (+4, 1d8+1 bludgeoning); **SA** divine eminence (bonus, expend slot, extra 3d6 radiant or necrotic, +1d6 per slot above 1st), spells (Wis +7, 9th, DC 15); **Str** +1, **Dex** +1, **Con** +2, **Int** +2, **Wis** +4, **Cha** +3; **Skills** Medicine +10, Persuasion +5, Religion +5; **AL** any good or evil; **CR** 5; **XP** 1800.

Spells (slot): 0 (at will)—*guidance, resistance, sacred flame, thaumaturgy;* 1st (4)— *bane, guiding bolt (necrotic), inflict wounds;* 2nd (3)—*blindness/deafness, hold person, spiritual weapon;* 3rd (3)—*animate dead, bestow curse, spirit guardians;* 4th (3)—*freedom of movement, guardian of faith;* 5th (1)—*contagion, insect plague.*

Equipment: scale mail, flail, belt pouch containing 126gp, 449sp, 1 ruby (200gp), warhorse, saddle

Lum's Ogre: **AC** 11; **HP** 59 (7d10+21); **Spd** 40ft;
Melee greatclub (+6, 2d8+4 bludgeoning); **Ranged** (+6, 30ft/120ft, 2d6+4 piercing); **Str** +4, **Dex** –1, **Con** +3, **Int** –3, **Wis** –2, **Cha** –2; **Senses** darkvision 60ft; **AL** CE; **CR** 2; **XP** 450.
Equipment: loincloth, greatclub, belt pouch containing full set of elven teeth, 29gp, small ivory statuette of a dog with ruby eyes (500gp)

Sir Thrant, Robber Knight: **AC** 18; **HP** 52 (8d8+16); **Spd** 30ft;
Melee greatsword (+5, 2d6+3 slashing); **SA** leadership (recharge after rest, 1 min, 30ft, if ally can hear and understand then add d4 to attack and save), multiattack (greatsword x2), parry (+2 AC vs. single melee); **Str** +3, **Dex** +0, **Con** +2 (+4), **Int** +0, **Wis** +0 (+2), **Cha** +2;
Traits brave (tactical advantage against saves against fright); **AL** CE; **CR** 3; **XP** 700.
Equipment: plate armor, greatsword, saddlebags with 3d6 x100gp (some in gems), warhorse, saddle

Bandit/Heretic (63): **AC** 12; **HP** 11 (2d8+2); **Spd** 30ft;
Melee shortsword (+3, 1d6+1 slashing); **Ranged** light crossbow (+3, 80ft/320ft, 1d8+1 piercing); **Str** +0, **Dex** +1, **Con** +1,
Int +0, **Wis** +0, **Cha** +0; **AL** CE; **CR** 1/8; **XP** 25.
Equipment: leather armor, shortsword, light crossbow, belt pouch with 1d10gp

Bandit Sergeant (3): **AC** 13; **HP** 22 (4d8+4); **Spd** 30ft;
Melee shortsword (+3, 1d6+1 slashing); **Ranged** shortbow (+3, 80ft/320ft, 1d6+1 piercing); **SA** multiattack (shortsword x2 or shortbow x2); **Str** +0, **Dex** +2, **Con** +1, **Int** +1, **Wis** +0, **Cha** +1; **AL** CE; **CR** 1/4; **XP** 50.
Equipment: leather armor, shortsword, shortbow, 20 arrows, belt pouch with 1d100gp

Heretic Fanatic (4): **AC** 13; **HP** 33 (6d8+6); **Spd** 30ft;
Melee dagger (+4, 1d4+2 piercing); **SA** spells (Wis +3, 4th, DC 11); **Str** +0, **Dex** +2, **Con** +1, **Int** +0, **Wis** +1, **Cha** +2;
Skills Deception +4, Persuasion +4, Religion +2; **Traits** dark devotion (tactical advantage against charm or fright); **AL** CE; **CR** 2; **XP** 450.
Spells (slots): 0 (at will)—*light, sacred flame, thaumaturgy;* 1st (4)—*bane, command, inflict wounds;* 2nd (3)—*hold person, spiritual weapon*
Equipment: leather armor, dagger, belt pouch with 1d100gp

Warhorse (chain barding) (3): **AC** 16; **HP** 19 (3d10+3); **Spd** 60ft; **Melee** hooves (+4, 2d6+4 bludgeoning); **SA** trampling charge (20ft move then hooves, DC 14 Str or knocked prone, if prone, bonus with hooves); **Str** +4, **Dex** +1, **Con** +1, **Int** –4, **Wis** +1, **Cha** –2; **AL** U; **CR** 1/2; **XP** 100.

Treasure in Bantar Prayershield's House

15 copies of the *Discordian Hymnal,* 10 *potions of healing* in a locked chest, a warrant for his own arrest with a reward of 1000gp if his head is brought to the Squires of the Ferret in Albor Broce, and a magic ring with a command word scribed on the outside. The ring is a *ring of demon summoning* that can be used to summon and command a vrock demon for 24 hours. Once the ring is used, its magic is lost. Prayershield is aware of

what the ring does and is horrified by it, but he still keeps it around for no reason that he can really pin down.

Treasure in King Lum's House

Lum has a large, locked chest holding his monetary treasure, which is a large percentage of the bandits' take. The chest contains 18,039gp, 40,938sp, 23,683cp, a jeweled goblet (5000gp), and 3 small diamonds (500gp each). Other treasure in the house includes 4 stolen tapestries (500gp each, on average), a set of golden eating utensils (200gp), and a golden crown set with turquoise and jade (5000gp).

2. Dilapidated Mill

A three-story mill stands beside the stream, its waterwheel broken and the top story collapsed.

Two sentries are always in place at the top of the mill to keep an eye out for intruders. They can see the entire clearing where the village is located, except the area directly blocked by the village buildings. At night, the sentries are not supposed to have a light since it shows their position and spoils night vision, but there is a 20% chance that they have a torch lit to allow them to see. They are alert, although if they have a lit torch at night, their ability to spot anything at a distance is very poor.

Sentry (2): **AC** 12; **HP** 11 (2d8+2); **Spd** 30ft; **Melee** shortsword (+3, 1d6+1 slashing); **Ranged** light crossbow (+3, 80ft/320ft, 1d8+1 piercing); **Str** +0, **Dex** +1, **Con** +1, **Int** +0, **Wis** +0, **Cha** +0; **AL** CE; **CR** 1/8; **XP** 25
Equipment: leather armor, shortsword, light crossbow, belt pouch with 1d10gp

3. Tents

A tent city is built here at the side of the village's stone buildings, along with various wooden sheds and other ramshackle hovels. Clotheslines are strung across many of the winding "streets," and mangy dogs run to and fro. The people of the tent city are skinny and poorly fed, but about three-quarters of them appear to be clean and energetic. The rest are filthy and dressed in tatters.

The tent city contains a total of **55 bandits and heretics**, in addition to **7 sergeants** and **1 heretic fanatic.** Another 100 noncombatants, including children and yapping dogs, are in the tent city, but they run in all directions if the village is attacked, getting in everyone's way. The dogs (about 20 of them) are not trained to fight, although they defend their owners if the owners are assaulted. The combatants do not simply pour forth fully armed if an alarm is sounded. They emerge in groups over the course of time as they manage to throw on their armor, grab their weapons, and fight through the chaos of non-combatants and dogs.

Bandit/Heretics (55): **AC** 12; **HP** 11 (2d8+2); **Spd** 30ft; **Melee** shortsword (+3, 1d6+1 slashing); **Ranged** light crossbow (+3, 80ft/320ft, 1d8+1 piercing); **Str** +0, **Dex** +1, **Con** +1, **Int** +0, **Wis** +0, **Cha** +0; **AL** CE; **CR** 1/8; **XP** 25
Equipment: leather armor, shortsword, light crossbow, belt pouch with 1d10gp

Sergeant (7): **AC** 13; **HP** 22 (4d8+4); **Spd** 30ft; **Melee** shortsword (+3, 1d6+1 slashing); **Ranged** shortbow (+3, 80ft/320ft, 1d6+1 piercing); **SA** multiattack (shortsword x2 or shortbow x2); **Str** +0, **Dex** +2, **Con** +1, **Int** +1, **Wis** +0, **Cha** +1; **AL** CE; **CR** 1/4; **XP** 50.
Equipment: leather armor, shortsword, shortbow, 20 arrows, belt pouch with 1d100gp

Heretic Fanatic: **AC** 13; **HP** 33 (6d8+6); **Spd** 30ft;
    Melee dagger (+4, 1d4+2 piercing); **SA** spells (Wis +3,
    4th, DC 11); **Str** +0, **Dex** +2, **Con** +1, **Int** +0, **Wis** +1, **Cha** +2;
    Skills Deception +4, Persuasion +4, Religion +2; **Traits** dark
    devotion (tactical advantage against charm or fright);
    AL CE; **CR** 2; **XP** 450.
        Spells (slots): 0 (at will)—*light, sacred flame,
        thaumaturgy*; 1st (4)—*bane, command, inflict wounds*;
        2nd (3)—*hold person, spiritual weapon*
        Equipment: leather armor, dagger, belt pouch with
        1d100gp

Concluding Matters

Everyone in Whitsun Measow other than the children is a damned soul. Magical or divine atonement could save them, but at this point merely recanting the heresy is not enough to cleanse their souls of Mathrigaunt's taint. The clerics of Vanitthu and Thyr in Albor Broce would simply burn them all at the stake to rescue their souls from the underworld. It is possible that if they undertook a pilgrimage to a powerful holy site, they could receive a mass absolution if they have sincerely renounced their belief in the *Discordian Hymnal*. There are two possibilities in the nearby area, if 100 to 150 miles can be considered nearby. The first option is the Ruined Chapel of St. Jorb, 100 miles to the northwest. The second is a sacred millstone located in the Well of Ceres to the south and west of Whitsun Measow, 150 miles distant. (See *Chapel of St. Jorb* and *Well of Ceres* for more details about these sites.)

Several of the heretics in Whitsun Measow are displaced refugees from villages near the Chapel of St. Jorb. If they are cooperating with the characters, they mention that the chapel is a holy place where a mass absolution might be granted. They can even lead the group there, although they also mention that the area has become very dangerous (the reason they became refugees in the first place).

It is less likely that the characters know of the lost millstone in the Well of Ceres. However, if they directly seek divine guidance about what to do with the heretics of Whitsun Measow, they might be guided there, possibly by a wild animal sent by Ceres. For a cleric character, it is not a hard-and-fast religious requirement that they round up the heretics and save their souls by any of the methods from pilgrimages to canon courts and executions. Nevertheless, higher-ups in most religious orders would frown on a cleric who failed to do anything at all about a large number of condemned souls, or simply decided to "kill them all and let the gods recognize their own."

Chapter Five: Gaelon River Valley

Gaelon River Valley

(GAYE-lun, or GUY-lun)

Overview

The Gaelon River Valley is a large area including the river's tributaries as well as the valley of the main river. It is a free land unclaimed by foreigners, with no central government. Many of the river valleys are inhabited, but the area also contains a considerable quantity of completely untamed wilderness. The great trading city of Endhome sits at the river mouth where it empties into the Sinnar Ocean.

General Information

Alignment: N
Capital: none (though Endhome exercises the greatest influence)
Notable Settlements: Beetlebridge (422), Deadfellows (1240), Endhome (35,000), Gaelon River Bridge (3251), Grimmsgate (46), Mirquinoc (7647)
Ruler: local village leaders and family heads (the Endhome Senate holds great sway when it wishes to)
Government: varies
Population: 1,815,840 (1,265,000 Foerdewaith; 301,000 Gaeleen; 135,500 halflings; 61,000 wood elves; 28,800 hill dwarves; 21,660 high elves; 1900 river giants; 980 Erskaelosi)
Humanoid: halfling (many), wood elf (many), hill dwarf (some), high elf (some), river giants (few)
Monstrous: wolf, water moccasin, giant animals (beaver, otter, and snapping turtle), lizardfolk, giant water strider, ratfolk, gnoll, merrow, vulchling, lycanthrope, undead, rusalka, water orm (river valley); goblin, kobold, giant scorpion, orc, ogre, manticore, hippogriff, dragon (Duskmoon Hills); bugbear, tiger, flind, dire wolf, undead, ogre, troll, wyvern, cave giant, bulette (Cretian foothills)
Languages: Common, Gaeling, Halfling, Elvish, Giant, Dwarvish, Erskin
Religion: Kamien, Telophus, Tykee, Pekko, Darach-Albith, Solanus, Vergrimm Earthsblood, Mick O'Delving, Jamboor, Narrah, The Horned God, Neriad
Resources: trade hub, fishing, foodstuffs, grain, pottery, timber, sugar, furs, dyes, gems (grades 1, 2, and 3), gold
Technology Level: High Middle Ages (major population centers), Dark Age (rural areas), Bronze Age (river giant settlements)

Borders and Lands

The geographical region defined by the watershed of the Gaelon River does not have precise political or cultural borders. The Gaelon originates in the Cretian Peaks where a vast waterfall of accumulated runoff roars down from the mountain heights. The river cuts almost due east to empty into the sea at Endhome. Along the way, it feeds from a web of tributary rivers and streams. The river basin is enormous: The northern edge begins its shallow downward slope no more than 50 miles south of the Estuary Road and only 20 miles south of the Trader's Way, and the river basin extends as far south and east as the King's Road. The edges of a river basin are not a natural boundary for the movement of armies or merchants, so adjoining lords and nations often claim or abandon, conquer, convert and fight over the lands at the periphery of the Gaelon River Valley. The farther one gets from the main river, the more lawless and dangerous the terrain becomes until reaching one of the patrolled roads that mark the approximate boundaries of the valley.

Thus, there is an important distinction between the "main river valley" and the "hinterlands" of the Gaelon River Valley, being the rest of the river basin, including the tributary rivers feeding the Gaelon itself. The main river valley is generally peaceful and well-ordered, with the military support of Endhome and a constant flow of river trade. The hinterlands, while they are still generally peaceful, are more sparsely populated and offer more risks to travelers.

The Valley of the Gaelon is mostly made up of rolling, grassy hills, with the tributaries running through wide valleys between these higher altitudes. Some of these valleys are entirely forested over, and many of the hills are limestone formations dotted with caves.

History and People

As noted earlier, the Gaelon Valley's lack of natural borders means that it has occasionally been a highway for armies on the move, or the site of other people's battles. The outer reaches of the valley are in constant political flux, moving from the control of one outside power to another. The main river area has been remarkably free of intruders and invaders, partly because the independent nature of the valleyfolk in the hinterlands makes it difficult for an invading army to reach the main river without suffering accidents, sabotage, and small ambuscades along the way.

Most of the people of the valley are ethnically Foerdewaith, but none of them consider themselves tied to the Kingdoms of Foere in any way. The river valley is also home to a population of riverfolk unrelated to the Foeredewaith who claim to have lived upon the river since time immemorial. The Gaeleen make their living as fishermen and sometimes hire out their flat skiffs as bargemen to skillfully carry cargoes from town to town. They are a colorful and vibrant people as they ply waters while singing their ancient songs and trading odds and ends found in old ruins whose locations only they know.

Solitary members of a few hereditary families of rangers also wander the Valley, mistrusted by the farm-folk they defend, but welcomed for short visits while closely watched with suspicious glances. No one really likes to host members of the Wayfarle clan or the Bristlebacks, but everyone acknowledges that the ranger families, small as they are, do a great deal to keep the perils of the wilderness at bay. But they are strange people, not proper folk like the villagers.

In addition, some of the wandering Erskaelosi remained in this area during their forced migration of an age ago and remained and settled in some of the more remote valleys of the river's tributaries to escape the persecution of their people. Unlike their warlike cousins that now reside in the Wildlands of the Sundered Kingdoms (see The Lost Lands: Cults of the Sundered Kingdoms for more information), instead of continuing to worship Bowbe these settlers turned to the more peaceful nature deity Cernunnos whom they worship in their cultural interpretation as The Horned God. The valley rangers find some of their staunchest allies among these Erskaelosi.

Perhaps the most unique and interesting of the valley's occupants are the river giants (a hill giant variant) who call the watershed home and perpetually travel up and down its waters on their crude rafts. These giantfolk are friendly enough but largely keep to themselves, except on market days in the smaller settlements when they frequently arrive with huge catches of fish that they sell for discount prices. Always willing to lend a hand to a riverman in need, they nonetheless tend to keep themselves, finding that the "little folk" are often mistrusting of them and their size.

Finally, many of the thickly forested tributary valleys branching from the Gaelon still hold primordial populations of wood elves. Here these isolated clans still live and cling to the old ways practiced since before the first Hyperboreans came. Unlike their wild elf kin far to the west, beyond the Great Sea, these elves do not consider humans to be enemies, though they do remain insular and aloof for the most part, with little contact beyond those few rangers that call them friend.

Trade and Commerce

A considerable amount of river traffic goes up and down the Gaelon River, as produce and farm goods are sailed or rowed downriver to the markets of Endhome. Occasional rafts of furs come down from trappers and hunters at the very highest source of the river in the Cretian Mountains themselves, but for the most part, the river valley's main trade goods are agricultural: hides to make vellum and leather, wool and textiles, cattle, beer, wheat, vegetables, and wine from the few highlands that support vineyards.

Loyalties and Diplomacy

The lands close to the banks of the main river consider themselves allies of the city of Endhome, which is a close trading partner and maintains a few armed keelboats to keep river piracy to a minimum. Beyond the close affiliation with the "Trade Capital of the Continent," the people of the Gaelon Valley consider themselves free folk, beholden to none.

Government

Officers of Endhome administer the small city at the Gaelon River Bridge and the even smaller camp town that perpetually exists at the King's River Bridge, but other than these exceptions, the communities of the river valley tend to be allied in mutually supporting groups rather than being part of a structured feudal system. Most of the small towns scattered through the region hire some soldiers as a defensive force to give backbone to the local militia, and several manor houses in the countryside are the independent fiefs of knights with their own small retinues of warriors. In general, any sort of defense is cobbled together, but the

people of the valley are fierce and steadfast when threatened, and the system ordinarily works well.

Government tends to be associations of village elders, local knights, town counselors, and freehold lords. The farther from the main river, and the more dangerous the land, the more likely that barons and lords are to be found with peasants working the fields in exchange for protection and castles.

Wilderness and Adventure

The Gaelon River Valley is rife with possibilities for adventure, from the relatively mundane guarding of caravans to the far more exotic exploration of ancient ruins in the forested and forgotten valleys of the smaller tributary rivers where clans of wood elves still live. Traveling up the Gaelon to the Cretian Mountains brings a group of adventurers into strange surroundings, for the Cretian Peaks are as ill-starred and dangerous here as they are on the other faces of the great mountain range. Trappers, gold panners, and outlaws inhabit the heights near the source of the river, keeping largely to themselves and harboring secrets.

Changing Times

The folk of the River Valley have been mostly unaffected by the changing political balance in the Borderland Provinces.

Beetlebridge

A village that raises unusual draft animals

N village
Government council of elders
Population 422 (422 humans)
Notable NPCs
  Bertrand the Elder (N male human **commoner**)
  Father Wheatfield (LN male human **Clr6** of Telophus)
Maximum Clerical Spell Level Good —, Neutral 4, Evil —
Purchase Maximum/Month 2000gp

Appearance

Beetlebridge is a village built beside a bridge where the Trader's Way crosses one of the Gaelon River's many tributaries, the river Windyforth.

Description

In most respects, Beetlebridge is an ordinary place with a 10ft stone wall around it, a council and mayor to govern, a small militia for protection, a volunteer town watch, and a market square for local peasants to sell their surplus crops. More unusual are the trained giant badgers that amble through the streets, and more unusual still are the large fields of churned-up earth a mile outside the town gates, alongside three large, sturdily walled corrals. The churned-up earth is a breeding and egg-laying field for massive giant beetles larger than horses that the citizenry train and sell for use as draft animals.

A few weeks after the breeding-stock of beetles lay their eggs in the great field, the trained giant badgers dig the eggs back up again, rooting in the earth to make sure all of them are recovered. The townsfolk destroy most of the eggs, but keep several to hatch. The young giant beetles are trained and sold to small villages in the countryside, where their tremendous strength is put to use. The beetles live longer than horses and oxen, and are less likely to be chosen as prey by large predators, which make them a good investment for peasants in isolated hamlets.

See "Beetle, Oxen" in the **Appendix F: New Monsters**.

Adventure

The council has learned that a plot is afoot to steal a number of beetle eggs in the next breeding season, presumably to be sold to another town that wants to get into the business of raising and training oxen beetles. They do not know any details of the plot other than the fact that it exists. They are willing to pay a group of sturdy adventurers to keep watch during the egg harvest to make sure that none of the eggs are taken. A particular worry is that beetles hatched from some of the eggs might turn out to be feral. The experts in Beetlebridge are able to identify these and destroy them, but improper egg selection could result in someone releasing a number of dangerously aggressive giant beetles into the wild. For obvious reasons, the town council does not want oxen beetles to get a reputation as dangerous creatures, and this concerns them much more than the possibility of losing a few eggs from their harvest.

One of the townsfolk, an ordinary fellow by the name of Leaman Carn, has been bribed by the Friendly Men (see **Chapter 1: Aachen Province, Taundre**) into helping them obtain a set of oxen-beetle eggs to sell as stock for a breeding operation. Leaman will be one of the corral guards at some point during the breeding period after the eggs are collected (the townsfolk are assigned to shifts), and he plans to open the corral door to allow 8 thugs hired by the Friendly Men to remove and escape with the eggs. These 8 people arrive in town several days early, and might pay too close an interest to the corral during that period of time. Leaman himself checked to make sure he would have a guard shift, and if the characters ask carefully about such things, it might jog the memory of the town official who set the schedule. Thus, there are a few clues if the characters investigate ahead of time, and if not, there might be a fight in the corral itself if the characters keep watch well enough to detect the theft while it is still going on.

Deadfellows

Highest navigable point on the Gaelon River, a rough frontier town

CN small town
Government anarchy

Population 1240 (862 humans; 316 hill dwarves; 62 halflings)
Notable NPCs
    Jolquet Maitzon, innkeeper of the Golden Jester (N male human **commoner**)
    Sineldia Sailflow (N female human **Clr9** of Kamien)
    Peigin Greenhowe (CG male human **Clr4** of Pekko)
    Father Headbreaker (CN male human **Clr4** of Bowbe)
    Big Walter Brown, fur trader (N male human **Ftr8**)
Maximum Clerical Spell Level Good 2, Neutral 5, Evil —
Purchase Maximum/Month 4000gp (lenders in Endhome finance the purchase of furs and gems for as much as 8000gp if the seller accepts a letter of credit on the House of Borgandy)

Appearance

A wooden stockade surrounds this small town, with three heads mounted on pikes outside the gate. The town has a river landing with a couple of shallow-draft keelboats sitting at the docks. The buildings in the town are half-timber and plaster, and they have a damaged look to them.

Description

Deadfellows is the highest upriver town on the Gaelon River. Even the shallowest-keeled boats can pass no farther without breaking up in the rapids and shallows of the fast-running torrent originating at the great waterfall in the mountains. Trappers and hunters routinely take makeshift rafts down through the violent waters upriver, bringing furs, tusks, and the occasional gem back from their camps to sell here, then return to the heights by foot.

This is a rough town, by any standards. Bulky hunters from the mountains rub shoulders with outlaws, misfits, and exiles here, carousing and drinking until the time comes to return to their assorted wilderness haunts. Furs, gold nuggets, and chunks of semi-precious stones are used for currency almost as often as coins. A death or two in tavern brawls is just part of the town's quaint charm.

The Golden Jester Inn is quite large since it houses a transient population of visitors, so rooms are generally available. The inn's name was once the "Golden Fool," but the innkeeper, Jolquet Maitzon, realized his attitude toward guests was showing a bit too prominently, and he changed the words beneath the sign's gold jester.

Deep Wake (Vulchlings)

Deep Wake is the broken remnant of an old castle. With the exception of a single tower, the walls have been reduced to no more than 3ft in height. The remaining tower is stable, although it has lost some of the crenellations from its flat roof, great stones that now lie at the base of the tower. The area around the ruined castle is sparsely forested, and the tower itself stands on a low hill.

Deep Wake is the home of the self-styled "Carrion King," a highly intelligent vulchling who has established himself as the leader of a large flock of fellow vulchlings. The vulchlings have attacked a number of small rafts and fishing vessels along the Gaelon River, which is roughly 10 miles to the south of the Deep Wake ruins. Thus far, no one has been able to determine where the attacking vulchlings came from, but concerns are rising.

The vulchling lair is not only protected by the vulchlings themselves, but the Carrion King has made an alliance with a manticore, 10 gnolls, and 2 hyaenodons that follow the gnoll pack. The group hunts as a pack: the vulchlings and the manticore scout for prey, and then attack with the help of the gnolls. They bring freshly killed carcasses back to Deep Wake to "age," eating them bit by bit in order of their culinary preferences. The manticore eats fresh meat, the gnolls eat slightly aged meat, and the vulchlings wait almost until the remainder of the flesh has started to rot before taking their share.

A badly ruined castle stands here in the hills, nothing but an unsteady-looking tower, collapsed walls, and some vast piles of rubble where a second tower and the keep once stood.

1. Outlook of the Manticore

Atop the tower, the **manticore** keeps a sleepy, not-very-alert watch over the ruins. The tower is 40ft tall and has 4 levels, all of which are used by the manticore as its lair. The tower levels are filled with trash, bones, and detritus, as well as numerous bits of stone that have broken away from the roof and walls.

Manticore: AC 14; HP 68 (8d10+24); Spd 30ft, fly 50ft; Melee bite (+5, 1d8+3 piercing), claw (+5, 1d6+3 slashing); Ranged tail spike (+5, 100ft/200ft, 1d8+3 piercing); SA multiattack (bite, claw x2 or tail spike x3); Str +3, Dex +3, Con +3, Int −2, Wis +1, Cha −1; Senses darkvision 60ft; Traits tail spike regrowth (up to 24); AL LE; CR 3; XP 700.

2. Gnoll Sentry (With Giant Hyena)

This fallen tower is nothing but rubble, a circular pile of broken masonry 4ft high on all sides. It is the sentry post for a **gnoll** and the **hyaenodon** tamed by the gnoll pack.

Gnoll: AC 15; HP 22 (5d8); Spd 30ft; Melee spear (+4, 1d6+2 piercing) or bite (+4, 1d4+2 piercing); Ranged longbow (+3, 150ft/600ft, 1d8+1 piercing); SA rampage (reduce target to 0hp with melee, bonus to move half speed and make a bite); Str +2, Dex +1, Con +0, Int −2, Wis +0, Cha −2; Senses darkvision 60ft; AL CE; CR 1/2; XP 100.

Hyena, Giant (Hyaenodon): AC 12; HP 45 (6d10+12); Spd 50ft; Melee bite (+5, 2d6+3 piercing); SA rampage (reduce target to 0hp with melee, bonus to move half speed and make a bite); Str +3, Dex +2, Con +2, Int −4, Wis +1, Cha −2; Skills Perception +3; AL U; CR 1; XP 200.

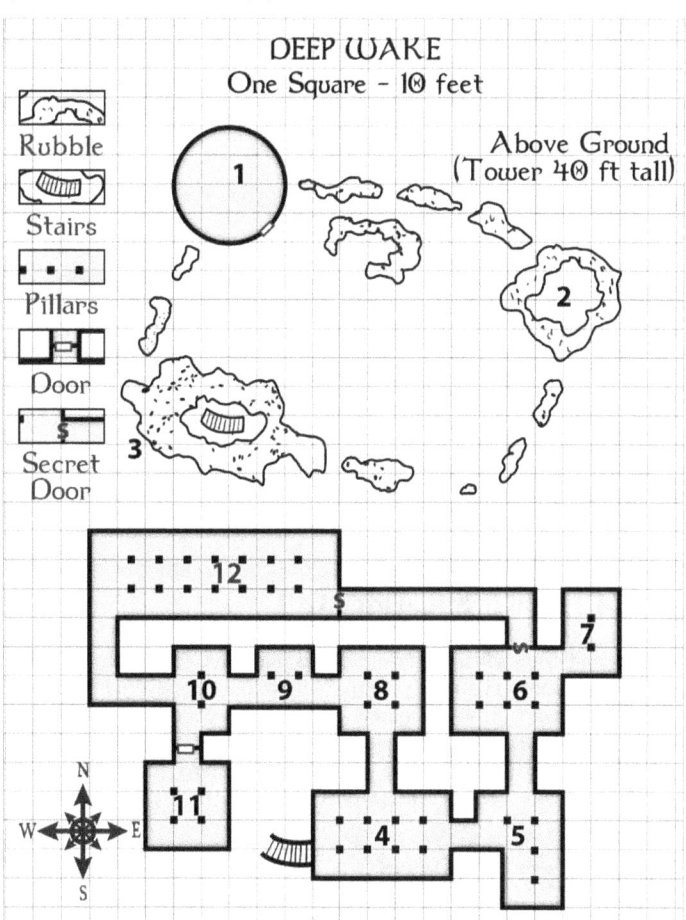

DEEP WAKE
One Square – 10 feet

Rubble
Stairs
Pillars
Door
Secret Door

Above Ground
(Tower 40 ft tall)

3. Remains of the Keep

This is a massive pile of rubble and broken masonry, 10ft in height. At the center, the vulchlings have dug through the rocks to uncover the stairway down into the keep's cellars and dungeon. The stair is guarded by a single **vulchling**.

Vulchling: AC 12; HP 9 (2d8); Spd 20ft, fly 50ft; Melee beak (+4, 1d4+2 piercing) or talons (+4, 1d6+2 slashing); Str −1, Dex +2, Con +0, Int −2, Wis +0, Cha +0; Senses darkvision 60ft; AL CE; CR 1/8; XP 25. (*Fifth Edition Foes* 243)

4. Main Cellar

The rock-strewn stairs lead down into what was once a cellar. The ceiling is barrel-vaulted, with numerous thick pillars supporting the arched vaults. The height of the ceiling at the pillars is only 5ft, and the top of the arched vaults is 8ft high. Mold covers the walls, although mold-free areas show where massive casks and bins once stood, presumably holding supplies for the old keep. The casks and bins are now gone, and the chamber stands empty. Inspecting the floor immediately reveals that various things have been walking around down here. Moreover, a barely visible trail of old blood leads to the arched opening in the north wall.

5. Side Cellar Room

This room is barrel-vaulted, with two low arches running north to south supported by heavy pillars. Some idiot has apparently spent time hacking at the pillars, and chunks of them have been broken off to lie beside the remains of the stone supports. Despite the damage, the ceilings still appear to be stable. A dwarf will note that this appearance is not entirely correct requiring a DC 10 Wis (Perception check) while others require a DC 15 Wis (Perception) check; the ceiling over the southern 10ft of the room is ready to collapse. Anyone walking to the south wall has a 25% chance of causing the entire ceiling to fall, causing 4d6 bludgeoning damage to anyone in the entire room. After a ceiling collapse, the room is still passable, but at a very slow rate of speed, since it involves climbing over fallen rocks and squeezing through gaps.

6. Wine Cellar

The ceiling is barrel-vaulted like the other rooms in the cellars. The ceiling is stable and the pillars undamaged. A latticework of diagonal shelves lines the walls of the room, obviously used for wine bottles. Indeed, about 20 bottles of wine are nestled in the diamond-shaped niches created by the shelves.

The gnolls left these wine bottles because the contents are visibly sludgy on the inside, nothing but sediment and vinegar. One of the bottles is supposed to look this way, however. It is a *potion of flying* and has always been a nasty sludge of sediment and some other liquid. The other 19 bottles are exactly what they appear to be.

7. Cellarer's Chamber

This smaller chamber is barrel-vaulted into three arches east to west. A very old wooden bedframe is here, badly rotted and covered in mold, a ring of keys hangs from a hook on the wall, and several pegs are driven between the stones of the wall, probably for clothing.

This was the sleeping chamber of the castle's cellarer, who was charged with the duty of keeping track of stores and wine.

8. Sentry Room

This square chamber has three ceiling arches running east to west. It contains no furnishings to indicate what it was once used for. This is a sentry point, the post of **2 gnolls**. If the gnolls hear any noise from the room to the south, they hide with their backs to the pillars in order to surprise anyone trying to enter the west corridor. They do not give an alarm until they attack from behind, so it may be possible to take them down quickly and quietly without alerting the inhabitants of the cellar's west wing.

Gnoll (2): AC 15; HP 22 (5d8); Spd 30ft; Melee spear (+4, 1d6+2 piercing) or bite (+4, 1d4+2 piercing); Ranged longbow (+3, 150ft/600ft, 1d8+1 piercing); SA rampage (reduce target to 0hp with melee, bonus to move half speed and make a bite); Str +2, Dex +1, Con +0, Int –2, Wis +0, Cha –2; Senses darkvision 60ft; AL CE; CR 1/2; XP 100.

Treasure: The gnolls have two burlap sacks containing the treasures they do not carry around with them. These include 2 human skulls painted blue, a necklace of glass beads (1gp), three rather smelly sets of tunics and trousers, some knucklebone dice, and a large iron fork. They carry belt pouches containing 25gp and 41gp.

9. Gnoll Chamber

This wide spot in the vaulted corridor is the sleeping chamber for **2 gnolls** (see stats above), who likely are present unless the inhabitants of Deep Wake know they are under attack, in which case they will already have gone out to fight the attackers.

Treasure: The gnolls have two burlap sacks containing the treasures they do not carry around with them. These include 2 human skulls painted blue, a necklace of glass beads (1gp), three rather smelly sets of tunics and trousers, some knucklebone dice, and a large iron fork. They carry belt pouches containing 23gp and 3gp with a jeweled medallion (200gp).

10. Gaoler's Room

This room no longer has any sign of its previous use, other than a ring of keys on a wall-hook. It was once the room belonging to the castle's jail-keeper. It is now the den of **4 gnolls** (see stats above). Their sleeping pallets are arranged in the side areas to the north, with one in the southeast corner as well. A sturdy door with a barred window is in an alcove of the south wall. It is possible to look through the window into **Area 11**. A very nasty smell emanates from behind it.

Treasure: Four burlap sacks stashed along the room's north wall contain the following: 23gp, 64sp, 10cp, a wooden disk painted blue (worthless), 8 sets of tunics and trousers, all gnoll-sized, two tin cups (worthless), an iron cleaver (worthless), a copper goblet chased with gold (20gp), and the skeleton of a pheasant held together with twine. The gnolls carry belt pouches containing 319gp, 527sp, 2 pieces of jade (10gp), 1 piece of crystal (5gp), a copper ring (1gp) and a piece of twine.

11. Dungeon Room

This room is now the larder for the carrion-eaters of Deep Wake. It contains the rotting bodies of 3 humans, a cow, and 5 quail. All have already been partly eaten (by the manticore) and are now "seasoning" for the gnolls and the vulchlings.

12. Lair of the Carrion King

This long chamber has a ceiling of three barrel arches running east to west supported by pillars like the other rooms in the cellars. The chamber has a cloying stench of death in it, and several human skeletons lie on the floor in piles of discarded, yellowing bone.

This is the lair of the **Carrion King** and **his 6 vulchling followers**. If a battle appears to be going badly, the Carrion King flees through the secret door in the east wall and tries to escape the area.

Carrion King (Vulchling Leader): AC 13; HP 33 (6d8+6); Spd 20ft, fly 50ft; Melee beak (+5, 1d4+3 piercing) or talons (+5, 1d6+3 slashing); Str –1, Dex +3, Con +1, Int –1, Wis +0, Cha +0; Senses darkvision 60ft; AL CE; CR 1/2; XP 100.
    Equipment: *wand of fear*, belt pouch containing 3 rubies (200gp) and 28gp.

Vulchling (6): AC 12; HP 9 (2d8); Spd 20ft, fly 50ft; Melee beak (+4, 1d4+2 piercing) or talons (+4, 1d6+2 slashing); Str –1, Dex +2, Con +0, Int –2, Wis +0, Cha +0; Senses darkvision 60ft; AL CE; CR 1/8; XP 25. (**Fifth Edition Foes** 243)
    Equipment: belt pouches with a total of 63gp and 528sp

Treasure: The vulchling treasure is simply piled up in the room's northeast corner. It consists of 497gp, 2548 sp, 4739cp, a golden goblet (50gp), a richly embroidered cloak with a tag reading: "Dlante" (300gp), and a *+1 dagger*.

Duskmoon Hills

The Duskmoon Hills are a large range of tall, jagged hills to the north of Endhome, the last stretch of the Trader's Way. Endhome patrols the Trader's Way through the hills, but the city has no particular interest in wasting time, gold, and people to tame these wild lands. Once travelers stray from the road, they are on their own. More information about the hills, and an alternate encounter table, are provided in *The Lost Lands: The Lost City of Barakus* published by **Frog God Games**.

01–30	No Encounter
31–65	Mundane Encounter
66–00	Dangerous Encounter

Mundane Encounters: Traders's Way (Duskmoon Hills)

1d100	Encounter
01–02	Baron and Retinue (Encounter #8)
03–05	Bear (Encounter #11)
06–15	Caravan (Endhome) (Encounter #16)
16–18	Cleric (Encounter #19)
19–30	Farmer (Encounter #36)
31–37	Foot Patrol (Encounter #37)
38–44	Herder (Encounter #51)
45–49	Heretic (Encounter #52)
50	High Noble (Encounter #53)
51	Kenckoo Vagrant (Encounter #55)
52–59	Knight and Retinue (Encounter #56)
60–63	Knight Challenger (Encounter #57)
64–66	Minstrel (Encounter #65)
67–71	Mounted Patrol (Encounter #67)
72–74	Peasant (Encounter #74)
75	Pilgrim (Encounter #78)
76–77	Small Trader (dwarf or halfling) (Encounter #86)
78–81	Small Trader (human) (Encounter #85)
82–84	Stag (Encounter #87)
85–90	Wild Horse or Pony (Encounter #103)
91–00	Wolf (Encounter #106)

Dangerous Encounters: Trader's Way (Duskmoon Hills)

1d100	Encounter
01–02	Ankheg (Encounter #2)
03–14	Bandit (Encounter #7)
15–16	Basilisk (Encounter #9)
17–18	Blood Hawk (Encounter #12)
19–30	Bugbear (Encounter #13)
31–32	Dragonfly, Giant (Encounter 26)
33–36	Dragon A (Encounter #27)
37–38	Drake, Fire (Encounter #30)
39–40	Eagle, Giant (Encounter #33)
41	Ettin (Encounter #35)
42–43	Giant, Cloud (Encounter #40)
44–46	Giant, Hill (Encounter #41)
47–50	Gnoll (Encounter #43)
51–52	Goblin Raider (Encounter #44)
53–54	Goblins, roaming (Encounter #45)
55–56	Griffon (Encounter #47)
57–58	Hag (Encounter #48)
59–60	Harpy (Encounter #50)
61–62	Korred (Encounter #58)
63–64	Lycanthrope (Encounter #61)

1d100	Encounter
65–68	Manticore (Encounter #63)
69–72	Ogre (Encounter #69)
73	Ogre Mage (Encounter #70)
74–75	Owlbear (Encounter #72)
76–80	Robber Knight (Encounter #80)
81	Roc (Encounter #81)
82	Satyr (Encounter #82)
83	Shambling Mound (Encounter #84)
84	Tangtal (Encounter #89)
85–88	Troll (Encounter #92)
89–90	Wasps, Giant (Encounter #99)
91–94	Weasel, Giant (Encounter #100)
95–96	Wight (Encounter #102)
97	Witherstench (Encounter #104)
98	Wizard (Encounter #107)
99–100	Wyvern (Encounter #108)

Endhome

Trading capital of the continent

LN metropolis
Government autocracy
Population 35,000 (28,000 humans; 1750 halflings; 1750 half-elves; 1750 hill dwarves; 1050 high elves; 700 other)
Notable NPCs
Ranlan Pool, Governor (CG male human **noble**)
Stylus Kant, Wizard's Academy Headmaster (CG male human **Wiz9**)
Bragger Bondhome, Captain of the Guard (LG male dwarf **Ftr8**)
High Priest Thaban (CG male human **Clr9** of Freya)
Maximum Clerical Spell Level Good 5, Neutral 5, Evil 2 (hidden, death-god Da-Jin)
Purchase Maximum/Month 64,000gp

Appearance

The port city of Endhome is surrounded by a 20ft stone wall with parapets and towers, split in two by the Gaelon River. Many sailing ships are docked here or moored in the river awaiting cargo.

> Certainly Endhome moves more bulk cargo, and that's why they call themselves the trade capital of the continent. But trade isn't about tonnage, it's about profits. Endhome's pet river supplies it with an excess of pigs and turnips. That's tonnage. I own a half share in a mine in the mountains, and a quarter share in a foundry downriver from the mine. By the time my cargo ever gets to Bard's Gate, I'm trading fine steel for armor and weapons. Pound for pound, that ingot steel is worth a lot more than turnips, friend. That's the difference between profit and tonnage, and it's why Bard's Gate is the real trading capital of the continent. We're merchants; they're nothing more than glorified longshoremen.
>
> —Unnamed merchant of Bard's Gate

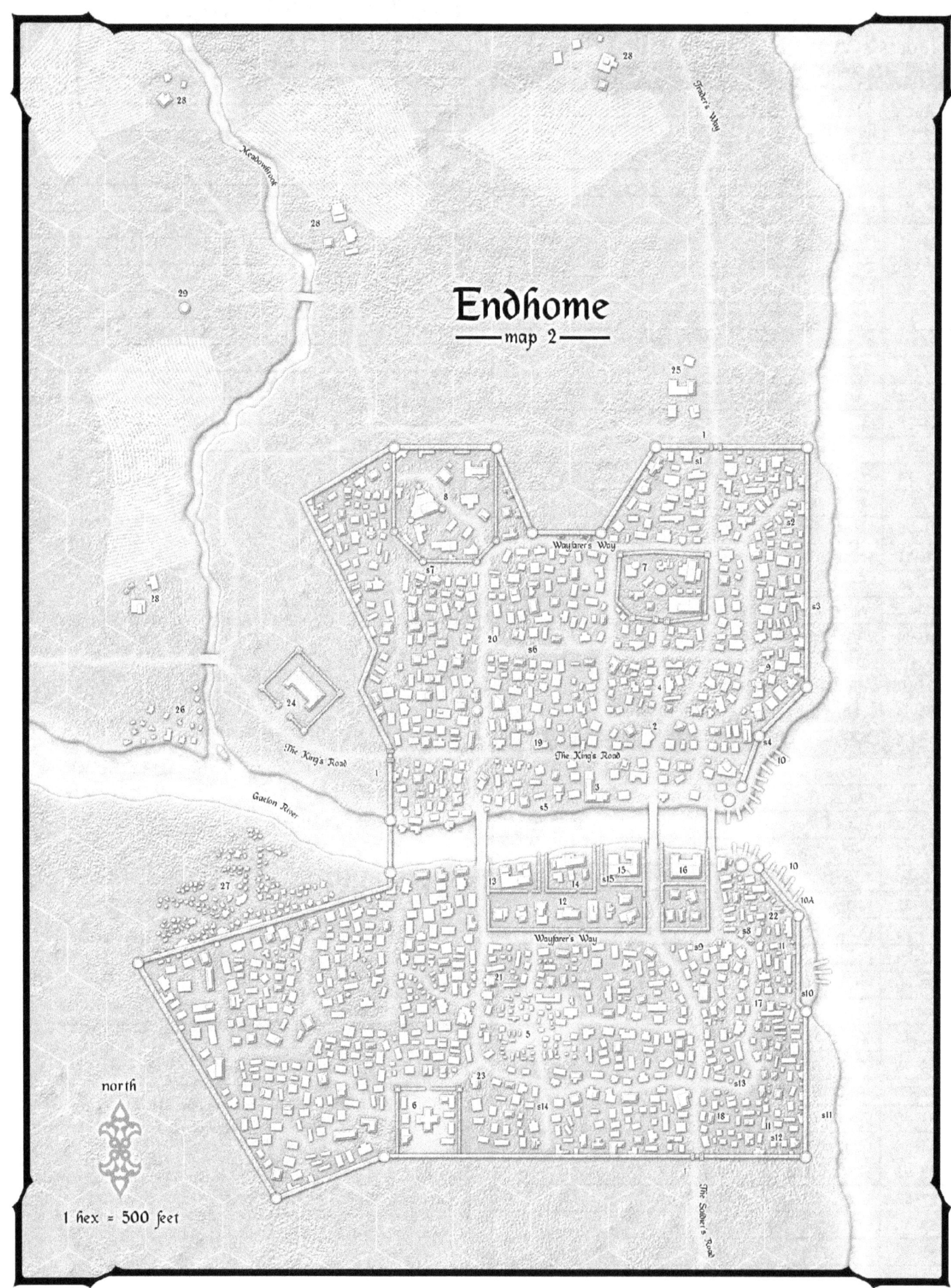

Endhome
—map 2—

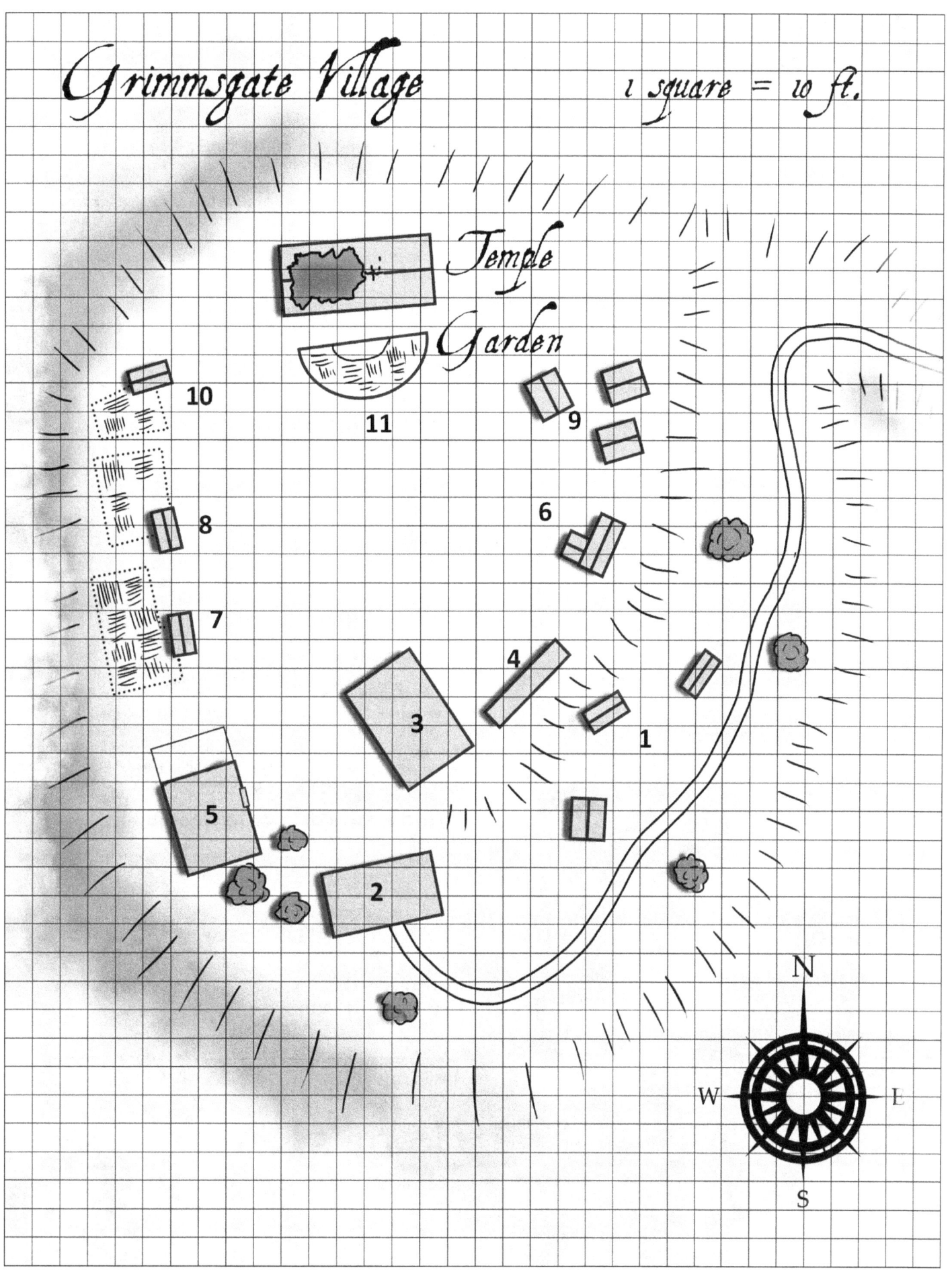

Grimmsgate Village

1 square = 10 ft.

Temple

Garden

10

11

9

8

6

7

4

3

1

5

2

N

W E

S

Description

The city of Endhome is widely known as the "Trade Capital of the Continent." Even though Bard's Gate is obviously a contender for the same claim, the fact of the matter is that Endhome, as a seaport, moves more trade through its docks on a daily basis than Bard's Gate. Endhome merchants scour the world for bargains, make long-term contracts, and jostle with the sharpest traders in the Lost Lands, and by doing so they still manage to remain ahead of Bard's Gate as a trading hub. Endhome does not engage in the sort of far-reaching political machinations that Bard's Gate does, and over time, it seems likely that Bard's Gate will eclipse Endhome for the role of the continent's trade capital. It is already possible, and even quite likely, that Bard's Gate's far-flung network of investments and businesses, seen as a whole, represents a larger role in commerce than Endhome's role as a center of trade.

The free city of Endhome is described in satisfyingly great detail in *The Lost Lands: The Lost City of Barakus* by **Frog God Games**.

Gaelon River Bridge

A large, busy town where the Trader's Way crosses the Gaelon River

N large town
Government autocracy (elected mayor)
Population 3251 (3110 humans; 68 half-elves; 48 hill dwarves; 25 halflings)
Notable NPCs
  Pivion Partridge, Emissary of Endhome (N male human **courtier**)
  Marquand Steersman, Head of the Keelcaptains' Guild (CN male human **Ftr4**)
  High Priestess Linnouine Fleuve (N female human **Clr9** of Kamien)
  High Priest Ephialtes (CG male human **Clr9** of Freya)
  Andray Hostler, owner of the Fat Farmer Tavern (LG male human **Ftr5**)
Maximum Clerical Spell Level Good 5, Neutral 5, Evil —
Purchase Maximum/Month 8000gp

Appearance

A massive stone bridge spans the river here, bisecting an un-walled town of half-timber houses, stone warehouses, and inns. There is an impressive wharf of wooden docks running the town's length along both sides of the river.

Description

The Gaelon River Bridge is a vast stone structure built by dwarves of old. It spans the Gaelon River at the Trader's Way crossing, and allows goods from the river's upper reaches to change hands with goods from the overland caravan trade. Not many caravan traders choose to cut across the river valley, simply because there are shorter roads from anywhere to everywhere, but wherever there is a major crossroad, one finds traders.

A fairly large, un-walled town has accumulated itself around the bridge to handle this commerce, including some tanneries that produce leather and vellum to sell in Endhome. For the most part, the docks of "Riverbridge," as it is locally called, run barges and keelboats up and downstream, including some of the nearby tributaries, to collect grain from the many granges lining the riverbanks, and deliver it to Endhome for sale abroad. The captains and owners of these boats are organized as the "Keelcaptains' Guild," which maintains warehouses and flophouses for cargos and crews. For a time, some investors from Endhome tried to set up a competing system of resources, but in a run of astounding good luck for the Keelcaptains' Guild, the Endhome buildings somehow caught fire and burned down three times in a row before the owners abandoned the competing enterprise.

Although the town elects its own mayor for local matters, officials from Endhome oversee the market and ensure the bridge is kept in good repair. A company of Endhome's soldiers is also stationed at the bridge to protect the city's interest in maintaining peaceful and honest trade here.

The Fat Farmer Tavern is a good place for wanderers to hear all the current rumors about things happening in the small villages and hamlets along the rivers many tributaries. Strange tales and outrageous lies fill the common room, so inquiring adventurers can usually hear all kinds of interesting tidbits of information. Unfortunately, small villages can't usually afford to pay for help, so the Fat Farmer isn't a very good source for paying work. On the other hand, the officials from Endhome occasionally pay wayfaring adventurers to look into any rumors that sound truly dangerous, since it is in Endhome's interest to maintain the flow of goods coming from those same small villages along the tributary rivers.

Adventures: The characters might hear about the vulchling attacks coming from Deep Wake, either from Pivion Partridge or in the Fat Farmer Tavern. Partridge is willing to offer a bounty for dead vulchlings, or a reward to anyone who can trace the vulchlings back to their lair and destroy them.

Grimmsgate

A thorp fading fast, built on a seldom-used road

N thorp
Government none
Population 46 (46 humans)
Notable NPCs
  Rhall the Priest (NG male human **priest** of Solanus)
  Ralmar Prath, innkeeper of the Silver Dagger (LG male human **veteran**)
Maximum Clerical Spell Level Good 2, Neutral —, Evil —
Purchase Maximum/Month 500gp

Grimmsgate is an isolated settlement on the now-unused trail that ran between the Free City of Mirquinoc and the Town of Keot, before Keot was destroyed in an earthquake. Now there is no more trade to sustain Grimmsgate: What was once a village has shrunken to a mere thorp of deteriorating buildings and dispirited inhabitants. According to rumor, an old, abandoned temple is located somewhere near the settlement.

Key to Grimmsgate map (See previous page):
1. Abandoned Farmhouses
2. Gatehouse
3. Silver Dagger Inn
4. Stables
5. Merchant Pantro Panga
6. Drunken Blacksmith
7. Farmhouse
8. Farmhouse
9. Abandoned Houses
10. Farmhouse
11. Dilapidated Temple of Solanus

Grimmsgate is fully described in *Quests of Doom 2* by **Necromancer Games**.

Heorm's Lair

See **Chapter 7: March of Mountains**, *Cretian Mountains, Heorm's Lair*.

King's Road
(Grollek's Grove to Endhome)

Edge of the Borderland Provinces — to the east lie the Sundered Kingdoms

Appearance

The King's Road is a stone highway built for the movement of troops. It is ancient, and this part of the road is in sometimes poor repair; most of those who might have kept it maintained have moved on from the area and Endhome and Rampartine repair crews are few and far between. Grass grows between the pavestones, and there are some large cracks where the ground has buckled over the centuries.

Description

This eastern portion of the King's Road runs along the outer extent of the Gaelon River's watershed. The lands to the east are considered to be part of the Sundered Kingdoms rather than the Borderland Provinces. It is a lonely road, although many caravans take this route to and from Endhome through the sparsely populated region, stopping at the trade community of Grollek's Grove to resupply and rest before or after this stretch of the run.

Encounter Chance: Make one encounter check in the morning, one in the afternoon, and one at night.

Risk Level: All encounters on the King's Road are at the Medium-Risk level, *except where it passes through the Gundlock Hills*, which are a High-Risk area. Inside the one-hex radius around Endhome, there is an additional automatic encounter check in the surrounding hex and the city's hex. All encounters in the city's hex and the surrounding hexes are at the Low-Risk level.

01–25	No Encounter
26–62	Mundane Encounter
63–00	Dangerous Encounter

Mundane Encounters:
King's Road (Grollek to Endhome)

1d100	Encounter
01–02	Baron and Retinue (Encounter #8)
03–05	Bear (Encounter #11)
06–11	Caravan (Endhome, Rampart, Suilleyn, possibly even Exeter) (Encounter #16)
12–13	Cleric (Encounter #19)
14	Druid (Encounter #31)
15–17	Dwarf (Encounter #32)
18–19	Elf (Encounter #34)
20–31	Farmer (Encounter #36)
32–37	Foot Patrol (Encounter #37)
38–44	Herder (Encounter #51)
45–49	Heretic (Encounter #52)
50	High Noble (Encounter #53)
51	Kenckoo Vagrant (Encounter #55)

1d100	Encounter
52–59	Knight and Retinue (Encounter #56)
60–63	Knight Challenger (Encounter #57)
64–66	Minstrel (Encounter #65)
67–71	Mounted Patrol (Encounter #67)
72–74	Peasant (Encounter #74)
75	Pilgrim (Encounter #78)
76–77	Small Trader (dwarf or halfling) (Encounter #86)
78–81	Small Trader (human) (Encounter #85)
82–84	Stag (Encounter #87)
85–90	Wild Horse or Pony (Encounter #103)
91–00	Wolf (Encounter #106)

Dangerous Encounters:
King's Road (Grollek to Endhome)

1d100	Encounter
01–02	Ankheg (Encounter #2)
03–14	Bandit (Encounter #7)
15–16	Basilisk (Encounter #9)
17–18	Blood Hawk (Encounter #12)
19–30	Bugbear (Encounter #13)
31–32	Dragonfly, Giant (Encounter 26)
33–36	Dragon A (Encounter #27)
37–38	Drake, Fire (Encounter #30)
39–40	Eagle, Giant (Encounter #33)
41	Ettin (Encounter #35)
42–43	Giant, Cloud (Encounter #40)
44–46	Giant, Hill (Encounter #41)
47–50	Gnoll (Encounter #43)
51–52	Goblin Raider (Encounter #44)
53–54	Goblin, Roaming (Encounter #45)
55–56	Griffon (Encounter #47)
57–58	Hag (Encounter #48)
59–60	Harpy (Encounter #50)
61–62	Korred (Encounter #58)
63–64	Lycanthrope (Encounter #61)
65–68	Manticore (Encounter #63)
69–72	Ogre (Encounter #69)
73	Ogre Mage (Encounter #70)
74–75	Owlbear (Encounter #72)
76–80	Robber Knight (Encounter #80)
81	Roc (Encounter #81)
82	Satyr (Encounter #82)
83	Shambling Mound (Encounter #84)
84	Tangtal (Encounter #89)
85–88	Troll (Encounter #92)
89–90	Wasp, Giant (Encounter #99)
91–94	Weasel, Giant (Encounter #100)

1d100	Encounter
95–96	Wight (Encounter #102)
97	Witherstench (Encounter #104)
98	Wizard (Encounter #107)
99–100	Wyvern (Encounter #108)

King's Road Bridge

A Toll of Two Cities

Appearance

The river is extremely wide and slow here, a thick muddy flow where it sometimes mixes with tidal backflow so close to the sea. A long wood-and-brick bridge spans the water, a timber and plaster building constructed at each end. A small tent city has spawned upon the road at either end of the span.

Description

Not a true settlement, King's Road Bridge is simply a bottleneck for travel to and from Endhome on the King's Road. A customs-house manned by officials from Endhome stands at each end of the bridge, and collects tolls from travelers and traders at whichever side they first enter. Southbound tolls are sent periodically to Courghais, and northbound tolls are the property of Endhome. The toll collectors are thorough and not known for their speed, so camps of caravans waiting their turn tend to spring up, as the wait can extend for several days in the busiest parts of the trade season.

From time to time when there is heavy rain upriver, the river around the bridge overflows, leaving the bridge standing 50ft from dry land. During such times, every local in possession of a boat comes to the bridge in hopes of getting work ferrying a caravan across the swollen river. The toll collectors can do nothing more than watch as their revenue travels cross-river on the improvised ferry system.

Mirquinoc

(MER-qwin-ock)

Fey-infested city, an odd and interesting place

N small city
Government autocracy (elected mayor)
Population 7647 (6231 humans; 853 high elves; 233 half-elves; 187 gnomes; 104 halflings; 39 hill dwarves; unknown number of fey)
Notable NPCs
Mayor Gandar Golson (CG male human **Ftr7**)
Captain of the Watch Tansinthe of Tertry (N female human **Ftr8**)
Guildmaster of Thieves Porsical Gnot (N male human **Rog10**)
High Priestess Taira (N female human **Clr17** of Narrah)
Priestess Arianwen (NG female human **Clr4** of Oghma)
Bishop Alaune of Mirquinoc (LN male human **Clr8** of Telophus)
Iolphezar (N male human **Wiz12**)
Rolbenad Windspeaker (N male human **Drd11**)
Maximum Clerical Spell Level Good 2, Neutral 9, Evil —
Purchase Maximum/Month 16,000gp

Appearance

This walled city comes upon travelers unexpectedly since it is not marked by any of the milestones along the road. The walls are uneven and the towers are crooked, but it is obviously quite a busy place, with peasants bustling about.

There is a very prominent sign at the city gate reading, "Ignore the sprites." Another, smaller, sign reads: "Drawing steel or iron weapons in the city is forbidden."

Description

The Free City of Mirquinoc stands just beyond the borders of Suilley, roughly a mile north of the King's Road. It stands at the tip of a range of hills that mark the geographical edge of the Gaelon watershed, locally known as the Keelstones, which run 15 miles wide and roughly 50 miles in length. The King's Road skirts around the edge of the hill line, at a mile's distance.

Mirquinoc is a walled city that has been conquered several times in the wars that have swept through the area, but no one has held it for more than a day or two without retreating in disarray.

Mirquin Shee

Mirquinoc is located at an ancient, pre-Hyperborean crossroad, so old that neither of the original roads can be seen. However, the conjunction of these roads fixed the city of Mirquinoc squarely into a shifting co-existence with the realm of a faerie queen and her fey court. Throughout the city, the fey are often visible for a few moments out of the corner of the eye, but seem to disappear when looked at directly. Humans cannot cross the boundaries into the fey realm for the most part, although it can happen by accident if a person trips off some fey spell, or happens to walk into just the right place at just the right moment. Many of the fey, on the other hand, are able to step through the barrier into the human world of the city. For the most part, only the sprites of Mirquin Shee actually come through the border, although on occasion a korred appears in town to purchase or sell things.

FREE CITY OF MIRQUINOC
One Square = 100 feet

Sprites

The sprites of Mirquin Shee are unpredictable and capricious, considering themselves as the protectors of the city. Unfortunately, their view of what constitutes protection is frequently not the same as that of the city's ordinary residents. Their sporadic vigilance has led to a beneficial outcome; the city contains no sinister necromancers or hidden demon cults. However, the sprites are haughty and proud, and on occasion they react badly to what they perceive as rude behavior to themselves. The city tries to minimize these misunderstandings by requesting that visitors completely ignore the sprites when encountering them. Encounters are not particularly common, but any visitor to the city will see two or three of them hiding behind chimneys or sitting on rooftops and windowsills.

The Fey Queen

Mirquin Shee is ruled by the faerie queen Twylinvere, a tall, slender figure with dragonfly wings who can occasionally be seen as a colorful but ghostly figure moving around in the city. She occasionally enters the human world to make agreements with the mayor or complain about certain humans that are behaving improperly. Again, her definition of "improper" can occasionally be a bit bizarre. Her relationship with the city's mayors has always been friendly, if a bit peremptory, and there are a few minor treaties in place that govern the dealings of her subjects with the city's citizens. Most prominently, everyone has agreed not to kill each other in disputes, and her sprites respect this limit on their ability to chastise and protect. Accidents happen on both sides from time to time, and the mayor and queen understand this, although it can cause tension.

Temple of Narrah

Mirquinoc holds one of the major temples of the goddess Narrah, the Lady of the Moon, a neutrally-aligned patroness of darkness, travel, and protection.

High Priestess Taira is perhaps the most powerful cleric of Narrah in the Borderland Provinces, and is rumored to be good friends with the faerie queen Twynlinvere. The temple often acts as an intermediary between the city's fey and human populations, and it is well-respected by the fey of the Mirquin Shee.

Map Key

1. City Gate. Guarded by 2 human guards and 1 sprite. Signs read "Ignore the Sprites," and "Drawing steel or iron weapons in the city is forbidden."
2. Druidic Enclosure.
3. Druid Spire. A 100ft tall sharp, conical tower grown from the living bedrock of the city. Precipitous stairs spiral up around it to the top, where there is a small academy of druids. The academy hauls supplies up to the top using cranes and winches.
4. Old Crossroad Market
5. Great Fane of Narrah
6. Grimalkin Square
7. Mummer's Meade
8. Fortnight Square
9. Citadel (the "Freehold")
10. Temple of Telophus
11. Temple of Oghma
12. King's Road Inn
13. Tower of Iolphezar
14. Thieves' Guild
15. Greentwine Inn
16. Ryhan's Jewelry
17. Armorers and Smiths

Government

Other than the strange co-existence with a fey realm, Mirquinoc is a relatively normal small city of the Borderland Provinces. The guilds elect a mayor, currently Gandar Golson, a well-known brewer; and a captain of the watch, currently Tansinthe of Tertry, a mercenary captain who settled here ten years ago when she decided to retire from a mercenary's traveling life.

The city contains several taverns, from the aristocratic Sword and Squire, to the Hart's Head, more favored by adventurers and mercenaries, to the Broken Pumpkin, a thieves' haunt. Inns include the Featherbed, the Noble Hound, and the Paupers' Hostel (to be avoided by anyone who dislikes fleas).

Mirquinoc has an active thieves' guild that makes forays into different towns along the King's Road. The guild engages in petty thievery in the city itself, but no violence lest the sprites become agitated and start causing problems. Since it operates only on any large scale outside the city walls, the thieves' guild is considered a legitimate organization that makes money for the town and pays its taxes. In consequence, the Guildmaster of Thieves sits in council with the other guildmasters to elect the mayor and discuss matters such as street drainage and minstrels' licenses.

Ruins of Keot

(KEE-ott)

Ghoul-haunted ruins

Appearance

This is the ruin of a town. Collapsed buildings and fallen town walls end abruptly at the bank of a lake, and the roofs of a few buildings poke up from the surface of the water.

Description

Keot was once a prosperous town in the Gaelon River Valley, located on one of the many tributaries leading down to the main river, with a trade road leading south toward the Free City of Mirquinoc. Twenty years ago, an earthquake shook Keot, collapsing the walls and most of the buildings. Worse, rockslides blocked the river that had connected Keot to the Gaelon River, creating a lake with a series of vicious rapids below. Half of the town flooded, and at a single stroke, Keot changed from a trade town into an isolated and un-walled settlement. The inhabitants moved away to safer places, and the road to Mirquinoc, also badly damaged in the vicinity of the town, fell into almost complete disuse.

The remnants of the town are now inhabited by ghouls, most of whom dwell underwater in the flooded part of the ruins where the dammed-up river rose to cover buildings and streets at the edge of the newly formed lake. As many as **50 ghouls** possibly live in the waters, but they usually hunt in smaller packs.

Ghoul (up to 50): AC 12; **HP** 22 (5d8); **Spd** 30ft; **Melee** claws (+4, 2d4+2 slashing plus paralysis for 1 min, DC 10 Con) or bite (+2, 2d6+2 piercing); **Immune** charm, exhaustion, poison; **Str** +1, **Dex** +2, **Con** +0, **Int** −2, **Wis** +0, **Cha** −2; **Senses** darkvision 60ft; **AL** CE; **CR** 1; **XP** 200.

Quaz Cantry

(Qwahz KAN-tree)

Birthplace of excellent minstrels and awful thespians

N small town
Government overlord
Population 405 (293 humans; 61 hill dwarves; 21 half-elves; 18 halflings; 7 high elves; 5 gnomes)
Notable NPCs
  Baron Wilyen Quaz (LN male human **Ftr9**)

Innkeeper of the Sleeping Bull and amateur playwright
  Tod Brushtail (N male human **commoner**)
Rebeccia Tanto (NG female human **Clr6** of Oghma)
Landry Hillpiper (N human male **Clr6** of Pan)
Maximum Clerical Spell Level Good 4, Neutral 4, Evil —
Purchase Maximum/Month 4000gp

Appearance

A small town stands on a low hill, walled with stone. It has a single gatehouse with the words "Quaz Cantry" inscribed over the archway. A stubby tower rises on each side of the gatehouse, and the top of a stone keep is only just visible on the far side of town from the road. The keep flies a flag showing a green dog on a yellow background with a wreath of green leaves around it. Around the bottom of the hill, fields and a few outlying farmhouses surround the town.

Trade

Quaz Cantry is a small town of 405 citizens ruled by the local baron. Most of its prosperity comes from travelers on the Trader's Way, but the town also has a small stable of "Suilleyn" warhorses that they breed and train for sale to knights. The warhorses are of excellent quality, although they bear a strange pattern of bluish stripes, like a tiger's.

The Cantry Citadel

The town's citadel, the keep visible on the far side from the road, was once a fortified temple of Oghma, but it was abandoned by its priests long ago and is now the castle of Baron Wilyen Quaz. It is still known as the Cantry since its great hall was used to sing praises to the god with complex choral arrangements and lyrics. The Cantry courtyard is used monthly for the Baron's court of justice. One priest of Oghma remains in the town, living in rooms in the Cantry Citadel. Rebeccia Tanto cultivates new minstrels in the town, and does not attend the play.

The Townsfolk

Even though the priests of Oghma are long departed from their fortified chantry, the townfolk still worship the god of music, and the place has an unusual number of excellent singers and musicians. Many youngsters from Quaz Cantry set out as minstrels to make their fortunes along the roads of the Borderland Provinces and even in great cities such as Manas, Troye, and Endhome. The city of Bard's Gate, far to the north and west along the Trader's Way, is seen as something of a legendary place here. To hear the townsfolk tell it, the streets of Bard's Gate are paved with gold, and all the city dwellers sing their conversations in rhyme and meter. Many of the oldsters here are retired minstrels returned to the city after years of traveling. Every single one of them claims to have made the journey to Bard's Gate, facing desperate risks and having exciting adventures along the way. Their claims are highly dubious at best, and obvious fiction at worst. Anyone stopping in Quaz Cantry with tales of Bard's Gate is welcomed here and drinks for free in the town's taverns.

Taverns and Accomodation

Two large taverns are in Quaz Cantry: the Bard's Head and the Grommet. Both are of equivalent quality, but the Bard's Head is known for having better music while the Grommet is known for having better beer. A preference for one tavern over the other is simply a matter of the customer's priorities, music or beer. Several of the farmers who live in the outlying farms make their way into the town's taverns during the evening.

If they see strangers in the tavern, the farmers sidle up to them to give them a whispered bit of advice: "Whatever you do, don't go to the play." The farmers are kindly souls and do not want to offend the townsfolk, so they say absolutely nothing more about the play, or why they are warning the characters not to go. "I've said all I'll say," is the response to any questions about the warning.

Only one inn operates within the town walls, although the town employs its civic dormitory for extra space when caravans arrive. The inn, which proudly displays the sign of the Sleeping Bull, offers reasonable rates and comfortable beds. Innkeeper Tod Brushtail is a great fan of the theater, and the town's celebrated playwright. He strongly encourages visitors to attend a performance. Performances are held every sixth day: Roll 1d6 to determine how soon the next play will be, with a "1" meaning that the play will be held that very night!

The Play

The townsfolk in Quaz Cantry are gifted with great musical talent. Their theatrical abilities? Not so much. Nevertheless, they delight in their performances, most of which are written by Tod Brushtail himself. The innkeeper is quite prolific, turning out a new play every month or so, and the amateur thespians of the town wait impatiently for each new masterpiece.

As it happens, the plays are awful. They are filled with inside jokes that only the townsfolk can understand, and the plots are tedious. The acting, moreover, is dismal. Watching a play in Quaz Cantry is akin to watching grass grow. The performances are more terrible than the worst school play performed by six-year-olds. Anyone other than one of the townsfolk must make a DC 10 (+1 per previous act) Wis save during each act of the three-act play, or fall into a complete stupor that lasts for 2d6 hours, unable to move or take any action. There is nothing sinister or magical about the effect of the play, it is simply boredom carried to the extent of human tolerance. Dwarves are immune, and greatly enjoy the performances, while elves are equally resistant, though only due to their unique long-view perspective on the passage of time.

If all the characters fall into a stupor, the townsfolk carry them to their quarters and leave them there. The townsfolk treat any character that makes it through the play without falling into a stupor favorably thereafter. On the other hand, the offended citizens treat anyone who leaves the play or becomes comatose during the performance with considerable dislike for the duration of their stay.

Skeorth Point

(skee-ORTH)

Safe, unlike everywhere else

Skeorth Point is built on a rock peninsula in the Gaelon River, a small village of 115 people. A wooden fence of sharpened tree trunks with a stout gate protects the village from attacks by land, but the side facing the river is undefended, just a wooden dock with three rickety piers jutting out over the water. Skeorth Point is hemmed in on all sides by woods and rocky outcroppings, getting most of its contact with the outside by way of the river. It is the home of the Venerable Seldorne, a **high priest** of Kamien, goddess of rivers. Seldorne retired eight years ago and returned to the small village where he was born and raised. It is a usual sight to see riverfolk from several different villages gathered here at dawn, waist-deep in the water, singing hymns to the river goddess. Riverboats en route from the Gaelon River Bridge to Endhome often moor here for the night, paying a few silver pieces to the villagers, for the river's dangers never seem to approach Skeorth Point.

Seldorne remains deeply in touch with the river's language, constantly gaining visions or impressions of events far upriver. Being old and somewhat infirm, he seldom acts on these, but he might serve as a useful source of information to travelers headed upstream.

Venerable Seldorne, High Priest of Kamien: AC 11; **HP** 58 (9d8+18); **Spd** 30ft; **Melee** flail (+4, 1d8+1 bludgeoning); **SA** divine eminence (bonus, expend slot, extra 3d6 radiant, + 1d6 per slot above 1st), spells (Wis +7, 9th, DC 15); **Str** +1, **Dex** +1, **Con** +2, **Int** +2, **Wis** +4 (+7), **Cha** +2; **Skills** Medicine +10, Persuasion +5, Religion +5; **AL** NG; **CR** 5; **XP** 1800.

> **Spells (slots):** 0 (at will)— *light, sacred flame, resistance, thaumaturgy*; 1st (4)— *cure wounds, guiding bolt, sanctuary*; 2nd (3)—*hold person, lesser restoration, spiritual weapon*; 3rd (3)—*dispel magic, remove curse, spirit guardians*; 4th (3)—*freedom of movement, guardian of faith*; 5th (1)—*greater restoration, raise dead*
>
> **Equipment:** robe, staff, holy symbol of Kamien, belt pouch containing 15cp.

Tatterdemalion's Manse

Archmage. Beware.

Appearance

This is a collection of three rustic-looking buildings and a large tower built between two small rivers. A stone pillar is carved with the words "Begone Forthwith."

Description

The Archmage Tatterdemalion makes his abode in a tower set between two small, isolated rivers originating in the Gundlock Hills that flow down to the Gaelon River. Only one of the rivers (the Bynewater) is navigable below the manse, and that only by small craft. The second river, the Dillybend, runs through stony rapids twenty miles to the northwest, preventing water travel to the Gaelon along that route.

Tatterdemalion's Manse is well protected by misdirectional magic to prevent the arrival of unexpected guests on the wizard's doorstep. When the mage wants to invite visitors, they are usually given some magical token that turns aside the spells and illusions of the manse's protective wards.

The Archmage is solitary and unconcerned with world events, preferring to read and experiment in the sprawling buildings of the manse, tended by a hundred minuscule servants made of animated clay. Very rarely, the temples of Jamboor or Belon the Wise are visited by one of these tiny clay men riding on the back of a thrush, bearing a particularly valuable gem as Tatterdemalion's contribution to the gods of magic. It is unknown whether the small clay men also make periodic visits to the dark temples of Hecate; one hopes not.

Tatterdemalion often needs "small" tasks performed on his behalf, and has been known to craft a magical item or two for those who run his often-not-insignificant errands. Having no agents in any of the great habitations of civilization, he literally blows into town when he needs assistance, arriving in places like Endhome, Eastgate, or Mirquinoc on a massive platform of pumice. The light stone platform bears a luxurious pavilion tent, which is protected for the journey by Tatterdemalion's "*Sphere of Placid Equilibrium*," and is borne at unthinkable speeds by a maelstrom of summoned air elementals.

Tatterdemalion himself resides in the tower. The other buildings are a stable, a guest-house, and a kitchen with a storage area. All are well maintained by Tatterdemalion's clay-men.

History of the Manse

The mystery-shrouded wizard who identifies himself as Tatterdemalion arrived at the manse twenty years ago, clearing out the magical traps and pernicious dweomers of the previous occupant, a fabulously powerful ogrish sorcerer by the name of Brocnolg, who had wrested the manse from Zaroun the Quintessential, who had in turn occupied it after the catastrophically pyrotechnic demise of Longoon the Alchemist. Before Longoon, the existence of the manse was unknown, but its foundations are said to date back to approximately a thousand to two thousand years after the Hyperborean Age. As a matter of caution to visitors, many ogres of greater or lesser magical powers still lurk in the valleys nearby, sons and daughters of Brocnolg, who resent the fact that Tatterdemalion took possession of the manse while it was still inhabited by the now-deceased Brocnolg.

As a final matter, an account of Tatterdemalion's mysterious contact with the ancient red dragon Heorm is detailed more fully under the entry for Heorm's Lair under the "March of Mountains," *Cretian Mountains, Heorm's Lair*.

The Archmage Tatterdemalion: AC 14 (17 with *mage armor*); **HP** 99 (18d8+18); **Melee** *staff of power* (+6, 1d8+2 piercing); **SA** spells (Int +9, DC 17); **Resist** normal weapons (from *stoneskin*); **Str** +0, **Dex** +2, **Con** +1, **Int** +5 (+9), **Wis** +2 (+6), **Cha** +3; **Skills** Arcana +13, History +13; **Traits** magic resistance, spell mastery (at will—*disguise self, invisibility*); **AL** N; **CR** 12; **XP** 8400.

> **Spells (slots):** 0 (at-will)—*fire bolt, light, mage hand, prestidigitation, shocking grasp*; 1st (4)—*detect magic, identify, mage armor*, magic missile*; 2nd (3)—*detect thoughts, mirror image, misty step*; 3rd (3)—*counterspell, fly, lightning bolt*; 4th (3)—*banishment, fire shield, stoneskin**; 5th (3)—*cone of cold, scrying, wall of force*; 6th (1)—*globe of invulnerability*; 7th (1)—*teleport*; 8th (1)—*mind blank**; 9th (1)—*time stop*
> *Pre-cast before combat

Trader's Way

(Gaelon River Valley, between Estuary Road Crossing and Grollek's Grove)

Appearance

The old stone high-road passes through pleasant lands here, with a few scattered inns, towns, and villages bridging multiple small rivers along the way. The terrain alternates between meadows deep with wildflowers and high, rocky ridges running parallel to the course of the rivers. In many places, the road's pathway has been cut directly through the ridges rather than climbing them.

Encounter Chance: Make one encounter check in the morning, one in the afternoon, and one at night.

Risk Level: All encounters on the Trader's Way in the Gaelon River Valley are at the Medium-Risk level.

01–40	No Encounter
41–65	Mundane Encounter
66–00	Dangerous Encounter

Mundane Encounters: Trader's Way (Gaelon Valley)

1d100	Encounter
01–02	Baron and Retinue (Encounter #8)
03–04	Bear (Encounter #11)

1d100	Encounter
05	Caravan (Bard's Gate, from Eastgate) (Encounter #15)
06–11	Caravan (Provincial) (Encounter #16)
12–13	Cleric (Encounter #19)
14	Druid (Encounter #31)
15–17	Dwarf (Encounter #32)
18–19	Elf (Encounter #34)
20–31	Farmer (Encounter #36)
32–37	Foot Patrol (Encounter #37)
38–45	Herder (Encounter #51)
46–49	Heretic (Encounter #52)
50	High Noble (Encounter #53)
51	Kenckoo Vagrant (Encounter #55)
52–59	Knight and Retinue (Encounter #56)
60–63	Knight Challenger (Encounter #57)
64–66	Minstrels (Encounter #65)
67–71	Mounted Patrol (Encounter #67)
72–74	Peasant (Encounter #74)
75	Pilgrim (Encounter #78)
76–77	Small Trader (dwarf or halfling) (Encounter #86)
78–81	Small Trader (human) (Encounter #85)
82–84	Stag (Encounter #87)
85–90	Wild Horse or Pony (Encounter #103)
91–00	Wolf (Encounter #106)

Dangerous Encounters: Trader's Way (Gaelon Valley)

1d100	Encounter
01–02	Ankheg (Encounter #2)
03–14	Bandit (Encounter #7)
15–16	Basilisk (Encounter #9)
17–18	Blood Hawk (Encounter #12)
19–30	Bugbear (Encounter #13)
31–32	Dragonfly, Giant (Encounter 26)
33–36	Dragon A (Encounter #27)
37–38	Drake, Fire (Encounter #30)
39–40	Eagle, Giant (Encounter #33)
41	Ettin (Encounter #35)
42–43	Giant, Cloud (Encounter #40)
44–46	Giant, Hill (Encounter #41)
47–50	Gnoll (Encounter #43)
51–52	Goblin Raider (Encounter #44)
53–54	Goblin, Roaming (Encounter #45)
55–56	Griffon (Encounter #47)
57–58	Hag (Encounter #48)
59–60	Harpy (Encounter #50)
61–62	Korred (Encounter #58)
63–64	Lycanthrope (Encounter #61)

1d100	Encounter
65–68	Manticore (Encounter #63)
69–72	Ogre (Encounter #69)
73	Ogre Mage (Encounter #70)
74–75	Owlbear (Encounter #72)
76–80	Robber Knight (Encounter #80)
81	Roc (Encounter #81)
82	Satyr (Encounter #82)
83	Shambling Mound (Encounter #84)
84	Tangtal (Encounter #89)
85–88	Troll (Encounter #92)
89–90	Wasp, Giant (Encounter #99)
91–94	Weasel, Giant (Encounter #100)
95–96	Wight (Encounter #102)
97	Witherstench (Encounter #104)
98	Wizard (Encounter #107)
99–100	Wyverns (Encounter #108)

Chapter Six:
Keston Province

Keston Province

(KEST-un, occasionally GAST-un)

Overview

Keston Province is no longer a province of the Kingdoms of Foere, having declared fealty to the Crown of Suilley. It has always been sparsely populated, and is still reeling from the devastation of the Wilderlands Clan War. The province is well-governed, but even before the war only the areas around the main roads were particularly safe or civilized, and at this point the province's interior is no more than a sparsely settled wilderness.

General Information

Keston Province

Alignment: N
Capital: Kingston (15,612)
Notable Settlements: Aljun (4,237), Caer Saliond (325), Notquite Inn (22)
Ruler: His Excellency the Lord-Governor of the Suilleyn Dominion of Keston Province, Baron Miltrin Cormien (LN male human **Ftr12**)
Government: feudalism (vassal of Suilley)
Population: 477,280 (385,150 Foerdewaith; 42,700 Heldring; 23,500 halflings; 17,680 half-elves; 4,100 hill dwarves; 2,060 high elves; 1,300 mountain dwarves; 790 half-orcs)
Humanoid: halfling (some), half-elf (some), hill dwarf (few), high elf (few), mountain dwarf (few); half-orc (few)
Monstrous: wolf, goblin, giant animal, hobgoblin, orc, aurochs, ogre-kin, ogres (plains); giant mosquito, lizardfolk, bugbear, shambling mound, undead, chuul, black dragon (The Creeping Mire); orc, ogre-kin, giant bat, undead, mobat, quickwood, witherstench, ogre, harpy, half-ogre, vulchling, minotaur, troll (highlands); giant animal, orc, ogre, mammoth, frost giant, ice troll, thunderbird, demon (mountains)
Languages: Common, Halfling, Dwarvish, Elvish, Orc
Religion: Dre'uain the Lame, Mitra, Freya, Mithras, Thyr, Pekko, Mick O'Delving, Muir, Pan, Dwerfater
Resources: wool, livestock (sheep), flax, foodstuffs (apples), grain, linen, quarry stone, coal, lead
Technology Level: High Middle Ages

Borders and Lands

The southern border of Keston Province runs due east from the intersection of the South Road with the Provincial Military Road, with an eastern boundary at the Trader's Way, 150 or so miles to the north of Albor Broce in Exeter Province. To the west, the province officially includes the eastern slopes of the Kal'Iugus and the southern half of the Meridian mountain ranges, but these are wild areas unpatrolled save at the very edges.

Between the two mountain ranges, the Keston Border extends through the high saddle of land along the Gap Road, all the way to the Duchy of Saxe (off map to west).

History and People

Keston is very lightly populated, with most of its folk living in the towns and villages along the length of the South Road and the Gap Road. Few settlements remain along the Trader's Way, after the ravages of the Wilderlands Clan War of 3506. There has never been more than a scattering of hamlets and freeholds in the Province's interior or along the edge of the mountain ranges.

Annexation by Foere

Before becoming a province of the Kingdoms of Foere, the lands of Keston were subject to waves of Heldring raiders over the course of thousands of years. As Foere expanded, it took steps to secure the region in 2803, establishing a garrison town at Kingston and drawing boundary lines for a royal province. Most of the area's inhabitants, scattered in their hamlets and tiny villages, remained completely unaware of this change in status. Local warlords were forced, one by one, to call themselves "knights" and enter the feudal hierarchy of the Foerdewaith by pledging fealty to the same chieftains they had always followed. These chieftains, in turn, discovered themselves actually to be "barons," who paid small amounts of tax to a distant governor in exchange for not being attacked. Once the concept of "taxes" had been gotten across by the burning of a few motte-and-bailey forts, the isolated settlements of the province settled into their new titles and life continued as before. In a very real sense, Keston Province was annexed by nomenclature rather than by armies.

Changed Allegiances

In 3336, Lord-Governor Fenevic Jaounehelm (JOWN-helm) switched his feudal allegiance from the Overking of Foere to the King of Suilley, following the lead of Count Catrebrasse of Toullen. This event is described in more detail under the entry for the County of Toullen.

Wilderlands Clan War of 3506

Keston Province's recent history is dominated by the events and effects of the recent Wilderlands Clan War. Some 10 years ago, early in the year of 3506, a great horde of raiders emerged from the Wilderland Hills, burning the village of Bynum and fortifying it to use as a base for ravaging the countryside. The Lord-Governor of Keston at that time, a veteran of several

petty border wars, began assembling his forces to counter the invasion, invoking the feudal duties of his four dukes and their barons to provide soldiers. The army of Keston, such as it was, consisted of a core of trained infantry with the various small cavalry units ordinarily responsible for patrolling the province's roads. Now, barons and their knights, accompanied by small levies of varying quality, assembled in the mustering-fields around Kingston underneath the colorful pennants of the feudal lords. Their numbers were small, and the then Lord-Governor chose to send the faster-moving elements of the army forward without the levies, ordering the less-organized and less-experienced militia force to follow behind the veterans and knights along the South Road to the Provincial Military Road, and then north to the borders of the Wilderland Hills.

In the first contact between the forward elements of the army of Keston and the raider horde, at the ill-fated battle of Sontanne Hill, the Kestonfolk engaged a mixed force of hill barbarians, orcs, and ogres. Sontanne Hill might have turned out to be a decisive victory for the more organized soldiery of Keston, but the humanoids turned out to have the unexpected support of several margoyles and their lesser gargoyle kin that flew over the human army, swooping in and out to the kill. Demoralized by the attacks from the air, the army of Keston retreated back to forested cover, leaving the raider horde in possession of the field. Perhaps even worse for morale, the Lord-Governor of the Province was badly wounded in the rearguard action, his leg crushed. The few prisoners taken from Sontanne Hill revealed that the army of raiders had been organized by a clan of margoyles from the Forlorn Mountains that hoped to seize a domain for themselves in the lowlands. Not particularly intelligent, for margoyles are not, this clan had nevertheless managed to use a mix of bad ideas, persuasiveness, and brute force to raise a truly massive horde of reavers to sweep down into the civilized lands.

When groups of lost or fleeing soldiers from the defeated regular army met the advancing militias and levies on the Trader's Way, and news spread through the militia, the second force evaporated, heading back to Kingston without officers, in a panic. The few barons that had been leading the levies were unable to rally them, and the army of Keston was effectively destroyed.

Drawn by the successes of the advance force, new tribes and clans poured out of the Wilderland Hills, some coming all the way from the Forlorn Mountains to join the pillaging. The Count of Toullen, always a good neighbor to Keston Province, immediately sent a contingent of his own knights and solders to shore up the collapsing defense of Keston. Too badly injured to take the field, the Lord-Governor appointed Sir Miltrin Cormien to reassemble and command the army of Keston, largely because the knight was related to all four of the Province's ducal families and had demonstrated great heroism in the Battle of Sontanne Hill. This turned out to have been a lucky decision, for as the war progressed, Sir Cormien's blood relation to the great nobles of the Province was far eclipsed by his unexpected military genius.

Making the correct assumption that his enemy was not a single army but rather a collection of independent clans, Cormien took the extremely unpopular step of ordering his knights off their prized Suilley destriers and out of their heavy armor, putting them in much lighter armor and onto lighter riding horses. This new force, small units of heavily armed light cavalry, fanned out across the contested area in eastern Keston guided by locals. By locating isolated clans and combining together for the battle, then splitting up again, Cormien's small army managed to check the advance of the horde, although the largest of the tribes remained undamaged by the light cavalry tactics.

By 3507, a small army raised by the King of Suilley finished mustering outside of Manas, and marched south along the Flatlander Road to assist in Keston's defense. With the arrival of these heavier troops, the war settled into a more traditional pattern, with the allied armies of Keston, Suilley, and Toullen attempting to bring the large tribes into a pitched battle where they could be decisively defeated. These attempts failed, mainly due to poor leadership of the allies by the commander of Suilley's army, the largest in the field. After a year of watching the army beaten back in petty defeat after petty defeat, the King of Suilley recalled his general and placed Keston's Sir Cormien at the head of all the allied forces. The disgraced Suilleyn general, Baron Nalsibert, drank himself to death on the road back to Manas, capping off a long and incompetent military career.

With Baron Nalsibert removed from command, and with a new influx of Foerdewaith troops from Vourdon and Exeter Provinces joining the allied army as a gesture from the Overking, Sir Cormien (now raised Baron Cormien) undertook a series of lighting advances against the horde, cutting off the army of the large Wormaganth Clan in a hamlet called Onjoun, and slaughtering them. The margoyle leadership of the horde now discovered that they actually had very little control over their "subjects," and were virtually unable to respond as Cormien severed and destroyed their army clan by clan. The final battle took place deep in the Wilderland Hills, as the clans retreated farther into their home territory. At the ancient fortifications of Broch Tarna, the allied armies broke and crushed the remaining hill clans, bringing an end to the bloody, three-year war and sending the few surviving margoyles fleeing back to their haunts high in the Forlorn Mountains. Cormien himself fought in the vanguard of the army, losing his left arm to the infection of a wound inflicted during the battle. When the former Lord-Governor eventually died from the lingering wounds suffered at Sontanne Hill, the King of Suilley elevated Keston's hero, Baron Cormien, to the position.

Trade and Commerce

The city of Kingston is well placed for trade, being at the crossroad of the Gap Road leading into the Kingdoms of Foere, the South Road which runs from Toullen to the Duchy of the Rampart, and controlling the Provincial Military Road leading to the Domain of Hawkmoon through Exeter Province. None of these routes is very heavily traveled, but together they make enough revenue to maintain the province well. If the province manages to rebuild the ravaged rural communities lost to the depredations of the Wilderland Clans, it will become a strong nation over time. At present, however, the province is still struggling with the loss of farmland, villages, and rural population from the war.

Loyalties and Diplomacy

Keston was once a province of Foere, but in 3336, along with the County of Toullen, Keston Province rescinded its feudal obligations to the Court of Courghais and offered fealty to the Crown of Suilley. It has been governed indirectly by the realm of Suilley ever since, as described below in "Government."

Government

Since declaring its independence from Foere, Keston Province has been governed as a feudal vassal to the Kingdom of Suilley, very much along the same model used by the Kingdoms of Foere with their subject states. The King of Suilley appoints a Lord-Governor for the province, but the feudal ranks below the Lord-Governor are hereditary. These nobles offer their fealty to the King of Suilley, but report to the Lord-Governor as the King's representative. Hence, travelers in the province find the usual mix of barons and knights, all with greater or lesser landholdings. Four dukes make up the governmental layer between the barons and the Lord-Governor, and these four dukes are extremely powerful in the province and even in Suilley. These four families, along with the Lord-Governor at the time, are the ones that delivered Keston into Suilley's hands by seceding from the Kingdoms of Foere. The Lord-Governor who engineered the secession became rich in land and titles himself, but his family is by no means as powerful as the dukes, and his descendants do not much involve themselves in the province's government other than as ordinary members of the nobility.

As described earlier, Keston's current ruler is the retired general Baron Miltrin Cormien, who was elevated to the position of Lord-Governor by the young King of Suilley, Ulrich IX. Cormien is a disciplined administrator, staunchly loyal to the Crown of Suilley, related by blood to all four of the Dukes of Keston, and a figure of legend among the common folk after his defeat of the Wilderland Clans.

Wilderness and Adventure

Other than along the roads, there is very little in Keston Province that is *not* wilderness. In the eastern part of the province, many secrets lie buried in the charred remains of forgotten villages. Wolves — and far worse things than wolves — howl unchallenged beneath the night skies of empty, rural Keston. Farms lie fallow, and forests claw their way back into the long-forgotten grounds of their ancestral growth. A few hardy settlements remain in these newly crafted wilds, and some new villages are springing up almost like colonies in a foreign land. Many of these new hamlets disappear in time, but some persevere and prosper.

Changing Times

Keston is relatively unaffected by the receding presence of Foere; it has its own troubles, and the province is occupied by the attempt to recover from the war. Times already changed for Keston in 3506, when the Wild Clans descended from the Wilderland Hills, and events beyond the borders seem very distant these days.

Abbot's Mercy

A hidden slaving operation

Abbot's Mercy is a monastery that was emptied and sacked by the Vanigoths during the Wilderlands Clan War. The buildings were left abandoned for three years after the war's conclusion, until a new monastic order petitioned the Lord-Governor to grant them the land, offering unusually generous tax payments to the Province's treasury. One

of the Lord-Governor's priorities has been the resettlement of the areas devastated by the war, and he readily agreed to the grant.

All is not what it seems here, as with many places in the Lost Lands. The so-called "monks" are not religious people at all, and the "Abbot" Rivaldo is a cleric of the demon-prince Fraz-Urb'luu, Master of Deception. Rivaldo and the other so-called monks are members of the Friendly Men, a widespread criminal operation (see **Chapter 1: Aachen Province, Taundre**). As "monks," they purchase the indentures of criminals held by various barons, promising to keep the prisoners working on the abbey farms until the indenture expires. The abbey does indeed put these convicts to work, but the place is actually the center for a slaving operation; the convicts are never released. This is one of the places where slaves are funneled into the system of clandestine markets the Friendly Men operate across most of the Borderland Provinces.

Approaching Abbot's Mercy

If the characters arrive during the daytime, they see small gangs of peasants working in the fields, each group with an overseer. They peasants do not look healthy. If the characters talk to one of the overseers, the man explains that the good religious folk of the abbey put prisoners to work out here in the open rather than leaving them to rot in city and town dungeons.

1. Gate

The gate of this pastoral abbey appears to be new, a solid construction of heavy beams and iron binding. It enters into a gatehouse through a portcullis.

2. Gatehouse

The abbey gatehouse has two levels. At the lower level, there is no connection between the towers, just an arched tunnel between them leading to a second portcullis and the entrance to the abbey courtyard. At the upper level, the towers are connected over the top of the tunnel, which has holes for firing arrows at any attackers trapped between the two portcullises. There are **2 guards** standing on the top of the gatehouse to greet visitors. The guards claim that the abbey is a hermitage whose inhabitants, other than the guards and lay members, are sworn to a vow of silence and do not wish to be disturbed by anything that might tempt them to speak. Please go away. The guards are both members of the Friendly Men. These two sleep in the gatehouse itself rather than in the abbey sanctum.

If the characters are asking for food and shelter, the guards offer to lower a basket of food down to them, but the abbey does not admit visitors.

If the characters are asking too many questions about the workers in the field, one of the guards explains, like the overseers, that the religious community here takes criminals from dungeons and puts them to work out in the fields where they can be productive until their sentences end, or the abbot commutes the sentence for good behavior.

Friendly Man Guard (2): AC 16; **HP** 22 (4d8+4); **Spd** 30ft;
  Melee longsword (+4, 1d10+2 slashing); **Ranged** shortbow (+3, 80ft/320ft, 1d6+1 piercing); **Str** +2, **Dex** +1, **Con** +1, **Int** +0, **Wis** +0, **Cha** +0; **Skills** Perception +2; **AL** CE; **CR** 1/4; **XP** 50.
    Equipment: chain mail, longsword, shortbow, dagger, belt pouch containing 1d100 x10gp

3. Courtyard

The abbey courtyard is essentially empty at night: the slave-laborers are locked in their silent roundhouses; the overseers are bedded down in their quarters; and the Friendly Men are either roistering inside the old abbey sanctum or sleeping off the day's portion of ale. However, the **4 ronuses** are set free from their kennel at nightfall to stalk the courtyard and kill any intruders.

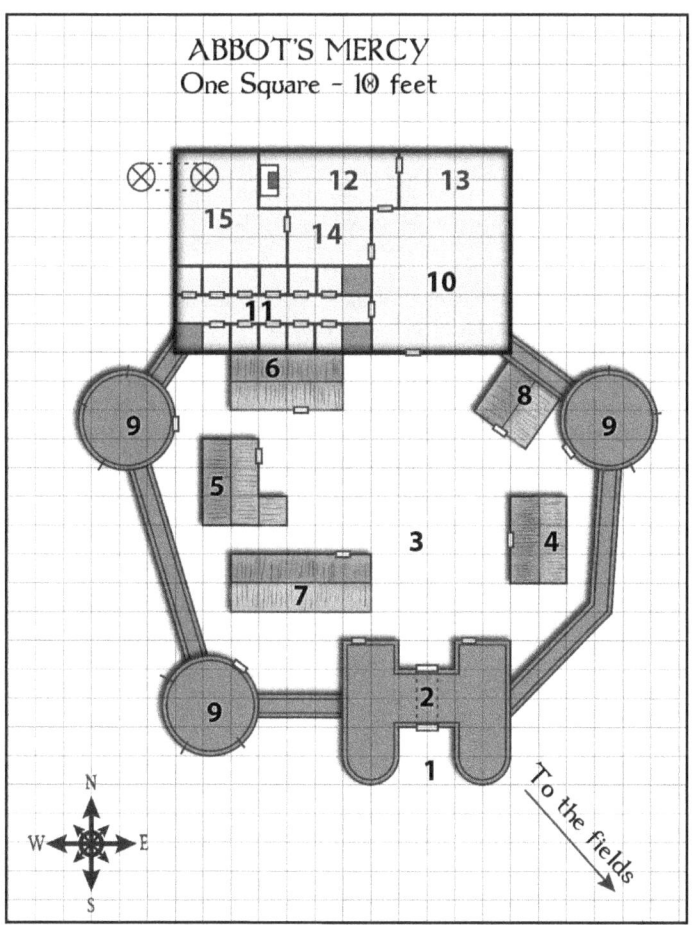

ABBOT'S MERCY
One Square - 10 feet

Ronus (4): AC 14; HP 16 (3d8+3); **Spd** 60ft; **Melee** bite (+5, 1d6+3 piercing); **Str** +2, **Dex** +3, **Con** +1, **Int** −3, **Wis** +1, **Cha** −2; **Skills** Perception +3, Stealth +5; **AL** U; **XP** 1/4; **XP** 50. (*Fifth Edition Foes* 193)

4. Stable

This is an ordinary stable, containing 4 oxen and 3 riding horses, along with pitchforks, saddles, ox-yokes, and the other items traditionally kept in a stable. Oddly, the pitchforks are all padlocked together with a chain.

5. Blacksmith

During the day, this building is a working forge operated by the abbey's **blacksmith**, Ort Smith, who is also one of the enforcers of the Friendly Men.

Ort Smith, Blacksmith: AC 15; HP 39 (6d8+12); **Spd** 30ft; **Melee** warhammer (+5, 1d10+3 bludgeoning); **Str** +3, **Dex** +1, **Con** +2; **Int** +1, **Wis** +0, **Cha** +0; **Skills** Perception +4; **AL** CE; **CR** 1/2; **XP** 100.

> **Equipment:** scale mail, warhammer, dagger, belt pouch containing 327gp

6. Overseers

This building is the sleeping quarters of the overseers **(commoner)** who work for the abbey, making sure that the slave-laborers work hard and do not escape. There are 5 beds in the building, which locks from the inside. The overseers carry their valuable possessions with them, so there is nothing valuable in the room. However, under one of the straw mattresses is a page of parchment showing common brands placed on convicts, and how to add additional branding lines to change some of the less serious offenses into the brand for a more serious one.

7. Barn

The abbey barn is used to store wheat and other foodstuffs produced in the fields. It is filled with produce of various kinds: turnips, potatoes, and bins of wheat.

8. Kennel

This stone building is usually kept locked from the outside during the day unless one of the laborers escapes from the abbey farms. It is the kennel for the **ronuses** (see stats above), ferocious creatures with the body of a wolf and a large falcon-head. Only Abbot Rivaldo can control these beasts.

9. Silent Roundhouses

These one-story roundhouses are only as tall as the curtain wall of the abbey's courtyard. They were once used for defense: Each of them has three arrow-slits that could be used to shoot at attackers hugging the walls. Now they are used as prisons for the abbey's slave-laborers, securely locked from the outside at night. Each of the roundhouses is enchanted with a permanent spell of *silence* that keeps the prisoners from shouting for help through the arrow-slits.

Each of the roundhouses imprisons 10 of the slave laborers after nightfall. All are **commoner** humans, with one exception. One of the roundhouses (it might be a different one on any given night) houses the witch-hunter Retribution deLac (unarmed **spy**) who was spying out matters in the prison of Alembretia, seeking word of a particularly noxious heretic last seen in that area. While still masquerading as a prisoner, deLac was suddenly transferred to a wagon filled with other convicts and brought here to Abbot's Mercy. Rather than fighting immediately, deLac decided

to follow along and see where he was being taken. He has been observing Abbot Rivaldo as best he can, and concluded that the man is a demon-worshipper. DeLac intends to break out soon and return to bring Abbot Rivaldo to his just end: a blazing pyre and a wooden stake.

There is one other fact about the roundhouses that the Friendly Men have overlooked. Although the places are silenced so that the prisoners cannot call out for help, they smell extremely foul. The captors have become so inured to the smell that they no longer think about it as a potential warning-sign for visitors that all is not as it seems here.

10. Chapel

The original inhabitants of the abbey were a contemplative order not dedicated to any one deity, but to the general harmonies and dictates of Law. Thus, no statue is to be found in the chapel area, and in any case, the Friendly Men removed the original furnishings. The chapel now resembles a low-quality tavern with some long tables set up and scattered with dice, cards, empty tankards, and unwashed plates. In addition to the domestic arrangements, an iron brazier in the northeast corner has several branding irons next to it.

Unless the abbey has been alerted, **4 Friendly Men** lounge in the room (including Ort Smith from **Area 5**, unless he has already been encountered in the courtyard).

11. Cells

The Friendly Men running this operation sleep in some of the old monastic cells along this corridor. Eight of the cells are in use as bedrooms, and if the abbey is not on alert, the **4 Friendly Men** not in the chapel are in their separate rooms.

Friendly Man (4): AC 16; HP 22 (4d8+4); **Spd** 30ft; **Melee** longsword (+4, 1d10+2 slashing); **Ranged** shortbow (+3, 80ft/320ft, 1d6+1 piercing); **Str** +2, **Dex** +1, **Con** +1, **Int** +0, **Wis** +0, **Cha** +0; **Skills** Perception +2; **AL** CE; **CR** 1/4; **XP** 50.
> **Equipment:** chain mail, longsword, shortbow, dagger, belt pouch containing 1d100 x10gp

Treasure:
Bedroom 1: Chest (locked) containing set of eating utensils, extra clothes, 22gp and 49sp.
Bedroom 2: Chest (unlocked) containing clothes and a lute (10gp)
Bedroom 3: Scattered clothes on floor, nothing of value
Bedroom 4: Chest with clothes and nothing of value, hidden flagstone hides pouch with 273gp and a ruby (200gp)
Bedroom 5: Chest with clothes and a pouch containing holy symbol of Moccavallo, 43gp, and a silver mirror (10gp)
Bedroom 6: Chest containing clothing, but nothing of value
Bedroom 7: Chest (locked) containing clothes and a box of valuable spices (250gp)
Bedroom 8: Chest (unlocked) containing clothing, sandalwood fan (10gp), an ivory statuette of a female human (100gp), and a *potion of healing*.

12. Kitchen

This is the kitchen for the abbey, where the overseers cook for the Friendly Men and the slave-laborers. It is filthy and rank, with glutinous bits of old food splashed on the counters and worktables, stains on the walls, and unwashed pots and pans stacked up near the fireplace waiting to be re-used. No one will be encountered in this room.

13. Storage

This is a storage room for the abbey, containing sacks of oats for the slaves and horses, along with containers of much more palatable fare for the Friendly Men.

14. Abbot's Office

This office is kept locked from the inside.

A large wooden desk dominates the room, which also has some large, now-empty bookcases against the walls. Unless the abbey has been alerted, **"Abbot" Rivaldo** is sitting at the desk doing paperwork. Rivaldo's first instinct is to escape into the open and then find out what followers he still has left alive. He tries to get into his bedroom, lock the door, and then get outside the walls through his escape tunnel.

"Abbot" Rivaldo, High Priest of Fraz-Urb'luu: AC 15; **HP** 58 (9d8+18); **Spd** 30ft; **Melee** flail (+4, 1d8+1 bludgeoning); **SA** divine eminence (bonus, expend slot, extra 3d6 radiant or necrotic, + 1d6 per slot above 1st), spells (Wis +7, 9th, DC 15); **Str** +1, **Dex** +1, **Con** +2, **Int** +2, **Wis** +4, **Cha** +3; **Skills** Medicine +10, Persuasion +5, Religion +5; **AL** any good or evil; **CR** 5; **XP** 1800.

> **Spells (slot):** 0 (at will)—*guidance, resistance, sacred flame, thaumaturgy;* 1st (4)— *bane, guiding bolt* (necrotic), *inflict wounds;* 2nd (3)—*blindness/deafness, hold person, spiritual weapon;* 3rd (3)—*animate dead, bestow curse, spirit guardians;* 4th (3)—*freedom of movement, guardian of faith;* 5th (1)—*contagion, insect plague.*
>
> **Equipment:** scale mail, flail, *rope of entanglement,* holy symbol of Fraz-Urb'luu

Treasure: No monetary treasure is in the room, but the paperwork on Rivaldo's desk reveals a considerable amount about what goes on at the abbey. There are piles of prisoner indentures from barons and jails showing the transfer of prisoners to the "religious brothers at the abbey." A scraping knife and parchment-shavings next to the documents make it obvious that the so-called abbot has been altering the starting dates and the length of the prison sentences on these indentures. He also has a book of "transactions" demonstrating that the abbey has been selling the convicts to buyers in Toullen, Exeter, Hawkmoon, Lowport, and lands beyond after altering the indentures.

15. Abbot's Bedroom

This room is well-furnished with a bed, wardrobe, chairs, carpets, and a locked treasure chest. Underneath a carpet in the northwest corner of the room is a trapdoor leading to a short escape tunnel that emerges under a false rock outside the abbey wall requiring a DC 20 Wis (Perception) check to locate.

In a locked chest in this bedroom, Rivaldo keeps his treasure: 7296gp, 12,971sp, 2 sapphires (250gp each), and a figurine of the demon prince Fraz-Urb'luu. There is also a blank face mask made of white ceramic and a roll of letters tied with a ribbon. Many letters are receipts for payment from prisons and jails. Some of these are clearly coming from people with no idea that the abbey's operations are anything other than a religious attempt to rehabilitate and train prisoners to become productive members of society. Other letters, many of which come from knights or barons with minor titles, are carefully worded and probably indicate that the author knows the abbey is involved with something questionable. Strangely enough, one of the suspicious-looking receipts comes from a royal gaoler in the city of Manas itself, an individual called Threlboc Gaolkeeper.

The only clue in the letters about the involvement of the Friendly Men is what appears to be a complaint from a buyer, which contains the line, *"I want my money back, or a healthier chattel to replace the diseased one. If this is the way the Friendly Men do business, I shall not be making any more purchases."*

Aljun

(AL-jun)

A peaceful place that could use some help clearing out the surrounding wilderness

N large town
Government council
Population 4237 (3728 humans, 322 halflings; 162 high elves; 25 hill dwarves)
Notable NPCs
    Watch-Commander Girard of Aljun (LG male human **Ftr6**)
    High Priestess Velunia Piper (NG female human **Clr8** of Pan)
    Jerralt Shield (LN male human **Clr7** of Mithras)
Maximum Clerical Spell Level Good 5, Neutral 5, Evil 2 (hidden, Oinodaemon)
Purchase Maximum/Month 8000gp

Appearance

This is a town with high stone walls surrounded by huge corrals with sheep milling around inside the enclosures. The wall-towers are all mounted with ballistas, and guards are keeping an alert watch on the skies as well as the nearby dirt road. In addition to the flags of Keston Province and the Kingdom of Suilley, the town flies its own banner of a sheep in a scale, topped by three red circles on a black field surrounded by red.

Description

Aljun is one of the few towns near the Wilderland Hills to have survived the Wilderlands Clan War without much damage to its buildings or surrounding farmlands. Spared by chance from the initial waves of the assault, Aljun became a mustering point for the Lord-Governor's knights and soldiery, which soon made it an unattractive target for casual pillaging. Once the war ended, Aljun prospered as the only surviving market in the area.

Aljun is ruled by a small town council made up of representatives from the Wool-Merchants' Guild, the Weavers' Guild, the Dyers' Guild, the Brewers' Guild, and the Guild of Smiths, the main industries here. For the last ten years, Aljun's flocks have been the main stock used to replenish the slaughtered sheep population as far as a hundred miles from the town itself. For a short period of time, the King of Suilley even provided a small subsidy to the town to assist with this task, but Suilley's own financial difficulties caused the subsidy to be withdrawn eight years ago. Nevertheless, Aljun is still the local center for sheep markets, with the villages and manors around the town making a good living by selling lambs to buyers from many miles away.

Given the likelihood of flying monsters trying to raid the sheep pens around the town, Aljun might be the only place on the continent to hold a regular archery contest in which the weapon is a ballista.

Adventure

The greatest obstacle to Aljun's growth is its distance from any high-quality, stone-paved roads. Getting to the town requires miles of travel along winding cart trails through areas that have now fallen into wilderness and lawlessness. It is common for sheep dealers and wool merchants to be robbed by bandits or attacked by monsters and wild beasts on their travels. The town is utterly incapable of patrolling an area more than a couple of miles beyond its gates. While the dangers of the region are by no means destroying the town's commerce, Aljun would be much more prosperous if it could secure the roads better, or counterattack against some of the more dangerous threats.

Caer Saliond

(KAYR SAL-ee-ond)

An excellent home base for those brave and/or foolish enough to contemplate expeditions into the mountainous wilds

Caer Saliond is a military fortress under the Lord-Governor's administration, bearing the primary responsibility for preventing incursions of raiders out of the Meridian Mountains. It is a concentric castle with an inner and outer bailey, housing two companies of 50 hill dwarf mountain fighters each, 100 human garrison troops, and two troops of 50 light cavalry. From time to time, a ranger will drift in for supplies, and two knights at a time are usually ordered to base a patrol from Caer Saliond as part of their feudal obligations. The Commander of the castle garrison is currently Hualtir Jabbott (LG male human **Ftr7**), a man of common birth whose fighting expertise comes from service in the Lord-Governor's army rather than from knightly combat. This occasionally causes tension with the knights assigned to his command, but he makes it a point to keep the sometimes-arrogant gentry out on the roads keeping an eye out for bandits.

Although Commander Jabbott has no budget to hire adventurers, his dwarven troops have identified several trouble spots in the mountains where predators and brigands tend to gravitate. He happily points any fortune-seekers to these areas, even providing dwarven guides to help them find the places. He asks for no share of any treasure they bring back, and even writes them a certification exempting them from any tax the guards of Manas might try to levy on the sale of items in that city.

Creeping Mire, The

Vast swamp, replete with swamp-denizens...and growing

Once a stark and beautiful moor in the center of Keston Province known as the Hearthglen, this area is the lowest-lying region between the March of Mountains and the highlands of the Wilderland Hills and Lorremachs. When the Fiend Rains unleased their ten-year deluge upon the eastern slopes of the March of Mountains, the surrounding lands for thousands of square miles drained into the Hearthglen, and though much of the water did slowly seep into the ground, the area became a vast, ever-expanding swamp nonetheless and swallowing an ancient shrine holy to pilgrims of the Church of Mitra. Lizardfolk and brutish swamp dwellers are rumored to lurk in the dark waters of the swamp, but they are seldom seen, and their true numbers are unguessed beyond the accumulated disappearances of travelers on the Swamp Road.

More detail about the Creeping Mire is contained in *The Mires of Mourning* in **Quests of Doom 2** published by **Necromancer Games**.

Gap Road

Bucolic and scenic, with pleasant inns and minimal casualties

Appearance

This is one of the old stone-paved high roads leading up into the hilly lands between the mountain ranges. It is relatively well-maintained, with milestones and a few places where the paving stones have been replaced. It passes through pleasant countryside.

Description

The Gap Road begins at Kingston's west gate, rises westward to cross the high saddle of land between the Kal'Iugus Mountains and the Meridians, then descends to the Duchy of Saxe (off the map to the west). A number of small roadside inns are to be found along the way, along with villages out of sight of the road but marked by cart trails leading to the thoroughfare. As long as wayfarers do not push on too aggressively, it is possible to spend each night of the journey at a coaching inn. It is a safe assumption that rooms are available unless a caravan or mule train happens to be present already. Lone travelers are seldom seen on the road, although this is not so much due to highwaymen as to the pure length of the journey: It is more than 200 miles from Kingston to the western side of the Gap, a long trip to make without companions. There are incidents of brigandage, of course, and monsters do come down from the cold southern heights to hunt, but this is one of the few areas that Keston Province can truly be said to govern, and it is well-patrolled.

Encounter Chance: Make one encounter check in the morning, one in the afternoon, and one at night.

Risk Level: All encounters on the Gap Road are at the Medium-Risk level. Inside the one-hex radius around Kingston, there is an additional automatic encounter check in the surrounding hex and the city's hex. All encounters in the city's hex and the surrounding hexes are at the Low-Risk level.

01–10	No Encounter
11–70	Mundane Encounter
71–00	Dangerous Encounter

Mundane Encounters: Gap Road

1d100	Encounter
01–02	Annoyance (Encounter #3)
03–04	Baron and Retinue (Encounter #8)
05–06	Bear (Encounter #11)
07–15	Caravan (Keston or Foerdewaith) (Encounter #16)
16–18	Cleric (Encounter #19)
19–20	Elf (Encounter #34)
21–36	Farmer (Encounter #36)
37–44	Foot Patrol (Encounter #37)
45–54	Herder (Encounter #51)
55–59	Heretic (Encounter #52)
60–61	High Noble (Encounter #53)
61	Kenckoo Vagrant (Encounter #55)
62–69	Knight and Retinue (Encounter #56)
70	Leper (Encounter #60)
71–74	Minstrel (Encounter #65)
75–77	Mountain Goat (Encounter #66)
78–82	Mounted Patrol (Encounter #67)
83	Outlaw (Encounter #71)
84–86	Peasant (Encounter #74)
87	Prisoner (Encounter #79)
88–89	Small Trader (halfling) (Encounter #86)
90–93	Small Trader (human) (Encounter #85)
94–95	Stag (Encounter #87)
96–98	Wandering Refugee displaced by Wilderlands Clan War, mainly migrant workers (Encounter #98)
99–00	Wolf (Encounter #106)

Dangerous Encounters: Gap Road

1d100	Encounter
01–02	Ankheg (Encounter #2)
03–10	Bandit (Encounter #7)
11	Basilisk (Encounter #9)
12–13	Bugbear (Encounter #13)
14–15	Bulette (Encounter #14)
16–17	Centaur (Encounter #17)
18–19	Cockatrice (Encounter #21)
20–23	Dragons A (Encounter #27)
24–27	Eagle, Giant (Encounter #33)
28–29	Ettin (Encounter #35)
30–32	Giant, Cloud (Encounter #40)
33–40	Gnoll (Encounter #43)
41–49	Goblin, Roaming (Encounter #45)
50–52	Hag (Encounter #48)
53–57	Lycanthrope (Encounter #61)
58–59	Manticore (Encounter #63)
60–61	Ogre Mage (Oni) (Encounter #70)
62–66	Owlbear (Encounter #72)
67–74	Robber Knight (Encounter #80)
75	Roc (Encounter #81)
76–78	Stirge (Encounter #88)
79–80	Troll (Encounter #92)
81–82	Undead A (Encounter #94)
83–86	Vulchling (Encounter #97)
87–88	Wasp, Giant (Encounter #99)
89–92	Weasel, Giant (Encounter #100)
93–94	Witherstench (Encounter #104)
95–96	Wizard (Encounter #107)
97–00	Wyvern (Encounter #108)

Kingston

Unevenly-built Capital City of Keston Province

LN large city
Government council
Population 15,612 (10,852 humans; 2340 halflings; 876 half-elves; 721 hill dwarves; 503 half-orcs; 259 gnomes; 61 high elves)
Notable NPCs
Lord-Governor Baron Miltrin Cormien (LN male human **Ftr12**)
Tauran Perziot, High Priest of Mithras (LN male human **Clr19**)
High Priest Binabantoo (N male gnome **Clr9** of Dre'uain the Lame)
Sebastio Velacaunt (CE male human **Clr7** of Fraz-Urb'luu)
Kallisthena of Keston (N female human **Wiz12**)
Magister Porgo (LE male human Wiz11)
Guacra Occlo, Dean of the Red Academy (LN male human **Ftr10**)
Maximum Clerical Spell Level Good —, Neutral 9, Evil 5 (hidden, Fraz-Urb'luu**)**
Purchase Maximum/Month 32,000gp

Appearance

Kingston is a high-walled city with a strangely lopsided appearance, for its foundations shifted slightly during the Fiend Rains. The citadel, in particular, leans visibly sideways, and has come to be known as the Tilting Citadel. As far as anyone can tell, the walls are still strong and stable, but entering the city with its crooked houses and uneven streets gives some travelers a distinct sense of vertigo.

Description

Kingston is the capital of Keston Province, and the seat of the Lord-Governor, currently Baron Miltrin Cormien.

Kingston is governed by a council of 10 citizens known as the Council of Listeners. Each of the four dukes of the realm appoints one Listener, the citizens of Kingston elect two, the city guilds elect two, and the Lord-Governor appoints two.

Religion and Temples

Temple of Mithras

Mithras, the warrior god of the ancient Hyperboreans (not to be confused with Mitra the sun god imported from distant Eastern realms), has a wide following in Keston, and his temple is the largest one in the capital city. The entrance to the temple complex is a massive stone bull's head, with the mouth forming the gateway. On the god's festival days, massive smoke-pots in the sides of the gatehouse cause the nostrils to belch colored smoke throughout the day, with occasional gouts of flame. Worship of the god is conducted in a number of different underground chambers in accordance with the season and various astrological confluences. Most of the chambers are accessed from stairwells and trapdoors in the main temple building, which also houses armories, training rooms, and the temple's administration.

Temple of Dre'uain the Lame

Dre'uain the Lame (DREY-oo-wain) is a god of industry and hard work; originally a god of the gnomes, and gnomish himself, his human following is quite large in recent centuries as a patron of industrious labor. In Keston he has become a symbol of recovering the once-settled areas emptied by the Wilderness Clan War that now lie wild and fallow in eastern Keston and has seen a surge in devotion in the last decade, becoming the pre-eminent faith in Keston among humans, halflings, dwarves, and gnomes alike. The priesthood is equally divided between gnomes and humans, and high priest Binabantoo (a gnome) has been very active in efforts to send settlers and refugees back into the wilderness to reclaim it. In service of this goal, he frequently hires adventurers and mercenaries to clear out dangerous areas and protect the young settlements he is trying to re-seed in the eastern parts of the province.

Unfortunately, Binabantoo has overly optimistic ideas about what can be achieved by a few straggling bands of refugees in an area that is rapidly devolving into a howling wilderness. He has piles of maps and crop-yield projections, charts of anticipated population growth, and stacks of reference manuals by well-regarded scholars, but his view of humanity has been formed by the sorts of people who seek out a god of hard work as their patron. The reliable, well-fed, resourceful worshippers who surround him in the city are a far cry from the beaten-down, ill-fed refugees and convicts he assumes will quickly transform themselves into sturdy yeoman farmers. He has certainly created more than one thriving village by his efforts, but several of his newly formed hamlets have simply disappeared, with a few battered survivors occasionally making their way to places like Aljun.

Other Matters of Interest

In addition to the various temples, Kingston has a number of other interesting places hidden away in its warren of uneven streets and tilted buildings.

Grey Rook Guild

A criminal brotherhood known as the Grey Rooks, or the "Grey Rook Guild," headquarters in the town of Durbenford across the mountains to the southwest in Toullen's transmontain holdings, and has some agents here in Kingston. Their activity here is small, mainly limited to fencing stolen goods. More detail about the Grey Rook Guild may be found in **Trouble in Durbenford** by **Necromancer Games**, but the guild's operation in Toullen is entirely separate from the petty criminals working in Kingston.

Sliding Scales Plaza

The largest open-air market in the city is the Sliding Scales, a circular plaza filled with tents and vendors' booths from dawn until noon each day. When the city's foundations were damaged by the Fiend Rains, the plaza developed a distinct slope. A ball could roll down the entire length of the market from west to east if not for the uneven cobblestones. A few permanent shops surround the plaza, and the Council-Hall of the Listeners stands at the western end of the market. A small theatre called The Moons stands across the plaza from the Council Hall, and is used for public announcements as well as performances. Kingston houses a number of semi-professional theater companies of widely varying quality. One of these companies, Manover's Players, is considered quite subversive, since many of their plays seem to advocate a return to the Kingdoms of Foere rather than continued allegiance to the Kingdom of Suilley.

Academy of Inquisitors (the "Red Academy")

The Academy of Inquisitors occupies an odd, sinister building in Kingston's poor quarter, the headquarters of what is effectively a guild of torturers and interrogators operating across many of the realms in the Borderland Provinces. Graduates of the Red Academy are hired by various governors, dukes, barons, and others who maintain dismal prisons, often traveling great distances to lucrative postings. Just as it is a point of pride and reputation for a ruler to have a priest of Jamboor as an adviser, it is also a matter of prestige to have a graduate of the Red Academy on a noble's staff to serve as an interrogator or spymaster. The Academy is not a religious organization, and serves no particular patron deity. The graduates are always of Lawful alignment, and for as long as they are under contract in a ruler's service they are utterly reliable and incorruptible.

The origins of the academy before it arrived in Kingston are vague, and the inquisitors are unwilling to discuss anything they might know about their past history. According to the city's records, a wain of six wagons, their contents hidden by red canopies, appeared at the city gates in the year 3199, the same year that Overking Oessum VIII called for the Fourth Great Crusade. No one except perhaps the Red Inquisitors knows whether the two events were in any way connected. The arrival of the caravan was taxed as coming from Foere, and the Red Inquisitors do not send their graduates into the Overking's realm, so there appears to have been some event that caused them to pick up and move across the mountains into Keston Province. What this event might have been, or how old the academy was before it moved into Kingston, are matters only of conjecture. Even the Red Inquisitors themselves might not have records dating back that far into the past. No one has ever tried to break into the academy building to find out.

Morninghaven Sanatorium

Prison for the criminally insane

Seven hundred and fifteen years ago, Overking Osbert II received a vision here from the foreign god, Mitra the Sun Father, predicting victory in a great battle. The prediction came to pass when Osbert's outmatched forces broke the power of the Heldring invaders at Oescreheit Downs and finally pacified the barbarians of the Helcynngae Peninsula after nearly 3000 years of warfare. In gratitude, the Overking built a shrine to Mitra on the site where the mystical vision came to him, and the resulting fame from the legacy of the battle played a large part in the faith of Mitra making great inroads in surpassing the Hyperborean church of Solanus in subsequent centuries; a usurpation that continues to this day.

Roughly 500 years later, the Church of Mitra built a convalescent home at the shrine, run by the Church's hospitalers. After the Fiend Rains, the sanatorium's foundations began to sink, and the Church sold the building

to a baronet who promised to keep the shrine in good repair. The baronet converted the hospital itself into a prison for the insane, and it came to be known colloquially as "Mourninghaven" for the horrors inflicted upon the inmates trapped within its walls. More detail on Mourninghaven and its sinister administration is available in adventure *The Mires of Mourning* in **Quests of Doom 2** published by **Necromancer Games**.

The Notquite Inn

A fortified inn located in a gap between country borders

N large roadhouse
Sign Wooden signboard with lettering: "The Notquite Inn"
Prices average; **Quality** average
Staff 13 (12 humans, 1 hill dwarf)
Notable NPCs
 Picardi of Notquite, Master of the Inn (N human male **Ftr6**)
 Torbin Blode, Blacksmith and Farrier (N male dwarf
  commoner)
Maximum Clerical Spell Level Good 2, Neutral 4, Evil —
Purchase Maximum/Month 1000gp

Appearance

A small, castle-like structure built on a triangular piece of land in the middle of a major crossroad of the South Road and the Provincial Military Road. It is walled in stone, and a large wooden sign hanging out front of the gate identifies it as "The Notquite Inn."

Description

The Notquite Inn is a fortified roadside inn located at the intersection of the borders of Exeter, Toullen, and Keston in a large island of land in the center of the crossroads where the Provincial Military Road intersects with the South Road. The roads do not meet in a cross, but form a large triangle, originally designed to allow one military unit to move off the road into the triangle so another unit could overtake if needed. At some point in the last 300 years or so, an enterprising innkeeper took advantage of the fact that the island of land in the center of this triangle was apparently unclaimed by all three of the adjoining realms, each of which defined their borders along the roads themselves, leaving out the "hole" in the middle.

This innkeeper proceeded to build a wooden stockade in the middle of the crossroad, with a blacksmith, a dormitory, and a stable to allow traveling merchants to shelter for a night while sleeping in a bed and getting their horses re-shod for the rest of the journey. Over the years, the little stockade has been re-walled with stone (albeit not nearly as powerfully as a castle), the buildings have been improved, and the available services expanded. The inn remains quite a rustic place, but it is secure and comfortable in its own way. In addition to housing traveling caravans, the Notquite Inn has become a meeting-place and re-provisioning point for wilderland adventurers such as rangers, ruin-plunderers, knights-errant, and adventuring parties. A broad assortment of these unconventional types can always be found in the inn's tavern building, the Three Crowns.

The triangle is generally accepted by all three adjoining realms to be ungoverned. Any attempt by one of the three powers to annex the land would be considered brash and illegal by the other two adjoining provinces. As a result, it is possible for a wanted criminal to gain sanctuary in the inn, although most such undesirables would be denied access or forcibly ejected by the Master of the Inn. Nevertheless, it has from time to time served as a place of refuge for those whom the Master of the Inn considers unjustly charged or worthy of protection.

The current Master of the Inn, for the title of "innkeeper" seems a bit understated, is Picardi of Notquite (N human male **Ftr6**), called "Master Picardi" in his professional role as innkeeper. He is jovial and friendly, welcoming to those who are often unwelcomed, and an excellent source of information about events both local and distant. The inn's beds are almost completely free of bedbugs, and massive lockboxes are available in each room to house valuable possessions, which are almost never stolen by other guests.

If adventurers inquire about current rumors at the inn, they may hear about troubles near Catten Moor to the southwest of the inn about a hundred miles or so, across the border in the County of Toullen (see **Chapter 10: Toullen,** *Catten Moor*).

1d100	Encounter
26–45	Ghoul (Encounter #39)
46–65	Giant Wasp (Encounter #99)
66–85	Lizardfolk (Encounter #59)
86–00	Robber Knight (Encounter #80)

South Road

See **Chapter 7: March of Mountains,** *South Road*.

Swamp Road

Appearance

The Swamp Road is desolate and obviously poorly maintained, especially during the spring rainy season when provincial repair crews are unwilling to brave the dangers of the Creeping Mire. Although it is one of the ancient stone-paved high roads built by the Hyperborean Empire. There are gaps where the stones have been washed out by floods and mudslides, sometimes miles long. These have been repaired many times by log corduroys in the past, but each spring, sections are washed out anew, requiring additional repair.

Description

The Swamp Road begins at the east gate of Kingston and extends as far as the Creeping Mire, where it becomes a raised earthen causeway leading to Morninghaven Sanatorium. The road is often washed out during storms, and Keston has much more pressing concerns than maintaining the quality of an old road that no longer leads anywhere important, so repairs are infrequent at best. People often disappear on the Swamp Road, and it is almost never traveled without armed escorts.

Encounter Chance: Make one encounter check in the morning, one in the afternoon, and one at night.

Risk Level: All encounters on the Swamp Road are at the Medium-Risk level. Inside the one-hex radius around Kingston, there is an additional automatic encounter check in the surrounding hex and the city's hex. All encounters in the city's hex and the surrounding hexes are at the Low-Risk level.

01–35	No Encounter
36–45	Mundane Encounter
46–00	Dangerous Encounter

Mundane Encounters

1d100	Encounter
01–10	Cleric (Encounter #19)
11–60	Farmer (Encounter #36)
61–70	Foot Patrol (Encounter #37)
71–80	Knight and Retinue (Encounter #55)
81–00	Outlaw (Encounter #70)

Dangerous Encounters

1d100	Encounter
01–20	Bandit (Encounter #7)
21–25	Dragon A (Encounter #27)

Chapter Seven: The March of Mountains

The March of Mountains

Overview

The March of Mountains is the name of a vast chain of mountain ranges, all part of the same geological formation as the Stonehearts. These ranges include the Kal'Iugus Mountains, the Meridian Range, the Ramparts, and the Cretian Mountains, in addition to the Mons Terminus range (although the Mons Terminus are generally considered to be the southern spur of the Stonehearts). The March of Mountains marked the eastern edge of the ancient Hyperborean Empire's heartland, and more recently has marked the eastern boundary of the true Kingdoms of Foere, as opposed to their subject provinces.

Cretian Mountains

(CREE-shin)

The Cretians are the northernmost range of the March of Mountains, and is also the largest. The peaks of the Cretians are unusually high, taller than any others of the highest mountains of the central Kal-Iugus range. Many dark rumors and superstitious stories surround the Cretians, from tales of ghosts, to invisible giants that fly on the wind, to the legends of Lost Boy Mountain on its northern end. The Cretians completely encircle the heavily wooded Yolbiac Vale, an isolated and inbred country with strange attitudes and motivations. The Yolbiac Vale has its own entry later in the book.

The heights of the Cretians are virtually unknown to geographers, scholars, and cartographers, with the exception of the outermost few miles around the periphery of the vast mountain range. Few venture into the interior, and fewer return. Those few hardy souls that have returned from deeper expeditions report that the mountains contain a number of small vales inhabited by folk even stranger than the eccentric citizenry of the Yolbiac Vale. Demon worship, cannibalism, and oddly tangled family trees are mentioned in most such accounts of the mountain folk. What is also spoken of is the number of ancient sites to be found in the deep Cretians, evidence that at one time there was a fairly large population dwelling in the mist-shrouded peaks. What drove these people into decay and decadence is not known, and those who have tried to investigate it seem to be overrepresented in the number of adventurers who have actually survived to return to civilization.

Around the mountain periphery one finds several "false passes," gaps in the more rugged terrain that eventually close off into dead ends several miles in. There are said to be a few high passes through the northern Cretians between Aachen Province and the Yolbiac Vale, but these are treacherous and difficult to follow without taking wrong turns, in addition to being impassable to wagons. The only truly reliable pass in the northern Cretians is the Ghostwind Pass that enters the mountain heights close to the Town of Elet.

Heorm's Lair

(HEE-yorm)

Heorm is an ancient red dragon whose lair is deep in the mountains, virtually inaccessible other than by air. The great wyrm seldom flies anymore, but the western Gaelon Valley still has old records of his depredations in the year of 3183, and again in the autumn of 3426. By these estimates, the dragon is at the very least 400 years old, for it was reported as fully grown in 3183. According to a few songs that cannot be considered completely reliable, Heorm is the sire of the dragons Hendrar, Gwairm, and the greatly feared female Graazaal of Ten-Falls Crag, whose lair is roughly 150 miles to the east of Heorm's in a highland ridge of the Gaelon Valley.

Heorm's hoard is, of course, legendary. It is no doubt exaggerated by the minstrels who take the dragon as a theme for songs or poetry, but a mere recitation of items taken in the great raids of 3183 and 3426 is enough to establish that the treasure is vast. There are few accounts of any meetings with Heorm other than that of Teskel Earme, apprentice to the wizard Tatterdemalion from the years 3497 to 3501. (See **Chapter 5: Gaelon River Valley**, *Tatterdemalion's Manse*). According to Earme,

Tatterdemalion paid a visit to Heorm's Lair in 3501, accompanied by Earme himself, arriving as normal in his maelstrom-borne pavilion tent. Apparently, the sheer flamboyance of the visit either roused the dragon's curiosity or caution, for no battle took place. The wizard and dragon engaged in conversation beyond the range of Earme's hearing, and an item of some sort changed hands. Earme was unable to tell whether the dragon gave something to the mage, or the mage to the dragon. No more information is available from this source, unfortunately, for Earme collapsed into a fit of nervous twitching shortly after penning his account, a debilitation that lasted until his death in 3503 in the city of Endhome. No foul play is suspected in his demise; the poor invalid suffered from a heart attack upon seeing a garden lizard in the Temple of Solanus where he was being tended. The Archmage Tatterdemalion has never volunteered information about his conversation with Heorm, or indeed anything about his visit to the wyrm's lair.

Heorm, Ancient Red Dragon Sor10: AC 22; **HP** 741 (28d20+252 plus 10d20+90); **Spd** 40ft, climb 40ft, fly 80ft; **Melee** bite (+18, 15ft, 2d10+10 piercing plus 4d6 fire), claw (+18, 10ft, 2d6+10 slashing) or tail (+18, 20ft, 2d8+10 bludgeoning); **SA** frightful presence (1 min, DC 23 Wis repeat), fire breath (recharge 5-6, 90ft cone, 26d6 fire, DC 25 Dex half), multiattack (frightful presence, bite, claw x2), spells (Cha +15, DC 23); **LA** detect, tail attack, wing attack (2, 15ft, 2d6+10 bludgeoning, knock prone, DC 26 Dex, fly up to half speed); **Immune** fire; **Str** +10, **Dex** +0 (+8), **Con** +9 (+17), **Int** +4, **Wis** +2 (+10), **Cha** +7 (+15); **Skills** Perception +18, Stealth +8; **Senses** blindsight 60ft, darkvision 120ft; **Traits** metamagic (empowered, heightened, quickened), legendary resistance (3/day), sorcery points (10); **AL** CE; **CR** 25; **XP** 75,000.

> **Spells (slots):** 0 (at will)—*blade ward, dancing lights, mage hand, mending, minor illusion, true strike;* 1st (4)—*detect magic, fog cloud;* 2nd (3)—*detect thoughts, hold person, mirror image;* 3rd (3)—*dispel magic, haste, slow;* 4th (3)—*greater invisibility, stoneskin;* 5th (1)—*cloudkill*

Treasure: 86,635gp, 173,936sp, 210,559cp, *mask of water breathing* (operates as a *potion of water breathing* 3 times per day, for 3 hours), arcane scroll (*arcane eye, dispel magic, knock),* 3 *potions of supreme healing,* divine scroll (*greater restoration, heal, lesser restoration, raise dead), adamantine plate armor, mace of terror, sentinel shield, sun blade,* 15 large rubies (500gp each).

Kal'Iugus Mountains
(KAL-eye-YOU-gus)

The Kal'Iugus Mountains are the second largest of the ranges of the March of Mountains after the Cretians. The meaning of the odd name Kal'Iugus is lost to history, but it is thought to predate the arrival of the Hyperboreans. The highest part of the range is its northern spur, where the massive Jerinot (Jair-i-no) Glacier lies over the peaks, and which is said to be the home of giants and reclusive tribes of barbarians who ride across its surface on sleds pulled by dogs. The King of Suilley is lately concerned with reports of a giantish invasion preparing to descend from these northern slopes into Keston and Toullen, but so far no solid evidence has been uncovered to confirm the danger.

The Kal'Iugus is home to several clans of mountain dwarves, hostile to lowlanders and possibly allied with the northern giants of the range. Other dwarves tend not to speak of them.

The southern reaches of the Kal'Iugus Range not covered by the great glacier are less dangerous, but still not a place for idle wandering. They are home to dragons of many ages, mostly of the terrifying red variety but including some white wyrms farther to the north. Several great orc-warrens are also known to exist in these reaches of the mountains, but they are high and remote, seldom posing a serious threat to the lowlands.

Meridian Range

In the year 43 I.R., the Imperial Court geographer Rasymius declared the central peak of this range to be the highest point upon the exact Prime Meridian of the world of Boros, based on a series of exacting calculations. The mountain was named "Primus," and the range containing it became the "Meridian Range." When the poles shifted in 2491 I.R. (1,026 years ago), the planet's north-south axis completely changed, thus making the venerable Rasymius' calculations no longer valid. Since then, political exigencies have caused the Prime Meridian to be administratively moved several more times, so that it now lies 350 miles to the west, running through the imperial city of Courghais.

The original name of the Meridian Range remains, and grim, sharp-peaked Primus still towers over the lesser mountains below it.

Mons Terminus

The Mons Terminus mountain range is the southernmost point of the Stoneheart Mountains beyond the Stoneheart Valley. The old imperial capital of Curgantium was built at the very tip of the Mons Terminus to symbolize the city's position as the core of the empire.

From the perspective of the Borderland Provinces, these mountains lie just across the Great Amrin River from Aachen Province, where they rise majestically to dominate the western horizon.

Rampart Mountains

The Rampart Mountains are so named because the central peaks of the range are steep and uniform like a castle wall. The mountains have always served as a bulwark defending the eastern flank of the Foerdewaith and the Hyperborean empires. The western verge of the Ramparts, entirely within the Duchy of the Rampart, has numerous mines that produce gold and iron. Many of these are dwarven excavations, but the mining towns serving them are predominantly human.

The western side of the Rampart Mountains, where most of the mining takes place, is contained within the borders of the Duchy of the Rampart, and the Duchy also rules the northern part of the range's eastern flanks.

Most of the dwarves of the western Ramparts are hill dwarves living in village-sized or smaller clan settlements high in the foothills. In addition to mining, they keep small herds of goats or sheep to supplement the grains and other farm produce they trade for in the mining towns lower down the slopes. The larger clans include the Hamarung, the Stoneshields, and the Timbercutters (who are, as one might surmise, engaged in a bit of lumbering activity as well as mining and herding). The Hamarungs can usually be identified by their long-tailed, yellow liripipe hoods, with the clan symbol of a yellow hammer. The Stoneshields wear different shades of gray, with no other color other than a cloak, which might be of any hue. The Timbercutters cannot be distinguished from other dwarves by their style of dress, but their clan symbol is a pair of crossed axes in front of a green tree. These three clans do not make up more than about 5% of the dwarves living in the western Ramparts, but they are considerably more numerous than any of the other clans.

South Road

The South Road runs north and south along the eastern rim of the March of Mountains, originating in Tuller on the south coast of Toullen, then passing northward through the County of Toullen, Keston Province, Vourdon, and the Duchy of the Rampart, and ending in the City of Troyes. In old documents, the road is called the "South Provincial Road," but common usage has shortened the name.

Merchants generally prefer taking the South Road rather than Trader's Way for moving their cargoes north or south through the Borderland

Provinces, for the Trader's Way passes through many areas of empty wilderness, and the South Road is at least lightly settled along its whole length. Even those on slow wagons only have to spend one or two nights under the stars rather than finding a roadside inn. Not necessarily a clean, honest, or comfortable one, but an inn nonetheless.

Encounter Chance: Make one encounter check in the morning, one in the afternoon, and one at night.

Risk Level: All encounters on the South Road are at the Medium-Risk level. Inside the one-hex radius around Tertry, Kingston, Olaric, and Troye, there is an additional automatic encounter check in the surrounding hex and the city's hex. All encounters in these city's hexes and the surrounding hexes are at the Low-Risk level.

01–17	No Encounter
18–65	Mundane Encounter
66–00	Dangerous Encounter

Mundane Encounters: South Road

1d100	Encounter
01–02	Annoyance (Encounter #3)
03–04	Baron and Retinue (Encounter #8)
05–07	Bear (Encounter #11)
08–12	Caravan (Toullen, Keston, Vourdon, or Rampart) (Encounter #16)
13–14	Cleric (Encounter #19)
15	Druid (Encounter #31)
16–18	Elf (Encounter #34)
19–30	Farmer (Encounter #36)
31–36	Foot Patrol local sheriff from the area (Encounter #37)
37–47	Herder (Encounter #51)
48–51	Heretic (Encounter #52)
52	High Noble (Encounter #53)
53–54	Kenckoo Vagrant (Encounter #55)
55–59	Knight and Retinue (Encounter #56)
60–61	Leper (Encounter #60)
62–65	Mountain Goat (Encounter #66)
66–69	Minstrel (Encounter #65)
70–74	Mounted Patrol (Encounter #67)
75–76	Outlaw (Encounter #71)
77–78	Peasant (Encounter #74)
79	Penitent (Encounter #76)
80	Prisoner (Encounter #79)
81–83	Small Trader (dwarf or halfling) (Encounter #86)
84–86	Small Trader (human) (Encounter #85)
87–91	Stags (Encounter #87)
92–95	Wandering Refugee (Encounter #98)
96–00	Wolf (Encounter #106)

Dangerous Encounters: South Road

1d100	Encounter
01	Ankheg (Encounter #2)
02–21	Bandit (Encounter #7)
22	Basilisk (Encounter #9)
23–27	Blood Hawk (Encounter #12)
28	Corpse Rook (Encounter #22)
29–33	Dragon A (Encounter #27)
34	Drake, Fire (Encounter #30)
35–36	Eagle, Giant (Encounter #33)
37	Ettin (Encounter #35)
38–40	Giant, Hill (Encounter #41)
41–42	Giant, Stone (Encounter #42)
43–47	Goblin Raider (Encounter #44) if near mountains; otherwise, Goblin, Roaming (Encounter #45)
48–50	Griffon (Encounter #47) near mountains only; otherwise, Owlbear (Encounter #72)
51–55	Harpy (Encounter #50)
56–58	Korred (Encounter #58) near mountains only; otherwise, Ankheg (Encounter #2)
59–60	Lycanthrope (Encounter #61)
61–65	Manticore (Encounter #63)
66–67	Ogre (Encounter #69)
68	Ogre Mage (Encounter #70)
69	Perytons (Encounter #77) near mountains only; otherwise, Tigers (Encounter #90)
70–73	Robber Knight (Encounter #80)
74–75	Rocs (Encounter #81)
76	Satyr (Encounter #82) near mountains only; otherwise, Tiger (Encounter #90)
77–78	Stirge (Encounter #88)
79	Tiger (Encounter #90)
80–81	Troll (Encounter #92)
82–83	Undead A (Encounter #94)
84–87	Vulchling (Encounter #97)
88–89	Wasp, Giant (Encounter #99)
90–91	Werewolf (Encounter #101) near mountains only; otherwise, Centaur (Encounter #17)
92–93	Witherstench (Encounter #104)
94–95	Wolverine, Giant (Encounter #105)
96	Wizard (Encounter #107)
97–00	Wyvern (Encounter #108)

Chapter Eight: Duchy of the Rampart

Duchy of the Rampart

Overview

The Duchy of the Rampart is a palatine dukedom, meaning that the title is hereditary and that the Duke reports to the Overking at the same level as one of the other rulers within the Kingdoms of Foere. It is a stable and well-guarded realm, with a strong sense of chivalry and feudal obligations. But a certain decay is setting in, and strange things lurk in the shadows. The creeping advance of dark and dangerous things is subtle and isolated here, but very much present. The people of the duchy know in the backs of their minds that the Rampart is declining, but they do not understand why, or how to counter the process.

General Information

Alignment: LN
Capital: Troye (44,600)
Notable Settlements: Metzel (2,876), Reliquary of Jamboor (2,274), Ristalt (6,781)
Ruler: His Most Noble Lordship, the Palatine Duke Claud VII, Battle-Duke of Foere and Sword of the Foerdewaith (LN male human **Ftr16**)
Government: feudalism (palatine duchy of Foere)
Population: 3,156,000 (2,850,000 Foerdewaith; 183,000 hill dwarves; 57,500 halflings; 43,000 high elves; 13,500 half-elves; 6,200 gnomes; 2,400 half-orcs; 400 other)
Humanoid: hill dwarf (many), halfling (many), high elf (some), half-elf (some), gnome (few), half-orc (few)
Monstrous: giant rat, giant ant, krenshar, kobold, kenckoo, giant boar, ankheg, owlbear, bulette (plains) dire wolf, goblin, orc, giant lizard, ogre, stone giant, bugbear, hill giant, wyvern, roc, dragon, yrthak (mountains)
Languages: Common, Gasquen, Dwarven, Halfling, Elven, Gnome, Orc, High Boros
Religion: Sefagreth, Vanitthu, Archeillus, Mithras, Vergrimm Earthsblood, Mick O'Delving, Thyr (declining), Mitra (rising), Darach-Albith, Jamboor, Muir, Solanus (declining), Quell
Resources: coal, iron, gems (grade 1), wool, quarry stone, cloth, timber, ironwork, gems (grade 3)
Technology Level: Medieval

Borders and Lands

On the eastern side of the March of Mountains, the borders of the Duchy of the Rampart extend roughly 200–250 miles from Troye to the south, southeast, and west. To the west, the border extends roughly 600 miles to the west, including all of the lands between the Cretian Mountains and the Rampart Mountains.

The Duchy was once much larger than it is now, reaching eastward as far east as the Gundlock Hills, and south nearly reaching the Lorremach Highhills (though this latter was a mix of Suilleyn and Rampartine nobles and villages that had no real delineation until the secession of the Suilleyn king). Most of these lands were lost to the Kingdom of Suilley during the Suilleyn rebellion from the Kingdoms of Foere, and there is no credible expectation that they will ever be retaken.

History and People

The Duchy of the Rampart was founded in 2802 I.R. when Overking Osbert II raised Claud Oberhammer, a war hero and the Overking's nephew, to the status of Duke of the Rampart, Battle-Duke of Foere, and Sword of the Foerdewaith. In accordance with the ancient Hyperborean custom of *dux bellorum*, the Battle-Duke is traditionally the marshal of the armies of Foere anywhere they fight. This custom has waned over the years, with Overkings or generals often leading armies into conflicts and crusades that occur far from the Rampart.

The earliest beginning of this break from custom came with a tragic occurrence, perhaps the Duchy's greatest shame. During the Second Great Crusade of 2970–2971, while the majority of Foere's military forces were engaged across the Sinnar Ocean in far Libynos, a powerful vampire lord known as the Singed Man arose in the western Kingdoms of Foere and conquered a great swath of territory in the distant Duchy of Kear, far to the west of the Borderland provinces and the Duchy itself. The Singed Man formed his own enslaved domain and named himself as its Infernal Tyrant. By the time the crusader forces returned from the East, the Infernal Tyrant was already well entrenched and ready for the attack of the war-weary soldiers.

Responsibility for dislodging the vampire lord from his hold and freeing the oppressed lands was given to Duke Ormand I, Palatine-Duke of the Rampart and Battle-Duke of Foere. Because of the scattered nature of the returning armies and the depleted resources of Foere, Duke Ormand had great difficulty in raising a new fighting force and properly equipping and supplying it. It was 2977 before Ormand finally marched on Kear, and in all those years the Singed Man had been carefully planning and preparing a response to just such an attack. Duke Ormand's forces trudged across the Plains of Eauxe, enduring the constant harassing tactics of the Singed Man's defenses, but was finally able to bring the Infernal Tyrant's forces to ground at Seilo Ford, trapped against the flooding Meander River. Unfortunately, it was also there that Ormand discovered the horrific preparations of the Infernal Tyrant: all the dead of Kear suddenly rose up

at one time simultaneously threatened and protected the entire provincial region of the Plains of Suilley.

The people of the Rampart are solidly and traditionally Foerdewaith, very loyal to the Overking in Courghais. Chivalry is still a strongly held value among the knightly class, although there are certainly many knights whose claim to chivalry is dubious at best, and scurrilous at worst. An ancient order of knights is based in the Rampart: the Order of the Swan, whose device is a white swan on a black background, framed by a circle of plumes. Knights of the Swan are generally knights-errant rather than in service to a feudal lord. They owe their loyalty to the Order, although they have often ridden to the defense of the Duchy when danger has threatened.

Trade and Commerce

The capital city of Troye benefits from an excellent strategic location for trade, although the city itself is not particularly mercantile. Caravans ascend the King's Road from the Kingdom of Foere, entering Troye's gates from the west. Southern trade arrives from Toullen, Keston, and Vourdon along the South Road, and the King's Road brings cargo from Endhome's seaport and the farms of the Gaelon River Valley. Many of these shipments change hands in Troye as the various different merchants buy each other's goods to take back on the return journey.

In general, the folk of the Rampart are not traders or merchants, but the Duchy makes efforts to foster trade and travel within its borders. In 3423 I.R., the Duchy of the Rampart acted in cooperation with Endhome, Sunderland, and Suilley to establish Grollek's Grove as a merchants' post on the Trader's Way to foster commerce among the four realms. Even though the Kingdom of Suilley tends to divert caravans onto its own Flatlander Road rather than the more-dangerous Trader's Way, the Duchy makes no protest about reducing trade to Grollek's Grove. The Flatlander Road, after all, eventually leads to Troye itself from which it can continue down the King's Road to Grollek's Grove, enriched from its time within the Duchy.

Loyalties and Diplomacy

The Duchy of the Rampart is the easternmost of the actual Kingdoms of Foere, the only one of the true Foerdewaith realms shown on this map or described in this book. The Duchy has stood for centuries as the eastern defense of the Foerdewaith homelands, and is fiercely loyal to the Overking and the heartlands to the west.

Government

The current ruler is Claud VII, Duke of the Rampart, Battle-Duke of Foere, and Sword of the Foerdewaith. He has a long and bloody history in petty wars on the wild fringes of civilization fighting on behalf of Foere, with the Duchy administered in his absence by the nobleman Traont, Baron Thulde under the title of Lord-Steward of the Rampart. In the recent campaign against the Huun in the lands of the Gulf of Akados and Irkaina, the Overking decided to lead the armies personally rather than placing the Duke in his traditional post of command, and Claud returned to his lands in the Rampart, clearly confused and insulted.

Having been established by decree, the Duchy is not a wild patchwork of feudal divisions like the provinces to its east. It is segmented into a regular system of equally sized counties (roughly 4 hexes each, by the map). The counts appoint sheriffs and other officials, and usually have at least four castled baronies in their lands, along with several knightly manors.

Wilderness and Adventure

The Duchy of the Rampart is well-settled, although pockets of wilderness are everywhere in between settlements. The southern verge of the Cretians is a wild and rugged place, much more sparsely inhabited, and correspondingly more dangerous for those who venture close to these strange peaks. Along the verges of the Rampart Mountains there are also fewer settlements, but this is an area where mining towns and settlements

from the ground on the banks of the Meander around the Duke's army and attacked from all sides.

Duke Ormand's army was decimated at Seilo Ford, the survivors fleeing east back towards Foere. The Battle-Duke himself was captured and turned into a vampire, an unholy slave of the Singed Man. Duke Ormand became the Singed Man's general and devoted servant, using his military prowess and experience to expand the wasted realm of the Infernal Tyrant to ever greater bounds. Foere's own armies were exhausted and crippled, unable to do anything but watch as the Infernal Tyrant ran rampant in the west. It was not until more than 50 years later that the paladin Sir Varral the Blessed was able to destroy the Singed Man, free the realm of Kear, and finally send the former Duke Ormand to his eternal rest. Ormand's name was stricken from the line of the Rampart by his grandson, Duke Claude III, and a taint lingered upon the Battle-Dukes in the eyes some of the Foerdewaith overkings due to the late duke's failure. This great shame only festered over the years, leading perhaps to an overly aggressive war doctrine among the line of Battle-Dukes that ultimately led to the Duchy's second-greatest shame at the Battle of Bullocks Bale some 94 years later (see **Chapter 9: Suilley**).

In the war between Oceanus and Foere, when the City of Endhome declared neutrality in 3217 I.R. and expelled its Foerdewaith garrison, the forces of the Rampart marched up the King's Road to retake the city, but sudden intervention by Burgundia caused the outflanked Foerdewaith army to withdraw to Troye without bloodshed. The Lord-General of the Army was dismissed in disgrace by the enraged Battle-Duke of the Rampart, but the event was the first real damage dealt to the legend of Foerdewaith military invincibility in the Provinces.

Only five years later, the forces of the Rampart were directly engaged in the war of Suilleyn independence of 3222 I.R. An aggressive new lord-general led his Foerdewaith army into western Suilley to bring the rebel barons to heel. Unfortunately for the Battle-Duke, who was returning from far afield in the battles of Matagost to the east, his Foerdewaith were virtually slaughtered at the Battle of Bullocks Bale, with only a few managing to escape. At this one stroke, the legend of the military power of the Duchy of the Rampart was ended. The Rampart maintains a powerful army in the present day, but it is no longer seen as the invincible force that

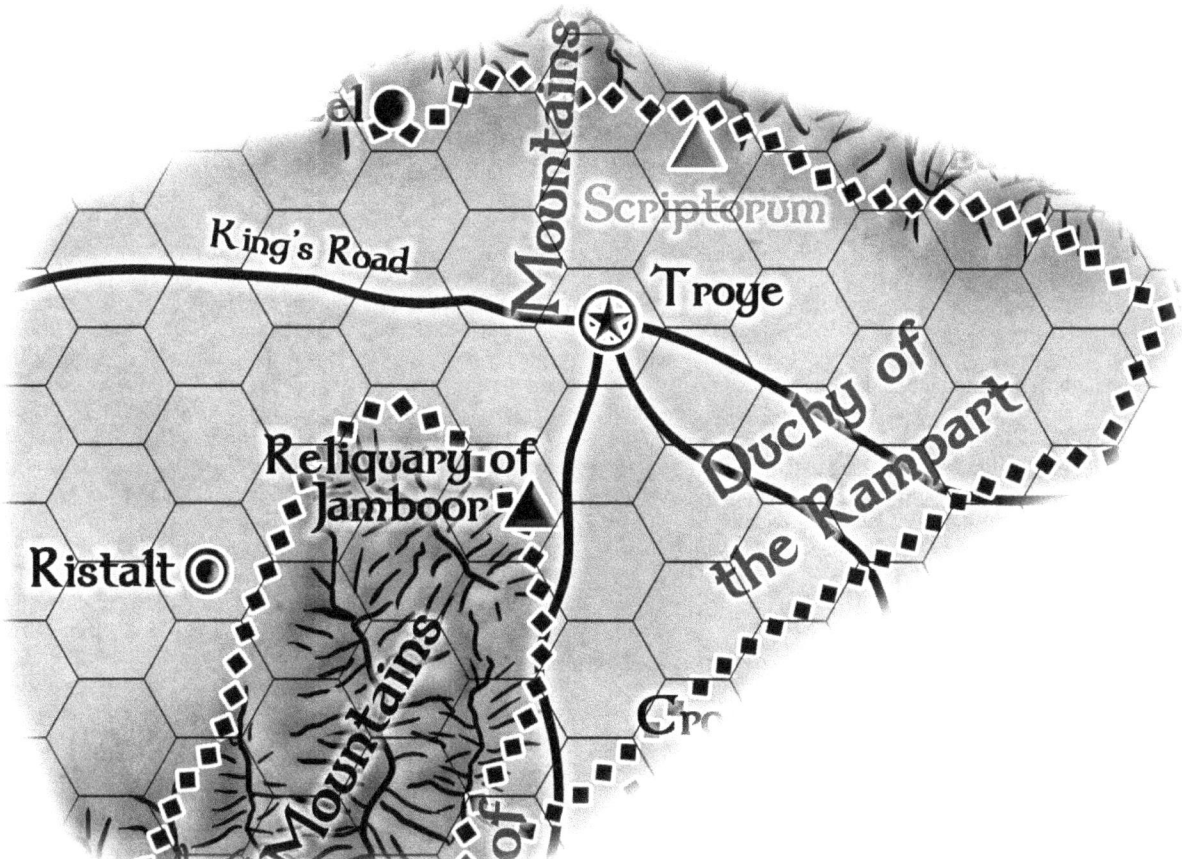

of hill dwarves can be found in the rugged foothills, and patrols are at least occasionally undertaken by actual troops, rather than a lone knight or a few volunteer yeomen with billhooks and crossbows.

Changing Times

A certain sense of ennui, decadence, and decay has been slowly creeping into the Duchy of the Rampart for many years. The tenets of chivalry are on the wane, roadside inns seem just a bit less well kept, and the pleasures of some of the nobility are a bit more jaded than in centuries past. Banquets sport increasingly elaborate dishes, carried to the table by poorly fed domestic servants. Heresy in on the rise, and small and secret covens of demon-worshippers have been uncovered in the rural countryside, their cults festering beneath the mask of a cheerful peasantry. The occasional savage murder goes unsolved, leaving people to look over their shoulders when walking alone. The touch of evil and decay is subtle, but its gentle pressure can be felt.

Cretian Mountains

See **Chapter 7: The March of Mountains, *Cretian Mountains*.**

Metzel

(METS-el)

A town of smelting, smugglers, and skullduggery

N small town
Government council
Population 2,876 (1,356 humans; 920 hill dwarves; 313

halflings; 152 half-elves; 77 gnomes; 58 high elves)
Notable NPCs
Mother Beatriz, smuggler and guide (N female human **Rgr7**)
Bishop Hoac of Metzel (LG male human **Clr8** of Thyr)
Yole Canter (N male human **Clr4** of Sefagreth)
Talakina Ramble (CN female gnome **Clr4** of Mocavallo)
Commander of the Watch Pietre Balmont (LN male human **Ftr8**)
Maximum Clerical Spell Level Good 5, Neutral 2, Evil —
Purchase Maximum/Month 4000gp

Appearance

This strong-walled town has several drum towers around the perimeter, and the buildings inside are so high and disorganized that the interior of the town looks like a pile of wood, plaster, stone, and shingle. The banner of the Duke of the Rampart flies over the gate, and a pall of stinking smoke from iron-smelting operations hangs over the entire town like a shroud.

Description

Metzel is located 10 miles from the base of the mountain pass into the Yolbiac Vale, and also benefits from several nearby coal and iron mines. Its main industry is smelting iron, and sturdy wagons containing pigs of iron and sacks of coal make their way down from Metzel to the forges of Troye, along with various products from the Yolbiac Vale.

Government and Law "Enforcement"

The town is chartered by the Palatine Duke, which allows it to be self-ruled, and is governed by a council of three: the Guildmaster of the Iron Smelters' Guild, the Trademaster of the Merchant Brotherhood, and the Commander of the Watch.

Metzel has a bad reputation for crime and questionable behavior. The guilds here are well organized, and have the feel of an extortion racket rather than a means of ensuring high-quality goods. The town imports the dream-apples of the Yolbiac Vale and even opium from Suilley. Miners consume these substances on long, drugged binges, and the town strips them clean of their money before they return to the mines. Even as far as Metzel is from Troye, "merchants" here are often buyers of stolen goods all the way from the capital. The most recognizable of these (unique pieces of jewelry and magic items, for the most part) are sometimes smuggled through the dangerous trails of the Yolbiac toward markets in Aachen Province, where they can be sold without attracting immediate attention.

Several Valesfolk come to Metzel each year to guide such smuggling operations through the Yolbiac, since the Vale has a tendency to lose people, either quietly murdered by villagers or eaten by the mysterious things that stalk the night. The smuggler-guide with the best reputation is Mother Beatriz, a corpulent peasant woman with a rude demeanor and a bad attitude. Despite these drawbacks, she has a good record of bringing jewelry-smugglers across the mountain passes and through the dark forests. Mother Beatriz is not a person to trifle with, having killed more than one thief who considered a short, fat, peasant woman in the town to be an easy mark. According to local tales, she once lifted a fully-grown horse to win a bet made in the Pickaxe Tavern.

Reliquary of Jamboor

(JAHM-boor)

Major religious center of the Hyperborean God of Magic, Knowledge, and Death

Appearance

The Reliquary is high in the foothills of the Rampart Mountains, but there is an excellent dirt road leading to the heights where the Reliquary is found. It is a massive fortress built into the side of a cliff, looking almost as if the sheer rock face had suffered an avalanche of carved stone walls and buildings.

Description

The fortress houses a large temple-complex to Jamboor, "He Who Hears the Secrets of the Dead," Hyperborean god of knowledge, magic, and death. The complex includes the main temple, a library, an academy of magecraft, and extensive burial catacombs in the depths of the cliff behind the cascade of buildings. It is the most significant temple to the god in the Borderland Provinces, and the High Reliquarian oversees the church's activities in the Rampart, Vourdon, Suilley, Keston, Toullen, Exeter, the Gaelon River Valley, Eastreach, and the Amrin Estuary.

The Reliquary is also the center of a considerable intelligence-gathering operation monitored by another high official who bears the title of "High Excriptor." The Reliquarian is considered senior to the Excriptor, but both are selected based on omens direct from the god: the Excriptor's role is more of an independent advisor to the Reliquarian than a subordinate.

In the world at large, the excriptors of Jamboor are a secretive and often dangerous group of individuals, including spies, thieves, agents, and groups of adventurers. These adventurer-groups are usually given the job of investigating rumors and mysteries brought to the High Excriptor's attention by other members of the organization. The ordinary priests of Jamboor, on the other hand, are generally clerics, mages, and adepts of various kinds engaged in the day-to-day business of operating temples and giving advice.

Many of these excriptors and ordinary priests are to be found at the Reliquary, whether training, visiting, or receiving instructions. However, the Reliquary is not just a larger version of a normal temple of Jamboor. Many of the church's higher religious operations are based here along with the merely administrative task of managing hundreds of priests and temples. Here, the red-robed members of the Order of Teeth inspect skeletons in the catacombs, using the *Book of Ossuic Marks* and the *Astrologicus Carnum* to identify where unknown patterns of magic and fate are taking place in the world. The ritually scarred members of the Order of Corollaries use the Seven Ciphers and the Forty Codes of Jamboor to interpret trends in bird migrations, manuscripts, and other records obtained for them by the Excriptors. The Order of Preservations moves through the libraries and catacombs, ensuring that both books and funereal remains are properly cared for and maintained. Most numerous of the Reliquary's staff are the Holy Scribes, expert copyists who copy manuscripts for distribution to the smaller libraries of Jamboor, re-copy worn books that can no longer be saved by the Order of Preservations, and prepare informatory letters for the priesthood throughout the Provinces, based on the bone-readings of the Order of Teeth, the reports from the Excriptors, and the omen-interpretations of the Order of Corollaries.

In the very deepest chambers of the catacombs, the dying bodies of the demon-listeners mutter words overheard in the councils of the Hells and underworlds, their eerie monologues recorded by the senior-most of the Holy Scribes as the murmuring bodies slowly rot away.

The High Reliquarian and the High Excriptor of Jamboor are both quite aware that the regions of the Borderland Provinces are precariously balanced between falling into chaos on the one hand, or, on the other hand, overcoming Foere's decline to build a new and stronger civilization. At the hub of a vast network of information, evaluating it without prejudice, these two servants of Jamboor have a much better perspective on current events than virtually anyone in the region. However, they are indifferent between the two outcomes. They will act to preserve knowledge if a dark age comes, but not to avert the dark age itself.

Many rulers employ priests of Jamboor as counselors, and these counselors are given a considerable amount of useful information by the Reliquary, but Jamboor ultimately has no preference between Law and Chaos, no preference between Good and Evil, no preference between Mercy and Tyranny. Whatever happens, the priests of Jamboor will preserve and interpret the record, continue to provide information to those who hire them, and continue to bury the dead in their great catacombs; they do not offer salvation. For an example of Jamboor's willingness to provide assistance to Evil as well as Good, see **Chapter 9: Suilley, Temple of Orchestration**).

King's Road

(From Foere in the west, through Troye, to Grollek's Grove)

An ancient stone road marking the northern border of Suilley, claimed as free passage by the Duchy of the Rampart

Appearance

The King's Road is one of the old Hyperborean high roads paved with stone and set with milestones. It passes through a variety of different terrains and countrysides. In general, travelers can find accommodation for the night in small coaching inns provided they do not press on too far in the evenings.

Description

The King's Road begins in Courghais and is more than a thousand years old. It crosses the Plains of Suilley to the mouth of the Gaelon River, where the city of Endhome now stands. Where the King's Road crosses the Gaelon a hundred miles west of Endhome, a wood-and-brick bridge spans the water, which is extremely wide as it reaches closer to the sea. A customs-house manned by officials from Endhome stands at each end of the bridge, and collects tolls from travelers and traders at whichever side they first enter. Southbound tolls are sent periodically to Courghais, and northbound tolls are the property of Endhome. From time to time when there is heavy rain upriver, the river around the bridge overflows, leaving the bridge standing 50ft from dry land. During such times, every local in possession of a boat comes to the bridge in hopes of getting work ferrying a caravan across the swollen river. The toll collectors can do nothing more than watch as their revenue travels cross-river on the improvised ferry system.

The King's Road runs east from Troye to leave the Duchy of the Rampart, skirts Suilley's northern border, and then passes through Grollek's Grove and the Gundlock Hills. See *The Lost Lands: Cults of the Sundered Kingdoms* for more information about these locales. The part of the King's Road from Grollek's Grove to Endhome is described in **Chapter 5: Gaelon River Valley,** *King's Road*.

Encounter Chance: Make one encounter check in the morning, one in the afternoon, and one at night.

Risk Level: All encounters on the King's Road are at the Medium-Risk level *except where it passes through the Gundlock Hills* (see **Chapter 5: Gaelon River Valley,** *King's Road*). Inside the one-hex radius around Troye and Mirquinoc, there is an additional automatic encounter check in the surrounding hex and the city's hex. All encounters in the city's hex and the surrounding hexes are at the Low-Risk level.

01–18	No Encounter
19–65	Mundane Encounter
66–00	Dangerous Encounter

Mundane Encounters: King's Road (Troye to Grollek)

1d100	Encounter
01–02	Baron and Retinue (Encounter #8)
03–04	Bear (Encounter #11)
05	Caravan (Bard's Gate, from Eastgate) (Encounter #15)
06–11	Caravan (Endhome, Rampart, Suilleyn) (Encounter #16)
12–13	Cleric (Encounter #19)
14	Druid (Encounter #31)
15–17	Dwarf (Encounter #32)
18–19	Elf (Encounter #34)
20–28	Farmer (Encounter #36)
29–34	Foot Patrol (Encounter #37)
35–45	Herder (Encounter #51)
46–49	Heretic (Encounter #52)
50	High Noble (Encounter #53)
51	Kenckoo Vagrant (Encounter #55)
52–59	Knight and Retinue (Encounter #56)
60–63	Knight Challenger (Encounter #57)
64	Military of Rampart (Encounter #64)
65–68	Minstrel (Encounter #65)
69–71	Mounted Patrol (Encounter #67)
72–74	Peasant (Encounter #74)
75	Pilgrim (Encounter #78)
76–77	Small Trader (dwarf or halfling) (Encounter #86)
78–81	Small Trader (human) (Encounter #85)
82–84	Stag (Encounter #87)
85–90	Wild Horse or Pony (Encounter #103)
91–00	Wolf (Encounter #106)

Dangerous Encounters: King's Road (Troye to Grollek)

1d100	Encounter
01–25	Bandit (Encounter #7)
26–30	Blood Hawk (Encounter #12)
31–40	Bugbear (Encounter #13)
41–43	Cockatrice (Encounter #21)
44–50	Dragon A (Encounter #27)
51–55	Giant, Hill (Encounter #41)
56–58	Hag (Encounter #48)
59–60	Harpy (Encounter #50)
61–70	Goblin, Roaming (Encounter #45)
71–75	Manticore (Encounter #63)
76–80	Ogre (Encounter #69)
81–85	Owlbear (Encounter #72)
86–90	Robber Knight (Encounter #80)
91–93	Wizard (Encounter #107)
94–00	Wyvern (Encounter #108)

Rampart Mountains

See **Chapter 7: The March of Mountains,** *Rampart Mountains*.

Rampart Road

A fairly safe high road through civilized regions, raised on a causeway anywhere from three to twenty feet in height depending on the surrounding terrain

Appearance

The Rampart is a raised causeway running from Troye to Manas and resembles a broad, short, wall of earth and rock with a road running along the top averaging 30ft in width. Small stone gatehouses at irregular intervals of 25 miles or so are used to block passage along the road, although the gates are kept open unless there is a serious threat that invaders may be on the road.

Description

The gatehouses range in size from a gate and gatehouse to small castles with archways over the road. The largest of these is Crossgate Hold (see **Chapter 9: Suilley,** *Crossgate Hold*). The small forts are not well-enough supplied or strongly enough garrisoned to hold out for long against a determined assault, but they would grievously delay a road-march upon Troye. Moreover, the raised causeway can be used as an actual wall in case of a pitched battle, a situation that has arisen more than once in the history of the Duchy.

The periphery of this road was the site of the Battle of Bullocks Bale, in which the Foerdewaith army was drawn onto treacherous ground by the Suilleyn forces, and decimated. The battle was perhaps the deciding factor in Suilley's successful rebellion from Foere.

Encounter Chance: Make one encounter check in the morning, one in the afternoon, and one at night.

Risk Level: All encounters on the Rampart Road are at the Medium-Risk level. Inside the one-hex radius around Troye and Manas, there is an additional automatic encounter check in the surrounding hex and the city's hex. All encounters in the city's hex and the surrounding hexes are at the Low-Risk level.

01–05	No Encounter
06–68	Mundane Encounter
69–00	Dangerous Encounter

Mundane Encounters: Rampart Road

1d100	Encounter
01–02	Annoyance (Encounter #3)
03–04	Baron and Retinue (Encounter #8)
05	Bear (Encounter #11)
06–16	Caravan (Provincial) (Encounter #16)
17–18	Cleric (Encounter #19)
19–20	Elf (Encounter #34)
21–36	Farmer (Encounter #36)
37–45	Foot Patrol (Encounter #37)
46–55	Herder (Encounter #51)
56–58	Heretic (Encounter #52)
59–60	High Noble (Encounter #53)
61	Kenckoo Vagrant (Encounter #55)
62–66	Knight and Retinue (Encounter #56)
67–69	Knight Challenger (Encounter #57)
70	Leper (Encounter #60)
71	Military (Encounter #64)
72–74	Minstrel (Encounter #65)
75–80	Mounted Patrol (Encounter #67)
81	Noble of the Realm (Encounter #68)
82–83	Peasant (Encounter #74)
84–85	Penitent (Encounter #76)
86–87	Pilgrim (Encounter #78)
88–89	Prisoner (Encounter #79)
90–91	Small trader (dwarf or halfling) (Encounter #86)
92–96	Small trader (human) (Encounter #85)
97–98	Stag (Encounter #87)
99–00	Wolf (Encounter #106)

Dangerous Encounters: Rampart Road

1d100	Encounter
01–04	Ankheg (Encounter #2)
05–19	Bandit (Encounter #7)
20–21	Bulette (Encounter #14)
22–25	Centaur (Encounter #17)
26	Cockatrice (Encounter #21)
27–30	Dragon A (Encounter #27)

1d100	Encounter
31–32	Eagle, Giant (Encounter #33)
33	Ettin (Encounter #35)
34	Giant, Hill (Encounter #41)
35–48	Gnoll (Encounter #43)
49–54	Goblin, Roaming (Encounter #45)
55–58	Lycanthrope (Encounter #61)
59–63	Manticore (Encounter #63)
64–67	Ogre (Encounter #69)
68	Ogre Mage (Oni) (Encounter #70)
69–73	Owlbear (Encounter #72)
74–77	Robber Knights (Encounter #80)
78–79	Roc (Encounter #81)
80–81	Stirge (Encounter #88)
82–84	Troll (Encounter #92)
85	Unicorn (Encounter #93)
86–88	Wasp, Giant (Encounter #99)
89–95	Weasel, Giant (Encounter #100)
96	Wizard (Encounter #107)
97–00	Wyvern (Encounter #108)

Ristalt
(riss-TAULT)

Known for adepts and an irrational dislike of elves

N small city
Government overlord
Population 6781 (3627 humans; 2895 hill dwarves; 251 halflings; 8 gnomes)
Notable NPCs
Mayor Sir Sorbat of Gulping Pond (N male human **courtier**)
Guard-Commander Jacques deNoir, (LN male human **Ftr7**)
Chief Constable Krail Mulekicker (LG female dwarf **Ftr6**)
Sun-Bishop Lorient Pas-Pairdu (LG male human **Clr9** of Mitra)
Honorary Bishop John Hieronymous (LG male human **Clr6** of Thyr)
High Priest Youlm Fetzredden (N male human **Clr7** of Sefagreth)
Maximum Clerical Spell Level Good 5, Neutral 4, Evil 2 (hidden, Orcus)
Purchase Maximum/Month 16,000gp

Appearance

The small city of Ristalt is walled with stone and surrounded by short, squat drum towers. The round citadel looks to be newer than the walls, and is quite beautifully constructed with protective symbols and realistic-looking vines sculpted as massive bas-relief decoration all around the wall. The city's flag, a circle of six gold coins on a purple background, flies proudly from the top of the stone-carved citadel, with its motto of "We Trust Our Strength" embroidered below the heraldic device.

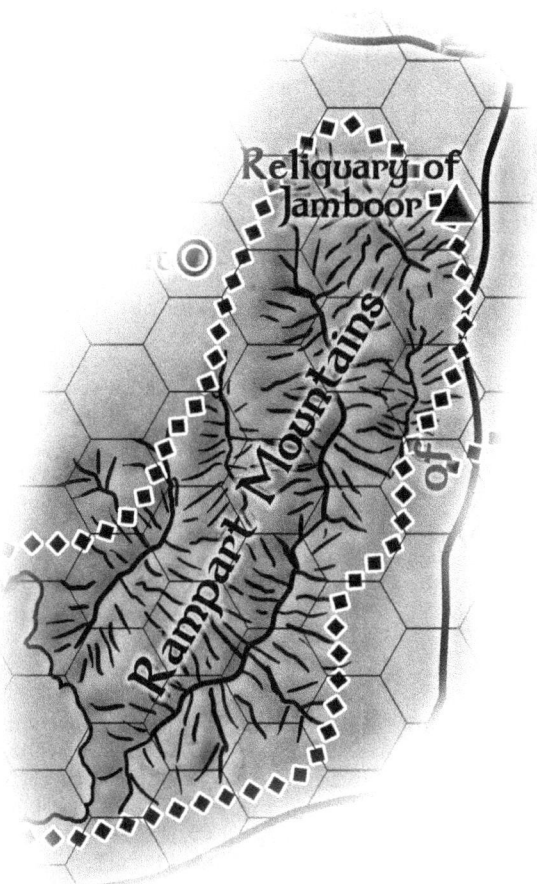

Description

Ristalt is the first destination of most products from the western face of the Rampart Mountains. The city turns some of the products into manufactured goods and sends the rest northward to the King's Road and thence to Troye. Dwarves are a common sight on the city streets, usually traders who live on the roads rather than actually dwelling in the mountains. For unknown reasons (possibly the dwarves), elves are greatly disliked here, and are considered to be thieves and leeches upon the prosperity of humankind.

The beautiful citadel here is mostly dwarven stonework quarried in the foothills of the Ramparts two centuries ago to replace and reinforce parts of the old citadel that had become structurally unsound. Numerous dwarves live and work in the city, and there is a large transient population of dwarven miners on holiday before they return to their mountain mines.

Ristalt is known for its adepts, although it does not provide the sort of intellectual resources required by actual mages. There are four "houses" of adepts: the House of Grey Adepts, the House of Moon Adepts, the House of Ten, and the House of Terce. None of them is specifically aligned with a particular deity; they just use different methods and rituals for their spellcasting. All four of the houses exert some influence in the communities beyond the city walls, and their rivalries always simmer in the background of the city's affairs.

Government and Law Enforcement

A mayor appointed by the Duke governs Ristalt. The mayor is responsible for keeping order and ensuring that the city pays its proper share of taxes. The current mayor is Sir Sorbat of Gulping Pond, a courtier more than a knight, but an adequate administrator nonetheless. Guard-Commander Jacques deNoir enforces the city's laws. DeNoir is assisted by his Chief Constable, a dwarf named Krail Mulekicker, and two constables (LN male or

human fighter 5). The city watch (who respond to criminal complaints and keep order) is 10 soldiers (N male or female guard) who can be reinforced by the citadel garrison if true violence breaks out.

Temples

Ristalt's patron god was once Thyr, but the city has shifted its official allegiance to Sefagreth, god of trade and commerce. The temple of Thyr has fallen upon hard times; not only has the deity been replaced as the city's patron, but the church of Mitra has arrived with splendor and fanfare.

Temple of Mitra (under construction)

The fashionable "new" sun god's worshippers are in the process of building a cathedral, although the work is likely to take a century to complete. The construction is, of course, a direct challenge to the church of Thyr. While their cathedral slowly rises stone by stone, the Mitrans have converted a large fieldstone warehouse beside the cathedral site into a good approximation of a prosperous temple. They have a big bronze bell to ring at dawn and nightfall and equipment to fit out large street processionals for the god's holy days. The high priest of Mitra is Sun-Bishop Lorient Pas-Pairdu, who trained in Courghais and is sleekly aristocratic.

Temple of Thyr

The temple of Thyr is large, stone, and almost empty. The chief priest of the god is an honorary bishop due to his role as a religious leader in a city, but he is only an ordinary priest. However, John Hieronymous is no ordinary priest. He is a renowned expert on the topic of heresy, and often consults on difficult cases with prosecutors and inquisitors of the church. Originally, Hieronymous was a professor in the University of Vermis in Aachen Province, but was reassigned as the Bishop of Ristalt when no one else of sufficient stature was available. Hieronymous is a mild-mannered, bespectacled man who still wears his professorial gown and hat. He is extremely sympathetic to the plight of heretics, and has diligently researched all he can about reclaiming lost souls without burning or executing the physical body. He has plenty of time to conduct his studies, for the temple followers have dwindled to only a couple hundred, and the services are poorly attended.

Temple of Sefagreth

The Temple of Sefagreth is booming. Rituals are crowded with worshippers, and the city is altogether enthusiastic about making money. The temple itself is fairly old and small, with decorative patterns dyed into the stone, but the priests are not yet considering any expansion. Essentially, they are waiting to see if they can buy part of the temple of Thyr at bargain-basement prices if John Hieronymous becomes too expensive for even the church of Thyr to support. Business is a waiting game, and the Temple of Thyr has a good location, definitely worth the investment.

Adventure

Ristalt is a good home base for adventuring into the western verges of the Rampart Mountains, although it is a bit too far away to serve as a true base camp. The small mining towns and villages closer to the mountains usually bring a steady stream of rumors about threats and opportunities there, some of which are credible, many of which are not. It is not in dispute, though, that the Rampart Mountains hide many opportunities for brave adventurers to find great riches if they dare.

Scriptorum of Discord

Festering stronghold of demonic madness

Appearance

This is a cluster of stone buildings in the high foothills of the mountains, an isolated hermitage to some deity, similar to many others.

Description

The Scriptorum of Discord is a small cluster of buildings in the foothills of the Cretian Mountains, an old monastery that has slowly turned into a holt of madness under the influence of the Demon Prince Mathrigaunt (see also **Chapter 6: Keston Province, *Abbot's Mercy*,** and **Chapter 9: Kingdom of Suilley, *Temple of Orchestration***). Here, Mathrigaunt's cultists are somber and decorous. Their madness is not immediately apparent, and a visitor could easily take the monastery to be a normal religious hermitage, but it is something quite different. Many of the "monks" are mountainfolk of the Cretians and converts from the Yolbiac Vale, strange people to begin with. Some are natives of the Duchy, and the remaining few are outsiders from other places in the Borderland Provinces who found their way here by the guidance of their own madness after making ill-advised pacts with Mathrigaunt.

The central building in the complex is the Scriptorum, where the insane scribes write down their dreams and ideas, chained to their desks until they die, sustaining themselves by eating the large white grubs that crawl everywhere in the room. In the middle of the chamber, a state-of-the-art printing press stamps out copies of the best visions produced by the scribes, preparing them to be left as pamphlets and handbills in Troye and other cities where the Scriptorum's riders might visit.

The monastery's outbuildings are the normal sort of places one might find in a monastic retreat: a blacksmith, some farms, and so on. Additionally, there are several empty rooms in "visitor" dormitories. Outsiders who are obsessed with traveling to the monastery will feel comfortable here, and are very likely to want to stay in the dormitories for a while, keeping close to the scriptorium. For those who remain over time, madness begins to set in, and the visitor eventually is admitted to the Scriptorum, chained to a desk, and becomes one of the mad scribes producing pamphlets for the outside world.

The supervisor of the Scriptorum is Praxis Gaunt (CE male human **high priest** of Mathrigaunt). A mostly burned scrap of parchment in his fireplace clearly contains orders and instructions from a superior named Malachord, but there is nothing on the remaining, unburned page to indicate Malachord's whereabouts. (See **Chapter 9: Suilley, *Temple of Orchestration***).

See the City of Troye for additional information about the effect of the pamphlets themselves.

Praxis Gaunt, High Priest of Mathrigaunt: AC 15; HP 117 (18d8+36); Spd 30ft; **Melee** dagger (+5, 1d4+2 piercing); **SA** spells (9th, Wis +7, DC 15); **Str** +0, **Dex** +2, **Con** +2, **Int** +2, **Wis** +4, **Cha** +2; **Skills** Deception +5, Medicine +7, Religion +5; **AL** CE; **CR** 6; **XP** 2300.

> **Spells (slots):** 0 (at will)—*light, mending, sacred flame, thaumaturgy;* 1st (4)—*bless, cure wounds, dissonant whispers, hideous laughter;* 2nd (3)—*blindness/deafness, crown of madness;* 3rd (3)—*fear, mass healing word, protection from energy;* 4th (3)—*confusion, freedom of movement;* 5th (1)—*geas, modify memory.*
>
> **Equipment:** chain shirt, dagger, belt pouch with 12gp and 3 rubies (250gp each)

Troye

(TROY)

A vast, sprawling metropolis, capital of the Duchy of the Rampart

N metropolis
Government overlord
Population 44,600 (36,760 humans; 4023 hill dwarves; 1910 halflings; 860 half-elves; 437 gnomes; 322 high elves; 160 half-orcs; 128 other)

Notable NPCs
> The Most Noble Claud VII, Duke of the Rampart, Battle-Duke of Foere, Sword of the Foerdewaith (LN male human **Ftr16**)
> High Counselor Traont, Baron Thulde, former Lord-Steward of the Rampart (LN male human **Ftr10**)
> Lady Yvonne Talaine, Lord-Mayor of Troye (N female human **Ftr9**)
> Cardinal Jordan Steadfast (LN male human **Clr17** of Vanitthu)
> Logan Wheat, Guildmaster of Troye Thieves Guild (N male human **Rog12**)
> Sir Terris Mallory, Chapter Commander of the Order of the Swan (LG male human **Ftr10**)
> Talisander, Master of the Guild of Magisters (N male human **Wiz12**)
> Sartir Yen Dar, Reliquarian of Jamboor (N male human **Clr9** of Jamboor)
> Olfred Venact, demon-worshipper (CE male human **Clr7** of Fraz-Urb'luu)

Maximum Clerical Spell Level Good —, Neutral 7, Evil 5 (known and tolerated)
Purchase Maximum/Month 64,000gp

Appearance

The high granite walls of Troye are resplendent with banners, and lines of colorful shields are affixed to the battlements, representing the various noble houses of the Duchy of the Rampart. Great towers stand at intervals above the walls, some crowned with trebuchets and ballistae, others with high, pointed roofs. Over it all rises the vast citadel of the Duke, greatest and most formidable structure in a city designed for war.

Description

Troye is the capital city of the Duchy of the Rampart, founded in the Hyperborean era. The city is a major destination city for caravans, whose merchants sell their cargos here to buy goods from faraway places for the return journey. Merchants planning on making the whole trek from the Kingdom of Foere into the provinces and back (most likely to Manas, but sometimes to Endhome) stop here to enjoy one last taste of city comforts before heading off into the wild.

This great metropolis at the far reaches of the Kingdoms of Foere offers a vast array of interesting sights, sounds, cultures, clothes, music, merriment, purchases, people, and pickpockets. It is wise to keep one hand on the belt pouch when walking through crowds in Troye. Tourist attractions include the University of Subtleties, the Great Stone Rabbit in Lapin Square, the smoke-snorting iron bull atop the temple of Mithras, the great Marchantal market, the dried remains of the six tall thieves (at the Citadel's Gate), and the Court of Thespians.

In any of the city's hundred small markets, mostly temporary affairs blocking crossroads, one can find herb-crusted breads, baskets of the dark purple, dream-inducing apples grown in the Yolbiac Vale, puppets, trained cats, dwarf-crafted trinkets, colorful surcoats, stolen items available for quick sale, clay idols painted with symbols, and all manner of merchandise culled from traveling merchants of the world.

Shells are a particularly popular item of jewelry, a curiosity in a city so far from the sea, and are often seen adorning wealthy merchants and nobles when they ride through the city's narrow streets. Pearls are also much more highly prized than mined gemstones.

Government

Troye is governed by a Lord-Mayor, whose position is equivalent in status to a count (in other words, higher than a baron but not ranked as high as a duke). The Duke Palatine appoints the Lord-Mayor, but a council of burgesses elected by the city's landowners handle most of the job of managing the city.

In the past, Lords-Mayor who continued to make unpopular decrees were stopped in their tracks by the citizens who shut down the gates, blocked streets, and started arresting people loyal to the unpopular mayor. So even though the city is not technically self-governed, there is a practical limit to what the Duke can impose upon his capital city without its consent.

Factions

Troye is the headquarters or an important area of operations for a number of different organizations. Principal among these, of course, is the city's government and city guard. Others include the Council of Guilds, which regulates the city's commerce; the Most Honorable Guild of Thieves, which regulates the city's crime and underworld; the Church of Vanitthu and the Temple of Jamboor, both important players in the city's politics and spiritual life; the city chapterhouse of the Order of the Swan (see **Chapter 13: Yolbiac Vale,** *Knights of the Swan*); and the Guild of Magisters.

Adventure

Troye is a large city containing many secrets, and many dangers for the unwary. Decadence is setting in, which is giving rise to a much higher level of murders and lesser crimes than in centuries — and even decades — past. The worst of the symptoms is the growth of demon-cults hiding within the city's walls that are conducting secret sacrifices and engaging in vicious plots to undermine the forces of law and mercy. Heresies are whispered in the shadows, and criminal gangs roam the streets at night, disappearing into the woodwork if challenged by the guards.

If a party of adventurers asks around about strange events, especially among city officials, they may hear about the bizarre posters, pamphlets, and handbills that have been finding their way into the city over the last couple of years. The texts of these writings are nonsensical and disturbing: visions of the underworld, pointless ramblings, and deranged advice. The city's officials have grave concerns about what seems at first glance to be nothing more than one more quirk of city life. They have observed that the printed materials have a certain fascination to them, and many citizens seem to be collecting them, even quoting them from time to time in ordinary discussions. Each time a new batch of pamphlets arrives, the city suffers a spate of unusual and pointless crimes, most of them completely petty. Signs are removed, turned upside down, or switched with those of other establishments. Horses are stolen from one stable, only to appear in another across the city. Bakeries report a tripling or quadrupling of the ordinary rate of pilfering. There seems to be no direct connection to the pamphlets, but the correlation is precise.

The source of the pamphlets is the Scriptorum of Discord (see the entry for the Scriptorum for more detail).

Reading the pamphlets in any detail can have a deleterious or even dangerous effect on the reader. Anyone who (a) has no settled home, or (b) is not loved by a person with a settled home might be affected; others are immune. Such a person must make a DC 10 Wis saving throw or be compelled to pick up and read more pamphlets when they appear. For each pamphlet read (and they show up at intervals of a week or so), a person who has failed the saving throw has a 1% chance to become mildly interested in traveling to the Scriptorum of Discord, where the victim eventually becomes caught in the web of madness there.

Chapter Nine: Kingdom of Suilley

Kingdom of Suilley

(SOO-lee)

Overview

Some three hundred years ago, the Kingdom of Suilley declared itself an independent kingdom and seceded from the Kingdoms of Foere. Since this time, other large regions of the Borderland Provinces have declared themselves vassals of the Suilleyn king, which has increased the kingdom's power by an order of magnitude but strained its resources to the utmost. It would be possible for Suilley to collapse under this pressure, in which case vast areas of the Borderland Provinces could be thrown into chaos.

General Information

Alignment: CG
Capital: Manas (28,420)
Notable Settlements: Alembretia (13,240), Cluin (3,213), Pfefferain (4,712), Stronghold Hjerrin (3,672)
Ruler: His Most Regal Majesty King Ulrich IX of Suilley, Sovereign of Keston and Toullen, Protector-Regent of the Lorremach.
Government: monarchy
Population: 2,449,600 (2,152,000 Foerdewaith; 202,500 halflings; 47,050 half-elves; 36,700 high elf; 7250 hill dwarves; 3280 gnomes; 820 other)
Humanoid: halfling (many), half-elf (some), high elf (some), hill dwarf (few), gnome (few)
Monstrous: hobgoblin, bugbear, hill giant, troll, manticore, roc, dragon (mainly Lorremach Highhills)
Languages: Common, Gasquen
Religion: Ceres, Sefagreth, Freya, Vanitthu, Mitra, Thyr, Muir, Archeillus, Mick O'Delving, Belon the Wise, Solanus, Darach-Albith, Yenomesh, Bowbe, The Father, Mathrigaunt the Mad
Resources: foodstuffs, livestock (horses), trade hub, grain, flax, spirits (ale), glass, manufactured goods, quarry stone, banking, copper, opium, gems (grade 2)
Technology Level: Medieval (cities), High Middle Ages (countryside)

Borders and Lands

The northern border of Suilley is the King's Road until it comes within 150 miles of the city of Troye; these 150 miles are within the Duchy of the Rampart. The western border with the County of Vourdon is roughly 100 miles east of Olaric, and although parts of it are disputed, it is considered to run due north and south along this line. The southern border is a line that runs northwest from the very southernmost extent of the Lorremach Highhills, with the Flatlander Road approximately 50 miles inside the border, then turning southwest 200 miles south of Manas to join a triple border-point with Keston and Vourdon 150 or so miles south of the city of Olaric.

History and People

Theft of a Kingdom

In the year 3222 I.R., the Lord-Governor of Suilley, Ghienvais Pas, had himself crowned as His Independent Majesty Ghienvais I, King of Suilley, Marquis of the Lorremach Highhills, and Warden of the Plains of Suilley. This event is still often called the "Theft of the Kingdom" in Foere, and Suilley the "Stolen Kingdom," although three centuries have turned the Suilleyn secession into an accomplished fact of history, legitimated by the passage of time. The rebellion's background can be explained in relatively simple terms, although the details are by definition more complex as it occurred within the larger tapestry of rebellion and secession that afflicted the Kingdoms of Foere during the Wars of Succession.

Essentially, the majority of the Suilleyn nobles had come to see themselves as a separate branch of the Foerdewaith, entitled to equal status with the nobility of the heartland kingdoms in terms of taxes and privileges. It is likely that many of them did not anticipate war at all, merely a long and ultimately successful wrangling of diplomats in the Court at Courghais. Thus, the noble class of Suilley united around the Lord-Governor, marshalled their legal arguments, sent a letter to the royal court explaining their grievances, and crowned a monarch who offered fealty to the Overking.

Despite the peacefulness of the intentions, a small civil war immediately broke out among barons in eastern Suilley, with loyalists and monarchists engaging each other in the plains near the Gundlock Hills, no doubt influenced by the struggles for independence occurring in Burgundia to the east.

Hopes of a peaceful secession were dashed, hwoever, when the Overking, watching his empire slip through his fingers as first Ramthion Island, then Pontos Island, and then Burgundia entered into rebellion, declared the King of Suilley to be a usurper and traitor to the crown, and his nobles to be stripped of their lands in favor of new, more faithful, vassals. By doing so, the Court at Courghais transformed a peaceful and ultimately still loyalist modification of feudal rights into a battlefield

war, with the Suilleyn nobles suddenly fighting for their lives rather than merely for lower taxes and greater social status.

With its back to the wall, Suilley stripped its fields of able-bodied peasants to form battalions of levied troops, mustered every knight who could straddle a horse and hold a lance, and prepared for an all-out war to the death. Blacksmiths' hammers rang through the night, couriers rode lathered horses from one manorial estate to the next, and even many of the originally loyalist barons came to realize that they would be executed alongside the rebels if Foere returned in victory to its former province. Surrender was no longer an option, and a soft resolve hardened into iron.

King Ghienvais realized the futility of trying to fight ardently loyalist barons in the east at the same time as a Foerdewaith army to the northwest, attempted to entice the loyalist nobles in the Gundlock Hills region and the surrounding plains with peace offerings of lucrative trade and influence, but to no avail. Many monarchist nobles of those areas soon fled to the Suilleyn heartlands as the jubilant loyalists held trials and burned accused traitors at the stake causing an eruption of civil war in eastern Suilley even as the western portion of the nascent kingdom prepared for an invasion by Foere.

Assembling the forces of Suilley would be greatly slowed by the muddy season, for the barons and supply wagons for the inevitable siege of Manas would have to fight their way down mud-soaked cart trails and sodden country lanes. But the new king also anticipated that the mustering of additional forces in the Duchy of the Rampart would take time, even though the higher lands of the Rampart did not face the obstacle of mired supply lines, since so many Foerdewaith troops had already been deployed to Matagost to put down the Burgundian rebellion and defend against Oceander invasion in the east. The new kingdom did what it could to protect the capital city in the meantime. Suilleyn troops occupied the nearby gatehouses along the Rampart without opposition from the garrisons, whose commanders elected to withdraw rather than die in a hopeless last stand, and the great road between the capital cities of Manas and Troye was turned into a fortification.

Battle of Bullocks Bale

Authorized for battle by the Overking, the aggressive general in charge of the army of the Rampart, a Lord-General Baron Cavodeill, moved into action immediately, not waiting for the arrival of the Battle-Duke from his deployment in Matagost, and not waiting for a full mustering of the barons. While the Suilleyn nobles were still organizing themselves in their rural manors and distant castles, or on the mud-wallowed roads to Manas, the Foerdewaith army marched down the Rampart against a kingdom that had barely started its preparations.

With siege engines in its train, and heavy infantry able to fight on the causeway far better than levied peasants or mounted knights, the Foerdewaith army crushed opposition at gatehouse after gatehouse along the Rampart, drawing nearer to the city of Manas day by day. Had the Lord-General of the Rampartine forces continued on this relentless march, the city of Manas might possibly have been taken at the outset of the war, although such an outcome would have been unlikely against a fortified city waiting for significant reinforcements to arrive from the countryside. In any case, the assault took a radically different turn when Rampartine scouts stumbled upon the main force of the small Suilleyn army circling around behind the Foerdewaith advance along the causeway. Correctly judging that the objective of the Suilleyn general was to retake the Rampart behind him, effectively cutting off his forces from reinforcement on the fortified road and allowing a hammer-and-anvil assault from behind when he reached the walls of Manas, the duchy's general moved his cavalry and main forces off the Rampart to prevent encirclement.

The Rampartine army caught and engaged the smaller Suilleyn force not more than a mile from the fortified causeway. In the open pastureland, the Foerdewaith knights and soldiery rapidly broke the smaller, hastily assembled array of Suilley's local knights and levies, forcing them back in disorder to a copse of trees near the pastures of Bullocks Bale. Unfamiliar with the muddy season in Suilley, the Lord-General of the Rampartine army immediately followed up his victory, pursuing the retreating Suilleyn into the muddy fields below the higher ground around the causeway. Suddenly bogged down in mud, and threatened with holes dug by the Suilleyn troops to break the legs of horses, the knights and cavalry of the Rampartine army died in droves from the missiles of archers and slingers sheltering in the copse of trees. The knights of Suilley circled entirely around the battle in the pasture to shatter the still-disorganized advance of the Foerdewaith infantry behind their mired cavalry, keeping to the higher ground near the causeway where their own charge could be delivered over dry, even ground. The army of the Rampart was utterly destroyed, and Suilley's "theft" into an independent monarchy free of the Overking's authority became an accomplished fact, though it ultimately withdrew from the civil war in its own eastern region and foreswore claim to any of the lands near the Gundlock Hills.

Growth of a Feudal Empire

As the power of Foere continued to decline in the provinces and the newly minted District of Sunderland beyond, the emerging Kingdom of Suilley found its power increasing by default. Although Suilley was forced to fight several more battles with the Foerdewaith after the first one, the cost of these conflicts was partially subsidized by other opponents of Foere, namely Endhome, Oceanus, and Burgundia. Captured territories between Manas and the duchy were granted to many of the monarchist nobility of eastern Suilley who had been forced to flee the loyalists, and this area continues to harbor considerable ill will toward the Kingdoms of Foere, remembering burning villages and executions by loyalist bands of marauders. This ill will is not directed at the Duchy of the Rampart, for the anti-monarchists were Suilleyn themselves, but the monarchists are quite hostile to any Foerdewaith from across the March of Mountains.

Two major provinces of Foere, the County of Toullen and Province of Keston, ultimately renounced their fealty to the Overking of Foere in the year 3336, and pledged themselves to the King of Suilley as vassal states. More detail about this dual secession is provided in the description of County of Toullen.

Treaty of Grollek's Grove

An example of Suilley's emerging power and authority is its participation in the establishment of a trading post at Grolle's Grove in 3423, in concert with the city of Endhome, the formerly hostile Duchy of the Rampart, and what representatives could be found to stand for the District of Sunderland (many of whom were former loyalists that battled against Suilley's secession).

Trade and Commerce

A great deal of caravan traffic passes through Suilley on the north-south Trader's Way from Exeter Province, the east-west route along the South County Road from Olaric toward Endhome, or on the Rampart Road to and from Foere itself. The Trader's Way route passes through wild and dangerous places, and the Flatlander Road diverts its traffic from a 300-mile stretch of the Lorremach Highhills, but the South County Road and the Manas-to-Troye Rampart Road are both well patrolled and served by towns and fortified inns along the way.

Although Suilley endures a season of rain and mud each year, farms are productive and pillaging is infrequent, especially in the regions up to 25 miles from one of the roads (with the exception of the Trader's Way). The uninhabited parts of the country's rural interior, and some wild regions such as the Lorremach Highhills, cannot be described as safe, but are not unduly dangerous for those who travel in large, well-armed groups.

Suilley has recently been making great efforts to entice northbound merchant caravans coming from Exeter Province to take the Flatlander Road through Manas rather than the Trader's Way. Given the dangers of the Trader's Way, even the small incentives offered are enough to persuade many merchants to take the Manas route. The result has been to make the Trader's Way between Grollek's Grove and Pfefferain even more sparsely traveled and more dangerous, but Suilley's main concern is the kingdom's coffers, not the safety of a road far at the realm's eastern border nor the lawless lands of the Sundered Kingdoms beyond that might suffer from this reduction in trade.

Loyalties and Diplomacy

Because the Overking has never officially recognized the independent status of Suilley, and the Court at Courghais continues to address the King of Suilley as "Our Subject," relations between Suilley and the Kingdoms of Foere are uneasy, but both realms are aware that the Kingdoms of Foere no longer have the wherewithal to successfully invade Suilley. Relations between the Kingdom of Suilley and the Duke of the Rampart are actually quite friendly, for the trade route between Manas and Troye is an important source of wealth for the duchy and the kingdom. Whatever the Overking and his court might think of Suilley, the Duchy of the Rampart would be exceedingly unhappy to find its trade relationship with Suilley impeded by war.

Many of the barons of northern Suilley have their eye on the periphery of the Gaelon River Valley, and a few freehold lords on the northern side of the King's Road have pledged fealty to the King of Suilley. But at this point, the incursion into the Gaelon River region remains small and scattered. The Kingdom of Suilley is aware that while the Duchy of the Rampart cares little about the Gaelon River Valley, it (along with Foere, beyond the March of Mountains) cares a great deal about who controls the King's Road. The one event that could lead to renewed hostility between the two realms would be if the Suilleyn border began to creep too far beyond the King's Road itself, putting the road firmly into Suilley's control.

Suilley's good relations with the County of Vourdon on its western border are a high priority for the monarchy. If there is ever another war with the Kingdoms of Foere, Vourdon would threaten Suilley's flank in a conflict with the Duchy of the Rampart, and although Suilley's army is strong, it is not strong enough to fight two separate conflicts on different fronts (as evidenced by its failure to curb the civil war in its own eastern territories at the time of its own inception). Keston Province is a vassal of the Suilleyn King, but is too weak to tie down the forces of Vourdon in case of a war. To this end, Suilley maintains an ambassador in the city of Olaric, whose task is to ensure that potential conflicts between the realms are quickly resolved.

Government

Suilley is a monarchy ruled by a hereditary king or queen, deriving descent from Ghienvais I, the first king to bear the crown in rebellion against Foere. The realm has eight ducal houses, which makes the king relatively strong compared with many of his peer monarchs, since it is rare for the dukes to agree long enough with each other to unite against the king in any way.

Only one queen has ruled Suilley in its history, for the succession traditionally goes to the oldest male offspring, and to the oldest female only if there is no male heir. The reign of Queen Dacinthe I was initially plagued by her uncle, Prince Huelbert, who claimed that no female could inherit the throne at all, making him the rightful king. Eventually one of Dacinthe's loyal dukes captured Huelbert in battle and sent his head to the queen in a large glass bottle. Dacinthe ordered the bottled head displayed as the centerpiece at her next royal banquet to the distress of many of the guests, especially those suspected of complicity with the would-be usurper. All ambiguities in the law were thus completely clarified.

The heraldry of the house of King Ulrich, and thus the device of Suilley, is a golden crown over two red lions rampant, back to back, on a green field.

Wilderness and Adventure

As with most of the Borderland Provinces, Suilley is far more settled, law-abiding, and prosperous in the regions surrounding its patrolled roads than in the rural areas beyond. Much of the interior resembles a thick scattering of villages and castles merging into an equally thick scattering of wilderness. Thus, there are always opportunities to find adventure, even in the country's heartlands. The Lorremach Highhills and the Wilderland Hills are both large wilderness regions with virtually no protection whatsoever, but they would be very dangerous for lower-level adventurers.

Changing Times

The largest problem facing Suilley at this time is actually the result of its own past successes in war and diplomacy. It has inherited the realms of Keston and Toullen, with all their problems, which means the King of Suilley now possesses, largely by default, a wide-ranging and disorganized feudal empire. The Suilleyn monarchy is being entreated from all sides to shoulder the burden of solving vast regional problems caused by the retreat of Foere. With a relatively independent nobility, the King of Suilley would have enough work just organizing his own domain. He is instead being forced into a constant juggling act trying to balance wilderness and depopulation in Keston; problems in the Lorremach Highhills; tax-rebels and petty wars among the barons of his own country; occasional tension with Foere over the King's Road or the Rampart border; and the task of turning his patchwork confederacy of feudal states into a functioning whole with unified laws and common defense. The core of Suilley, a hundred or so miles around Manas, is a very stable domain, but one cannot rule a vast empire from such a small base, and this is what the King of Suilley faces. The resources simply do not exist to protect, subdue, rebuild, and organize all the things in Suilley's far-flung domains that need to be protected, subdued, rebuilt, and organized. Very few people realize how tenuous King Ulrich's situation actually has become. The treasury is emptied as soon as it is filled, his personal wealth is tied up in maintaining the army, and his soldiery is stretched thin as a wire. Suilley is a growing empire that could falter and fail simply from a run of bad luck, or any significant catastrophe.

Aen Vani

(een VAH-nee)

CE large town
Government overlord
Population 3281 (2328 humans; 503 ogre-kin; 212 half-ogres; 91 half-orcs; 67 ogres; 48 orcs; 23 orogs; 9 ogrillons)
Notable NPCs
Saldevic II, King of the Vanigoths (CE male half-ogre **Ftr12**)
Theomar Fatherson (CE male human **Clr12** of The Father)
Maximum Clerical Spell Level Good —, Neutral —, Evil 6
Purchase Maximum/Month 8000gp

Deep in the Wilderland Hills, the Vanigothic town of Aen Vani falls into the territory of Suilley only upon maps drawn in the civilized realms. In reality, the Vanigoths have their own king and do not acknowledge any other rulership. Indeed, they barely acknowledge their own king, being organized into independent tribes ruled by a Rohalac. The Rohalac of a Vanigoth tribe is essentially a hereditary chieftain, although the tribe can vote to remove a Rohalac in favor of another Vanigoth of any Rohalac bloodline, including one from another tribe.

Aen Vani is the seat of the Vanigoth King, currently a seasoned warrior by the title of Saldevic II. At the age of 20, Saldevic led several Vanigoth tribes into Keston Province during the Wilderlands Clan Wars and managed to avoid the slaughter at Broch Tarna. His forces in Aen Vani are small in number, perhaps 200 raiders, but most of these are trained and experienced fighters rather than mere tribal warriors. Moreover, the Highland Vanigoths appear to have a strong strain of ogrish blood, for some of the Highlanders are utterly massive by human standards. Saldevic himself is one of these apparent half-breeds, standing 7ft tall and roped in muscle. The Vanigoths of the Lowlands, by contrast, do not appear to have the strain of ogre blood that runs in the Vanigoths of the Highlands.

Aen Vani itself is a trading town and meeting point for different Vanigoth tribes. The outskirts are "decorated" with heads on pikes, and outriders circle at a distance, watching for intruders. The town is built within the ruins of an old stone fort. The old walls rise to only half their original height, and only circle half the town, but they are supplemented with walls of sharpened logs and some wooden watchtowers. Given the fighting strength of the Vanigoths living here, most monsters give the town a very wide berth in any case.

Most of the Vanigoths worship an ancient god referred to only as "The Father," a violent, primitive deity whose worship dates back to the Neolithic era of Akados at least. He has a large number of shamans scattered throughout the Vanigoth tribes, and his high priest in Aen Vani is a true cleric of high level.

Outsiders are curiosities here, and quite well tolerated as long as the Vanigoths do not consider them to be spies. Those who appear to be warriors may be challenged to contests of strength or combat prowess, but these are seldom lethal.

Alembretia

(ah-lem-BREE-shah)

A highly fashionable city known for manufacturing exquisite glassware

LE large city
Government council
Population 13,240 (10,575 humans; 1085 hill dwarves; 740 gnomes; 460 half-elves; 380 halflings)
Notable NPCs
  Riobert Nev, Grand Master of the Glassmakers' Guild of Alembretia (LE male human **commoner**)
  Lumiere Laval, Master Lensmaker (LG male human **Wiz5**)
  High Priest Vhembardo Luc (N male human **Clr9** of Sefagreth)
  High Priestess Olivienne Ralan (LG female human **Clr8** of Ceres)
Maximum Clerical Spell Level Good 5, Neutral 5, Evil 5 (known, Mathrigaunt)
Purchase Maximum/Month 32,000gp

Appearance

This obviously rich city has conical towers with blue-painted roofs all along the outer stone wall. The Flatlander Road passes directly through the city's two gates, which are brightly painted with the symbol of a purple wineglass over red flames. The guards standing beside the gates wear brightly polished armor with high feather plumes on their helmets. The city's symbol, visible on numerous banners flying from the battlements, is a purple wineglass over red flames, on a gold field.

Description

Alembretia is a large city on the Flatlander Road some 10 miles from the base of the Lorremach Highhills, and perhaps 50 miles from

---

The Father, Primeval God of Violence, Strength, and Warfare (Lost)

Alignment: NE
Domain: Tempest, War
Symbol: A triangle
Garb: Skins of hunted animals or enemies
Favored Weapon: Stone greataxe
Form of Worship and Holidays: Blood sacrifices at solstices and equinoxes, before and after battles, and upon the birth or death of a chieftain
Typical Worshippers: Neolithic tribes (mostly extinct), Vanigoths of the Wilderland Hills, some Wildmen of the Mistwood, possibly others

The Father has existed as long as there has been life on the world now known as Lloegyr and has often been associated as an embodiment of the world itself or its primordial oceans. He has been known by many names through the ages, The Father simply being the most universal and enduring. To the ancient Phoromyceans who knew of him only through their own ancient legends, he was known as the Demiurge. To the Hyperboreans, who came along an age later, he was known as Boros and represented the planet upon which they lived as well as their home continent to the north. To the ancient peoples of the North before the coming of the Northlanders he was Buri, the grandfather of Wotan. To the Khemitite priest-kings of old he was Nun. The even more ancient Ashurians called him Engur or Abzu. The most ancient writings of Far Jaati refer to him as Dyaus Pitra, and to the Ancient Folk of Akados he was Lir.

Worship of The Father predated the formation of pantheons and culturally defined religions; in fact, the existence of The Father seems to predate the concept of worship or even the existence of humanoid life on Lloegyr. To these early cultures, The Father was known as patron of tribal warfare, competition for scarce resources, survival, dominance, and rulership by might, and he was seen as a primal creator of the world, life, and the gods themselves. The Father was typically not so much revered as feared, for the savage world was harsh and unforgiving with an equally harsh and unforgiving god for the strong to cling to and the weak to perish before. Ritual bloodshed marked the holy times and sites of The Father, and human sacrifice became a standard practice under his stern gaze.

Despite this near hegemony of devotion in the earliest ages of the world, worship for and even memory of The Father eventually died out, supplanted by belief in younger, gentler gods, many of whom are believed to be his children or even their offspring. Only in the most ancient records and esoteric circles is mention of The Father even found and usually then only disjointed and incomplete references. To those few with the depth of scholarship or requisite age (a few of the oldest elves and assorted dragons and undead beings) to even know of The Father, it is believed his eventual decline and erasure from the consciousness of humanity was in large part to the heroic and selfless actions of an equally primeval creator deity known only as The Goddess, mother of many of the oldest gods and both mate and mortal enemy of The Father. Thanks to her efforts, knowledge of The Father was forgotten from the world to the point that he is now considered a "lost" deity. None in this day and age revere The Father, nor is there liturgy available to revive his worship, except among a very few small and scattered tribal societies that exist as holdovers from those most ancient of times. Even in these cultures worship of The Father is corrupted and inexact due to lack of any written record, and such peoples themselves are in decline is well so that it is only a matter of time until The Father ceases to exist as a deific entity upon Lloegyr.

the crossroad where the Flatlander Road meets the Trader's Way in the highlands. It is justly famous for the elaborate clothes worn by the city's wealthier classes: extravagant plumes, tall fur hats, cloaks 10ft in length, bejeweled doublets of velvet and damask silk; all of these are an everyday sight in the more fashionable streets of Alembretia. Anyone dressed in ordinary garb is understandably treated as a rank commoner, and on no account taken seriously.

The city makes considerable revenue from travelers on the Flatlander Road, but its main product is blown glass. The sandy hills of the Lorremach include several deposits of colored sand that can be incorporated into the glassmaking process. Alembretia's glass-makers and glassblowers are thus able to produce glassware in a variety of beautifully rich hues, or clear glass with graceful swirls of color. In addition to the high artistry of Alembretia's most-skilled artisans, the city also produces glass beads and plates of colored glass for stained-glass windows and mosaic tile (which is somewhat out of fashion, but still a steady trade item). In addition to the decorative glass products, some of Alembretia's artisans are highly skilled at more precision work. These experts produce such things as crystalline spheres, finely ground lenses, and cut prisms suitable for use by alchemists and practitioners of the arcane. Although the city is far from being a center of magical knowledge, it is fairly common to see the envoys and couriers of many great wizards cooling their heels in the city taverns, waiting through the many days required for the city's artisans to finish custom-made glassworks of the highest grade.

For the most part, Alembretia is a manufacturing city, not a trading city. Glass merchants arrive here from Manas and even from as far as Endhome to purchase the city's wares in bulk, and most of Alembretia's merchants are simply no match for the competition from the great trading cities.

Government

The city is self-ruled under a charter dating back to Ghienvais I, when the Glassblower's Guild offered to recruit and equip a full battalion of soldiers for the King's royal army. After a flurry of swift negotiations, the King granted a charter to the city in exchange for the offered troops, a quantity of gold and several wagons of glassware, plus an annual tax to be paid into the royal coffers. Since that time, a Council of Guilds was established to regulate the city's economy and government, but the council is effectively controlled by the Glassmakers' Guild, whose members elect the majority of the council seats.

Citizenry

The citizens of Alembretia's upper class are a rather unpleasant lot, greedy and somewhat cruel. Much of the city's glass molding is done in manufactories, whose workers are ill-paid and denied membership in the guild itself, being considered laborers rather than artisans.

Recent Events

As the Kingdom of Suilley has been steadily increasing taxes to fund its increasingly precarious finances, the guilds of Alembretia have been just as steadily passing along the costs to the laboring classes of the city, reducing pay and lengthening hours. As standards of living for the city's non-guild workers continued to fall, the high priestess of Ceres, Olivienne Ralan, began demanding that the guilds absorb some portion of the tax increases. Matters came to a head a year ago, when Olivienne finally threatened to ban the city's guild members — apprentices to masters — from the graces of the goddess. Many of the city laborers in the glass manufactories went on strike, and fought street-battles with armed apprentices of the guild. Finally, the high priest of Sefagreth stepped in to mediate the dispute and bring the city back to normal business operations. The guilds agreed to re-establish some of the original pay scales for the laborers, and Olivienne agreed not to use the force of her authority to shut the city down.

Tensions are still running high, not only between the laborers and the guilds, but between the Temple of Ceres and the city's government.

Broch Tarna
(BROCK TARN-ah)

Ancient Fortress in the Wilderland Hills, reputedly cursed

This ancient edifice is thought to be the oldest still-extant fortification in all of Akados. The Daanites of Ynys Cymragh would argue that some of the mountain fortresses on their island are older, but these are not technically on the mainland, and no one can be entirely sure about histories reaching so far back. There is no record at all of the people who originally built the broch; it was already an abandoned ruin when Oerson led his Legion through this area in –88 I.R. (3,605 years ago). Since then it has been rebuilt, occupied, and abandoned many times; so many times, in fact, that the broch has gained a reputation for being cursed in some way. The Hyperboreans chose to build a new fortress at Albor Broce rather than claim this one in the highlands, and a goodly number of those who have occupied Broch Tarna have died either in battle or for seemingly entirely unrelated reasons (an outbreak of plague, treachery from within, a well gone bad to poison the occupants, or everyone simply disappearing one night). The last known occupants were the margoyle overlords of the human hill clans of the Wilderland Hills, who were defeated there in the final battle of that war. Lately, wandering rangers have reported that the walls are repaired once again, and that spearmen walk the battlements once more. But no banner flies above its ramparts, so who (or what) these new occupiers are, and what their purpose is in garrisoning the fortress, remains unknown as of now.

Caer Silecia
(KAYR sil-AY-see-uh)

Country Seat of the King of Suilley

N small town
Government overlord
Population 621 (approx. 1500 when Royal Court is present) (565 humans; 32 halflings; 17 half-elves; 7 hill dwarves)
Notable NPCs
  Castellan Martin Surtiera (LN male human **Ftr4**)
  Commander of Guards Sir Lohendor of Lohen (LN male human **Ftr10**)
Maximum Clerical Spell Level Good 7 (when King is present, otherwise 5), Neutral 5 when King is present, otherwise —), Evil —
Purchase Maximum/Month 16,000gp when King is present; otherwise, 2000gp

Appearance

A vast fortress, bristling with guards, catapults, and banners of the king.

Description

Caer Silecia is the personal castle of King Ulrich, ancestral seat of the royal family since the nobles of Suilley originally granted it as royal lands to Ghienvais I. It is a medium-sized fortress on a high promontory that overlooks the large village of Silecia. The combined population of garrison and village equates to a small town, although the village sees little commerce other than weekly market days. What Silecia does see, however, is the arrival of the Royal Court of Suilley once per year during the kingdom's mud season. When the city of Manas becomes choked with mud following the seasonal rains, and the clogged gutters begin turning into pools of filth, the King retreats to Silecia until the pungent odors of the capital city are carried away on the breezes of the next season. During such time, although the unfortunate officials in Manas continue to run the country's day-to-day business amid the mud and stench, the official seat of government moves with the King, and Silecia technically becomes the capital of the realm until the King departs again.

The court travels with a great retinue, including family members of all eight ducal houses. It would be uncouth, but true, to observe that these wives, heirs, and children would not fare well if the patriarchs of their families were to do something untoward such as raise a rebellion against the king. This is a mere precaution, and common practice; there is no inclination on the part of the dukes to revolt. As great nobles of Suilley during its rise toward empire, they are unquestionably on the right side of history at the moment.

Caer Silecia is extremely well defended, with a year-round garrison of 400 men-at-arms, many of whom are 1st-level fighters or higher. The King's retinue usually includes another 500 soldiers or more, so the fortress becomes virtually impregnable while the King is present. During the royal retreat here, the castle and even the village become a hotbed of intrigue as various factions try to influence the kingdom's policies, obtain lucrative trading-rights, and sabotage the efforts of their rivals.

Cluin

(CLOO-in)

A popular pilgrimage destination, with a nice miracle and a bit of religious radicalism

N large town
Government overlord
Population 3213 (2730 humans, 480 half-elves, 3 gnomes)
Notable NPCs
  Mayor Oswalt of Cluin (LN human male **courtie**r)
  Sigilline, High Priestess of Yenomesh (N female human **Clr9** of Yenomesh)
  Palmadoc, Priest of Thyr (LG male human **Clr7** of Thyr)
Maximum Clerical Spell Level Good 5, Neutral 5, Evil 2 (hidden, Mathrigaunt)>>
Purchase Maximum/Month 8000gp

Appearance

The South County Road passes through the center of this walled town, although there is a well-worn path around the edge of the wall from both gates that leads to the town's cemetery. A large, rune-covered rock stands in the middle of the gravestones.

Description

Cluin is one of the main towns along the road from Manas to Grollek's Grove. An elected mayor governs the town, and all citizens are entitled to vote. The current mayor is Oswalt of Cluin, a prominent merchant who has managed the town diligently and well, having handed the management of his business over to his son and daughter. Most of the town's basic industry is centered on producing manufactured goods for the wealthier members of the surrounding rural communities: an armorer for the knights, a jeweler for finery, a tannery for producing leather, and other such crafts. Only a very small amount of trade comes from caravans passing to and from Manas, although many of them stop here for the night, and the town is not authorized to tax travelers on the road. It is not a rich place, nor is it a poor place. What is unusual about the town is not Cluin itself: It is the miracle that transpired here.

The Rock of Yenomesh

Cluin is a major pilgrimage destination in the area due to an event that took place here roughly a hundred years ago. A man rode into town soaked in blood, slumped over the back of his horse, with several bandit-arrows embedded deep in his back. No one knew the man; his purse had been taken and his horse died before it could be sold. The townsfolk buried him in an unmarked common grave, a lime-pit where the town's paupers are buried. The few possessions he still wore were sold to pay for the burial, and one of the items, a copper medallion, came into the hands of the town's only cleric at that time, a priest of Thyr. The medallion had a curious glyph on it and, being interested in such things, the priest hung it on his wall as a decoration.

A year or so later, a learned cleric of Thyr was passing through Cluin, en route to Manas from Endhome, in the company of a caravan of merchants. Invited to have dinner with the resident cleric, the learned man immediately remarked upon the ancient holy symbol of Yenomesh on the wall, for he recognized the sign of the Hyperborean god of glyphs and writing. Of particular interest, and the reason no one else had recognized the sigil as belonging to Yenomesh, was that the glyph was an earlier — much earlier — form of the symbol than the one currently in use. Such things were found only in the possession of those greatly favored by Yenomesh himself. The astonished town cleric told the tale of how he came by the medallion, and that very evening the two clerics sought an audience with the mayor, offering to pay for the body to be exhumed and reburied in a more suitable grave. At this second funeral, the Endhome cleric read aloud some holy words of Yenomesh he found in one of his tomes of theology, there being no actual priest of Yenomesh available to preside. Once the words were spoken, the earth shook, and a great stone rose from the ground beside the grave. As the townsfolk watched in awe, glyphs and runes began to trace themselves into the stone, circling and spiraling with unearthly beauty. This rune-etched pillar is now called the Rock of Yenomesh, and it is still shrouded with mystery. To this very day, *even the priests of Yenomesh do not know who is buried beside the stone.* No priest was found missing, no devotee of the god had disappeared in the area, and it was certainly not the sort of hero who would merit the god's direct attention in the way it was shown.

The glyphs inscribed on the rock have implications of gratitude and protection, and it has healed some pilgrims of curses and diseases when they touched it. Pilgrims travel from all corners of Suilley to see and touch the rock, which is considered to be something of a holy site for Thyr as well as Yenomesh given the role played by the two clerics of Thyr. The town priest lived to a ripe old age in Cluin, drinking free in any tavern he chose. The learned priest continued his journey to Manas, where he died soon afterward while picking marigolds in a meadow where an ankheg had made its lair since the previous winter.

Other Places of Interest

Temples of Yenomesh and Thyr

A fairly new temple of Yenomesh is to be found in Cluin, as one might expect, although it is small; and the temple of Thyr is well regarded, with statues of the two clerics responsible for the miracle placed outside the front gates. Sigilline, the high priestess of Yenomesh, is a smooth performer with a flair for performance. Her services are the last thing one would expect from a follower of the dry-as-dust god of writing and glyphs. Instead of lectures and contemplation, Sigilline tells stories of adventures and miracles like the one here in Cluin. To hear her tell it, Yenomesh and his followers have thwarted dark forces to the left and right, faced the darkness eye to eye and driven it back, preserved the light of civilization when it seemed all but lost. She keeps her audiences on the edge of their seats, rapt with the drama, and free with their cash when the services are over.

Sigilline is one of a very small number of radical clerics in the Church of Yenomesh who believe that their mission is to preach the word of the god rather than just passively accept worshippers when they happen to show up. Members of Sigilline's faction have a strong moral tendency toward good rather than evil, and their focus on educating peasants equally with the higher classes makes them politically dangerous in areas where the social order depends on the peasantry being kept down. Many of the traditionalist clerics of Yenomesh are highly suspicious of these radicals who follow the writings of an obscure Yenomeshite priest named Verician, who wrote and died centuries in the past. Verician's writings resurfaced only fifty years ago, so most of the Verician radicals are younger clerics who found the new, charismatic, populist approach to make far more sense than settling passively in towns, contemplating mysteries, and teaching only a select few members of the upper classes.

Sigilline's goal is to build a library here in Cluin, although so far all her resources have been taken to build the temple itself. She envisions a place where peasants can be taught to read and write, and where followers of Belon, Jamboor, and even Hecate can trade and expand knowledge, putting it in writing rather than keeping it secret. Her first vision is perhaps workable; but the idea of getting clerics of those three particular deities to work together illustrates that the youthful Sigilline is still a bit naïve about the world beyond the cloisters of Yenomesh. She also has no idea that her teachings in Cluin are aggravating some of the nearby nobles almost to the point of violence, for they are losing serfs to the town and facing opposition from peasants who are suddenly getting glimpses of the outside world through increasing literacy.

Inns and Accommodations

In addition to putting up visiting pilgrims, the town of Cluin sees a fair amount of traffic from ordinary merchants and travelers, although true caravans from Manas to Grollek's Grove only pass through every few days or so. The town has two large inns to handle visitors, and these are not ordinarily filled unless a large caravan or pilgrimage is in town. The better of the two inns is the Runic Rock, and the less expensive is the Glyph and Gauntlet.

Adventure

Sigilline's Cause: Sigilline is, so far, the most successful of the Verician radicals in the church of Yenomesh, and she corresponds with several other radical preachers. They tend to fall into trouble with local nobles unfriendly to having their serfs or peasants learning to read and write, and their tendency to wander around in rural areas puts them at a great deal of risk from monsters as well. Adventurers willing to help the cause may be entreated to rescue one or another of these priests from imprisonment, capture, or disappearance in distant places such as Manas, the unsettled regions east of Cluin, or the Gaelon River Valley.

The Friendly Men: The criminals of the Friendly Men (see **Chapter 1: Aachen Province,** *Taundre*) have taken note of the pilgrimages to Cluin and identified a ripe opportunity. They have installed a roving agent in the Gaelon River Valley who claims to be organizing small pilgrimages to Cluin, but is actually leading small groups of naïve peasants from the valley into ambushes where agents of the Friendly Men take them into captivity and sell them as serfs to isolated baronies deep in the rural countryside. So far, the number of disappearances has not been noticed as an epidemic, but Sigilline and the villagers of the Gaelon Valley have started to pay attention to the unusually large number of small groups that never make it to Cluin.

Crossgate Hold

Accommodations on the Rampart Road

Crossgate Hold is the largest of the gate-fortresses along the Rampart, once a veritable fortress that travelers passed through. The army of the Rampart reduced the stronghold during the Suilleyn Secession, and most of it now lies to either side of the causeway in the form of rubble and crushed bone. However, one walled stone platform still stands to the side of the causeway, the foundation for stone stables and the Causeway Inn. The King of Suilley, as a protection against the Foerdewaith troops, rebuilt two towers, one on each side of the high causeway, and the stone bridge between them. Suilleyn troops garrison here. The commander of the Hold

is Sir Hual Benis (LN male human **Ftr6**), who commands 50 soldiers and a crew of catapult engineers.

Innkeeper Jarel Muggs owns and manages the Causeway Inn. His family has held a charter to operate the inn for the last seventy years, and they have done it well. Jarel, however, has unfortunately gotten into significant debt after becoming addicted to opium, and the inn's finances are precarious. If anyone mentions opium to him, he immediately suggests that they go see his friend Luam Ghere in the city of Manas, whom he says is a dealer in "the finest opium." Jarel emphasizes that they should mention his name as the person making the referral, for he hopes to gain some credit with the man who supplies him with the drug.

Elfingate

An elven community with an ancient relic

Elfingate is to be found in the middle of an old forest that has remained undamaged by fires, droughts, and floods since the days predating even the Hyperborean Empire. It is a semi-sacred place to the elves who live here, and elves from far away occasionally arrive to stay for months at a time in the shadowy trees of the forest. The elves do not have a particular name for the forest since they consider it to still be a part of the greater forest that once grew unbroken across the continent. The few humans that have mapped the area named it arbitrarily as the Greenfallen Wold.

Elfingate itself is a ruined stone structure dating back to the pre-Hyperborean Age, built around a stone disk that was once capable of teleporting people between Elfingate and a location, now also ruined, near Chantry in the present-day Kingdom of Foere. The stone disk remains, inscribed with elegant elvish script that forms an inward-leading spiral to the center. Surrounding it at a distance are the remnants of delicate stone columns and lace-like walls, now broken and ruined. The structures were ruined by forest-troops of the attacking Hyperboreans during the war between Polemarch Oerson's legion and the defending elven nobles of the Great Akadonian Forest. The Hyperborean soldiers had no idea, and never learned, that they had dealt a severe blow to the elven side by destroying a magical *gate* that had been bringing a steady stream of reinforcements from the west to the eastern reaches of the forest.

Near the ruins there are still high elf settlements, "hamlets" as they might be called by humans, but actually the halls of extended elven clans. These elves consider themselves guardians of the Elfingate ruins, and do not allow any non-elf to look upon the disk or the broken stones of the ancient elf-halls that surround it. The ruins themselves are maintained by priestesses of Darach-Albith, the foremost god of the elves. Although the site is not considered sacred, the elves deem it significant enough to be tended by those who are most reverent and spiritual among the community.

The elves of the Greenfallen Wold deter humans and others from entering the forest at all. If anyone should attempt to use force against the forest's protectors, they find that the elves have allies in the forest's depths. There are **3 treants** who live here in alliance with the elves, and **8 giant owls** that also come to the forest's defense. Any battle with these guardians would most likely be a series of encounters in different places along the way to the ruins, unless the intruders stop long enough to allow the defenders time to assemble. The forest contains a total of 200 high elves, but they are too scattered to come swiftly to the defense of the ruins. No more than 50 are likely to be involved in a defense of the ruins if they are attacked.

Elven Priestess of Darach-Albith (5): AC 14; **HP** 27 (5d8+5); Spd 30ft; **Melee** shortsword (+3, 1d6+1 slashing); **SA** divine eminence (bonus, expend slot, extra 3d6 radiant, + 1d6 per slot above 1st), spells (Wis +6, 5th, DC 14); **Str** +0, **Dex** +1, **Con** +1, **Int** +1, **Wis** +4, **Cha** +1; **Skills** Medicine +7, Perception +6, Persuasion +3, Religion +4; **Senses** darkvision 60ft; **Traits** fey ancestry (tactical advantage on saves against charm and sleep; **AL** CG; **CR** 2; **XP** 450.

    Spells (slots): 0 (at will)— *light, sacred flame, resistance, thaumaturgy;* 1st (4)— *cure wounds, guiding bolt, sanctuary;* 2nd (3)—*hold person, lesser restoration, spiritual weapon;* 3rd (3)—*dispel magic, remove* curse, *spirit guardians*; 4th (3)—*freedom of movement, guardian of faith*; 5th (1)—*greater restoration, raise dead*.

Equipment: chain shirt, shortsword, holy symbol of Darach-Albith, scroll of *cure wounds* (5th), belt pouch containing 1d10 100gp gems

Treant (3): AC 16; HP 138 (12d12+60); Spd 30ft; Melee slam (+10, 3d6+6 bludgeoning); Ranged rock (+10, 60ft/180ft, 4d10+6 bludgeoning); SA animate trees (1/day, 60ft, 1 or 2 trees), multiattack (slam x2); Resist bludgeoning, piercing; Vulnerable fire; Str +6, Dex −1, Con +3, Int +1, Wis +3, Cha +1; Traits false appearance (tree), siege monster; AL CG; CR 9; XP 5000.

Owl, Giant: (8): AC 12; HP 19 (3d10+3); Spd 5ft, fly 60ft; Melee talons (+3, 2d6+1 slashing); Str +1, Dex +2, Con +1, Int −1, Wis +1, Cha +0; Skills Perception +5, Stealth +4; Senses darkvision 120ft, keen hearing and sight; Traits flyby (no opportunity attack when flying out of reach); AL N; CR 1/4; XP 50.

Elven Guardians (50): AC 16; HP 22 (4d8+4); Spd 30ft; Melee shortsword (+4, 1d6+2 piercing); Ranged shortbow (+4, 80ft/320ft, 1d6+2 piercing); SA multiattack (shortsword x2 or shortbow x2); Str +1, Dex +2, Con +1, Int +0, Wis +1, Cha +1; Skills Perception +3; Senses darkvision 60ft; Traits fey ancestry (tactical advantage on saves against charm and sleep; AL CG; CR 1/2; XP 100.

Equipment: scale mail, shortsword, shortbow, belt pouch with 1d10gp

Fairbridge

Just beyond the edge of the Borderlands, a not-nice place awaits travelers

NE large town
Government overlord
Population 2212 (1354 humans; 628 half-elves; 230 halflings)
Notable NPCs
  Pythorus Kroon, Magistrate (CE male human **Clr9** of Jubilex)
  Artel Splunk, Chief Constable (NE male human **Ftr8**)
  Shumwe, Priestess of Kudrak (LN female human **Ftr4**)
Maximum Clerical Spell Level Good —, Neutral 2, Evil 5 (hidden, Jubilex)
Purchase Maximum/Month 8000gp

The town of Fairbridge is located on the Sunderland side of the Suilley/ Sunderland border, but is included for reference in **Borderland Provinces** in case the characters travel along the Trader's Way.

Fairbridge stands where the Trader's Way crosses a small muddy river called the Granis by the locals, though it does not appear on any maps. Workers out of Grollek's Grove maintain and repair the bride every few years to keep it sturdy and to repair washouts. The town's magistrate collects tolls for crossing the bridge from travelers that look like they can be intimidated, though he has no authority to do so since the town does not maintain it. Next to the bridge is a crow cage that usually has the picked-over skeleton of some petty criminal that the locals like to point out to discourage miscreants. Unbeknownst to the town, the magistrate is a member of the Cult of the Faceless Lord, though only occasionally are rituals held in the cow shed behind his small manor. Lairing at the bottom of the town well is a semi-sentient vampiric ooze that is allied with the magistrate and which comes out only at night to hunt.

Flatlander Road

The main southern road between Manas and Exeter Province

Appearance

The Flatlander Road is not one of the stone-paved Hyperborean high roads. It turns and wanders, and much of it is nothing more than a wide dirt trail. During Suilley's mud season, parts of the road are almost impassable, and during this season, bandits come out of the woodwork, some of them sponsored by local knights who desire a bit more revenue.

Description

The Flatlander Road is a relatively recently built path that breaks away from the Trader's Way north of the Suilleyn city of Pfefferain. It leads down from the Lorremach Highhills to the plains of Suilley (at the city of Alembretia), then turns toward the capital city of Manas. The road's quality improves dramatically once it descends from the rocky highland, offering a decently fast journey (except during the mud season) for wagons and caravans to reach the city markets approximately 300 miles by road to the north. A small fort has been built at the crossroad itself, where a royal agent tries to convince traveling merchants to head for Manas rather than continue along the Trader's Way. The fort's garrison is small, and does not patrol more than a mile from its walls.

Encounter Chance: Make one encounter check in the morning, one in the afternoon, and one at night.

Risk Level: All encounters on the Flatlander Road are at the Medium-Risk level. Inside the one-hex radius around Manas, there is an additional automatic encounter check in the surrounding hex and the city's hex. All encounters in the city's hex and the surrounding hexes are at the Low-Risk level.

01–15	No Encounter
16–67	Mundane Encounter
68–00	Dangerous Encounter

Mundane Encounters: Flatlander Road

1d100	Encounter
01–02	Annoyance (Encounter #3)
03–04	Baron and Retinue (Encounter #8)
05	Bear (Encounter #11)
06–16	Caravan (Provincial) (Encounter #16)
17–18	Cleric (Encounter #19)
19–20	Elf (Encounter #34)
21–36	Farmer (Encounter #36)
37–45	Foot Patrol (Encounter #37)
46–55	Herder (Encounter #51)
56–58	Heretic (Encounter #52)
59–60	High Noble (Encounter #53)
61	Kenckoo Vagrant (Encounter #55)
62–66	Knight and Retinue (Encounter #56)
67–69	Knight Challenger (Encounter #57)
70	Leper (Encounter #60)
71	Military (Encounter #64)
72–74	Minstrel (Encounter #65)

1d100	Encounter
75–80	Mounted Patrol (Encounter #67)
81	Noble of the Realm (Encounter #68)
82–83	Peasant (Encounter #74)
84–85	Penitent (Encounter #76)
86–87	Pilgrim (Encounter #78)
88–89	Prisoner (Encounter #79)
90–91	Small Trader (dwarf or halfling) (Encounter #86)
92–96	Small Trader (human) (Encounter #85)
97–98	Stag (Encounter #87)
99–00	Wolf (Encounter #106)

Dangerous Encounters: Flatlander Road

1d100	Encounter
01–04	Ankheg (Encounter #2)
05–06	Ant (Encounter #4)
07–21	Bandit (Encounter #7)
22	Basilisk (Encounter #9)
23	Blood Hawk (Encounter #12)
24–26	Bugbear (Encounter #13)
27	Bulette (Encounter #14)
28–29	Cockatrice (Encounter #21)
30–34	Dragons A (Encounter #27)
35–37	Giant, Hill (Encounter #41)
38–47	Gnoll (Encounter #43)
48–53	Goblin, Roaming (Encounter #45)
54–56	Lycanthrope (Encounter #61)
57–61	Manticore (Encounter #63)
62–66	Ogre (Encounter #69)
67–72	Owlbear (Encounter #72)
73–80	Robber Knight (Encounter #80)
81–85	Stirge (Encounter #88)
86–88	Troll (Encounter #92)
89–90	Unicorn (Encounter #93)
91	Undead A (Encounter #94)
92–93	Wasp, Giant (Encounter #99)
94–95	Weasel, Giant (Encounter #100)
96–00	Wyvern (Encounter #108)

Mirquinoc

See **Chapter 5: Gaelon River Valley,** *Mirquinoc*. The city of Mirquinoc is roughly a mile outside the Suilleyn Border.

Lorremach Highhills
(LORE-eh-mock)

A dangerous region indeed. Also, the main source of poppies for Suilley's increasing opium trade.

Description

The Highhills are a rugged, savannah highland, very dry and riven with uncounted gullies and canyons. It receives little of the rainfall associated with the lowlands to the west. Winds blow violent dust storms through the area, carving the rocks into strange shapes, many of which are somehow eerie, others of which are dramatically beautiful. Farming is poor, although corn and opium poppies seem to thrive, and there are many hidden fens in the valleys or shaded by cliffs the locals call "florelgartens." The Lorremach is home to numerous tribes and communities of very diverse types. Halfling villages surround shaded farmland in the dells, their goats grazing on the scrub and sparse vegetation on the higher ground. Gnomes, also, have many settlements in the Lorremachs, living in caves around the edges of a florelgarten region and fishing in the deep wells and streams found in many of the cave systems. Several gnomish settlements have extensive mines and quarries deep in the hills, and from time to time groups of the gnomes march their products out to Pfefferain to sell. In general, however, the Lorremarch Highhills are a dangerous place, home to hobgoblins and ogres as well as the friendlier folk. The cave systems below the hills are prime territory for small clans of these brutes, and the area teems with them. Moreover, numerous different dragons, most of them blue or green, have been seen circling in gyres high over the hills, a matter of concern to most visitors.

For the most part, other than around Pfefferain and Stronghold Hjerrin, the Kingdom of Suilley leaves the Highhills to its inhabitants and does not interfere in the area.

Travel Note

The portion of the Trader's Way passing through the Lorremach Highhills is treated as a High-Risk area for purposes of random encounters.

Manas
(mah-NASS)

Behind the power and energetic activity of the burgeoning capital of Suilley is a desperately strained treasury and a growing problem with the opium trade.

N metropolis
Government council
Population 28,420 (21,500 humans; 3030 halflings; 1700 half-elves; 950 high elves; 680 hill dwarves; 400 gnomes; 160 other)
Notable NPCs
Ulrich IX, King of Suilley (N male human **noble**)
Sir Orlando Cormont, Commander of the Corps of Wardens (LN human male **Ftr8**).
Sun-Priest Ozoon Heliophar (LG male human **Clr17** of Mitra)
High Priest Besondar the Cognate (N male human **Clr9** of Belon the Wise)
High Priest Grobalond the Mighty (CN male human **Clr9/Ftr5** of Bowbe

Guildmaster of Thieves Casmir Dark (N male human **Rog12**)
Veril of Tourne (N female human **Sor16**)
Ciosceppio (CN male human **Wiz12**)
Pytharian the Mystical (N male human **Wiz11**)
The Notable Rhomenides (N male human **Wiz11**)
Luam Ghere, opium dealer of the Friendly Men (N male human **Rog9**)
Maximum Clerical Spell Level Good 9, Neutral 5, Evil —
Purchase Maximum/Month 64,000gp

Appearance

Manas is a sprawling metropolis that has outgrown its city walls, with cottages and other buildings extending in all directions around the central walled precincts. There has been a project to build an outer wall around these settlements, but construction has been stalled for some time.

Description

Manas is the capital city of Suilley, housing the court of King Ulrich at Palaz Terondel within the city walls, along with various other institutions of the country's government. The city prospers from trade and from the stability of the surrounding region, being at the very heart of the King's authority and power. At the same time, however, the treasury is badly strained as the city helps to fund the King's distant landholdings and vassal nations.

History

Like Troye, Manas is an ancient city, charting its history back to the days of the Hyperboreans, although it grew as a trading town rather than originating as a fortress. The city's stone walls are of great antiquity, but they were built to replace wooden walls that had protected the city for centuries before quarrying ever began for the stronger fortifications. Below the city is a vast Hyperborean-era series of vaults, passageways, and tombs. Why a tomb complex would require such a wealth of rooms, galleries, and winding tunnels beneath Manas is a secret lost with the Hyperboreans, for it is not a common feature of Hyperborean city-building. Throughout the city, a number of holes have been dug deeply enough to break into the vaulted corridors and labyrinthine tunnels below so that sewage and storm water can drain down from the city streets and be dispersed in the labyrinth.

Citizenry

Manas has the vibrant, almost frenetic, atmosphere of a place at the center of events, and this is indeed the case, for the kingdom is more and more becoming the main center of gravity in the Borderland Provinces. The kingdom's trade roads are safer than average, its guilds are less venal than many, its courts of justice are fairer and less corrupt than one might expect, its coins are well minted, its troubadours have little trouble finding wealthy patrons, and its nobility still considers chivalry to be something more than a fashionable lie. Demolition of old buildings and the construction of larger ones clog the city's thoroughfares with stone and lumber as the city continues to expand to fit its emerging role as a major power. New merchant houses, not only from Suilley but from places as far as Bard's Gate and Endhome, are opening their doors for business. Famous troubadours and jongleurs travel to the city from as far as Troye and Vermis to seek audiences and noble patronage. Manas has even begun to export some of its court fashions, perhaps the most significant mark of any city's pre-eminence. There are limits, of course; when Manas fashions are worn in Troye, the days of the Kingdoms of Foere will truly be ended, and that day has not yet come.

Map Key — City of Manas

1. The Caerronde Citadel
2. Palaz Terondel (Royal Palace)
3. Damozel Square
4. Seven Widows Market
5. Urbantine Square
6. House of Burgesses (City Government)
7. Feathermarket
8. Thieves' Guild
9. Trade Embassy of Bard's Gate
10. Trading-Consulate of Endhome
11. Palaz Tourne
12. Mansion of Cioseppio
13. Rune-Bull Square
14. Fane Court
15. Temple of Belon the Wise
16. Temple of Yenomesh
17. Temple of Jamboor
18. Consulates of Toullen and Keston
19. Consulate of Foere
20. Headquarters of the Corps of Wardens
21. The Court of Armorers
22. Temple of Mitra
23. Temple of Bowbe
24. Temple of Thyr
25. Temple of Telophus
26. Courtyard of Seasons
27. Pytharian's Tower
28. Tower of the Notable Rhomenides
29. Temple of Freya

Currency of the Borderlands Provinces

Unlike the rest of the Borderlands Provinces that still use the standard Foerdewaith-minted coins of the old empire, Suilley has established its own mints and its own coinage which circulates within that kingdom and its vassal states.

Currency of Foere

The coin denominations of the Kingdoms of Foere and their outlying holdings, and their game value, are listed below. This currency is common even outside the Kingdoms of Foere and is accepted in virtually any land at face value.

Emperor – 1 pp (10 gp)Sovereign – 1 gp (10 sp)
Noble – 1 sp (10 cp)
Silver Penny – 1/2 sp (5 cp)
Penny – 1 cp

Currency of Suilley

The coin denominations of the Kingdom of Suilley and its vassals, as well as their game value is listed below. Currency of Suilley is rejected within the Kingdoms of Foere and must be exchanged with a moneylender at a 90% exchange rate. Despite this prohibition many merchants, especially in Troye and Olaric, readily accept Suilley coinage at face value and use it in their own dealings with their Suilleyn counterparts. Coinage of Foere is accepted in Suilley, though merchants in Manas tend to frown on it and have been known to add a small (1–2%) surcharge on purchases using money of the old empire.

Bale – 1 pp (10 gp)
Liberty – 1 gp (10 sp)
Chapter – 1 sp (10 cp); intended to celebrate the organized guilds of Manas but is more commonly referred to as "bullocks" or "steers" in counterpart to the platinum bale.
Spoke – 1 cp

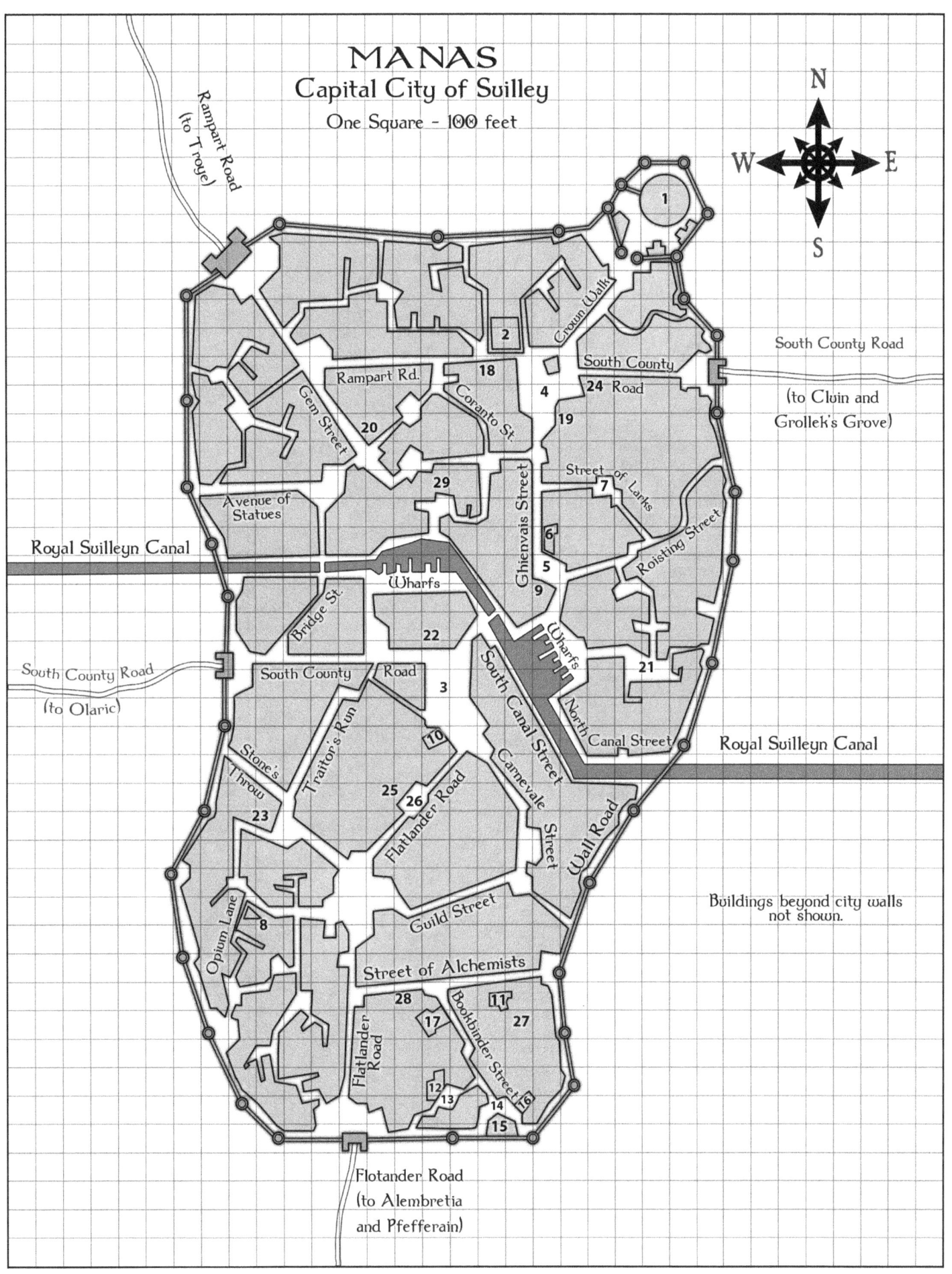

MANAS
Capital City of Suilley
One Square - 100 feet

N
W   E
S

Rampart Road
(to Troye)

South County Road

(to Cluin and
Grollek's Grove)

Crown Walk

South County
Road

2

18

Rampart Rd.

4

24

Coranto St.

Gem Street

20

19

Street of Larks

29

7

Avenue of
Statues

Ghienvais Street

6

Roisting Street

Royal Suilleyn Canal

5

9

Wharfs

Bridge St.

22

Wharfs

South County   Road

3

21

South County Road

(to Olaric)

North Canal Street

Royal Suilleyn Canal

Traitor's Run

10

South Canal Street

Stone's
Throw

25

26

Flatlander Road

Carnevale Street

23

Wall Road

Buildings beyond city walls
not shown.

Opium Lane

8

Guild Street

Street of Alchemists

28

11

17

27

Bookbinder Street

Flatlander
Road

12

13

16

14

15

Flotander Road
(to Alembretia
and Pfefferain)

115

Mages and Magic

At present, Manas has no formal college of magecraft but it is home to several wizards and sorcerers of note who live in formidable palazzi with arcane wards upon the doors and strange guardians prowling their halls by night. The sorceress Veril of Tourne lives in the crumbling Palaz Tourne, former home of her now-deceased father, the sorcerer Beinad of Tourne, son of Ylaine of Tourne, the Courghais-born sorceress who advised Ghienvais I when he was still a mere Lord-Governor, and was an early advocate of the Suilleyn secession. The family is long-lived, and not entirely sane. There is also Ciosceppio, who seems to disdain any surname, and whose rune-tattooed bull is, by specific decree of the King himself, not allowed into the city streets any more. The mystical Pytharian and the notable Rhomenides also number among the city's great mages, both of them solemn and long-bearded, quite satisfactory to the expectations of the citizens of Manas in terms of how wizards should look and behave.

Factions and Politics

Various factions operate within the city of Manas, especially now that the kingdom has become a major power in the provinces. The trade embassies of Bard's Gate and Endhome are both making considerable numbers of allies among the city's mercantile classes. The thieves' guild supervises criminal activities, and several small opium guilds are involved in a savage battle to control sales of opium from Pfefferain. A diplomat from Courghais, while never referring to Suilley as a kingdom, works diligently to ensure that Foere's interests are represented in the court at Palaz Terondel. Representatives from the vassal courts in Kingston and Tertry promote caravan trade to their countries and petition Ulrich for funds and troops to assist in the interests of Keston and Toullen respectively. Temples of various gods jostle for influence with the citizenry (especially those who are wealthy and/or noble). The quantity of intrigue as all these factions interact is mind-boggling.

Defense and Law Enforcement

The city maintains a small standing garrison, mostly to watch and guard the walls, but also a ceremonial bodyguard for the King, a troop of ranger-outriders, and a few spellcasters to supplement the city Wardens, described below.

Additionally, units of the Royal Army are stationed in the citadel, the city's last defense, a round tower called the Caerronde (which also contains the royal dungeon). The standing army of Suilley is much smaller than in days past when the Duchy of the Rampart represented a real threat, and many of its units are constantly on dispatch in Keston and even as far as Toullen trying to assist these vassal realms with the daunting task of keeping order. The army also patrols roads and maintains small garrisons throughout the kingdom, so the King's force here in Manas is not much larger than the city's own army. It usually is composed of a levied force of 200 trained peasants, 50 men-at-arms, and 5 mounted knights representing the feudal obligation of one or two barons to provide the King periodically with troops. Additionally, there is one battalion made up of 100 archers and 200 lightly armored infantrymen, and a second battalion of 300 heavy infantrymen. The King's Cavalry comprises 5 troops of 20 riders, plus their officers, one unit of 50 heavy cavalry, and a third unit of 20 knights together with their soldiers (a number varying from 30 to 50). All of these forces are supplemented by the private standing forces of the eight dukes, and by a small corps of more-powerful individuals who shift from unit to unit as needed. This corps is often referred to as the King's Scepters, and includes sorcerers, powerful fighters, clerics, and often a paladin or two. It is a mixed and often-changing group, but the Scepters are in many ways the troubleshooters and backbone of an otherwise relatively weak army.

The King has the ability to muster a massive army by calling up barons and knights, so the size of the standing army should not be seen as a measure of Suilley's true power. This is merely the group of professional, full-time soldiers who are ready to respond at a moment's notice if the King or country is threatened.

The Corps of Wardens is a separate contingent of guards maintained by the city who patrol the streets responding to disorder and crimes. As with the Royal Army, the Wardens are mostly no more than trained but ordinary individuals who answer mundane problems such as thefts and tavern brawls. For larger matters such as Ciosceppio's rune-tattooed bull, the Wardens have a small number of spellcasters and clerics who can support the ordinary Wardens with considerably more unusual resources. The Commander of the Corps of Wardens is currently the knight Sir Orlando Cormont.

Government

The city's symbol is three white circles arranged as a triangle around a badger on a blue field. This is distinct from the King's Royal arms, representing only Manas itself, and it is proudly displayed on banners flown atop the houses of the city's wealthy merchants, the towers around the city wall, and the House of Burgesses.

The burgesses are prominent leaders elected by the citizens for terms of two years. It is the burgesses who elect the mayor, pass municipal laws, and undertake specific responsibilities such as the Minister of Justiciars (courts), Minister of the Curtilage (the walls and defenses), and Minister of Revenues (gate and sales taxes).

Places of Interest

It is obviously impossible to list all the places of interest in a city the size of Manas, but a short list follows. First, of course, is the Palaz Terondel, where the King resides and holds court, and the Caerronde, the city's massive citadel tower. The city's greatest market is the Damozel Square, with the great merchants buying and selling large lots in the center, and small vendors selling to ordinary shoppers around the square's periphery. Every oddment and tidbit of the world seems to be available here, from diamonds and opium to turnips and flax. In addition to the wonders of the Damozel Square, there is the Court of Armorers, the Street of Alchemists, and the Avenue of Statues. All of these are usually crowded with busy citizens and gawking peasants.

One place is unlikely to come to the attention of anyone other than those asking questions specifically about opium or slaves: the Blue Dragonfly Tavern. The Blue Dragonfly is a drinking room with eight large tables, two upstairs rooms that can be rented for a few hours at a time, and a side room that serves as the offices of Luam Ghere (see *Crossgate Hold*). The tavernkeeper is Humbalto Roarc, a fat and unpleasant-looking man with a lazy eye.

Luam Ghere, the inhabitant of the side room office, is an opium merchant who purchases the material from the Lorremach Highlands and resells it to caravans passing through Manas. The business is not illegal in Suilley, but it is a dangerous game due to the number of gangs battling to control the trade. Luam, like many others, has the objective of forming (and controlling) an opium guild for the city, thereby controlling the bloodshed and increasing the profits of all concerned. In the meantime, he is careful to preserve his own life from his rivals. Luam's chances are better than most, for he is connected to a widely spread organization of drug-traders, slavers, and enforcement brokers known as the Friendly Men.

The Friendly Men provide Luam with access to a group of enforcement racketeers known as the Kindhearts. These individuals operate under license from the thieves' guild in the city, maintaining a business in which they charge small fees to merchants and households in their territory to protect them from robberies and criminal violence. It is an unstated but obvious fact that anyone not paying the Kindhearts could encounter criminal violence from the Kindhearts themselves. This small-time racketeering operation employs thugs for its dirty work when necessary, but also helps Luam by protecting him from rival opium dealers, and occasionally putting a stop to the operations of such rivals. Luam does not pay the Kindhearts for this service; rather, he works with the Friendly Men's chief agent in the town, an aristocrat with a country estate by the name of Sir Foscoun of Tallvine. Sir Foscoun's manor is a common meeting place for those who run caravans for the Friendly Men, or engage in larger-scale operations.

Adventure

Manas is an excellent place for adventurers to hear rumors, find employment, and ferret out interesting opportunities. Representatives of the eight dukes are often looking for mercenaries who can solve problems in the countryside such as dealing with dragons and mysterious events. The city's wizards always require tasks and travels that would be too dangerous for ordinary people. The temples extend their benevolent reach as far into the realm as they can, usually offering such rewards as raising the dead or removing curses instead of paying money, but even the temples dip into their coffers to handle truly strange and threatening events, whether inside or outside the walls of Manas. Caravans always need guards, and merchants always seek unusual items to sell. Even within the city, there are strange mysteries, secret cults, sabotage, bodyguarding, and other interesting chances for gold and renown. Manas is a place where many possibilities converge.

Dealing with the Kindhearts is one possible adventure in the city itself, or becoming involved with the savage conflict between rival opium gangs.

Pfefferain

(FEF-er-ain)

"Crown of the Lorremach," the center of the opium trade in Suilley

N large town
Government autocracy
Population 4712 (2686 humans; 754 gnomes; 613 halflings; 377 high elves; 236 half-elves; 46 hill dwarves)
Notable NPCs
Mayor Arellias auf der Henneschlieden (CG male half-elf **courtier**)
Justicator Joanna Lynne 'JL' Hilltopper (NG female halfling **Clr4/Ftr4** of Mick O'Delving)
Guard Commander Symsycks the IV (NG male human **Ftr10**)
High Priest Wairran Enceptus (LG male human **Clr5** of Muir)
Emerral Fnored (NG male gnome **Clr9** of the Hammer Mittelschmerz)
Ritarra auf der Lorremach (NG female human **Clr7** of Diana)
Oizwix Pnai Pfanglooi, Guildmistress of the Revered Sorcerers and Wizards Guild (N female gnome **Wiz11**)
Maximum Clerical Spell Level Good 3, Neutral 5, Evil —
Purchase Maximum/Month 8000gp

Appearance

The town is sited in the middle of four hills that form a rough triangle, joined to each other by great ramparts of stone and dirt. Quarried stone walls have been built around both the hills and the ramparts to create a sheer, cliff-like protective wall on all sides. Three gates pierce the ramparts to allow entry and exit. The banner of a golden griffon rampant over a wand, discharging flames, on a field of green is displayed proudly on many buildings within the city's manmade protective valley.

Description

Known to its citizens as the "Crown of the Lorremach," the hill-walled town of Pfefferain is part of the Kingdom of Suilley but has a charter allowing it to govern itself rather than being ruled by a local lord. A justicator (essentially a magistrate) from the King's court in Manas supervises the town's court of law and serves as the voice of the King's authority if needed, but the royal court does not interfere with any matters other than law and taxation. Pfefferain is left to itself on all local matters.

In this generally unhospitable region, Pfefferain benefits from its position in the middle of a large plot of fertile savannah territory near a spring-fed stream. The tillable land nearby supports corn, wheat, flax, soybeans, vegetables, and fruit trees, and grasslands supply grazing for herds of cattle, pigs, sheep, and horses. However, its main trade product is processed opium from the poppies that grow wild in the surrounding highlands. The town itself does not manufacture the opium; this is done, for the most part, by the hillfolk who gather or grow the poppies, and bring the paste to the town to sell.

The town is extremely friendly to users of magic, and is home to the "Revered Sorcerers and Wizards Guild of Pfefferain."

Government

"His Most Exalted Authority" Mayor Arrellias, a half-elven individual known for his hatred of dwarves and his mercurial personality, rules the town. By his decree, no armor may be worn and no weapons carried within the walls of the city. There are no exceptions to this law.

Adventure

For those wishing to travel the dangerous route between Pfefferain and Stronghold Hjerrin, experienced local mercenaries known as "hillbreakers" can be employed as guards for that portion of the Trader's Way. The road is not patrolled at all, and attempted banditry by hobgoblins is very common. Dragon attacks are rarer, or, at least, the ones where someone survives to report the attack are fairly rare. Take it for what you will.

More information about Pfefferain and the Lorremach Highhills is available in module *F1: Vindication* published by **Necromancer Games** as a d20 supplement. The digital copy is available and useful as a campaign tool.

Remballo

(rem-BAH-low)

A small trading city dominated by a far-reaching banking house that subtly opposes organized crime

LN small city
Government autocracy
Population 6722 (5382 humans; 623 halflings; 421 hill dwarves; 180 half-elves; 116 high elves)
Notable NPCs
Mayor Catherine of House Borgandy (N female human **noble**)
High Priest Bruno Fortinbras (LG male human **Clr7** of Thyr)
High Priestess Eliana Arjente (N female human **Clr8** of Sefagreth)
Romero Borgandy, Head of House Borgandy (LN male human **noble**)
Ghristoph Borgandy, Spymaster of House Borgandy (N male human **Rog10**)
Gorvais Borgandy, Vicar of Remballo Cathedral (LN male human **courtier**)
Maximum Clerical Spell Level Good 4, Neutral 4, Evil 2 (hidden)
Purchase Maximum/Month 32,000gp (this is double the normal purchasing power of a normal city of this size due to presence of the House of Borgandy)

Appearance

Milestones along the road count down the distance to the city of Remballo for the last five miles. When the city comes into view, it has

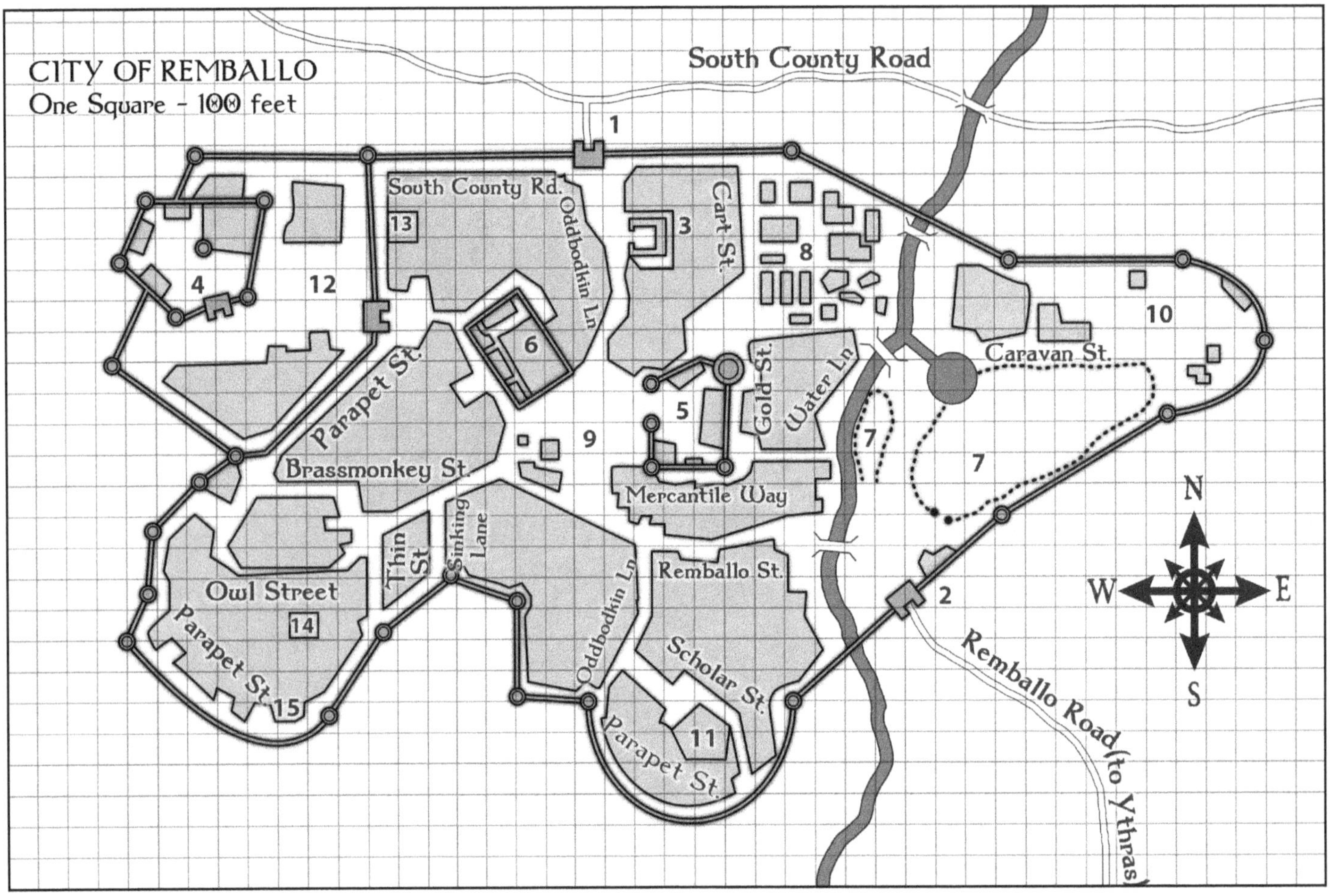

CITY OF REMBALLO
One Square – 100 feet

South County Road

1

South County Rd.

13

Oddbodkin Ln

Cart St.

3

8

4

12

Parapet St.

6

10

Caravan St.

Gold St.

Water Ln

5

7

Brassmonkey St.

9

7

Mercantile Way

Thin St.

Sinking Lane

Remballo St.

Owl Street

14

Oddbodkin Ln

2

Scholar St.

Parapet St.

15

11

Parapet St.

Remballo Road (to Ythras)

N
W E
S

City of Remballo Map Key

1. County Road Gate
2. Remballo Road Gate
3. Red Jongleur Inn
4. Citadel
5. Counting-House of the Borgandy family
6. Cathedral of Thyr and Sefagreth
7. Corrals and Enclosures for animals
8. Warehousing District
9. Cathedral Square
10. Caravansary (caravans assemble in these fields)
11. University of Remballo
12. Citadel Courtyard (municipal buildings)
13. Public Baths
14. Thieves' Guild
15. Dead Fiddler Square

the look of a fortification rather than a settlement, with high stone walls and substantial towers. Two flags fly over the gatehouse, one of them a mounted merchant on an orange background, and the other a triangle of three coins on a field of black.

General Information

Remballo is a small city along the South County Road between the capital cities of Olaric and Manas, where a wide cart-road from the kingdom's rural interior joins the high road. The town is filled with merchants, petty traders, carters, caravan guards looking for employment, and others who make their livelihood along major trade roads. Much of the area inside Remballo's walls is given over to warehouses and caravan yards, large inns, and animal corrals, all the requirements of a commercial city.

History

Remballo is not built upon Hyperborean ruins, as many of the cities of the Borderland Provinces are. It was founded in 3027 — at roughly the same time as Bard's Gate — as a small trading post to take advantage of increasing trade from the southern cart road. The southern trail is usually called the Remballo Road, even though it is not paved in any way and winds drunkenly through the countryside, making sharp curves around woodlands and hillsides. To call it a "road" is quite an overstatement of the facts. Nevertheless, the Remballo Road is one of the longest decent trails through this part of the kingdom's interior. A fairly steady stream of farm produce and other rural goods arrive at Remballo from the south, except during the mud season when rural travel becomes tremendously difficult for carts and wagons.

The House of Borgandy

The Borgandy family are a house of investors and bankers headquartered in Remballo. Rather than engaging in trade themselves, they finance caravans, expeditions, and land purchases for others. They do invest in town real estate, not only in Remballo but also in Manas and Olaric, but the only reason they would hold farmland is if they had foreclosed on a noble's estate. The patriarch of the Borgandy Family is Romero Borgandy, and much of the family's business is also managed by his daughter, Isobel Borgandy Razaan (the Razaan family is closely allied with the Borgandys).

The Borgandys provide a few services that might be useful to adventurers. First of these is simply to hold money safe for travelers unwilling to carry huge sums with them on the dangerous roads of the Borderland Provinces. The Borgandys do not pay interest on deposits: ensuring the safety of large sums of money is considered value enough in these uncertain times. Second, the Borgandys issue "letters of credit" that can be redeemed with other moneylenders in distant cities on the strength of the Borgandy family's assets. Such letters of credit are extremely specific, with a description of the holder given in the letter itself, making them useless to thieves (other than shapechangers, perhaps). Moreover, the paper used for the letters bears a very specific magical watermark, difficult to forge even for a high-level spellcaster. The downside of these letters is that they cost 10% of the face value (a 1000gp letter of credit requires a payment of 1100gp), which is how the Borgandys make their profits and pay their distant affiliates for cashing the letters in.

The Counting House is, for obvious reasons, well fortified. A robbery would by no means bankrupt the family since they have extensive real-estate holdings, loans to nobles, and shares of caravan cargos, but there is still a formidable quantity of treasure stored away here.

One might expect the Borgandy family to be motivated purely by self-interest, and there are unquestionably a few of them that fit the mold of a greedy banker. Most of them, however, are dedicated to the proposition that if they foster a more productive world, one that is governed by Law and mercy (commercially reasonable mercy, at least), their own trade will prosper. For a family that lives a thousand miles from any sea, their oddly maritime motto is that "a rising tide lifts all boats." The family has informants and agents in several of the great cities, and in addition to the commercial information they get from this network, they have been piecing together information about larger-scale criminal activity. Unlike the counts and dukes and kings of the Provinces, the Borgandys assemble information that is not cut off by political boundaries, and they have a much broader picture of the threats facing the Borderland Provinces as a whole. They understand many of the implications of Foere's withdrawal from the region, and have also discerned that the northern-based Friendly Men appear to be a very far-ranging criminal syndicate. They even surmise that the headquarters of the Friendly Men is probably somewhere in Aachen Province.

Although they cannot pay well for purely altruistic missions, the Borgandys might be willing to hire traveling adventurers for a number of different tasks. They often have foreclosures in distant lands, investments that seem to be going bad for no discernable reason, and people they suspect of being dishonest in business dealings. They handle their own problems in Manas and Olaric for the most part, but always have need of trustworthy help in places such as Kingston, Troye, Alembretia, and even the distant city of Endhome. In particular, they are very concerned about the fact that one of the Borgandy cousins, Savario Borgandy, has disappeared (see *Rogues in Remballo*, below).

They do not engage in the opium trade that has started to develop in the area, not for moral reasons but because they want to avoid the violence involved in the opium-related gang wars that are simmering in Manas and elsewhere. "Violence is unprofitable business," as they say.

Although it is not a common occurrence, the House of Borgandy occasionally does business with Loom Ché, a denizen of Leng who resides in the Unclaimed Lands. Loom Ché captains a ship that can sail through the misty seas between dimensions. For a price, he sometimes ships supplies of gold coin to the family's offices in Mirquinoc and Endhome. Loom Ché and his associates are very, very dangerous and unpredictable, not to mention bizarre. Lower-level characters would be at great risk to even board the ship. However, a higher-level group of characters might have a chance to interact with Loom Ché through the Borgandy family. See **Chapter 11: The Unclaimed Lands**, *Court of Loom Ché*.

Places of Interest

The Red Jongleur Inn

Wealthier travelers in Remballo are directed in particular to the Inn of the Red Jongleur. The Jongleur offers ordinary accommodations to farmers and pilgrims, but their luxury rooms at the top of a large round tower are spectacular. For a (large) price, the Jongleur produces gourmet foods of a quality that would impress even the King of Suilley. The top rooms have their own common room for small gatherings, and the inn is frequently host to diplomatic gatherings of dignitaries from Olaric and Manas, allowing these nobles and luminaries to meet midway and live in luxury while their discussions are in progress.

Cathedral of Thyr and Sefagreth

The cathedral of Thyr and Sefagreth is a splendid, graceful stone building with the left side dedicated to Sefagreth and the right side to Thyr. It was originally just a small temple to Thyr, financed by the city fathers at the time of the city's founding. When the first members of the Borgandy family arrived a hundred or so years ago, they began financing the temple and later arranged for the sanctuary to maintain a shrine to Sefagreth as well. The Borgandys take both of these gods as their patrons, without preference between the two. Since the cathedral has a dual nature, it is not maintained by the priests of either of the two deities venerated in its halls. Rather, it is managed by a Vicar neutral to both gods who is appointed by the Borgandy family. The current Vicar is Gorvais (gor VAY iss) Borgandy, a family member who showed more talent for managing real estate than money. In addition to supervising the cathedral grounds and building, Gorvais manages several of the warehouses and caravan-yards in Remballo on the family's behalf.

The priests of Thyr and Sefagreth are generally content with the role of tenants, even though it is a bit unorthodox. The Borgandys do not interfere with religious practices, and handle the sort of administrative tasks that the priests view as a distraction anyway.

Adventure

Ghristoph Borgandy is always willing to pay for information, and he occasionally handles the family's dirty work, some of which is kept secret from the other members of the family. Ghristoph could send a party of adventurers on all kinds of missions, from recovering lost collateral to gaining information about mercantile and political operations in Manas or Olaric, to tracking down rumors about the Friendly Men or the Wheelwrights.

Rogues in Remballo

This book contains an introductory adventure to the Lost Lands set in the city of Remballo. See the section **Rogues in Remballo**.

South County Road

A stone-paved high road, well traveled, peaceful, and pleasantly bucolic

The South County Road is well patrolled, well settled, and peaceful. Most of the journey from Manas to Olaric passes through orchards and fields of flax; farm wagons laden with produce are a constant sight as they make their way to the various market towns and inns along the road.

Encounter Chance: Make one encounter check in the morning, one in the afternoon, and one at night.

Risk Level: All encounters on the South County Road are at the Medium-Risk level. Inside the one-hex radius around Manas, Remballo, and Olaric, there is an additional automatic encounter check in the surrounding hex and the city's hex. All encounters in a city's hex and the surrounding hexes are at the Low-Risk level.

01–07	No Encounter
08–68	Mundane Encounter
69–00	Dangerous Encounter

Mundane Encounters: South County Road

1d100	Encounter
01–02	Annoyance (Encounter #3)
03–04	Baron and Retinue (Encounter #8)
05–06	Bear (Encounter #11)
07–16	Caravan (Provincial) (Encounter #16)
17–18	Cleric (Encounter #19)
19–20	Elf (Encounter #34)
21–36	Farmer (Encounter #36)
37–45	Foot Patrol (Encounter #37)
46–53	Herder (Encounter #51)
54–58	Heretic (Encounter #52)
59–60	High Noble (Encounter #53)
61	Kenckoo Vagrant (Encounter #55)
62–66	Knight and Retinue (Encounter #56)
67–69	Knight Challenger (Encounter #57)
70	Leper (Encounter #60)
71	Military (Encounter #64)
72–74	Minstrel (Encounter #65)
75–80	Mounted Patrol (Encounter #67)
81	Noble of the Realm (Encounter #68)
82–83	Peasant (Encounter #74)
84–85	Penitent (Encounter #76)
86–87	Pilgrim (Encounter #78)
88–89	Prisoner (Encounter #79)
90–91	Small Trader (dwarf or halfling) (Encounter #86)
92–96	Small Trader (human) (Encounter #85)
97–98	Stag (Encounter #87)
99–00	Wolf (Encounter #106)

Dangerous Encounters: South County Road

1d100	Encounter
01–04	Ankheg (Encounter #2)
05–20	Bandit (Encounter #7)
21–22	Bulette (Encounter #14)
23–25	Cockatrice (Encounter #21)
26–30	Dragon A (Encounter #27)
31–32	Eagle, Giant (Encounter #33)
33	Ettins (Encounter #35)
34	Giants, Hill (Encounter #41)
35–48	Gnoll (Encounter #43)
49–54	Goblin, Roaming (Encounter #45)

1d100	Encounter
55–58	Lycanthrope (Encounter #61)
59–63	Manticore (Encounter #63)
64–67	Ogre (Encounter #69)
68	Ogre Mage (Oni) (Encounter #70)
69–73	Owlbear (Encounter #72)
74–77	Robber Knight (Encounter #80)
78–79	Roc (Encounter #81)
80–81	Stirge (Encounter #88)
82–84	Troll (Encounter #92)
85	Unicorn (Encounter #93)
86–88	Wasp, Giant (Encounter #99)
89–95	Weasel, Giant (Encounter #100)
96	Wizard (Encounter #107)
97–00	Wyvern (Encounter #108)

Stronghold Hjerrin

(JAYR-in)

An ancient fortress held by the Kingdom of Suilley

LN large town/fortress
Government overlord (military commander)
Population 3672 (3120 humans; 330 hill dwarves; 179 gnomes; 43 halflings)
Notable NPCs
  Fortress-Commander Sir Oessum Keenblade (LN male human **Ftr9**)
  Guardian-Sacrist Lars Medovar (LG male human **Clr7** of Vanitthu)
Maximum Clerical Spell Level Good 4, Neutral —, Evil —
Purchase Maximum/Month 8000gp

Appearance

Stronghold Hjerrin occupies the tops of two adjacent mesas, and is built up between them to create a stone tunnel through which caravans may pass without entering the stronghold itself. The fortress is a vast construction of drum towers and thick walls, designed to pour destruction down onto the road below. It flies a huge banner of the Kingdom of Suilley over the highest tower.

History

Built by the Hyperboreans 88 years before the start of the Imperial Record, Stronghold Hjerrin is more than 3500 years old and still remains formidable, a testament to the engineering skills of the ancient empire. Its original role was to defend against Heldring raids from the south, but it is now important for its role in protecting the Trader's Way and the Lorremach Highhills. The fortress is heavily garrisoned by the Suilleyn army, and capable of withstanding a long siege.

Description

In the vast, shaded underpass through the fortress, one finds two inns, stables, a store selling general supplies, and the forge of an experienced blacksmith, all to allow caravans a safe rest stop and supplies for the next leg of their journey. The long, arched tunnel is as ancient as the stronghold it passes through, but the stonework remains as sound as the day the Hyperboreans built it.

Only travelers of very high station or fame are admitted to the stronghold itself for reasons of security. Most visitors are limited to the small community in the huge, arched underpass beneath the fortifications.

Temple of Orchestration

Main Temple of the Demon-Prince Mathrigaunt in the Provinces

Appearance

This temple is a bizarre structure of towers, ramps, and strangely shaped buildings. The main building of the temple complex is shaped like a beehive with an acropolis-like level at the top, open to the air, the domed roof supported by pillars.

Description

This temple-complex is the headquarters of the Cult of Mathrigaunt the Mad, a demon-prince. It is one of the few places in the Borderland Provinces where a demon-prince is openly worshipped mainly due to the protection of its local baron and its remote location. The Temple of Orchestration is situated in a small valley of the Barony of Lorip, a territory long known for its iniquity and lawlessness. Baron Lorip does not personally worship the demon-prince, but he is a renegade and occasionally a bandit; moreover, Mathrigaunt's cultists pay him well for his protection.

Map Locations

1. Main Gate

Immediately upon arriving at the main gate, or anywhere directly adjacent to the walls, the angelic sound of a singer becomes clearly audible. This is the song of one harpy in the temple-top (**Area 12**), but it will not take full effect until visitors enter the complex itself. If the time is between midnight and dawn, all of the harpies will be singing, and visitors must make saving throws to ignore the effect of harpy-song immediately upon reaching the gate.

This is a large, bronze, double door in the stone wall of the temple complex. Two guards stand on the catwalk over the top of the gate where a large winch is used to open the gates at midnight. The guards are both **ogres**, and they will not open the gates for anyone, although if characters are persuasive, one of the ogres goes to fetch a priest. There is a large bell on the catwalk over the gate so the ogres can sound an alarm to rouse the rest of the temple complex.

Ogre (2): AC 11; **HP** 59 (7d10+21); **Spd** 40ft; **Melee** greatclub (+6, 2d8+4 bludgeoning); **Ranged** (+6, 30ft/120ft, 2d6+4 piercing); **Str** +4, **Dex** −1, **Con** +3, **Int** −3, **Wis** −2, **Cha** −2; **Senses** darkvision 60ft; **AL** CE; **CR** 2; **XP** 450.

2. Garden

Anyone entering the temple through the main gate must walk through the garden to the second gate, which is usually open unless the temple is under attack. The garden is thickly planted with dark purple flowers that fill the garden with a deep, rich scent that sticks to clothes like smoke. Anyone passing through the garden must make a saving throw or become vulnerable to charms and mental control, including the choir of harpies in **Area 12**, the top of the main temple. Saving throws against such magic are made at −2.

3. Concealed Gate

A gate enters the temple complex here, but it is cunningly crafted to look exactly like the stone of the surrounding wall. It can be found by

---

Mathrigaunt the Mad, Demon Prince of Insanity, Evil Music, and Orchestration

Alignment: CE
Domain: Trickery
Symbol: Five-stringed rebec
Garb: Colorful minstrel clothes
Favored Weapon: shortsword
Form of Worship and Holidays: Nights of the new moon, solar and lunar eclipses, anniversaries of natural disasters (the beginning of the Fiend Rains in the Borderland Provinces, for instance) as a celebration of the "Crescendo"
Typical Worshippers: Nihilists, insane musicians, harpies, debased satyrs and korreds, redcaps, sirens, exiled Leng-men, shantaks, cambions, gallu-demons, nabasu, skitterdarks

The demon-prince Mathrigaunt "the Mad" is a patron of insanity, evil music, and orchestration. While "orchestration" might seem to be a strange obsession for a creature of Chaos, it is the best way to describe a love of madly complex plans, intricately crafted for their complexity as much as for their intended effect. The temple of Mathrigaunt funds and supports many distant criminals, madmen, and bizarre conspiracies in accordance with the *Apocalyptic Epiphanies of Mathrigaunt the Mad,* a tome of Mathrigaunt's forty-seven different ways in which the world can be toppled into ultimate destruction. Supposedly, Mathrigaunt has scribed a similar book for each world in existence, each book crafted in accordance with the different possible endings for that specific world. His priesthoods generally have plans to support as many of these apocalyptic outcomes as possible; the Temple of Mathrigaunt in Lorip claims to be working on twenty-two of them simultaneously.

Mathrigaunt resembles a human of ordinary build, although he is as tall as an ogre. Great bat wings rise from his back, and ram's horns curl outward from the sides of his head. He is traditionally depicted in elegant clothes suitable to a minstrel, usually with riding boots to hide his cloven hooves, and carrying a five-stringed rebec (similar to a violin). His cultists dress in similar, colorful fashion. The symbol of the demon-prince is the rebec he carries, and most of his cultists wear a medallion bearing this innocuous symbol. The rebec Mathrigaunt carries, depicted as his symbol, is a powerful item of Evil said to originate from the realms of mad Azathoth. In many other ways, too, Mathrigaunt seems to be far more connected to the ageless powers of the ancient, elder beings than most demon-princes.

His highest priests speak of the ultimate destruction of all reality as the "Crescendo," the day when a final apocalypse destroys the last of worlds and the cosmos devolves into ultimate entropy, filled only with the mad piping of Azathoth's inhuman minstrels. Some even conjecture that Mathrigaunt is actually one of the musicians of Azathoth, fallen somehow into demonic flesh and made conscious of his personal existence, unlike his brother beings that play eternally for the god of Evil. He is in many respects the opposite of a fallen angel, a creature raised somehow from the madness of churning chaos into a self-aware demon-prince. Other demon-princes consider him eerie, and try to avoid becoming embroiled in his intricate machinations.

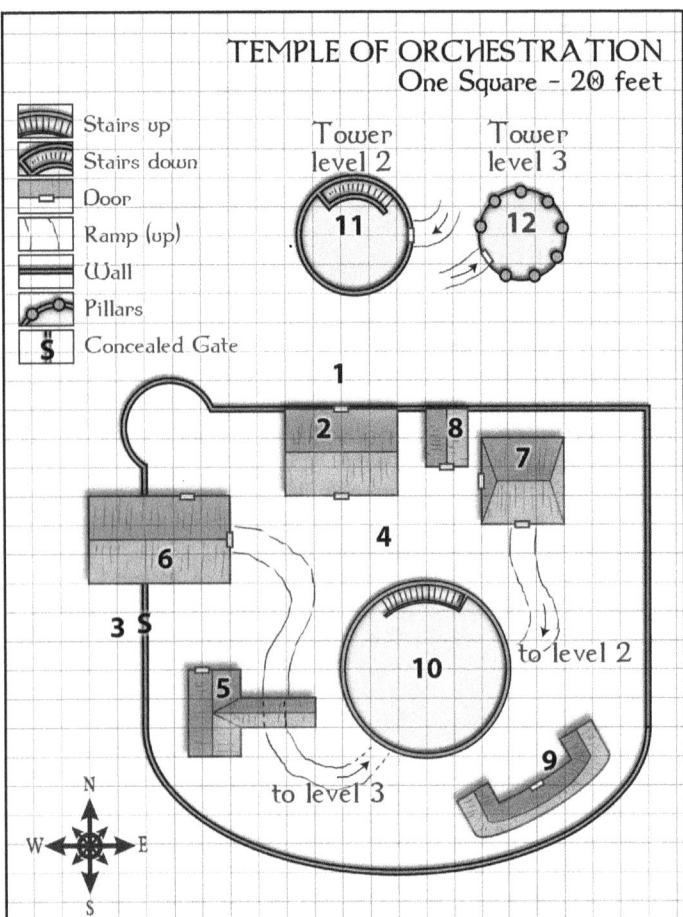

TEMPLE OF ORCHESTRATION
One Square - 20 feet

Stairs up
Stairs down
Door
Ramp (up)
Wall
Pillars
Concealed Gate

Tower level 2 — 11
Tower level 3 — 12

1
2
8
7
4
6
3 S
5
10
9
to level 2
to level 3

N
W — E
S

Ogre (2): AC 11; HP 59 (7d10+21); Spd 40ft; Melee greatclub (+6, 2d8+4 bludgeoning); Ranged (+6, 30ft/120ft, 2d6+4 piercing); Str +4, Dex −1, Con +3, Int −3, Wis −2, Cha −2; Senses darkvision 60ft; AL CE; CR 2; XP 450.

Treasure: There are four ogre treasures in the building (the two who are present and the two guarding the main gate). These are all in large sacks, and contain a total of 1200gp in various denominations of coin. The peasants and the guards have no treasure other than what they carry.

6. Antechamber to the Choir

This building serves as a combination stable and storage room. Steps lead up to the door in the east wall, which in turn lead up to the curving ramp toward top floor of the tower, the pillar-supported roof.

Two guard dogs (**mastiff**) are kept in this building along with the six horses kept by the temple.

Mastiff (2): AC 12; HP 5 (1d8+1); Spd 40ft; Melee bite (+3, 1d6+1 piercing plus knock prone, DC 11 Str); Str +1, Dex +2, Con +1, Int −4, Wis +1, Cha −2; Skills Perception +3; Senses keen hearing and smell; AL U; CR 1/8; XP 25.

7. Antechamber to the Temple

The inside walls of this building are painted with pictures of dancing demons playing harps and violins. Steps lead up to a door in the south wall, which leads onto the temple's eastern ramp. The ramp leads to the middle floor of the temple building.

8. Study and Office of Bas-Baldra, wizard of Jamboor

The inside of this building is filled with neatly arranged books, several skulls mounted on wooden pedestals with pins and labels sticking from them, a desk, chair, and a comfortable-looking feather bed.

Unless some sort of alarm has been given in the temple, Bas-Baldra the **mage** is in here, probably reading. He is an agent of the church of Jamboor, rendering political and arcane advice to High Priest Malachord, in exchange for information and payment. Bas-Baldra enjoys the game of chess he is waging against his own brother clerics, himself advising a servant of Chaos and evil while they advise protectors of civilization and Law. Nevertheless, he hopes that his next assignment will be to protect civilization, largely because the food is better.

Bas-Baldra (Mage): AC 12 (15 with *mage armor*); HP 40 (9d8); Spd 30ft; Melee dagger (+5, 1d4+2 piercing); SA spells (Int +6, 9th, DC 14); Str −1, Dex +2, Con +0, Int +3 (+6), Wis +1 (+4), Cha +0; Skills Arcana +6, History +6; AL N; CR 6; XP 2300.
   Spells (slots): 0 (at will)—*fire bolt, light, mage hand, prestidigitation*; 1st (4)—*detect magic, mage armor, magic missile, shield*; 2nd (3)—*misty step, suggestion*; 3rd (3)—*counterspell, fireball, slow*; 4th (3)—*greater invisibility, ice storm*; 5th (1)—*cone of cold*.
   Equipment: robes, staff, holy symbol of Jamboor, *carpet of flying*

Treasure: Bas-Baldra keeps his possessions in a locked chest hidden under the floorboards of the building. His spellbook is here, along with 3 scrolls of spells, a holy symbol of Jamboor, a *bone-rattle of Jamboor*, a box containing 72gp and a letter of credit for 2000gp drawn on the House of Borgandy in the name of any priest or agent of Jamboor, and the key to a house in the city of Troye (Bas-Baldra's ordinary residence when he is not on assignment).

The three scrolls are scribed with the following spells:
Scroll #1: *cloudkill, clairvoyance, charm person*
Scroll #2: *magic missile* (x5)
Scroll #3: *antimagic field, legend lore, project image*

ordinary means if anyone gets close enough to search the wall here, but it is difficult to spot from a distance. The gate is not guarded.

4. Main Courtyard

Anyone entering this area during the hours between midnight and dawn hears the choir of harpies in **Area 12**. Saving throws should be made at this point, and those failing the save head toward **Area 6** to enter the western ramp. Four **cult guards** patrol the courtyard, and there is a 25% chance for them to be in the area where any intruders go. Eventually, of course, the patrol covers the entire grounds of the complex; they are not stationed anywhere in particular.

5. Lay Dormitories

This building is essentially a barracks for the less-important followers of the demon-prince. A pair of **ogres** (the other guard shift for the main gate) sleep here in sturdy beds. Another 5 **peasant cultists** live here, sleeping on straw pallets. These demon-cultists are the cooks and servants of the priests. In the eastern wing of the building, where the ramp passes over the roof, are another **6 cult guards** who serve Malachord in various tasks, from defending the temple complex to riding as couriers. Four of these fighters are usually patrolling the temple grounds at any given time; they are described in **Area 4**.

Peasant Cultists (5): AC 10; HP 4 (1d8); Spd 30ft; Melee dagger (+2, 1d4 piercing); Str +0, Dex +0, Con +0; Int +0, Wis +0, Cha +0; Traits dark devotion (tactical advantage against charm and fright); AL CE; CR 0; XP 10.
   Equipment: clothing, dagger, belt pouch with 1d4gp

Cult Guards (6): AC 16; HP 11 (2d8+2); Spd 30ft; Melee longsword (+3, 1d8+1 slashing); Str +1, Dex +1, Con +1, Int +0, Wis +0, Cha +0; Skills Deception +2, Perception +2, Religion +2; Traits dark devotion (tactical advantage against charm and fright); AL CE; CR 1/8; XP 25.
   Equipment: chain shirt, shield, longsword, dagger, belt pouch with 1d20gp

Bone Rattle of Jamboor

Rare Wondrous Item

This rather grisly magic item is a rattle made from human bone. When the user shakes it at a dead body (no more than 72 hours dead), the rattle has the effect of a *speak with dead* spell. It can be employed by any cleric, or by a wizard in the service of the god Jamboor. The rattle has 10 charges; each time it is used, a charge is expended. When the charges are all used, the rattle becomes an ordinary bone rattle.

Additional charges can be expended to speak with bodies that have been dead longer than 3 days. Two charges may be expended to add an additional 24 hours (for a total of 4 days), 3 charges for an additional 48 hours (for a total of 4 days), 3 charges for an additional week, 4 charges for an additional week, 5 charges for an additional month, or 6 charges for three additional months. Three months and three days represent the maximum duration of death that the rattle can affect with its spell.

9. Dormitory of Priests

This building contains the dormitories of the priests of Mathrigaunt, in addition to the temple's kitchens. There are **4 priests of Mathrigaunt** and **7 acolytes** living in the building at present.

In addition to the dormitory area, there is a scriptorium in the southwest wing where **6 scribes** sit at tall desks copying books. One is making a new copy of the *Apocalyptic Epiphanies* and the other five are copying out new Hymnals of Discord (see the **Heresy Appendix** for details about the Hymnal of Discord). A seventh desk is empty, with the body of a scribe lying next to it, dead for at least the last 8 hours to judge from the smell. This scribe is skeletally gaunt, and apparently just dropped dead while copying a hymnal. The scribes are quite mad, drooling and moaning as they work. They offer no threat, but they are definitely tainted with the mark of the demon-prince.

Priest of Mathrigaunt (4): AC 13; HP 27 (5d8+5); Spd 30ft; Melee mace (+2, 1d6 bludgeoning); SA divine eminence (bonus, expend slot, extra 3d6 necrotic, + 1d6 per slot above 1st), spells (Wis +5, 5th, DC 13); Str +0, Dex +0, Con +1, Int +1, Wis +3, Cha +1; Skills Medicine +7, Persuasion +3, Religion +4; AL CE; CR 2; XP 450.
  Spells (slots): 0 (at will)—*guidance, resistance, sacred flame, thaumaturgy;* 1st (4)— *bane, guiding bolt (necrotic), inflict wounds;* 2nd (3)—*blindness/deafness, spiritual weapon;* 3rd (2)—*bestow curse, spirit guardians.*
  Equipment: chain shirt, mace, unholy symbol of Mathrigaunt, belt pouch containing 1d20gp

Acolyte (7): AC 10; HP 9 (2d8); Spd 30ft; Melee club (+2, 1d4 bludgeoning); SA spells (Wis +4, 1st, DC 12); Str +0, Dex +0, Con +0, Int +0, Wis +2, Cha +0; Skills Medicine +4, Religion +2; AL CE; CR 1/4; XP 50.
  Spells (slots): 0 (at will)—*resistance, sacred flame, thaumaturgy;* 1st (2)—*bane, guiding bolt (necrotic), inflict wounds*
  Equipment: club, holy symbol, belt pouch containing 2d10gp

Treasure: In addition to the materials carried by the cult-priests, a small amount of treasure is stashed away in the building in 11 unlocked chests. Most of their possessions are clothing, but the trove includes a total of 632gp, 1825sp, and jewelry worth a total of 300gp.

10. Lower Temple and High Priest's Chamber

High Priest Malachord lives in the vast, windowless ground floor of the temple, surrounded by tables, maps, charts, numerous pentagrams, and a variety of musical instruments. Malachord is completely insane, but he is also frenetically busy trying to keep an eye on all of his projects, plots, and plans. He has a tendency to forget several of them for weeks at a time, returning to them only to discover that minions have died, made bad decisions, or been captured by the authorities. On the other hand, Malachord's inventive mind continues to dream up new ideas faster than the forces of Law can respond to the old ones. It adds to the high priest's success that some of his plans are so deranged and out of the blue that no one could possibly have been expected to foresee them.

Lurking around the periphery of the chamber are Malachord's servitors, **4 vrock demons**. They carry messages on his behalf, rescue his less-intelligent minions for him, and protect him from harm. They respond quickly to anything that threatens him.

Demon, Vrock (4): AC 15; HP 104 (11d10+44); Spd 40ft, fly 60ft; Melee beak (+6, 2d6+3 piercing), talons (+6, 2d10+3 slashing); SA multiattack (beak, talons), spores (recharge 6, 15ft radius, poisoned, DC 14 Con repeat, then take 1d10 poison each turn), stunning screech (1/day, 20ft, stunned until end of vrock's next turn, DC 14 Con); Str +3, Dex +2 (+5), Con +4, Int −1, Wis +1 (+4), Cha −1 (+2); Immune poison; Resist cold, fire, lightning, normal weapons; Senses darkvision 120ft; Traits magic resistance; AL CE; CR 6; XP 2300

High Priest Malachord: AC 16; HP 78 (12d8+24); Spd 30ft; Melee *+1 flail* (+5, 1d8+2 bludgeoning); SA divine eminence (bonus, expend slot, extra 3d6 necrotic, + 1d6 per slot above 1st), spells (Wis +8, 12th, DC 16); Str +1, Dex +1, Con +2, Int +2, Wis +5 (+8), Cha +3 (+6); Skills Medicine +11, Persuasion +6, Religion +5; AL CE; CR 8; XP .
  Spells (slots): 0 (at will)—*guidance, resistance, sacred flame, thaumaturgy;* 1st (4)— *bane, guiding bolt (necrotic), inflict wounds;* 2nd (3)—*blindness/deafness, hold person, spiritual weapon;* 3rd (3)—*animate dead, bestow curse, spirit guardians;* 4th (3)—*death ward, freedom of movement, guardian of faith;* 5th (2)—*contagion, flame strike, insect plague;* 6th (1)—*blade barrier, harm*
  Equipment: half plate, *+1 flail,* unholy symbol of Mathrigaunt, *staff of charming,* belt pouch containing 217gp and 3 diamonds worth 1000gp each.

Treasure: In addition to the coins and gems, Malachord has a *scroll of recall* that he can use to escape into the castle of Baron Lorip where he can get a horse and ride for the hills. He has a half-written letter with delivery instructions for a courier to deliver it to a place called the "Scriptorum" in the Duchy of the Rampart, addressed to someone named Praxis Gaunt. (See **Chapter 8: Duchy of the Rampart**, *Scriptorum of Discord*). The letter seems to be nothing more than a question about how many scribes Praxis Gaunt currently has working on "pamphlets."

11. Temple Level

The ramp from **Area 7** leads to the temple level, where there is a huge statue of the demon-prince, an offering bowl, an altar, and several musical instruments hanging from the walls for use during the demon's nighttime rituals. The ordinary ritual, if characters should spy upon it, is simply a matter of playing wild music and dancing until the celebrants drop to the floor in exhaustion. The demon prince's darker rituals take place on specific dates and at specific times, and are not likely to be seen.

12. Choir of Harpies

The top level of the temple is the lair of a flock of **6 harpies** dedicated to the service of Mathrigaunt and the high priest. The floor of their circular dome is covered in filth and discarded bones, its reek carried away onto the wind. One of the harpies sings at all times, a sweet, lilting melody carried upon the same breezes that dispel the foul stench of the lair. At midnight, when the temple opens for services, the voices of all six harpies rise like a choir of angels into the night.

If the temple is attacked, four of the harpies fly to assist the other cultists in combat, and two remain in the tower, trying to entice the intruders to this high place where they can be lured off the edge of the roof.

Harpy (6): AC 11; HP 38 (7d8+7); Spd 20ft, fly 40ft; **Melee** claws (+3, 2d4+1 slashing), shortsword (+3, 1d6+1 piercing); **SA** luring song (300ft, DC 11 Wis or charmed, continue singing as bonus), multiattack (claws, shortsword); **Str** +1, **Dex** +1, **Con** +1, **Int** −2, **Wis** +0, **Cha** +1; **AL** CE; **CR** 1; **XP** 200.

Treasure: the harpies have bits of valuable material scattered in with the refuse and rotting garbage of the temple top. If they root through the garbage and noisome filth, the characters find 32gp, 4274sp, 5629cp, a golden necklace (100gp), a jade bracelet (100gp), a bag of 3 opals (200gp each), and a jewel-encrusted unholy symbol of Mathrigaunt (1000gp).

Tower of Corredrix

(CORE-eh-drix)

The abandoned tower of a wizard with a long history of tenants

The Tower of Corredrix stands at the edge of the Lorremach Highhills, now named for its current occupant, the wizard Corredrix (CG male half-elf **high mage**). The tower itself is much older than the wizard, who took it by force from a hobgoblin chieftain and his band of brigands. It is an isolated place, and adventurers are very unlikely to stumble upon it unless they already know of its existence and approximate whereabouts.

It is possible to learn about the tower from outside sources, for it is mentioned, although not as the "Tower of Corredrix," in several historical tomes about the Plains of Suilley. Most of these may be found in the library of the University at Vermis, but obscure references are made to the tower in some of the books of the Revered Sorcerers and Wizards Guild of Pfefferain. It is of Hyperborean construction, although not quite so old as Stronghold Hjerrin, and has been occupied by different wizards throughout much of its thousands of years of existence. Apparently it is located in an area where certain magical convergences are at their strongest, making the construction of magical items somewhat more reliable and less exhausting. Although Corredrix took the place more for its value as a conveniently isolated spot, he unknowingly followed a long tradition of wizards who have resided here.

The most famous of these wizards was Yejipann, who appeared apparently out of nowhere, perhaps from another plane of existence entirely. Yejipann scribed the now-lost tome known as the *Tenth Lexicon*, and tall jaguar-men are said to have guarded the tower during his tenancy.

Another of the tower's inhabitants, less known than Yejipann, was Tual Jannarc, cursed to be a voracious eater by his rival Merivarjun, a vengeful sorcerer of Troye. Apparently the cause of the dispute had to do with the ownership of a particular rosebush, both mages being avid horticulturalists in their spare time, unless "rosebush" was some sort of cipher indicating something other than an actual rosebush.

Trader's Way

(Suilley, from Grollek's Grove to the Wilderland Hills)

The longest road in the Borderland Provinces runs through Suilley into dangerous places

The Trader's Way, insofar as it concerns the Kingdom of Suilley, extends from beyond Suilley's southern border into Exeter Province, runs northward through the town of Pfefferain, through the Lorremach

Highhills to Stronghold Hjerrin, and then forms the country's eastern border with the District of Sunderland until it reaches Grollek's Grove at the base of the Gundlock Hills.

This reach of the Trader's Way runs through wild and untamed regions, for neither Suilley nor Sunderland has many settlements in the area. There are a small number of fortified inns along the road, of course, for caravans are willing to pay good gold for a safe night's rest, but these are few and far between. One of the inns, the Grey Genie, occupies a true, abandoned castle once called Grezjinn Keep. The Grey Genie is known for its safety, and has most of the amenities a tired caravan might need, although not much in the way of luxuries.

Encounter Chance: Make one encounter check in the morning, one in the afternoon, and one at night.

Risk Level: All encounters on the Trader's Way are at the Medium-Risk level *except the portion running through the Lorremach Highhills and the Gundlock Hills, which are both High-Risk areas*. Inside the one-hex radius around Eastgate, there is an additional automatic encounter in the surrounding hex and the city's hex. All encounters in the radius of the city are at the Low-Risk level.

01–25	No Encounter
26–62	Mundane Encounter
63–00	Dangerous Encounter

Mundane Encounters: Trader's Way (Suilley)

1d100	Encounter
01–02	Baron and Retinue (Encounter #8)
03–05	Bear (Encounter #11)
06–11	Caravan (Endhome, Rampart, Suilleyn, Exeter) (Encounter #16)
12–13	Cleric (Encounter #19)
14	Druid (Encounter #31)
15–17	Dwarf (Encounter #32)
18–19	Elf (Encounter #34)
20–31	Farmer (Encounter #36)
32–37	Foot Patrol (Encounter #37)
38–45	Herder (Encounter #51)
46–49	Heretic (Encounter #52)
50–51	Kenckoo Vagrants (Encounter #55)
52–59	Knight and Retinue (Encounter #56)
60–63	Knight Challenger (Encounter #57)
64–66	Minstrel (Encounter #65)
67–71	Mounted Patrol (Encounter #67)
72–74	Peasant (Encounter #74)
75	Pilgrim (Encounter #78)
76–77	Small Trader (dwarf or halfling) (Encounter #86)
78–81	Small Trader (human) (Encounter #85)
82–84	Stag (Encounter #87)
85–90	Wild Horse or Pony (Encounter #103)
91–00	Wolf (Encounter #106)

Dangerous Encounters: Trader's Way (Suilley)

1d100	Encounter
01–02	Ankheg (Encounter #2)
03–14	Bandit (Encounter #7)
15–16	Basilisk (Encounter #9)
17–18	Blood Hawk (Encounter #12)
19–30	Bugbear (Encounter #13)
31–32	Dragonfly, Giant (Encounter 26)
33–36	Dragon A (Encounter #27)
37–38	Drake, Fire (Encounter #30)
39–40	Eagle, giant (Encounter #33)
41	Ettin (Encounter #35)
42–43	Giant, Cloud (Encounter #40)
44–46	Giant, Hill (Encounter #41)
47–50	Gnoll (Encounter #43)
51–52	Goblin Raider (Encounter #44)
53–54	Goblin, Roaming (Encounter #45)
55–56	Griffon (Encounter #47)
57–58	Hag (Encounter #48)
59–60	Harpy (Encounter #50)
61–62	Korred (Encounter #58)
63–64	Lycanthrope (Encounter #61)
65–68	Manticore (Encounter #63)
69–72	Ogre (Encounter #69)
73	Ogre Mage (Oni) (Encounter #70)
74–75	Owlbear (Encounter #72)
76–80	Robber Knight (Encounter #80)
81–82	Roc (Encounter #81)
83	Shambling Mound (Encounter #84)
84	Tangtal (Encounter #89)
85–88	Troll (Encounter #92)
89–90	Wasp, Giant (Encounter #99)
91–94	Weasel, Giant (Encounter #100)
95–96	Wight (Encounter #102)
97	Witherstench (Encounter #104)
98	Wizard (Encounter #107)
99–100	Wyvern (Encounter #108)

Wennesalar (Ruins)

(win-ES-a-lar)

A destroyed village

Wennesalar was an old village of the Highhills that was recently destroyed and its population scattered. A wizard known as the "Darkmage" is widely considered to be responsible for the destruction, and the garrison at the crossroads chooses not to investigate what happened here.

More information about the ruins of Wennesalar may be found in the

d20 module *F1: Vindication* published by **Necromancer Games** and available digitally at froggodgames.com.

Wilderland Hills

Description

Although the Wilderland Hills are generally considered to be a part of the Kingdom of Suilley, no real attempt is made by anyone to lay claim over these wild, desolate lands, other than a few patrols in the western reaches that keep the Trader's Way from becoming utterly infested with bandits and humanoid raiders. It was the hill clans and humanoid tribes from this desolate region that invaded Keston Province in 3506 I.R. (11 years ago), and it was at the ancient fortress of Broch Tarna at the center of the hills where the final, decisive battle was fought to end the war (for more detail, see **Chapter 6: Keston Province, History**). Some scattered clan remnants are still known to roam the highlands here, so few travelers dare to intrude too closely in the area.

Ythras Village

(YITH-rus)

A village that hosts periodic expeditions to ancient ruins

N village
Government overlord
Population 728 (410 humans; 112 half-elves; 73 halflings; 52 hill dwarves; 48 high elves; 18 gnomes; 8 half-orcs; 7 other)
Notable NPCs
Benou the Bald, Sheriff of Ythras (LN male human **Ftr7**)
Hugo Eyeballs (CN male human **Clr2** of Yenomesh)
Aurian Lamasu (LG human male **Clr7** of Solanus)
Maximum Clerical Spell Level Good 4, Neutral 1, Evil —
Purchase Maximum/Month 2000gp

The Village

Ythras Village is a modest place with ancient stone walls and a single gate, located near a high but short range of hills in the Suilleyn countryside. It is not a particularly remarkable settlement other than for its proximity to an ancient construction in the nearby hills, a place called Ythras Tower. No one knows whether the tower eventually borrowed its name from the village, or vice versa; the tower is older by far, but might have rested unknown for years, its original name forgotten. And, in truth, the town's original name stands in some question as well, since scholars have turned up alternate spellings for it including: Yrthus, Yrbys, Myrbyus, Mithrus, and others, calling further into question the true ancient origin of the name for both town and tower.

During the mud season, the hillsides are virtually impassable due to the potential for lethal mudslides, and during the winter a dreadful cold surrounds the hills, apparently pulling coldness from the surrounding air as far away as the town itself. As a result of the hills' cold-pulling effect, Ythras Village enjoys a considerably warmer climate during winter than any of its neighbors.

The entire Ythras region is a part of the Barony of Paribas. The community is governed by the Sheriff of Ythras Town on behalf of Baron Lundric of Paribas, who resides in the castle of Caer Paribas three miles to the south. The current Sheriff is Benou the Bald, a bearded fellow with a prodigious capacity for pear brandy (one of the town's best products).

The Tower of Ythras

The mysterious tower stands in a range of high hills that runs 30 miles east-west and 10 miles wide from north to south, five miles from Ythras Town. It is the only remnant of an ancient system of forts, once joined by labyrinthine tunnels that have been expanded over the centuries by a succession of monstrous denizens. The corridors below the tower are apparently pre-Hyperborean according to the few remaining records of the elves who lived here while the area was surrounded by the Great Akadonian Forest, but these manuscripts fail to mention the tower itself, leading to the supposition that the structure atop the labyrinths was built at some time after the coming of the Hyperboreans.

> *Forbidden are the coldening ruins of the high hills, forbidden to the forest peoples, by staunch decree and high deliberation;*
> *Forgotten shall the mouldering halls below them lie, forgotten by the forest peoples, to memory and all consideration.*
>
> —Fragment of Elven manuscript apparently referencing Ythras Tower, considered to be pre-Hyperborean

Each year, Sheriff Benou leads an expedition into the hills to clear monsters out of the labyrinths below Ythras Tower. Adventurers come from far and wide to participate in this odd, subterranean hunting season, usually making a number of forays into the depths over time. Neither Benou nor the townsfolk actually participate in the underground exploration; the Sheriff and a small garrison of his soldiers stay aboveground in the crumbling tower to protect horses and other necessary features of a base camp, while the assorted adventurers of the expedition delve into the vast tunnels and vaults below. Great treasure troves have been recovered from the massive dungeons, but Baron Lundric has no intention of trying to loot the dungeons on his own behalf. The expedition's death toll each year is enough to remind locals that the gold beneath Ythras Tower is not easily taken, and it keeps down the monster population at no cost to the Baron.

A stone formation greatly resembling a ship (including two internal decks) stands near the Tower. During the month-long expedition, the bottom cargo deck is operated by townsfolk as an inn, while the upper deck serves as a tavern. A strange fellow by the name of Hugo Eyeballs seems to be in charge, although he claims to be working on behalf of undisclosed "owners." During the off-season, Hugo lives in the town, muttering and drawing maps in a small shop where he sells bits and pieces of treasure he buys at a discount from returning adventurers each year.

Chapter Ten: County of Toullen

County of Toullen

(TOO-len, antique: too-lain)

Overview

Toullen is now a feudal vassal of Suilley, essentially a palatine realm ruled by the Count, who has pledged his personal fealty to the Suilleyn king. It is a very rural country, still recovering from long-term damage caused by the Fiend Rains. The main attraction of Toullen for most people of the Borderland Provinces is the Tournament of Lilies and the highly competitive jousting competitions of the county. Most of the county's revenue comes from logging and mining operations on the western slopes of the Kal'Iugus Mountains.

General Information

Alignment: LG
Capital: Tertry (13,593)
Notable Settlements: Tuller (8,840), Durbenford (7,073)
Ruler: The Honorable Luthien I, Count-Palatine of Toullen, Protector of the Southern Marches (NG male human Ftr6)
Government: feudalism (palatine county of Suilley)
Population: 1,292,000 (789,600 Foerdewaith; 198,000 half-elves; 93,700 halflings; 59,100 high elves; 54,000 hill dwarves; 42,550 Heldring; 28,000 wood elves; 19,800 mountain dwarves; 4,950 gnomes; 2,300 other)
Humanoid: half-elf (many), halfling (many), high elf (many), hill dwarf (many), wood elf (some), mountain dwarf (some); gnome (few)
Monstrous: giant boar, kobold, giant weasel, goblin, dire wolf, goblin snake, swan maiden (plains); orc, hill giant, troll, trollhound, winter wolf, mammoth, frost giant, chimera, thunderbird, red dragon, white dragon (Kal'Iugus Mountains); giant animal, worg, giant spider, fey, ettercap, tangtal, wood giant, forest drake, lycanthrope, treant (Wiltangle Forest)
Languages: Common, Halfling, Elvish, Dwarvish, Gnomish
Religion: Freya, Thyr, Mick O'Delving, Muir, Pan, Darach-Albith, Dwerfater, Vergrimm Earthsblood, Quell, Sefagreth, Shae'loegn, Path of the Shattered Sword
Resources: timber, flax, linen, foodstuffs, livestock (swine), copper, furs, gems (grade 2), fishing, shipbuilding supplies, shipbuilding
Technology Level: High Middle Ages, Medieval (Tertry and Tuller)

Borders and Lands

Much of the County of Toullen extends to the south of the Sinnar Coast Region Map, for the vassal state of Suilley reaches all the way to the seaport of Tullen, the only port within Suilley's domains. The County is a narrow realm bordered to the west by the Kal'Iugus Mountains, although a small annex exists beyond the mountains in a forested area dominated by the city of Durbenford that is reached by means of a mountain pass. The County's eastern border is the Wiltangle Forest, and its southern border is Tywyl Bay. Its northern border with Keston Province is the crossroad of the Provincial Military Road and the South Road, 200 miles by road from the capital city of Tertry.

History and People

Founding of the County

The County of Toullen was established in 2856 during the period of time when Foere made great strides in organizing and consolidating its vassal states beyond the March of Mountains. In that year, the Overking raised High Baron Trosvoun to the rank of Count, granting him the vast region of Toullen as a feudal realm, and charging him with the task of uniting the local warlords and petty chieftains into an organized system of vassalage and fealty. Count Trosvoun established his seat of authority in the small town of Tertry on the South Road, thereby allowing reinforcements and supplies to travel swiftly to his assistance from Foere, if need be. Over the years, the mandated system of vassalage and fealty slowly developed outward from Tertry as one warlord after another eventually chose to join the County's march toward unification and centralized power, represented by the Count and his distant, omnipotent Overking.

Secession

In the year 3336, 181 years ago from the current year, Count Catrebrasse II of Toullen declared that he was retracting his feudal loyalties from the Kingdom of Foere, and would pay fealty instead to the Kings of Suilley. Emboldened by this development, the Lord-Governor of Keston Province similarly shifted his allegiance to Suilley not more than a month after the Count of Toullen's decree. It is evident an agreement was made between the two rulers so Toullen's troops would help defend Keston across the Gap Road in case of a counter-invasion by Foere. A large contingent of knights of Toullen was already present in Keston Province with a battalion of crossbowmen when the town criers of Kingston began ringing their bells to announce that the King of Kingston had changed.

Most likely the first discussions took place during the Tournament of Lilies in Tertry, which the Lord-Governor of Keston Province attended to witness a much-anticipated joust between Sir Rolvin of Dwarnhold and Sir Corin of Kingston (the victor being Sir Rolvin). Thereafter, Count Catrebrasse and the Lord-Governor remained in contact, making use of a magic mirror known as the *Ormoulande* that allowed them to use two mirrors to speak to each other at a distance. As all know, the legendary

thief Morwin, also known as the "Golden Crescent," stole the *Ormou-lande* from the palace of the Count of Toullen some months later.

Catastrophe and Cowardice

The catastrophic year of 3439 brought the Fiend Rains, torrential downpours along the March of Mountains that flooded the easternmost of Foere's provinces, principally the Duchy of the Rampart, the Kingdom of Suilley, Keston Province, and the Counties of Vourdon and Toullen. Although the city of Tertry was spared most of the destruction by being on somewhat higher ground near the mountains, the entire realm became a shallow river, the regions north of Tertry draining toward Keston, and the regions to the south draining slowly toward Tywyl Bay. Count Rolomair, who was wavering and indecisive and already suffering the disrespect of his subject nobility, failed to marshal any sort of response to the disaster, and has since been given the appellation "Rolomair the Wetself." The deluge thus affected Toullen somewhat worse than the other provinces, and set the County back by many years. Many barons declared themselves freeholders rather than vassals of the Wet Count, and petty wars against these barons occupied Rolomair's successors for a decade thereafter.

Recovery

In the interim between the Fiend Rains and the present day, Toullen has struggled to recover its prosperity. It is somewhat aided by its possession of Suilley's only seaport, even though most of Suilley's trade goes north to Endhome or Eastgate.

Jousting

It might seem like a strange thing for a nation to have a separate entry for a sport, but in Toullen's case, leaving out mention of the sport of jousting would be a serious omission. In addition to hosting the Tournament of Lilies at Tertry, which is the most prestigious tournament in the provinces and brings contestants from as far as Eastreach and even Courghais, Toullen is obsessed with the sport. From knights on their Suilleyn destriers in elaborate plate armor, all the way to peasants on donkeys riding at each other with quarterstaffs and barrel lids, the County of Toullen is universally addicted to the lists.

Under the auspices of Count Quelovic II, the first Tournament of Lilies was held in Tertry in 3119 as a melee tournament with 25 knights to each side, and was resolved in a single mock battle that resulted in two deaths and a number of serious wounds. Members of the victorious side received chaplets of lilies, and all the knights — save two — declared that the mock battle had been a tremendous success. The Count's popularity greatly increased, and on the spot he declared that the tournament would be repeated the following year on the same day (the day before the first full moon) in the same month. From that time, the Tournament of Lilies has evolved to become more a competition of individual jousts rather than of the melee, and a system of qualifications developed to ensure that the tournament would not drag on for weeks due to the number of participants.

Trade and Commerce

Virtually all of Toullen's wealth comes from two sources: merchants on the South Road, and the extensive mining and logging efforts in the Kal'Iugus Mountains. Caravans on the South Road are fairly common as they make short legs of the route between the port at Tuller through Toullen and then beyond to Keston, Vourdon, the Duchy of the Rampart, and Manas. Caravans along this route are often quite large, but carry cargoes of relatively low value compared with the riches that traverse the north. Toullen gains more of its revenue from the Kal'Iugus Mountains, mainly along the western flanks, which are reached through the Toullen Pass 100 miles to the southwest of Tertry. On the far side of the mountains is the region of Durbenford, an area that renounced its fealty to Foere at the same time as Keston and Toullen, but instead pledged itself to the Count of Toullen. Durbenford has extensive logging and mining resources, and has proven to be a great financial boon to the County's limited coffers.

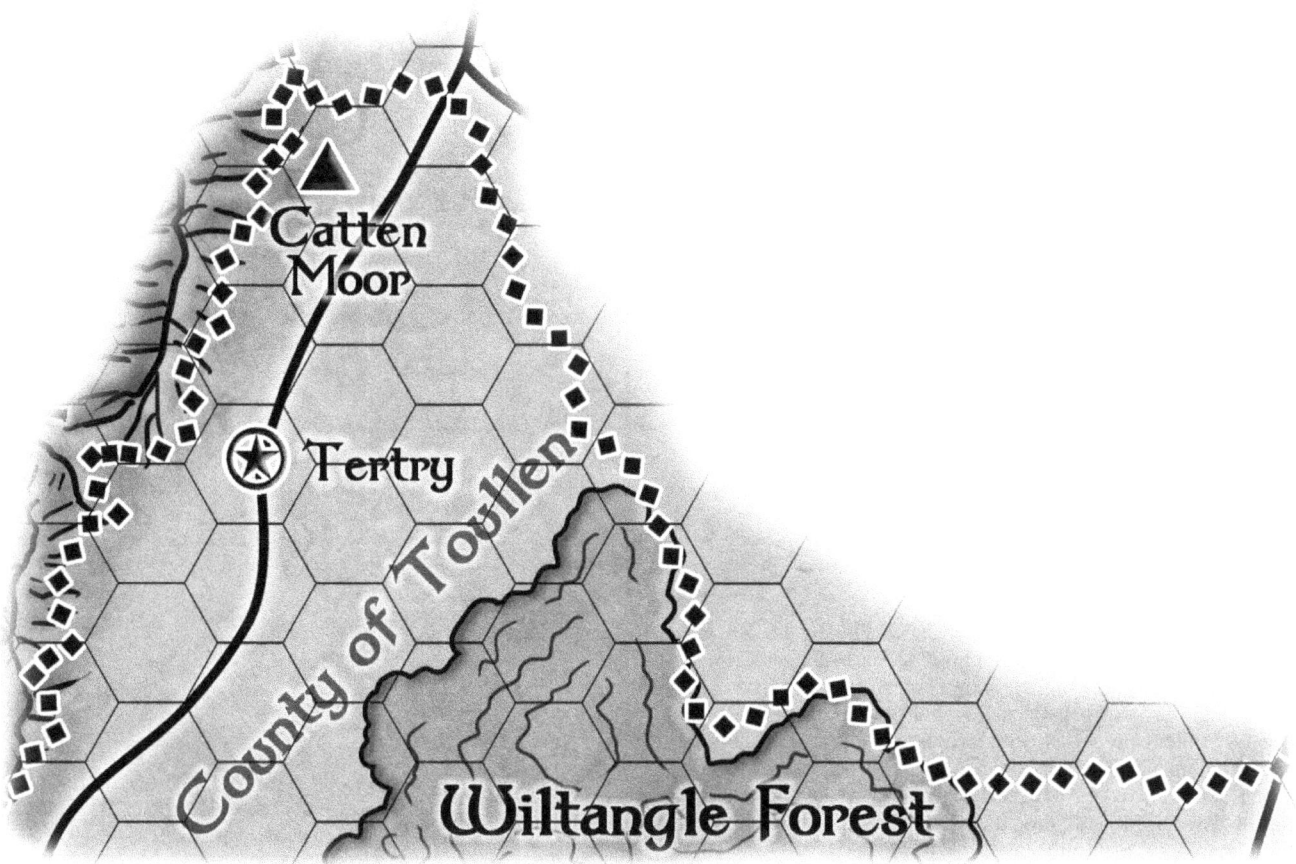

Loyalties and Diplomacy

Toullen has been subject to the Kingdom of Suilley since 3336, and is on particularly good terms with the Province of Keston to its north. The only connection between Toullen and Suilley is through Keston, and at present, no good road leads directly from the two vassal states to that kingdom, although the Court of Manas is definitely contemplating one. No one is hostile to the County, and the County minds its own business in the regional politics of the Provinces.

Government

A hereditary Count, currently Luthien, first of his name to rule, governs Toullen. Count Luthien is a fat, friendly man, much loved by his subjects. His popularity is greatly enhanced by the independent fame of his younger sister, the Demoiselle Cyrilinde the Lance, a champion tournament jouster, grand victor at one Tournament of Lilies, finishing in the top ten jousters for the last three years, and taking the laurel crown in two of the last three Tournaments of the Realm.

Below the level of Count, Toullen has a stratum of nobility called High Barons to whom ordinary barons pledge fealty, most knights in turn pledging fealty to one of the ordinary barons. Fifteen high baronial houses form an advisory council of sorts to the Count, but the council has no actual governmental powers. Of all the realms in the Borderland Provinces, the Count of Toullen exerts more direct power over his subjects than the ruler of any other realm. For Toullen, a weak ruler means a weak County (see, e.g., Count Rolomair "Wetself"), but a strong ruler can make dramatic improvements without facing much opposition from great noble houses serving their own agendas. Count Luthien is a strong and popular ruler, and the County is benefitting greatly from his reign.

The 15 High Baronial Houses are the Aulzevern, Caer Nor, Grellec, Saltfalcon, Gloun, Nantres, Hleen, Jormorel, Tauntirion, Mothcandle, Cascat, Porthiliot, Greenwine, Liscondel, and Vanj. In addition, Lord Durben of Durbenford has been campaigning hard for the elevation of a sixteenth High Baronial House for the last several years.

Wilderness and Adventure

In general, Toullen appears to be quite well settled, with villages and hamlets throughout the County's narrow band of territory. Yet these settlements all have much-smaller populations than one would expect, for the Fiend Rains turned a great deal of the County's tillable land to marsh and fen, something from which Toullen's former vast fields of grain have never recovered. Depopulated as it is, the countryside has few broad expanses of primeval wilderness, which makes for fewer threats to civilization. On the other hand, the Kal'Iugus Mountains to the west, and the Wiltangle Forest to the east, are quite wild and dangerous, indeed. Adventurers seeking their fortunes in Toullen will most likely be seeking out treasure and fame in one of these two places and should be prepared for unpleasant surprises in the wilderness of Toullen's marches.

Changing Times

As with the Province of Keston, the County of Toullen is not greatly affected by the retreat of Foere's power. These vassal states of Suilley threw off the yoke of Foere relatively early, and Foere was doing little to benefit them in the first place. They experienced the rough edge of Foerdewaith culture far more than the civilized edge; other than a countryside interpretation of chivalric principles, and an invader's language, they have little to show for their temporary role as vassal states to the Overking in Courghais.

For the Toullenese, the changing times have more to do with growth and stability, building connections with Suilley to benefit their people, and reclaiming fens and marshes that have stood fallow since the Fiend Rains decades ago.

Barren Forest

The southern and western border of Toullen, south of the Sinnar Coast Region Map

The Harwood Forest is the single greatest remaining woodland and largest-surviving remnant of the Great Akadonian Forest east of the Crescent Sea. The forest's easternmost reaches are known as the Barren Forest and are little explored and even less settled, though some logging towns do exist.

More information concerning the Barren Forest is provided in the adventure *Timber Rivalry*, in **Quests of Doom 3**, published by **Necromancer Games**.

Catten Moor

(KAT-en MOOR)

Home of a green hag coven

Catten Moor is a remote highland near the foothills of the Kal'Iugus Mountains where the soil is too poor for farming. There are numerous peat bogs throughout the area, and ferns grow in profusion along with gorse bushes and high thistle. The moor is roughly thirty miles from north to south, and ten miles across from east to west. It is often obscured by deep, gray mist, a natural phenomenon common to such areas. The locals do not allow their animals to graze here, although large groups of well-armed peasants occasionally venture onto the moors to cut peat for their hearth fires. No one wanders the heath alone.

The locals do not know exactly why the moor is so dangerous, but they know animals and people disappear there with alarming frequency. In the deep mists, it is easy to become lost or get mired in a peat bog, but the ordinary risks of wandering on moorlands cannot account for the number of animals and people that have gone missing over the years.

The moor is home to a coven of three green hags, horrible non-human creatures of a profoundly evil nature who eat human flesh with relish. The three hags are sisters: Gretchen, Wretchen, and Sheare. They have lived in their house on the moor for almost a hundred years, preying occasionally upon the nearby villages but also hunting in the foothills for mountain cats, which they consider a delicacy. In recent years, the hag called Sheare has been overcome with a voracious appetite, foregoing the delicious pottage of cat to hunt down humans and steal babies. Sheare's uncontrollable appetites are a great annoyance to her sisters, who have become worried that her forays beyond the moor will draw too much attention to them, possibly even calling forth knights and soldiers with sharp blades and a lack of sympathy.

1. Peat Bog

The entire area surrounding the hags' cottage is a peat bog that pulls people down like quicksand if they step onto it. Use quicksand rules per 5e DMG. If anyone becomes stuck in the bog before any contact with the hags, one of the hags discovers the character within an hour, especially if assisted by cries for help.

2. Causeway

The trail leading to the hags' cottage is firm ground, and can be safely followed.

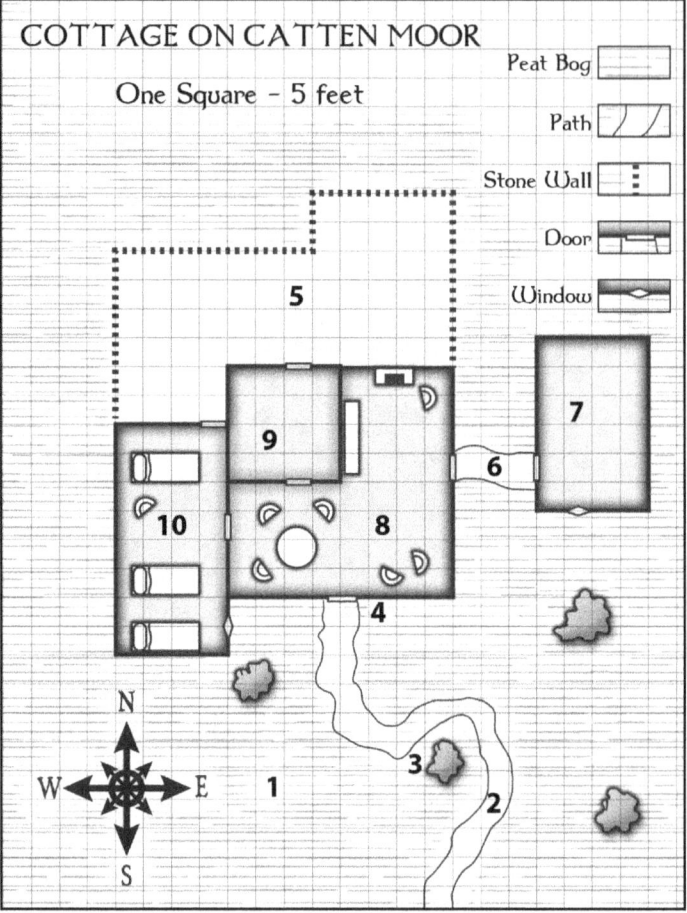

COTTAGE ON CATTEN MOOR

One Square – 5 feet

Peat Bog
Path
Stone Wall
Door
Window

3. Tree Trap

Four willow trees grow from the dark, muddy soil around the cottage, each of them about 20ft tall. One **tree** is different from the others, for it is quasi-sapient and animated, although it stands quietly unless someone steps off the path nearby. It has claimed more than one victim; people sneaking toward the hut have a tendency to notice the window in the outbuilding (**Area 7**) and duck off the path behind the tree for cover. If this happens, the tree knows that it is facing intruders and it reacts quickly and violently.

Animated Tree: AC 15; **HP** 114 (12d10+48); **Spd** 0ft; **Melee** slam (+8, 3d6+5 bludgeoning); **SA** multiattack (slam x2); **Resist** bludgeoning, piercing; **Vulnerable** fire; **Str** +5, **Dex** −2, **Con** +4, **Int** −5, **Wis** +2, **Cha** −5; **Traits** false appearance (tree); **AL** NE; **CR** 5; **XP** 1800.

4. Door

The cottage door is old and fragile, made of now-rotting planks of wood and covered in mold. A single rune is painted upon it. The rune is a *symbol of death*, but it is so moldy and weather beaten that it has almost no effect. Anyone other than one of the hags passing through the door takes 10 necrotic damage as the paint of the symbol seethes and disappears.

5. Garden

The garden is also on stable ground, and is surrounded by a three-foot-tall stone wall. The hags grow completely mundane vegetables here (all stew vegetables) that include potatoes, celery, carrots, and onion. A scarecrow hangs on a wooden frame in the middle of the garden to scare away birds.

The **scarecrow** is an animated monster that defends its garden from anyone other than one of the hags. The hags' treasure is buried directly underneath the scarecrow's post.

Scarecrow: AC 11; **HP** 36 (8d8); **Spd** 30ft; **Melee** claw (+3, 2d4+1 slashing plus fright, DC 11 Wis); **SA** multiattack (claw x2), terrifying glare (30ft, paralyzed fright, DC 11 Wis); **Immune** charm, exhaustion, fright, paralysis, poison, unconscious; **Resist** normal weapons; **Vulnerable** fire; **Str** +0, **Dex** +1, **Con** +0, **Int** +0, **Wis** +0, **Cha** +1; **Senses** darkvision 60ft; **AL** CE; **CR** 1; **XP** 200.

Treasure: Underneath the scarecrow's post the hags have hidden away a trove of 14,000gp and 48,325sp. In addition to the coins, a few other interesting items are buried in the trove underneath the scarecrow, all of them from the hoard of a manticore the sisters rendered into stew many years ago. Somehow, the manticore had come into possession of items plundered from a temple of Ceres in Exeter Province, long before the manticore could have been born. These items include a holy symbol (a small millstone), a well-stoppered stone potion bottle, a *cloak of invisibility* and a book. The liquid in the bottle is a *potion of raising the dead*: If it is poured over a body that has not been dead for more than a few days, the potion calls back the missing soul, and the body is returned to life.

The book is bound in leather, and has been well-preserved in the peat-rich soil. It is apparently a record-book kept by a religious community of Ceres, since the very first line begins with, "By the Grace of Ceres, in the lands of Exeter …" The book is not filled, but the very last page has been used for a scrawled map to show the location of something labeled "well," and also "millstone." The map and book are meaningless to anyone outside a temple of Ceres, but priestesses of Ceres are likely to realize that this map shows approximately where one of the goddess's temple-millstones may have been hidden for security. By perusing old maps and records, they can make a guess as to which old temple it might have been, and give the characters an approximate location where their map might be useful. They most certainly offer the characters a reward if the temple-millstone is recovered; the older ones can be a strong focus for the goddess's attention, and this books suggests that the millstone in question might be very old indeed.

Further detail on this lost temple-millstone may be found under "Well of Ceres" in **Exeter Province**.

6. Safe Path

This is a narrow path between the cottage and its only outbuilding. It is safe to walk on.

7. Outbuilding

The hags use this building to store their vegetables, gardening tools, human bones, and similar things. The **green hag** Sheare is usually found in this building, hissing melodiously to herself and using human skulls as hand puppets to talk to each other about how beautiful Sheare is.

Sheare, Green Hag: AC 17; **HP** 82 (11d8+33); **Spd** 30ft; **Melee** claws (+6, 2d8+4 slashing); **SA** illusory appearance, innate spells (Cha, DC 12), invisible passage; **Str** +4, **Dex** +1, **Con** +3, **Int** +1, **Wis** +2, **Cha** +2; **Skills** Arcana +3, Deception +4, Perception +4, Stealth +3; **Senses** darkvision 60ft; **Traits** amphibious, mimicry—imitation detect on DC 14 Wis (Insight); **AL** NE; **CR** 3; **XP** 700.
    Innate Spells: at will—*dancing lights, minor illusion, vicious mockery*
    Green Hag Coven: When all three members are within 30ft of each, they have additional spellcasting abilities but must share the spell slots among themselves. The caster level is at 12th with Int +5, DC 13.
    Spells (slots): 1st (4)—*identify, ray of sickness*; 2nd (3)—*hold person, locate object*; 3rd (3)—*bestow curse, counterspell, lightning bolt*; 4th (2)—*phantasmal killer, polymorph*; 5th (2)—*contact other plane, scrying*; 6th (1)—*eyebite*

8. Main Room

This is obviously the cottage's main room, a combination kitchen and eating area with rushes strewn on the floor, some chairs, and a sturdy round dining table. A large fireplace with an iron spit and a big cauldron rises from the north wall, and two doors lead into other parts of the cottage. The **green hag** Gretchen is usually in the kitchen area near the fireplace, knitting.

Gretchen, Green Hag: AC 17; **HP** 82 (11d8+33); **Spd** 30ft; **Melee** claws (+6, 2d8+4 slashing); **SA** illusory appearance, innate spells (Cha, DC 12), invisible passage; **Str** +4, **Dex** +1, **Con** +3, **Int** +1, **Wis** +2, **Cha** +2; **Skills** Arcana +3, Deception +4, Perception +4, Stealth +3; **Senses** darkvision 60ft; **Traits** amphibious, mimicry—imitation detect on DC 14 Wis (Insight); **AL** NE; **CR** 3; **XP** 700.
    Innate Spells: at will—*dancing lights, minor illusion, vicious mockery*

9. Back Room

This room contains a few gardening tools and a large burlap sack, but it its otherwise empty. The sack contains only potatoes.

10. Bedroom

This is the bedroom for the three hag sisters. It contains three long beds and a comfortable rocking chair. The **green hag** Wretchen is usually in this room in the comfortable chair, reading and re-reading a book called *"Proper Methods for the Breeding of Cats."* If Wretchen hears any unusual noise in the cottage, garden, or out front, she whisks out the bedroom's backdoor to see if a threat is in the garden, then scrabbles rapidly up the cottage wall to the roof, where she slithers around quickly and quietly, sniffing her way, to see if she can find the source of the disturbance.

Wretchen, Green Hag: AC 17; **HP** 82 (11d8+33); **Spd** 30ft; **Melee** claws (+6, 2d8+4 slashing); **SA** illusory appearance, innate spells (Cha, DC 12), invisible passage; **Str** +4, **Dex** +1, **Con** +3, **Int** +1, **Wis** +2, **Cha** +2; **Skills** Arcana +3, Deception +4, Perception +4, Stealth +3; **Senses** darkvision 60ft; **Traits** amphibious, mimicry—imitation detect on DC 14 Wis (Insight); **AL** NE; **CR** 3; **XP** 700.
    Innate Spells: at will—*dancing lights, minor illusion, vicious mockery*

Durbenford
(DERB-in-furd)

A rural city with criminal problems

LN small city
Government overlord
Population 7073 (5446 humans; 637 halflings; 354 high elves; 212 hill dwarves; 141 gnomes; 71 half-elves; 53 half-orcs; 159 other)
Notable NPCs
    Marcus Durben, Lord of Durbenford (LE male human **veteran**)
    The Fat Man, Master of Durbenford Thieves' Guild (NE male half-orc **Rog11**)
    Maegena, Guildmistress of the Grey Rook Guild (LE female human **Rog14**)
    Mother Tara, High Priestess of the Shattered Sword (LG female human **Clr9** of the Shattered Sword)

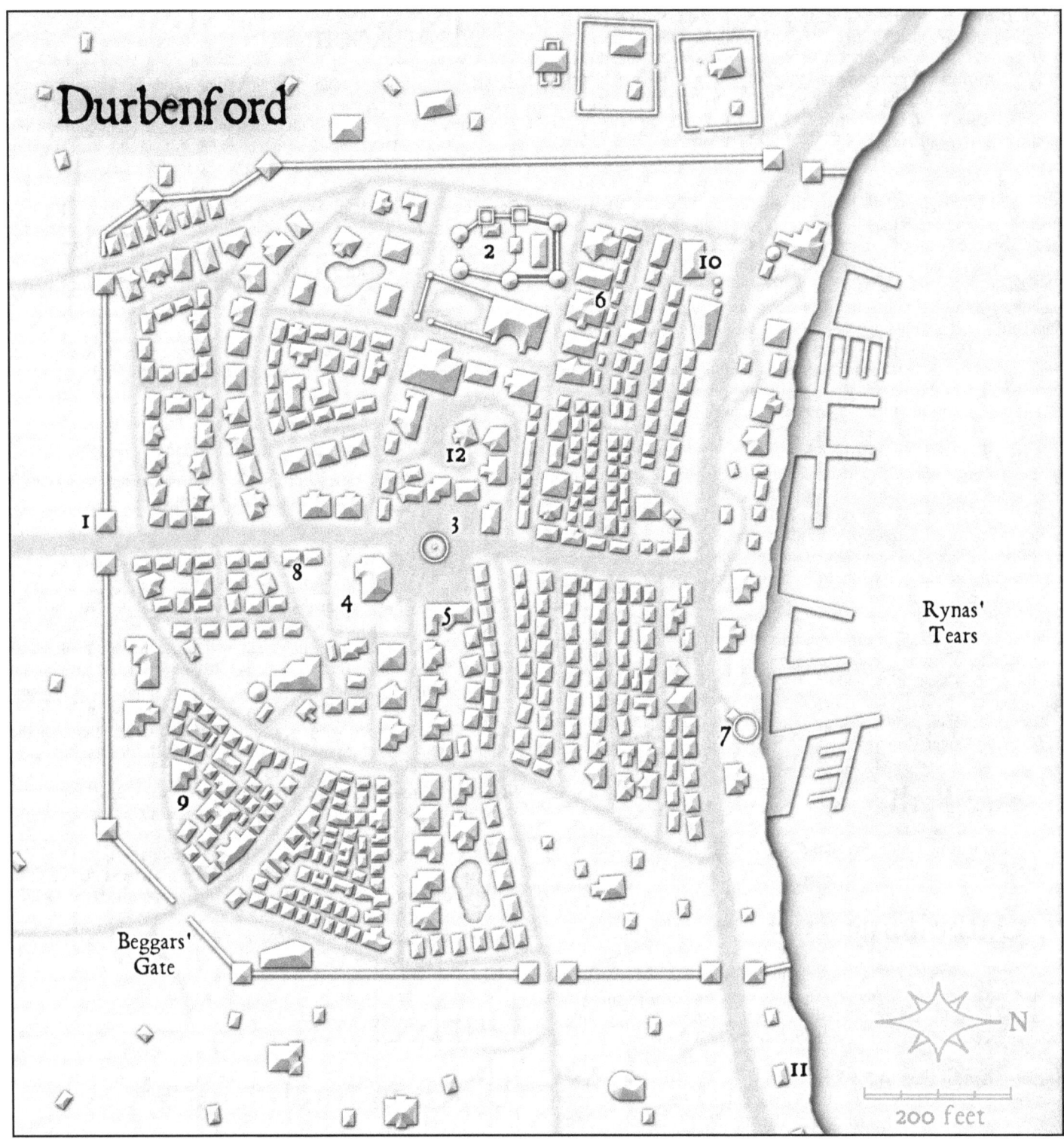

Durbenford

Beggars'
Gate

Rynas'
Tears

200 feet

Maximum Clerical Spell Level Good 5, Neutral 5, Evil 2
(hidden)
Purchase Maximum/Month 16,000gp

Durbenford is primarily a lumbering town, but it provides a very significant benefit to the County of Toullen to which it declared fealty (seceding
from the Duchy of Saxe) when Toullen changed fealty to the Kingdom of
Suilley. Durbenford is the most remote possession of the Kingdom of Suilley, which the folk of Durbenford refer to simply as "The Northern Kingdom." The particular species of pine tree native to the Durbenford region
grows extremely straight, making them highly desirable for ship's masts
and other specific uses. More information about Durbenford is available
in the d20 adventure ***Trouble in Durbenford*** published by **Necromancer
Games**. The module is available digitally at froggodgames.com.

Kal'Iugus Mountains

See **Chapter 7: The March of Mountains, *Kal'Iugus Mountains***.

The Notquite Inn

See **Chapter 6: Keston Province, *The Notquite Inn***. The Notquite Inn
is located at the intersection of three borders, Keston, Exeter, and Toullen,
and is not ruled by any of the three.

Tertry

(TER-tree)

A backwater capital, but host to the most prestigious tournament in the Borderlands

NG large city
Government overlord
Population 13,593 (10,003 humans; 1312 half-elves; 880 halflings; 526 high elves; 442 hill dwarves; 350 other)
Notable NPCs
 Luthien I, Count-Palatine of Toullen (NG male human **Ftr6**)
 Cyrilinde the Lance, sister of Luthien (LG female human **Pal12** of Muir)
 Sir Gillobert Omphry, Master of the Revels (N male human **Brd4**)
 Lord Parzalon Mothcandle, Commander of the Guard (LN male human **Ftr7**)
 Ruthenvais the Fair (LG male human **Clr9** of Thyr)
 Quilverin Opaque (N male human **Clr8** of Pan)
 Parale Greenguild, Guildmaster of Thieves (N female human **Rog12**)
Maximum Clerical Spell Level Good 5, Neutral 4, Evil 3 (hidden)
Purchase Maximum/Month 32,000gp

Appearance

The city of Tertry is a forest of small towers bounded by a strong stone wall, with a river running through the middle of the city. A large, permanent field of tournaments and jousting is laid out beyond the city walls.

Description

Tertry is the capital of the County of Toullen, but far more importantly to the Toullenese, it is the site of the annual Tournament of Lilies on the great lists and fields beyond the city walls.

Government

The Count's palace is located in the city, and the Count reserves the power to veto any decisions made by the city for its own government, although this feudal privilege is seldom invoked. Subject to the Count's veto, a council made up of an unusually diverse group governs the city. The Master of Revels, who is responsible for the tournament, is one of the members of the city's council. The Count's official jester is also a member of the council. More prosaic members are two council seats appointed by the city's guilds, one commoner popularly elected by the people, one member of noble descent also selected by popular vote, one representative of the King of Suilley, and the city's High Priest of Thyr.

The Tournament of Lilies

The annual Tournament of Lilies is the highest event in the calendar of all Toullen. The fields around the city begin filling up a month before the tournament with knights from all over the Provinces, far beyond Toullen's own borders. Pavilion tents fly long banners proclaiming the heraldry and lineages of the knights within, minstrels compose songs extolling the skills of their patrons, bookmakers stroll from one area to another taking bets, and the Master of Revels employs twice his normal staff just keeping matters from devolving into utter chaos.

The Tournament is composed of several different contests, divided into three categories. The first category allows knights from any realm to participate in the individual jousts, and is the main event of the Tourney. Winning the Crown of Lilies is a matter of pride for provinces as far as Eastreach. Foreign knights participate in a number of qualifying jousts to limit the number of contestants once the true tournament begins.

The second category is the least of the events, being competitions other than jousting, and is open to the peasantry. Such competitions include wrestling, archery, quarterstaff, pig-hurling, and horse racing, to name but a few.

The third category is often called the Tournaments of the Realm, for only the Count's subjects may participate in these jousts. Patronage from one of the 15 High Barons or from the Count himself is required in order to allow a knight to enter the Tournaments of the Realm. The least prestigious of the Tournaments of the Realm is the Peasants' Tourney, once held for comedic value, but which has become so serious that the Toullenese High Barons now sponsor talented rural jousters by providing loaned armor and warhorses. Victory in the Peasants' Tourney leads to immediate offers of employment from barons in their personal forces, and represents a tremendous improvement in the life of whatever talented peasant managed to defeat all others.

The next most prestigious Tournament of the Realm is the Warriors' Tourney, limited to members of the class "at arms," generally professional soldiers of all kinds, from city guards to royal or baronial regular troops. The winner in this Tournament is invariably knighted on the jousting field.

The third and most prestigious Tournament of the Realm is almost as important to the folk of Toullen as the Crown of Lilies. This is the "Count's Tournament," and it is open only to Toullenese of the noble or knightly classes. As with the other Tournaments of the Realm, the Count's Tournament requires patronage by one of the High Barons of the Realm, and also requires that a contestant has placed high in the lists of a qualifying lesser tournament in one of the County's towns.

Victories and placing in the Tournaments of the Realm (including the lesser ones) has become a matter of incalculable prestige for the High Barons. All the country perceives a High Baron's sponsored contestants as a kind of team, even though they all compete separately. The audiences at the Tournament carry flags of their faction, engage in brawls with followers of other factions, and generally show an almost-religious fervor. The importance of winning and placing in the tournament now translates directly into political power; barons have switched allegiances from one High Baron to another based on consistently poor results in the lists. Moreover, the High Barons whose sponsored contestants win first, second, and third place in a tournament each exempt all the High Baron's vassals from one of nine taxes levied by the Count. The tournament exemptions are generally divided among different High Barons, for it is highly unusual for a single faction to sweep first through third place in all three divisions of the Tournaments of the Realm, but it has happened a few times in the County's history. Thus, even the peasantry benefits when their High Baron's faction wins one or more divisions of the Tournaments.

Adventure

High-Baron Lucard of Saltfalcon is concerned that there is a plan underway by local gamblers, or possibly one of the other high baronial houses, to sabotage the horses of his jousters in the next Tournament of Lilies. He wants to hire some people (probably low-level characters) who cannot be recognized as members of his entourage to keep an eye on the stables, and ensure that no one other than his own handlers and jousters gain access to them. There is indeed a plot to sabotage the horses, and the characters will have to deal with a stealthy attempt to gain access to the stables by hired rogues.

Toullen Pass

A heavily patrolled mountain pass connecting east and west Toullen

The Toullen Pass lies 100 miles southwest of Tertry, and provides a fairly level, low-altitude crossing of the Kal'Iugus Mountains to reach

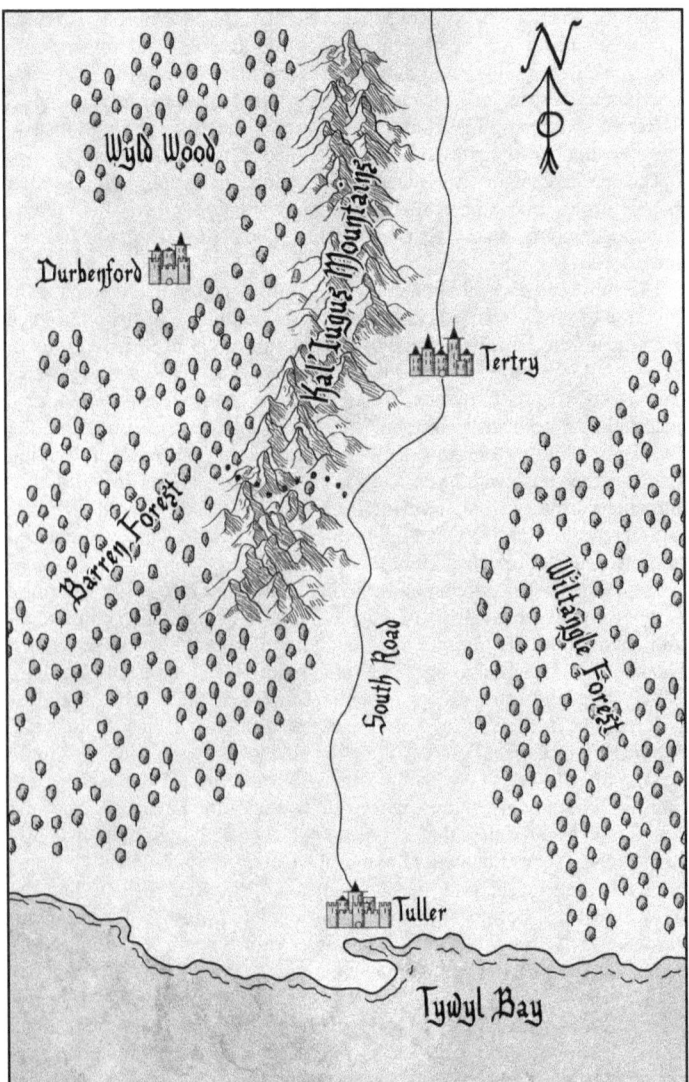

Merchant's Map of southern Toullen,
ink on parchment, circa 3509 I.R.

the mines and quarries of its western flanks, and the timbering industry around Durbenford. The County of Toullen employs local rangers to maintain watchposts and waystations along the pass, providing security for the vitally important caravans making their way to Tertry and beyond.

Tuller

(TULL-er)

The only seaport in Suilley's feudal empire, Tuller is barely under anyone's authority

N small city
Government council
Population 6840 (4126 humans [Foerdewaith]; 1854 humans [Heldring]; 833 half-elves; 27 other)
Notable NPCs
　Mayor Bendigond Lune (LN male human **noble**)
　Jules Canard, Minister of Law (N male human **noble**)
　Tseshion Tash, High Priest of Quell (N male human **Clr9** of Quell)
　Jeralynd Seaforth, High Priestess of Sefagreth (N female human **Clr9** of Sefagreth)

Loramorthius, prominent wizard (N male human **Wiz11**)
Maximum Clerical Spell Level Good 5, Neutral 5, Evil 2
Purchase Maximum/Month 16,000gp

Appearance

Tuller is a seaport city located on a small, deep harbor. It has high walls of a green-tinged stone, and a round citadel flying the flag of Toullen: a yellow jousting helm on a black field, with a green fleur-de-lis in the corner. A small island lies in the harbor, its land area completely occupied by a pillared temple with attached outbuildings, all made of stone.

Description

Though Tuller is the only seaport accessible to the Kingdom of Suilley, and a small flotilla is maintained there to fend off pirates on Tywyl Bay, the kingdom nevertheless conducts very little trade through the port. There is a modest stream of seaborne trade between Tuller and the western ports of the Helcynngae Peninsula to the east, and with some ports of the Southern Reach to the west, but the merchants of Manas generally prefer to send their goods overland to ports such as Endhome or Eastgate where prices are higher.

Government and Law Enforcement

Tuller elects a mayor, but the city is governed by a council of ministers also elected by the city's landowners. There is a Harbor Minister, a Minister of Taxes, a Minister of Buildings and Land, and so forth. Characters in the city might fall afoul of the Minister of Law, Jules Canard, who runs the city guard and the courts. Canard is willing to take bribes to release people from minor crimes, but if there was any sort of publicity to the crime, he considers it too much of a risk to let culprits walk free.

Tuller is so distant from the authority of Suilley's king that the city operates virtually free of foreign law, even the laws of the Count in Tertry. It tends to have the lax attitude of a free city, overlooking obvious pirates, smugglers, and even slavers, so long as they are foreigners and add to the city's trade. Tuller is not a pirate base, but it offers a haven to many pirate vessels as long as they are well behaved and not known for attacking ships flying the banners of Tuller itself.

Interesting Places

Temple of Quell

The priests of Quell are uninterested in the politics of the largely inland Borderland Provinces, and occupy themselves only with the veneration of their sea god. The temple is built on an island in the harbor, and the priesthood maintains that they are not subject to any secular authority, neither the laws of Suilley nor even of the Count of Toullen. The temple fronts on the sea; half of it is built lower than the rest, open to the water under a stone-pillared roof, and floods during high tide up to chest height. A large statue of the sea god stands in this lower area, washed by the seawater with each change in the tide. Offerings are left with the statue while the sea portico is dry; they are carried away on the sea when the waves recede from the flooded chamber.

In the past, the Temple of Quell has granted sanctuary to criminals from "the mainland," leading to strong protests from the city's small temple of Thyr. The clerics of Quell simply ignore such complaints, considering themselves above and beyond all landlocked authority.

Dockmarket

A large market surrounds the city's modest docks, and is one of the most cosmopolitan places in the southern half of the Borderlands. Merchants and sea captains from Farshore in Tywyl Bay, the Kingdom of the Helcynngae, Swordport in the Domain of Hawkmoon, and even Endhome can be found rubbing shoulders in the Dockmarket. Slave-rowed galleys from the Coredor Belt are studiously ignored as they sit in the harbor, and elves from the Wiltangle and Barren Forests both venture into the city to trade. Trade-goods from distant places can be found here, including strange items and rare spices. Captains with foreign names such as "Quanool Thra," "Gundr Wavejarl," and "Kelwa Phaizeng" barter for supplies with Tuller's Foerdewaith merchants. It is a good place to obtain bargains, and also a good place to negotiate sea-passage away from the Borderlands, if one has a pressing need to depart quickly.

Wiltangle Forest
(WILL-tangle)

A primordial forest of legend, deadly and vast

The Wiltangle Forest is one of the last eastern remnants of the Great Akadonian Forest, which once covered most of the continent. The majority of the Great Akadonian Forest was slowly broken up by a series of catastrophes, and by woodcutting intended to free up farmland or burn out monsters. The Wiltangle, unaffected by the fate of the rest of the continental forest, is primordial and wild, and only little explored. The folk of Toullen engage in very little woodcutting on their side of the forest, but there are a few villages and logging camps along the eastern reaches of the forest, in Cerediun Province.

Deep in the forest, more than one stone circle dating back to antiquity remain as holy sites to many druidic sects. Villages along the forest's periphery are almost universally druidic, although various gods are recognized and some even have small temples that live alongside the influence of the druids. All attempts to actually subdue the druidic faith have met utter failure in this area, not always peaceful and often

mysteriously. Such is true of the forest-edge communities in all the realms abutting the Wiltangle: Toullen, Exeter, and Cerediun.

In the days before the coming of the Hyperboreans, there were several elven kingdoms in the Wiltangle, and the Heldring referred to the forest by a name translating to "northern woodland kingdoms." A fey and deadly place for intruders, the southern reaches of the Wiltangle (farther south of the map) restricted the Heldring to their peninsula until the arrival of the Hyperboreans. Even then, the Heldring took care never to enter the forest in force.

To this day, the Wiltangle is a forest of legends: a witch queen who ruled until being transformed into a tree; ancient ruins along the riverbanks of the interior; cairns and holds of some diminutive race; and fabulous jewels recovered from a few upriver expeditions. Such tales may, of course, be exaggerated. The question, however, is not whether ancient treasures are in the Wiltangle, for there certainly are: The question is whether they are ripe for the taking or whether they are a fool's errand for those fated to die beneath leaf-green shadows.

Wyld Wood
(WILD WOOD)

The tail-end of Toullen, infested with fey creatures and pernicious druidism

The Wyld Wood is the northernmost extent of the Barren Forest, heavily lumbered by the folk of Durbenford. It is also known for its reputation as a haven for often-unfriendly druidic powers, so the loggers are ever wary of fey or wildmen who claim to protect the forest. The superstitious folk want no truck with such things of the Otherworld.

Chapter Eleven: Unclaimed Lands

The Unclaimed Lands

Overview

The Unclaimed Lands are the uncontrolled feudal lands north of the Great Amrin River and west of the Glimmrill Run until it reaches the Forest Kingdoms to the north. A few self-styled counts and barons rule in castles over a scattering of manor houses and small villages, and small groups of nomadic Erskaelosi wander here and there, but the region is mostly given over to wild forests, unexplored hills, and uncultivated meadowland. Several small tributaries flow from the Unclaimed Lands to the Great Amrin and the Glimmrill, some of which are deep enough to allow trade by raft or even keelboat.

General Information

Alignment: CE
Capital: none
Notable Settlements: Turpin (812)
Ruler: none (local freeholders and robber knights)
Government: none
Population: 337,400 (238,000 Foerdewaith; 61,200 Erskaelosi; 26,300 half-orcs; 8,700 high elves; 3,200 hill dwarves)
Humanoid: half-orc (some), high elf (some), hill dwarf (few)
Monstrous: lion, giant snake, goblin dog, centaur, goblin, giant falcon, orc, gnoll, hyaenodon, fey, ratfolk, jack-o-lantern, ogre, inphidian (plains); giant catfish, giant snake, fuath gremlin, nixie, water weird (waterways)
Languages: Common, Erskin, Orc, Elvish, Dwarvish
Religion: Freya, Bowbe, Tykee, Archeillus, Moccavallo, Pan, Grotaag, Bacchus-Dionysus
Resources: grain, mercenaries, livestock (sheep), wool, plunder
Technology Level: Dark Age

Borders and Lands

The Unclaimed Lands have no defined borders, representing an area unclaimed by any of its neighboring states. As a general rule, it is considered to be the area north of the Great Amrin and west of the Glimmrill Run, extending westward along the coast toward Bard's Gate.

History and People

The Unclaimed Lands were conquered by Oerson in the early days of the Hyperborean invasion, and benefited greatly from Hyperborean government under the Empire. However, after the dark years following the Empire's fall, the civilizing influence of the Kingdoms of Foere never sufficiently reached across the Great Amrin River to the Unclaimed Lands, and the region has remained little improved throughout the Foerdewaith hegemony. New roads were never built, taxes were never standardized, no common currency was introduced, and trade never rebuilt itself. With a few exceptions, the Unclaimed Lands remains a window upon the dark age following the Fall of the Hyperborean .

Court of Loom Ché

(loom CHAY)

Loom Ché is a denizen of Leng, once the captain of a black ship that traveled the skies of strange worlds and sailed across the boundaries of the planes of existence. Unfortunately, he caught a strange disease while the ship was resting in this isolated part of the Unclaimed Lands. Whenever he tries to cross any of the major planar boundaries, millions of tiny spiders form within his body and erupt from his every orifice, an extraordinarily unpleasant symptom that lasts for hours. With no desire to continue traveling across the planes of existence under these conditions, Loom Ché has embarked upon a career as what he considers a "local" trader.

The Court of Loom Ché has become a base of operations for those who shift between dimensions, those who stalk the boundaries of reality, and those who journey beyond materiality into other planes of existence. It is a place where few humans dare to tread, for the morals and intentions of the Court's other visitors are bizarre and often entirely alien. The oni known as ogre magi are always the largest population in the Court, although there are also often creatures of mixed supernatural bloodlines (tieflings), hags, rakshasas, Leng-denizens, and the occasional neh-thalggu. Loom Ché dislikes the company of demons and fey creatures, so these are not found at the Court, although he tolerates humans of diluted demonic and fey bloodlines. For some reason, Loom Ché finds halflings immensely entertaining, and the very few who are willing to go anywhere remotely near the Court are welcomed into Loom Ché's presence to tell him stories while he chuckles and claps his hands with glee.

From time to time, Loom Ché travels from one place to another in his black ship, a massive, sailing ship that resembles a Chinese junk. His debilitating disease does not flare up badly from mere dimensional travel within the same plane of existence, so he is able to make rapid trips to several places in the Lost Lands that are located along the dimensional streams near his home "port." The ship can fly, but it is relatively slow when not being used to traverse gaps between dimensions. The other "ports" where Loom Ché trades are in Lower Khemit far to the east (a journey of two weeks through the misty seas of the dimensions), the City of Endhome (a one-week journey), Mirquinoc (a one-week journey), Remballo (a one-week journey) and Bard's Gate (a one-week journey). He also, very infrequently, brings a cargo of food and alchemical materials to a mage called Jupiter Kwan who lives in a dimensional rift that Loom Ché can reach without causing his symptoms to flare up more than they do from a trip from point to point in the ordinary world (a one-week journey).

Travel over the misty seas of the dimensional rifts is not perfectly accurate, and Loom Ché's navigation is imprecise, so the ship's arrival in the skies of the targeted destination may be off-target by as much as 100 miles, requiring material-plane flight to reach the exact location sought.

Given the unpleasant side effects of any travel on the ship, Loom Ché tends to remain at the Court most of the time, buying and selling commodities from other traders and taking a share of their transactions with each other.

The Court itself is a massive edifice built of dinosaur-like bones Loom Ché bought cheaply from a Leng-ship captained by an inexperienced merchant who badly misread the market demand for such things. The tower of bones rises 200 feet in the air, and has long flanges at the top where up to three flying vessels can moor at a time for unloading cargo. The ground level of the tower and an outside courtyard are the "market" of the Court, the five lower levels of the tower are guest rooms for visitors, and the rest of the tower is Loom Ché's domain.

Most of the commerce in Loom Ché's Court consists of slaves, souls, gems (especially rubies), strange furs of distant origin, magical items, bizarre spices, drugs, and pets (some of which can be staggeringly dangerous). Another business he engages in is to move money around for the House of Borgandy (see **Chapter 9: Kingdom of Suilley,** *Remballo*). Their letter of credit business can cause shortfalls of actual gold coins in the different cities where they operate, and Loom Ché transports supplies of gold to the family's counting-houses in Endhome, Mirquinoc, and Bard's Gate.

produce goods for the rural countryside and the outlying baronial villages. The rest of the village's business, however, is sinister and reprehensible, depending on pirate loot and occasional overland banditry.

A variety of traders in Turpin buy the stolen cargo of the pirates after Count Ranquin takes his share, and then travel forth to sell the merchandise, usually within the borders of the Unclaimed Lands, where no law follows them. Some are brazen enough to place cargoes on their own keelboats and proceed down the Great Amrin into the port of Eastgate, selling the stolen goods as if they had come all the way from Bard's Gate with the cargo.

Turpin
(TERP-en)

A megalomaniacal nobleman and his pirate followers

CE village
Government overlord
Population 812 (422 humans [Foerdewaith]; 196 humans [Erskaelosi]; 123 half-orcs; 37 hill dwarves; 24 half-elves; 10 high elves)
Notable NPCs
   Count Jonas Ranquin (CE male human **Ftr9**)
   Bandas, Erskaelosi war captain (CN male human **Bbn8**)
   Runefarc, Erskaelosi shaman (NE male human **Clr5** of Bowbe)
Maximum Clerical Spell Level Good —, Neutral 2, Evil 3
Purchase Maximum/Month 2000gp

The village of Turpin is the comitial seat of the self-styled "Count" Jonas Ranquin, who holds three vassal baronies within 25 miles of the town. Count Ranquin is the mastermind and the financier behind many of the river-pirate operations on the Great Amrin River, owning several small keelboats of his own. The Count's symbol, a fish speared on a trident, is prominently displayed on the sails of these ships, marking them as pirates but also signaling that if a merchant surrenders to them immediately and does not attempt to flee, they reliably accept half of the riverboat's cargo and allow the boat to go free with the remainder and without harm or loss of life.

Turpin is located on the banks of one of the Great Amrin's tributaries, a small but navigable waterway called the Dwellerflow. Count Ranquin's keelboats make their way down to the Great Amrin along the Dwellerflow, strike at their targets, and then return to town to sell the loot. Bard's Gate and the Province of Eastreach know the Count's name and his approximate whereabouts from captured raiders, but thus far the only punitive expeditions have been fought off by Count Ranquin's forces.

Despite its small size, Turpin is a walled village. The Count's Keep forms the citadel, and curtain walls 20ft tall surround the town. The only other towers along the wall are those flanking the gatehouse. Much of the town's business is the everyday commerce of a county seat: a weekly market day, a fair day every two months, the Count's court held every second week, and so forth. Cobblers, potters, blacksmiths, and weavers

Chapter Twelve: County of Vourdon

County of Vourdon

(VORE-dun)

An independent vassal-state of the Foerdewaith overking, caught between the receding empire and the growing power of Suilley

Overview

The County of Vourdon is a vassal state of the Overking in Foere, with a great deal of independence from the distant rule of Courghais. It is a peaceful and productive land, enjoying good diplomatic and trade relations with its neighbors on either side of the March of Mountains.

General Information

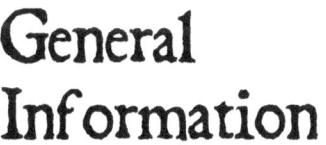

COUNTY OF VOURDON

Alignment: LN
Capital: Olaric (19,297)
Notable Settlements: Shullcross (3,100), Yllec (982)
Ruler: His Excellency Peilorth Rhombard I, Count-Palatine of Vourdon, Earl of the South Rampart Marches (LN male human Ftr9)
Government: feudalism (palatine county of Foere)
Population: 914,400 (768,000 Foerdewaith; 68,500 hill dwarves; 50,100 halflings; 21,000 half-elves; 6400 high elves)
Humanoid: hill dwarf (many), halfling (many), half-elf (some), high elf (some)
Monstrous: ankheg, goblin, fey, smilodon (valley); spider-eye goblin, giant stag and boar, smilodon, forlarren, forest troll, owlbear, dryad, green dragon (forest); cave lion, hill giant, griffon, giant eagle, cave moray (mountains)
Languages: Common, Gasquen, Dwarvish, Halfling, Elvish
Religion: Telophus, Ceres, Sefagreth, Thyr (declining), Pan, Hester, Archeillus, Freya, Stryme, Dwerfater, Bacchus-Dionysus, Moccavallo
Resources: spirits (wine, brandy), flax, grain, foodstuffs (grapes, apples, pears), linen, livestock (sheep, swine), wool
Technology Level: Medieval

Borders and Lands

The County of Vourdon extends through the gap between the Meridian and Rampart ranges, from the verge of the Shadrack Forest (just west of Shullcross) to approximately 100 miles east of Olaric, 100 miles north of Olaric, and 150 miles south of Olaric.

History and People

The County of Vourdon was established by decree of the Overking in the year 2822, thus incorporating a region that had been a largely ungoverned expanse since the days of Hyperborea that lay between the Kingdom of Foere and the outlying Province of Suilley. Lords and barons with their bloodlines dating back to the Hyperborean Age were required to pledge fealty to the new Count, whose seat of government would be Caer Sferic near the thriving market town of Olaric. When the Archmage Quaoule destroyed Caer Sferic in a fit of pique, the Count's surviving retainers brought the Throne of Harts to the town of Olaric itself, eventually building the Comital Palace to house it properly. In default of living heirs to the Countship, the Overking appointed a new great house to the position, and so began the still-surviving dynasty of the House of Rhombard.

In the Fiend Rains of 3439, Vourdon was subjected to massive flooding, its rivers becoming deluges, and its lower-lying pastures becoming stagnant lakes. Unlike the catastrophic failure in Toullen, the County of Vourdon, under the leadership of Count Lorn of House Rhombard, responded immediately to the catastrophe. All the great mages of the country were summoned to Olaric to hear the Edict of Rains, which ordered them to different tasks in accordance with their capabilities, knowledge, and prestige. By means of great magicks, and an unprecedented level of cooperation, the mages excavated a number of deep weirs along the March of Mountains, raised ramparts and dykes around many of the larger towns, and bound earth elementals to the task of cutting massive drainage canals to channel the mountain runoff down to the lower-lying regions of Suilley and Keston. The wizards Thylimeles, Fernijan, and Xolobar worked together (reportedly using the lost secrets of Alycthron and Margon) to raise the city of Olaric itself to an altitude 10ft higher than its original standing. All but the owners of the numerous collapsed buildings considered this a small price to pay for such security. The mages also created great terraces carved from the mountain rock east of the capital (using the same unknown magic) to stop rockslides and to abate surges of water during the heaviest rain.

Due to this orderly and expansive reaction to the flooding, the Fiend Rains affected Vourdon considerably less than they damaged the surrounding regions. Some of the canals are still in use, connecting towns by waterway. The artificial mountain terraces are now home to fertile vineyards that produce the mediocre vintages of wine for which Olaric is justifiably not famous but sells in great quantity across the continent to establishments and wine cellars less interested in quality and more interested in price and availability.

In the year 3222, when the Lord-Governor of Suilley declared himself to be an independent monarch, the Count of Vourdon declined the Overking's demand to send troops against the rebellious new kingdom, citing obscure matters of feudal law. As a result, diplomatic relations between the County of Vourdon and the Kingdom of Suilley have always been friendly and amicable.

> *"Many sages, myself included, hold that the miserable quality of the Vourdon grape comes from magical residue. The grape is grown on mountain terraces carved out by earth elementals and other great magic during the floods, and it is possible that the earth contains strange, unnatural minerals as a result. Perhaps the magical residues will fade, and the quality of the grapes improve over time. One can only hope."*
>
> —*Essay Upon Wine*, by Mondrat of High Ribbon, Court Sage of Vourdon in the City of Olaric, submitted to the University of Vermis in 3507.

Trade and Commerce

The County of Vourdon is an exclusively agricultural region, and initiates very little trade beyond its borders other than linen, bad wine, brandy, and small quantities of flax oil. A number of merchant caravans pass through Olaric on the way into and out of Foere along the South County Road, which is a safe and pleasant route. The length of the road from Olaric to Shullcross, while very hilly, is a pleasant journey, lined with fields of flax that turn into a sea of blue during the flowering season. Orchards cover the hillsides, and great terraces carved into the mountains are overburdened with the yellow grapes of Vourdon. Fortified stone chateaux may be seen in the distance, usually on hilltops from which the owner can look over the lands and farms of the fiefdom.

Olaric and Shullcross are both below the highland gap between the Rampart Mountains and the Meridians. Shullcross is a lumbering town, and Olaric is surrounded by fields of golden wheat. Other than farming, Olaric's main industries are manufacturing linen from flax, selling barrels of "cask-quality" wine, and distilling brandy. Distillation in Olaric is a primitive process of mixing grain alcohol into wine, then distilling the mixture. The brandy is consumed in sailors' taverns and questionable dives across the Provinces, just as the wine is imbibed in the manors of impoverished knights and the houses of miserly merchants.

The linen industry in Olaric produces fabrics with a wide variety of quality, some of which are suitable to be worn by kings. The lowest-quality flax fibers are woven into rope and twine, and the long ropewalk in Olaric is always a hive of activity.

Loyalties and Diplomacy

The County of Vourdon is an independent feudal state, subject to the Overking of Foere.

Diplomatic relations with the adjacent Kingdom of Suilley are extremely good, partially based on the fact that Vourdon never attacked Suilley during Suilley's war of secession, but also due to trade along the South County Road directly between the capitals, and general sense that the two realms are quite similar in culture and outlook.

The King of Suilley constantly attempts to woo the Count of Vourdon into switching their allegiance from Foere to Suilley, making lucrative trade agreements and bestowing gifts. Thus far, all diplomatic efforts in this regard have failed, albeit very cordially. Vourdon's status as an independent feudal realm under Foere's protection is a comfortable situation for the Counts of Vourdon, and they see no need to go through the turmoil of changing their fealty.

Of late, however, Foere has made some onerous demands upon the County, calling up a number of troops to join the Overking's army, and levying several new taxes. If the trend continues, too many demands from Foere might certainly cause the Count to rethink his current loyalties.

Government

The Countship of Vourdon is a hereditary title currently held by Count Peilourth Rhombard, second of his name. Below the rank of Count, the country has High Barons as in Toullen, with barons below the high barons and knights below the barons. The Count of Vourdon has only 5 high barons in his council, which means that the high barons exert considerable power in the country. On one occasion, four of the high barons threatened a civil war if the Count enacted a particular law, forcing the Count to withdraw the proposal.

Wilderness and Adventure

Vourdon is safe enough that wandering the villages looking for adventure yields relatively poor results, although there are always small groups of bandits to chase, and the occasional predator from the adjoining mountain ranges. Most adventurers in the country are drawn to the mountain terraces, for when these were carved from the mountainsides, some few of them revealed ancient catacombs that had been underground until the removal of countless tons of rock. There are not many of these, but a few expeditions into some have discovered that many of the passageways are of worked stone, their origins completely unknown. Moreover, they are home to a number of dangerous predators and contain ancient treasures. Little organized exploration of these catacombs has been attempted; their terraces are left unfarmed, and the folk of the mountainsides avoid them. It is possible that some of these catacombs are the source of predators that emerge from the mountains, although the high peaks of the mountains certainly house a variety of fell beasts.

Changing Times

Vourdon has not suffered excessively from the retreat of Foere's influence, although the demands of the Overking are increasing as their taxes and military power wane. Large numbers of troops have been requested, although so far the Count has avoided sending more than the bare minimum. The tax burden is a bit more serious, and causes consternation among the nobles. Thus far, the County's status as an independent vassal has allowed it to dodge or reduce several tax levies, but demands from the Court of Courghais are becoming more strident and threatening.

At the same time, diplomatic overtures from the Kingdom of Suilley continue, offering potentially enormous benefits to the County if it were to throw off the reins of Foere and offer its fealty to the Suilleyn king. The concern, however, is that even as weak as the Kingdoms of Foere have become, they could still potentially overwhelm Vourdon before any help could arrive from Suilley. The County of Vourdon is no warrior nation, much as its knights believe otherwise, and its peaceful lands provide a desperately needed flow of gold and food into the Foerdewaith heartlands. The Count is justifiably concerned that if Vourdon shifted its allegiance, Foere might not just accept the situation as it did with the secessions of Keston Province and the County of Toullen. War would be a definite possibility, and Vourdon is not prepared for such a conflict. Even more vexing, if Suilley's power continues to expand, while that of Foere weakens, the friendly persuasions of the King of Suilley might change their tone into demands or threats.

Caught between kingdoms, given choices of an increasingly demanding overlord, the potential of ruinous war against that overlord, or possibly waiting too late to join with Suilley on good terms, the Count of Vourdon waits. With good luck, some new event will arise to give him better leverage against the demands of the Overking. With bad luck, some new event may force his hand and require him to rush to Suilley, risking bloody retribution from Foere.

Meridian Range

See entry under **March of Mountains**.

Olaric

(oh-LAR-ic)

Peaceful provincial capital in the midst of a holy cold war

N large city
Government overlord
Population 19,297 (18,102 humans; 995 halflings; 170 half-elves; 30 other)
Notable NPCs
 Count-Palatine Peilorth Rhombard (LN male human **Ftr9**)
 Lord-Mayor Margaine Fleur (N female human **noble**)
 Olarine of Misc, Justiciar of Vourdon (LN female human **courtier**)
 Archbishop Gerald Harvesttide (LN male human **Clr9** of Telophus)
 Loraldo Mnemodoc, Court Advisor (N male human **Clr8** of Jamboor)
 Trevin the Puppeteer, High Priest of Moccavallo (NE male human **Clr7** of Moccavallo)
 Magister Yaunte, Court Mage (N male human **Wiz11**)
 Aureilia the Resplendent, Prominent Sorceress (N female human **Sor11**)
Maximum Clerical Spell Level Good —, Neutral 5, Evil 4
Purchase Maximum/Month 32,000gp

Approach

Olaric's walls are not high, but they are serviceable enough to protect the city against any attacks short of a true siege. Slender towers around the wall rise to dramatic, conical roofs where the banner of Olaric (a bunch of yellow grapes on a field of green) and the Rhombard family (a red lion on black and white) fly proudly over the city. Four gates lead into the city to admit the high roads from the realms surrounding Vourdon, which cross in the city center.

Description

Olaric, also often spelled Olaaric, is the capital of Vourdon and seat

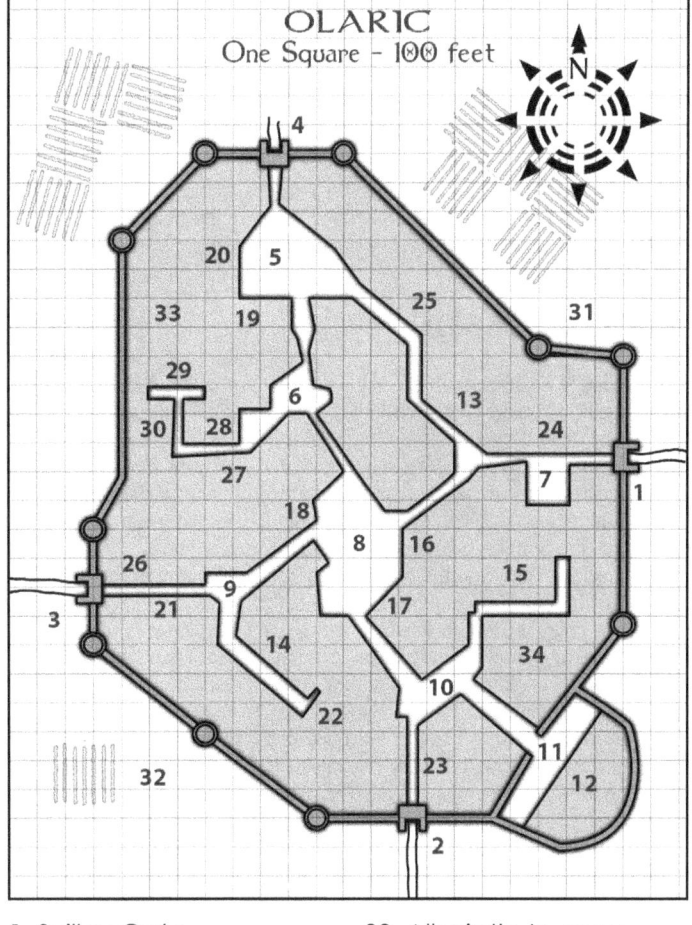

OLARIC
One Square - 100 feet

1. Suilley Gate
2. Kestongate
3. Shullsgate
4. Northgate
5. Flaxmarket Plaza
6. Pork Plaza
7. Tater Square
8. Grand Market Square
9. Cowpiddle Court
10. Citadel Square
11. Petitioners' Yard
12. Citadel
13. Warehouse Way
14. Shortfellow's Walk
15. Distillery Lane
16. Ropemakers' Guild (ball of twine)
17. Temple of Telophus
18. Comital Palace
19. Priory of Sefagreth (accommodations)
20. Albaird's Journey Supplies
21. Temple of Moccavallo
22. Temple of Hester and Ceres
23. The Bacon-Eater Inn
24. The Troll's Tankard Inn
25. Warehouses
26. The Good Knight Inn
27. Temple Way
28. Temple of Thyr
29. Shrines of Freya, Tykee, and Solanus
30. Chapel-Crypt of Jamboor
31. Paupers' Graveyard
32. Fairgrounds
33. Aureilia's Tower
34. Palazzo Yaunte

of Count Peilorth Rhombard. The city is quite provincial, but pleasant. Indeed, the royal family of Ulrich, king of Suilley, has on more than one occasion summered in the upland wine country of the County, and guested at the Comital Palace here.

Olaric's main industries are wheat-farming, manufacturing linen from the flax fields of the West Country, and distilling low-quality brandy. A few merchant houses are based here, but the majority of buying and selling is conducted by factors from merchant houses in Troye and Manas. As a flax-producer, the city also boasts the largest ball of twine in all of Foere, which is likely an accurate claim. It is displayed in the hall of the Ropemakers' Guild, for those who wish to see it; admission is free.

Recent Events

At the moment, there is a moratorium on arresting heretics in Olaric. The reasons are complex, and described in the "Adventure" section below. If characters are just passing through the city, it is enough to know that witch-hunters are not allowed to arrest heretics at the moment, and that several heretics from the countryside are enjoying the temporary sanctuary offered by the city's internal religious squabbling.

Map of Olaric

1. *Suilley Gate* The South County road enters into the gatehouse, where customs-officials and guards collect the gate-tax. Two gibbets are set up outside the gate, both containing bones of traitors to the Count.

2. *Kestongate* The South Road enters the city here through a gatehouse, with guards and tax-collectors stationed in the tunnel-like archway through the gatehouse. Three heads are mounted on pikes at the top of the gatehouse, the remains of thieves who were convicted here.

3. *Shullsgate* The South County Road between Olaric and Shullcross enters the city here, where gate-taxes are collected.

4. *Northgate* The South Road to and from Troye enters the city here through a strong gatehouse. Customs officials collect taxes.

5. *Flaxmarket Plaza* A large market mostly dedicated to buying and selling massive bales and wagon-loads of flax from the countryside.

6. *Pork Plaza* This square is surrounded by slaughterhouses, and the flagstones often run with blood. The city is trying to force the slaughterhouses to move farther away from the city center, but so far they have had no success.

7. *Tater Square* Once a market for potatoes and other crops, trade with Suilley has turned the open area into a market for other goods as well.

8. *Grand Market Square* This is the center of the city, and it is usually crowded with wagons and merchants. This is where most of the permanent shops of the city are to be found, including jewelers, fur traders, high-quality clothiers, and armorers. This is also where heretics are burned and criminals hanged. The gallows is in the center of the plaza, and the Temple of Telophus has built a large pyre of wood with four posts for burning heretics as a threat to the Temple of Moccavallo.

9. *Cowpiddle Court* This small market is in the process of being enlarged, and buildings around it are being demolished.

10. *Citadel Square* This square is surrounded by the offices of lawyers, scribes, and accountants who are not permitted to operate businesses anywhere else in the city.

11. *Petitioners' Yard* This is the courtyard of the citadel where those with lawsuits and complaints wait to be admitted to the citadel.

12. *Citadel* The citadel is a massive fortress, and also contains the municipal courts, the offices of the Lord-Mayor, city tax-offices, the treasury, the mint, the dungeon, and the office of the Justiciar of Vourdon.

13. *Warehouse Way* This long avenue passes through a lightly populated part of the city where the closely-packed townhouses of the city center give way to cottages with large gardens and several large warehouses.

14. *Shortfellow's Walk* This street runs through an area preferred by the city's halflings. A number of burrow-houses and low-ceilinged taverns are interspersed with buildings sized for taller folk.

15. *Distillery Lane* Several different businesses operate along this street, but brandy distillers are specifically limited to working along this street, so there are a number of small distilleries and brandy warehouses down the length of the lane.

16. *Ropemakers' Guild* The Ropemakers' Guild has the largest ball of twine in the world available for display free of charge.

17. *Cathedral of Telophus* This soaring stone building has a large courtyard behind it where various outbuildings house clerics, acolytes, a school, and the home of Archbishop Harvesttide himself.

18. *Comital Palace* The palace of the Count-Palatine of Vourdon. This is a square of fortified buildings around a pleasant garden courtyard.

19. *Priory of Sefagreth* The priory of Sefagreth offers rooms at reasonable rates, along with a chapel to the god of trade and commerce and a minimum of proselytizing. The priory maintains a list of caravan guards available for hire in the city.

20. *Albaird's Journey Supplies* Most of the basic supplies needed for adventuring are sold here as caravan supplies. It is a convenient one-stop shop.

21. *Temple of Moccavallo* This is a small temple, with a banner outside advertising a play called "Falsehood of Seasons" performed daily in the temple courtyard.

22. *Temple of Hester and Ceres* A traditional temple of the two goddesses.

23. *The Bacon-Eater Inn* A safe and secure inn known for the quality of its bacon.

24. *The Troll's Tankard Inn* A rough inn with low rates frequented by visiting farmers who can't afford better.

25. *Warehouses* Betrando's Warehouse is here, where the players of the "Falsehood of Seasons" are concealed, along with several other warehouses, mostly holding flax or linen.

26. *The Good Knight Inn* This inn has a sign of a glowing paladin on horseback, and at night the paladin actually glows. It is a decent-quality inn, with a common dormitory for farmers and several private rooms for wealthier visitors.

27. *Temple Way* This street contains several temples and small shrines, as marked.

28. *Temple of Thyr* The temple of Thyr once occupied several buildings here, but most of them are now leased to law-abiding craftsmen: candlemakers and the like. The temple itself is falling into disrepair, but is still an impressive building.

29. *Shrines of Freya, Mitra, Tykee, and Solanus* These one-room chapels are separated along the street by residences. The shrines of Mitra and Freya are both in negotiations to buy surrounding buildings so that they can expand, but the sellers are holding out for higher prices.

30. *Chapel-Crypt of Jamboor* This large building has extensive crypts and catacombs below, and stores the bones of those who can afford to be housed there. There is an attached library building and a school that teaches basic reading, writing, and math to future clerks.

31. *Paupers' Graveyard* This is where the city's poor are buried.

32. *Fairgrounds* When the city holds a fair, every three months or so, this area is crowded with peasants, tents, and the pavilions of knights who attend the tournaments.

33. *Aureilia's Tower* This is the tower of the powerful sorceress Aureilia.

34. *Palazzo Yaunte* This sprawling mansion is the home and workshop of Magister Yaunte, who advises the Count on arcane matters and conducts secret experiments in his workshops.

Adventure: Heretical per Fiat Canonical

Although Olaric is generally a peaceful place interested only in bucolic matters, there is a bit of religious excitement going on at the moment: a dispute between the Church of Telophus and the Temple of Moccavallo. At the heart of the dispute is a passion play sponsored by the Temple of Moccavallo called the "Falsehood of Seasons," which is seen as a direct attack on the doctrines of Telophus and includes a character obviously representing Archbishop Harvesttide himself. Searching in the city's charter, the Archbishop discovered an aggressive solution. The ancient city charter of Olaric places all witch-hunting and arrests of heretics under control of the clergy of Muir and Thyr, but establishes the Church of Telophus as the authority empowered to conduct the trials and determine what constitutes heretical behavior. No doubt influenced by his own personal rage at the play, the Archbishop has recently issued a declaration of *Heretical per Fiat Canonical*, ruling that followers of Moccavallo, provided they are found within the city walls, are to be considered heretics under the law based on their behavior, regardless of their actual beliefs.

The Justiciar of Vourdon has been forced to admit that the Church of Telophus is within its ancient rights, although it is extraordinarily rare for the fiat to be used against traditional followers of a major deity. Matters are currently at an impasse, for the clerics of Moccavallo are amused by the chaos, and the Temple of Telophus is restricted from actually capturing heretics unless permitted by the clergy of Thyr (the temple of Muir has closed since the time of the charter). The Count refuses to arrest the Moccavallans without the approval of the temple of Thyr, and the clergy of Thyr have completely stopped granting authorization to witch-hunters in the city while they wait for a ruling from superiors in their own hierarchy. The upper echelons of the Church of Thyr, far from Olaric in distant Bard's Gate, are not pleased to be handed what looks like a squabble between two other religions, and are not hurrying to give any instruction to their clerics in Olaric. And so the matter stands. No heretics are being hunted here, and several heretics have fled here for refuge. The temple of Moccavallo still performs its play, to much-larger audiences than before, although, mindful of the declaration of heresy, people have begun to avoid the actual religious services at the Moccavallan temple. Few are willing to risk being burned as heretics if matters swing in the Archbishop's favor.

The Archbishop does have a plan to end the stalemate. He has found an elderly witch-hunter in the countryside who in his youth received a strangely worded witch-hunting charter from a barely-literate village priest who wrote it out himself, from memory. The charter authorizes the witch-hunter to "arrest heretics wherever they may be found." What is crucial about this, to the Archbishop, is that the village priest was a priest of Thyr, meaning that this stooped, 80-year-old witch-hunter already has the proper authorization to arrest heretics in Olaric, and can go after the Moccavallans. Unfortunately, Grandfather Mowch (the witch-hunter) can barely hobble along with the aid of his crutch. The Archbishop needs to find him some reinforcements, and cannot use the city's resources or citizens. Thus, what he needs is a group of tough, well-armed non-citizens. Adventurers.

If the characters agree to work with the Archbishop for a healthy reward, he hires them as Grandfather Mowch's deputies. All Grandfather Mowch needs to do is touch one of the heretics for the arrest to be legal. Once the heretic is legally arrested, Archbishop Harvesttide becomes the person in control of the entire judicial process from that point on. The Archbishop's target is not the temple building of Moccavallo, which would be going too far. But he thinks he knows — vaguely — where the actors of "Falsehood of Seasons" are being hidden away. The hiding place is in a warehouse on Warehouse Way (**Location 25** on the city map) but he has not been able to learn which one.

If the characters are able to follow people, conduct surveillance, or otherwise detect the location of the hiding place, they can try to arrest the actors. The hiding place is a one-story warehouse located on Warehouse Way that is guarded by 2 clerics of Moccavallo, 4 hired guards, and 4 guard dogs.

A low garden wall made of stone surrounds the warehouse, creating an open space 40ft around the building on the north, west, and east sides. The south side of the building abuts directly on the street. The eastern half of the warehouse garden is a goose-run where 15 geese are kept in coops at night and allowed to roam the yard during the day. The western half of the garden is just a vegetable plot. The two halves are separated by a wooden fence to keep the geese out of the vegetables. There is a gate from the street into each of the two halves of the gardens, and the warehouse has only the one front entry, a high double door large enough for a wagon to enter the storage area.

Another warehouse stands across the street with a similar layout of gardens and buildings, although the other building is two stories in height, with the owner's residence on the top floor and the warehouse space below.

The other possibility, of course, is to try to arrest the actors during or after the play. The difficulty involved in the arrest, wherever the characters might attempt it, is the possibility of civilian casualties. The Archbishop is not willing to sanction murder of townsfolk. However, anyone directly guarding the "heretics" is engaged in a capital crime, and could be legally killed. The Archbishop wants the actors alive so he can threaten to burn them if the temple of Moccavallo does not knuckle under.

Shullcross

(SHULL-cross)

Quiet charter town in the midst of political upheaval

NG large town
Government autocracy
Population 3100 (2763 humans; 282 high elves; 55 halflings)
Notable NPCs
    Mayor Jormandh Sawyer (LG male human **courtier**)
    Huilliam of Saxe, Bishop of Thyr (LN male human **Clr8** of Thyr)
    Philosopher Heriodopolis (LG male human **Clr4** of the Shattered Sword)
    Sevilard Fane (N male human **Clr4** of Sefagreth)
Maximum Clerical Spell Level Good 2, Neutral 4, Evil —
Purchase Maximum/Month 8000gp

Appearance

Shullcross is a walled town where flowering ivy covers the walls and many of the buildings in the city. The town's heraldic shield depicts a green ivy leaf centered in a red pale, on a field of white.

Description

A medium-sized town at the western border of Vourdon, Shullcross stands where the South County Road turns southward and becomes the Saxen Road to the Duchy of Saxe. Shullcross has traditionally been licensed by the Throne to conduct logging in the royal forest of Shadrack ever since the days of the Hyperborean Empire, with the tradition carrying on through the rise of the Kingdoms of Foere. The timber industry is the mainstay of Shullcross' small economy, with some flax farming, and the remainder coming from merchants crossing the gap to and from the provinces.

Government and Law

Shullcross is a chartered town allowed to govern itself in exchange for taxes and providing soldiers to the Count's army. The town elects a mayor and a commander of the watch by popular vote of the city's landowners. Unfortunately, the town is currently split between the politics of the craft guilds and the timber guild, a conflict that has given rise to street fights and highly contested mayoral elections. Characters are unlikely to get embroiled in the dispute, but they will definitely perceive that the town is in a state of high political tension. The guards are unusually alert, and the mayor has authorized street-searches of anyone, including foreigners, who look like they might cause trouble.

South County Road

The South County Road is described under the entry for the Kingdom of Suilley. Perhaps the only important additional point to make about the road concerns the fact that it passes through the gates of Olaric. This is important, because it means that the troops of Suilley cannot move from this road to the South Road without traveling through Olaric (and Olaric will not allow troops of a foreign nation to do so). Neither can vassal troops from Keston or Toullen reinforce Suilley. Any military movement connecting the Kingdom of Suilley with its southwestern vassals requires an arduous trek down cart trails and through potentially deep mud, fording streams rather than crossing bridges, and losing considerable time in the process. This is one of the reasons the King of Suilley would desperately like to bring the County of Vourdon into his growing feudal empire. A side road is under construction to bypass Olaric, but Suilley's resources are so strained that the construction has stopped several times, and has not progressed far at all.

Encounter Chance: Make one encounter check in the morning, one in the afternoon, and one at night.

Risk Level: All encounters on the South County Road within Vourdon are at the Medium-Risk level. Inside the one-hex radius around Olaric itself, there is an additional automatic encounter check in the surrounding hex and the city's hex. All encounters in Olaric's hex and the surrounding hexes are at the Low-Risk level.

01–07	No Encounter
08–68	Mundane Encounter
69–00	Dangerous Encounter

Mundane Encounters: South County Road (Vourdon)

1d100	Encounter
01–02	Annoyance (Encounter #3)
03–04	Baron and Retinue (Encounter #8)
05–06	Bear (Encounter #11)
07–16	Caravan (Provincial) (Encounter #16)
17–18	Cleric (Encounter #19)
19–20	Elf (Encounter #34)
21–36	Farmer (Encounter #36)
37–45	Foot Patrol (Encounter #37)
46–54	Herder (Encounter #51)
55–58	Heretic (Encounter #52)
59–60	High Noble (Encounter #53)
61	Kenckoo Vagrant (Encounter #55)
62–66	Knight and Retinue (Encounter #56)
67–69	Knight Challenger (Encounter #57)
70	Leper (Encounter #60)
71	Military (Encounter #64)
72–74	Minstrel (Encounter #65)
75–80	Mounted Patrol (Encounter #67)
81	Noble of the Realm (Encounter #68)
82–83	Peasant (Encounter #74)
84–85	Penitent (Encounter #76)
86–87	Pilgrim (Encounter #78)
88–89	Prisoner (Encounter #79)
90–91	Small Trader (dwarf or halfling) (Encounter #86)
92–96	Small Trader (human) (Encounter #85)
97–98	Stag (Encounter #87)
99–00	Wolf (Encounter #106)

Dangerous Encounters: South County Road (Vourdon)

1d100	Encounter
01–04	Ankheg (Encounter #2)
05–20	Bandit (Encounter #7)
21–22	Bulette (Encounter #14)
23–25	Cockatrice (Encounter #21)
26–30	Dragons A (Encounter #27)
31–32	Eagle, Giant (Encounter #33)
33	Ettin (Encounter #35)
34	Giant, Hill (Encounter #41)
35–48	Gnoll (Encounter #43)
49–54	Goblin, Roaming (Encounter #45)
55–58	Lycanthrope (Encounter #61)
59–63	Manticore (Encounter #63)
64–67	Ogre (Encounter #69)
68	Ogre Mage (Oni) (Encounter #70)
69–73	Owlbear (Encounter #72)
74–77	Robber Knight (Encounter #80)
78–79	Roc (Encounter #81)
80–81	Stirge (Encounter #88)
82–84	Troll (Encounter #92)
85	Unicorn (Encounter #93)
86–88	Wasp, Giant (Encounter #99)
89–95	Weasel, Giant (Encounter #100)
96	Wizard (Encounter #107)
97–00	Wyvern (Encounter #108)

South Road

See South Road entry under *March of Mountains*.

Yllec

(EE-lek)

Criminal exiles of a strong religion bent

N village
Government autocracy
Population 982 (888 humans; 94 half-elves)
Notable NPCs
Mayor Falco Querard (N male human **noble**)
Godefroy Anquin, War-Priest of Mithras (LN male human **Clr6** of Mithras)
Lujard Wise, Keeper of Records (NG male human **Clr4** of Belon the Wise)
Maximum Clerical Spell Level Good 2, Neutral 3, Evil —
Purchase Maximum/Month 2000gp

Appearance

Yllec is a village with stone walls but no citadel. The towers around the wall fly banners of Foere and Vourdon, and there is a prominent sign just outside the city gates. The sign reads: *"All priests not of Mithras, Freya, or Wise Belon must adhere to the town's ancient laws, and register with guards at the gate."*

History

Yllec is a walled village about 50 miles inside the borders of Vourdon on the South Road. Exiled criminals from the Kingdoms of Foere originally settled Yllec when the Duke of Saxe decided to empty the prisons of Saxentry in the year 2825. The ragged band of exiles was marched to Olaric where the Count of Vourdon refused them entry but granted them a small patch of land in the north of his domain. After another march of 125 miles, the survivors of the harrowing journey arrived in the relative wilderness of northern Vourdon and were put to the task of building a wooden road-fort on the Count's behalf. Once the task was completed, they established a small settlement and began farming.

The village eventually grew, being the first settled community in the area, and received a charter to elect their own council and mayor. At this time, Yllec is still a relatively isolated place, but serves as a market town for the surrounding hamlets and villages, along with providing a convenient stopping-point for travelers between Troye and Olaric.

Description

Yllec is very insular; only those of at least half Foerdewaith lineage are acknowledged as citizens. The vast majority (750 or so) of the town's inhabitants are citizens, and the rest are countryside laborers of "tainted" provincial bloodlines. Many of the citizens speak Gasquen as well as the common tongue, and their sense of superiority is highly obnoxious. One other expression of the militant way the Yllecaines cling to the traditions of Old Foere is their religious rules. The town maintains a small temple to Mithras (War God of the ancient Hyperboreans), which also contains shrines to Freya and Belon the Wise. Clerics of all other gods are barred from the town unless they agree not to speak the name of their patron deities within the walls. The temple priest makes official waivers to this rule on behalf of other gods of the Foerdewaith pantheon, and their clerics are actively welcomed once their religious affiliations are confirmed as orthodox "Old Foerdewaith." Yllec's extreme religious bias is not based upon any kind of theological bias; the citizens cheerfully admit the existence and the power of gods other than the ones of Old Foere. They simply prefer that the town be dedicated solely to the specifically Foerdewaith deities, or those (such as Mithras) whose association with the Hyperborean Empire is so ancient that they are considered to be as much a part of Foere's pantheon as any other.

Chapter Thirteen: Yolbiac Vale

Yolbiac Vale

(YOLE-bee-ack)

Overview

The Yolbiac Vale is a dark and forested realm, barely populated, ruled by independent barons and a scattering of local nobles claiming higher status than baronial. Villages are far apart, roads are dangerous, peasants are secretive, and dangers lurk in the omnipresent forests. The people of the Yolbiac Vale are considered to be strange and unpredictable.

General Information

Alignment: CN
Capital: none (though Coelum is usually considered the First City of the Vale)
Notable Settlements: Coelum (2,848), Roulune (507)
Ruler: none (13 "Ducal" families rule most of the area)
Government: decentralized feudalism
Population: 85,800+ (79,000 Foerdewaith; 3,800 hill dwarves; 3,000 half-elves; unknown number of wood elves)
Humanoid: wood elf (some), hill dwarf (few), half-elf (few)
Monstrous: giant wolf, fey, ogre, lycanthrope, wight, treant, dullahan, hag, hangman tree, groaning spirit, vampire (Yolbiac Vale and passes); lycanthrope, adlet, frost drake, lamia, nightmare creature, yeti, wind walker, Leng spider (high peaks)
Languages: Common, Gasquen, Elvish, Dwarvish, Druidic
Religion: Narrah, Thyr, The Green Father, Cybele, druidism, Hecate, Bilis
Resources: livestock (swine), timber, foodstuffs (dream-apples), spirits (wine), alchemical reagents
Technology Level: Dark Ages

Borders and Lands

The Yolbiac Vale is a deep indentation in the middle of the Cretian Mountains that runs from Coelum to about a hundred miles south of the town of Elet. It has several wide river valleys extending to the west that curl into the deep heart of the mountains. The strange folk of the Yolbiac populate these remote areas. The territory comprises approximately 10 hexes on the Sinnar Coast Region Map, an area of 22,000 square miles. The majority of the region is heavily forested, but not with a single, contiguous growth of trees. Instead, the region has many primordial forests that run five to ten miles across. Ridges of stone, or infertile ground, divide the forests, for this is high and broken terrain.

As the teaching rhyme suggests, the great forest of the Scal Farnu is a dominating feature in the Yolbiac Vale. Irregularly shaped, it has long, narrow extents that most certainly shift their locations by

The Gurmenadh possesses blackest bark,
And Olcabar the Deep is dryad-marked.
Nevezeld holds close its standing stones,
And Grim Canoct shall hoard its whitened bones.
Beware the Wargenwold of Tamril Shee;
Wear green in Lengis Lorme of restless trees.
In Faunwood Fey the wildest satyrs pipe,
While murderous fruits in Mouldenarc grow ripe.
The Father Forest, first that ever grew
Is the primeval wild of Scal Farnu.

Ending stanzas of the
"Teaching-Rhyme of the Druids of Leagan Cairn"

The Translator's Note to the Teaching-Rhyme, by the scholar Nonadh Bleyir, reads as follows:

"In the Cant of the Druids, the iambic pentameters of the Teaching-Rhyme contain a number of nuances and double-meanings which do not translate well into the Westerling tongue. Moreover, each of the stanzas has a sub-poem associated with it; I must confess that my understanding of the Cant proved insufficient to convey the interwoven implications of any of the sub-poems, and I have abandoned the task of translating these."

several miles each lunar month beneath the waning gibbous moons. Common folk avoid the Scal Farnu, not because it is inherently deadly, as with the Mouldenarc, but because strange and unpredictable things — often life changing — happen in the forest. Such events are by no means always maleficent, but peasants are conservative folk and choose not to risk the shifting pathways that entice travelers into the shadowy, green depths of the Scal Farnu. The Scal Farnu is said to contain the manse of Hautmarlune, a mysterious archmage. It is also thought to contain the sacred groves of the druidess Rowena of the Hounds (as distinguished from the famous Rowena of Greatstone Cairn). Two supernatural hounds, Aubrei and Simain, prowl the forest, apparently immortal beasts that may guide a party of lost adventurers back to the safer paths if they follow. The hounds travel separately, and mortal weapons and magic cannot harm them. They are patient and not vindictive, but they depart if attacked, melting away into the trees. According to legend, these are the hounds of Rowena, but none knows for certain.

In the deepest forests of the lower peaks surrounding the Vale are known to dwell a reclusive tribe of wood elves known to the Valefolk only as The Eldest. What tragedy or turmoil this people may have suffered in the past is not known, but they are seldom seen by the folk of the Vale and when they are spotted they remain distant and quickly disappear into the trees. Attempts to make contact with them have universally met with stony silences and hasty withdrawals, but so far they have shown no inclination over the years for hostilities towards the humans of the Vale. To most of the Yolbiac's inhabitants, they are simply one more evidence of the Vale's fey nature. Hints at a tragic history of these elven folk can be found, however, in the few elven ruins to be found in the lowland parts of the valley and in the unusual preponderance of groaning spirits that are known to haunt some of the surrounding mountain slopes.

History and People

The Yolbiac Vale is a land of dark alpine forests, independent villages, isolated abbeys, bizarre superstitions, and strange perils. Its people are widely varied in attitudes and customs, for few of them ever leave the environs of their home villages. Such wanderers are highly suspect, and even though they bring back fascinating news and tales of other villages, they might be doppelgangers or shape-changed faeries. It is best to always be careful; some returning travelers merely receive a sound thrashing before being sent back on their way.

Trade and Commerce

The Yolbiac region produces many strange commodities such as a variety of dark-purple apples that induce strange dreams and a dark grape, almost black, from which they ferment a potent, bitter wine that stains the lips and teeth of those who indulge frequently. Fey items are often brought down from the Vale, and include twists of hair or painted sticks that have magical powers, or finely chased goblets of hypnotic beauty. Purchasers of such items are cautioned; occasionally, their original owners have imbued them with unanticipated consequences.

The Vale may be reached either through the Coelum Pass in the Duchy of the Rampart, or by the Ghostwind Pass near Elet in Aachen Province. During the summer months, there is a considerable amount of trade with the folk of the Yolbiac Vale, but when the winter snows set in, they are left to themselves. The Ghostwind Pass is completely inaccessible during the depths of winter, and the Coelum Pass is treacherous at best.

Loyalties and Diplomacy

As noted, outsiders consider the Yolbiac Vale to be an annex of Foere, but it is strangely ignored and appears to have no ruling authority whatsoever. As such, the Vale cannot be said to have any loyalties to, or diplomacy with, other nations. At one point, a baron of Aachen Province led a small army into the Yolbiac with the intention of seizing a fiefdom, but there is no historical record of the event beyond the army's departure from Elet.

Government

The Vale is considered a part of the Kingdoms of Foere, but no one seems to rule it; there is no capital and no governor, just the occasionally tyrannical law of a few barons, some of whom pay fealty to one of the thirteen so-called "Ducal" families, more commonly referred to as the "Old Families." Unruled lands separate the baronies and duchies, but the barons make no attempt whatsoever to expand their territories, staying strictly within their traditional landholdings. This is a general tendency in the Vale: Strange traditions and odd customs are seemingly more binding upon the folk of the Yolbiac than any decree of authority.

Old writings refer to the Vale as the "Canton" of the Yolbiac, but even these records seem not to mention any sort of authority over the area, which is exceedingly unusual, perhaps unique. The folk of the Yolbiac Vale refer only to "Good King Oersen," as if the ancient Hyperborean emperor still lived and ruled. They smile and nod when hearing about the Kingdoms of Foere, as if the entire sweep of post-Hyperborean history were a fairy tale for gullible children.

Wilderness and Adventure

There is essentially nothing *but* wilderness and adventure in the Yolbiac Vale. Many villages find themselves in times of crisis without the help of anyone, and monster lairs are virtually everywhere in the high crags and deep forests of the region. Off the top of one's head, one can list Ysoolte's Weir, the caves of Quarvel, the lair of Borovendal, the Tor of the Yellow

147

Witch, and many others. Adventuring in the Scal Farnu is possible for those of stout heart, and fur hunting in the Ghostwind Pass could leave a group of hunters with a nice bag full of gold afterward. It is more difficult to avoid adventure here than to seek it out.

Changing Times

Events in the Yolbiac Vale proceed unchanged since time immemorial. Stories accumulate and are forgotten, heroes live and heroes die, strange and supernatural events occur, others are warded off by the proper hand gestures and taboos. Darkness abides, and life goes on. Such is the Yolbiac Vale.

Coelum

(SEE-lum)

N small town
Government overlord
Population 2848 (2602 humans; 181 hills dwarves; 65 half-elves)
Notable NPCs
High Mayor Riaundo Groon (N male human **noble**)
Watchmeister Gustav Lampert, Husjaeger Commander (LE male human **Ftr13**)
Tholberon of Thyr (LG male human Clr9 of Thyr)
Blind Cynthiene, High Priestess of Narrah (N female human **Clr12** of Narrah)
Luald the Witch-Hunter (LG male human **Pal7** of Thyr)
The Drogas Mondu (N male human **Drd12**)
Cithinvere of Coelum (CE female human **Clr7** of Hecate)
Augus Monticylaire, Vinter (N male human **courtier**)
Maximum Clerical Spell Level Good 5, Neutral 6, Evil 4 (hidden)
Purchase Maximum/Month 4000gp

Appearance

High, dark stone walls dominate this large town. The walls are so old that they are uneven and buckle between the towers. The buildings within are tall, overshadowing the mud streets that wind between them into alleyways and small courtyards. The roofs are steeply pitched, shingled with molding wood. Chains of garlic and other strange charms are securely nailed over all the doorways.

Description

Coelum is not a political capital, but as the main town in the Yolbiac Vale, it is where most of the trade goods go to market, and where the local nobles go for their larger meetings. The thirteen "Ducal Houses" of the Vale, which are the old noble families whose bloodlines date back past any recorded history, elect a High Mayor for the town every ten years or so. The High Mayor oversees the town's trade, maintenance of walls, and a small (but extremely well-armed and dangerous) city guard called the Husjaegers.

As with much of the Yolbiac Vale, the town seems, to outsiders, at least, to be ruled more by its customs and superstitions than by any sort of actual law. Many of the inhabitants practice druidism. The Drogas Mondu, an extremely old druid who dresses in white robes, oversees a grove and cromlech stone outside the walls where he intones prayers to gods that sound strange to the ears of visitors: names like Bel, Myrddin, and Annawn.

Another religious edifice in the town is a tall and rather shaky-looking temple of Thyr. The high priest of Thyr in Coelum, Tholberon of Thyr, is the highest religious authority in the Vale, supervising 10 itinerant priests,

2 priests of the temple, 2 acolytes in training, and the Witch-hunter. The Witch-hunter, Luald the Witch-Hunter has the divine sense to detect evil. He is surly and unpleasant, seldom bathes, and is not generally impressed with adventurers. He wears a dented, rusty breastplate and carries *+1 longsword* named *Deadman. Deadman* exerts a constant *protection from good and evil* around its bearer when it is unsheathed. Luald has no budget to hire assistance, but if some characters ask to work for free, he can usually direct them to some rumor or another that bears looking into.

Blind Cynthiene, High Priestess of Narrah, is the third religious power in Coelum. Narrah is the ancient (possibly Neolithic) goddess associated with the primary moon, known in various places as The Lady of the Moon, or the Pale Sister. Her small temple is a square of modest buildings surrounding a courtyard, but Blind Cynthiene's subtle influence over the Yolbiac Vale is considerable. Relations between the Temple of Thyr and the Temple of Narrah can be described only as vitriolic: Cynthiene and Tholberon dislike each other intensely, and have significantly different goals. Cynthiene sees her task as warding the people of the Vale from its outward dangers, whereas Tholberon is utterly dedicated to the task of burning out heresy and chaos from society, and purging the Vale's wilderness of its strange, evil nature when possible.

Heorm's Lair

See **Chapter 7: March of Mountains,** *Heorm's Lair.*

Knights of the Swan

The Knights of the Swan have no exact location, for they are an order of itinerant knights who range through the Yolbiac Vale, usually alone or with a couple of armed retainers. Many of the knights are paladins, although the majority are fighters dedicated to protecting civilization — such as it is — in the Vale. At times members of this Order go abroad to a new adopted home where they establish chapterhouses to continue their duty in the protection of other civilized lands (see Sir Terris Mallory, **Chapter 8: Duchy of the Rampart,** *Troye*).

A few rangers are also attached to the Order, but those not of the knightly class are not full members. The Order of the Swan is not attached to any particular religious denomination with paladins representing several different holy faiths, although they are universally of lawful good alignment. The Grand Master of the Order of the Swan is Sir Thyrian de Swan (LG male human **Pal12** of Muir), who generally convenes any necessary meetings of the knights at the tournament of Coelum. His castle, which often serves as the ad hoc headquarters of the Order, is roughly twenty miles to the north of Coelum Town.

Although many of the Knights of the Swan decry the often-tyrannous rule of the local lords in the Vale, they do not ever interfere with the feudal structure, confining their efforts to eliminating monsters. More than once members of the Order have come near to blows with the brutal Husjaegers of Coelum, though to date cooler heads have always prevailed. By the same token, they do not interfere with, or assist, the witch-hunters who track down heretics in the Vale.

Chapter Fourteen: Points Beyond

Points Beyond

Overview

The Borderland Provinces stretch from one end of the lands of the Sinnar Coast to the other, but these lands are vast and even the Provinces do not compass their entire breadth. Detailed here are some of those peripheral areas that are not a part of the Borderland Provinces but lie close enough to constitute points of interest for those residing in or traveling through the nearby provinces. Where available, sources for more specific information about these places is included in their entires.

Byrn

(BERN)

This small village stands deep in the southern hills of the Stoneheart Valley at the very feet of Lost Boy Mountain. The village has long known the tragedy and danger of living in the shadow of that ill-starred peak, but its work-hardened folk have persevered nonetheless and continue to scratch out a life in the stony soil of the lower slopes.

For more information on the village of Byrn, see *The Lost Lands: Bard's Gate Complete*, forthcoming in 2016 from **Frog God Games**.

District of Sunderland

The "District of Sunderland" is the name given by the Kingdoms of Foere to the ungoverned region from the King's Road to the Matagost Peninsula, excluding the almost-equally ungoverned wilderness of Old Burgundia. Sunderland is a sea of dry, rolling plains scattered with small villages and hamlets. Even the smallest actual towns are exceedingly rare on these plains, mostly supported by the influence of various Endhome merchant houses.

Shepherds and their flocks are the main tenants of the grasslands, and the hills support vineyards and orchards as well as more than their share of predators — natural and unnatural alike.

The kings of Suilley have, from time to time, cast their gaze across the Trader's Way at the southern reaches of Sunderland, thinking of conquest to regain the eastern lands lost to rebellion during their own war of secession, but once they begin calculating the actual costs involved in such an endeavor their ardor for those lands inevitably dies down again. The independence of the villages in south Sunderland has essentially continued only because Suilley's forces and treasuries are already overextended beyond the point of stability.

For more information on the District of Sunderland, see *The Lost Lands: Cults of the Sundered Kingdoms* by **Frog God Games**.

Forest Kingdoms

The northernmost expanse of the primeval Great Akadonian Forest that once blanketed the continent stands here as a woodland bracketed by the Glimmrill Run to the east, the Tradeway to the north, the Unclaimed Lands to the south, and the suzerainty of Bard's Gate to the west. Here in this hardwood forest, trees still stand that existed when Oerson marched and when the great ancient kingdom of the elves fell. Likewise here remains the last true remnant in the East of that great sylvan realm. What was once the elven Kingdom of Parnuble exists now as a number of small elven realms known collectively as the Forest Kingdoms. Unlike the wild elves of the Green Realm far to the west where humans are unwelcome and hidden archers fire barbed arrows on sight, the high elves and wood elves of the Forest Kingdoms have found peace with the descendants of the long ago human invaders. Bard's Gate in particular maintains friendly relations with the elven folk to the extent that the primary tradeway across the chasm-bridging city of Derindin and on to their port of Freegate in the east runs directly through the forest and the sylvan trade city of Arendia where human and elven merchants and travelers are able to exist in mutual peace and accord in a way that they were rarely able to achieve throughout history.

For more information on the Forest Kingdoms, see *The Lost Lands: Bard's Gate Complete*, forthcoming in 2016 from **Frog God Games**.

Forlorn Mountains

This vast mountain range is one of the largest other than the Stonehearts, and once served as the ancestral home of the Great Mountain Clan of Targ, although these dwarves are now widely scattered after the fall of the citadel at Hazad-Burgh in 3160 to giant invaders. Giants haunt the eastern reaches of the mountains in great numbers, on the far side of the range, but Exeter Province is spared from the worst threat the mountains offer. Nevertheless, the province still has to cope with giantish raids from time to time, for the entire mountain range is rife with them. In recent years, the Lord-Governor of Exeter Province has done an excellent job of staving off the giant incursions, although some of the local nobles have voiced the opinion that rooting out trouble at the source might do more to stop the problem.

> *"Not to give insult, but your statement is arrant nonsense, Baron Korl. A good offense makes no contribution to a good defense; to say so is patently a contradiction of terms. It is obviously a good defense that constitutes the best defense. Good walls make strong lands, I always say."*
>
> —Benevic of Lortsbar, Lord-Governor of Exeter Province,
> to Baron Korl of Trollheart Haven, at the Tournament of Lancefield.

Legends speak of a strange and powerful wizard called the Mechanician who is said to have a fortress in the southern Forlorn Mountains where he keeps one of the fabled *Bells of Heaven*, though no one has been able to confirm this rumor. The margoyle creche that once led the hill clans of

the Wilderlands to war is thought to still exist high in the western slopes, nursing their wounds after their defeat at Broch Tarna and plotting their revenge against the earthbound manlings.

For more information on the Forlorn Mountains, see *The Lost Lands: Cults of the Sundered Kingdoms* by **Frog God Games**.

Grollek's Grove
(GRAHL-ecks GROVE)

Grollek's Grove, population 853, is a small town and trading post at the crossroad of the King's Road and the Trader's Way. Most of its trade is with Endhome, which purchases the excellent wines produced here. The town was founded a century or so ago with the cooperation of the surrounding regions and governments, and is self-governed.

For more information on Grollek's Grove, see *The Lost Lands: Cults of the Sundered Kingdoms* by **Frog God Games**.

Gundlock Hills
(GUND-lok)

There are a number of villages in the western vicinities of these hills, especially in the areas near the Trader's Way and King's Road. The eastern reach of the hills is much less populated and quite wild. The western hills have many orchards and fine vineyards, though many of these are overgrown, having been abandoned after raids and skirmishes in the past. Humanoids roam the eastern hills in small bands, but have yet to gather into any tribes large enough to pose a threat to anything but

isolated farmsteads. Small dragons also breed in the eastern hills, but few of them have attained a dangerous enough age to be either far-ranging or highly destructive.

For more information on the Gundlock Hills, see *The Lost Lands: Cults of the Sundered Kingdoms* by **Frog God Games**.

Kingdom of Oceanus
(OH-see-an-es, or OH-she-an-es)

Founded on the Island of Pontos by the Grand Admiral of the Foerdewaith Fleet, the Kingdom of Oceanus has declared itself sovereign over the oceans of the world and named its king as Emperor of the Oceans Blue. This audacious claim was initially mocked in foreign courts, but the efficiency and advanced weapons of the Oceanic Navy have prevented anyone from actively challenging their supremacy since the disastrous Battle of Kapichi Point exactly three centuries. For its part, Oceanus rules its maritime empire with a light hand, generally not interfering with the peaceful shipping of other nations, only asserting their alleged authority when it is expedient to do so. Most ships of other nations simply avoid an Oceanic man-o-war when sighted upon the high seas or accede to its demands if it wishes to board and search the craft. Denying an Oceanic warship's demands is done at a captain's own risk. Oceanus's current policy is to not interfere with the warships of other nations as it does not see an open naval conflict to be in its best interests at this time. Those interests are currently to amass a colonial empire throughout the oceans of Lloegyr, and the Empire of Oceanus administered from Pontus Tinigal is already grown vast and rich.

For more information on the Kingdom of Oceanus, see *The Lost Lands: Cults of the Sundered Kingdoms* by **Frog God Games**.

Old Burgundia
(burr-GUN-dee-ah)

In the past, Burgundia was an affluent and well-reputed kingdom to the east of the Borderland Provinces, which declared its independence from the Overking earlier than the Kingdom of Suilley. However, unlike Suilley's rapid expansion into a vacuum of power, Burgundia faced staunch opposition on all of its borders, and eventually collapsed in the face of a determined assault by Oceander armies. The capital was reduced to ruins, and the population was decimated by the famines and diseases that inevitably follow upon military disaster. At the present time, the lands of Old Burgundia are little more than wild and ungoverned territories, with scattered handfuls of independent walled towns and packs of roving humanoids and barbarians.

For more information on Old Burgundia, see *The Lost Lands: Cults of the Sundered Kingdoms* by **Frog God Games**.

Stoneheart Forest

To the north of the Borderland Provinces beyond the Great Amrin Bridge, lies the southern fringes of the Stoneheart Forest. This forest stands at the eastern end of the Stoneheart Valley and marks the true southern extent of the demesne of Bard's Gate. The forest is quite thick and wild, and the great trade city can hardly claim to have fully tamed its interior, but the trade road that cuts through its eastern fringe is well patrolled and largely safe and the river traffic on the Stoneheart River that flows through its heart remains unmolested as well. Recently, the city has conquered the difficulties in river transport once presented by the Stoneheart Falls with the construction of Karling's Contraption, a great waterwheel-powered lift capable of carrying an entire keelboat from the top or bottom of the falls in a matter of minutes, ending the days of tedious portage around the falls of entire cargoes. Like the river traffic, this river outpost likewise remains undisturbed by the forest's residents. The deep denizens of the forest may not bow to the authority of the High Burgess in Bard's Gate, but they have well learned the lesson that attacks on that city's trade brings swift and deadly reprisals of steel and spell.

For more information on the Stoneheart Forest, see *The Lost Lands: Sword of Air* now available from **Frog God Games** and *The Lost Lands: Bard's Gate Complete*, forthcoming in 2016 from **Frog God Games**.

Chapter Fifteen: Rogues in Remballo

A 5e adventure by Matt Finch

Rogues in Remballo is a **Fifth Edition** adventure for 4–6 first level characters, a city adventure that gets the characters embroiled in strange plots, sinister intrigue, and fierce battles. Is the thieves' guild of Manas encroaching on the territory of the Remballo guild? What is hidden in the sanctuary-courtyard known as the Four Corners? How is the powerful banking house of Borgandy involved with all of it? What starts as a straightforward mission actually involves a host of complications — some of which can be deadly if the characters don't play their cards right.

Introduction

Rogues in Remballo is an adventure for first-level characters, but is not intended as an adventure for a first-time game master or players. The adventure is not difficult to run, but pacing an adventure like this one requires a game master with some experience. There is a large area for information-gathering, which can slow down the adventure if it is not well controlled, and assaults on a location like the Four Corners frequently bog down in excessive planning and discussion. The experienced game master should encounter no difficulties here, but keeping the action moving could prove to be a problem for a first-timer. Frog God Games publishes a number of introductory adventures suitable for learning how to run a game for the first time, and if you have never run an adventure before, one of these would be a better introduction to the art.

Rogues in Remballo takes place in the neighborhood of Dead Fiddler Square. It is a starting adventure for 1st-level characters, designed to get them a few experience points and establish relationships (good or bad) with some possible patrons who can point them to more adventures in the future. By the end of the adventure, the characters will most likely have contacts with the Borgandy family, the Thieves' Guild of Remballo, and the City Watch.

Like most cities, Remballo has a tangled mess of strange laws and land rights. Case in point, a small courtyard in the Dead Fiddler Square neighborhood called the Four Corners is not subject to search or seizure by city authorities. It has become a place where stolen goods and renegade people can be hidden from the law, and the courtyard's tenants are known to be a criminal fraternity of some kind. The situation has become more a matter of concern not only to the neighbors but also to the city watch and the Thieves' Guild.

Ordinarily, this is exactly the sort of situation the Thieves' Guild would handle for the city; the reason the guild is allowed to exist is because it helps control and regulate crime. However, in this case, the Thieves' Guild believes (a) it has a traitor in its midst, and (b) the operation going on in the Four Corners is being run by the Thieves' Guild of Manas. If the Manas Thieves' Guild is involved, it creates a serious problem. First, there is a strict policy of nonviolence between the guilds, formalized in an actual treaty. Second, the Manas Thieves' Guild is much more violent and numerous than the one in Remballo, which makes keeping to the treaty a matter of self-preservation as well as honor. However, if the Manas thieves are fencing goods or operating in Remballo, the Remballo thieves would very much like to put a stop to it, preferably involving the death of the Manas thieves who are invading their territory.

A Tale of Two Thieves Guilds

The Thieves' Guild of Remballo is virtually an extension of the city government. Thieves are forbidden to act with violence, pickpockets and thieves all pay dues to the guild, and a cut is paid into the city coffers as a tax. The number of authorized burglaries is limited to a certain number, and the number of thieves allowed in the guild is also limited. Guild thieves are tried in the city courts (with a guild attorney), but if convicted they are sentenced not by the city but by the guild, which assesses monetary damages rather than hangings, brandings, and mutilation. On the other hand, the Thieves' Guild actively hunts down freelance thieves, handing them over to the city or trying them in the Court of Thieves (which invariably hangs the freelancers they convict). As such, the Remballo Thieves' Guild not only reduces crime in the city but ensures that it is nonviolent, and helps the city to police all other thefts.

The Thieves' Guild of Manas is an altogether different animal. The City of Manas allows their Thieves' Guild to remain in operation not because of a friendly relation but because any attempts to close it down result in an all-out crime wave, not only of theft but of murder and arson as well. The guild makes it very clear that war means war. Just as with the Remballo guild, the Manas guild hunts down freelance thieves in its territory and limits its numbers. Unlike the Remballo guild, the thieves of Manas are not barred from violence, and rather than paying the city's government, they pay bribes to selected government officials. The city of Manas and its Thieves' Guild have a much more adversarial relationship than the peaceful situation in Remballo, and the Manas guild has a correspondingly more-violent approach. Since they are already a technically illegal operation, the Manas guild dabbles in crimes other than thieving and fencing, getting into extortion, kidnapping, and even assassination, while the traditionalist Remballo guild absolutely forbids such expansions.

What is Happening in the Four Corners?

The Thieves' Guild of Manas is not officially running a secret operation in Remballo as feared by the Remballo Thieves' Guild. However, thieves from the Manas Guild are involved here, without the knowledge of their own guild. They are acting as renegades, an activity that can get them executed by either one of the guilds involved. The Remballo Guild is working from reliable information — that there is a Manas connection to the Four Corners — they just reached an incorrect conclusion that it was the Manas *guild* behind it rather than renegade *members* of the guild. This could become important in the events following the adventure.

There are actually two criminal activities based in the Four Corners, and they are not related except for their location and the fact that they know about each other. The first is the fencing and smuggling operation run by the renegade Manas guildmembers. The second is a kidnapping plot by the actual owner of the Four Corners: a man by the name of Doctor Remora, once a professor at the University of Remballo. Remora is a magic-user of small talent, but with a flair for audacious crime. He has kidnapped a member of the Borgandy family, and with the coerced assistance of the banker is producing fake letters of credit.

Getting Involved

The characters might get involved with the Four Corners in a number of ways: the Thieves' Guild, the City Watch, and the Borgandy Family. The Borgandys are quietly searching for their kidnapped relative, Savario, aware that he could be fashioning letters of credit; they do not know if he has been kidnapped, or if he has turned to a life of crime. The City Watch knows nothing of the possible involvement of the Manas Thieves' Guild or of the missing Borgandy relative. These are secrets the thieves and the Borgandys are keeping to themselves. However, the City Watch knows that something is going on in the Four Corners, wants to stop it, and has no way to do so — not officially, at least. The Thieves' Guild, believing that the Manas guild is involved, wants to kill everyone in Four Corners without leaving a trail back to themselves. This is made more difficult by the fact that they believe they have a traitor in their midst.

The City Watch: If the characters come into contact with the City Watch, they meet with Captain Gustave Bouchard, who explains that the city cannot enter the Four Corners. But if the characters were to break in and find out what is happening, the City Watch also cannot prosecute the characters if they were to take everything in the place. The guards would prefer that the characters capture any wrongdoers and take them out of the Four Corners for arrest, but they won't lose sleep if there are a few deaths. Because of their legal constraints, they cannot pay for the characters' work, but they have talked to the House of Borgandy about some sort of secret payment from the city's premier family. They just don't want to know about it. Captain Gustave gives them a letter of introduction to speak to Romero Borgandy, head of the family. He also gives them a copy of the player map of the Dead Fiddler Square neighborhood so they don't have to waste time scouting it out.

The House of Borgandy: If the characters come into contact with the House of Borgandy and appear to be reliable, they are brought before the aged Romero Borgandy and his daughter Isobel, who explains that their cousin Savario has disappeared and must be recovered. They believe that he disappeared in the vicinity of Dead Fiddler Square, and willingly give this information, but they do not mention the possibility that he might be forging letters of credit. It is possible that this contact happens because the City Watch sends the characters to get the promise of a reward from the family. If this is the case, the Borgandys offer a reward of 1000gp for handling the situation in Four Corners, and 2000gp if they can recover Savario — keep in mind that at this point, no one knows that the two missions are connected. If the characters agree to help, the Borgandys give them a copy of the player map.

The Thieves' Guild: Finally, it is possible that the Thieves' Guild will contact the characters. This will be done in secret by the guild's second in command because the guild does not want to alert a possible traitor in their midst. The agent, Master Thief Leonora Spider (N female human **Rog8**) will of course not mention the possibility of a Thieves' Guild traitor, but will caution the characters not to talk to anyone in the Thieves' Guild other than herself. If the characters are obviously concerned about this, she explains the traitor problem. If the characters agree to undertake the mission for the Thieves' Guild, the guild pays 1000gp for a successful mission, and 500gp toward raising any casualties from the dead at the

Cathedral of Thyr and Sefagreth. They give the characters a copy of the player map.

Investigating the Neighborhood

The City Watch and the Thieves' Guild have both been keeping an eye on the Four Corners, and can tell the characters that there is not much passage in and out of the place, even though several people seem to be living there. They prefer that the characters be extremely discreet about asking questions, and definitely don't want to see a door-to-door investigation going on. A quick scout-around is fine, but they want the place cleared out regardless of who is in there, so there isn't much mystery (or so they think). A bit of discreet inquiry of the neighbors could help the characters, but it can also slow the adventure down, so try to move them along if they are playing police detectives.

The only person who seems to go in and out on a regular basis is the owner, a Doctor Remora who once taught at the University of Remballo. Doctor Remora is described as a tall man, bald except for a long, red-dyed braid (a queue) that lies down his back. He usually wears professorial robes, and he talks to himself. No one in the university knew him well, and he was removed from the faculty for accepting bribes from students. If the characters visit the university, they gain a piece of information no one originally told them: Doctor Remora is a magic-user, although not a very good one. No other useful information comes from the university; do not let the characters get bogged down there.

Temporary Surveillance on the Characters

Whether the City Watch or the Thieves' Guild (or both) hire the characters, the patron has someone shadow the characters to make sure they are remaining discreet. Moreover, if the characters were hired only by the City Watch, they almost immediately gain a shadow from the Thieves' Guild and vice versa. Within a day, **spies** will follow them, one from each organization. The spies notice each other, and report to the characters that they are being followed. This can lead to all sorts of complications; if the characters handle it well, they may come into peaceful — or non-lethal, at least — contact with another patron, and get more reward money for the same task. If they kill a thief or a guard, on the other hand, they will be in trouble with a powerful organization in the city. *Under no circumstances will either of the two tails assist the characters in any way within the boundaries of the Four Corners.* Their organizations do not want to be implicated in anything: that's what the characters are for. If both the city watch and the Thieves Guild end up hiring the characters, the two organizations decide that there is no need to keep tailing the characters and withdraw their agents for more useful pursuits.

Spy (2): **AC** 12; **HP** 27(6d8); **Spd** 30ft; Melee shortsword (+4, 1d6+2 piercing); **Ranged** hand crossbow (+4, 1d6+2 piercing); **SA** cunning action (dash, disengage, or hide as bonus), multiattack (shortsword x2), sneak attack (1/day, extra 2d6 with weapon with tactical advantage or 5ft of an ally); **Str** +0, **Dex** +2, **Con** +0, **Int** +1, **Wis** +2, **Cha** +3; **Skills** Deception +5, Insight +4, Investigation +5, Perception +6, Persuasion +5, Sleight of Hand +4, Stealth +4; **AL** N; **CR** 1; **XP** 200.

Dead Fiddler Square Map Key

Unless otherwise noted, all of the NPCs encountered in the city are human **commoners**. The player map shows the number of floors in each building.

1. Four Corners Courtyard

See separate map.

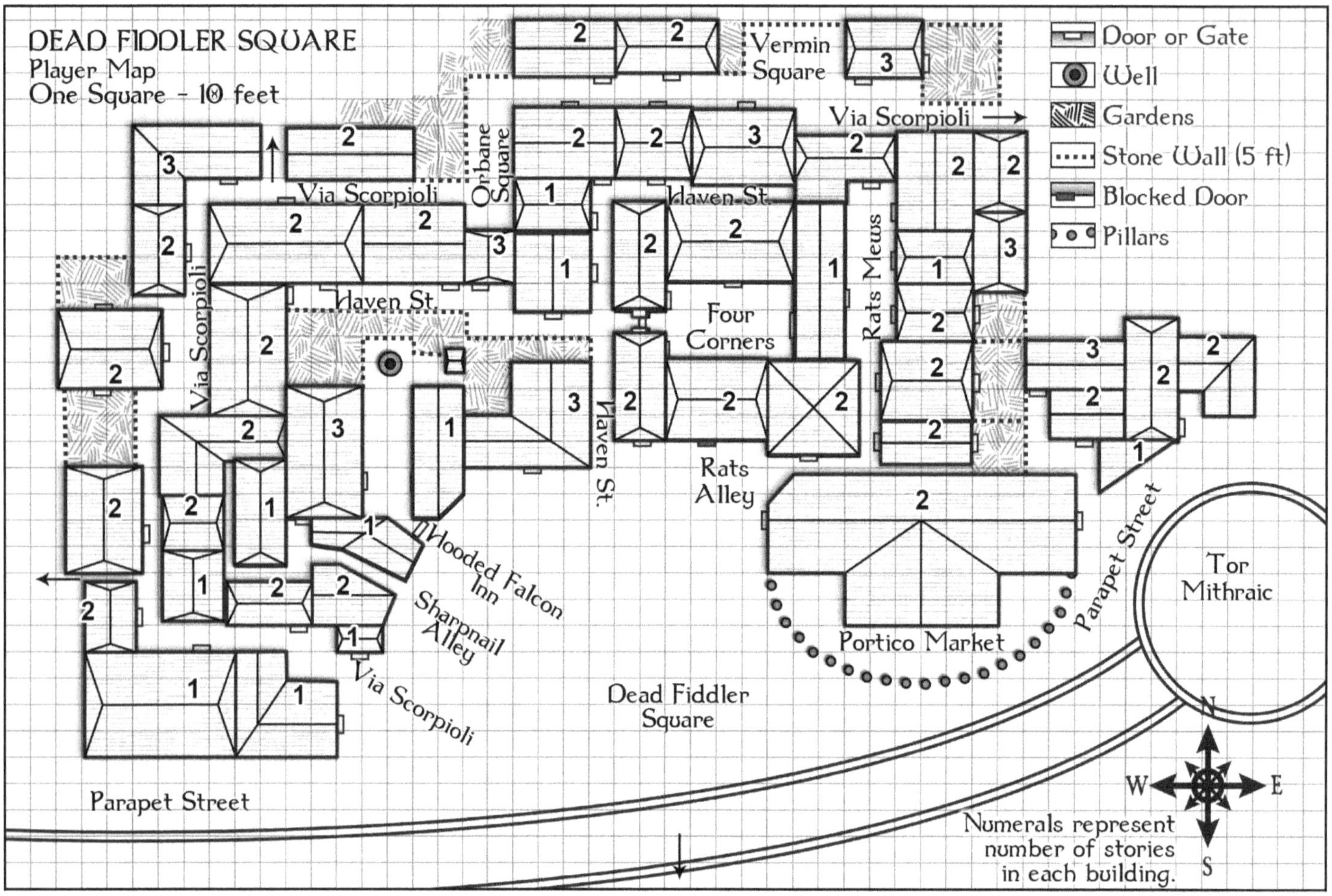

DEAD FIDDLER SQUARE
Player Map
One Square - 10 feet

Legend:
- Door or Gate
- Well
- Gardens
- Stone Wall (5 ft)
- Blocked Door
- Pillars

Vermin Square

Via Scorpioli

Orbane Square

Haven St.

Four Corners

Rats Mews

Rats Alley

Hooded Falcon Inn

Sharpnail Alley

Via Scorpioli

Haven St.

Portico Market

Dead Fiddler Square

Parapet Street

Tor Mithraic

Numerals represent number of stories in each building.

W — E
N / S

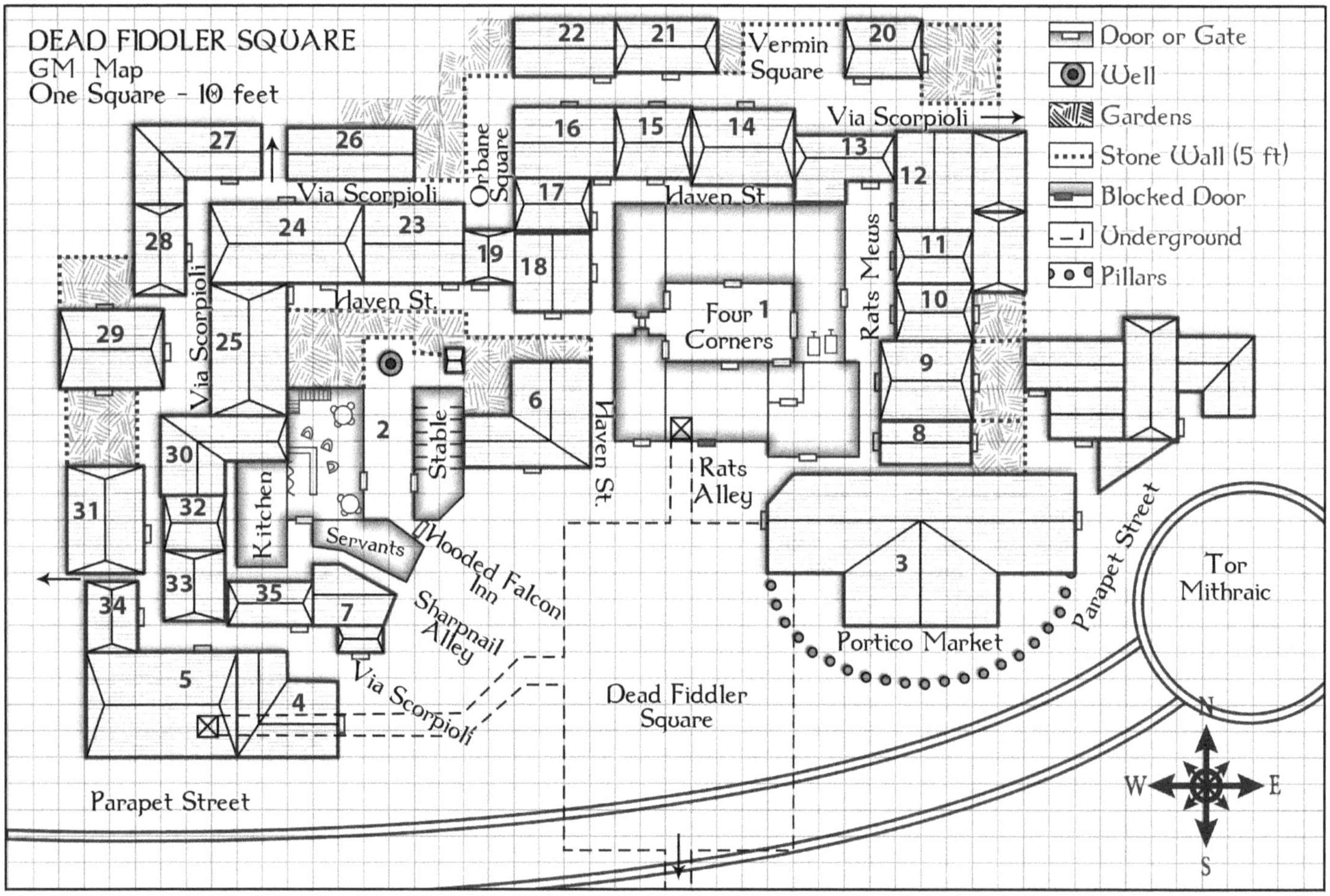

DEAD FIDDLER SQUARE
GM Map
One Square - 10 feet

Legend:
- Door or Gate
- Well
- Gardens
- Stone Wall (5 ft)
- Blocked Door
- Underground
- Pillars

22 21 Vermin Square 20

27 26 16 15 14

Via Scorpioli

Orbane Square

13

12

17

24 23

19 18

Haven St.

11

10

28

Via Scorpioli

Haven St.

Four Corners 1

Rats Mews

29

25

6

9

Stable

30

Kitchen

2

8

Haven St.

Servants

Rats Alley

31

32

Hooded Falcon Inn

33

35

Sharpnail Alley

34

7

Via Scorpioli

5

4

Dead Fiddler Square

Portico Market

3

Parapet Street

Tor Mithraic

W — E
N / S

2. Hooded Falcon Inn

This is a large inn with the sign of a hooded falcon over the entry gate. The gate leads into a courtyard surrounded by inn's various buildings.

Owned by Jirander and Jauntline Lamarc, the Hooded Falcon offers rooms at a reasonable rate, food included. The common room is generally filled with an ordinary tavern crowd until 10 p.m. (the "tenth hour non," as it is said here). The other buildings in the inn's courtyard are a stable, an outhouse, the kitchen (attached to the common room through a curtained door, and the residence building where the Lamarcs live on the top floor, with servants and staff on the ground floor. The inn's gate closes at midnight, but porter Firkin Fortbeard (a dwarf) remains on watch by the gate to let guests in and out — and to keep an eye out for burglars. Asking about the Four Corners here will automatically give characters the information that the red-haired Doctor Remora is the only inhabitant of the place who is ever seen in the streets.

3. Portico Market

This is a busy market covered by a large wooden roof supported by old stone pillars at the front and a two-story stone warehouse at the back.

The Portico Market is run by a group of merchants who keep their wares in the large building behind the covered area. Several of the street vendors who push carts through the city streets buy their stock at wholesale in the warehouse, but the stalls under the portico itself offer their goods at normal prices to passers-by.

A successful DC 10 Cha (Persuasion) check allows the characters to find a talkative vendor at the portico market who knows Doctor Remora well, although he does not know the name of the robed man with the long braid. The vendors were all quite interested when the braided man purchased (from three different sellers) a set of window bars, some manacles, and a chamber pot. Doctor Remora failed to realize that the vendors gossip among themselves. In the end, they decided it was none of their business.

4. Curganon's Warehouse

This is a one-story stone building with a slate-shingled roof and a securely locked double door in front. There is no sign to indicate what the building contains, but there is a single window in the front with a window box of yellow geraniums.

This warehouse offers space to a variety of small merchants, and is also the home of Leo and Veldiss Curganon and their 3 children. The window, which is securely locked at night (DC 15 with thieves' tools to open), opens into the residential portion of the building.

5. Ozzerd's Warehouse

A dark, slate-shingled roof tops this one-story stone building. There is no sign outside, and the wooden double doors are closed.

Space is not available for general rent in this warehouse, which stores the property of the merchant Feodric Ozzerd (See area 18). It is also one of the hidden outlets for the Four Corners, with a hidden tunnel leading to the lair.

6. Aralt's Warehouse

This is a three-story building. The ground floor is built of stone, and the upper two stories are half-timbered. The only windows in the building are on the top floor, looking out over the square. These have stout wooden shutters and are painted in a cheery blue color. A sign over the double wooden doors reads: "General Warehousing."

This warehouse stores general goods for several small merchants. It is also the home of the owners, Timon and Liriel Aralt (who live on the top floor). They don't know anything about the Four Corners, but it happens they have a very useful piece of information linking Remora to the thieves. If asked about man with a red braid, Liriel Arault remembers him: he and another man with a strong Manas-city accent once made fun of the Araults' blue-painted shutters. She doesn't remember any details about the man from Manas, but she remembers him saying, "We should train to pains; it could be another source of income." (This was Rafael the Cur.)

7. Doctor Escalous, Alchemist

This is a two-story building with a one-story extension built onto the main building as a store. A sign over the shop entrance has a painting of a mortar and pestle, and reads: "Doctor Escalous, Alchemist and Apothecary."

Doctor Escalous is an apothecary and a minor alchemist. His house and workshops are in the main part of the building, and his shop is the 10-foot-by-20-foot extension. A successful DC 10 Cha (Persuasion) check gets him to reveal that he has met the man with the long red braid (Doctor Remora, although he does not know the name), and recalls selling him various concoctions that help people sleep. These concoctions cost 5gp each and although they will not knock out a person, they will knock out any of the dogs labeled as a "little dog" in the adventure.

8. Shoemaker Huron Cordonyr

This is a two-story wooden building in poor repair, with a faded red roof of uneven wood shingles. The picture of a shoe is painted over the door.

Cordonyr supplies shoes to various different merchants. This building is his home and workshop. His wife Jocelyn does various odd jobs, mostly working as a seamstress. They don't know anything useful to the characters, but offer to repair their boots for a fair price.

9. Bertran Limner

This is a two-story, half-timbered building. It is newly painted and has a roof of wooden shingles. A paintbrush hangs over the door.

Bertran is a housepainter who works for various contractors. A successful DC 10 Cha (Persuasion) check gets him to reveal he recently painted the inside of the Four Corners courtyard (the exteriors, not the insides of the buildings). He knows where the doors in the courtyard are located, but not much more. A DC 15 check means that he thinks to mention that the man who hired him was a halfling with Manas-city accent, who said something strange when Bertran asked about painting over the boarded up door in the south wall of the Corners. He said, "Paint it over, cracks will show if anyone tampers with it.". Bertran asked why anyone would tamper with the door when there was a perfectly good one around the corner, and the halfling told him rudely to get on with his work, and not to ask stupid questions.

10. Arnault Porter

This is a two-story house, half-timbered but weathered and ill-kept. The roof is shingled in wood, and there is no sign out front.

This is the home of the Porter family, all of whom are day laborers working for builders, warehouses, or caravans. They know nothing useful about the Four Corners, red-haired men with braids, or people with accents from the City of Manas. They also don't like to be bothered by nosy busybodies who obviously don't have gainful employment.

11. Giles Woodmonger

This is a one-story house with a roof made of moldy-looking wooden planks. A less-weathered rectangular patch next to the door must have once been covered by a sign, but it is no longer there.

Giles Woodmonger and his wife Parrille buy firewood and charcoal by the wagonload in the wholesale markets, and sell it door to door. They have delivered to the Four Corners once or twice, but remember nothing useful about it. Someone bought wood. People do that. After the characters talk to them, they inform the city guard that the characters are asking suspicious questions. The guards know what is happening, but will quickly inform the characters that their inquiries are raising suspicions.

12. Everil the Scribe

This is a two-story building made of plaster-covered wood and brick; the roof is shingled with slates. A quill pen is painted over the door.

Everil is a freelance copyist, serving the needs of various businesses in the city that need copies of contracts, letter, etc. A successful DC 10 Cha (Persuasion) check gets him to reveal that he remembers the man with the red braid, and knows his name is Doctor Remora because of a curious incident. Doctor Remora came to Everil's little office with a piece of paper. It had writing on it, but the doctor did not show it to him. What Remora wanted was to see if any of Everil's supply of paper matched with the one Remora was carrying. None of Everil's paper seemed right, and Remora went on his way, tipping Everil with a silver piece for his time. If the characters offer him some money to help his recollection, Everil remembers Remora seemed to be checking the heavier-weight paper, like that used for legal documents. He was talking to himself, and kept saying, "Borgandy, Borgandy, Borgandy… where do they get it?"

13. Valry Tailor

This is a two-story building at the end of the alley. The building is plaster-and-wood, with a sharply-pitched roof of wooden shingles. The sign of a needle hangs over the door.

Valry is a tailor who sews garments to order for the city's middle class of small merchants and guild-members.

14. Bordac Gilere

This is a half-timbered building of three stories, with a wood-shingle roof and a balcony ten feet above the street level. While it is by no means a rich residence, it is obviously the home of someone who is well employed.

Bordac is a messenger for House Borgandy, one of several employees whose only duty is to locate and give messages to people the Borgandys need to contact during the business day. Bordac helped with the kidnapping of Savario Borgandy, giving him a "message" to meet a client in the Four Corners. If asked about a man with a red braid he becomes visibly nervous, but still says nothing. Bordac won't say anything about the event unless intimidated (DC 10) or if the characters seem to already know what happened, in which case his *story* is that a man with long red braid paid him a modest tip and asked if Savario Borgandy could be bothered to meet him as potential new client. In *actuality*, he was paid a very healthy bride and sent with the message that is was another member of the House Borgandy who wanted an urgent meeting — a story that was obviously invented by the robed man (who name he does not know, but the characters likely do). If threatened further (DC 15 or possibly *charmed*), he will tell the whole story and beg the characters not to tell anyone because he has a starving aunt and feed beggars regularly (quite obviously not true). If he reveals any information at all to the characters, he goes on the run and leaves the city as soon as the characters depart from his house, barely taking the time to pack a bag.

15. Honore Berrioc

This two-story house is half-timbered with a slate roof, very well-built. There are glass-paned windows in the top floor, and the house's beams are carved with decorative patterns and small gargoyle-faces.

Honore is a freelance accountant who helps businesses total up their books of account. Unbeknownst to Honore, his wife Beatrice is a Non-Substantialist heretic, one who believes that the gods are unable to act directly in the world other than by granting clerical spells. She owns a pamphlet by the scholar Crasmus of Troyes called "The Limitations of the Divine," setting forth his arguments for Non-Substantiation, a book that carries the death penalty if it is discovered (and if the owner does not recant the heresy).

16. Ardaal Parsine

This is a two-story building, well maintained and neat. It is built of half-timber construction, with a wooden-shingled roof. There is no sign to indicate anything about the building other than the word "Parsine" above the door.

Ardaal Parsine is a journeyman in the Guild of Cheesemakers. He works elsewhere in the city and is not present during the day. His wife Claudette does not work, since Ardaal is a relatively well-off member of the middle class, even though he is not yet a master cheesemaker.

17. Gilbert Toullenese

This is a one-story building of half-timber and plaster, with a wood-shingled roof.

Gilbert (N male human **Ftr3**) is an attendant at the city baths where he acts, essentially, as a bouncer. His wife Nancie is a bookkeeper who works with Honore Berrioc (see area **15**) on larger tasks.

18. Residence of Feodric Ozzerd, Merchant

This one-story residence is obviously owned by someone rich. The roof is slate and the building is of stone. The windows are barred and stoutly shuttered.

The Ozzerd family are merchants and own their own warehouse (see area **5**). They are complicit in the smuggling operation being carried on in the Four Corners, but do not know about the kidnapping or the fact that the tunnels under Dead Fiddler Square extend beneath the city wall. As far as Ozzerd knows, goods come in through the tunnels, and leave his warehouse by wagon.

19. Isarn Jarn

This three-story house is built of cheap wood and plaster, an obvious fire hazard. There is no sign outside.

Isarn Jarn is a laborer for one of the city's brickmakers, and sublets the rest of the house to other workers.

20. Coribald Nightwatch

This three-story building is half-timbered and has a wood-shingled roof. There are shuttered windows along the top floor, and a walled garden beside the house.

Coribald works as a freelance torchbearer/guard for people making their way through the city streets after dark. He sleeps during the day, and is not happy to be awakened by people knocking on his door. It requires a successful DC 20 Cha (Persuasion) check to get anything useful out of him, and his only contribution to the party's knowledge is that he remembers once at about midnight that he saw someone climbing down a ladder from the roof of the Four Corners' eastern building, "the low one." He didn't ask questions, and cannot describe the person.

21. Cabinetmaker

This two-story house has a small walled garden to the side, with a neatly lettered sign reading, "keep out." The roof is neatly shingled with wood, and the windows on the top floor have beautifully carved shutters.

Tharthibal Groone is a freelance cabinetmaker, a master member of the Carpenters' Guild, who works to order for households that hire him. He is not wealthy because he dislikes people, does not hire apprentices, and tends to insult his customers. He will also insult the characters.

22. Lobright Gorm, Teamster

This is a two-story house, half-timbered and well-kept. The roof is tiled with slates, and there is a walled yard beside the house.

Lobright and his 2 sons have a wagon (kept in the garden to the side of the house) and hire themselves out to deliver goods throughout the city or even into the countryside for short trips. Mistress Gorm is a phenomenal cook, and occasionally works as a caterer. None of them know anything of value about the Four Corners, but the characters will be offered a jam tart.

23. Warehouse Workers

This is a two-story building, drab and not very well-kept. It is built of plastered brick, and has a wood-shingled roof.

This house is rented out to a group of 5 peasants from the countryside, two of whom work in the adjacent warehouse.

24. Warehouse

This sturdy, two-story building is made of stone, and has a roof of slate tiles. A sign over the woor reads, "Warehouse," and there is a second sign beside the door reading, "For sale, contact House Borgandy."

This small warehouse on the Via Scorpioli is partitioned for the use of several small merchants. It is operated by a manager (Ilgor Manat) on behalf of the Borgandy family at the moment, for they foreclosed on an unpaid mortgage three months ago. The place is for sale, if there are any buyers.

25. Sir Vodivaine of Remballo (Landlord)

This two-story building is decorated with carved and painted beams, and the windows of the top floor are paned with glass. The roof is of wooden shingles, painted a rich, red color.

Sir Vodivaine's family has resided in the city for four generations, owning several houses that they rent to tenants. Sir Vodivaine is fat and not particularly greedy, but he has a hot temper. Dame Rillian Vodivaine is friendly but very aware of her high social status. The Vodivaines own the vacant building at area **27**. They know nothing of value to the characters, whom they perceive to be of low social status in any case. "Please go away, we contribute at the temple for the welfare of beggars, we don't give food to them at the front door."

Sir Vodivaine: AC 10 or 20; **HP** 32 (5d8+10); **Spd** 30ft;
   Melee longsword (+3, 1d8+1 slashing);; **SA** multiattack (longsword x2); **Str** +1, **Dex** +0, **Con** +2; **Int** +0, **Wis** +1, **Cha** +1; **Skills** Perception +3, Intimidation +3; **AL** LN; **CR** 1/2; **XP** 100.
   Equipment: plate mail and shield (in house), longsword (worn on belt), dagger, belt pouch containing 2 gems (100gp each), 14gp, and house key.

26. Ulric Plasterer

This is a two story building, half-timbered and well built. The roof is shingled in wood, and there are shuttered windows (not with glass) in the top floor.

Ulrich is a contract plaster-worker with various builders. He doesn't even know where the Four Corners is, since he walks north to his place of employment from here.

27. Vacant Building

This three-story building is half-timbered, and has a roof of slate tiles. The windows are shuttered and locked, and the place looks disused.

Sir Vodivaine (see area **25**) owns this building.

28. Bartlet of Ruece

This is an old stone building, probably from early in the city's history, built of fieldstone rather than mortared blocks. It has two stories and the roof is made of unpainted wood shingles. There are shuttered windows in the top floor.

Bartlet is a day laborer from the countryside (a hamlet called Ruece). A successful DC 10 Cha (Persuasion) check reveals the he works with a red-haired man in robes who ties back his hair. The man is a massive brute named Ulbrogar, who can often be found in the Hooded Falcon. This is true, but Ulbrogar has a full head of hair and does not wear robes. No one anywhere else has even remotely connected Ulbrogar to the party's questions because he simply does not fit the description. Except, apparently, to Bartlet.

29. Rodrion Carpenter

This is a pleasant, well-built house with walled gardens beside it. The construction is half-timber, and the roof is shingled with wood. The building has two stories, and there is a small placard near the door with a picture of a hammer, sign of the Carpenters Guild.

Rodrion is a journeyman carpenter in the Carpenters' Guild, a house-framer. Like Beatrice Berrioc (area **15**), Rodrion is a Non-Substantialist heretic, but he does not know Beatrice. He meets with similarly heretical friends from the Carpenters' Guild elsewhere in the city. A successful DC 20 Int (Religion) check allows a character to notice a pattern of wood in the door-placard that looks like a secret sign used by many Non-Substantialist heretics. The bounty is 100gp, if the party decides to take action on this, but if they get involved with a heresy investigation it will completely blow their cover in the neighborhood.

30. Opium Den

This two-story building is a rickety construction of wood and plaster, with a wood-shingled roof. The picture of a smoking pipe is crudely drawn over the top of the door.

This building is an opium den where the drug is sold by the pipe to users who then sleep it off on one of the pallets that cover the floor. The building itself is rented, but the operator of the den is a man named Porthos Quaine (CE male human **Ftr5**), who is a member of the Five Circles opium gang. The Five Circles are not a significant group: two of them travel to Manas to buy the opium, and the other three members of the gang run opium dens in different parts of the city (this being one of them). They are actually quite terrified that one of the Manas opium gangs might start trying to consolidate business here in Remballo, for the Manas gangs are extremely violent. Porthos is the only member of the Five Circles Gang who can swing a sword reliably, and his four partners all distrust him.

Porthos himself is worried because he has recently spotted someone he knows from his occasional visits to purchase opium in Manas: a member of the Manas Thieves' Guild named Gedriz the Legbreaker. Porthos has reached the uncomfortable conclusion that Gedriz might be planning to extort money from opium dens, and Porthos' den is right in the area he assumes Gedriz is scouting. He happens to know one useful thing about Gedriz, which is that the Manas thief is considered one of the rising stars in the Manas guild, although he is known to be reckless and rebellious.

31. Hauvoc the Teamster

This building is well maintained, a two-story structure of plastered brick and timber beams. The roof is made of wooden shingles painted black. A small sign over the door bears the picture of a wagon, and beneath it the word "Haulage" has been neatly lettered in black paint.

Hauvoc owns a wagon (kept in the caravansary on the east side of the city), and hires out for whatever sort of haulage is needed by various contractors. He once hauled a lot of dirt and rubble from the Four Corners, a whole wagonload a day for 5 days.

32. Bolti Ghar, Wine Deliverer

This is a two-story building of whitewashed bricks, turned grey with the weather. The roof is wood shingled and needs repair. Two windows on the top floor are painted blue, but the paint is faded and peeling.

Bolti delivers casks of wine from a wine merchant to various taverns and households in the city. He does not own his own wagon, nor does he deliver to the Four Corners.

33. Luco Fortinbras

This corner building has only one floor, with two shuttered windows that look like they have taken considerable damage from passers-by, including the name "Bertrand" carved into one of them. The building is made of brick covered in plaster, which has been broken away in spots. The roof is of wooden shingles.

Luco is a caravan guard who finds work as a night watchman if he is not traveling between Remballo and Olaric or Manas.

34. Yanno the Pastry Seller

The top floor of this two-story house is built out over the top of the alleyway running beside it, turning the narrow street into a tunnel between the adjacent buildings. The structure is a mix of whitewashed stone and black timber beams, with two windows in the top floor looking out over the Via Scorpioli.

Yanno and his wife Erissa own two handcarts, which they push through the streets selling pastries (bought from bakers in the Portico Market). They also, once per day, make a delivery to the Haven Street Gate of the Four Corners. They are not delivering pastries; they are making a delivery of horse meat purchased from a butcher outside the Dead Fiddler Square neighborhood. If asked about the deliveries, they will be completely forthcoming since they have no suspicions about the Four Corners. The people want horse meat, and Yanno and Erissa sell them horse meat at a nice profit. It does seem to be an awful lot of meat, though, they must admit.

35. Ilander the Potter

This is a two-story building with an open-fronted potter's workshop on the ground floor. The building is half-timbered, and the roof is shingled with wood. There are three windows on the top floor, all wood-shuttered.

Ilander makes pottery and sells it to the merchants of the Portico Market. A successful DC 10 Cha (Persuasion) check gets him to reveal he recalls the man with the red braid because he sold him a chamber pot. He also remembers that other merchants sold him a set of window bars and some manacles the same day.

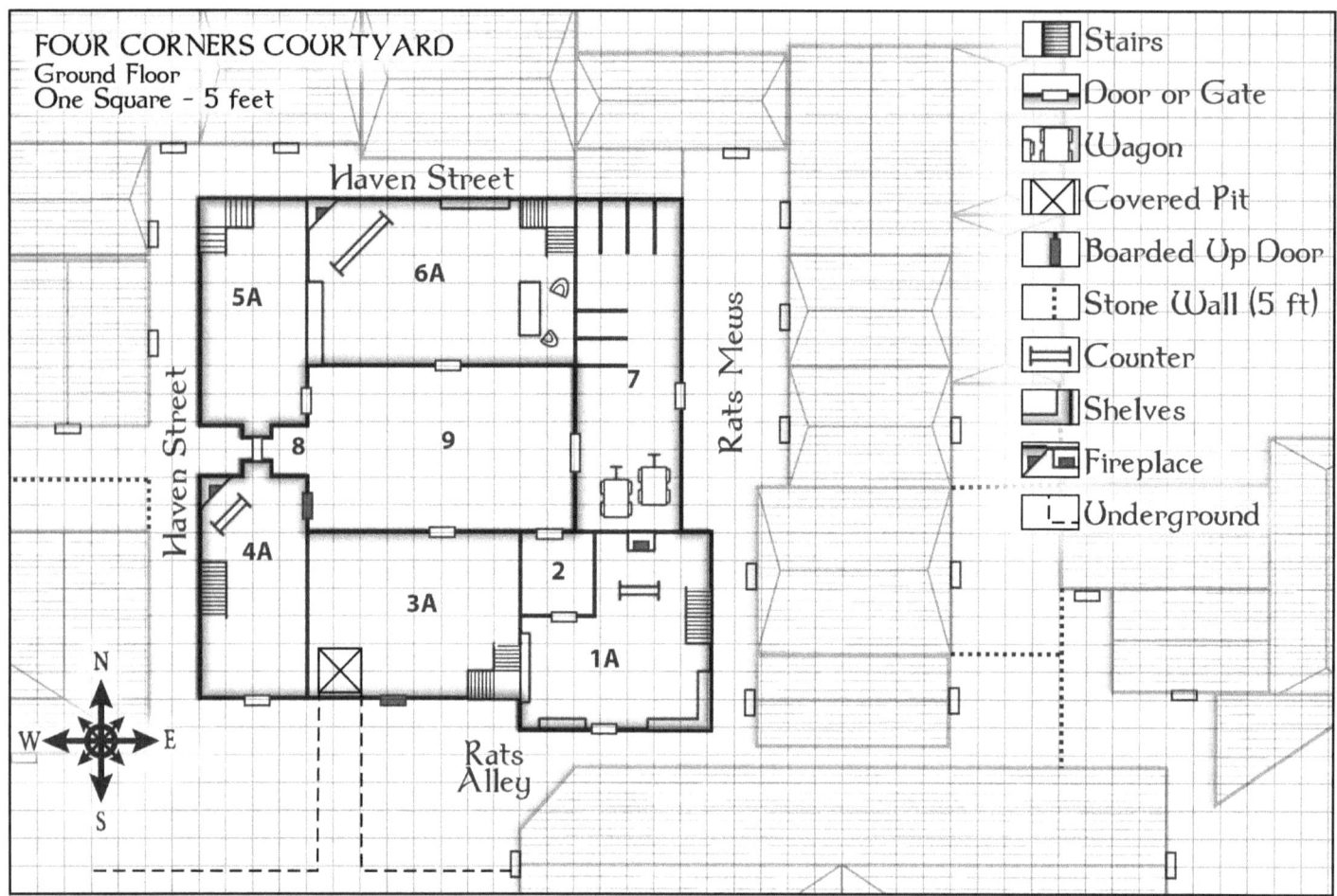

FOUR CORNERS COURTYARD
Ground Floor
One Square - 5 feet

Haven Street

Haven Street

Rats Mews

Rats Alley

Stairs
Door or Gate
Wagon
Covered Pit
Boarded Up Door
Stone Wall (5 ft)
Counter
Shelves
Fireplace
Underground

The Four Corners

Remember the Upper Floors

Before starting the adventure, take note that there are some balconies on the second level that the characters will notice, and also that some of the adjoining buildings are built slightly over the street, making them closer to the buildings of the Four Corners than they are at street level. Also take note of the locations of the windows. There are no windows at ground level, even in the surrounding buildings, for at the time these structures were built, the area was quite dangerous.

Visitors and Deliveries

The characters might stake out the gate on Haven Street or the door in Rat's Mews. If so, they will learn the following information about those who visit the Four Corners. A successful DC 10 Wis (Perception) check allows the characters to notice the first important point is that none of the thieves, or Doctor Remora, apparently ever leave the place. If the stakeout lasts more than a day, this becomes quite suspicious. The second visitor is Widow Tarcy, who prepares lots of cooked food. She delivers the pots of stew and such twice per day to the Haven Street gate. Gedriz the Legbreaker opens the gate, pays her a couple of silver pieces, gives her the pots from her last visit, and takes the ones with food. The third visitor to the Haven Street gate is Yanno or Erissa, the pastry sellers, delivering horse meat (see area **34** on the Dead Fiddler Square neighborhood map). The final visitor arrives at night, usually about ten o'clock, preceded by a foul smell. This is Bodo the Night-soil dealer, who picks up the contents of chamber pots along his route (free!), then takes them to mix with dirt and sell as fertilizer. Naladir the Elf opens the gate for him and hands chamber pots through, which Bodo empties into the large clay pots in his wagon. Bodo himself does not live in the neighborhood. He knows nothing at all about the Four Corners, he just picks up the night-soil and moves on to other houses.

There is one other outside contact with the Four Corners, but it will not be seen in a stakeout of the complex. The Remballo thief Caron Brun, a traitor to the guild working with the Manas thieves, delivers information to them through the tunnel leading from Ozzerd's Warehouse at area **5** on the neighborhood map. The messages are usually just about the times when the Thieves' Guild sends an observer to check on the courtyard, but occasionally he passes on some very sensitive information about the Remballo Guild's activities. Since the Manas thieves burn the letters, none of the seriously incriminating letters currently exist.

Ground Floor

1. Glassware Shop

1A. Ground Floor Shop

This building looks like a shop, with shelves of glassware against the wall. A skinny man with a pockmarked face stands behind a counter near the back of the room, and smiles to see you enter. Stairs on the east wall lead to a second floor, and a back door stands closed in the western corner of the north wall.

This is indeed an ordinary, innocent shop rented to Blaroin Adaloc by the sinister Doctor Remora. Blaroin knows absolutely nothing about anything illegal going on in the courtyard. He has no access to the courtyard itself; the door of his back room is locked from the inside of the courtyard (as are his upstairs balcony door and his upstairs window looking out over the stable).

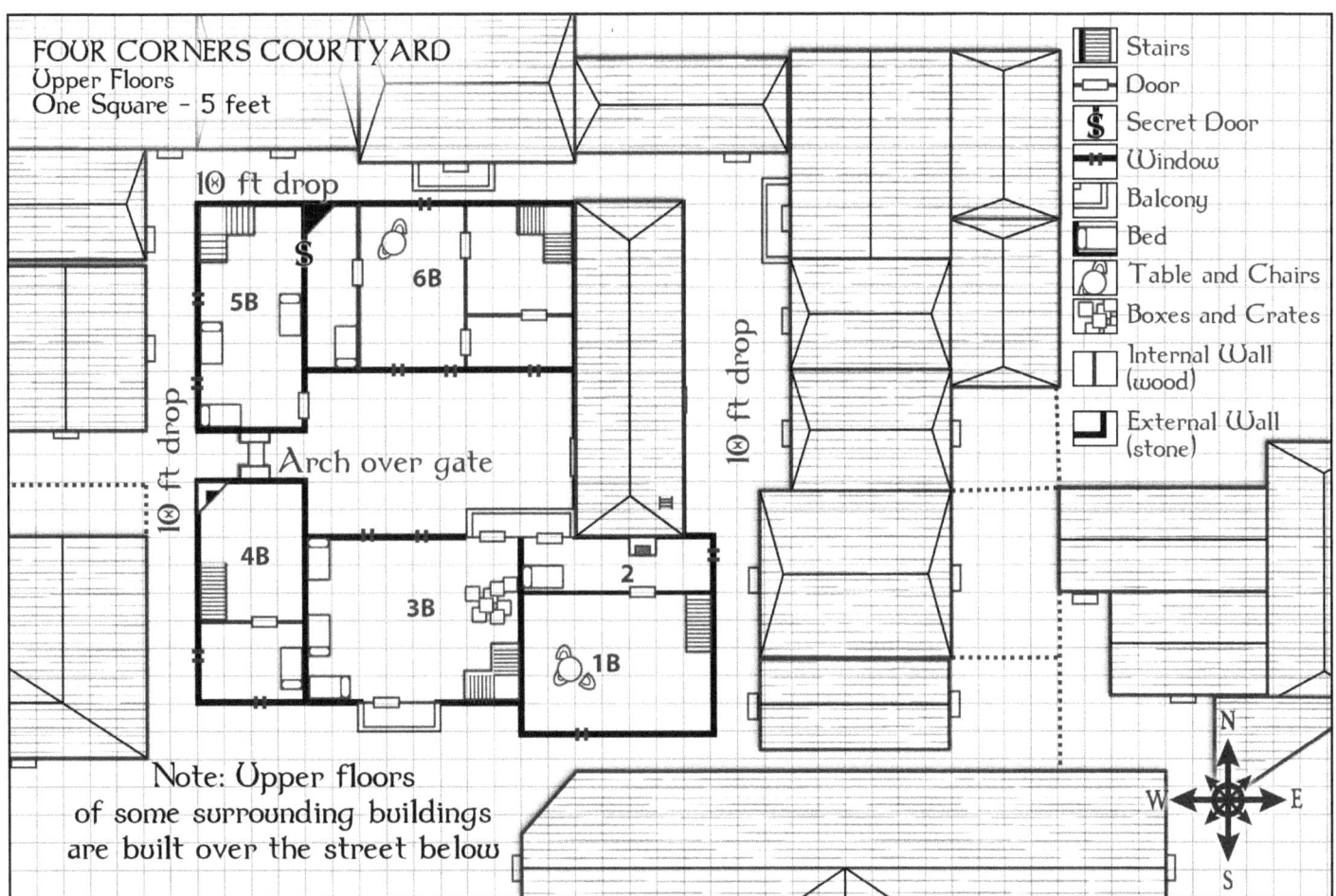

FOUR CORNERS COURTYARD
Upper Floors
One Square - 5 feet

10 ft drop

Arch over gate

Note: Upper floors
of some surrounding buildings
are built over the street below

	Stairs
	Door
$	Secret Door
	Window
	Balcony
	Bed
	Table and Chairs
	Boxes and Crates
	Internal Wall (wood)
	External Wall (stone)

Other than his inventory of glassware and a wooden box containing 5gp and 39sp, there is nothing of interest in Blaroin's shop. The stairs lead up to area **1B**.

1B. Blaroin Adaloc's Bedroom

Blaroin's upstairs chambers are unremarkable and standard for the living quarters of a modest shopkeeper. He keeps a lockbox under his bed (DC 15 with thieves' tools) containing 22gp and 439sp.

2. Back Room

This is the back room of Blaroin's shop, where he stores extra glassware. The door in the north wall is securely locked (DC 20 with thieves' tools to open) from the outside.

3. Tunnel Building

3A. Ground Floor and Tunnel
Note: The door into this building is a wooden double door large enough to accommodate a wagon. The door is of recent construction, and broken masonry around the edges indicates that it replaced a much smaller door.

The interior of the building is a single room with a rickety wooden staircase leading up to the second floor in the southeast corner. Large wooden crates and bales of wool and hay fill most of the room, but a pathway between the stored items is open to the southwest corner. The interior of the building is quite dark, since there are no windows.

At night, one of the dogs (**mastiff**) sleeps here, and sounds an alarm if not dealt with quickly.

Mastiff: **AC** 12; **HP** 5 (1d8+1); **Spd** 40ft; **Melee** bite (+3, 1d6+1 piercing plus knock prone, DC 11 Str); **Str** +1, **Dex** +2, **Con** +1, **Int** –4, **Wis** +1, **Cha** –2; **Skills** Perception +3; **Senses** keen hearing and smell; **AL** U; **CR** 1/8; **XP** 25.

The open area in the southwest corner is a very important place. It is a very large trapdoor, not hinged, but a removable section of the floor that can be located with a DC 20 Int (Investigation) check requires two people to lift it away from the top of the pit below. The pit descends 20ft underground to a tunnel leading south. Heavy bales of wool block the boarded-up door the characters may have seen from the outside.

The stairs lead up to area **3B**.

3B. Thieves and Storage

The upper floor of this building is single, large room containing three wooden beds and a large pile of boxes and crates. Doors lead through the north and south walls, both of which must lead to balconies. There are two windows in the north wall overlooking the courtyard, both of which are open and un-shuttered (although there are locking shutters that can be closed).

This is the room of three of the Manas thieves, including the ringleader of the operation, Jamais Vue. Jamais is a rising star in the Manas Thieves' Guild, and a potential rival to the guildmaster within a few years. Jamais wants to reduce the number of those years, so he has started this operation to provide himself with funding for an eventual takeover. Now that the smuggling and fencing operation is well under way, he plans to return to Manas from the "vacation" he has been taking, resuming his ordinary role in the Manas guild while money rolls in here in Remballo.

Only one of the thieves (Fandiff Quickfingers) is likely to be present at any given time, since Jamais is usually down in the lair, and one of the two others (assume it's Selardy Doland) is always on guard in area **16** of the Lair.

Fandiff Quickfingers, Male Human Rog3: AC 15; **HP** 23 (3d8+6); **Spd** 30ft; **Melee** shortsword (+5, 1d6+3 piercing); **SA** cunning action (bonus to dash, disengage, or hide), sneak attack (+2d6 with tactical advantage or ally within 5ft of target); **Str** +0, **Dex** +3 (+5), **Con** +2, **Int** +2 (+4), **Wis** +1, **Cha** +0; **Skills** Investigation +4, Perception +3, Stealth +5, Sleight of Hand +7; **Traits** expertise (sleight of hand, thieves' tools), fast hands; **AL** NE; **CR** 1/4; **XP** 50.

> **Equipment:** studded leather armor, short sword, necklace (10gp), belt pouch with thieves' tools, key and 12gp.

Treasure: Each of the three beds has a locked chest (DC 20 with thieves' tools to open) underneath, along with a chamber pot.

Fandiff's Chest: This chest contains ordinary clothing plus a small stash of opium (50gp), a bag of 28gp, and a small silver chime (10gp). The chime is not magical, but the dogs have been trained not to bark when they hear it. This has been necessary because, for some reason, dogs absolutely hate Fandiff. He also has a small medallion showing the image of a hand with two fingers removed (this is the medallion of the Manas Thieves' Guild).

Selardy's Chest: This chest contains ordinary clothing, a bag of 45gp, and a turquoise gem worth 100gp). Selardy's chest, like Fandiff's has one of the Manas guild medallions.

Jamais's Chest: Jamais' chest contains clothing and one of the Manas guild medallions, like the others. There is nothing else in here since he stashes his treasure in a box in area **16** in the lair.

4. Widow Tarcy's House

4A. Ground Floor Living Room

> The ground floor of this building appears to be unoccupied, but someone lives here. There are comfortable-looking chairs and a kitchen in the north end of the room, along with a small wooden table. Stairs along the room's west wall lead to an upper floor. There is a door in the northeast wall, which must lead to the courtyard. A large stone fireplace is built into the room's northwest corner, and is surrounded by very large pots and pans, together with a countertop piled high with meat and vegetables.

This building is the home of the Widow Tarcy, a very grumpy old lady who has been living here for more than forty years. She is currently upstairs. The widow knows nothing about any sort of strange doings in the courtyard, and she is quite convinced that nothing could possibly be going on without her knowledge. If pressed, she admits that she does the cooking for the courtyard's inhabitants, delivering food to the gate twice per day, and gets paid for it.

The door in the room's northeast corner is securely barred and boarded up from the outside, preventing access to the courtyard. The stairs lead up to area **4B**.

4B. Widow Tarcy's Rooms

> The upper floor is obviously a residence. The walls are decorated with knitted wall-hangings with pictures of cats.

The Widow Tarcy will most likely be encountered in one of the two upper rooms. She will scream for assistance if anyone enters the area, and this will certainly alert the thieves that something is amiss.

5. Kennels and Storage

5A. Ground Floor Dog Kennels

> The room is dark, and something snarls.

This room contains **2 small dogs** and a big dog **(mastiff)** that begin barking if they are not immediately handled in some way. They stop and eat meat without barking if any is fed to them. Only one of the dogs is an attack dog; the others are small mongrels. Several food dishes are in the room, and if anyone bothers to count, there are five of them, plus one big water dish.

The stairs in the room, which can be seen once the dogs are dealt with, lead up to area **5B**.

Mastiff: AC 12; **HP** 5 (1d8+1); **Spd** 40ft; **Melee** bite (+3, 1d6+1 piercing plus knock prone, DC 11 Str); **Str** +1, **Dex** +2, **Con** +1, **Int** −4, **Wis** +1, **Cha** −2; **Skills** Perception +3; **Senses** keen hearing and smell; **AL** U; **CR** 1/8; **XP** 25.

Small Dog (2): AC 12; **HP** 3 (1d6); **Spd** 30ft; **Melee** bite (+2, 1d4 piercing); **Str** +0, **Dex** +2, **Con** +0, **Int** −4, **Wis** +0, **Cha** −2; **Skills** Perception +2; **Senses** keen hearing and smell; **AL** U; **CR** 0; **XP** 10.

5B. Thieves' Quarters

> This floor of the building is a single room with three beds.

One of the beds belongs to Rafael the Cur, one belongs to Gedriz the Legbreaker, and the third belongs to Naladir the Elf. Gedriz and Naladir are the gate guards, so only one of them will is present in this room at a time. Their information is given in area **8**. Rafael is here during the night, but he usually goes out into the city during the day, leaving through the exit in Ozzerd's Warehouse. If the characters attack the Four Corners during the day, Rafael might escape the net.

Rafael the Cur, Animal Trainer: AC 14; **HP** 11 (2d8+2); **Spd** 30ft; **Melee** longsword (+3, 1d8+1 slashing); **Str** +1, **Dex** +2, **Con** +1, **Int** +0, **Wis** +2, **Cha** +0; **Skills** Animal Handling +4, Perception +4; **AL** NE; **CR** 1/8; **XP** 25

> **Equipment:** studded leather armor, longsword, belt pouch with key, 3gp, 13sp.

If the characters speak to Rafael rather than killing him outright, he tells them that he is being kept prisoner here (not entirely true), and try to bargain for his freedom if they let him out of the courtyard (a rope out the window, or exit through the gate, he doesn't care). In exchange, he tells them that there is a secret tunnel (area **3**). He claims not to know anything about what is in the tunnels, and also does not disclose that he is the trainer for the dogs in the courtyard, although if asked, he admits that the dogs do not bark at his presence. He explains the wooden mallet away as a tool used for hammering spikes into the walls for digging.

Treasure: All three beds have locked chests (DC 20 with thieves' tools to open) beneath them (and a chamber pot).

Rafael's Bed: In addition to the chest and chamber pot, there is a large wooden mallet with a five-foot-handle under the bed (used to discipline the bulette, since it would not feel a whip at all). Along with clothes, the chest contains a bag of 32gp and 27sp.

Gedriz's Bed: Gedriz's chest contains ordinary clothing, along with a false mustache and beard. A small bag contains 102gp and an emerald (250gp). Additionally, there is a small medallion showing the image of a hand with two fingers removed (this is the medallion of the Manas

Thieves' Guild, which is the last thing Gedriz wants to advertise here in Remballo, since he is a renegade).

Naladir's Bed: The chest under Naladir's bed is locked and contains a needle trap with a poison that causes 1d6 poison damage. The chest contains ordinary clothing, a medallion of the Manas Thieves Guild identical to the one in Gedriz's chest, a bag of 272gp, and a *cloak of elvenkind.*

6. House of Doctor Remora

6A. Ground Floor Workshop

Note: Door is locked.

The ground floor of this building is a single room, the floor strewn with sand. A counter in the northwest corner holds various bottles and jars of liquid. Shelves on the north and south walls are stacked high with books, bird skeletons, glass jars of dried herbs, measuring scales, and alchemical equipment. A table and chairs are set up in the southeast corner, stacked with dirty dishes. A wooden staircase in the northeast corner leads to the second floor.

This is Doctor Remora's workshop and living room. The doctor is upstairs, but there is a good chance he hears anyone moving around down here.

The shelves contain the sorts of things a magic-user keeps in a workshop, but there is nothing of unusual value. The whole lot could probably be sold for no more than 200gp. The stairs lead to area **6B.**

6B. Doctor Remora's Chambers

Stair Room: The entry chamber is empty, with the exception of a cheap, canvas wall hanging painted with floral patterns on the north wall. There are doors on the south and west walls of the room. The west door is normal, and can be locked from the other side (it is). The south door has a recently installed bar across it, allowing it to be securely locked from this side.

Southeast Room: This is the room where Doctor Remora imprisoned Savario Borgandy until the captive started shouting for help through the window. There is a door in the west wall and the north wall, both of which can be barred from the outside. The window in the south wall has recently installed metal prison bars, a single grating that is attached across the outside of the window. There is a chamber pot in the southeast corner but no furniture.

Central Room: The main features of this room are a wooden table, the three doors, and three windows. There is a door in the west wall, and two doors in the east wall. (It is also possible that the characters encounter Doctor Remora in this room.) All of the windows are shuttered and locked from the inside during the night. A stack of paper and writing implements are on the table (see treasure, below).

West Bedroom: The west bedroom is Doctor Remora's. It contains a bed with two wooden chests underneath it, along with a half-full chamber pot.

Doctor Remora, Male Human Wiz4: AC 12 (15 with *mage armor*); **HP** 20 (4d6+4); **Spd** 30ft; **Melee** dagger (+4, 1d4+2 slashing); **SA** spells (Int +6, DC 14); **Str** +0, **Dex** +2, **Con** +1, **Int** +4 (+6), **Wis** +2 (+4), **Cha** +0; **AL** NE; **CR** 1; **XP** 200.
  Spells (slots): 0 (at will)—*blade ward, fire bolt, ray of frost, shocking grasp*; 1st (4)— *mage armor, magic missile, sleep, witch bolt*; 2nd (3)— *flaming sphere, invisibility, mirror image, web.*
  Equipment: robes, dagger, belt pouch containing 4sp and 18cp.

Treasure: Two interesting treasures are found in Doctor Remora's Chambers. The first is the stack of papers on the table in the central room, and the second is one of the chests in Doctor Remora's bedroom.

The Papers: The papers at the top of the stack are blank, but anyone rifling through them finds that the bottom pages have been written upon.

The bottom pages appear to be much sturdier and higher-quality paper than the ones on top. Several of the bottom pages are titled "Letter of Credit by the House of Borgandy," filled out with different small amounts of money: five written for 25gp, two written for 100gp, and three written for 500gp. The lines for "Description of Holder" and for a signature are blank on all of the documents. There is also a ring, apparently a signet ring of some kind, hidden behind the papers. It shows residue of blue sealing wax. Characters could potentially use these to collect money from the House of Borgandy in other cities, but a forged signature is very likely to be detected.

One of the wooden chests under the bed contains ordinary clothing, items of personal hygiene, and two bottles of white powder (sleeping draughts from Doctor Escalous — see area **7** on the map of Dead Fiddler Square). The sleeping draughts only have the effect of creating a slight lassitude; they do not force a person into sleep. The second chest contains 57gp, 1284sp, and 94cp, along with Doctor Remora's spellbook, 2 sapphires worth 300gp each, and three rental contracts. Two of the contracts are for the widow Tarcy and for the glass shop. The third is less of a rental contract and more of a contract to share profits, since it grants "General use of the Four Corners in exchange for 5%." It is not stated what the five percent is actually from. In addition to Doctor Remora's signature, the document also bears the signature of "Casmir Dark, Guildmaster of the Thieves' Guild of Manas." The signature is a bad forgery, which will be detected by anyone familiar with Casmir's handwriting (or by comparing it with his original signature). This document is dated two months ago.

Spellbook: Doctor Remora's spellbook is bound in gray leather and stamped with his name and the symbol of a moon and stars. It contains all of the above prepared first level spells plus *charm person, detect magic, identify,* and *protection from evil and good.* The second level spells in the book are prepared ones listed above.

7. Stables

Note: The door leading into this building from Rats Mews is locked, but not blocked off. The denizens of Four Corners use it from time to time for shoveling horse dung into the alley.

This one-story building is a stable with stalls for six horses, three of which are occupied by large draft horses. Two wagons sit in the southern part of the room. Various bits of tack and harness hang from wooden pegs in the walls.

The three horses are accustomed to people, and do not react to the characters' presence.

8. Gate

This is a wide wooden gate, large enough to accommodate a wagon. The gate is eight feet high, and is topped by a stone archway between the buildings to the north and south. There is a peephole in the gate that can be opened from the inside.

The gate is guarded day and night. During the day, the gatekeeper is Gedriz the Legbreaker, one of the Manas thieves, unless he is away on other business. At night, the gatekeeper is Naladir the Elf. Naladir sleeps very little, if at all, and is usually awake during the day as well.

Gedriz the Legbreaker, Male Human Rog3: AC 15; **HP** 26 (3d8+9); **Spd** 30ft; **Melee** shortsword (+5, 1d6+3 piercing); **SA** cunning action (bonus to dash, disengage, or hide), sneak attack (+2d6 with tactical advantage or ally within 5ft of target); **Str** +0, **Dex** +3 (+5), **Con** +3, **Int** +0 (+2), **Wis** +2, **Cha** +0; **Skills** Perception +3, Stealth +7, Sleight of Hand +5, Survival +4; **Traits** expertise (stealth, thieves' tools), fast hands; **AL** NE; **CR** 1/4; **XP** 50.

    Equipment: studded leather armor, short sword, bracelet (25gp), belt pouch with thieves' tools, key and 22gp.

Naladir, Male Elf Rog3: AC 16; **HP** 23 (3d8+6); **Spd** 30ft; **Melee** shortsword (+6, 1d6+4 piercing); **SA** cunning action (bonus to dash, disengage, or hide), sneak attack (+2d6 with tactical advantage or ally within 5ft of target); **Str** +0, **Dex** +4 (+6), **Con** +2, **Int** +2 (+4), **Wis** +2, **Cha** +0; **Skills** Insight +4, Perception +4, Stealth +6, Sleight of Hand +8; **Senses** darkvision 60ft; **Traits** expertise (sleight of hand, thieves' tools), fast hands, fey ancestry, trance; **AL** NE; **CR** 1/4; **XP** 50.

    Equipment: studded leather armor, short sword, belt pouch with thieves' tools, key, 6gp, 15sp.

Naladir has a scrap of folded parchment in his belt pouch with "Burn" written on the outside. He got the note only recently, so he has not yet burned it. The inside simply says, "Thief patrol at 9th hour; leaves 9th hour, 3 glass; free from third glass to midnight, then next check." The handwriting is flowery and fancy, but the note is not signed. If the note is given to the Remballo thieves, they will immediately be able to tell which one of their members has been betraying them, since the handwriting is distinctive.

    GM Note: 9th hour, 3 glass is 9:30 p.m. as any resident of the Lost Lands would know.

9. Courtyard of the Four Corners

The courtyard has nothing interesting in it other than some muddy wagon tracks leading from the door of one building (area **3**) to the gate (area **8**). It is overlooked by several windows and by a wooden-railed balcony, although the thieves seldom go out to sun themselves on the balcony.

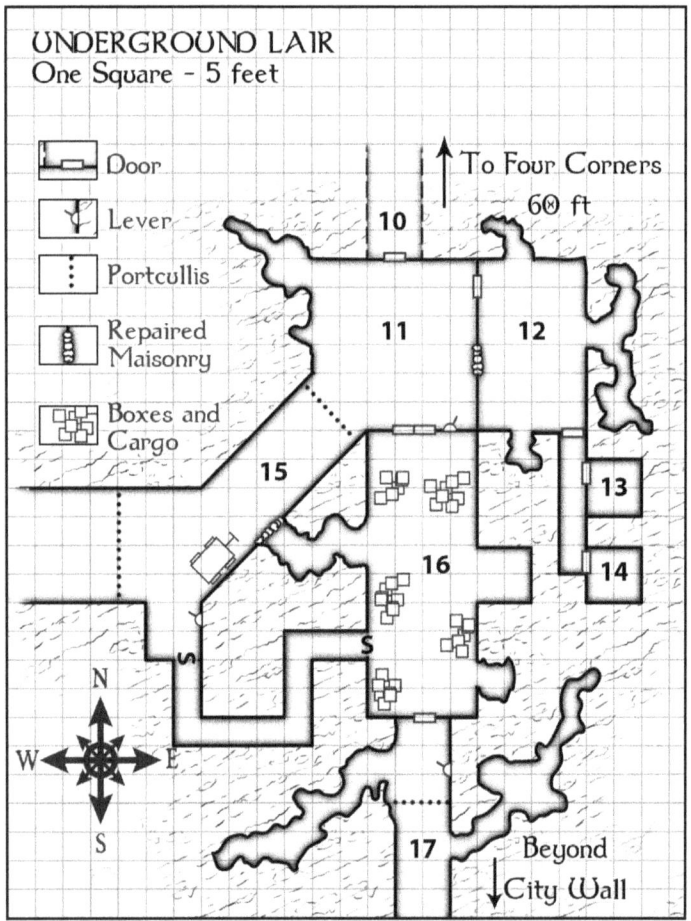

The Lair

The lair can be reached only through the tunnel (area **3A**) or from Ozzerd's Warehouse (area **5** on the map of Dead Fiddler Square).

10. Entry Door

A large gate blocks the underground corridor, which must be at least twenty feet underground by this point due to the downward slope from north to south. The gate is large enough for a wagon to pass through when it is open. It is currently closed, however.

The gate is not barred from the inside, and it can be pushed open easily. However, the hinges are old and make a loud squealing sound.

11. Main Room

This 30-foot-by-30-foot underground chamber is obviously the central room for some sort of cellar complex, for it has a number of different exits leading to other chambers. In addition to the large door in the north wall, which you now see can be barred from the inside, there are two other large doors, one in the east wall and one in the south wall. A very large open passageway leads southwest from that corner of the room. A lever is in the wall beside the south door, which is currently in the "up" position. The oddest feature of the room, though, is that the walls have been damaged almost everywhere, up to a height of five feet. Deep scratches are gouged into the stone, the entire northwest corner of the room has been tunneled away to quite some distance, and part of the east wall has apparently been repaired with bricks and mortar where something dug through it.

One odd item in the room is a massive, 5ft-long iron bar with 10ft-long chains attached to each side of it. The chains end in large iron hooks.

The iron bar and chains are actually a bit and harness for the bulette in area **12**, allowing the creature to be attached to a wagon. If the characters inspect it, they discover deep toothmarks in the iron bar.

The wide tunnel to the southwest has a portcullis in the roof, which is spotted only if the characters inspect the tunnel entrance. The lever in the room's south wall raises and lowers the portcullis.

If the characters inspect the south door, they discover a peephole, a little metal cover that slides up and down. If they open it, they get a partial view of area **16**, since Selardy has a light. They will be able to see the dog, but not Selardy himself.

Any significant noise in this room (and definitely if there is a fight with the bulette in area **12**) alerts Selardy, who checks the peephole to see what is happening, and Jamais Vue in area **15**, who sneaks forward to see what is happening through the tunnel entrance. Even quiet noises in here have a 50% chance to warn Jamais Vue that there are intruders in the lair. Vue may try to link up with Selardy if the characters look wounded or few in number, or he might try to escape.

12. Bulette Room

Like the room outside, the walls of this room are all deeply gouged and even tunneled away. There are short tunnels in the north and south walls, and a deeper one in the east wall. There is a door in the south wall barred from this side that also seems to have suffered some damage. The source of the damage is right before you in the middle of the room, an armadillo-type creature with long claws and a large, toothy mouth. An armor plate like a dorsal fin rises from the middle of its back. It is quite small, only four feet in length, but its response to your arrival is a ferocious charge.

This creature is a very young **bulette** the renegade Manas thieves purchased when some peasants (who are lucky to be alive) captured it at an even younger age. The beast has been trained (somewhat) by Rafael the animal trainer, and it will not attack any of the denizens of the Four Corners. The bulette is perfectly happy to pull things around underground, unlike horses or mules. It has finally been trained not to dig through the walls, but the damage throughout the cellar complex testifies to how destructive it was in the early stages of training. With anyone other than the Manas thieves and Doctor Remora, the beast is utterly feral. It still regards people in general as nothing more than food.

As with area **11**, noise here alerts the Manas thief Selardy, who is on guard in area **16**.

Bulette (Young): AC 15; HP 67 (9d8+27); **Spd** 30ft, burrow 30ft; **Melee** bite (+4, 4d8+2 piercing); **SA** deadly leap (move at least 20ft, land in space, knocked prone, 3d4+2 bludgeoning plus 3d4+2 slashing, DC 13 Str or Dex half not prone pushed 5ft); **Str** +2, **Dex** +0, **Con** +3, **Int** −4, **Wis** +0, **Cha** −3; **Skills** Perception +4; **Senses** darkvision 60ft, tremorsense 60ft; **Traits** standing leap (20ft long, 10ft high); **AL** U; **CR** 2; **XP** 450.

13. Empty Cell

The door to this chamber has a barred window in it, showing the inside of the room on the other side.

This room is a featureless, empty prison cell.

14. Savario Borgandy

The door to this chamber has a barred window in it, like the one to the north. However, as you draw near, someone inside begins shouting for help.

The person in the cell is Savario Borgandy (**commoner**). He is dressed in the rags of rich clothing and chained to the wall. He explains to his rescuers that he is a member of the Borgandy family, kidnapped to write false letters of credit on behalf of a man with a red-dyed queue of hair. He knows that he has been forced to write several letters under the influence of mental domination magic, and is frantic to get loose to warn his family about the letters.

If Savario is returned safely to the Borgandys, they pay a substantial reward. If the characters kill him, and the Borgandys somehow learn about it, then the characters will be facing the anger of the city's most powerful merchant family.

15. Tunnel to Ozzerd's Warehouse

This is a broad, diagonal corridor leading to the southwest. Part of the tunnel's south wall appears to have been broken through and repaired. At the southwest end of the tunnel it appears to fork to the west and south. A sturdy iron portcullis blocks the west fork.

The south "fork" in the tunnel is a guard post containing the lever to open and close the portcullis in the tunnel's west fork. The lever is in the down position, and the portcullis is thus closed.

Unless the thieves have been alerted, the operation's ringleader, Jamais Vue, is counting up several boxes of stolen goods in the cart, getting them ready to go to Ozzerd's Warehouse (area **5** on the map of Dead Fiddler Square). Unlike the other thieves, he will be cautious if he hears a potential attack, and he may attempt to escape from the lair without reinforcing his associates. Based on what he hears, he might head for Ozzerd's Warehouse through the west tunnel, or might go through the secret door to area **16**, planning to escape through the southern tunnel beyond the city walls (area **17**). If he escapes, the party will have made an enemy, although Vue is likely to have much bigger problems than hunting down the characters if his renegade operation is brought to light either in Manas or in Remballo.

Jamais Vue, Ringleader, Male Human Rog4: AC 15; HP 33 (4d8+12); **Spd** 30ft; **Melee** *+1 shortsword* (+7, 1d6+5 piercing); Ranged shortbow (+6, 80ft/320ft, 1d6+4 piercing) **SA** cunning action (bonus to dash, disengage, or hide), sneak attack (+2d6 with tactical advantage or ally within 5ft of target); **Str** +0, **Dex** +4 (+6), **Con** +3, **Int** +2 (+4), **Wis** +2, **Cha** +1; **Skills** Perception +3, Stealth +7, Sleight of Hand +5, Survival +4; **Traits** expertise (stealth, thieves' tools), fast hands; **AL** NE; **CR** 1/2; **XP** 100.
    Equipment: studded leather armor, *+1 short sword*, dagger, shortbow, 20 arrows, *potion of healing*, 25gp gems (x5), key, 47gp.

Contents of Cart: The cart contains several boxes of stolen cloth, bound for resale in the city since it is not easily recognizable. There are 55 bolts of woolen cloth, worth 10gp each.

16. Underground Warehouse

This chamber is stacked high with boxes, crates, bolts of cloth, barrels, and pottery jars. There is a large wooden gate in the south wall, a couple of the roughly gouged tunnels you have already seen elsewhere in the cellars, and a much better constructed tunnel leading to the east.

This is the storage room for the smuggling and fencing operation run by the renegade Manas thieves. The "tunnel" in the west wall is actually a guard post occupied by one of the thieves at all times. For purposes of convenience, assume that it is always Selardy Doland. In addition to the guard, a **small dog** sleeps here and barks at intruders. The sound carries in the lair, but will not be heard all the way back in the Four Corners, although it will alert Jamais Vue in area **15**.

Selardy Doland, Male Human Rog3: AC 15; HP 26 (3d8+9); **Spd** 30ft; **Melee** shortsword (+5, 1d6+3 piercing); **SA** cunning action (bonus to dash, disengage, or hide), sneak attack (+2d6 with tactical advantage or ally within 5ft of target); **Str** +0, **Dex** +3 (+5), **Con** +3, **Int** +0 (+2), **Wis** +2, **Cha** +0; **Skills** Perception +3, Stealth +7, Sleight of Hand +5, Survival +4; **Traits** expertise (stealth, thieves' tools), fast hands; **AL** NE; **CR** 1/4; **XP** 50.

Equipment: studded leather armor, short sword, belt pouch with thieves' tools, key, fake beard, 7gp, 3sp.

Small Dog: **AC** 12; **HP** 3 (1d6); **Spd** 30ft; **Melee** bite (+2, 1d4 piercing); **Str** +0, **Dex** +2, **Con** +0, **Int** −4, **Wis** +0, **Cha** −2; **Skills** Perception +2; **Senses** keen hearing and smell; **AL** U; **CR** 0; **XP** 10.

Selardy Doland hears any substantial noise made in area **11**, and most certainly hears it if there is a fight with the bulette in area **12**. He checks the peephole into area **11**, and if it is not occupied, he dashes out of the storage room, headed for the tunnel back to the Four Corners. If he is allowed to reach the courtyard, he warns all of the inhabitants that there is trouble in the lair.

Treasure: The boxes here contain a large and valuable assortment of merchandise, which totals as high as 7000gp. However, it is all very recognizable stolen merchandise (things with monograms and engraved letters) or massively bulky material like bolts of cloth. It would be possible for the characters to smuggle these goods out themselves, but they immediately recognize that, unlike the personal possessions of the thieves, the cargo here is going to get confiscated if they try to sell it openly in Remballo. As they are picking through the boxes, they find a locked one (DC 25 with thieves' tools to open) that is marked "personal property of Jamais Vue."

Jamais Vue's chest: This chest contains 427gp, and a short letter reading, "Have a good time on your vacation. We expect you back in three months." It is signed with the name Casmir Dark (who is the Guildmaster of the Manas Thieves' Guild). The signature is absolutely nothing like the "Casmir Dark" signature Doctor Remora has on his lease.

17. Tunnel Beyond the Walls

On the far side of the wooden gate is a ten-foot-wide tunnel leading south into the darkness. A lever on the east wall is in the "down" position, which might be related to a massive iron portcullis blocking the tunnel fifteen feet south of the door. As with other places in this cellar complex, the walls are gouged with scratches, and roughly dug tunnels lead away from the main corridor.

This tunnel leads outside the city walls, continuing for almost a mile before ending at a trapdoor in the ceiling. The trapdoor emerges in a "vacant" peasant cottage purchased by Doctor Remora two months ago. The renegade Manas thieves have been using the tunnel to smuggle goods in and out of the city without paying a gate tax, and — more importantly — not allowing the guards at the city gate to identify the more unique items as being stolen in other cities.

Concluding the Adventure

By the time the adventure finishes, if the characters are still alive, they will have the means to get treasure from both the Thieves' Guild and the Borgandy Family, not to mention the gratitude of the City Watch. Any of these connections can be parlayed into future adventures, for all three of these groups generally have some sort of work, or know someone who does. On the other hand, if the characters try to fence the stolen goods, they end up in very hot water with the City Guard. If they misinform the Thieves' Guild that the Manas Guild is behind this operation, they eventually (although not immediately) end up in hot water with the thieves. If they kill Savario Borgandy, they end up in trouble with the House of Borgandy. Regardless of the outcome, these connections (and possibly problems) can easily move the characters toward further adventures and set a framework for their interaction with the rest of the campaign world.

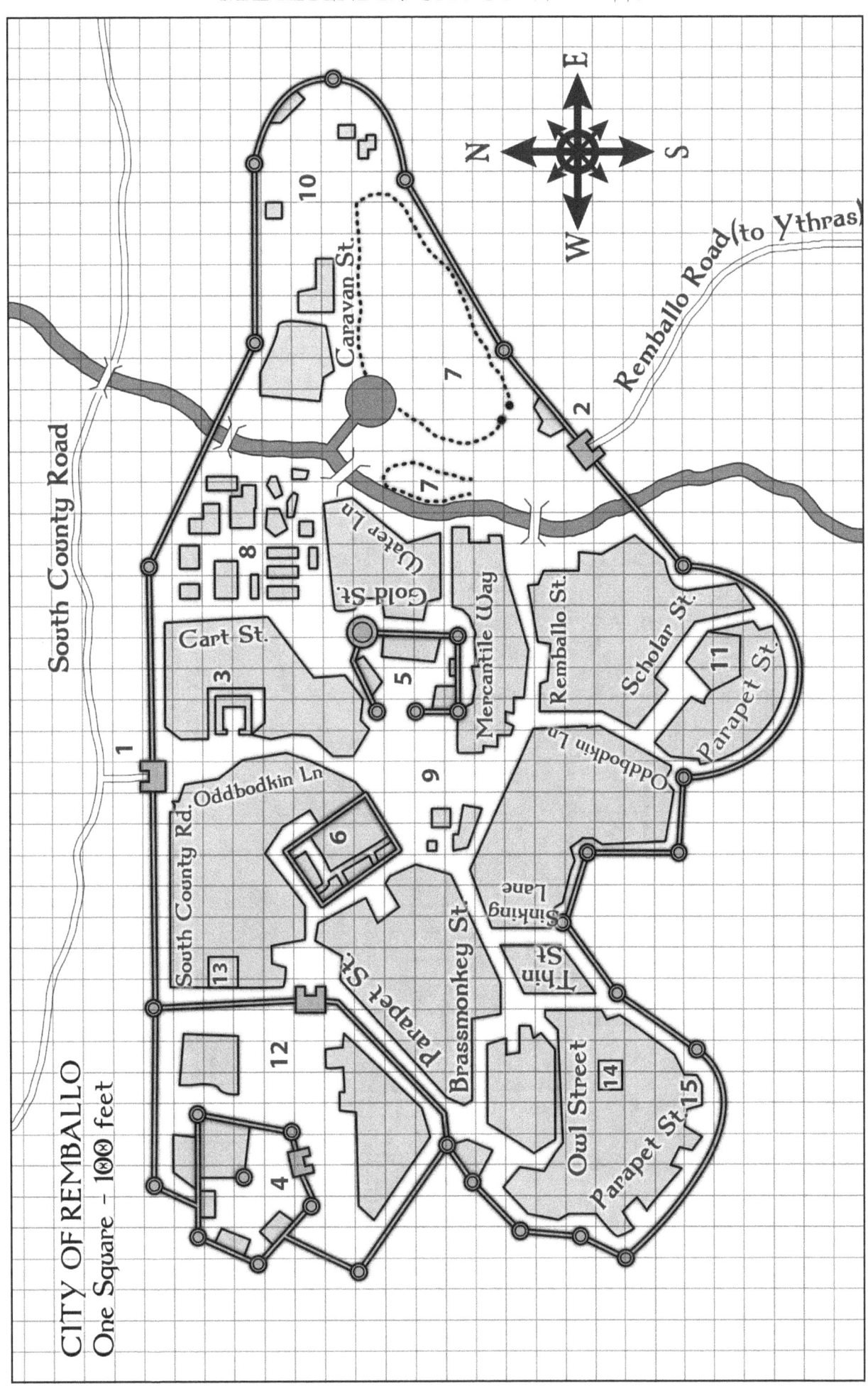

CITY OF REMBALLO
One Square – 100 feet

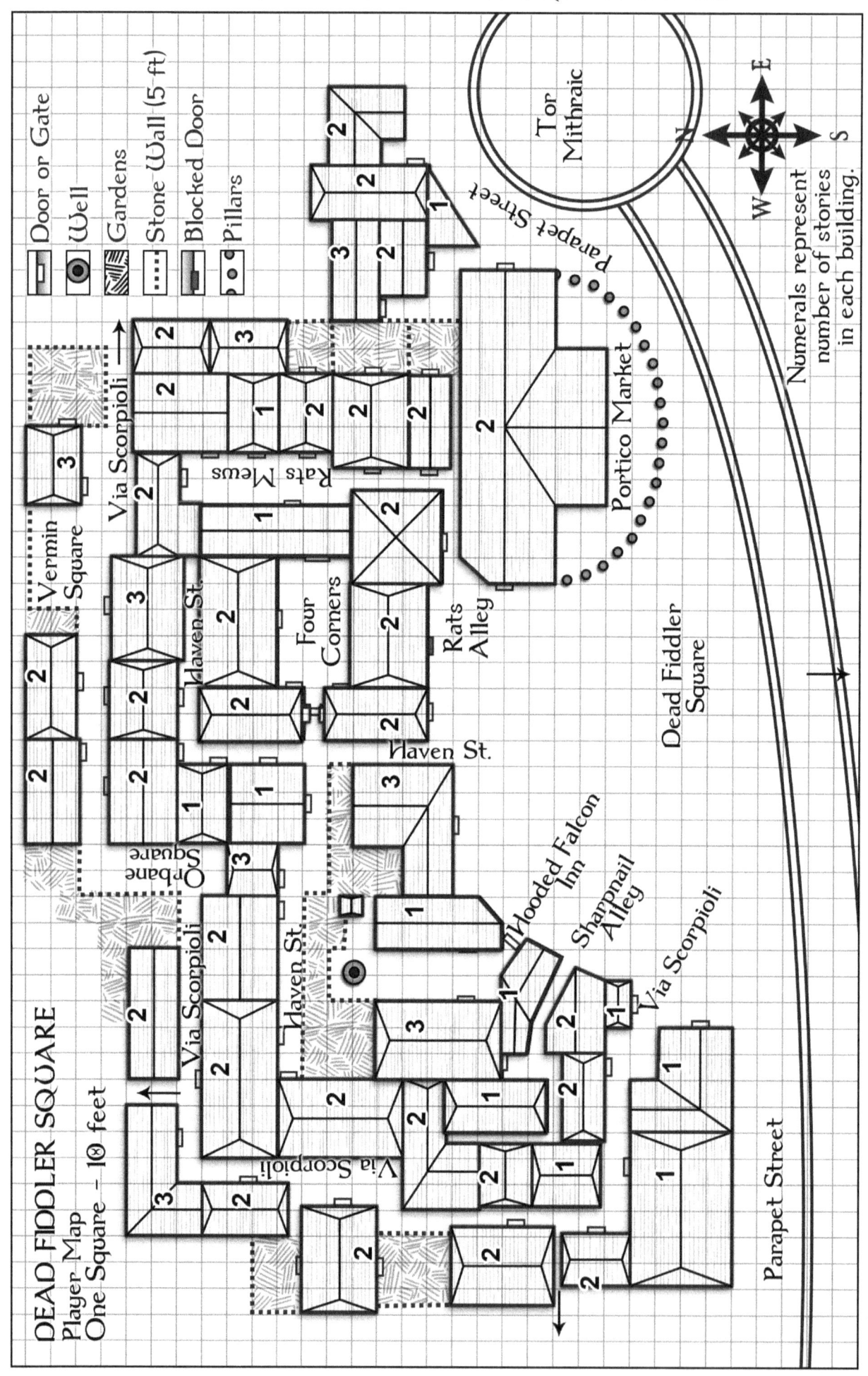

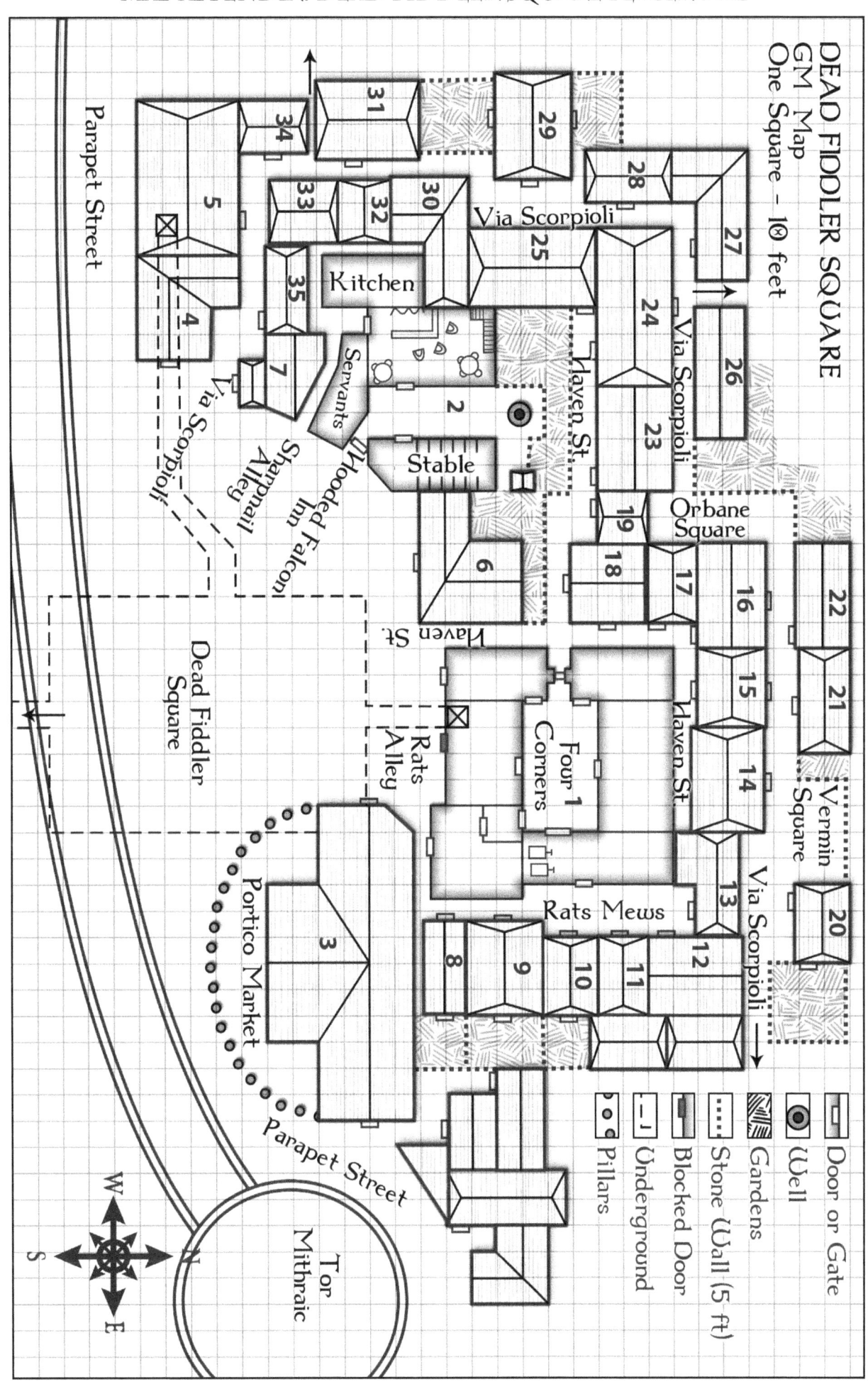

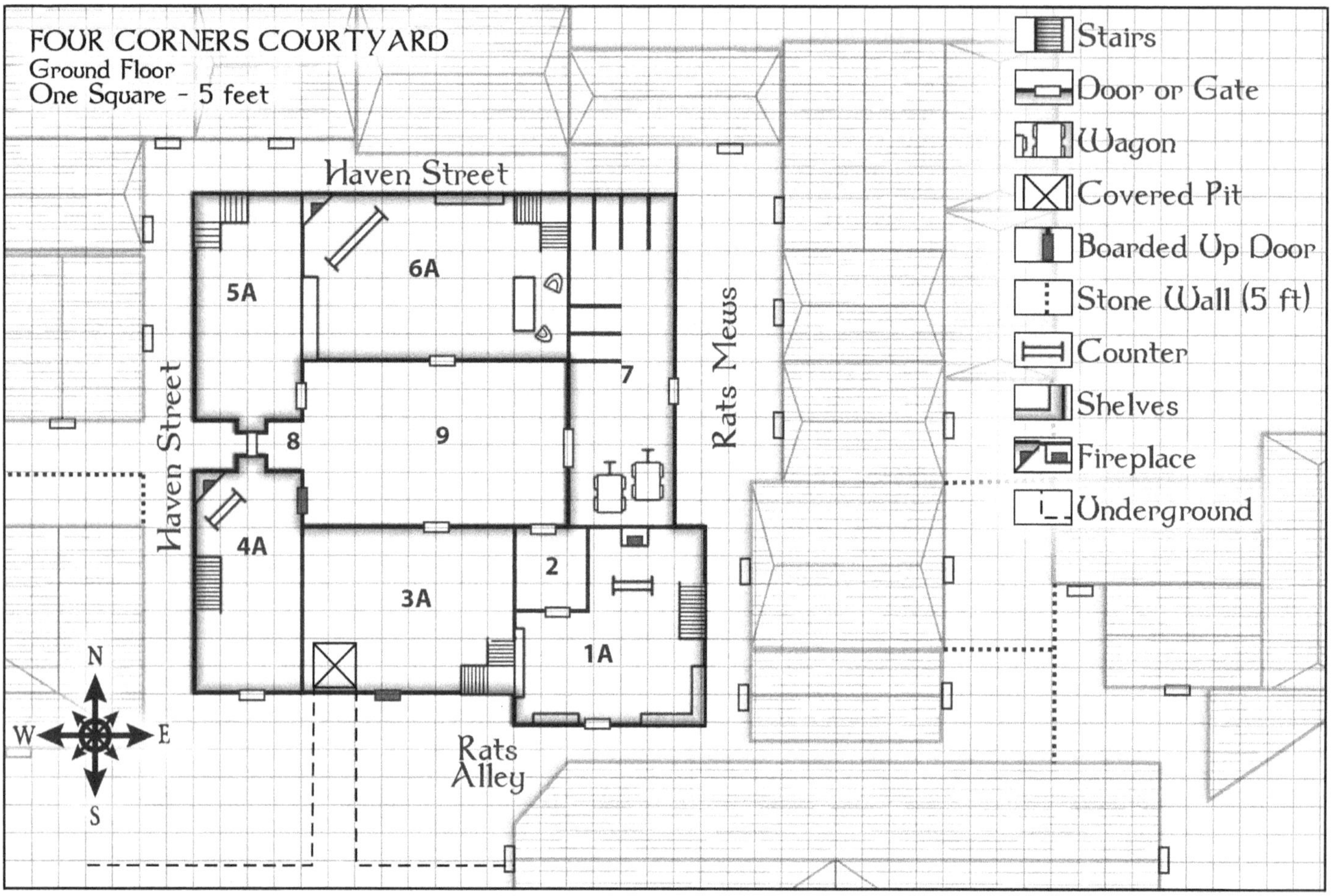

MAP APPENDIX: FOUR CORNERS COURTYARD GROUND AND UPPER FLOORS

FOUR CORNERS COURTYARD
Ground Floor
One Square - 5 feet

Haven Street

Haven Street

Rats Mews

5A

6A

7

8

9

4A

3A

2

1A

Rats Alley

N
W   E
S

Stairs
Door or Gate
Wagon
Covered Pit
Boarded Up Door
Stone Wall (5 ft)
Counter
Shelves
Fireplace
Underground

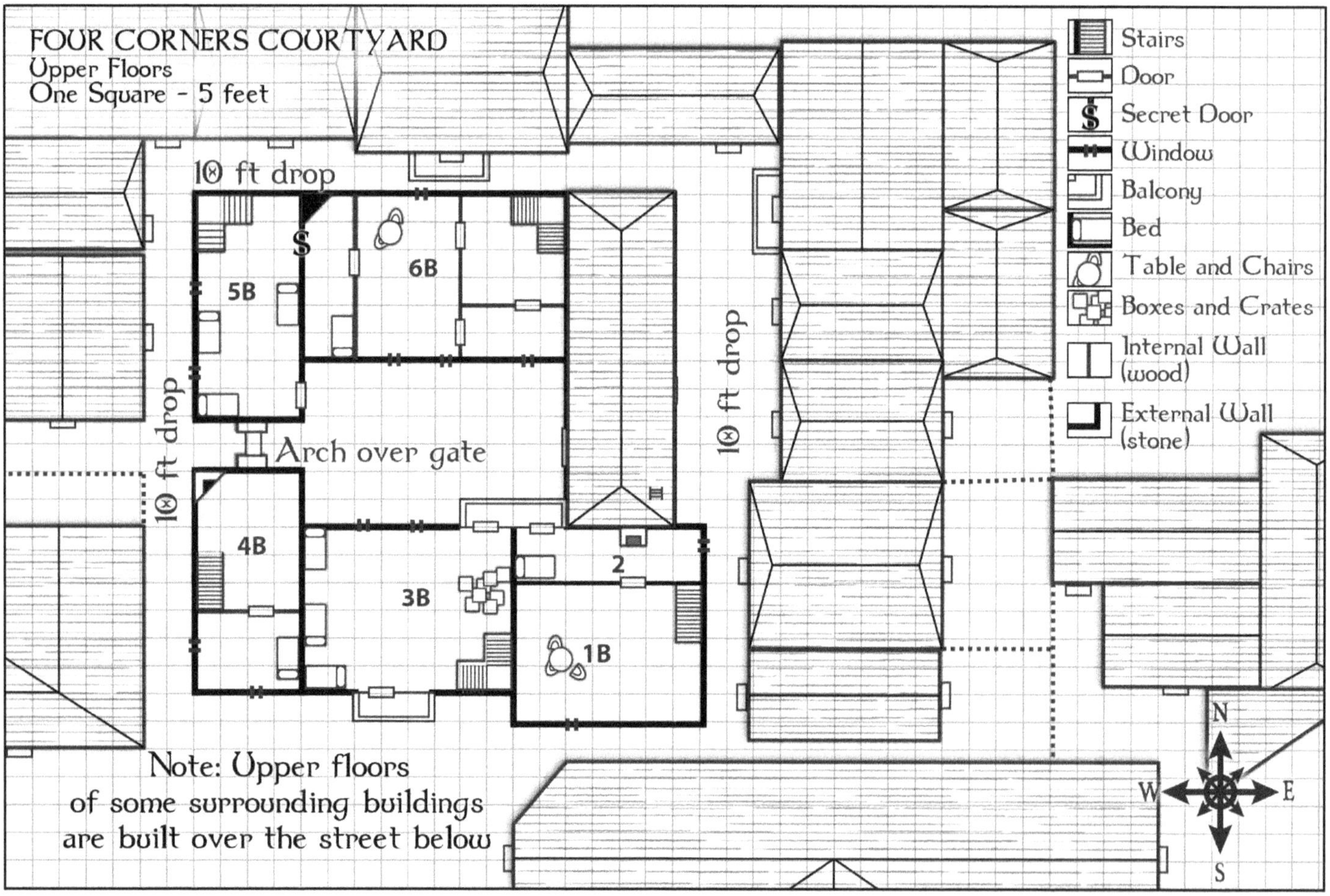

FOUR CORNERS COURTYARD
Upper Floors
One Square - 5 feet

10 ft drop

S

5B

6B

10 ft drop

10 ft drop

Arch over gate

4B

3B

2

1B

Note: Upper floors
of some surrounding buildings
are built over the street below

N
W   E
S

Stairs
Door
Secret Door
Window
Balcony
Bed
Table and Chairs
Boxes and Crates
Internal Wall (wood)
External Wall (stone)

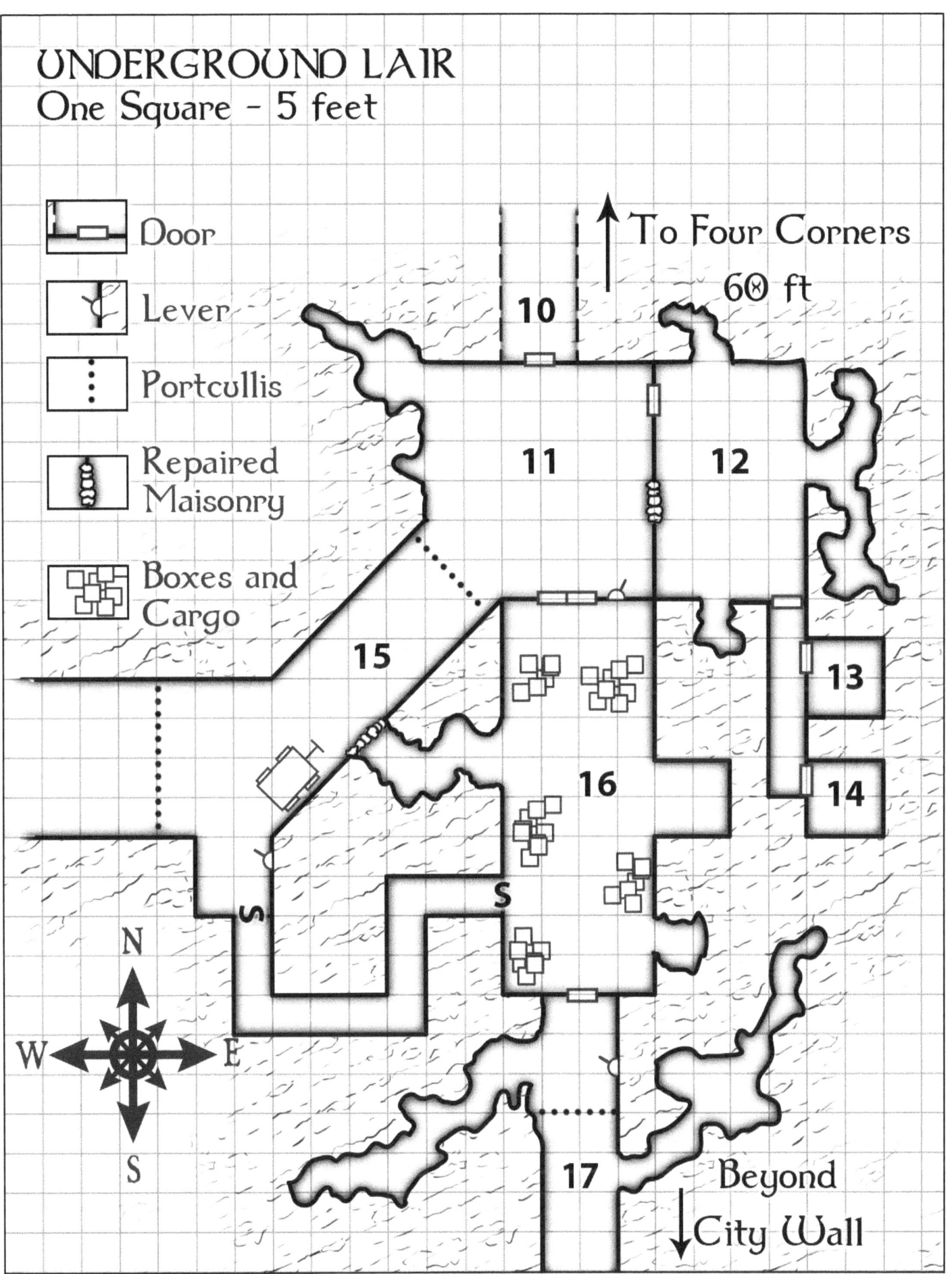

UNDERGROUND LAIR
One Square – 5 feet

Door

Lever

Portcullis

Repaired
Maisonry

Boxes and
Cargo

To Four Corners
60 ft

10

11

12

13

14

15

16

17

Beyond
City Wall

N
W — E
S

Appendices

Appendix A: Personal Names

The Borderland Provinces share a common linguistic background, the overlaying of Hyperborean on top of a tribal language, followed by a second overlay of Foere's Gasquen dialect and the resulting Westerling common tongue on top of that. Eastreach, the Amrin Estuary, the Gaelon River Valley, and Exeter Province have less Gasquen influence on their original dialects since they either escaped Foerdewaith occupation entirely, or have been exposed to it to a lesser degree than in the rest of the Provinces.

The table of personal names is designed for quick use since it is a resource for coping with the sudden need for a non-player character's name in the midst of an adventure. The table contains common first names and surnames for the two linguistic regions in the Provinces. Roll 1d100 to find the first name (one of the two first columns) and 1d100 to find a surname (one of the last 2 columns). Thus, if you rolled a 1 and a 1, you would have either Adjan Azur if you were rolling for a person in the Suilley-Rampart dialect-group, or Adward Abbitry if you were rolling for

a person in the Eastreach-Exeter dialect-group. Yolbiac Vale is something of an oddity in and of itself, so its names do not neatly conform to those on this table, bearing influences of other peoples, possibly much older. Nevertheless, if you're needing a quick NPC name for Yolbiac Vale, feel free to use the Suilley-Rampart columns, just keep in mind that you can diverge from those as you see fit to capture the more exotic alpine feel of the Valefolk.

Surnames are not the only way that people in the Provinces name themselves. The use of a family surname is now common in all the Provinces, but in rural areas it can still cause confusion, the reason being that there are only a few family names in the area. Thus, a village might have several people named "Adward Abbitry" if the Abbitry family has been living in the area since time immemorial. Thus, rural folk often use nicknames or place names to distinguish all the "Adwards." This can lead to names like "Tall Adward," Awkward Adward," "Adward the Smith," and "Adward of Carterscroft." The naming tables presented here don't take nicknames into account, simply because it's faster to use a single table when you're at the gaming table. Simplicity is of primary importance. Nevertheless, feel absolutely free to substitute nicknames for surnames. This is a common practice, and the tables shouldn't be read to suggest that surnames are the only naming convention the Provinces use.

Common Male Names in the Provinces

1d100	First Name Aachen, Rampart, Vourdon, Suilley, Keston, Toullen	First Name Eastreach, Amrin Estuary, Gaelon Valley, Exeter	Last Name Aachen, Rampart, Vourdon, Suilley, Keston, Toullen	Last Name Eastreach, Amrin Estuary, Gaelon Valley, Exeter
1	Adjan	Adward	Azur	Abbitry
2	Aimery	Alan	Barakeen	Ardensman
3	Alain	Albert	Bezentier	Banter
4	Albair or Alberto	Almaric	Bonfilh	Bantry
5	Althien	Alwin	Bordelan	Bardiman
6	Arnault	Ambrose	Briarc	Bargol
7	Asemar	Arnold	Burguniot	Broave
8	Balthazart	Atson	Campania	Burgess
9	Baudoin	Barthelby	Capet	Chark
10	Beneset	Beal	Carinzac	Clevistoke
11	Bernart	Bertrand	Carnelot	Cooper
12	Bernart	Bill	Chenard	Croaten
13	Bertran	Bindle	Chioc	Cromwail
14	Bertran	Bodwyn	Contretu	Crowcatcher
15	Carfot	Borneod	Corbin	Daan
16	Cercamont	Botho	Corenza	Deacon
17	Ciamel	Brogan	Cortil	Drandle
18	Clasculac	Bruno	Dalfinet	Falzabond
19	Claud	Clarth	Defoere	Fauble
20	Cleeljat	Cormac	Delac	Faudily
21	Clement	Courtland	Drampart	Firkin
22	Cleomarc	Dunald	Esrevaine	Fisherdawn

1d100	First Name *Aachen, Rampart, Vourdon, Suilley, Keston, Toullen*	First Name *Eastreach, Amrin Estuary, Gaelon Valley, Exeter*	Last Name *Aachen, Rampart, Vourdon, Suilley, Keston, Toullen*	Last Name *Eastreach, Amrin Estuary, Gaelon Valley, Exeter*
23	Clespiar	Duncan	Fintz	Forester
24	Cluvien	Duthwin	Fogelvide	Gaelonder
25	Dalfot	Eddar	Freyathier	Garrison
26	Danyel	Emery	Galondier	Gaunt
27	Dormert	Eoden	Ghendirac	Glimrill
28	Emeric	Fergus	Gherier	Gortboat
29	Etienne	Galt	Gonfaloneer	Grangit
31	Felip	Geoffrey	Gornault	Hawkins
32	Felquet	Gesper	Huebit	Heldring
33	Foerdi	Giles	Huillot	Heuldown
34	Galtier	Gort	Jalatar	Highcourt
35	Gaspart	Gwion	Jamac	Highlander
36	Gaston	Halwin	Jeyquayt	Hoondy
37	Gaucelm	Harken	Jolien	Horntile
38	Girault	Hart	Kanticleer	Innskelling
39	Guardamon	Helmorth	Keltrantz	Ishenbeck
40	Guilcamon	Henry	Keston	Iudarc
41	Guilhaut	Herswith	Kilsanje	Jeems
42	Guilhelm	Hestle	Le Mar	Jessop
43	Guillaume	Hugh	Leocurt	Jorpen
44	Guillem	Hugh	Leot	Kets
45	Guy	Hugo	Letranj	Lanternlight
46	Henri	Ian	Manasin	Littleward
47	Hugh	Jack	Marcalt	Lowlander
48	Huicat	Jacob	Marroy	Lowwater
49	Huilienj	Jerss	Meer	Lurrible
50	Hurtold	John	Melhor	Macobert
51	Isarn	Jory	Meratz	Magnus
52	Jacalt	Kay	Meridian	Marcher
53	Jacques	Keffin	Merlott	Markoom
54	Jean	Lud	Ocseval	Medley
55	Jocat	Markin	Octaj	Melcott
56	Joffrey	Markle	Oris	Mitrand
57	Jogues	Melfyn	Ormaloon	Morcam
58	Juliac	Melgin	Ortalan	Muiriman
59	Julian	Mellon	Ortaliot	Naisby
60	Kyot	Milo	Pairdiou	Oerson or Orson
61	Louis	Neal	Palindar	Opty
62	Marcabrun	Nicolas	Parvantine	Orfendil
63	Martin	Nye	Pavan	Ormian
64	Martin	Odo	Peregrin	Osbert
65	Maurice	Oswyn	Perroket	Parlendale
66	Melcamont	Oxibur	Poulett	Pennyworthy
67	Meljat	Pagan	Provensall	Penperthy
68	Meljian	Parthit	Quillarc	Pepperman

1d100	First Name Aachen, Rampart, Vourdon, Suilley, Keston, Toullen	First Name Eastreach, Amrin Estuary, Gaelon Valley, Exeter	Last Name Aachen, Rampart, Vourdon, Suilley, Keston, Toullen	Last Name Eastreach, Amrin Estuary, Gaelon Valley, Exeter
69	Miquel	Peter or Petry	Redmont	Ploutin
70	Moulienj	Philip	Rohelain	Ploverdill
71	Olivier	Pracken	Rondemeer	Porterman
72	Oth	Prospect	Rovenac	Quarin
73	Oton	Quinn	Sanzalot	Quindle
74	Paul	Randwin	Sketre	Rambert
75	Peyrot	Redwyn	Sondrelan	Rood
76	Pierlou	Robert	Sul	Rooster
77	Pierol	Seeler	Sulerat	Saltwater
78	Pierre or Piers	Seren	Sulien	Shield
79	Polbasc	Siamon	Sulien	Shiresman
80	Porthos	Spindle	Surlenetz	Smith
81	Raielh	Swain	Talacar	Spindler
82	Raimon	Thaddeus	Talaric	Stubble
83	Raimond	Thomas	Tarquin	Swithin
84	Robert or Roberto	Todric	Tarsentier	Swithin
85	Savario	Turbert	Teliondra	Swynn
86	Savort	Tywen	Toullen	Thane
87	Sebastian	Urman	Traval	Thyrriman
88	Selerm	Valman	Troubeyl	Torrin
89	Stroul	Vossin	Turcott	Trackle
90	Suarvier	Wallen	Turin	Tunion
91	Talbot	Walter	Ulbrec	Twines
92	Tallac	Warren	Vaun	Ushery
93	Tellac	Wat	Ventador	Venipp
94	Tomas	Wergeld	Venzac	Waldwater
95	Toussaint	Wickett	Vidal	Waxish
96	Tristan	William	Vismarc	Weir
97	Valentin	Wulfred	Vourdon	Wenter
98	Vasvier	Yard	Yllac	Yambles
99	Vidal	Yodel	Yolbiac	Yarne
100	Walter	Zellard	Ystin	Zorbicks

Common Female Names in the Provinces

Use the same method as for male names above. Roll 1d100 for the first name on one of the first 2 columns (depending on the dialect-group), and 1d100 for a surname on the appropriate one of the last 2 columns. The list of surnames is the same as in the male-name table, since both the males and females are drawn from the same common set of families.

1d100	First Name Aachen, Rampart, Vourdon, Suilley, Keston, Toullen	First Name Eastreach, Amrin Estuary, Gaelon Valley, Exeter	Last Name Aachen, Rampart, Vourdon, Suilley, Keston, Toullen	Last Name Eastreach, Amrin Estuary, Gaelon Valley, Exeter
1	Adjanie	Aliana	Azur	Abbitry
2	Aimelle	Alice	Barakeen	Ardensman
3	Alaina	Almarinda	Bezentier	Banter
4	Alitzia	Alyria	Bonfilh	Bantry
5	Althiena	Atsaine	Bordelan	Bardiman
6	Aseile	Barthil	Briarc	Bargol
7	Auril	Bealdrun	Burguniot	Broave
8	Balthazine	Beladine	Campania	Burgess
9	Beguille	Bertianne	Capet	Chark
10	Beldienne	Bessilia	Carinzac	Clevistoke
11	Belletelia	Biniss	Carnelot	Cooper
12	Benetzelle	Bornaliss	Chenard	Croaten
13	Bertrandel	Briana	Chioc	Cromwail
14	Carfarine	Carmen	Contretu	Crowcatcher
15	Cercamelle	Claress	Corbin	Daan
16	Ciamela	Claudia	Corenza	Deacon
17	Clascaile	Cormacine	Cortil	Drandle
18	Claudette	Courtney	Dalfinet	Falzabond
19	Cleira	Dalarin	Defoere	Fauble
20	Clejacinde	Dunwynn	Delac	Faudily
21	Clemesinthe	Dythren	Drampart	Firkin
22	Clespia	Eduine	Esrevaine	Fisherdawn
23	Cluvienne	Elaine	Fintz	Forester
24	Daania	Emily	Fogelvide	Gaelonder
25	Dalencia	Eowynn	Freyathier	Garrison
26	Danyelle	Faradila	Galondier	Gaunt
27	Dormerinne	Galtania	Ghendirac	Glimrill
28	Esylt	Gessivere	Gherier	Gortboat
29	Eylaran	Gilliana	Gonfaloneer	Grangit
31	Falasinthe	Gorlana	Gornault	Hawkins
32	Fierann	Guindara	Huebit	Heldring
33	Foerdia	Guinivere	Huillot	Heuldown
34	Freyat	Gwien	Jalatar	Highcourt
35	Galiatia	Halwen	Jamac	Highlander
36	Gallerine	Harklinn	Jeyquayt	Hoondy
37	Ghirmine	Hartsvere	Jolien	Horntile
38	Gialmia	Hayla	Kanticleer	Innskelling
39	Giselle	Helena	Keltrantz	Ishenbeck
40	Guilcamet	Herswen	Keston	Iudarc
41	Guilhera	Heslieth	Kilsanje	Jeems
42	Guillemin	Ianeria	Le Mar	Jessop

1d100	First Name *Aachen, Rampart, Vourdon, Suilley, Keston, Toullen*	First Name *Eastreach, Amrin Estuary, Gaelon Valley, Exeter*	Last Name *Aachen, Rampart, Vourdon, Suilley, Keston, Toullen*	Last Name *Eastreach, Amrin Estuary, Gaelon Valley, Exeter*
43	Guinevere	Ingril	Leocurt	Jorpen
44	Halia	Isarne	Leot	Kets
45	Halline	Jaclinn	Letranj	Lanternlight
46	Henriett	Jeanette	Manasin	Littleward
47	Hermienne	Jesslyn	Marcalt	Lowlander
48	Iocasta	Joy	Marroy	Lowwater
49	Isarnia	Kay	Meer	Lurrible
50	Jacaltia	Kylaina	Melhor	Macobert
51	Jacqueline	Kyllera	Meratz	Magnus
52	Jeanne	Louisa	Meridian	Marcher
53	Jenivere	Markleia	Merlott	Markoom
54	Jillienne	Marlena	Ocseval	Medley
55	Jocasta	Melfianna	Octaj	Melcott
56	Joffrine	Melginia	Oris	Mitrand
57	Julia	Mellara	Ormaloon	Morcam
58	Julienne	Milimara	Ortalan	Muiriman
59	Katrinne	Miribelle	Ortaliot	Naisby
60	Kylivere	Nialda	Pairdiou	Oerson or Orson
61	Lienja	Nicole	Palindar	Opty
62	Louette	Nylaine	Parvantine	Orfendil
63	Marcabrine	Odwina	Pavan	Ormian
64	Martina	Olivia	Peregrin	Osbert
65	Martinette	Oscela	Perroket	Parlendale
66	Mauricelle	Ossine	Poulett	Pennyworthy
67	Melisse	Pagana	Provensall	Penperthy
68	Meljathia	Parthitelle	Quillarc	Pepperman
69	Meljiette	Piresse	Redmont	Ploutin
70	Miqueline	Praccania	Rohelain	Ploverdill
71	Oersia	Prosperine	Rondemeer	Porterman
72	Olivia	Raniss	Rovenac	Quarin
73	Othine	Rediss	Sanzalot	Quindle
74	Otonnie	Rilriss	Sketre	Rambert
75	Palcinet	Seelserynn	Sondrelan	Rood
76	Peyrovanne	Serenia	Sul	Rooster
77	Piera	Siamone	Sulerat	Saltwater
78	Pierlanne	Sisterill	Sulien	Shield
79	Pieroline	Spinilen	Sulien	Shiresman
80	Piertinne	Swanille	Surlenetz	Smith
81	Polbasinne	Teliandra	Talacar	Spindler
82	Raielha	Tessina	Talaric	Stubble
83	Raimelie	Thadlaine	Tarquin	Swithin
84	Raimona	Thomasine	Tarsentier	Swithin
85	Rosbertine	Turceline	Teliondra	Swynn
86	Saavia	Tyweness	Toullen	Thane
87	Savariette	Valwen	Traval	Thyrriman

1d100	First Name Aachen, Rampart, Vourdon, Suilley, Keston, Toullen	First Name Eastreach, Amrin Estuary, Gaelon Valley, Exeter	Last Name Aachen, Rampart, Vourdon, Suilley, Keston, Toullen	Last Name Eastreach, Amrin Estuary, Gaelon Valley, Exeter
88	Sebaette	Vossille	Troubeyl	Torrin
89	Selecine	Walwynn	Turcott	Trackle
90	Seleia	Wendria	Turin	Tunion
91	Strallinne	Wicwynn	Ulbrec	Twines
92	Talberie	Wilaina	Vaun	Ushery
93	Tallacine	Wylfrieda	Ventador	Venipp
94	Tomasine	Wyrwyth	Venzac	Waldwater
95	Toussaintine	Yardcyl	Vidal	Waxish
96	Tristalle	Yscalie	Vismarc	Weir
97	Valentina	Yssende	Vourdon	Wenter
98	Valeria	Yssila	Yllac	Yambles
99	Videnne	Zellriss	Yolbiac	Yarne
100	Wistrianne	Aliana	Ystin	Zorbicks

Appendix B: Place Names in the Borderland Provinces

The "formula" for place names isn't as easy to boil down into fast-moving tables because the result will be too many places with the same type of name, even if the words are different. Just to show the sort of variation one finds in medieval place names, for example, consider the different formulas of the following: Abbot's River, Abbot's House, Red River, Red House, Oak River, Oak House, and House-by-the-River. All of these are different: You have a person and place, person and building, adjective and place, adjective and building, noun and place, noun and building, and finally a descriptive phrase. A good set of place names needs to change up these different formulas, and not only that, if it's going to be an evocative setting for adventure it also needs to be salted with names that aren't any formula at all, just a good one or two word "name," like "Troy." So the task of filling in your adventure areas on the big map can be a challenge if you're not particularly good at coming up with names — and most people aren't. Even for those who are good at naming, probably particularly these people, there's also the issue of making the names sound good for the particular area, since it's part of the world-builder's art to avoid making everywhere in the fantasy world sound exactly like everywhere else.

We mentioned above that in the Borderland Provinces there are two main areas where there are different flavors to the language, the group of Eastreach, the Gaelon River Valley, the Amrin Eastuary, and Exeter Province (the areas that had less Foerdewaith influence), and then the areas that have had more Foerdewaith influence, being Aachen, Rampart, Suilley, Vourdon, Keston, and Toullen.

For the Suilley-Rampart language group, structure the name as follows:

1–4	Roll a 2-part word, then a geographical feature from the Suilley-Rampart Group (examples: Adzir Faletz, Calec Pont)
5	Roll a first syllable for the first word of the name, then a 2-syllable word for the second word (Tretz Ormec, Re Carral)
6	Roll a first syllable for the first word of the name, then a 3-syllable word for the second word of the name (Tram Aziryt, Tas Adzalon)
7	Roll a 2-syllable word for the first word of the name, then a 1-syllable word for the second word of the name (Talaf Cal, Tremel Tas)
8	Roll a 3-syllable word followed by a geographical feature (Caloba Ruad)
9	Roll a first syllable, but then use a geographical feature as the second part of the word (Tascastel, Adzribiere)
10	Roll a 3-syllable word as the first word, then a geographical word from the *Eastreach* list, not the Suilley-Rampart list (Calelut Cliff, Arjobat Forest).

For the Eastreach-Exeter language group, structure the name as follows:

2 parts + Geographical Feature as one word (Gandigbrook, Scalik Slade)
2 parts + Geographical feature as 2 separate words (Gandig Brook, Scalikslade)
3 parts + Geographical feature (Perebyl River, Oppyfot Mire)
Geographical feature +2 parts (Brook Drasyl, Tower Crewac)
Geographical feature + 3 parts (Brook Drasylon, Tower Crewacelas)

1d100	Part 1 (Suilley/Eastreach) Note: When word has only one part, add a vowel at the end)	Part 2 (Suilley/ Eastreach)	Part 3 (Suilley/ Eastreach)	Geographical feature in Suilley-Rampart	Geographical feature in Eastreach-Exeter
1	A/As	-ab	-a	Ej	Bank
2	Abil/Abel	-ac	-ac	Bassin	Basin
3	Adz/Ade	-ac	-ail	Bas	Botham (valley)
4	Adz/At	-ad	-ail	Hilsej	Bray or Brae (hillside)
5	Alj/A	-adj/-ul	-air	Pont	Bridge
6	Amar/Amr	-af	-air	Ribiere	Brook
7	Andr/An	-ag	-air	Broc	Brook
8	Arj/Art	-agh	-ais	Cair	Cairn (stone pile)
9	Art	-aj/-ug	-ais	Caer	-caster or -cester (town)
10	At/Ath	-ak	-ais	Castel	Castle
11	Ats/Eigh	-al	-ais/-ors	Gleisa	Church
12	Aul/Al	-al	-ais/-urs	Chiria	Clearing
13	Av/Af	-am	-al	Faletz	Cliff
14	Az/Arn	-an	-al	Val	Coomb, combe (valley)
15	Bar	-ap	-alas	Faletz	Crag
16	Beal/Bet	-ar	-alont/-alond	Patiaj	Croft (enclosure)

1d100	Part 1 (Suilley/Eastreach) Note: When word has only one part, add a vowel at the end)	Part 2 (Suilley/ Eastreach)	Part 3 (Suilley/ Eastreach)	Geographical feature in Suilley-Rampart	Geographical feature in Eastreach-Exeter
17	Bej/Berle	-as	-an	Travessar	Cross (crossing or crossroad)
18	Bel/Be	-at/-up	-an	Val	Dean(e) (valley)
19	Bel/Bur	-av	-at	Boule	Dell (hollow)
20	Ber	-e/-ud	-aud	Ronde	Down (hill)
21	Berj/Berg	-eb	-aud	Ej	Edge
22	Bor	-ec	-e	Ej	Edge (border)
23	Caj/Crew	-ec	-ec	Fair	Fair
24	Cal	-ed	-eil	Fel	Fell
25	Cal/Kal	-ef	-el	Valt or falt	Firth (forest)
26	Carn	-eg	-elas	Guet	Ford
27	Carr	-egh	-elond	Forett	Forest
28	Cel	-ej/-uc	-et	Bifurc	Fork
29	Cer	-ej/-uh	-etre/-uen	Fort	Fort
31	Chall	-ek	-i	Petival	Glen (valley)
32	Cren	-el	-ic	Bocage	Grove
33	Cron	-el	-ic	Redenza	Hall
34	De/Doth	-em	-ic	Villa	Ham (homestead)
35	Ders/Dars	-en	-iles	Stoc	Harrow (temple)
36	Dlar/Diar	-ep	-ilond	Lande	Heath
37	Dor	-er	-in	Haut (high)	Heights
38	Dras	-es	-in	Colline	Hill
39	El/E	-ev	-in/-yn	Boule	Hollow
40	Escl-El	-ib	-ioc	Holt	Holt (forest)
41	Fal	-ic	-ioc	Ostal or Ostalas (mansion)	House
42	Far or Phar	-ic	-ioc	-nel	-howe (hill)
43	Fen	-ict	-ir	Stoc	Kirk (temple)
44	Gant/Gand	-id	-ir	Nel	Knoll
45	Ghel/Gell	-if	-ir	Lac	Lake
47	Guen	-ig	-it	Barcasej	Landing
48	Iac/P	-igh	-it	Lane	Lane
49	Ial/Hal	-ik	-it	Pasture	Lynch (plain/ pasture)
50	Iel/Yel	-il	-ith	Bord	March (border)
51	Ier/Her	-il	-ith	Marc or March	Mark (border)
52	Jhel/Jell	-im	-ith	Mercat	Market
53	Lar	-in	-iwyn	Maraiz	Marsh
54	Leol	-ip	-iwyn	Champ or campa	Meadow
55	Leor	-ir	-iya	Molie	Mill
56	Lyth	-ir	-li	Mine	Mine
57	Mal/Mass	-is	-li	-fan (as in "fane")	-minster (temple)
58	Mar	-iv	-li	Mire	Mire
59	Mer	-ob/-obb	-o	Tourbietz	Moor
60	Nar	-oc	-oan	Mont	Mound

1d100	Part 1 (Suilley/Eastreach) Note: When word has only one part, add a vowel at the end)	Part 2 (Suilley/ Eastreach)	Part 3 (Suilley/ Eastreach)	Geographical feature in Suilley-Rampart	Geographical feature in Eastreach-Exeter
61	Occ	-oct/-uk	-oc	Montagne, mont	Mountain
62	Ocl/Opp	-od	-oc	Boc	Mouth or –moth
63	Oll	-of	-oc	Mud	Mud
64	Or/Orr	-og	-od	Noc	Nook
65	Orl	-ogh	-od	Champ or campa	Pasture
66	Orm/Arm	-ok	-odh/od	Pec	Peak
67	Pal	-ol	-ol	Pit	Pit
68	Par	-ol	-ol	Ponj	Pond
69	Paras	-old	-olas	Etaang	Pool
70	Pent	-om	-olh/ol	Ridj	Ridge
71	Perl	-on	-olind/ish	Marc or March	Riding (border)
72	Pier/Per	-op	-olio/ish	Riu	River
73	Qual/Quall	-or	-oliond/ish	Ruad	Road
74	Quarr/Quarth	-os	-olond	Escarp	Scarp
75	Quill	-osc	-on	-side	-side
76	Ral/Rath	-otc/-uf	-on	Ej	Slade (slope)
77	Raul/Raith	-our	-on	Val	Slade (valley)
78	Re	-ov	-on	Slope	Slope
79	Risp	-ub	-ond	Font	Spring
80	Ros/Red	-um	-ond	Stoc	Stoke (temple)
81	Sel	-un	-ool	Caer	Stone
82	Shel	-ur	-oon	Stoc	Stow(e) (temple)
83	Suir/Scall	-ur	-or	Rajol	Stream
84	Taj/Tarr	-us	-ot	Valt of falt	Thicket
85	Tal	-uv	-ot	Villa	Thorpe
86	Tas	-ux	-ot	-ton	-ton (town)
87	Tasc/Tan	-yb	-ot	Top	Top
88	Tasc/Tesc	-yc	-u	Tor	Tower
89	Ter	-yd	-uc	Vil or –ton	Town
90	Tes	-yf	-ulain/-uen	Sentir	Trail
91	Tram	-yg	-ulas	Bifurc	Twitchel (fork)
92	Trass	-yh	-ut	Val	Valley
93	Trej/Treb	-yk	-y	Vor or voir	View
94	Trem	-yl	-yc	Eau	Water
95	Tresc/Trisc	-ym	-yl	Puit	Well
96	Tretz/Tras	-yn	-ylas	Ferme	-wich (farm)
97	Ts/Tes	-yp	-yls	Ferme	Wick (farm)
98	Ul	-yr	-yr	Foret	Wold (forest)
99	Yl	-ys	-yr	Granja	Worth (farm)
100	Yss/Iss	-yv	-yt	Patiaj	Yard (enclosure)

A slight warning for mapmakers about fantasy words: the Suilley-Rampart dialect is based on the Occitan of Langue d'oc and Catalan, and will sound more foreign to the ear of English-speakers than the Eastreach-Exeter names. Yolbiac names tend towards the Langue d'oc-Catalan group but sometimes include a Germanic influence. Don't overdo the unusual names. Players will very shortly give up on remembering names if every single one is difficult. Use the unusual names sparingly.

Appendix C: Encounter Quick-Reference

Many of the encounter tables in the book have repeating entries (all roads have bandits, for example), so for economy of space we have placed all the encounter information here in the back of the book. For random encounters from a table, where the encounter is the main event and doesn't refer back to the book's text, the problem of page-flipping isn't really an issue. Monsters described in *lairs* still have their statistical information side-by-side with the text itself to avoid too much page-flipping in the middle of an adventure.

Risk Levels

Monsters are usually listed at four levels of Risk, as follows:

• Low-Risk Areas: In the Borderland Provinces, only the hexes immediately surrounding a city are considered Low-Risk areas. There is no distinction between traveling on or off roads within a city's patrolled radius unless the characters are in an area where the GM has designed specific encounter tables.
• Medium-Risk Areas: This is the normal level of risk for traveling along a high road once the characters leave behind the one-hex radius guarded by a city's patrols.
• High-Risk Areas: This is the normal level of risk for wilderness travel off-road in an area beyond a city's patrolled radius.
• Extreme-Risk Areas: Unusually dangerous, offering even greater risks than ordinary wilderness travel. Such places should not be traversed other than by high-level characters.

In each case, it is possible that an area will be more or less dangerous than the norm.

1. Air Elemental

These are ordinarily airborne encounters.
Low-Risk Area: 1 **air elemental**
Medium- and High-Risk Areas: Roll 1d6, and if the encounter is over mountains, add +1 to the roll.

1d6	Encounter
1	1 air elemental
2–6	1d2 air elementals
7	1d3 air elementals

Extreme-Risk Area: Roll 1d6, and if the encounter is over mountains, add +1 to the roll.

1d6	Encounter
1	2 air elementals
2-3	1d2+1 air elementals
4–6	1d3+1 air elementals
7	1d4+1 air elementals

Elemental, Air: AC 15; **HP** 90 (12d10+24); **Spd** 0ft, fly 90ft (hover); **Melee** slam (+8, 2d8+5 bludgeoning); **SA** multiattack (slam x2), whirlwind (recharge 5–6, 3d8+2 bludgeoning, flung up to 20ft and knocked prone, DC 13 Str half only); **Immune** exhaustion, grapple, paralysis, petrify, poison, prone, restraint, unconscious; **Resist**

lightning, normal weapons, thunder; **Str** +2, **Dex** +5, **Con** +2, **Int** –2, **Wis** +0, **Cha** –2; **Senses** darkvision 60ft; **AL** N; **CR** 5; **XP** 1800.

2. Ankheg

Ankhegs encountered on roads usually burrow underground by the roadside, awaiting the arrival of sumptuous morsels. If the characters have a local guide, these individuals are often good at spotting new ankheg mounds, and might be able to warn the morsels before disaster ensues.

Ankheg Encounters

1d6	Low Risk	Medium Risk	High Risk	Extreme Risk
1	1 ankheg	2 ankhegs	3 ankhegs	4 ankhegs
2-3	1d2 ankhegs	1d2+1 ankhegs	1d2+2 ankhegs	1d2+3 ankhegs
4-5	1d4 ankhegs	1d4+1 ankhegs	1d4+2 ankhegs	1d4+3 ankhegs
6	1d6 ankhegs	1d6+1 ankhegs	1d6+2 ankhegs	1d6+2 ankhegs

Ankheg: AC 14 or 11 while prone; **HP** 39 (6d10+6); **Spd** 30ft, burrow 10ft; **Melee** bite (+5, 2d6+3 slashing plus 1d6 acid plus grapple—tactical advantage until escape DC 13); **SA** acid spray (recharge 6, 30ft long 5ft wide line, 3d6 acid, DC 13 Dex half); **Str** +3, **Dex** +0, **Con** +1, **Int** –4, **Wis** +1, **Cha** –2; **Senses** darkvision 60ft, tremorsense 60ft; **AL** U; **CR** 2; **XP** 450.

3. Annoyance

Annoyance does not vary by an area's Risk. Roll 1d6:

1–4	A roadside preacher accosts the characters, accusing them of heresy, fornication, possession, and rapacious greed. There is also a 10% chance that the preacher tries to follow along with the characters if the encounter takes place between villages. In this case, the accusations are usually muttered rather than shouted. There is a 5% chance that the preacher is actually a heretic (see the "Heresy" Appendix)
5	Bees swarm the characters, stinging them badly enough that all rolls for the next 2 days are made with a penalty of –1, and spells have a 5% chance of failing (although the spell is not lost, just not cast). An ordinary peasant beekeeper from the area is watching, aghast, as his bees attack a group of dangerous-looking travelers, and runs away in terror.
6	The characters encounter a traveling seller of printed pamphlets ranging from religious tracts to manuals of noble etiquette, to licentious (possibly illegal) materials. The seller will not go away until someone buys something; the characters are by far the best customer-prospects of the seller's entire day.

181

4. Ant

Daytime:

Low-Risk Area: 1d6 **giant ants**
Medium-Risk Area: 2d6 **giant ants** (including 1 warrior per 6 workers)
High-Risk Area: 3d6 **giant ants** (including 1 warrior per 6 workers)
Extreme-Risk Area: 4d6 **giant ants** (including 1 warrior per 6 workers)

Night:

Low-Risk Area: If the characters scout around their proposed campsite during daylight hours, they have a 90% chance to simply avoid this encounter by shifting the camp's location away from the anthills (treat as "no encounter"). Otherwise, normal ants from a nearby anthill make their way into the camp. It is virtually impossible for a guard to detect them. Everyone in the camp has a 25% chance to awaken with numerous ant bites. Characters that are bitten suffer badly for 2 days, with all attack and damage rolls at −1, and spellcasters having a 5% chance of spell failure (although the spell is not lost; it is simply not cast).

Medium-Risk Area: As per the Low-Risk Area, but 1d6 giant ants accompany the ants as well.

High-Risk Area: 3d6 giant ants (including 1 warrior per 6 workers)
Extreme-Risk Area: 4d6 giant ants (including 1 warrior per 6 workers)

Ant, Giant Warrior: AC 15; HP 13 (3d6+3); Spd 30ft; Melee bite (+4, 1d6+2 piercing plus 1d6 poison); Str +2, Dex +1, Con +1, Int −4, Wis −3, Cha −4; AL U; CR 1/4; XP 50.

Ant, Giant Worker: AC 15; HP 9 (2d6+2); Spd 30ft; Melee bite (+4, 1d6+2 piercing); Str +2, Dex +1, Con +1, Int −4, Wis −3, Cha −4; AL U; CR 1/8; XP 25.

5. Assassin Bug

Aerial encounters are with 1d6 **assassin bugs**.

If the bugs are encountered on the ground, determine the numbers by the area's risk level:

Low-Risk Area: 1 **assassin bug**
Medium-Risk Area: 1d2 **assassin bugs**
High Risk-Area: 1d3 **assassin bugs**
Extreme-Risk Area: 1d4+1 **assassin bugs**

Assassin Bug: AC 16; HP 120 (16d8+48); Spd 30ft, climb 20ft, fly 50ft; Melee claws (+6, 2d6+3 slashing plus grapple, DC 13 Dex avoids); SA grapple bite (auto, 2d6+3 piercing plus 1d8 poison drains hp max); Immune charm; Str +2, Dex +3, Con +3, Int −5, Wis +1, Cha −1; Senses darkvision 60ft; AL U; CR 5; XP 1800. (*Fifth Edition Foes* 17)

6. Badger

Low-Risk Area: 1d4 **badgers** are rooting around, making a bit of noise. They flee if attacked. 10% chance that they are accompanied by 1 giant badger.

Medium-Risk Area: 1d4 **badgers** rooting around, but with a 90% chance to be accompanied by 1d2 **giant badgers**

High-Risk Area: 1d4 **badgers** rooting around, but with a 30% chance to be accompanied by 1d3 **giant badgers**

Extreme-Risk Area: 1d6 **giant badgers**

Badger: AC 13; HP 7 (2d4+2); Spd 20ft, swim 30ft; Melee bite (+2, 1d3 piercing); Str +0, Dex +1, Con +1, Int −4, Wis −2, Cha +0; AL U; CR 0; XP 10.

Badger, Giant: AC 13; HP 22 (5d6+5); Spd 20ft, swim 30ft; Melee bite (+3, 1d6+1 piercing), tail (+3, 1d4+1 bludgeoning); SA multiattack (bite, tail); Str +1, Dex +1, Con +1, Int −4, Wis −2, Cha +0; AL U; CR 1/2; XP 100.

7. Bandit

Bandit forces usually have a specified number of "regular" bandits. For every 5 bandits there will be a **sergeant**. For every 50 bandits, there will also be a **leader**. For every band of 100+, a **bandit captain** is present. Some bandits may have been legally hired by a baron to act as tax collectors or simply posing as tax collectors.

Low-Risk Area: 1d12 **bandits**
Medium-Risk Area: 4d6 **bandit**s (80%); otherwise, 1d100 **bandits**
High-Risk Area: 1d100 **bandits**
Extreme-Risk Area: 1d100 **bandits**

Bandit: AC 12; HP 11 (2d8+2); Spd 30ft; Melee shortsword (+3, 1d6+1 slashing); Ranged light crossbow (+3, 80ft/320ft, 1d8+1 piercing); Str +0, Dex +1, Con +1, Int +0, Wis +0, Cha +0; AL any non-L; CR 1/8; XP 25.

Bandit Sergeant: AC 13; HP 22 (4d8+4); Spd 30ft; Melee shortsword (+3, 1d6+1 slashing); Ranged shortbow (+3, 80ft/320ft, 1d6+1 piercing); SA multiattack (shortsword x2 or shortbow x2); Str +0, Dex +2, Con +1, Int +1, Wis +0, Cha +1; AL any non-L; CR 1/4; XP 50.

Bandit Leader: AC 14; HP 44 (8d8+8); Spd 30ft; Melee scimitar (+4, 1d6+2 slashing); Ranged shortbow (+4, 8ft/320ft, 1d6+2 piercing); SA multiattack (scimitar x2 or shortbow x2); Str +1 (+3), Dex +2 (+4), Con +1, Int +1, Wis +0, Cha +1; Skills Athletics +3; AL any non-L; CR 1; XP 200.

Bandit Captain: AC 15; HP 65 (10d8+20); Spd 30ft; Melee scimitar (+5, 1d6+3 slashing), dagger (+5, 1d4+3 piercing); Ranged dagger (+5, 20ft/60ft, 1d4+3 piercing); SA multiattack (scimitar x2, dagger or ranged dagger x2), parry (reaction, +2 AC vs. single melee); Str +2 (+4), Dex +3 (+5), Con +2, Int +2, Wis +0 (+2), Cha +2; Skills Athletics +4, Deception +4; AL any non-L; CR 2; XP 450.

8. Baron (and retinue)

This encounter does not vary by risk level.

Barons generally rule three or more villages' worth of peasants, not to mention knightly manor-houses; this makes them important people, worthy of ransom. Sending pieces of barons to potential ransom-payers in order to accelerate negotiations is a good way to have high-level characters hired to find you (and kill you); so moderation, as in all things, is advisable. Most barons are fighters, although some are mere noble-types, so two "standard" barons are provided here.

The retinue contains the baron (50% chance between veteran and noble), 1d3 **knights**, 1d6+4 **cavalry**, 1 **serjeant of horse**, 1d6 courtiers (**noble**), 1d2 minstrels (**commoner**), 1d2 falconers (**commoner**), 1d4 **mastiffs**.

Baron, Veteran: AC 18; HP 78 (12d8+24); Spd 30ft; Melee longsword (+5, 1d8+3 slashing), shortsword (+5, 1d6+3 piercing); Ranged heavy crossbow (+4, 1d10+2 piercing); SA multiattack (longsword x2, shortsword); Str +3, Dex +2, Con +2, Int +0, Wis +0, Cha +1; Skills Athletics +5, Perception +2; AL LN; CR 3; XP 700.

Baron, Noble: AC 15; HP 18 (4d8); Spd 30ft; Melee rapier (+3, 1d8+1 piercing); SA parry (reaction, +2 AC vs. single melee); Str +0, Dex +1, Con +0, Int +1, Wis +2, Cha +3; Skills Deception +5, Insight +4, Persuasion +5; AL LN; CR 1/4; XP 50.

Retainers:
Commoner: AC 10; HP 4 (1d8); Spd 30ft; Melee club (+2, 1d4

bludgeoning); **Str** +0, **Dex** +0, **Con** +0; **Int** +0, **Wis** +0, **Cha** +0; **AL** any; **CR** 0; **XP** 10.

Knight: AC 18; **HP** 52 (8d8+16); **Spd** 30ft; **Melee** greatsword (+5, 2d6+3 slashing); **SA** leadership (recharge after rest, 1 min, 30ft, if ally can hear and understand then add d4 to attack and save), multiattack (greatsword x2), parry (+2 AC vs. single melee); **Str** +3, **Dex** +0, **Con** +2 (+4), **Int** +0, **Wis** +0 (+2), **Cha** +2; **Traits** brave (tactical advantage against saves against fright); **AL** LN; **CR** 3; **XP** 700.

Cavalry: AC 16; **HP** 22 (4d8+4); **Spd** 30ft; **Melee** lance (+3, 10ft, 1d10+1 piercing); **Ranged** shortbow (+3, 80ft/320ft, 1d6+1 piercing); **Str** +1, **Dex** +1, **Con** +1; **Int** +0, **Wis** +0, **Cha** +0; **AL** LN; **CR** 1/4; **XP** 50.

Serjeant of Horse: AC 16; **HP** 32 (5d8+10); **Spd** 30ft; **Melee** spear (+4, 1d8+2 piercing); **Ranged** shortbow (+4, 80ft/320ft, 1d6+2 piercing); **SA** multiattack (spear x2 or shortbow x2); **Str** +2, **Dex** +2, **Con** +2; **Int** +0, **Wis** +1, **Cha** +1; **Skills** Perception +3, Intimidation +3; **AL** LN; **CR** 1/2; **XP** 100.

Mastiff: AC 12; **HP** 5 (1d8+1); **Spd** 40ft; **Melee** bite (+3, 1d6+1 piercing plus knock prone, DC 11 Str); **Str** +1, **Dex** +2, **Con** +1, **Int** –4, **Wis** +1, **Cha** –2; **Skills** Perception +3; **Senses** keen hearing and smell; **AL** U; **CR** 1/8; **XP** 25.

Warhorse (chain barding): AC 16; **HP** 19 (3d10+3); **Spd** 60ft; **Melee** hooves (+4, 2d6+4 bludgeoning); **SA** trampling charge (20ft move then hooves, DC 14 Str or knocked prone, if prone, bonus with hooves); **Str** +4, **Dex** +1, **Con** +1, **Int** –4, **Wis** +1, **Cha** –2; **AL** U; **CR** 1/2; **XP** 100.

9. Basilisk

Low-Risk Area: 1 **basilisk**
Medium-Risk Area: 1d2 **basilisks**
High-Risk Area: 1d2+1 **basilisks**
Extreme-Risk Area: 1d4+1 **basilisks**

Basilisk: AC 15; **HP** 52 (8d8+16); **Spd** 20ft; **Melee** bite (+5, 2d6+3 piercing plus 2d6 poison); **Str** +3, **Dex** –1, **Con** +2, **Int** –4, **Wis** –1, **Cha** –2; **Senses** darkvision 60ft; **Traits** petrifying gaze (30ft, restrained then petrified, DC 12 Con repeat); **AL** U; **CR** 3; **XP** 700.

10. Bat

Low-Risk Area: 2d6 bats
Medium-Risk Area: 1d6 bats, 10% chance to be accompanied by 1 giant bat
High-Risk Area: 1d6 bats, 25% chance to be accompanied by 1d2 giant bats
Extreme-Risk Area: 1d6 bats, 50% chance to be accompanied by 1d3 giant bats

Bat: AC 12; **HP** 1 (1d4–1); **Spd** 5ft, fly 30ft; **Melee** bite (+0, 1 piercing); **Str** –4, **Dex** +2, **Con** –1, **Int** –4, **Wis** +1, **Cha** –3; **Senses** blindsight 60ft, keen hearing; **Traits** echolocation; **AL** U; **CR** 0; **XP** 10.

Bat, Giant: AC 13; **HP** 22 (4d10); **Spd** 10ft, fly 60ft; **Melee** bite (+4, 1d6+2 piercing); **Str** +2, **Dex** +3, **Con** +0; **Int** –4, **Wis** +1, **Cha** –2; **Senses** blindsight 60ft, keen hearing; **Traits** echolocation; **AL** U; **CR** 1/4; **XP** 50.

11. Bear

Note that the encounter table may already have specified the type or number of bears.

Low-Risk Area: 1 **black bear** (75%); otherwise 2 **black bears**
Medium-Risk Area: 1d4 **black bears** (90%); otherwise, 1d2 **brown bears**
High-Risk Area: 1d4+2 **black bears** (60%); otherwise, 1d4 **brown bears**
Extreme-Risk Area: 1d6+1 **black bears** (50%); otherwise, 1d4 **brown bears**

Bear, Black: AC 11; **HP** 19 (3d8+6); **Spd** 40ft, climb 30ft; **Melee** bite (+3, 1d6+2 piercing), claws (2d4+2 slashing); **SA** multiattack (bite, claws); **Str** +2, **Dex** +0, **Con** +2, **Int** –4, **Wis** +1, **Cha** –2; **Skills** Perception +3; **Senses** keen smell; **AL** U; **CR** 1/2; **XP** 100.

Bear, Brown: AC 11; **HP** 34 (4d10+12); **Spd** 40ft, climb 30ft; **Melee** bite (+5, 1d8+4 piercing), claws (+5, 2d6+4 slashing); **SA** multiattack (bite, claws); **Str** +4, **Dex** +0, **Con** +3, **Int** –4, **Wis** +1, **Cha** –2; **Skills** Perception +3; **Senses** keen smell; **AL** U; **CR** 1; **XP** 200.

12. Blood Hawk

Low-Risk Area: 1d4 **blood hawks**
Medium-Risk Area: 1d10 **blood hawks**
High-Risk Area: 1d10+2 **blood hawks**
Extreme-Risk Area: 1d10+4 **blood hawks**

Blood Hawk: AC 12; **HP** 7 (2d6); **Spd** 10ft, fly 60ft; **Melee** beak (+4, 1d4+2 piercing); **Str** –2, **Dex** +2, **Con** +0, **Int** –4, **Wis** +2, **Cha** –3; **Skills** Perception +4; **Senses** keen sight; **Traits** pack tactics; **AL** U; **CR** 1/8; **XP** 25.

13. Bugbear

Low-Risk Area: 1d2+1 **bugbears**
Medium- to Extreme-Risk Area: Roll on table below:

1–3	1d2+1 **bugbears**
4–6	1d6+3 **bugbears**
7	2d6+3 **bugbears** accompanied by 1d3 human slaves
8	3d6+3 **bugbears** accompanied by 1d4 human slaves
9	3d6+3 **bugbears** accompanied by a **bugbear chief** and 1d2 **brown bears**
10	3d6+3 **bugbears** accompanied by a **bugbear chief** and 2d6 **goblins**

Bugbear: AC 16; **HP** 27 (5d8+5); **Spd** 30ft; **Melee** morningstar (+4, 2d8+2 piercing); **Ranged** javelin (+4, 30ft/120ft, 1d6+2 piercing); **Str** +2, **Dex** +2, **Con** +1, **Int** –1, **Wis** +0, **Cha** –1; **Skills** Stealth +6, Survival +2; **Senses** darkvision 60ft; **Traits** brute, surprise attack (extra 2d6); **AL** CE; **CR** 1; **XP** 200.

Bugbear Chief: AC 17; **HP** 65 (10d8+20); **Spd** 30ft; **Melee** morningstar (+5, 2d8+3); **Ranged** javelin (+5, 30ft/120ft, 1d6+3 piercing; **SA** multiattack (morningstar x2); **Str** +3, **Dex** +2, **Con** +2, **Int** +0, **Wis** +1, **Cha** +0; **Skills** Intimidation +2, Stealth +6, Survival +3; **Senses** darkvision 60ft; **Traits** brute, surprise attack (extra 2d6), warrior's heart (save tactical advantage against charm, fright, paralysis, poison, stun, and sleep); **AL** CE; **CR** 3; **XP** 700.

Bear, Brown: AC 11; **HP** 34 (4d10+12); **Spd** 40ft, climb 30ft; **Melee** bite (+5, 1d8+4 piercing), claws (+5, 2d6+4 slashing); **SA** multiattack (bite, claws); **Str** +4, **Dex** +0, **Con** +3, **Int** −4, **Wis** +1, **Cha** −2; **Skills** Perception +3; **Senses** keen smell; **AL** U; **CR** 1; **XP** 200.

Goblin: AC 15; **HP** 7 (2d6); **Spd** 30ft; **Melee** scimitar (+4, 1d6+2 slashing); **Ranged** shortbow (+4, 80ft/320ft, 1d6+2 piercing); **SA** nimble escape (Disengage or Hide as bonus); **Str** −1, **Dex** +2, **Con** +0, **Int** +0, **Wis** −1, **Cha** −1; **Skills** Stealth +6; **Senses** darkvision 60ft; **AL** NE; **CR** 1/4; **XP** 50.

14. Bulette

Low-Risk Area: 50% chance of 1 **bulette**; otherwise, no encounter
Medium-Risk Area: 1 **bulette** (75%); otherwise, 2
High-Risk Area: 1d2 **bulettes**
Extreme-Risk Area: 1d2 **bulettes** (90%); otherwise, nest of 2d4.

Bulette: AC 17; **HP** 94 (9d10+45); **Spd** 40ft, burrow 40ft; **Melee** bite (+7, 4d12+4 piercing); **SA** deadly leap (jump at least 15ft into space of one or more; 3d6+4 bludgeoning plus 3d6+4 slashing and knocked prone, DC 16 Str or Dex half and pushed 5ft); **Str** +4, **Dex** +0; **Con** +5, **Int** −4, **Wis** +0, **Cha** −3; **Skills** Perception +6; **Senses** darkvision 60ft, tremorsense 60ft; **Traits** standing leap (long 30ft, high 15ft); **AL** U; **CR** 5; **XP** 1800.

15. Caravan (Bard's Gate)

Caravans from Bard's Gate are larger and better armed than the average group of traveling merchants. Three pre-generated caravans are described, as well as a formula for generating more. Bard's Gate caravans are centered on a caravan master who has been approved by the Wheelwrights' Guild to assemble and lead caravans of merchants. This independent contractor is essentially nothing more than a provider of guards, navigation, and know-how for long journeys. Some businesses in Bard's Gate hire the caravan-master to deliver specific cargos under the protection of the Wheelwright's Guild, so the caravan master may have a wagon or two marked as "Wheelwright's Guild" containing such shipments. The majority of a caravan, though, is made up of the traveling merchants who pay the caravan-master a fee to be included in the caravan's complement.

Generating Bard's Gate Caravans:

Roll 3d6 to determine how many wagons are in the Bard's Gate caravan. This determines the rest of the caravan's composition:

03–06	4 wagons
07–09	5 wagons
10–12	6 wagons
13	7 wagons
14	8 wagons
15	9 wagons
16	10 wagons
17	11 wagons
18	12 wagons

Each wagon provides the caravan's total composition with:
1 merchant (**warrior**)
2 **cavalry**
1 teamster (**commoner**)
1 **archer**
1 **foot soldier**
1 **mastiff** (trained for attack with foot soldier as handler)

Each Bard's Gate caravan is accompanied by a caravan master (**veteran**), a **mage**, a battle-wagon, 2 **archers**, and 6 **foot soldiers**. The battle-wagon has sturdy wooden sides and arrow-slits for up to 6 **archers**, and a small ballista to deter flying monsters.

Archer: AC 14; **HP** 11 (2d8+2); **Spd** 30ft; **Melee** shortsword (+3, 1d6+1 piercing); **Ranged** longbow (+3, 150ft/600ft, 1d8+2 piercing); **Str** +1, **Dex** +1, **Con** +1, **Int** +0, **Wis** +0, **Cha** +0; **Skills** Perception +2; **AL** LN; **CR** 1/8; **XP** 25.

Cavalry: AC 16; **HP** 22 (4d8+4); **Spd** 30ft; **Melee** lance (+3, 10ft, 1d10+1 piercing); **Ranged** shortbow (+3, 80ft/320ft, 1d6+1 piercing); **Str** +1, **Dex** +1, **Con** +1, **Int** +0, **Wis** +0, **Cha** +0; **AL** LN; **CR** 1/4; **XP** 50.

Commoner: AC 10; **HP** 4 (1d8); **Spd** 30ft; **Melee** club (+2, 1d4 bludgeoning); **Str** +0, **Dex** +0, **Con** +0, **Int** +0, **Wis** +0, **Cha** +0; **AL** any; **CR** 0; **XP** 10.

Foot Soldier: AC 16; **HP** 11 (2d8+2); **Spd** 30ft; **Melee** longsword (+3, 1d8+1 slashing); **Str** +1, **Dex** +1, **Con** +1, **Int** +0, **Wis** +0, **Cha** +0; **Skills** Perception +2; **AL** LN; **CR** 1/8; **XP** 25.

Mage: AC 12 (15 with *mage armor*); **HP** 40 (9d8); **Spd** 30ft; **Melee** dagger (+5, 1d4+2 piercing); **SA** spells (Int +6, 9th, DC 14); **Str** −1, **Dex** +2, **Con** +0, **Int** +3 (+6), **Wis** +1 (+4), **Cha** +0; **Skills** Arcana +6, History +6; **AL** any; **CR** 6; **XP** 2300.
>   **Spells (slots):** 0 (at will)—*fire bolt, light, mage hand, prestidigitation*; 1st (4)—*detect magic, mage armor, magic missile, shield*; 2nd (3)—*misty step, suggestion*; 3rd (3)—*counterspell, fireball, fly*; 4th (3)—*greater invisibility, ice storm*; 5th (1)—*cone of cold*.

Mastiff: AC 12; **HP** 5 (1d8+1); **Spd** 40ft; **Melee** bite (+3, 1d6+1 piercing plus knock prone, DC 11 Str); **Str** +1, **Dex** +2, **Con** +1, **Int** −4, **Wis** +1, **Cha** −2; **Skills** Perception +3; **Senses** keen hearing and smell; **AL** U; **CR** 1/8; **XP** 25.

Veteran: AC 18; **HP** 78 (12d8+24); **Spd** 30ft; **Melee** longsword (+5, 1d8+3 slashing), shortsword (+5, 1d6+3 piercing); **Ranged** heavy crossbow (+4, 1d10+2 piercing); **SA** multiattack (longsword x2, shortsword); **Str** +3, **Dex** +2, **Con** +2, **Int** +0, **Wis** +0, **Cha** +1; **Skills** Athletics +5, Perception +2; **AL** any; **CR** 3; **XP** 700.

Warhorse (chain barding): AC 16; **HP** 19 (3d10+3); **Spd** 60ft; **Melee** hooves (+4, 2d6+4 bludgeoning); **SA** trampling charge (20ft move then hooves, DC 14 Str or knocked prone, if prone, bonus with hooves); **Str** +4, **Dex** +1, **Con** +1, **Int** −4, **Wis** +1, **Cha** −2; **AL** U; **CR** 1/2; **XP** 100.

Warrior: AC 16; **HP** 33 (6d8+6); **Spd** 30ft; **Melee** longsword (+4, 1d10+2 slashing); **Ranged** longbow (+4, 150ft/600ft, 1d8+2 piercing); **SA** multiattack (longsword x2 or longbow x2); **Str** +2 (+4), **Dex** +2, **Con** +1 (+3), **Int** +0, **Wis** +1, **Cha** +0; **Skills** Athletics +4, Perception +3; **AL** any; **CR** 1/2; **XP** 100.

Cargo: Each wagon contains, on average, 1500gp worth of varied cargo. The bulk of a caravan's cargo is most likely in only two or three of the wagons, the ones belonging to the real merchants. The rest of the wagons in a caravan belong to farmers and small traders carrying bulk goods over a small distance, with many of these constantly joining and leaving the caravan along the whole distance of the route.

Pregenerated Bard's Gate Caravans:

Lowell's Company

Contingent:

Caravan Master: Thanister Lowell (N male human **veteran**)

7 wagons, 14 oxen, 2 **yak-beasts**

1 passenger wagon, 4 draft horses

1 battle-wagon, 4 oxen

4 **mastiffs**

16 **cavalry**, 16 **warhorses**

8 teamsters (**commoner**)

10 **archers**

14 **foot soldiers**

4 Bard's Gate Merchants: Crawton Pearly (NE male human **warrior**), Lemmison Mersil (N male human **warrior**), Lyessen Tawl (N female human **warrior**), and Gunderk Boreballum (LN male dwarf **warrior**).

1 Local Merchant: Terralt Quayle (N male human **warrior**)

2 Farmers: Hoot Rayburne (N male human **commoner**), Carylore Hissop (N female human **commoner**)

1 Wizard: Touerne Magister (N male human **mage**)

2 Passengers: Lady Mara (LN female human **warrior**) and her servant Dilla (LN female human **commoner**). Lady Mara is married to a local knight, but is not yet knighted herself.

Cargo: 2 wagons of turnips (100gp total), half-wagon of printed books (1000gp), 1 wagon of almonds (2000gp), 1 wagon of rugs and woven textiles (3500gp), 1 half-empty wagon (0gp), 1 half-wagon assorted trinkets, ribbons, candles, etc. (300gp), 1 wagon of semi-rare spices (2000gp).

Cash-Box: 1652gp in coins of various denominations, 1 letter of credit for Lemmison Mersil drawn on the Borgandy Family of Remballo (in Suilley) in the amount of 561gp.

Wheelwrights Number Nine

Contingent:

Caravan Master David Wheelwright (N male human **veteran**)

10 wagons, 20 oxen. 2 **yak-beasts**

1 battle-wagon, 1 **yak-beast**

2 **mastiffs**

20 **cavalry**, 20 **warhorses**

10 teamsters (**commoner**)

12 **archers**

16 **foot soldiers**

4 Bard's Gate Merchants: Clinkem Darley (N male human **warrior**), Ombert Shave (N male human fighter 3), Guenivere Bartley (N male human **warrior**), Peter Miller (N male human **warrior**)

Bartholomew Bown (CG male human **mage**)

Cargo: One-and-a-half wagons' worth of empty space (0gp), one-half wagon of local trinkets (200gp), 2 wagons of full wine casks (2000gp total), half-wagon of rare spices (3000gp), 2 wagons of semi-rare spices (5000gp total), half-wagon of paper and parchment (500gp), 2 wagons of dyes (1000gp total), half-wagon of barreled nuts (500gp), half-wagon of carpets (2000gp)

Cash-box: 1038gp in varying denominations.

Kimalyn's Road Warriors

Contingent:

Caravan Master Kimalyn Forthe (N female human **veteran**)

9 wagons, 18 oxen, 2 **yak-beasts**

1 battle-wagon, 4 oxen

3 **mastiffs**

18 **cavalry**, 18 **warhorses**

9 teamsters (**commoner**)

11 **archers**

15 **foot soldiers**

5 Bard's Gate merchants: Carlen Winter (N female human **warrior**), Burgum of Bard's Gate (N male human **warrior**), Yane Candle (N male human **warrior**), Leo Perdilian (N male human **warrior**), Sattry Noriss (N male human **warrior**)

2 local merchants: Ghorvis Tradesman (N male human **warrior**), Rinaldo Blanc (N male human **warrior**)

2 farmers: Huillem Freedman (N male human **commoner**), Bert Yeoman (N male human **commoner**)

Doctor Needles (N male human **mage**)

Cargo (13,500): One wagon's worth of empty space, 2 wagons of assorted farm produce (200gp total), half-wagon of good mead (700gp total), half-wagon of embroidery from Dlante, in Aachen Province (2000gp), half-wagon of pickled purple dream-apples from the Yolbiac Vale (1800gp), 1 wagon of well-tanned hides (1000gp), box of opium paste from Suilley (1000gp), half-wagon of woolen cloth (300gp), half-wagon of spools of thread (400gp), 2 wagons of pottery and ceramics (3000gp total), half-wagon of locally-produced trinkets and beadwork (300gp).

Cash Box: 2947gp worth of coins in various denominations.

16. Caravan (Provincial)

Generating Provincial Caravans

Roll 3d6 to determine how many wagons are in the caravan. This determines the rest of the caravan's composition:

03–06	2 wagons
07–09	3 wagons
10–12	4 wagons
13	5 wagons
14	6 wagons
15	7 wagons
16	8 wagons
17	9 wagons
18	10 wagons

Each wagon provides the caravan's total composition with:

1 merchant (**warrior**)

2 cavalry

1 teamster (**commoner**)

1 archer

Each caravan of 5 or more wagons is also accompanied by a caravan master (**veteran**) with 2 **foot soldiers** with 2 **mastiffs**.

Archer: AC 14; HP 11 (2d8+2); Spd 30ft; **Melee** shortsword (+3, 1d6+1 piercing); **Ranged** longbow (+3, 150ft/600ft, 1d8+2 piercing); **Str** +1, **Dex** +1, **Con** +1, **Int** +0, **Wis** +0, **Cha** +0; **Skills** Perception +2; **AL** LN; **CR** 1/8; **XP** 25.

Cavalry: AC 16; HP 22 (4d8+4); Spd 30ft; **Melee** lance (+3, 10ft, 1d10+1 piercing); **Ranged** shortbow (+3, 80ft/320ft, 1d6+1 piercing); **Str** +1, **Dex** +1, **Con** +1; **Int** +0, **Wis** +0, **Cha** +0; **AL** LN; **CR** 1/4; **XP** 50.

Commoner: AC 10; HP 4 (1d8); Spd 30ft; **Melee** club (+2, 1d4 bludgeoning); **Str** +0, **Dex** +0, **Con** +0; **Int** +0, **Wis** +0, **Cha** +0; **AL** any; **CR** 0; **XP** 10.

Mastiff: AC 12; HP 5 (1d8+1); Spd 40ft; **Melee** bite (+3, 1d6+1 piercing plus knock prone, DC 11 Str); **Str** +1, **Dex** +2, **Con** +1, **Int** −4, **Wis** +1, **Cha** −2; **Skills** Perception +3; **Senses** keen hearing and smell; **AL** U; **CR** 1/8; **XP** 25.

Veteran: AC 18; **HP** 78 (12d8+24); **Spd** 30ft; **Melee** longsword (+5, 1d8+3 slashing), shortsword (+5, 1d6+3 piercing); **Ranged** heavy crossbow (+4, 1d10+2 piercing); **SA** multiattack (longsword x2, shortsword); **Str** +3, **Dex** +2, **Con** +2, **Int** +0, **Wis** +0, **Cha** +1; **Skills** Athletics +5, Perception +2; **AL** any; **CR** 3; **XP** 700.

Warhorse (chain barding): AC 16; **HP** 19 (3d10+3); **Spd** 60ft; **Melee** hooves (+4, 2d6+4 bludgeoning); **SA** trampling charge (20ft move then hooves, DC 14 Str or knocked prone, if prone, bonus with hooves); **Str** +4, **Dex** +1, **Con** +1, **Int** −4, **Wis** +1, **Cha** −2; **AL** U; **CR** 1/2; **XP** 100.

Warrior: AC 16; **HP** 33 (6d8+6); **Spd** 30ft; **Melee** longsword (+4, 1d10+2 slashing); **Ranged** longbow (+4, 150ft/600ft, 1d8+2 piercing); **SA** multiattack (longsword x2 or longbow x2); **Str** +2 (+4), **Dex** +2, **Con** +1 (+3), **Int** +0, **Wis** +1, **Cha** +0; **Skills** Athletics +4, Perception +3; **AL** any; **CR** 1/2; **XP** 100.

Cargo: Roughly 1000gp per wagon

Pregenerated Provincial Caravans:

Caravan of Lucius Palejohn

Contingent:
Caravan Master Lucius Palejohn (LN male human **veteran**)
5 wagons, 10 oxen, 2 **yak-beasts**
2 **mastiffs**
10 **cavalry**, 10 **warhorses**
5 teamsters (**commoner**)
5 **archers**
2 **foot soldiers**
5 merchants: Perault Vane (N male human **warrior**), Gillaina Fenberry (N female human **warrior**), Guraldo Silvercoin (N male human **warrior**), Hugh Featherstock (N male human **warrior**), Louis Ambrose (N male human **warrior**).

Cargo: Half-wagon of cheap wine (200gp), half-wagon of expensive wine (600gp), 1 wagon of hazelnuts (500gp), 1 wagon of cloth tapestries (2000gp), half-wagon of cheap spices (700gp), half-wagon of leather shoes (500gp).

Coin Box: 416gp in coins of various denominations.

The Wandering Wardens

Contingent:
Caravan Master Palkin Warden (N male human **veteran**)
6 wagons, 14 oxen, 2 **yak-beasts**
5 **mastiffs**
12 **cavalry**, 12 **warhorses**
6 teamsters (**commoner**)
6 **archers**
2 **foot soldiers**
6 merchants: Oliver Treforde (N male human **warrior**), Huilline Baltro (N female human **warrior**), Stephin Louard (N male human **warrior**), Zinnalt Redrobin (N male human **warrior**), Gervis Goldminder (N male human **warrior**), Giles of Crossroad (N male human **warrior**)

Cargo: 1 wagon of local foodstuffs (50gp), 1 wagon of pottery (700gp), 1 wagon of beer (800gp), 1 wagon of assorted merchandise (1000gp), 1 wagon of woolen bales (800gp), and 1 wagon of barreled wines (1200gp).

Cash Box: 1450gp in coins of assorted denominations.

Porpentine's Escorteers

Contingent:
Caravan Master Porpentine (N male human **veteran**)
7 wagons, 15 oxen, 2 **yak-beasts**
1 passenger wagon, 4 draft horses
2 **mastiffs**

14 **cavalry**, 14 **warhorses**
8 teamsters (**commoner**)
7 **archers**
2 **foot soldiers**
7 merchants: Pfalgen Trustworthy (N male human **warrior**), Belinda Trader (N male human **warrior**), Dennys Balcourtney (N male human **warrior**), Robardo Groat (N male human **warrior**), Purleaf Dwindle (N male halfling **warrior** with shortsword and shortbow), Bartholde Getz (N male human **warrior**), Randall of Hillside (N male human **warrior**).

2 passengers: Devion and Pelliria Espaire (**commoners**), the teenage son and daughter of a local knight, traveling to visit their uncle Tilnius at his castle twenty miles away.

Cargo: 1 wagon of local foodstuffs (50gp), 1 wagon of brandies and liqueurs (2500gp), 2 wagons of barreled beer (1000gp total), 1 wagon of colorful songbirds (400gp), 1 wagon of bolts of cloth (900gp), 2 wagons of jars of honey (1000gp total).

Cash Box: 650gp in coins of assorted denominations, 1 sapphire (500gp).

17. Centaur

Encounter with 1d6+3 **centaurs**. Does not vary by Risk Level of the area.

Centaur: AC 12; **HP** 45 (6d10+12); **Spd** 50ft; **Melee** pike (+6, 10ft, 1d10+4 piercing), hooves (+6, 2d6+4 bludgeoning); **Ranged** longbow x2 (+4, 150ft/600ft, 1d8+2 piercing); **SA** charge (least 30ft and hit with pike, extra 3d6 piercing), multiattack (pike, hooves or longbow x2); **Str** +4, **Dex** +2, **Con** +2, **Int** −1, **Wis** +1, **Cha** +0; **Skills** Athletics +6, Perception +3, Survival +3; **AL** NG; **CR** 2; **XP** 450.

18. Chimera

As an airborne encounter, an encounter over mountains is with 1d2 **chimerae**, and encounters over non-mountain terrain is with a single one.

Chimera: AC 14; **HP** 114; **Spd** 30ft, fly 60ft; **Melee** bite (+7, 2d6+4 piercing), horns (+7, 1d12+4 bludgeoning), claws (+7, 2d6+4 slashing); **SA** fire breath (recharge 5–6, 15ft cone, 7d8 fire, DC 15 Dex half), multiattack (bite, horns, claws; fire breath can replace bite or horns); **Str** +4, **Dex** +0, **Con** +4, **Int** −4, **Wis** +2, **Cha** +0; **Skills** Perception +8; **Senses** darkvision 60ft; **AL** CE; **CR** 6; **XP** 2300.

19. Cleric

For purposes of encounters, all clerics follow the generic example below. If they join the characters, you may wish to individualize them more. Encounters with a lone cleric are with priests .

1d20	Encounter
1–2	1d6 Good **acolytes**
3	1d6 Evil **acolytes**
4–9	1 Good **priest** with 1d2 **acolytes**
10–13	1 Evil **priest** with 1d2 **acolytes**
14	1 Evil **priest** with 1d4+1 **knights**
15–16	1 Good **priest** with 1d2+1 **acolytes**, accompanied by a **knight**
17	1 Evil **priest** with 1d2+1 **acolytes**, accompanied by a **knight**

1d20	Encounter
18–19	1 Good **high priest** with 1d2 **priest**s, 1d3+2 **acolytes**, 2 knights, and 8 foot soldiers
20	1 Evil **high priest** with 1d2 **priests**, 1d3+2 **acolytes**, 2 knights, and 8 **foot soldiers**

Clerics traveling together will virtually always be followers of the same god. There are innumerable possibilities, but the most common gods of clerics who would be traveling roads in the Borderland Provinces are as follows:

Gods of Traveling Clerics

1d12	Good Deities	Evil Deities
1	Solanus (sun, healing)	Oinodaemon (disease)
2–3	Freya (love, harvest)	Orcus (undeath)
4–6	Kamien (rivers, travel)	Demogorgon (earth, fate)
7	Telophus (crops, seasons)	Inoculist Heretic (Hel)*
8	Mitra (law, sun)	Mirkeer (shadows, night)
9	Oghma (song, bards)	Orcus (undeath)
10	Thyr (law, justice)	Hecate (dark magic)
11	Belon the Wise (travel, magic)	Idolist Heretic (Fraz-Urb'luu)**
12	Ceres (healing, mercy)	Fraz-Urb'luu (deception)

* Cleric who believes him/herself to still be a cleric of Freya, but who is actually worshipping the goddess Hel by following the dictates and rituals of the Inoculist heresy.

** Cleric who embraces the Idolist Heresy, thereby unknowingly venerating the demon prince Fraz-Urb'luu. The cleric believes him/herself to be a cleric of Thyr dedicated to "purifying" doctrinal mistakes being made by most of Thyr's true clerics.

Acolyte: AC 10; HP 9 (2d8); Spd 30ft; Melee club (+2, 1d4 bludgeoning); SA spells (Wis +4, 1st, DC 12); Str +0, Dex +0, Con +0, Int +0, Wis +2, Cha +0; Skills Medicine +4, Religion +2; AL any good or evil; CR 1/4; XP 50.

Foot Soldier: AC 16; HP 11 (2d8+2); Spd 30ft; Melee longsword (+3, 1d8+1 slashing); Str +1, Dex +1, Con +1, Int +0, Wis +0, Cha +0; Skills Perception +2; AL LN; CR 1/8; XP 25.

High Priest: AC 15; HP 58 (9d8+18); Spd 30ft; Melee flail (+4, 1d8+1 bludgeoning); SA divine eminence (bonus, expend slot, extra 3d6 radiant or necrotic, + 1d6 per slot above 1st), spells (Wis +7, 9th, DC 15); Str +1, Dex +1, Con +2, Int +2, Wis +4 (+7), Cha +2; Skills Medicine +10, Persuasion +5, Religion +5; AL any good or evil; CR 5; XP 1800.

Knight: AC 18; HP 52 (8d8+16); Spd 30ft; Melee greatsword (+5, 2d6+3 slashing); SA leadership (recharge after rest, 1 min, 30ft, if ally can hear and understand then add d4 to attack and save), multiattack (greatsword x2); parry (+2 AC vs. single melee); Str +3, Dex +0, Con +2 (+4), Int +0, Wis +0 (+2), Cha +2; Traits brave (tactical advantage against saves against fright); AL LN; CR 3; XP 700.

Priest: AC 13; HP 27 (5d8+5); Spd 30ft; Melee mace (+2, 1d6 bludgeoning); SA divine eminence (bonus, expend slot, extra 3d6 radiant or necrotic, + 1d6 per slot above 1st), spells (Wis +5, 5th, DC 13); Str +0, Dex +0, Con +1, Int +1, Wis +3, Cha +1; Skills Medicine +7, Persuasion +3, Religion +4; AL any good or evil; CR 2; XP 450.

Good Spell List

Acolyte Spells (slots): 0 (at will)—*light, sacred flame, thaumaturgy;* 1st (2)—*bless, cure wounds, sanctuary.*

Priest Spells (slots): 0 (at will)—*guidance, light, sacred flame, thaumaturgy;* 1st (4)—*cure wounds, guiding bolt, sanctuary;* 2nd (3)—*lesser restoration, spiritual weapon;* 3rd (2)—*dispel magic, spirit guardians.*

High Priest Spells (slots): 0 (at will)— *light, sacred flame, resistance, thaumaturgy;* 1st (4)— *cure wounds, guiding bolt, sanctuary;* 2nd (3)—*hold person, lesser restoration, spiritual weapon;* 3rd (3)—*dispel magic, remove curse, spirit guardians;* 4th (3)—*freedom of movement, guardian of faith;* 5th (1)—*greater restoration, raise dead.*

Evil Spell List

Acolyte Spells (slots): 0 (at will)—*resistance, sacred flame, thaumaturgy;* 1st (2)—*bane, guiding bolt (necrotic), inflict wounds.*

Priest Spells (slots): 0 (at will)—*guidance, resistance, sacred flame, thaumaturgy;* 1st (4)— *bane, guiding bolt (necrotic), inflict wounds;* 2nd (3)—*blindness/deafness, spiritual weapon;* 3rd (2)—*bestow curse, spirit guardians.*

High Priest Spells (slots): 0 (at will)—*guidance, resistance, sacred flame, thaumaturgy;* 1st (4)— *bane, guiding bolt (necrotic), inflict wounds;* 2nd (3)—*blindness/deafness, hold person, spiritual weapon;* 3rd (3)—*animate dead, bestow curse, spirit guardians;* 4th (3)—*freedom of movement, guardian of faith;* 5th (1)—*contagion, insect plague.*

20. Cloud Giant Tower

This airborne encounter is with a single-tower castle built on a cloud and inhabited by cloud giants. The castle contains 1d4+2 **cloud giants** and 1 **roc**.

Giant, Cloud: AC 14; HP 200 (16d12+96); Spd 40ft; Melee morningstar x2 (+12, 10ft, 3d8+8 piercing); Ranged rock (+12, 60ft/240ft, 4d10+8 bludgeoning); SA innate spells, multiattack; Str +8, Dex +0, Con +6 (+9), Int +1, Wis +3 (+7), Cha +3 (+7); Skills Insight +7, Perception +7; Senses keen smell; AL NE; CR 9; XP 5000.
    Innate Spells: at will—*detect magic, fog cloud, light;* 3/day—*feather fall, fly, misty step, telekinesis;* 1/day—*control weather, gaseous form*

Roc: AC 15; HP 248 (16d20+80); Spd 20ft, fly 120ft; Melee beak (+13, 10ft, 4d8+9 piercing), talons (+13, 4d6+9 slashing plus grapple, target restrained, escape DC 19); SA multiattack (beak, talons); Str +9, Dex +0 (+4), Con +5 (+4), Int −4, Wis +0 (+4), Cha −1 (+3); Skills Perception +4; Senses keen sight; AL U; CR 11; XP 7200.

21. Cockatrice

Low-Risk Area: 1 **cockatrice**
Medium-Risk Area: 1d3 **cockatrices**
High-Risk Area: 1d6 **cockatrices**
Extreme-Risk Area: 1d4+2 **cockatrices**

Cockatrice: AC 11; HP 27 (6d6+6); Spd 20ft, fly 40ft; Melee bite (+3, 1d4+1 piercing plus petrifying touch); Str −2, Dex

+1, **Con** +1, **Int** –4, **Wis** +1, **Cha** –3; **Senses** darkvision 60ft; **Traits** petrifying touch (restrained then petrified for 24 hours, DC 11 Con repeat); **AL** U; **CR** 1/2; **XP** 100.

22. Corpse Rook

Low-Risk Area: 1 **corpse rook**
Medium-Risk Area: 1d2 **corpse rooks** (90%); otherwise, 1d6+1
High-Risk Area: 1d2+1 **corpse rooks** (90%); otherwise, 1d8+1
Extreme-Risk Area: 1d4+1 **corpse rooks** (90%); otherwise, 1d12+1

Corpse Rook: AC 14; **HP** 45 (6d10+12); **Spd** 10ft, fly 60ft; **Melee** bite x3 (+5, 1d10+3 piercing), claws (+5, 2d8+3 slashing); **SA** multiattack (bite x3, claws); **Str** +3, **Dex** +2, **Con** +2, **Int** –3, **Wis** +0, **Cha** +0; **Senses** darkvision 60ft, all-around vision; **Traits** combat mobility (opportunity attacks have tactical disadvantage); **AL** NE; **CR** 4; **XP** 1100. (**Fifth Edition Foes** 66)

23. Couatl

This aerial encounter is with a single **couatl**.

Couatl: AC 19; **HP** 97 (13d8+39); **Spd** 30ft, fly 90ft; **Melee** bite (+7, 1d6+5 piercing plus unconscious poison, DC 13 Con) or constrict (+5, 10ft, 2d6+3 bludgeoning plus restrained, escape DC 15); **SA** change shape, innate spells (Cha, DC 14); **Immune** normal weapons, psychic; **Resist** radiant; **Str** +3, **Dex** +5, **Con** +3 (+5), **Int** +4, **Wis** +5 (+7), **Cha** +4 (+6); **Senses** truesight 120ft; **Traits** magic weapons, shielded mind; **AL** LG; **CR** 4; **XP** 1100.

> **Innate Spells**: at will—detect evil and good, detect magic, detect thoughts; 3/day—bless, create food and water, cure wounds, lesser restoration, protection from poison, sanctuary, shield; 1/day—dream, greater restoration, scrying.

24. Demon

Low-Risk Area: Leaves rustle, and there is a sense of evil, but nothing more.
Medium-Risk Area: 1d6 **manes**
High-Risk Area: 1 **vrock**
Extreme-Risk Area: 1d3+1 **vrock**

Demon, Manes: AC 9; **HP** 9 (2d6+2); **Spd** 20ft; **Melee** claws (+2, 2d4 slashing); **Immune** charm, fright, poison; **Resist** cold, fire, lightning; **Str** +0, **Dex** –1, **Con** +1, **Int** –4, **Wis** –1, **Cha** –3; **Senses** darkvision 60ft; **CR** 1/8; **XP** 25.

Demon, Vrock: AC 15; **HP** 104 (11d10+44); **Spd** 40ft, fly 60ft; **Melee** beak (+6, 2d6+3 piercing), talons (+6, 2d10+3 slashing); **SA** multiattack (beak, talons), spores (recharge 6, 15ft radius, poisoned, DC 14 Con repeat, then take 1d10 poison each turn), stunning screech (1/day, 20ft, stunned until end of vrock's next turn, DC 14 Con); **Str** +3, **Dex** +2 (+5), **Con** +4, **Int** –1, **Wis** +1 (+4), **Cha** –1 (+2); **Immune** poison; **Resist** cold, fire, lightning, normal weapons; **Senses** darkvision 120ft; **Traits** magic resistance; **AL** CE; **CR** 6; **XP** 2300.

25. Djinni

This airborne encounter is with 1 or 2 **djinni** (90%/10%).

Genie, Djinni: AC 17, **HP** 161 (14d10+84); **Spd** 30ft, fly 90ft; **Melee** scimitar x3 (+9, 2d6+5 slashing plus 1d6 lightning or thunder damage); **SA** create whirlwind (5ft radius, 30ft tall, 120ft range, restrained, DC 18 Str avoid or free), innate spells (Cha +9, DC 17), multiattack; **Immune** lightning, thunder; **Str** +5, **Dex** +2 (+6), **Con** +6, **Int** +2, **Wis** +3 (+7), **Cha** +5 (+9); **Senses** darkvision 120ft; **Traits** elemental demise; **AL** CG; **CR** 11; **XP** 7200.

> **Innate Spells**: at will—detect evil and good, detect magic, thunderwave; 3/day—create food and water (can create wine instead of water), tongues, wind walk; 1/day—conjure elemental (air only), creation, gaseous form, invisibility, major image, plane shift

26. Dragonfly, Giant

Low-Risk Area: 1 **giant dragonfly**
Medium-Risk Area: 1d3 **giant dragonflies**
High-Risk Area: 1d3+1 **giant dragonflies**
Extreme-Risk Area: 1d4+2 **giant dragonflies**

Dragonfly, Giant: AC 15; **HP** 52 (8d8+16); **Spd** 10ft, fly 50ft; **Melee** bite (+5, 1d10+3 piercing); **Str** +3, **Dex** +4, **Con** +2, **Int** –5, **Wis** +1, **Cha** –2; **Skills** Perception +3; **Senses** darkvision 60ft; **AL** U; **CR** 1; **XP** 200.

27. Dragon A

Although there is a wide variety of possible dragon encounters, this encounter number is with an insignificant and common wyrm, youthful ones that still hunt actively and fairly indiscriminately. The GM may substitute any type of dragon or age category, by whatever means desired, but the standard dragon encounter along roads or in the countryside is with a young green or red dragon.

Dragon, Young Green: AC 18; **HP** 136 (16d10+48); **Spd** 40ft, fly 80ft, swim 40ft; **Melee** bite (+7, 10ft, 2d10+4 piercing plus 2d6 poison), claw (+7, 2d6+4 slashing); **SA** multiattack (bite, claw x2), poison breath (recharge 5–6, 30ft cone, 12d6 poison, DC 14 Con half); **Immune** poison; **Str** +4, **Dex** +1 (+4), **Con** +3 (+6), **Int** +3, **Wis** +1 (+4), **Cha** +2 (+5); **Skills** Deception +5, Perception +7, Stealth +4; **Senses** blindsight 30ft, darkvision 120ft; **Traits** amphibious; **AL** LE; **CR** 8; **XP** 3900.

Dragon, Young Red: AC 18; **HP** 178 (17d10+85); **Spd** 40ft, climb 40ft, fly 80ft; **Melee** bite (+10, 10ft, 2d10+6 piercing plus 1d6 fire), claw (+10, 2d6+6 slashing); **SA** fire breath (recharge 5–6, 30ft cone, 16d6 fire, DC 17 Dex half), multiattack (bite, claw x2); **Immune** fire; **Str** +6, **Dex** +0 (+4), **Con** +5 (+9), **Int** +2, **Wis** +0 (+4), **Cha** +4 (+8); **Skills** Perception +8, Stealth +4; **Senses** blindsight 30ft, darkvision 120ft; **AL** CE; **CR** 10; **XP** 5900.

28. Dragon B

This is an airborne encounter with one adult black or green dragon over a non-mountainous area.

Dragon, Adult Black: AC 19; **HP** 195 (17d12+85); **Spd** 40ft, fly 80ft, swim 40ft; **Melee** bite (+11, 10ft, 2d10+6 piercing plus 1d8 acid), claw (+11, 2d6+6 slashing); **SA** acid breath (recharge 5–6, 60ft line 5ft wide, 12d8 acid, DC 18 Dex half), frightful presence (120ft, frightened for 1 min, DC 16 Wis repeat), multiattack (frightful presence, bite, claw x2); **LA** detect, tail (+11, 15ft, 2d8+6 bludgeoning), wing (2 actions, 10ft, 2d6+6 bludgeoning, knock prone, DC 19 Dex, flies up to half speed); **Immune** acid; **Str** +6, **Dex** +2 (+7), **Con** +5 (+10), **Int** +2, **Wis** +1 (+6), **Cha** +3 (+8);

Skills Perception +11, Stealth +7; **Senses** blindsight 60ft, darkvision 120ft; **Traits** amphibious, legendary resistance (3/day); **AL** CE; **CR** 14; **XP** 11,500.

Dragon, Adult Green: AC 19; **HP** 207 (18d12+90); **Spd** 40ft, fly 80ft, swim 40ft; **Melee** bite (+11, 10ft, 2d10+6 piercing plus 2d6 poison), claw (+11, 2d6+6 slashing); **SA** frightful presence (120ft, frightened for 1 min, DC 16 Wis repeat), multiattack (frightful presence, bite, claw x2), poison breath (recharge 5–6, 60ft cone, 16d6 poison, DC 18 Con half); **LA** detect, tail (+11, 15ft, 2d8+6 bludgeoning), wing (2 actions, 10ft, 2d6+6 bludgeoning, knock prone, DC 19 Dex, flies up to half speed); **Immune** poison; **Str** +6, **Dex** +1 (+6), **Con** +5 (+10), **Int** +4, **Wis** +2 (+7), **Cha** +3 (+8); **Skills** Deception +8, Insight +7, Perception +12, Persuasion +8, Stealth +7; **Senses** blindsight 60ft, darkvision 120ft; **Traits** amphibious, legendary resistance (3/day); **AL** LE; **CR** 15; **XP** 13,000.

29. Dragon C

This is an airborne encounter with one adult red or white dragon over a mountainous area.

Dragon, Adult Red: AC 19; **HP** 256 (19d12+133); **Spd** 40ft, climb 40ft, fly 80ft; **Melee** bite (+14, 10ft, 2d10+8 piercing plus 2d6 fire), claw x2 (+14, 2d6+8 slashing); **SA** fire breath (recharge 5–6, 60ft cone, 18d6 fire, DC 21 Dex half), frightful presence (120ft, frightened for 1 min, DC 19 Wis repeat), multiattack (frightful presence, bite, claw x2); **LA** detect, tail (+11, 15ft, 2d8+6 bludgeoning), wing (2 actions, 10ft, 2d6+6 bludgeoning, knock prone, DC 21 Dex, flies up to half speed); **Immune** fire; **Str** +8, **Dex** +0 (+6), **Con** +7 (+13), **Int** +3, **Wis** +1 (+7), **Cha** +5 (+11); **Skills** Perception +13, Stealth +6; **Senses** blindsight 60ft, darkvision 120ft; **AL** CE; **CR** 17; **XP** 18,000.

Dragon, Adult White: AC 18; **HP** 200 (16d12+96); **Spd** 40ft, burrow 30ft, fly 80ft, swim 40ft; **Melee** bite (+11, 10ft, 2d10+6 piercing plus 1d8 cold), claw (+11, 2d6+6 slashing); **SA** cold breath (recharge 5–6, 60ft cone, 12d8 cold, DC 19 Con half), frightful presence (120ft, frightened for 1 min, DC 14 Wis repeat), multiattack (frightful presence, bite, claw x2); **LA** detect, tail (+11, 15ft, 2d8+6 bludgeoning), wing (2 actions, 10ft, 2d6+6 bludgeoning, knock prone, DC 19 Dex, flies up to half speed); **Str** +6, **Dex** +0 (+5), **Con** +6 (+11), **Int** −1, **Wis** +1 (+6), **Cha** +1 (+6); **Skills** Perception +11, Stealth +5; **Traits** icy walk (move across icy with extra movement or checks), legendary resistance (3/day); **AL** CE; **CR** 13; **XP** 10,000.

30. Drake, Fire

This encounter is with 1d6 **fire drakes**, regardless of an area's Risk Level.

Drake, Fire: AC 13; **HP** 27 (6d6+6); Spd 20ft, fly 60ft; **Melee** bite (+3, 1d8+1 piercing), claws (+3, 2d6+1 slashing); **SA** fiery breath (recharge 6, 20ft cone, 2d10 fire, DC 11 Dex half), multiattack (bite, claws); **Immune** fire, paralysis, sleep; **Vulnerable** cold; **Str** +1, **Dex** +1, **Con** +1, **Int** −3, **Wis** +0, **Cha** +0; **Skills** Stealth +3; **Senses** darkvision 60ft; **Traits** pyrophoric blood (attack with melee slashing or piercing weapon, DC 11 Dex or take 1d6 fire); **AL** CE; **CR** 1; **XP** 200. (**Fifth Edition Foes** 86)

31. Druid

Unlike cleric encounters, in which the clerics are generally moving from one inhabited place to another as travelers, druids met on a road are usually taking part in a religious procession of some kind. Most ordinary druidic travel in the get-from-place sense is done cross-country.

If the encounter tables specify a lone druid on the other hand, the druid is simply a traveler, possibly a preacher. Encounters specified to be with a lone druid are with a druid of 4th level.

Otherwise, roll on the table below to determine the makeup of a druidic procession:

1–3	1 **druid** with 1d6+2 druidic worshippers (**commoner**) in white robes, carrying branches tied with ribbons
4–6	1 **druid** with 1d4+1 **acolytes** singing chants.
7	1 **druid** with 2 **acolytes**, 2 **brown bears**, and 3d6 druidic worshippers (**commoner**) in white robes.
8	1 **master druid** with 2 **druids**, 2 **acolytes**, 2 **brown bears**, 3d6 druidic worshippers (**commoner**), and 2d6 **druidic foot soldiers**

Acolyte Druid: AC 10; **HP** 9 (2d8); **Spd** 30ft; **Melee** club (+2, 1d4 bludgeoning or +4, 1d8+2 bludgeoning with *shillelagh*); **SA** spells (Wis +4, 1st, DC 12); **Str** +0, **Dex** +0, **Con** +0, **Int** +0, **Wis** +2, **Cha** +0; **Skills** Medicine +4, Nature +2; **AL** any N **CR** 1/4; **XP** 50.
   Spells (slots): 0 (at will)—*druidcraft, shillelagh*; 1st (2)—*entangle, faerie fire, thunderwave*.

Bear, Brown: AC 11; **HP** 34 (4d10+12); **Spd** 40ft, climb 30ft; **Melee** bite (+5, 1d8+4 piercing), claws (+5, 2d6+4 slashing); **SA** multiattack (bite, claws); **Str** +4, **Dex** +0, **Con** +3, **Int** −4, **Wis** +1, **Cha** −2; **Skills** Perception +3; **Senses** keen smell; **AL** U; **CR** 1; **XP** 200.

Druid: AC 11 (16 with *barkskin*); **HP** 27 (5d8+5); **Spd** 30ft; **Melee** quarterstaff (+2, 1d6 bludgeoning or +5, 1d8+3 bludgeoning with *shillelagh*); **SA** spells (Wis +5, 4th, DC 13); **Str** +0, **Dex** +1, **Con** +1, **Int** +1, **Wis** +3, **Cha** +0; **Skills** Medicine +5, Nature +3, Perception +5; **AL** any N; **CR** 2; **XP** 450.
   Spells (slots): 0 (at will)—*druidcraft, produce flame, shillelagh*; 1st (4)—*entangle, faerie fire, speak with animals, thunderwave*; 2nd (3)—*barkskin, flaming sphere, hold person*.

Druidic Foot Soldiers: AC 13; **HP** 11 (2d8+2); **Spd** 30ft; **Melee** greatclub (+3, 1d8+1 bludgeoning); **Ranged** sling (+3, 30ft/120ft, 1d4+1 bludgeoning); **Str** +1, **Dex** +1, **Con** +1, **Int** +0, **Wis** +0, **Cha** +0; **Skills** Perception +2; **AL** N; **CR** 1/8; **XP** 25.

Master Druid: AC 12 (16 with *barkskin*); **HP** 78 (12d8+24); **Spd** 30ft; **Melee** quarterstaff (+3, 1d6 bludgeoning or +6, 1d8+4 bludgeoning with *shillelagh*); **SA** spells (Wis +7, 11th, DC 15); **Str** +0, **Dex** +2, **Con** +2, **Int** +1, **Wis** +4, **Cha** +1; **Skills** Medicine +7, Nature +4, Perception +7; **AL** any N; **CR** 5; **XP** 1800.
   Spells (slots): 0 (at will)—*druidcraft, produce flame, shillelagh, thorn whip*; 1st (4)—*entangle, faerie fire, speak with animals, thunderwave*; 2nd (3)—*barkskin, flaming sphere, hold person*; 3rd (3)—*call lightning, dispel magic*; 4th (3)—*blight, confusion, stoneskin*; 5th (2)—*conjure elemental, insect plague*; 6th (1)—*conjure fey*.

32. Dwarf

This encounter is with a group of hill dwarves that are not traveling traders. They might be messengers, mercenaries, or miners on their way to a new dig. Their numbers are not determined by threat level. Roll 1d10 to determine the composition of a dwarven band:

1d10	Composition of Group
1–7	1d6 **dwarves**
8	2d6 **dwarves** with a leader (**warrior**) mounted on a pony
9	3d6 **dwarves** with 2 leaders (**warrior**) mounted on ponies
10	4d6 **dwarves** with 3 leaders (**warrior**) mounted on ponies

Dwarf: AC 16; **HP** 13 (2d8+4); **Spd** 30ft; **Melee** battleaxe (+4, 1d8+2 slashing); **Ranged** handaxe (+4, 20ft/60ft, 1d6+2 slashing); **Str** +2, **Dex** +1, **Con** +2, **Int** +0, **Wis** +0, **Cha** +0; **Skills** Perception +2; **Senses** darkvision 60ft; **Traits** dwarven resilience; **AL** LN; **CR** 1/8; **XP** 25.

Dwarven Warrior: AC 16; **HP** 39 (6d8+12); **Spd** 30ft; **Melee** battleaxe (+5, 1d10+3 slashing); **Ranged** handaxe (+5, 20ft/60ft, 1d6+3 slashing); **SA** multiattack (battleaxe x2 or handaxe x2); **Str** +3 (+5), **Dex** +2, **Con** +2 (+4), **Int** +0, **Wis** +1, **Cha** +0; **Skills** Athletics +5, Perception +3; **Senses** darkvision 60ft; **Traits** dwarven resilience; **AL** LN; **CR** 1/2; **XP** 100.

33. Eagle, Giant

Low-Risk Area: 1 **giant eagle**
Medium-Risk Area: 1 **giant eagle** (60%); otherwise, 1d4
High-Risk Area: 1d6 **giant eagles**
Extreme-Risk Area: 1d6+3 **giant eagles**

Eagle, Giant: AC 13; **HP** 26 (4d10+4); **Spd** 10ft, fly 80ft; **Melee** beak (+5, 1d6+3 piercing), talons (+5, 2d6+3 slashing); **SA** multiattack (beak, talons); **Str** +3, **Dex** +3, **Con** +1, **Int** –1, **Wis** +2, **Cha** +0; **Skills** Perception +4; **Senses** keen sight; **AL** NG; **CL** 1; **XP** 200.

34. Elf

A group of elves (high elves or wood elves) consists of 3d6 **elves** and a leader who is an **elven war mage**.

Elven Warrior: AC 15; **HP** 33 (6d8+6); **Spd** 30ft; **Melee** longsword (+4, 1d10+2 slashing); **Ranged** longbow (+4, 150ft/600ft, 1d8+3); **SA** multiattack (longsword x2 or longbow x2); **Str** +2 (+4), **Dex** +2, **Con** +1 (+3), **Int** +0, **Wis** +2, **Cha** +0; **Skills** Athletics +4, Perception +4; **AL** CG; **Senses** darkvision 60ft; **CR** 1/2; **XP** 100.

Elven War Mage: AC 16; **HP** 66 (12d8+12); **Spd** 30ft; **Melee** scimitar (+5, 1d6+3 slashing); **SA** multiattack (scimitar x2), two weapon fighting (bonus, 2nd scimitar), spells (Int +5, 6th, DC 13); **Str** +1, **Dex** +3 (+5), **Con** +1, **Int** +3 (+5), **Wis** +2, **Cha** +1; **Skills** Arcana +5, Acrobatics +5, Perception +4; **AL** CG; **Senses** darkvision 60ft; **CR** 4; **XP** 1100.
> **Spells (slots):** 0 (at will)—*blade ward, fire bolt, ray of frost, true strike*; 1st (4)—*magic missile, thunderwave, witch bolt*; 2nd (3)—*cloud of daggers, mirror image*; 3rd (3)—*fireball, fly, haste.*

35. Ettin

Low-Risk Area: 1 **ettin**
Medium-Risk Area: Roll 1d6: 1–4, 1 **ettin**; 5, 2 **ettins**; 6, 1d6+1 **ettins**.
High-Risk Area: 1d8+1 **ettins**
Extreme-Risk Area: 1d10 **ettins**

Ettin: AC 12; **HP** 85 (10d10+30); **Spd** 40ft; **Melee** battleax (+7, 2d8+5 slashing), morningstar (+7, 2d8+5 piercing); **SA** multiattack (battleax, morningstar); **Str** +5, **Dex** –1, **Con** +3, **Int** –2, **Wis** +0, **Cha** –1; **Skills** Perception +4; **Senses** darkvision 60ft; **Traits** two heads—tactical advantage on Wis (Perception) checks and on saves against blinded, charmed, deafened, frightened, stunned, and unconsciousness), wakeful (one head is always awake); **AL** CE; **CR** 4; **XP** 1100.

36. Farmer

Farmers (**commoner**) are generally locals traveling with produce to a market town or village. They are accompanied by 1d4 dogs (**mastiff**). Roll 1d6. On a roll of 1–5, there is only one farmer and one wagon. On a roll of 6, there are 1d3+1 farmers, each with a wagon and dogs.

Mastiff: AC 12; **HP** 5 (1d8+1); **Spd** 40ft; **Melee** bite (+3, 1d6+1 piercing plus knock prone, DC 11 Str); **Str** +1, **Dex** +2, **Con** +1, **Int** –4, **Wis** +1, **Cha** –2; **Skills** Perception +3; **Senses** keen hearing and smell; **AL** U; **CR** 1/8; **XP** 25.

Farmers in rural areas have a 5% chance to be members of a heretical sect, most likely not one of the Great Heresies, just a heretical set of rituals that offer no benefit to whatever deity the farmer thinks is actually being worshipped. Among farmers, the most likely heresy is the "Secret Rituals of Telophus," a completely invented book of rituals believed to be more powerful than the actual rituals of the God of Crops. Followers of this heresy call themselves "Second Ritualists." They are hard to convince of their own heresy because they believe the true priests of Telophus keep the Second Rituals a closely guarded secret, so *of course* the priesthood denies the legitimacy of the Second Rituals.

37. Foot Patrol

A foot patrol is usually under the command of a local sheriff (who might have a different title such as "constable" in a city). For this encounter number, the sheriff is technically a deputy working for the true sheriff, who is usually of noble birth and is responsible for enforcing law and tax collection in a rural area. The patrol consists of 1 mounted **sheriff**, 2 **sergeants**, and 10 **foot soldiers**.

Sheriff: AC 18; **HP** (10d8+20); **Spd** 30ft; **Melee** lance (+6, 10ft, 1d12 +3), greatsword (+6, 2d6+3 slashing); **SA** leadership (recharge after rest, 1 min, 30ft, if ally can hear and understand then add d4 to attack and save), multiattack (greatsword x2); **Str** +4, **Dex** +0, **Con** +2 (+4), **Int** +1, **Wis** +1 (+3), **Cha** +3; **Skills** Perception +3, Persuasion +5, Intimidation +3; **Traits** brave (tactical advantage against fright); **AL** LN; **CR** 3; **XP** 700

Sheriff's Warhorse (plate barding): AC 18; **HP** 19 (3d10+3); **Spd** 60ft; **Melee** hooves (+4, 2d6+4 bludgeoning); **SA** trampling charge (20ft move then hooves, DC 14 Str or knocked prone, if prone, bonus with hooves); **Str** +4, **Dex** +1, **Con** +1, **Int** –4, **Wis** +1, **Cha** –2; **AL** U; **CR** 1/2; **XP** 100.

Sergeant: AC 17; **HP** 32 (5d8+10); **Spd** 30ft; **Melee** longsword (+4, 1d8+2 slashing); **Ranged** longbow (+4, 150ft/600ft, 1d8+2 piercing); **SA** multiattack (longsword x2 or longbow x2); **Str** +2, **Dex** +2, **Con** +2; **Int** +0, **Wis** +1, **Cha** +1; **Skills** Perception +3, Intimidation +3; **AL** LN; **CR** 1/2; **XP** 100.

Foot Soldier: AC 16; **HP** 11 (2d8+2); **Spd** 30ft; **Melee** longsword (+3, 1d8+2 slashing); **Str** +1, **Dex** +1, **Con** +1, **Int** +0, **Wis** +0, **Cha** +0; **Skills** Perception +2; **AL** LN; **CR** 1/8; **XP** 25.

38. Gargoyle

Airborne encounters with gargoyles over non-mountainous terrain are with 1d4 gargoyles. Encounters over mountains are with 1d6+1 gargoyles, and have a 10% chance to be accompanied by 1d2 margoyles, a deadlier variety of the beasts.

Ground encounters with gargoyles are as follows:
Low-Risk Area: 1 **gargoyle**
Medium-Risk Area: 1d4 **gargoyles**
High-Risk Area: 1d6 **gargoyles** plus 1 **margoyle**
Extreme-Risk Area: 1d8 **gargoyles** plus 1d2 **margoyles**

Gargoyle: AC 15; **HP** 52 (7d8+21); **Spd** 30ft, fly 60ft; **Melee** bite (+4, 1d6+2 piercing), claws (+4, 1d6+2 slashing); **SA** multiattack (bite, claws); **Immune** exhaustion, petrify, poison; **Resist** normal weapons that aren't adamantine; **Str** +2, **Dex** +0, **Con** +3, **Int** −2, **Wis** +0, **Cha** −2; **Senses** darkvision 60ft; **Traits** false appearance (statue); **AL** CE; **CR** 2; **XP** 450.

Margoyle: AC 17; **HP** 114 (12d8+60); **Spd** 30ft, fly 60ft; **Melee** bite (+6, 1d8+3 piercing), claws (2d8+3 slashing), horns (+6, 1d8+3 piercing); **SA** multiattack (bite, claws, horns); **Immune** exhaustion, petrify, poison; **Resist** normal weapons that aren't adamantine; **Str** +3, **Dex** +2, **Con** +5, **Int** −1, **Wis** +1, **Cha** −1; **Senses** darkvision 60ft, tremorsense 60ft (motionless); **Traits** false appearance (statue); **AL** CE; **CR** 5; **XP** 1800. (*Fifth Edition Foes* 116)

39. Ghoul

Low-Risk Area: 1d3 **ghouls**
Medium-Risk Area: 1d6 **ghouls** (75%); otherwise, 2d6 **ghouls** and 1d2 **ghasts**
High-Risk Area: 2d6 **ghouls**, 75% chance for 1d2 **ghasts**
Extreme-Risk Area: 3d6 **ghouls**, 1d4 **ghasts**

Ghoul: AC 12; **HP** 22 (5d8); **Spd** 30ft; **Melee** claws (+4, 2d4+2 slashing plus paralysis for 1 min, DC 10 Con) or bite (+2, 2d6+2 piercing); **Immune** charm, exhaustion, poison; **Str** +1, **Dex** +2, **Con** +0, **Int** −2, **Wis** +0, **Cha** −2; **Senses** darkvision 60ft; **AL** CE; **CR** 1; **XP** 200.

Ghast: AC 13; **HP** 36 (8d8); **Spd** 30ft; **Melee** claws (+5, 2d6+3 slashing plus paralysis for 1 min, DC 10 Con repeat) or bite (+3, 2d8+3 piercing); **Immune** charm, exhaustion, poison; **Resist** necrotic; **Str** +3, **Dex** +3, **Con** +0, **Int** +0, **Wis** +0, **Cha** −1; **Senses** darkvision 60ft; **Traits** stench (5ft, poisoned until start of next turn, DC 10 Con), turning defiance (30ft, tactical advantage on saves against turn effects); **AL** CE; **CR** 2; **XP** 400.

40. Giant, Cloud

Low-Risk Area: 1 **cloud giant**
Medium-Risk Area: 1 **cloud giant** with 50% chance to be accompanied by 1d4 **lions**
High-Risk Area: 1d2 **cloud giants** with 50% chance to be accompanied by 1d2+1 **lions**

Extreme-Risk Area: 1d4 **cloud giants** with 1d4 **lions**

Giant, Cloud: AC 14; **HP** 200 (16d12+96); **Spd** 40ft; **Melee** morningstar x2 (+12, 10ft, 3d8+8 piercing); **Ranged** rock (+12, 60ft/240ft, 4d10+8 bludgeoning); **SA** innate spells, multiattack; **Str** +8, **Dex** +0, **Con** +6 (+9), **Int** +1, **Wis** +3 (+7), **Cha** +3 (+7); **Skills** Insight +7, Perception +7; **Senses** keen smell; **AL** NE; **CR** 9; **XP** 5000.
    Innate Spells: at will—*detect magic, fog cloud, light*; 3/day—*feather fall, fly, misty step, telekinesis*; 1/day—*control weather, gaseous form*

Lion: AC 12; **HP** 26 (4d10+4); **Spd** 50ft; **Melee** bite (+5, 1d8+3 piercing) or claw (+5, 1d6+3 slashing); **SA** pounce (20ft straight then hit with claw, DC 13 Str or knocked prone then bite as bonus); **Str** +3, **Dex** +2, **Con** +1, **Int** −4, **Wis** +1, **Cha** −1; **Skills** Perception +3, Stealth +6; **Senses** keen smell; **Traits** pack tactics, running leap (10ft start, 25ft jump); **AL** U; **CR** 1; **XP** 200.

41. Giant, Hill

If the encounter description dos not state a random number of giants, then there are 1d4 of them. Hill giants have a 25% chance to be encountered with 1d2+1 pet cave bears

Low-Risk Area: **1 hill giant**
Medium-Risk Area: Roll 1d3:

1	1d2 **hill giants**
2	1d2 **hill giants** with 1d2 **cave bears**
3	1d2 **hill giants** with 1d3 **ogres**

High-Risk Area Roll: 1d3:

1	1d3 **hill giants**
2	1d3 **hill giants** with 1d2 **cave bears**
3	1d3 **hill giants** with 1d3 **ogres**

Extreme-Risk Area Roll: 1d3:

1	1d6 **hill giants**
2	1d4 **hill giants** with 1d2 **cave bears**
3	1d4 **hill giants** with 1d3 **ogres**

Bear, Cave: AC 12; **HP** 42 (5d10+15); **Spd** 40ft, swim 30ft; **Melee** bite (+7, 1d8+5 piercing), claws x2 (2d6+5); **SA** multiattack (bite, claws x2); **Str** +5, **Dex** +0, **Con** +3, **Int** −4, **Wis** +1, **Cha** −2; **Skills** Perception +3; **Senses** darkvision 60ft, keen smell; **AL** U; **CR** 2; **XP** 450.

Giant, Hill: AC 13; **HP** 105 (10d12+40); **Spd** 40ft; **Melee** greatclub x2 (+8, 10ft, 3d8+5 bludgeoning); **Ranged** rock (+8, 60ft/240ft, 3d10+5 bludgeoning); **Str** +5, **Dex** −1, **Con** +4, **Int** −3, **Wis** −1, **Cha** −2; **Skills** Perception +2; **AL** CE; **CR** 5; **XP** 1800.

Ogre: AC 11; **HP** 59 (7d10+21); **Spd** 40ft; **Melee** greatclub (+6, 2d8+4 bludgeoning); **Ranged** (+6, 30ft/120ft, 2d6+4 piercing); **Str** +4, **Dex** −1, **Con** +3, **Int** −3, **Wis** −2, **Cha** −2; **Senses** darkvision 60ft; **AL** CE; **CR** 2; **XP** 450.

42. Giant, Stone

Low-Risk Area: 1 **stone giant**
Medium-Risk Area: 1d2 **stone giants**
High-Risk Area: 1d3 **stone giants**
Extreme-Risk Area: 1d4 **stone giants**

Giant, Stone: AC 17; **HP** 126 (11d12+55); **Spd** 40ft; **Melee** greatclub x2 (+9, 10ft, 3d8+6 bludgeoning); **Ranged** rock (+9, 60ft/240ft, 4d10+6 bludgeoning plus knock prone, DC 17 Str); **SA** multiattack, rock catching (reaction, catch take no damage, DC 10 Dex); **Str** +6, **Dex** +2 (+5), **Con** +5 (+8), **Int** +0, **Wis** +1 (+4), **Cha** −1; **Skills** Athletics +12, Perception +4; **Senses** darkvision 60ft; **Traits** stone camouflage (tactical advantage to hide in rocky terrain); **AL** N; **CR** 7; **XP** 2900.

43. Gnoll

Low-Risk Area: 1d6+1 **gnolls**
Medium-Risk Area: Roll on gnoll table, below, at −2
High-Risk Area: Roll on gnoll table below, at +2
Extreme-Risk Area: Roll on gnoll table below at +4

Gnoll Encounters (1d20):

<1 to 6	1d6 **gnolls**
7–10	1d6+3 **gnolls**
11–15	2d10+3 **gnolls**
16–17	3d10 **gnolls** and a **gnoll pack lord**
18	4d10 **gnolls** and a **gnoll pack lord**
19	5d10 **gnolls**, **gnoll pack lord**, **gnoll fang**, and 1d3 **giant hyenas**
20+	6d10 **gnolls** with **gnoll pack lord**, 2 **gnoll fangs**, and 1d4+1 **giant hyenas**

Gnoll: AC 15; **HP** 22 (5d8); **Spd** 30ft; **Melee** spear (+4, 1d6+2 piercing) or bite (+4, 1d4+2 piercing); **Ranged** longbow (+3, 150ft/600ft, 1d8+1 piercing); **SA** rampage (reduce target to 0hp with melee, bonus to move half speed and make a bite); **Str** +2, **Dex** +1, **Con** +0, **Int** −2, **Wis** +0, **Cha** −2; **Senses** darkvision 60ft; **AL** CE; **CR** 1/2; **XP** 100.

Gnoll Pack Lord: AC 15; **HP** 49 (9d8+9); **Spd** 30ft; **Melee** glaive (+5, 10ft, 1d10+3 slashing) or bite (+5, 1d4+3 piercing); **Ranged** longbow (+4, 150ft/600ft, 1d8+2 piercing); **SA** incite rampage (recharge 5–6, 30ft, rampage trait target that can hear then make melee attack as reaction), multiattack (incite rampage, glaive x2 or longbow x2), rampage (reduce target to 0hp with melee, bonus to move half speed and make a bite); **Str** +3, **Dex** +2, **Con** +1, **Int** −1, **Wis** +0, **Cha** −1; **Senses** darkvision 60ft; **AL** CE; **CR** 2; **XP** 450.

Gnoll Fang: AC 14; **HP** 65 (10d8+20); **Spd** 30ft; **Melee** bite (+5, 1d6+3 piercing plus DC 12 Con or 2d6 poison, claw (+5, 1d8+3 slashing); **SA** multiattack (bite, claw x2), rampage (reduce target to 0hp with melee, bonus to move half speed and make a bite); **Str** +3, **Dex** +2, **Con** +2 (+4), **Int** +0, **Wis** +0 (+2), **Cha** +1 (+3); **Senses** darkvision 60ft; **AL** CE; **CR** 4; **XP** 1100.

Hyena, Giant (Hyaenodon): AC 12; **HP** 45 (6d10+12); **Spd** 50ft; **Melee** bite (+5, 2d6+3 piercing); **SA** rampage (reduce target to 0hp with melee, bonus to move half speed and

make a bite); **Str** +3, **Dex** +2, **Con** +2, **Int** −4, **Wis** +1, **Cha** −2; **Skills** Perception +3; **AL** U; **CR** 1; **XP** 200.

44. Goblin Raider

Goblin raiding parties are relatively organized forces, usually led by bugbears.
Low-Risk Area: 2d6 **goblins**
Medium-Risk Area: Roll 1d4:

1	3d6 **goblins**
2	4d6 **goblins** with 1 **bugbear**
3	5d6 **goblins** with 1d3 **bugbears**
4	5d6 **goblins** with 1d6 additional **goblins** on **worgs**, 1d4 **bugbears**

High-Risk Area: 1d100 **goblins** with 1 **bugbear** per 15 **goblins**, 1d8 additional **goblins** on **worgs**.
Extreme-Risk Area: 1d100+10 **goblins**, with 1 **bugbear** per 15 **goblins** and 1d10 additional **goblins** on **worgs**.

Goblin: AC 15; **HP** 7 (2d6); **Spd** 30ft; **Melee** scimitar (+4, 1d6+2 slashing); **Ranged** shortbow (+4, 80ft/320ft, 1d6+2 piercing); **SA** nimble escape (bonus, disengage or hide); **Str** −1, **Dex** +2, **Con** +0, **Int** +0, **Wis** −1, **Cha** −1; **Skills** Stealth +6; **Senses** darkvision 60ft; **AL** NE; **CR** 1/4; **XP** 50.

Bugbear: AC 16; **HP** 27 (5d8+5); **Spd** 30ft; **Melee** morningstar (+4, 2d8+2 piercing); **Ranged** javelin (+4, 30ft/120ft, 1d6+2 piercing); **Str** +2, **Dex** +2, **Con** +1, **Int** −1, **Wis** +0, **Cha** −1; **Skills** Stealth +6, Survival +2; **Senses** darkvision 60ft; **Traits** brute, surprise attack (on first round, extra 2d6); **AL** CE; **CR** 1; **XP** 200.

Worg: AC 13; **HP** 26 (4d10+4); **Spd** 50ft; **Melee** bite (+5, 2d6+3 piercing plus knock prone, DC 13 Str); **Str** +3, **Dex** +1, **Con** +1, **Int** −2, **Wis** +0, **Cha** −1; **Skills** Perception +4; **Senses** darkvision 60ft, keen hearing and smell; **AL** NE; **CR** 1/2; **XP** 100.

45. Goblin, Roaming

Roaming goblins are disorganized, leaderless bands looking for pillage and mayhem.
Low-Risk Area: 2d6 **goblins**
Medium-Risk Area: 3d6 +20 **goblins**
High-Risk Area: 4d6 +20 **goblins**
Extreme-Risk Area: 2d100 **goblins**

Goblin: see **44** above for stats.

46. Gray Ooze

Encounter is with 1 **gray ooze** regardless of the area's inherent Risk.

Gray Ooze: AC 8; **HP** 22 (3d8+9); **Spd** 10ft, climb 10ft; **Melee** pseudopod (+3, 1d6+1 bludgeoning plus 2d6 acid plus corrode metal); **Immune** blind, charm, deafen, exhaustion, fright, prone; **Resist** acid, cold, fire; **Str** +1, **Dex** −2, **Con** +3, **Int** −5, **Wis** −2, **Cha** −4; **Skills** Stealth +2; **Senses** blindsight 60ft (blind beyond); **Traits** amorphous, corrode metal (damage for weapons and AC for armor, cumulative −1 for each contact with normal metal, at −5 weapon and AC 10 armor destroyed); **AL** U; **CR** 1/2; **XP** 100.

47. Griffon

Land encounters:

Low-Risk Area: 1 **griffon**
Medium-Risk Area: 1d3 **griffons**
High-Risk Area: 1d4+1 **griffons**
Extreme-Risk Area: 1d6+1 **griffons**

Airborne Encounters:

For airborne encounters over non-mountain terrain, unless otherwise stated, roll 1d3 to determine the number of **griffons**. For airborne encounters over mountains, roll 1d6+1.

Griffon: AC 12; **HP** 59 (7d10+21); **Spd** 30ft, fly 80ft; **Melee** beak (+6, 1d8+4 piercing), claws (+6, 2d6+4 slashing); **SA** multiattack (beak, claws); **Str** +4, **Dex** +2, **Con** +3, **Int** −4, **Wis** +1, **Cha** −1; **Skills** Perception +5; **Senses** darkvision 60ft, keen sight; **AL** U; **CR** 2; **XP** 450.

48. Hag

Low-Risk Area: 1 **green hag**
Medium-Risk Area: 1 **green hag** (60%) or else **green hag** coven
High-Risk Area: **green hag** coven (60%) or else 1 **night hag**
Extreme-Risk Area: 1 **night hag** (60%) or **night hag** coven

Hag, Green: AC 17; **HP** 82 (11d8+33); **Spd** 30ft; **Melee** claws (+6, 2d8+4 slashing); **SA** illusory appearance, innate spells (Cha, DC 12), invisible passage; **Str** +4, **Dex** +1, **Con** +3, **Int** +1, **Wis** +2, **Cha** +2; **Skills** Arcana +3, Deception +4, Perception +4, Stealth +3; **Senses** darkvision 60ft; **Traits** amphibious, mimicry—imitation detect on DC 14 Wis (Insight); **AL** NE; **CR** 3; **XP** 700.
> **Innate Spells:** at will—*dancing lights, minor illusion, vicious mockery*

Hag, Night: AC 17; **HP** 112 (15d8+45); **Spd** 30ft; **Melee** claws (+7, 2d8+4 slashing); **SA** change shape, etherealness, innate spells (Cha +6, DC 14), nightmare haunting (1/day); **Immune** charm; **Resist** cold, fire, non-silver normal weapons; **Str** +4, **Dex** +2, **Con** +3, **Int** +3, **Wis** +2, **Cha** +3; **Skills** Deception +9, Insight +8, Perception +8, Stealth +8; **Senses** darkvision 120ft; **Traits** magic resistance; **AL** NE; **CR** 5; **XP** 1800.
> **Innate Spells:** at will—*detect magic, magic missile*; 2/day—*plane shift* (self only), *ray of enfeeblement, sleep*.

49. Hamster

These nocturnal creatures can be a problem. A group of them is called a "horde."

Low-Risk Area: A horde of hamsters comes upon the camp, and infiltrates the food. Each guard must make a successful saving throw to notice them. If they are not noticed, they eat 50% of the rations in the camp. They can be frightened away with loud noises and attacks (roll 1d20 to see how many attacks are required to scare off the horde). The noise required to frighten off a hamster horde causes a second roll for an encounter, as nearby creatures are attracted to the furor.

Medium-Risk Area: As above, but the undetected hamsters are numerous and large enough to eat all the food. There is a 10% chance that a giant hamster accompanies the hamster horde.

High-Risk Area: Horde of hamsters as described for the Medium-Risk Area, accompanied by 1d4+2 **giant hamsters**.

Extreme-Risk Area: Horde of hamsters as described for the Medium-Risk Area, accompanied by 2d6+2 **giant hamsters**.

Hamster, Giant: AC 12; **HP** 7 (2d6); **Spd** 30ft; **Melee** bite (+4, 1d4+2 piercing); **Str** −2, **Dex** +2, **Con** +0, **Int** −4, **Wis** +0, **Cha** −3; **Senses** darkvision 60ft, keen smell; **Traits** pack tactics; **AL** U; **CR** 1/8; **XP** 25.

50. Harpy

Low-Risk Area: 1 **harpy**
Medium-Risk Area: 1d4 **harpies** with 20% chance to be accompanied by 1d3 **blood hawks**
High-Risk Area: 1d6+1 **harpies** with 30% chance to be accompanied by 1d4 **blood hawks**
Extreme-Risk Area: 2d10 **harpies** with 1d6 **blood hawks**

Harpy: AC 11; **HP** 38 (7d8+7); **Spd** 20ft, fly 40ft; **Melee** claws (+3, 2d4+1 slashing), club (+3, 1d4+1 bludgeoning); **SA** luring song (300ft, DC 11 Wis or charmed, continue singing as bonus), multiattack (claws, club); **Str** +1, **Dex** +1, **Con** +1, **Int** −2, **Wis** +0, **Cha** +1; **AL** CE; **CR** 1; **XP** 200.

Blood Hawk: AC 12; **HP** 7 (2d6); **Spd** 10ft, fly 60ft; **Melee** beak (+4, 1d4+2 piercing); **Str** −2, **Dex** +2, **Con** +0, **Int** −4, **Wis** +2, **Cha** −3; **Skills** Perception +4; **Senses** keen sight; **Traits** pack tactics; **AL** U; **CR** 1/8; **XP** 25.

51. Herder

This is an encounter with a local herder (**commoner** with quarterstaff) and a herd of animals.

Low-Risk Area: 1d4 herders each with 1d6+1 animals and 1 dog (**mastiff**)
Medium-Risk Area: 1d4 herders each with 1d6+1 animals and 1 dog (**mastiff**)
High-Risk Area: 1d4 herders each with 1d4 animals and 2 dogs (**mastiff**)
Extreme-Risk Area: pile of mixed bones and scraps of meat

Herd Animals (roll 1d8)

1	Cattle
2–4	Goats
5	Draft Horses
6	Yak-beasts (1d2 per herder only)
7–8	Sheep
9–10	Pigs

Commoner: AC 10; **HP** 4 (1d8); **Spd** 30ft; **Melee** quarterstaff (+2, 1d8 bludgeoning); **Str** +0, **Dex** +0, **Con** +0; **Int** +0, **Wis** +0, **Cha** +0; **AL** any; **CR** 0; **XP** 10.

Mastiff: AC 12; **HP** 5 (1d8+1); **Spd** 40ft; **Melee** bite (+3, 1d6+1 piercing plus knock prone, DC 11 Str); **Str** +1, **Dex** +2, **Con** +1, **Int** −4, **Wis** +1, **Cha** −2; **Skills** Perception +3; **Senses** keen hearing and smell; **AL** U; **CR** 1/8; **XP** 25.

52. Heretic

See the Heresy Appendix for more information about heretics and heresies. Encounters with heretics are not altered by an area's Risk Level. The problem with encountering heretics usually isn't that they are dangerous to traveling adventurers. Rather, the problem is what to *do* with them if a cleric is in the adventuring party who detects the presence of the heresy. Most clerics don't have the religious authority to burn or otherwise slaughter heretics on the spot without a trial. Capturing them and bringing them to justice is the approved method for dealing with heretics, but this could necessitate a side trip. It is up to the cleric to decide what to do.

193

Roll 1d10 to determine the composition of a group of heretics:

1–4	1 heretic preacher (**commoner**), traveling alone. 20% chance to be mounted, otherwise on foot. There is a 75% chance that the preacher is a follower of a Lesser Heresy; otherwise, one of the Great Heresies.
5	1 heretical **priest** of one of the Great Heresies, traveling alone.
6	1d6+1 heretical believers (**commoner**) who are local farmers. They have 1d2 wagons of farm produce and 1d4 dogs with them. There is a 75% chance that they are followers of one of the Lesser Heresies; otherwise, they are followers of a Greater Heresy.
7–8	1 heretical believer who is a traveling peddler, usually selling trinkets such as pots, pans, cheap necklaces, and pamphlets containing stories or pictures. There is a 90% chance that the peddler's wares contain something connected with the heresy. Heretics of the Discordian Hymnal will have copies of the hymnal to sell or distribute. Inoculist heretics will have anti-disease charms mixed in with ordinary trinkets. Idolist Heretics will be selling their deceptive little idols. Eternalists and True Penitents are less likely to be carrying anything incriminating.
9	1d8+2 heretical believers (**commoner**) of a Greater Heresy led by a heretical **priest** on a "pilgrimage" to a false "holy" site that is actually dedicated to a demon.
10	2d6 heretical **bandits**. This is an armed group of heretics that has set themselves against all opposing secular and religious authority. The spread of violent zealots is a symptom of a widely spread heresy, and indicates to any cleric that the surrounding area has deep, deep, problems. There is a 25% chance that the bandits are members of a Lesser Heresy; otherwise, they are followers of one of the Great Heresies.

Great Heresies

If the encounter is with followers of one of the Great Heresies, determine which one by rolling 1d6:

1	Canticalist Heresy
2	Eternalist Heresy
3	Idolist Heresy
4	Inoculist Heresy
5–6	True Penitence Heresy

Commoner: AC 10; **HP** 4 (1d8); **Spd** 30ft; **Melee** club (+2, 1d4 bludgeoning); **Str** +0, **Dex** +0, **Con** +0; **Int** +0, **Wis** +0, **Cha** +0; **AL** any; **CR** 0; **XP** 10.

Heretical Bandit: AC 12; **HP** 11 (2d8+2); **Spd** 30ft; **Melee** shortsword (+3, 1d6+1 slashing); **Ranged** light crossbow (+3, 80ft/320ft, 1d8+1 piercing); **Str** +0, **Dex** +1, **Con** +1, **Int** +0, **Wis** +0, **Cha** +0; **AL** any non-L; **CR** 1/8; **XP** 25

Heretical Priest: AC 13; **HP** 27 (5d8+5); **Spd** 30ft; **Melee** mace (+2, 1d6 bludgeoning); **SA** divine eminence (bonus, expend slot, extra 3d6 necrotic, + 1d6 per slot above 1st), spells (Wis +5, 5th, DC 13); **Str** +0, **Dex** +0, **Con** +1, **Int** +1, **Wis** +3, **Cha** +1; **Skills** Medicine +7, Persuasion +3, Religion +4; **AL** any evil; **CR** 2; **XP** 450.

Spells (slots): 0 (at will)—*guidance, resistance, sacred flame, thaumaturgy;* 1st (4)— *bane, guiding bolt (necrotic), inflict wounds;* 2nd (3)—*blindness/deafness, spiritual weapon;* 3rd (2)—*bestow curse, spirit guardians.*

53. High Noble, with Retinue

A high noble is a duke, count, or (in Foerdewaith-ruled areas) a Regional Governor. Note: This does not include the Duke of the Rampart or the Counts of Toullen or Vourdon, who are nobles of the *realm*, not merely high nobility. The dukes and counts in an encounter with high nobility are rulers of a large division of a country but not the country itself (this is why the Duke of the Rampart and the Counts of Toullen and Vourdon are called "Palatine" nobles, to distinguish them from ordinary dukes and counts).

High Noble (**veteran**)
Baron (1d3) (**veteran**)
Courtier (1d6+6) (**noble**)
Captain (1 per 2 knights) [these are same stats for a sheriff]
Knight (3d6+3)
Sergeant (1 per 10 foot soldiers and archers)
Archer (1d6 x20)
Foot Soldier (1d6 x25)
Serjeant of Horse (1 per 10 cavalry)
Cavalry (1d4 x25)
Priests (2)
Court Warlock (**mage**)
Entertainer (5) (**commoner**)

Baggage train: 4d10 servants and laborers (**commoner**) in 1d6+6 supply wagons. The support staff for the nobles do not mix with the support staff for the soldiers, of course.

Archer: AC 14; **HP** 11 (2d8+2); **Spd** 30ft; **Melee** shortsword (+3, 1d6+1 piercing); **Ranged** longbow (+3, 150ft/600ft, 1d8+2 piercing); **Str** +1, **Dex** +1, **Con** +1, **Int** +0, **Wis** +0, **Cha** +0; **Skills** Perception +2; **AL** LN; **CR** 1/8; **XP** 25

Captain: AC 18; **HP** (10d8+20); **Spd** 30ft; **Melee** lance (+6, 10ft, 1d12 +3), greatsword (+6, 2d6+3 slashing); **SA** leadership (recharge after rest, 1 min, 30ft, if ally can hear and understand then add d4 to attack and save), multiattack (greatsword x2); **Str** +4, **Dex** +0, **Con** +2 (+4), **Int** +1, **Wis** +1 (+3), **Cha** +3; **Skills** Perception +3, Persuasion +5, Intimidation +3; **Traits** brave (tactical advantage against fright); **AL** LN; **CR** 3; **XP** 700

Cavalry: AC 16; **HP** 22 (4d8+2); **Spd** 30ft; **Melee** lance (+3, 10ft, 1d10+1 piercing); **Ranged** shortbow (+3, 80ft/320ft, 1d6+1 piercing); **Str** +1, **Dex** +1, **Con** +1; **Int** +0, **Wis** +0, **Cha** +0; **AL** LN; **CR** 1/4; **XP** 50.

Commoner: AC 10; **HP** 4 (1d8); **Spd** 30ft; **Melee** club (+2, 1d4 bludgeoning); **Str** +0, **Dex** +0, **Con** +0; **Int** +0, **Wis** +0, **Cha** +0; **AL** any; **CR** 0; **XP** 10.

Foot Soldier: AC 16; **HP** 11 (2d8+2); **Spd** 30ft; **Melee** longsword (+3, 1d8+1 slashing); **Str** +1, **Dex** +1, **Con** +1, **Int** +0, **Wis** +0, **Cha** +0; **Skills** Perception +2; **AL** LN; **CR** 1/8; **XP** 25.

Knight: AC 18; **HP** 52 (8d8+16); **Spd** 30ft; **Melee** greatsword (+5, 2d6+3 slashing); **SA** leadership (recharge after rest, 1 min, 30ft, if ally can hear and understand then add d4 to attack and save), multiattack (greatsword x2); parry (+2 AC vs. single melee); **Str** +3, **Dex** +0, **Con** +2 (+4), **Int** +0, **Wis** +0 (+2), **Cha** +2; **Traits** brave (tactical advantage against saves against fright); **AL** LN; **CR** 3; **XP** 700.

Mage: AC 12 (15 with *mage armor*); HP 40 (9d8); Spd 30ft; **Melee** dagger (+5, 1d4+2 piercing); **SA** spells (Int +6, 9th, DC 14); **Str** −1, **Dex** +2, **Con** +0, **Int** +3 (+6), **Wis** +1 (+4), **Cha** +0; **Skills** Arcana +6, History +6; **AL** N; **CR** 6; **XP** 2300.

> **Spells (slots):** 0 (at will)—*fire bolt, light, mage hand, prestidigitation*; 1st (4)—*detect magic, mage armor, magic missile, shield*; 2nd (3)—*misty step, suggestion*; 3rd (3)—*counterspell, fireball, fly*; 4th (3)—*greater invisibility, ice storm*; 5th (1)—*cone of cold*.

Noble: AC 15; HP 18 (4d8); **Spd** 30ft; **Melee** rapier (+3, 1d8+1 piercing); **SA** parry (reaction, +2 AC vs. single melee); **Str** +0, **Dex** +1, **Con** +0, **Int** +1, **Wis** +2, **Cha** +3; **Skills** Deception +5, Insight +4, Persuasion +5; **AL** LN; **CR** 1/4; **XP** 50.

Priest: AC 13; HP 27 (5d8+5); Spd 30ft; **Melee** mace (+2, 1d6 bludgeoning); **SA** divine eminence (bonus, expend slot, extra 3d6 radiant, + 1d6 per slot above 1st), spells (Wis +5, 5th, DC 13); **Str** +0, **Dex** +0, **Con** +1, **Int** +1, **Wis** +3, **Cha** +1; **Skills** Medicine +7, Persuasion +3, Religion +4; **AL** LG; **CR** 2; **XP** 450.

> **Spells (slots):** 0 (at will)— *light, sacred flame, resistance, thaumaturgy*; 1st (4)— *cure wounds, guiding bolt, sanctuary*; 2nd (3)—*hold person, lesser restoration, spiritual weapon*; 3rd (3)—*dispel magic, remove curse, spirit guardians*; 4th (3)—*freedom of movement, guardian of faith*; 5th (1)—*greater restoration, raise dead*.

Serjeant of Horse: AC 16; HP 32 (5d8+10); **Spd** 30ft; **Melee** spear (+4, 1d8+2 piercing); **Ranged** shortbow (+4, 80ft/320ft, 1d6+2 piercing); **SA** multiattack (spear x2 or shortbow x2); **Str** +2, **Dex** +2, **Con** +2; **Int** +0, **Wis** +1, **Cha** +1; **Skills** Perception +3, Intimidation +3; **AL** LN; **CR** 1/2; **XP** 100.

Sergeant: AC 17; HP 32 (5d8+10); **Spd** 30ft; **Melee** longsword (+4, 1d8+2 slashing); **Ranged** longbow (+4, 150ft/600ft, 1d8+2 piercing); **SA** multiattack (longsword x2 or longbow x2); **Str** +2, **Dex** +2, **Con** +2; **Int** +0, **Wis** +1, **Cha** +1; **Skills** Perception +3, Intimidation +3; **AL** LN; **CR** 1/2; **XP** 100.

Veteran: AC 18; HP 78 (12d8+24); **Spd** 30ft; **Melee** longsword (+5, 1d8+3 slashing), shortsword (+5, 1d6+3 piercing); **Ranged** heavy crossbow (+4, 1d10+2 piercing); **SA** multiattack (longsword x2, shortsword); **Str** +3, **Dex** +2, **Con** +2, **Int** +0, **Wis** +0, **Cha** +1; **Skills** Athletics +5, Perception +2; **AL** any; **CR** 3; **XP** 700.

Warhorse (chain barding): AC 16; HP 19 (3d10+3); **Spd** 60ft; **Melee** hooves (+4, 2d6+4 bludgeoning); **SA** trampling charge (20ft move then hooves, DC 14 Str or knocked prone, if prone, bonus with hooves); **Str** +4, **Dex** +1, **Con** +1, **Int** −4, **Wis** +1, **Cha** −2; **AL** U; **CR** 1/2; **XP** 100.

54. Hippogriff

Low-Risk Area: 1 **hippogriff**
Medium-Risk Area: 1d6 **hippogriffs**
High-Risk Area: 2d4 **hippogriffs**
Extreme-Risk Area: 1d6+3 **hippogriff**s

Airborne encounters are with 1d6+3 **hippogriffs**.

Hippogriff: AC 11; HP 19 (3d10+3); **Spd** 40ft, fly 60ft; **Melee** beak (+5, 1d10+3 piercing), claws (+5, 2d6+3 slashing); **SA** multiattack (beak, claws); **Str** +3, **Dex** +1, **Con** +1, **Int** −4, **Wis** +1, **Cha** −1; **Skills** Perception +5; **Senses** keen sight; **AL** U; **CR** 1; **XP** 200.

55. Kenckoo Vagrant

Low-Risk Area: 1d3 **kenckoos**
Medium-Risk Area: 1d6 **kenckoos**, with 20% chance of a **leader** in the group.
High-Risk Area: 1d6+4 **kenckoos** with 1 **leader**
Extreme-Risk Area: Kenckoos are *far* too cautious to be in an area like this; treat as "No Encounter"

Kenckoo: AC 13; HP 13 (3d8); **Spd** 30ft; **Melee** shortsword (+5, 1d6+3 piercing); **Ranged** shortbow (+5, 80ft/320ft; 1d6+3 piercing); **Str** +0, **Dex** +3, **Con** +0, **Int** +0, **Wis** +0, **Cha** +0; **Skills** Deception +4, Perception +2, Stealth +5; **Traits** ambusher (tactical advantage on attack from surprise), mimicry—(detection of imitation with DC 14 Wis (Insight); **AL** CN; **CR** 1/4; **XP** 50. (**Monster Appendix**)

Leader Kenckoo: AC 14; HP 27 (6d8); **Spd** 30ft; **Melee** shortsword (+6, 1d6+4 piercing); **Ranged** shortbow (+6, 80ft/320ft; 1d6+4 piercing); **SA** cunning action (bonus to take Dash, Disengage, or Hide), multiattack (shortsword x2 or shortbow x2), sneak attack (1/turn, extra 2d6 on hit with tactical advantage or within 5ft of ally); **Str** +0, **Dex** +4, **Con** +0, **Int** +1, **Wis** +2, **Cha** +3; **Skills** Deception +7, Insight +4, Investigation +5, Perception +6, Persuasion +5, Sleight of Hand +6, Stealth +6; **Traits** ambusher (tactical advantage on attack from surprise), mimicry—detection of imitation with DC 14 Wis (Insight); **AL** CN; **CR** 1; **XP** 200.

56. Knight(s) with Retinue

This is an encounter with a knight and the knight's mounted soldiers. Most likely they are patrolling the knight's territory, but they might also be traveling to a tournament or to a mustering of soldiers called by the knight's feudal overlord.

Low-Risk Area: 1 **knight** and 4 **cavalry** only (50%); otherwise, add 1d4 servants (**commoner**) and a wagon.
Medium-Risk Area: 1 **knight** and 4 **cavalry** only (75%); otherwise, add 1d4 servants (**commoner**) and a wagon.
High-Risk Area: 1d3 **knights** with 4 **cavalry** each
Extreme-Risk Area: 1d3+1 **knights** with 4 **cavalry** each

Knight: AC 18; HP 52 (8d8+16); **Spd** 30ft; **Melee** greatsword (+5, 2d6+3 slashing); **SA** leadership (recharge after rest, 1 min, 30ft, if ally can hear and understand then add d4 to attack and save), multiattack (greatsword x2); parry (+2 AC vs. single melee); **Str** +3, **Dex** +0, **Con** +2 (+4), **Int** +0, **Wis** +0 (+2), **Cha** +2; **Traits** brave (tactical advantage against saves against fright); **AL** LN; **CR** 3; **XP** 700.

Cavalry: AC 16; HP 22 (4d8+2); **Spd** 30ft; **Melee** lance (+3, 10ft, 1d10+1 piercing); **Ranged** shortbow (+3, 80ft/320ft, 1d6+1 piercing); **Str** +1, **Dex** +1, **Con** +1; **Int** +0, **Wis** +0, **Cha** +0; **AL** LN; **CR** 1/4; **XP** 50.

Warhorse (chain barding): AC 16; HP 19 (3d10+3); **Spd** 60ft; **Melee** hooves (+4, 2d6+4 bludgeoning); **SA** trampling charge (20ft move then hooves, DC 14 Str or knocked prone, if prone, bonus with hooves); **Str** +4, **Dex** +1, **Con** +1, **Int** −4, **Wis** +1, **Cha** −2; **AL** U; **CR** 1/2; **XP** 100.

57. Knight Challenger

A **knight** (see stats above) blocks the road. Anyone in plate or half-plate receives a challenge to joust, and the knight will not allow the group to pass unless the challenge is accepted. The knight does not fight to the death: Victory is a matter of making the opponent yield. By the same token, a defeated knight expects that yielding is enough to end the battle. If a character accepts the challenge and is beaten, the knight allows the characters to continue on their way.

58. Korred

Korreds are not usually found wandering around on the high roads of civilization, but in areas where the wilderness reaches close to the road, travelers may occasionally meet one.

Low-Risk to High Risk Areas: 1 **korred**
Extreme-Risk Area: 1d3 **korreds**

Korred: AC 13; HP 27 (6d6+6); Spd 30ft; **Melee** club (+4, 1d6+2 bludgeoning), shears (+4, 1d8+2 slashing, critical on natural 18-20); **Ranged** stone (+4, 20ft/60ft, 1d4+2 bludgeoning); **SA** animated hair (restrained, DC 12 Dex or Str), innate spells (Cha, DC 12), laugh (recharge 5–6, 60ft, stunned for 1d3 rounds, DC 12 Wis), stone stride (30ft); **Immune** charm, stun, unconscious; **Resist** normal weapons; **Str** +2, **Dex** +2, **Con** +1, **Int** +1, **Wis** +1, **Cha** +2; **Skills** Sleight of Hand +4, Stealth +4; **Senses** darkvision 60ft; **Traits** mobility (tactical disadvantage against opportunity attacks); **AL** CN; **CR** 1; **XP** 200. (*Fifth Edition Foes* 158)
Innate Spells: at will—*animate object* (stone only), *shatter*, *speak with stone* (like with *speak with plants*), *stone shape*

59. Lizardfolk

Very few of the high roads in the Borderland Provinces run through areas inhabited by lizardfolk (roads sink and disappear in swamps), but in some cases the road might pass closely enough to a marsh that lizardfolk are a possible encounter. The Swamp Road in Keston is the only place where this is particularly common; most encounters with lizardfolk will be deeper into the countryside where there are larger fens or marshes.

Low-Risk Area: 1d6 **lizardfolk**
Medium-Risk Area: 1d10+2 **lizardfolk** with 20% chance of **shaman** (75%); otherwise, 3d10 **lizardfolk** with 20% chance of **shaman** and 20% chance of **chieftain**
High-Risk Area: 3d10 **lizardfolk** with 25% chance of **shaman** and 25% chance of **chieftain**
Extreme-Risk Area: 4d10 **lizardfolk** with 40% chance of **shaman** and 40% chance of **chieftain**

Lizardfolk: AC 15; HP 22 (4d8+4); Spd 30ft, swim 30ft; **Melee** bite (+4, 1d6+2 piercing), heavy club (+4, 1d6+2 bludgeoning), spiked shield (+4, 1d6+2 piercing); **SA** multiattack (melee x2, each different); **Str** +2, **Dex** +0, **Con** +1, **Int** −2, **Wis** +1, **Cha** −2; **Skills** Perception +3, Stealth +4, Survival +5; **Traits** hold breath (15 min); **CR** 1/2; **XP** 100.

Lizardfolk Shaman: AC 13; HP 27 (5d8+5); Spd 30ft, swim 30ft; **Melee** bite (+4, 1d6+2 piercing), claws (+4, 1d4+2 slashing); **SA** change shape (1 hour, crocodile, only bit, 1d10+2 piercing plus grapple, DC 12 to escape restraint), multiattack (bite, claws), spells (Wis +4, DC 12); **Str** +2, **Dex** +0, **Con** +1, **Int** +0, **Wis** +2, **Cha** −1; **Skills** Perception +4, Stealth +4, Survival +6; **Traits** hold breath (15 min); **CR** 2; **XP** 450.
Spells (slots): 0 (at will)—*druidcraft, produce flame, thorn whip*; 1st (4)—*entangle, fog cloud*; 2nd (3)—*heat metal, spike growth*; 3rd (2)—*conjure animals* (reptiles only), *plant growth*.

Lizardfolk Chieftain: AC 16; HP 58 (9d8+18); Spd 30ft, swim 30ft; **Melee** bite (+6, 1d6+4 piercing), battleaxe (+4, 1d8+4 slashing), spiked shield (+6, 1d6+4 piercing); **SA** multiattack (battleaxe x2 plus spiked shield or bite); **Str** +4, **Dex** +1, **Con** +2, **Int** −1, **Wis** +1, **Cha** +0; **Skills** Athletics +5, Perception +3, Stealth +5, Survival +5; **Traits** hold breath (15 min); **CR** 3; **XP** 700.

60. Leper

The encounter is with 1d6 highly contagious, diseased people (not necessarily actual leprosy, and possibly something even worse, such as a slow-acting plague). They are exiled from any settlement, and have to beg for food and alms. Anyone coming within 10ft of the lepers (**commoners**) must make a DC 15 Con save or be afflicted with it; however, the disease is curable by *lesser restoration*. Leper encounters do not vary by risk level.

61. Lycanthrope

The encounter is with lycanthropes (see table), all of the same type and probably in human form.

Low-Risk Area: treat as no encounter
Medium-Risk Area: 1d3 lycanthropes
High-Risk Area: 1d6 lycanthropes
Extreme-Risk Area: 2d6 lycanthropes

Lycanthropes

1	Wererat
2	**Weretiger** (Aachen and Eastreach Provinces only; otherwise, **wereboar**)
3	Wereboar
4	Werebear
5-6	Werewolf

Wererat: AC 12; HP 33 (6d8+6); Spd 30ft; **Melee** bite (+4, 1d4+2 piercing plus lycanthropy, DC 11 Con), shortsword (+4, +1d6+2 piercing); **Ranged** hand crossbow (+4, 30ft/120ft, 1d6+2 piercing); **SA** multiattack (attack x2, only one bite), shapechanger; **Immune** non-silver normal weapons; **Str** +0, **Dex** +2, **Con** +1, **Int** +0, **Wis** +0, **Cha** −1; **Skills** Perception +2, Stealth +4; **Senses** darkvision 60ft (rat only), keen smell; **AL** LE; **CR** 2; **XP** 450.

Weretiger: AC 12; HP 120 (16d8+48); Spd 30ft, as tiger 40ft; **Melee** bite (+5, 1d10+3 piercing plus lycanthropy, DC 13 Con), claw (+5, 1d8+3 slashing), scimitar (+5, 1d6+3 slashing); **Ranged** longbow (+4, 150ft/600ft, 1d8+2 piercing); **SA** multiattack (claw x2 or scimitar x2 or longbow x2), pounce (15ft move, claw, DC 14 Str or knocked prone, bite as bonus), shapechanger, **Immune** non-silver normal weapons; **Str** +3, **Dex** +2, **Con** +3, **Int** +0, **Wis** +1, **Cha** +0; **Skills** Perception +5, Stealth +4; **Senses** darkvision 60ft, keen hearing and smell; **AL** N; **CR** 4; **XP** 1100.

Wereboar: AC 11; HP 78 (12d8+24); Spd 30ft, as boar 40ft; **Melee** maul (+5, 2d6+3 bludgeoning), tusks (+5, 2d6+3 slashing plus lycanthropy, DC 12 Con); **SA** charge (15ft move, tusks, DC 13 Str or knocked prone), multiattack (attack x2, only one tusks), shapechanger; **Immune** non-silver normal weapons; **Str** +3, **Dex** +0, **Con** +2, **Int** +0, **Wis** +0, **Cha** −1; **Skills** Perception +2; **Traits** relentless (recharge after rest, damage of 14 or less would reduce to 0, reduce to 1hp instead); **AL** NE; **CR** 4; **XP** 1100.

Werebear: AC 11; HP 135 (18d8+54); Spd 30ft, as hybrid or bear 40ft, climb 30ft; **Melee** bite (+7, 2d10+4 piercing plus lycanthropy, DC 14 Con), claw (+7, 2d8+4 slashing), greataxe (+7, 1d12+4 slashing); **SA** multiattack (claws x2 or greataxe x2), shapechanger; **Immune** non-silver normal weapons; **Str** +4, **Dex** +0, **Con** +3, **Int** +0, **Wis** +1, **Cha** +1; **Skills** Perception +7; **Senses** keen smell; **AL** NG; **CR** 5; **XP** 1800.

Werewolf: **AC** 12; **HP** 58 (9d8+18); **Spd** 30ft, 40ft (wolf); **Melee** bite (+4, 1d8+2 piercing plus lycanthropy, DC 12 Con), claws (+4, 2d4+2 slashing); **SA** multiattack (bite, claws), shapechanger; **Immune** non-silver normal weapons; **Str** +2, **Dex** +1, **Con** +2, **Int** +0, **Wis** +0, **Cha** +0; **Skills** Perception +4, Stealth +3; **Senses** keen hearing and smell; **AL** CE; **CR** 3; **XP** 700.

62. Mantari

The encounter is with 1d10 **mantaris** regardless of Risk Level or type of terrain.

Mantari: **AC** 12; **HP** 4 (1d8); **Spd** 5ft, fly 50ft; **Melee** sting (+4, 10ft, 1d8+2 piercing); **Str** +1, **Dex** +2, **Con** +0, **Int** −4, **Wis** +0, **Cha** −2; **Skills** Perception +4, Stealth +4; **Senses** darkvision 60ft; **AL** NE; **CR** 1/8; **XP** 25. (*Fifth Edition Foes* 169)

63. Manticore

Low-Risk Area: 1 manticore
Medium-Risk Area: Solitary male (70%); otherwise, mated pair
High-Risk Area: Solitary male (25%); otherwise, 1d3 manticores
Extreme-Risk Area: 1d4+1 manticores

Manticore: **AC** 14; **HP** 68 (8d10+24); **Spd** 30ft, fly 50ft; **Melee** bite (+5, 1d8+3 piercing), claw (+5, 1d6+3 slashing); **Ranged** tail spike (+5, 100ft/200ft, 1d8+3 piercing); **SA** multiattack (bite, claw x2 or tail spike x3); **Str** +3, **Dex** +3, **Con** +3, **Int** −2, **Wis** +1, **Cha** −1; **Senses** darkvision 60ft; **Traits** tail spike regrowth (up to 24); **AL** LE; **CR** 3; **XP** 700.

64. Military

This encounter is with a true military unit on the march. In most cases, this is not going to be a combat encounter because a military unit is not only very dangerous but lacks significant treasure and is not going to stop even to deal with bandits (who keep away from them for obvious reasons).

The composition of the average military unit is as follows:
Commander (**veteran**)
Baron (1d3) (**veteran**)
Knight (3d6+3)
Archer (1d3 x50)
Foot Soldier (1d10 x100)
Cavalry (1d4 x50)
Sergeant (1 per 10 foot soldiers and archers)
Serjeant of Horse (1 per 10 cavalry)
Captain (1 per 2 knights)
Priest (2)
Court Warlock (**mage**)
4d10 camp followers (**commoner**) in 1d6+6 supply wagons, including at *least* 2 blacksmiths and 2 leatherworkers. Others include the spouses of soldiers, servants of officers, drovers with flocks of sheep or goats, tinkers, fletchers, and paid companions.

Archer: **AC** 14; **HP** 11 (2d8+2); **Spd** 30ft; **Melee** shortsword (+3, 1d6+1 piercing); **Ranged** longbow (+3, 150ft/600ft, 1d8+2 piercing); **Str** +1, **Dex** +1, **Con** +1, **Int** +0, **Wis** +0, **Cha** +0; **Skills** Perception +2; **AL** LN; **CR** 1/8; **XP** 25

Captain: **AC** 18; **HP** (10d8+20); **Spd** 30ft; **Melee** lance (+6, 10ft, 1d12 +3), greatsword (+6, 2d6+3 slashing); **SA** leadership (recharge after rest, 1 min, 30ft, if ally can hear and understand then add d4 to attack and save), multiattack (greatsword x2); **Str** +4, **Dex** +0, **Con** +2 (+4), **Int** +1, **Wis** +1 (+3), **Cha** +3; **Skills** Perception +3, Persuasion +5, Intimidation +3; **Traits** brave (tactical advantage against fright); **AL** LN; **CR** 3; **XP** 700

Cavalry: **AC** 16; **HP** 22 (4d8+2); **Spd** 30ft; **Melee** lance (+3, 10ft, 1d10+1 piercing); **Ranged** shortbow (+3, 80ft/320ft, 1d6+1 piercing); **Str** +1, **Dex** +1, **Con** +1, **Int** +0, **Wis** +0, **Cha** +0; **AL** LN; **CR** 1/4; **XP** 50.

Commoner: **AC** 10; **HP** 4 (1d8); **Spd** 30ft; **Melee** club (+2, 1d4 bludgeoning); **Str** +0, **Dex** +0, **Con** +0; **Int** +0, **Wis** +0, **Cha** +0; **AL** any; **CR** 0; **XP** 10.

Foot Soldier: **AC** 16; **HP** 11 (2d8+2); **Spd** 30ft; **Melee** longsword (+3, 1d8+1 slashing); **Str** +1, **Dex** +1, **Con** +1, **Int** +0, **Wis** +0, **Cha** +0; **Skills** Perception +2; **AL** LN; **CR** 1/8; **XP** 25.

Knight: **AC** 18; **HP** 52 (8d8+16); **Spd** 30ft; **Melee** greatsword (+5, 2d6+3 slashing); **SA** leadership (recharge after rest, 1 min, 30ft, if ally can hear and understand then add d4 to attack and save), multiattack (greatsword x2); parry (+2 AC vs. single melee); **Str** +3, **Dex** +0, **Con** +2 (+4), **Int** +0, **Wis** +0 (+2), **Cha** +2; **Traits** brave (tactical advantage against saves against fright); **AL** LN; **CR** 3; **XP** 700.

Mage: **AC** 12 (15 with *mage armor*); **HP** 40 (9d8); **Spd** 30ft; **Melee** dagger (+5, 1d4+2 piercing); **SA** spells (Int +6, 9th, DC 14); **Str** −1, **Dex** +2, **Con** +0, **Int** +3 (+6), **Wis** +1 (+4), **Cha** +0; **Skills** Arcana +6, History +6; **AL** N; **CR** 6; **XP** 2300.
   Spells (slots): 0 (at will)—*fire bolt, light, mage hand, prestidigitation*; 1st (4)—*detect magic, mage armor, magic missile, shield*; 2nd (3)—*misty step, suggestion*; 3rd (3)—*counterspell, fireball, fly*; 4th (3)—*greater invisibility, ice storm*; 5th (1)—*cone of cold.*

Noble: **AC** 15; **HP** 18 (4d8); **Spd** 30ft; **Melee** rapier (+3, 1d8+1 piercing); **SA** parry (reaction, +2 AC vs. single melee); **Str** +0, **Dex** +1, **Con** +0, **Int** +1, **Wis** +2, **Cha** +3; **Skills** Deception +5, Insight +4, Persuasion +5; **AL** LN; **CR** 1/4; **XP** 50.

Priest: **AC** 13; **HP** 27 (5d8+5); **Spd** 30ft; **Melee** mace (+2, 1d6 bludgeoning); **SA** divine eminence (bonus, expend slot, extra 3d6 radiant, + 1d6 per slot above 1st), spells (Wis +5, 5th, DC 13); **Str** +0, **Dex** +0, **Con** +1, **Int** +1, **Wis** +3, **Cha** +1; **Skills** Medicine +7, Persuasion +3, Religion +4; **AL** LG; **CR** 2; **XP** 450.
   Spells (slots): 0 (at will)— *light, sacred flame, resistance, thaumaturgy*; 1st (4)— *cure wounds, guiding bolt, sanctuary*; 2nd (3)—*hold person, lesser restoration, spiritual weapon*; 3rd (3)—*dispel magic, remove curse, spirit guardians*; 4th (3)—*freedom of movement, guardian of faith*; 5th (1)—*greater restoration, raise dead.*

Serjeant of Horse: **AC** 16; **HP** 32 (5d8+10); **Spd** 30ft; **Melee** spear (+4, 1d8+2 piercing); **Ranged** shortbow (+4, 80ft/320ft, 1d6+2 piercing); **SA** multiattack (spear x2 or shortbow x2); **Str** +2, **Dex** +2, **Con** +2; **Int** +0, **Wis** +1, **Cha** +1; **Skills** Perception +3, Intimidation +3; **AL** LN; **CR** 1/2; **XP** 100.

Sergeant: **AC** 17; **HP** 32 (5d8+10); **Spd** 30ft; **Melee** longsword (+4, 1d8+2 slashing); **Ranged** longbow (+4, 150ft/600ft, 1d8+2 piercing); **SA** multiattack (longsword x2 or longbow x2); **Str** +2, **Dex** +2, **Con** +2; **Int** +0, **Wis** +1, **Cha** +1; **Skills**

Perception +3, Intimidation +3; **AL** LN; **CR** 1/2; **XP** 100.

Veteran: AC 18; **HP** 78 (12d8+24); **Spd** 30ft; **Melee** longsword (+5, 1d8+3 slashing), shortsword (+5, 1d6+3 piercing); **Ranged** heavy crossbow (+4, 1d10+2 piercing); **SA** multiattack (longsword x2, shortsword); **Str** +3, **Dex** +2, **Con** +2, **Int** +0, **Wis** +0, **Cha** +1; **Skills** Athletics +5, Perception +2; **AL** any; **CR** 3; **XP** 700.

Warhorse (chain barding): AC 16; **HP** 19 (3d10+3); **Spd** 60ft; **Melee** hooves (+4, 2d6+4 bludgeoning); **SA** trampling charge (20ft move then hooves, DC 14 Str or knocked prone, if prone, bonus with hooves); **Str** +4, **Dex** +1, **Con** +1, **Int** −4, **Wis** +1, **Cha** −2; **AL** U; **CR** 1/2; **XP** 100.

65. Minstrel

If the encounter table does not specify the number of minstrels (**commoner**), determine the composition of the minstrel troupe on the table below. Minstrel encounters do not vary by Risk Level.

1d6	Encounter
1–2	1d2+1 minstrels
3–4	1d2+1 minstrels, 1 juggler, 1 trained bear, with house-wagon (the bear, of course, is not in the wagon)
5	Locally famous troubadour with 1d2 minstrels
6	Band of 1d6+3 minstrels, in house-wagon.

66. Mountain Goat

These encounters are with 1d6+1 **mountain goats** regardless of Risk Level in the area, with a 10% chance for the goats to be accompanied by a giant mountain goat.

Mountain Goat: AC 10; **HP** 4 (1d8); **Spd** 40ft; **Melee** ram (+3, 1d4+1 bludgeoning); **SA** charge (20ft move, ram, extra 1d4 bludgeoning, DC 11 Str or knocked prone); **Str** +1, **Dex** +0, **Con** +0, **Int** −4, **Wis** +0, **Cha** −3; **Traits** sure-footed (tactical advantage against knocked prone); **AL** U; **CR** 0; **XP** 10.

Giant Mountain Goat: AC 11; **HP** 19 (3d10+3); **Spd** 40ft; **Melee** ram (+5, 2d4+3 bludgeoning); **SA** charge (20ft move, ram, extra 2d4 bludgeoning, DC 13 Str or knocked prone; **Str** +3, **Dex** +0, **Con** +1, **Int** −4, **Wis** +0, **Cha** −2; **Traits** sure-footed (tactical advantage against knocked prone); **AL** U; **CR** 1/2; **XP** 100.

67. Mounted Patrol

Low-Risk to Medium-Risk Areas: 10 **cavalry**, 1 **serjeant of horse**, 1 **knight**

High-Risk to Extreme-Risk Areas: 20 **cavalry**, 2 **serjeants of horse**, 2 **knights**

Cavalry: AC 16; **HP** 22 (4d8+2); **Spd** 30ft; **Melee** lance (+3, 10ft, 1d10+1 piercing); **Ranged** shortbow (+3, 80ft/320ft, 1d6+1 piercing); **Str** +1, **Dex** +1, **Con** +1; **Int** +0, **Wis** +0, **Cha** +0; **AL** LN; **CR** 1/4; **XP** 50.

Knight: AC 18; **HP** 52 (8d8+16); **Spd** 30ft; **Melee** greatsword (+5, 2d6+3 slashing); **SA** leadership (recharge after rest, 1 min, 30ft, if ally can hear and understand then add d4 to attack and save), multiattack (greatsword x2); parry (+2

AC vs. single melee); **Str** +3, **Dex** +0, **Con** +2 (+4), **Int** +0, **Wis** +0 (+2), **Cha** +2; **Traits** brave (tactical advantage against saves against fright); **AL** LN; **CR** 3; **XP** 700.

Serjeant of Horse: AC 16; **HP** 32 (5d8+10); **Spd** 30ft; **Melee** spear (+4, 1d8+2 piercing); **Ranged** shortbow (+4, 80ft/320ft, 1d6+2 piercing); **SA** multiattack (spear x2 or shortbow x2); **Str** +2, **Dex** +2, **Con** +2; **Int** +0, **Wis** +1, **Cha** +1; **Skills** Perception +3, Intimidation +3; **AL** LN; **CR** 1/2; **XP** 100.

Warhorse (chain barding): AC 16; **HP** 19 (3d10+3); **Spd** 60ft; **Melee** hooves (+4, 2d6+4 bludgeoning); **SA** trampling charge (20ft move then hooves, DC 14 Str or knocked prone, if prone, bonus with hooves); **Str** +4, **Dex** +1, **Con** +1, **Int** −4, **Wis** +1, **Cha** −2; **AL** U; **CR** 1/2; **XP** 100.

68. Noble of the Realm

This is an encounter with a Lord-Governor, King, Duke-Palatine, or Count-Palatine, who is named as the ruler in the region's description. If the area has no ruler, such as the Gaelon River Valley, treat this as an encounter with High Nobility (Encounter #52).

Noble: See the country's description for the ruler's level and class.
Baron (1d4+3) (**veteran**)
Courtier (2d6+6) (**noble**)
Knight (4d6+3)
Archer (1d6 x50)
Foot Soldier (1d6 x50)
Cavalry (1d4 x50)
Sergeant (1 per 10 foot soldiers and archers)
Serjeant of Horse (1 per 10 cavalry)
Captain (1 per 2 knights)
Priests (2)
Court Warlock (**mage**)
Entertainer (5) (**commoner**)
Baggage train: 5d10 servants and laborers (**commoner**) in 1d6+6 supply wagons.

See Encounter **64** for stats.

69. Ogre

Low-Risk Area: 1 **ogre** (60%); otherwise, 2 **ogres**
Medium-Risk Area: 1d6 **ogres** with 25% chance to be accompanied by a pet **cave bear**.
High-Risk Area: 1d6+3 **ogres** with 30% chance to be accompanied by a pet **cave bear**.
Extreme-Risk Area: 2d10 **ogres** with 35% chance to be accompanied by a pet **cave bear**.

Ogre: AC 11; **HP** 59 (7d10+21); **Spd** 40ft; **Melee** greatclub (+6, 2d8+4 bludgeoning); **Ranged** (+6, 30ft/120ft, 2d6+4 piercing); **Str** +4, **Dex** −1, **Con** +3, **Int** −3, **Wis** −2, **Cha** −2; **Senses** darkvision 60ft; **AL** CE; **CR** 2; **XP** 450.

Bear, Cave: AC 12; **HP** 42 (5d10+15); **Spd** 40ft, swim 30ft; **Melee** bite (+7, 1d8+5 piercing), claws x2 (2d6+5); **SA** multiattack (bite, claws x2); **Str** +5, **Dex** +0, **Con** +3, **Int** −4, **Wis** +1, **Cha** −2; **Skills** Perception +3; **Senses** darkvision 60ft, keen smell; **AL** U; **CR** 2; **XP** 450.

70. Ogre Mage (Oni)

Low-Risk Area: 1 **ogre mage**, probably engaged with his own business rather than hunting, but a snack is always welcome if it looks tasty and poorly defended.

Medium-Risk Area: 1 **ogre mage** (90%); otherwise, 1d3. 25% chance to be accompanied by 1d4 **wolves**, and 25% chance to be accompanied by a **worg** as well.

High-Risk Area: 1d2 **ogre mages** (80%); otherwise, 1d3+1. 50% chance to be accompanied by 1d4 **wolves**, and 50% chance to be accompanied by a **worg** as well.

Extreme-Risk Area: 1d4 **ogre mages** (70%); otherwise, 1d4+2. 75% chance to be accompanied by 1d4 **wolves**, and 75% chance to be accompanied by a **worg** as well.

Aerial encounters are with 1 **ogre mage**.

Ogre Mage (Oni): AC 16; HP 110 (13d10+39); Spd 30ft, fly 30ft; **Melee** claw (+7, 1d8+4 slashing) or glaive (+7, 10ft, 2d10+4 or 1d10+4 slashing in S/M form); **SA** change shape, innate spells (Cha, DC 13), multiattack (claw x2 or glaive x2); **Str** +4, **Dex** +0 (+3), **Con** +3 (+6), **Int** +2, **Wis** +1 (+4), **Cha** +2 (+5); **Skills** Arcana +5, Deception +8, Perception +4; **Senses** darkvision 60ft; **Traits** magic weapons, regeneration (10/turn with at 1hp); **AL** LE; **CR** 7; **XP** 2900.
  Innate Spells: at will—*darkness, invisibility*; 1/day—*charm person, cone of cold, gaseous form, sleep*

Wolf: AC 13; HP 11 (2d8+2); Spd 40ft; **Melee** bite (+4, 2d4+2 piercing plus knock prone, DC 11 Str); **Str** +1, **Dex** +2, **Con** +1, **Int** –4, **Wis** +1, **Cha** –2; **Skills** Perception +3, Stealth +4; **Senses** keen hearing and smell; **Traits** pack tactics; **AL** U; **CR** 1/4; **XP** 50.

Worg: AC 13; HP 26 (4d10+4); Spd 50ft; **Melee** bite (+5, 2d6+3 piercing plus knock prone, DC 13 Str); **Str** +3, **Dex** +1, **Con** +1, **Int** –2, **Wis** +0, **Cha** –1; **Skills** Perception +4; **Senses** darkvision 60ft, keen hearing and smell; **AL** NE; **CR** 1/2; **XP** 100.

71. Outlaw

2d10 refugees (**commoner**) from the law, tattered, destitute, and furtive. They are pathetic rather than aggressive, and most are armed only with clubs or daggers for self-defense.

72. Owlbear

Low-Risk Area: 1 **owlbear**
Medium-Risk Area: 2 **owlbears**
High-Risk Area: 4 **owlbears**
Extreme-Risk Area: 6 **owlbears**

Owlbear: AC 13; HP 59 (7d10+21); Spd 40ft; **Melee** beak (+7, 1d10+5 piercing), claws (+7, 2d8+5 slashing); **SA** multiattack (beak, claws); **Str** +5, **Dex** +1, **Con** +3, **Int** –4, **Wis** +1, **Cha** –2; **Skills** Perception +3; **Senses** darkvision 60ft, keen sight and smell; **AL** U; **CR** 3; **XP** 700.

73. Patrol of Waymark Cavalry

Waymark cavalry are troops from the Waymarch that are employed by Bard's Gate and stationed at Eastgate and Telar Brindel. They are found patrolling Eastgate's portion of the Estuary Road, the Lowwater Road on the north side of the Amrin Estuary, and along the part of the Trader's Way running between Eastgate and Telar Brindel. A patrol is composed of 10 **cavalry** and one **serjeant of horse**.

Cavalry: AC 16; HP 22 (4d8+4); Spd 30ft; **Melee** lance (+3, 10ft, 1d10+1 piercing); **Ranged** shortbow (+3, 80ft/320ft, 1d6+1 piercing); **Str** +1, **Dex** +1, **Con** +1, **Int** +0, **Wis** +0, **Cha** +0; **AL** LN; **CR** 1/4; **XP** 50

Serjeant of Horse: AC 16; HP 32 (5d8+10); Spd 30ft; **Melee** spear (+4, 1d8+2 piercing); **Ranged** shortbow (+4, 80ft/320ft, 1d6+2 piercing); **SA** multiattack (spear x2 or shortbow x2); **Str** +2, **Dex** +2, **Con** +2, **Int** +0, **Wis** +1, **Cha** +1; **Skills** Perception +3, Intimidation +3; **AL** LN; **CR** 1/2; **XP** 100.

74. Peasant

This is an encounter with a single, ordinary peasant (**commoner**), regardless of the area's Risk Level. Roll 1d6:

1	The peasant is insane and raving
2	The peasant is looking for something lost, probably a sheep, possibly a relative
3	The peasant is terrified, running from something (roll another dangerous encounter to see what is nearby)
4	The peasant is completely drunk, and has already passed out
5	The peasant is lost and far from home, probably returning from a pilgrimage, a prison, or migrant labor
6	The peasant is dead and half-eaten

75. Pegasus

Low-Risk Area: 1d2 **pegasi**
Medium-Risk Area: 1d4 **pegasi**
High-Risk Area: 1d6+2 **pegasi**
Extreme-Risk Area: 1d6+2 **pegasi**

Airborne encounters are always with 1d6+3 **pegasi**.

Pegasus: AC 12; HP 59 (7d10+21); Spd 60ft, fly 90ft; **Melee** hooves (+6, 2d6+4 bludgeoning); **Str** +4, **Dex** +2 (+4), **Con** +3, **Int** +0, **Wis** +2 (+4), **Cha** +1 (+3); **Skills** Perception +6; **AL** CG; **CR** 2; **XP** 450.

76. Penitent

The encounter is with 1d6 penitents (**commoner**), who lash their backs occasionally with small whips, or hit themselves with wooden boards. Some of these groups (5% chance) are World's Pain heretics (see the **Heresy Appendix**. For more information about the n'gathau who are behind this heresy, see *The Tome of Horrors Complete* by **Frog God Games**.)

Penitents who are not World's Pain heretics are usually (90% chance) atoning for a heretical past, expiating their sin by order of one of the various priesthoods of the Borderlands Provinces. Their heresy would have been one of the lesser heresies, since members of one of the Great Heresies are usually burned at the stake rather than being sent on a penitentiary pilgrimage.

If the penitents are neither active heretics nor reformed heretics, they are atoning for a lesser religious crime at the orders of a High Priest.

77. Peryton

Low-Risk Area: 1 **peryton**
Medium-Risk Area: 1d2 **perytons**
High-Risk Area: 2 **perytons** (50%); otherwise, small flock of 1d3+2
Extreme-Risk Area: flock of 1d6+2 **perytons**

Peryton: AC 13; HP 33 (6d8+6); Spd 20ft, fly 60ft; **Melee** gore (+5, 1d8+3 piercing), talons (+5, 2d4+3 piercing);

SA dive attack (30ft, hit with attack then deal extra 2d8), multiattack (gore, talons); **Resist** normal weapons; **Str** +3, **Dex** +1, **Con** +1, **Int** −1, **Wis** +1, **Cha** +0; **Skills** Perception +5; **Senses** keen sight and smell; **Traits** flyby; **AL** CE; **CR** 2; **XP** 450.

78. Pilgrim

Roll 1d3 to determine the size of a pilgrimage. The size of a pilgrimage does not depend on the Risk Level of an area, although the success of it might.

Composition of Pilgrimage

1d3	Pilgrims
1	1 **priest**, 2 **knights**, 30 pilgrims (**commoner**)
2	1 **knight**, 1d3+10 pilgrims (**commoner**)
3	1d6+1 pilgrims (**commoner**)

Commoner: AC 10; **HP** 4 (1d8); **Spd** 30ft; **Melee** club (+2, 1d4 bludgeoning); **Str** +0, **Dex** +0, **Con** +0; **Int** +0, **Wis** +0, **Cha** +0; **AL** any; **CR** 0; **XP** 10.

Knight: AC 18; **HP** 52 (8d8+16); **Spd** 30ft; **Melee** greatsword (+5, 2d6+3 slashing); **SA** leadership (recharge after rest, 1 min, 30ft, if ally can hear and understand then add d4 to attack and save), multiattack (greatsword x2); parry (+2 AC vs. single melee); **Str** +3, **Dex** +0, **Con** +2 (+4), **Int** +0, **Wis** +0 (+2), **Cha** +2; **Traits** brave (tactical advantage against saves against fright); **AL** LN; **CR** 3; **XP** 700.

Priest: AC 13; **HP** 27 (5d8+5); Spd 30ft; **Melee** mace (+2, 1d6 bludgeoning); **SA** divine eminence (bonus, expend slot, extra 3d6 radiant, +1d6 per slot above 1st), spells (Wis +5, 5th, DC 13); **Str** +0, **Dex** +0, **Con** +1, **Int** +1, **Wis** +3, **Cha** +1; **Skills** Medicine +7, Persuasion +3, Religion +4; **AL** LG; **CR** 2; **XP** 450.

> **Spells (slots):** 0 (at will)— *light, sacred flame, resistance, thaumaturgy*; 1st (4)— *cure wounds, guiding bolt, sanctuary*; 2nd (3)—*hold person, lesser restoration, spiritual weapon*; 3rd (3)—*dispel magic, remove curse, spirit guardians*; 4th (3)—*freedom of movement, guardian of faith*; 5th (1)—*greater restoration, raise dead.*

Where are they going?

1d4	Destination
1	To the small shrine of a saint in a town
2	The nearest large city to a temple
3	The birthplace of a religious leader, hero, or saint somewhere in a rural village
4	To view a religious relic kept in a remote abbey

What are they bringing?

1d6	Accompanied by
1	Children (1d4+4)
2	Herd animals for blessing (2d4+4)
3	A symbolic item of their home for blessing
4	A body in a coffin for blessing and burial
5–6	Nothing

Sample Pilgrimages

Second Pilgrimage of Sir Matthieu the Corpulent

(1 knight, 12 pilgrims): Sir Matthieu the Corpulent is making a pilgrimage to the nearest city where he seeks healing for a case of gout. He is bringing 12 of his villagers along in an effort to improve their piety (they are not very pious, and at least one is drunk). Sir Matthieu's last pilgrimage was an attempt to persuade the gods to reduce his substantial weight, and was not successful. The knight has brought along a necklace worth 400gp, which he plans to place around the neck of the goddess's statue in the temple of Ceres (healing, mercy, and patience). The priestesses of the goddess of patience view Sir Matthieu's visits as a test of faith, for he strains even their tolerance for idiocy.

Jaunt's Pilgrimage of Early Opportunity

(8 peasants): The peasants, led by one Wormian Jaunt, are on their way to touch the scorched and mummified sword-hand of a martyred paladin from a nearby village, Sir Baldivere, who almost fought off a demon. They consider the paladin to be a future saint, and plan on getting themselves into Baldivere's favor before the rush. Wormian Jaunt is the originator of this unusual theological interpretation, and is willing to explain it at very great length. The peasants are not bringing any offering other than a couple of copper pieces each.

79. Prisoner

A foot patrol is bringing a wagon-full of prisoners to be burned, hanged, tried, or incarcerated.

The cart contains 1d4+2 prisoners (**commoner**). Their crimes and status may be determined below:

d100	Accusation
1–8	Accused of heresy: guilty
9–10	Accused of heresy: innocent

d100	Accusation
11–25	Accused of theft: guilty
26–28	Accused of theft: innocent
29–35	Accused of demon worship: innocent
36–37	Accused of demon worship: guilty
38–45	Accused of impiety (minor crime): guilty
46–47	Accused of impiety (minor crime): innocent
48–57	Accused of murder: guilty
58–61	Accused of murder: innocent
62–75	Accused of poaching on a noble's land: guilty
76–80	Accused of poaching: innocent
81–90	Accused of fraudulent selling: guilty
91–93	Accused of fraudulent selling: innocent
94–99	Accused of banditry: guilty
00	Accused of banditry: guilty

Foot Soldier: AC 16; **HP** 11 (2d8+2); **S**pd 30ft; **Melee** longsword (+3, 1d8+1 slashing); **Str** +1, **Dex** +1, **Con** +1, **Int** +0, **Wis** +0, **Cha** +0; **Skills** Perception +2; **AL** LN; **CR** 1/8; **XP** 25.

Sergeant: AC 17; **HP** 32 (5d8+10); **Spd** 30ft; **Melee** longsword (+4, 1d8+2 slashing); **Ranged** longbow (+4, 150ft/600ft, 1d8+2 piercing); **SA** multiattack (longsword x2 or longbow x2); **Str** +2, **Dex** +2, **Con** +2; **Int** +0, **Wis** +1, **Cha** +1; **Skills** Perception +3, Intimidation +3; **AL** LN; **CR** 1/2; **XP** 100.

Sheriff: AC 18; **HP** (10d8+20); **Spd** 30ft; **Melee** lance (+6, 10ft, 1d12 +3), greatsword (+6, 2d6+3 slashing); **SA** leadership (recharge after rest, 1 min, 30ft, if ally can hear and understand then add d4 to attack and save), multiattack (greatsword x2); **Str** +4, **Dex** +0, **Con** +2 (+4), **Int** +1, **Wis** +1 (+3), **Cha** +3; **Skills** Perception +3, Persuasion +5, Intimidation +3; **Traits** brave (tactical advantage against fright); **AL** LN; **CR** 3; **XP** 700

Sheriff's Warhorse (plate barding): AC 18; **HP** 19 (3d10+3); **Spd** 60ft; **Melee** hooves (+4, 2d6+4 bludgeoning); **SA** trampling charge (20ft move then hooves, DC 14 Str or knocked prone, if prone, bonus with hooves); **Str** +4, **Dex** +1, **Con** +1, **Int** −4, **Wis** +1, **Cha** −2; **AL** U; **CR** 1/2; **XP** 100.

80. Robber Knight

Unless otherwise stated in the encounter table, this is an encounter with 1d3 robber knights, accompanied by 2d6 bandits. There is also a 10% chance that a **mage** accompanies the group.

Bandit: AC 12; **HP** 11 (2d8+2); **Spd** 30ft; **Melee** shortsword (+3, 1d6+1 slashing); **Ranged** light crossbow (+3, 80ft/320ft, 1d8+1 piercing); **Str** +0, **Dex** +1, **Con** +1, **Int** +0, **Wis** +0, **Cha** +0; **AL** NE; **CR** 1/8; **XP** 25.

Robber Knight: AC 18; **HP** 52 (8d8+16); **Spd** 30ft; **Melee** greatsword (+5, 2d6+3 slashing); **SA** leadership (recharge after rest, 1 min, 30ft, if ally can hear and understand then add d4 to attack and save), multiattack (greatsword x2); parry (+2 AC vs. single melee); **Str** +3, **Dex** +0, **Con** +2 (+4), **Int** +0, **Wis** +0 (+2), **Cha** +2; **Traits** brave (tactical advantage against saves against fright); **AL** NE; **CR** 3; **XP** 700.

Mage: AC 12 (15 with *mage armor*); **HP** 40 (9d8); **Spd** 30ft;

Melee dagger (+5, 1d4+2 piercing); **SA** spells (Int +6, 9th, DC 14); **Str** −1, **Dex** +2, **Con** +0, **Int** +3 (+6), **Wis** +1 (+4), **Cha** +0; **Skills** Arcana +6, History +6; **AL** NE; **CR** 6; **XP** 2300.

> **Spells (slots):** 0 (at will)—*fire bolt, light, mage hand, prestidigitation;* 1st (4)—*detect magic, mage armor, magic missile, shield;* 2nd (3)—*misty step, suggestion;* 3rd (3)—*counterspell, fireball, fly;* 4th (3)—*greater invisibility, ice storm;* 5th (1)—*cone of cold.*

81. Roc

Low to Medium-Risk Areas: 1 **roc**
High to Extreme-Risk Area: 1d2 **rocs**

Airborne encounters with rocs: over non-mountainous regions, the encounter is with 1 roc. Encounters over mountainous terrain are with 1d2 rocs.

Roc: AC 15; **HP** 248 (16d20+80); Spd 20ft, fly 120ft; **Melee** beak (+13, 10ft, 4d8+9 piercing), talons (+13, 4d6+9 slashing plus grapple, target restrained, escape DC 19); **SA** multiattack (beak, talons); **Str** +9, **Dex** +0 (+4), **Con** +5 (+9), **Int** −4, **Wis** +0 (+4), **Cha** −1 (+3); **Skills** Perception +4; **Senses** keen sight; **AL** U; **CR** 11; **XP** 7200.

82. Satyr

If not specified in the encounter table, the encounter is with 1d6 satyrs. Risk Level does not affect the number of satyrs encountered.

Satyr: AC 14; **HP** 31 (7d8); **Spd** 40ft; **Melee** ram (+3, 2d4+1 bludgeoning) or shortsword (+5, 1d6+3 piercing); **Ranged** shortbow (+5, 80ft/320ft, 1d6+3 piercing); **Str** +1, **Dex** +3, **Con** +0, **Int** +1, **Wis** +0, **Cha** +2; **Skills** Perception +2, Performance +6, Stealth +5; **Traits** magic resistance; **AL** CN; **XP** 1/2; **XP** 100.

83. Shadow

Low-Risk Area: 1 **shadow**
Medium-Risk Area: 1d3 **shadows** (75%); otherwise, 1d6 **shadows**
High-Risk Area: 1d6 **shadows**
Extreme-Risk Area: 1d10 **shadows**

Shadow: AC 12; **HP** 16 (3d8+3); **Spd** 40ft; **Melee** touch (+4, 2d6+2 necrotic plus 1d4 Str drain); **SA** shadow stealth (in dim light darkness, hide as bonus); **Immune** exhaustion, fright, grapple, necrotic, paralysis, petrify, poison, prone, restraint; **Resist** acid, cold, fire, lightning, normal weapons, thunder; **Vulnerable** radiant; **Str** −2, **Dex** +2, **Con** +1, **Int** −2, **Wis** +0, **Cha** −1; **Skills** Stealth +4 (+6 in dim light or darkness); **Senses** darkvision 60ft; **Traits** amorphous, sunlight weakness; **AL** CE; **CR** 1/2; **XP** 100.

84. Shambling Mound

Low-Risk Area: Treat as "No Encounter"
Medium-Risk Area: 1 **shambling mound**
High-Risk Area: 2 **shambling mounds**
Extreme-Risk Area: 3 **shambling mounds**

Shambling Mound: AC 15; **HP** 136 (16d10+48); **Spd** 20ft, swim 20ft; **Melee** slam (+7, 2d8+4 bludgeoning); **SA** engulf (grappled target is blinded, restrained, and unable to breathe, DC 14 Con or 2d8+4 bludgeoning), multiattack (slam x2, if both hit, then grappled then engulf, escape

DC 14); **Immune** blind, deaf, exhaustion, lightning; **Resist** cold, fire; **Str** +4, **Dex** –1, **Con** +3, **Int** –3, **Wis** +0, **Cha** –3; **Skills** Stealth +2; **Senses** blindsight 60ft (blind beyond); **Traits** lightning absorption; **AL** U; **CR** 5; **XP** 1800.

85. Small Trader (human)

Small traders are essentially small-scale caravans, usually moving from town to town on a circuit rather than crossing hundreds of miles from one major market to another. Roll 1d3 to determine the composition of the group:

1	Mule train of 2d6 mules with 1d6 **small traders**
2	2 wagons with 1d6 small traders and 2 **archers**
3	3 wagons with 1d6+1 **small traders**, 2 **archers** and 1 **cavalry** as scout

Small Trader: AC 16; **HP** 11 (2d8+2); **Spd** 30ft; **Melee** longsword (+3, 1d8+1 slashing); **Str** +1, **Dex** +1, **Con** +1, **Int** +0, **Wis** +0, **Cha** +0; **Skills** Perception +2; **AL** N; **CR** 1/8; **XP** 25.

Archer: AC 14; **HP** 11 (2d8+2); **Spd** 30ft; **Melee** shortsword (+3, 1d6+1 piercing); **Ranged** longbow (+3, 150ft/600ft, 1d8+2 piercing); **Str** +1, **Dex** +1, **Con** +1, **Int** +0, **Wis** +0, **Cha** +0; **Skills** Perception +2; **AL** LN; **CR** 1/8; **XP** 25.

Cavalry: AC 16; **HP** 22 (4d8+4); **Spd** 30ft; **Melee** lance (+3, 10ft, 1d10+1 piercing); **Ranged** shortbow (+3, 80ft/320ft, 1d6+1 piercing); **Str** +1, **Dex** +1, **Con** +1, **Int** +0, **Wis** +0, **Cha** +0; **AL** LN; **CR** 1/4; **XP** 50

Cargo: Most small trader cargoes are a mix of pottery, ribbons, tin and pewter ware, and other items purchased in towns to sell in the country. Each small trader carries roughly 2d6x10gp worth of goods.

86. Small Trader (dwarf or halfling)

Dwarf and halfling traders tend to be the same in terms of numbers. These groups are usually either all hill dwarves or all halflings, not a mix. Roll 1d2 to determine the composition of the group:

1	Mule train of 2d6 mules with 1d6 **dwarf/halfling traders**
2	2 wagons with 1d6 **dwarf/halfling traders**, 2 **guards**, and 50% chance of 2d6 herd animals :(roll 1d3: 1, goats; 2, donkeys; 3, sheep)

Dwarf Trader: AC 16; **HP** 13 (2d8+4); **Spd** 30ft; **Melee** battleaxe (+4, 1d8+2 slashing); **Ranged** handaxe (+4, 20ft/60ft, 1d6+2 slashing); **Str** +2, **Dex** +1, **Con** +2, **Int** +0, **Wis** +0, **Cha** +0; **Skills** Perception +2; **Senses** darkvision 60ft; **Traits** dwarven resilience; **AL** LN; **CR** 1/8; **XP** 25.

Dwarf Guard: AC 17; **HP** 32 (5d8+10); **Spd** 30ft; **Melee** battleaxe (+4, 1d8+2 slashing); **Ranged** handaxe (+4, 20ft/60ft, 1d6+2 slashing); **SA** multiattack (longsword x2 or handaxe x2); **Str** +2, **Dex** +2, **Con** +2, **Int** +0, **Wis** +1, **Cha** +1; **Skills** Perception +3, Intimidation +3; **Senses** darkvision 60ft; **Traits** dwarven resilience; **AL** LN; **CR** 1/2; **XP** 100.

Halfling Trader: AC 16; **HP** 13 (2d8+4); **Spd** 30ft; **Melee** shortsword (+4, 1d6+2 slashing); **Str** +1, **Dex** +2, **Con** +2, **Int** +0, **Wis** +0, **Cha** +1; **Skills** Perception +2, Persuasion +3; **Traits** brave, lucky, nimbleness; **AL** LG; **CR** 1/8; **XP** 25.

Halfling Guard: AC 17; **HP** 27 (5d6+10); **Spd** 25ft; **Melee** shortsword (+5, 1d6+3 slashing); **Ranged** shortbow (+4, 20ft/60ft, 1d6+3 slashing); **SA** multiattack (shortsword x2 or shortbow x2); **Str** +1, **Dex** +3, **Con** +2, **Int** +0, **Wis** +1, **Cha** +1; **Skills** Perception +3, Persuasion +3; **Traits** brave, lucky, nimbleness; **AL** LG; **CR** 1/2; **XP** 100.

Treasure:

Each dwarf trader carries roughly 2d6x100gp worth of crafted metal goods.

Most halfling trader cargoes are a mix of pottery, ribbons, tin and pewter ware, and other items purchased in towns to sell in the country. Each small trader carries roughly 2d6x50gp worth of goods.

87. Stag

Roll 1d6 to determine how many deer:

1–3	lone **stag**
4	1d3+1 **stags**
5–6	1d6 **does** and 1 **stag**

Stag: AC 13; **HP** 5 (1d8+1); **Spd** 50ft; **Melee** bite (+3, 1d4+1 piercing); **Str** +1, **Dex** +3, **Con** +1, **Int** –4, **Wis** +2, **Cha** –3; **AL** U; **CR** 0; **XP** 10.

Doe: AC 13; **HP** 4 (1d8); **Spd** 50ft; **Melee** bite (+2, 1d4 piercing); **Str** +0, **Dex** +3, **Con** +0, **Int** –4, **Wis** +2, **Cha** –3; **AL** U; **CR** 0; **XP** 10.

88. Stirge

Low-Risk Area: 1d4 **stirges**
Medium-Risk Area: 2d6 **stirges**
High-Risk Area: 2d6+3 **stirges**
Extreme-Risk Area: 3d6 **stirges**

Stirge: AC 14; **HP** 2 (1d4); **Spd** 10ft, fly 40ft; **Melee** proboscis (+5, 1d4+3 piercing plus attach, blood drain 1d4+3/turn); **Str** –3, **Dex** +3, **Con** +0, **Int** –4, **Wis** –1, **Cha** –2; **Senses** darkvision 60ft; **AL** U; **CR** 1/8; **XP** 25.

89. Tangtal

These great cats are surrounded by *mirror images* of themselves.
Low-Risk Area: Treat this as an encounter with ants rather than a tangtal
Medium-Risk Area: 1 tangtal (90%); otherwise, a mated pair
High-Risk Area: 1d2+1 tangtals
Extreme-Risk Area: 1d4+2 tangtals

Tangtal: AC 13; **HP** 22 (4d8+4); **Spd** 50ft, climb 40ft; **Melee** bite (+5, 1d6+3 piercing), claws (+5, 1d8+3 slashing); **SA** duplicate (1/day per *mirror image*); multiattack (bite, claws); **Str** +3, **Dex** +3, **Con** +1, **Int** +1, **Wis** +2, **Cha** +0; **Skills** Perception +4, Stealth +7; **Senses** darkvision 60ft, keen smell; **AL** NE; **CR** 1; **XP** 200. (*Fifth Edition Foes* 221)

90. Tiger

Low-Risk Area: 1 **tiger**
Medium-Risk Area: Roll 1d6:

1–4	1 **tiger**
5	2 **tigers**
6	1d6 **tigers**

High-Risk Area: 1d8 **tigers**
Extreme-Risk Area: 1d6+2 **tigers**

Tiger: AC 12; **HP** 37 (5d10+10); **Spd** 40ft; **Melee** bite (+5, 1d10+3 piercing), claw (+5, 1d8+3 slashing); **SA** pounce (20ft move then claw, DC 13 Str or knocked prone, bonus bite); **Str** +3, **Dex** +2, **Con** +2, **Int** −4; **Wis** +1, **Cha** −1; **Skills** Perception +3, Stealth +6; **Senses** darkvision 60ft, keen smell; **AL** U; **CR** 1; **XP** 200.

91. Treant

Treants are generally uninterested in humans unless a great deal of woodcutting is in progress. They occasionally make their way into human camps to listen to news of the world. They often bring berries or some other type of food when making such intrusions.

Low-Risk Area: 1 **treant**
Medium-Risk Area: 1 **treant**
High-Risk Area: 1d2 **treants**
Extreme-Risk Area: 1d3 **treants**

Treant: AC 16; **HP** 138 (12d12+60); **Spd** 30ft; **Melee** slam (+10, 3d6+6 bludgeoning); **Ranged** rock (+10, 60ft/180ft, 4d10+6 bludgeoning); **SA** animate trees (1/day, 60ft, 1 or 2 trees), multiattack (slam x2); **Resist** bludgeoning, piercing; **Vulnerable** fire; **Str** +6, **Dex** −1, **Con** +3, **Int** +1, **Wis** +3, **Cha** +1; **Traits** false appearance (tree), siege monster; **AL** CG; **CR** 9; **XP** 5000.

92. Troll

Low-Risk Area: 1 **troll**
Medium-Risk Area: Roll 1d6:

1–3	1 **troll**
4–5	2 **trolls**
6	3 **trolls**

High-Risk Area: 1d3+1 **trolls**
Extreme-Risk Area: 1d8 **trolls**

Troll: AC 15; **HP** 84 (8d10+40); **Spd** 30ft; **Melee** bite (+7, 1d6+4 piercing), claw (+7, 2d6+4 slashing); **SA** multiattack (bite, claw x2); **Str** +4, **Dex** +1, **Con** +5, **Int** −2, **Wis** −1, **Cha** −2; **Skills** Perception +2; **Senses** darkvision 60ft, keen smell; **Traits** regeneration (10hp/turn); **AL** CE; **CR** 5; **XP** 1800.

93. Unicorn

Unicorn encounters do not vary by an area's Risk Level. The encounter is with 1 **unicorn**.

Unicorn: AC 12; **HP** 67 (9d10+18); **Spd** 50ft; **Melee** hooves (+7, 2d6+4 bludgeoning), horn (+7, 1d8+4 piercing); **SA** charge (20ft move, horn, extra 2d8 piercing, DC 15 Str or knocked prone), healing touch (3/day, 2d8+2 hp, all diseases and poisons), innate spells (Cha, DC 14), multiattack (hooves, horn), teleport (1/day, 5ft, up to 3 to a familiar location up to 1 mile); **LA** hooves, shimmering shield (2, 60ft, +2 AC until end of next turn), heal self (3, 2d8+2 hp); **Immune** charm, paralysis, poison; **Str** +4, **Dex** +2, **Con** +2, **Int** +0, **Wis** +3, **Cha** +3; **Senses** darkvision 60ft, telepathy 60ft; **Traits** magic resistance, magic weapons; **AL** LG; **CR** 5; **XP** 1800.

94. Undead A

Low-Risk Area: 1d6 **skeletons** (60%); otherwise, 1d6 **zombies**
Medium-Risk Area: Roll 1d6:

1–3	1d12 **skeletons**
4–5	2d6 **zombies**
6	Ghoul (**Encounter #39**)

High-Risk Area: Roll 1d6:

1–3	3d6 **skeletons**
4–5	3d6 **zombies**
6	Ghoul (**Encounter #39**)

Extreme-Risk Area: Treat as ghoul encounter (**Encounter #39**)

Skeleton: AC 13; **HP** 13 (2d8+4); **Spd** 30ft; **Melee** shortsword (+4, 1d6+2 piercing); **Ranged** shortbow (+4, 80ft/320ft, 1d6+2 piercing); **Immune** exhaustion, poison; **Vulnerable** bludgeoning; **Str** +0, **Dex** +2, **Con** +2, **Int** −2, **Wis** −1, **Cha** −3; **Senses** darkvision 60ft; **AL** LE; **CR** 1/4; **XP** 50.

Zombie: AC 8; **HP** 22 (3d8+9); **Spd** 20ft; **Melee** slam (+3, 1d6+1 bludgeoning); **Immune** exhaustion, poison; **Str** +1, **Dex** −2, **Con** +3, **Int** −4, **Wis** −2 (+0), **Cha** −3; **Senses** darkvision 60ft; **Traits** undead fortitude (upon 0hp, Con save with DC 5 + damage taken, then drop to 1hp); **AL** NE; **CR** 1/4; **XP** 50.

95. Undead B

Low-Risk Area: 1d2 **shadows**
Medium-Risk Area: 1d2 **shadows** and 1 **wight**
High-Risk Area: 1d3 **shadows** and 1d2 **wights**
Extreme-Risk Area: 1d6 **wights**

Shadow: AC 12; **HP** 16 (3d8+3); **Spd** 40ft; **Melee** touch (+4, 2d6+2 necrotic plus 1d4 Str drain); **SA** shadow stealth (in dim light darkness, hide as bonus); **Immune** exhaustion, fright, grapple, necrotic, paralysis, petrify, poison, prone, restraint; **Resist** acid, cold, fire, lightning, normal weapons, thunder; **Vulnerable** radiant; **Str** −2, **Dex** +2, **Con** +1, **Int** −2, **Wis** +0, **Cha** −1; **Skills** Stealth +4 (+6 in dim light or darkness); **Senses** darkvision 60ft; **Traits** amorphous, sunlight weakness; **AL** CE; **CR** 1/2; **XP** 100.

Wight: AC 14; **HP** 45 (6d8+18); **Spd** 30ft; **Melee** touch (+4, 1d6+2 necrotic plus life drain, DC 13 Con or max hp reduction), longsword (+4, 1-H 1d8+2 or 2-H 1d10+2 slashing); **Ranged** longbow (+4, 150ft/600ft, 1d8+2 piercing); **SA** multiattack (longsword x2 or longsword, touch or longbow x2); **Immune** exhaustion, poison; **Resist** necrotic, non-silver normal weapons; **Str** +2, **Dex** +2, **Con** +3, **Int** +0, **Wis** +1, **Cha** +2; **Skills** Perception +3, Stealth +4; **Senses** darkvision 60ft; **Traits** sunlight sensitivity; **AL** NE; **CR** 3; **XP** 700.

96. Undead C

Low-Risk Area: 1d3 **shadows** (see stats above)
Medium-Risk Area: 1d3 **wights** (see stats above) and 1d2 **wraiths**
High-Risk Area: 1d4 **wraiths**
Extreme-Risk Area: 1d6 **wraiths**

Wraith: AC 13; **HP** 67 (9d8+27); **Spd** 0ft, fly 50ft (hover); **Melee** touch (+6, 4d8+3 necrotic plus life drain, DC 14 Con or max hp reduction); **Immune** charm, exhaustion, grapple, necrotic, paralysis, petrify, poison, prone, restraint; **Resist** acid, cold, fire, lightning, non-silver normal weapons, thunder; **Str** −2, **Dex** +3, **Con** +3, **Int** +1, **Wis** +2, **Cha** +2; **Senses** darkvision 60ft; **Traits** incorporeal movement, sunlight sensitivity; **AL** NE; **CR** 5; **XP** 1800.

97. Vulchling

Low-Risk Area: 1d12 **vulchlings**
Medium-Risk Area: 2d10 **vulchlings**
High-Risk Area: 3d10 **vulchlings**
Extreme-Risk Area: 4d10 **vulchlings**

Vulchling: AC 12; **HP** 9 (2d8); **Spd** 20ft, fly 50ft; **Melee** beak (+4, 1d4+2 piercing) or talons (+4, 1d6+2 slashing); **Str** −1, **Dex** +2, **Con** +0, **Int** −2, **Wis** +0, **Cha** +0; **Senses** darkvision 60ft; **AL** CE; **CR** 1/8; **XP** 25. (*Fifth Edition Foes* 243)

98. Wandering Refugee

Viewed on the large scale, the Borderlands Provinces are relatively stable in the sense that none of the countries are at war with one another, and that there is no large-scale raiding such as the Heldring raids of centuries past, or the more recent Wilderlands Clan War in Keston. However, by this late point in the book, the reader is fully aware that at the microscopic level of towns and peasantry, there is a great seething of unrest, violence, and social collapse currently threatening most of the Borderlands region.

This encounter is with a band of displaced peasants (**commoner**) who no longer have settled homes. The reason might vary depending on the location: Keston still has a large population of peasants that were refugees from the Wilderlands Clan War; Eastreach Province and Aachen Province are slowly taxing their most vulnerable subjects into destruction; Exeter Province is no longer adequately protecting its rural population from the threats of monsters and banditry. Across the Borderlands, barons fight petty wars that destroy villages and crops, and everywhere there are scattered feudal masters who are tyrannical and unjust. Sometimes the remnants of entire villages are on the roads seeking homes or work.

Low-Risk Area: 1d6 landless peasants seeking work
Medium-Risk Area: 1d6 landless peasants with 1d2 wagons and 1d4 dogs (60%); otherwise, 1d100 peasants from an entirely destroyed hamlet or village are on the road with 1d4+1 wagons and 1d6 dogs.
High-Risk Area: 1d6 landless peasants
Extreme-Risk Area: pile of bones, no encounter

99. Wasp, Giant

Low-Risk Area: 1d3 **giant wasps**
Medium-Risk Area: 1d8 **giant wasps**
High-Risk Area: 1d6+3 **giant wasps**
Extreme-Risk Area: 1d10+3 **giant wasps**
Aerial encounters: 1d8 **giant wasps**

Wasp, Giant: AC 12; **HP** 13 (3d8); **Spd** 10ft, fly 50ft; **Melee** sting (+4, 1d6+2 piercing plus 3d6 poison, DC 11 Con half, at 0hp stable but paralyzed); **Str** +0, **Dex** +2, **Con** +0, **Int** −5, **Wis** +0, **Cha** −4; **AL** U; **CR** 1/2; **XP** 100.

100. Weasel, Giant

Low-Risk Area: 1 **giant weasel**
Medium-Risk Area: 1d4 **giant weasels**
High-Risk Area: 1d6 **giant weasels**
Extreme-Risk Area: 1d10 **giant weasels**

Weasel, Giant: AC 13; **HP** 9 (2d8); **Spd** 40ft; **Melee** bite (+5, 1d4+3 piercing); **Str** +0, **Dex** +3, **Con** +0, **Int** −3, **Wis** +1, **Cha** −3; **Skills** Perception +3, Stealth +5; **Senses** darkvision 60ft, keen hearing and smell; **AL** U; **CR** 1/8; **XP** 25.

101. Werewolf

Low-Risk Area: 1 **werewolf**
Medium-Risk Area: 1d4 **werewolves**
High-Risk Area: 1d10 **werewolves**
Extreme-Risk Area: 2d6 **werewolves**

Werewolf: AC 12; **HP** 58 (9d8+18); **Spd** 30ft, as wolf 40ft; **Melee** bite (+4, 1d8+2 piercing plus lycanthropy, DC 12 Con), claws (+4, 2d4+2 slashing); **SA** multiattack (bite, claws), shapechanger; **Immune** non-silver normal weapons; **Str** +2, **Dex** +1, **Con** +2, **Int** +0, **Wis** +0, **Cha** +0; **Skills** Perception +4, Stealth +3; **Senses** keen hearing and smell; **AL** CE; **CR** 3; **XP** 700.

102. Wight

Low-Risk Area: 1 **wight**
Medium-Risk Area: 1 **wight** (40%); otherwise, 1d4
High-Risk Area: 1 **wight** (10%); otherwise, 1d6
Extreme-Risk Area: 1d8 **wights**

Wight: AC 14; **HP** 45 (6d8+18); **Spd** 30ft; **Melee** touch (+4, 1d6+2 necrotic plus life drain, DC 13 Con or max hp reduction), longsword (+4, 1-H 1d8+2 or 2-H 1d10+2 slashing); **Ranged** longbow (+4, 150ft/600ft, 1d8+2 piercing); **SA** multiattack (longsword x2 or longsword, touch or longbow x2); **Immune** exhaustion, poison; **Resist** necrotic, non-silver normal weapons; **Str** +2, **Dex** +2, **Con** +3, **Int** +0, **Wis** +1, **Cha** +2; **Skills** Perception +3, Stealth +4; **Senses** darkvision 60ft; **Traits** sunlight sensitivity; **AL** NE; **CR** 3; **XP** 700.

103. Wild Horse or Pony

1d10+5 **wild horses** or **ponies**. If the encounter does not specify horses or ponies, roll to determine which type of animal (equal chance). These encounters are the same at all Risk Levels.

Horse, Wild: AC 10; **HP** 15 (2d10+4); **Spd** 60ft; **Melee** hooves (+3, 2d4+3 bludgeoning); **Str** +3, **Dex** +0, **Con** +2, **Int** −4, **Wis** +0, **Cha** −2; **AL** U; **CR** 1/4; **XP** 50.

Pony, Wild: AC 10; **HP** 11 (2d8+2); **Spd** 40ft; **Melee** hooves (+2, 2d4+2 bludgeoning); **Str** +2, **Dex** +0, **Con** +1, **Int** −4, **Wis** +0, **Cha** −2; **AL** U; **CR** 1/8; **XP** 25.

104. Witherstench

Unless specified on the encounter table, the encounter is with 1d2 **witherstenches**. The encounter does not vary by Risk Level.

Witherstench: AC 12; **HP** 1 (1d6−2); **Spd** 20ft; **Melee** claws (+4,

2 slashing); **Str** −2, **Dex** +2, **Con** −2, **Int** −4, **Wis** +0, **Cha** −4; **Senses** darkvision 60ft; **Traits** stench (30ft, incapacitated, DC 8 Con); **AL** U; **CR** 0; **XP** 10. (*Fifth Edition Foes* 249)

105. Wolverine, Giant

Low-Risk Area: 1 **giant wolverine**
Medium-Risk Area: 1 **giant wolverine** (75%); otherwise, 2 **giant wolverines**
High-Risk Area: 1d4 **giant wolverines**
Extreme-Risk Area: 1d6 **giant wolverines**

Wolverine, Giant: AC 15; **HP** 51 (6d10+18); **Spd** 30ft, climb 10ft; **Melee** claws (+6, 2d10+4 slashing), bite (1d8+4 piercing); **SA** multiattack (claws, bite); **Str** +4, **Dex** +3, **Con** +3; **Int** −4, **Wis** +1, **Cha** +0; **Skills** Athletics +6, Perception +5; **Senses** keen smell; **Traits** rage (on next turn after damage, tactical advantage on Str checks and saves, resist weapon damage); **AL** U; **CR** 4; **XP** 1100.

106. Wolf

Low-Risk Area: 1d6 **wolves**
Medium-Risk Area: Roll 1d6:

1–3	1d12+1 **wolves**
4–5	1d6+1 **wolves** and 1 **worg**
6	1d10+1 **wolves** and 1d2 **worgs**

High-Risk Area: 1d10+1 **wolves** and 1d4 **worgs**
Extreme-Risk Area: 3d6 **wolves** and 1d6 **worgs**

Wolf: AC 13; **HP** 11 (2d8+2); **Spd** 40ft; **Melee** bite (+4, 2d4+2 piercing plus knock prone, DC 11 Str); **Str** +1, **Dex** +2, **Con** +1, **Int** −4, **Wis** +1, **Cha** −2; **Skills** Perception +3, Stealth +4; **Senses** keen hearing and smell; **Traits** pack tactics; **AL** U; **CR** 1/4; **XP** 50.

Worg: AC 13; **HP** 26 (4d10+4); **Spd** 50ft; **Melee** bite (+5, 2d6+3 piercing plus knock prone, DC 13 Str); **Str** +3, **Dex** +1, **Con** +1, **Int** −2, **Wis** +0, **Cha** −1; **Skills** Perception +4; **Senses** darkvision 60ft, keen hearing and smell; **AL** NE; **CR** 1/2; **XP** 100.

107. Wizard

Road Encounters are with a mage (9th level), with a retinue (unless stated otherwise in the encounter tables). Airborne encounters with a high mage (11th level). Mages are not ordinarily encountered in the wilderness unless they are flying over it.

Road Encounters
1d4+5 **cavalry**
1d3 wagons (50%); otherwise, 1d4 peasants (**commoner**) carrying huge packs of the wizard's baggage

1d3 servants (**commoner**)
1 bodyguard (**sergeant**)
1 **mage** on road

Airborne Encounter
High Mage (11th)

Commoner: AC 10; **HP** 4 (1d8); **Spd** 30ft; **Melee** club (+2, 1d4 bludgeoning); **Str** +0, **Dex** +0, **Con** +0; **Int** +0, **Wis** +0, **Cha** +0; **AL** any; **CR** 0; **XP** 10.

Cavalry: AC 16; **HP** 22 (4d8+4); **Spd** 30ft; **Melee** lance (+3, 10ft, 1d10+1 piercing); **Ranged** shortbow (+3, 80ft/320ft, 1d6+1 piercing); **Str** +1, **Dex** +1, **Con** +1; **Int** +0, **Wis** +0, **Cha** +0; **AL** LN; **CR** 1/4; **XP** 50

High Mage: AC 12 (15 with *mage armor*); **HP** 49 (11d8); **Spd** 30ft; **Melee** dagger (+5, 1d4+2 piercing); **SA** spells (Int +7, 11th, DC 15); **Str** −1, **Dex** +2, **Con** +0, **Int** +4 (+7), **Wis** +2 (+5), **Cha** +0; **Skills** Arcana +7, History +7; **AL** any; **CR** 6; **XP** 2300.
  Spells (slots): 0 (at will)—*fire bolt, light, mage hand, prestidigitation;* 1st (4)—*detect magic, mage armor, magic missile, shield;* 2nd (3)—*misty step, suggestion;* 3rd (3)—*counterspell, fireball, fly;* 4th (3)—*greater invisibility, ice storm;* 5th (1)—*cone of cold.*

Mage: AC 12 (15 with *mage armor*); **HP** 40 (9d8); **Spd** 30ft; **Melee** dagger (+5, 1d4+2 piercing); **SA** spells (Int +6, 9th, DC 14); **Str** −1, **Dex** +2, **Con** +0, **Int** +3 (+6), **Wis** +1 (+4), **Cha** +0; **Skills** Arcana +6, History +6; **AL** any; **CR** 6; **XP** 2300.
  Spells (slots): 0 (at will)—*fire bolt, light, mage hand, prestidigitation;* 1st (4)—*detect magic, mage armor, magic missile, shield;* 2nd (3)—*misty step, suggestion;* 3rd (3)—*counterspell, fireball, fly;* 4th (3)—*greater invisibility, ice storm;* 5th (1)—*cone of cold.*

Sergeant: AC 17; **HP** 32 (5d8+10); **Spd** 30ft; **Melee** longsword (+4, 1d8+2 slashing); **Ranged** longbow (+4, 150ft/600ft, 1d8+2 piercing); **SA** multiattack (longsword x2 or longbow x2); **Str** +2, **Dex** +2, **Con** +2; **Int** +0, **Wis** +1, **Cha** +1; **Skills** Perception +3, Intimidation +3; **AL** LN; **CR** 1/2; **XP** 100.

108. Wyvern

Low-Risk Area: 1 **wyvern**
Medium-Risk Area: 1d2 **wyverns** (50%); otherwise, 1d6
High-Risk Area: 1d6 **wyverns**
Extreme-Risk Area: 1d8 **wyverns**

Wyvern: AC 13; **HP** 110 (13d10+39); **Spd** 20ft, fly 80ft; **Melee** bite (+7, 10ft, 2d6+4 piercing), claws (+7, 2d8+4 slashing), stinger (+7, 10ft, 2d6+4 piercing plus 7d6 poison, DC 15 Con half); **SA** multiattack (bite, stinger or in flight, claws for one attack); **Str** +4, **Dex** +0, **Con** +3, **Int** −3, **Wis** +1, **Cha** −2; **Skills** Perception +4; **Senses** darkvision 60ft; **AL** U; **CR** 6; **XP** 2300.

Appendix D: Flying Encounters

Mid-level and some higher-level characters will travel the Borderland Provinces by road, which is generally faster and safer than overland travel through the wilderness. Higher-level characters might choose to travel as the crow flies, winging their way through the skies as a shortcut from place to place. We've provided encounter tables for roads in the main part of the book, since the encounters are often specific to the territory the characters are moving through. The dangers of the sky, however, are less connected to politics or terrain than what characters encounter along a road. Instead, flying monsters have much broader territories, and the sky has no physical barriers (such as mountains or forests), so the skies tend to be more similar across wide areas than the land. Thus, airborne encounters anywhere in the Borderland Provinces may be determined using the tables below.

Quick-use "Rules" for Airborne Travel

These "rules" are intended as a way of abstracting whatever your game-system's rules for flying might be. They are not a binding or an official part of the **Lost Lands** campaign world; they are just a method for simplifying any official flying rules to make things go faster, designed to work with the scale of the Borderland Provinces map.

Base Speeds

Base speed depends purely on the motive force behind the travel: the mode of propulsion. These numbers are abstract, of course, and may be modified to reflect the nature of an unusually constructed craft. Note that base speeds do not depend on a craft's wind resistance or ability to take advantage of sails in high winds.

Magically propelled travel (e.g., a carpet, broom, flying spell, etc.):	25 miles per hour
Physically propelled travel (e.g., winged mounts, winged characters):	10 miles per hour
Wind-driven conveyances (e.g., blimp, airborne sailing-ship):	5 miles per hour

Wind Effect on Base Speed

To determine wind effects, roll on the table below each hour. Note that all base wind speeds are divisible by five.

01–05	Very strong headwinds. Travel is one-fifth normal speed for magic and physical propulsion; no forward progress possible for wind-driven conveyances.
06–10	Strong headwinds reduce speed to two-fifths normal speed; one-fifth for wind-driven craft
11–25	Minor headwinds reduce speed to four-fifths normal speed; three-fifths for wind-driven craft
26–30	Calm. Lack of any measurable wind has no effect on magically powered or physically powered travel, but wind-driven craft are becalmed and cannot move.
31–75	Winds vary; average base speed during travel is unaffected
76–80	Tailwinds increase speed by two-fifths; three-fifths for wind-driven craft
85–95	Strong tailwinds increase speed by four-fifths, and increase the base speed for wind-driven craft to two and one-fifth of normal.
96–00	Very strong tailwinds increase speed by 100% for magic and physically powered travel, and quadruple the base speed of wind-powered vehicles.

Note: For purposes of simplicity, the rules assume that minor use of sails ("I'm holding out a sheet to increase my magic carpet's speed in the wind!") have no measurable effect unless they are *quite* significant. Significant use of sails on a magically powered craft allow the craft to use the better of the two speeds, not the cumulative effect of both wind and magic.

Other Considerations

Fast-moving travel on a flying carpet or other magical conveyance can cause great discomfort over time if the character is not shielded from the wind of movement at 20 miles per hour or more without some sort of windscreen. Goggles are advisable. This possibility is listed as a hazard on the encounter tables.

Secondly, it is worth remembering that winged mounts get exhausted just as ordinary mounts become tired in the course of land travel. It is actually possible to ride a mount to the point of injury, although most mounts (horse-types being the main exception) will not allow themselves to be ridden to the point of death. Assume that a flying mount smaller than a roc or dragon must rest for an hour after every four hours of travel.

Encounter Tables

The tables below are divided based on altitude and terrain. There are only two possibilities for each: (1) high and low altitude, and (2) normal or mountainous terrain. Low-altitude is a simple question of whether the characters are flying above or below the cloud level, and the only terrain-type that really affects the danger of flying is mountain ranges.

Encounter Chance

Check for an encounter once per hour traveled. Encounter type and likelihood is the same regardless of altitude.

Normal Terrain (all non-mountain)	Mountains	Result
01–70	01–60	No encounter
71–90	61–80	Hazard
91–00	81–00	Encounter

Hazards

If the result is "Hazard," roll on the appropriate table below (Mountainous Terrain or Non-Mountainous Terrain).

Hazards for Non-Mountainous Flight

Die Roll High Altitude	Die Roll Low Altitude	Result
01–05	01–05	Flock of Geese
n/a	06–16	Precipitation (general)
06–30	16–35	Uncertain Navigation
31–50	n/a	Lost!
51–70	36–45	Turbulence, Major
71–00	46–00	Turbulence, Minor

Hazards for Mountain Flight

Die Roll High Altitude	Die Roll Low Altitude	Result
n/a	01–05	Flock of Geese
01–30	06–25	Uncertain Navigation
n/a	26–50	Precipitation, snow
n/a	51–55	Precipitation, hail
31–40	56–60	Lost!
41–50	61–75	Turbulence, Major
51–00	76–00	Turbulence, Minor

Description of Hazards

Flock of Geese: Flocks of geese are the bane of airborne travelers. The stupid things can fly right into you, and impacts can be quite dangerous.

Uncertain Navigation: This can occur when the countryside below fails to offer good landmarks, or produces confusing landmarks. The hazard may be ignored *only* if the characters are following the edge of a mountain range: even forests, rivers, and hills can produce confusing patterns. Roll 1d6 to determine if the characters have become Lost, adding 2 to the die roll if the characters are above the clouds, 1 if they are flying extremely high, and subtracting 1 if the characters are following specific landmarks such as a river or a forest edge.

1–4	Not lost, no problem, just a moment of concern
5–6	Lost (see description of "Lost!")

Lost: Oops. It's not always easy to navigate from the air, especially if you were over the cloud level. It can even happen if you're trying to trace natural contours. Fortunately, if you can fly, it isn't nearly as difficult to regain your bearings as it is for travelers on the ground. Getting lost while traveling by air simply means that the characters lose 1 hour of useful travel time if they have a map and a compass, 2 hours if they have only a map or compass, or 3 hours if they are traveling without the benefit of either navigational tool.

Precipitation (General): The characters are flying into either rain or snow, depending on the season. Travel cannot continue below the clouds, and if they wish to proceed, they must fly above the clouds, immediately rolling another encounter check when they ascend. They also have a 10% chance to become Lost.

Precipitation (Hail): A sudden hailstorm causes 1d6+1 hit points of damage to everyone and everything flying through it. Further progress is impossible unless the characters ascend above the clouds, immediately making another encounter check.

Precipitation (Snow): The characters are flying into snowfall. Travel cannot continue below the clouds, and if the characters wish to proceed, they must ascend above the clouds, immediately rolling another encounter check when they ascend. They also have a 25% chance to become Lost in the process.

Turbulence (Major): Major turbulence creates a 25% chance of becoming Lost, and each flying character must make a saving throw at –4 or become seasick. A seasick character cannot function other than throwing up, but can descend to the ground for a rest of 1 hour, or keep going while otherwise helpless. The character remains seasick until resting on the ground for an hour, even after the turbulence is left behind. Further, if a character is holding an item in hand (such as a map or compass), there is a 10% chance (per such item) that it is torn out of the character's hands and blown away.

Turbulence (Minor): Minor turbulence creates a 5% chance of becoming Lost, and each flying character must make a saving throw or become seasick. A seasick character cannot function other than throwing up, but can descend to the ground for a rest of 1 hour, or keep going while otherwise helpless. The character remains seasick until resting on the ground for an hour, even after the turbulence is left behind.

Encounters

Non-Mountain Airborne Encounters

High Altitude	Low Altitude
01–05: Air Elemental (Encounter #1)	**01–02:** Air Elemental (Encounter #1)
06–11: Blood Hawk (Encounter #12)	**03–06:** Assassin Bug (Encounter #5)
12–16: Chimera (Encounter #18)	**07–10:** Blood Hawk (Encounter #12)
17–20: Couatl (Encounter #23)	**11–13:** Chimera (Encounter #18)
21: Cloud Giant Tower (Encounter #20)	**14–17:** Couatl (Encounter #23)
22–23: Djinni (Encounter #25)	**18–19:** Corpse Rook (Encounter #22)
24–30: Dragon B (Encounter #28)	**20–21:** Djinni (Encounter #25)
31–40: Eagle, Giant (Encounter #33)	**22–26:** Dragon B (Encounter #28)
41–50: Griffon (Encounter #47)	**27–28:** Drake, Fire (Encounter #30)
51–55: Hippogriff (Encounter #54)	**29–31:** Eagle, Giant (Encounter #33)
56–60: Mantari (Encounter #62)	**32–36:** Gargoyle (Encounter #38)
61–65: Ogre Mage (Encounter #70)	**37–46:** Griffon (Encounter #47)
66–75: Pegasus (Encounter #75)	**47–53:** Hippogriff (Encounter #54)
75–83: Roc (Encounter #81)	**54–56:** Mantari (Encounter #62)
84–85: Wizard (Encounter #107)	**57–66:** Manticore (Encounter #63)
86–00: Wyvern (Encounter #108)	**67:** Ogre Mage (Encounter #70)
	68–74: Pegasus (Encounter #75)
	75–77: Roc (Encounter #81)
	78–83: Wasp, Giant (Encounter #99)
	84: Wizard (Encounter #107)
	85–00: Wyvern (Encounter #108)

207

Mountain Airborne Encounters

High Altitude	Low Altitude
01–08: Air Elemental (Encounter #1)	**01–03:** Air Elemental (Encounter #1)
09–14: Blood Hawk (Encounter #12)	**04–09:** Blood Hawk (Encounter #12)
15–21: Chimera (Encounter #18)	**10–16:** Chimera (Encounter #18)
22–26: Couatl (Encounter #23)	**17–21:** Couatl (Encounter #23)
27: Cloud Giant Tower (Encounter #20)	**22:** Djinni (Encounter #25)
28–29: Djinni (Encounter #25)	**20–27:** Dragon C (Encounter #29)
30–40: Dragon C (Encounter #29)	**28–29:** Drake, Fire (Encounter #30)
41–50: Eagle, Giant (Encounter #33)	**30–36:** Eagle, Giant (Encounter #33)
51–60: Griffon (Encounter #47)	**37–42:** Gargoyle (Encounter #38)
61–64: Hippogriff (Encounter #54)	**43–53:** Griffon (Encounter #47)
65: Mantari (Encounter #62)	**54–59:** Hippogriff (Encounter #54)
66–70: Ogre Mage (Encounter #70)	**60–65:** Mantari (Encounter #62)
71: Pegasus (Encounter #75)	**66–75:** Manticore (Encounter #63)
72–85: Roc (Encounter #81)	**76:** Ogre mage (Encounter #70)
86: Wizard (Encounter #107)	**77:** Pegasus (Encounter #75)
87–00: Wyvern (Encounter #108)	**78–83:** Roc (Encounter #81)
	84–85: Wasp, Giant (Encounter #99)
	86–00: Wyvern (Encounter #108)

Appendix E: Night Encounters

To keep things simple, there is a single table for Night Encounters across the Borderland Provinces. Night tends to be its own "place." Roll once per night.

Night Encounter Chance

Road (camped out)	Wilderness	Result
01–85	01–75	No encounter
86–00	76–00	Encounter

Night Encounters

1d100	Encounter
01–15	Ant (Encounter #4)
16–25	Badger (Encounter #6)
26–40	Bat (Encounter #10)
41–42	Demon (Encounter #24)
43–50	Goblin (Encounter #45)
51	Gray Ooze (Encounter #46)
52–53	Hag (Encounter #48)
54–60	Hamster (Encounter #49)
61–65	Lycanthrope (Encounter #61)
66–68	Owlbear (Encounter #72)
69	Shambling Mound (Encounter #84)
70–76	Stirge (Encounter #88)
77–78	Tangtal (Encounter #89)
79–80	Treant (Encounter #91)
81–86	Troll (Encounter #92)
87–90	Undead A (Encounter #94)
91–93	Undead B (Encounter #95)
94	Undead C (Encounter #96)
95–00	Witherstench (Encounter #104)

Appendix F: New Monsters

Beetle, Oxen

XP 200 (CR 1)
Unaligned Large beast
Init +0

DEFENSE
AC 14
HP 60 (8d10+16)

OFFENSE
Speed 20ft
Melee gore (+6, 2d8+4 piercing)

STATISTICS
Str 18 (+4), **Dex** 10 (+0), **Con** 15 (+2),
Int 1 (–5), **Wis** 10 (+0), **Cha** 9 (+0)
Languages none

ECOLOGY
Environment temperate
Organization solitary, pair, or cluster (1d6)

Oxen beetles are domesticated giant beetles raised only in the town of Beetlebridge in the Gaelon River Valley, and in a few other places that have obtained breeding stock from the Beetlebridgers over the years. The beetles are massive creatures standing 6ft tall and 10ft long, with a dull black and red carapace. At least one horn protrudes from an oxen beetle's head, often more. The curving horns can be used as weapons, but the townsfolk of Beetlebridge have trained most aggression out of the bloodline, and the beetles only use their natural weapons in self-defense against predators.

The beetles are used as draft animals in the area around Beetlebridge, for they are long-lived, sturdy, and strong, not to mention that predators such as wyverns and manticores find them dangerous and unappetizing. Oxen beetles are far less intelligent than other draft animals, so they have not supplanted mules, oxen, and horses even in the area around Beetlebridge itself. Most villages need no more than one of the hulking beasts to handle the heavy work.

Oxen beetles eat grass, trees, and occasionally rocks, so they are as economical as other farm animals; very occasionally, one of them eats a pig, and the townsfolk of Beetlebridge are still trying to breed out this one inconvenient trait.

Kenckoo

XP 50 (CR 1/4)
CN Medium humanoid (kenckoo)
Init +3

DEFENSE
AC 13
HP 13 (3d8)
Immune charm

OFFENSE
Speed 30ft
Melee shortsword (+5, 1d6+3 piercing)
Ranged shortbow (+5, 80ft/320ft, 1d6+3 piercing)

STATISTICS
Str 10 (+0), **Dex** 16 (+3), **Con** 10 (+0),
Int 11 (+0), **Wis** 10 (+0), **Cha** 10 (+0)
Languages understand Auran and Common, speak only through mimicry
Skills Deception +4, Perception +2, Stealth +5

TRAITS
Ambusher Tactical advantage on attack against any creature surprised.
Mimicry Any sounds heard including voices. A creature can tell heard sounds are imitations with a successful DC 14 Wis (Insight) check.

ECOLOGY
Environment temperate mountains or urban
Organization solitary, pair, or conspiracy (3d4)

A human-sized creature resembling a crow, with feathers and a cruel beak. It has no wings, and is dressed in the worn cloak and hood of a traveler, but without shoes to cover its clawed bird-feet.

The kenckoo are flightless, avian humanoids who often live at the borders of civilization, and occasionally venture into towns or cities as traders (or thieves). They tend to be capricious and unpredictable in their actions, and they are very much willing to take advantage of others. As a result, they are not much liked or trusted by anyone.

Kenckoo do not have souls; they have spirits that are reborn in later kenckoo at some point after they die. They do not remember their prior lives, but their spirit-nature does have some influence on their material reality. They are immune to charms and mental domination, and also cannot be magically forced to sleep. Moreover, they have an unerring ability to mimic sound, like a mockingbird or parrot. Conversing with them is a bit bizarre, since they learn language by precise mimicry. Their speech is a jumble of different voices delivered exactly in the voice and tenor of the person from whom the kenckoo learned it: usually entire quotes they have heard, which seem to apply to the situation. As a result, a kenckoo usually seems to be switching back and forth between the voices of several different people while talking, with strange pauses, inflections, and often entire quotations that might or might not be exactly what the tengu means to convey. From its speech alone, it is virtually impossible to tell a kenckoo's emotions or detect if it is lying: A kenckoo delivers a sentence in exactly the same pattern of mimicry whether it is furious, sorrowful, sincere, or lying through its teeth (beak, actually). It is equally difficult to tell if a kenckoo's sentence is a statement or a question.

Hence, conversations like the following are the norm for ordinary kenckoo. For example, if they meet some characters on the road, and want to join them to the next village:

Kenckoo (monotone): "We come along yes."
Character: "What?"
Kenckoo (cheerfully): "Let's go, children, time for temple!"
Character: "You want to go with us?"
Kenckoo (monotone): "We come along yes."
Character: "No thieving, or we'll string you up by the side of the road."
Kenckoo (pompous): "You wound me, sir. I am utterly innocent of these charges."
Character: "Fine, you can come along."
Kenckoo (cheerfully): "Let's go, children, time for temple!"

The bizarre kenckoo speech lulls some people into assuming that the kenckoo is foolish or unperceptive. To the contrary, kenckoo are *extraordinarily* good at reading other peoples' emotions and meaning; they simply cannot express their own in human speech. Among themselves, kenckoo communicate with very subtle chirrups and mimicked sounds. The language is difficult to learn, and impossible for anyone (other than a bird) to actually reproduce the required sounds.

Occasionally one encounters kenckoo of higher social rank, or who are experienced adventurers with years of wandering. These kenckoo are usually of 6 hit dice, and have the abilities of a thief of sixth level. They are also usually much better at ordinary speech, having learned a wider variety of quotes and words.

A final note: Kenckoo originate in Japanese mythology, but the ones in the Borderland Provinces are culturally similar to the regions where they live; they do not have a pseudo-Japanese culture

Yak-beast

XP 100 (CR 1)
Unaligned Large beast
Init +0

___

DEFENSE
AC 13
HP 51 (6d10+18)

___

OFFENSE
Speed 20ft
Melee gore (+6, 2d8+4 piercing)

___

STATISTICS
Str 18 (+4), **Dex** 10 (+0), **Con** 16 (+3),
Int 2(–4), **Wis** 10 (+0), **Cha** 9 (+0)
Languages none

___

ECOLOGY
Environment temperate
Organization solitary, pair, or cluster (1d6)

___

Yak-beasts are massive bovine creatures used in the Borderland Provinces as draft beasts or pack animals where they are often referred to as great-oxen. Technically, since they are bovine draft animals, they could be described accurately as an ordinary ox, but they are quite different from ordinary cows and bulls. Their legs are proportionally longer, which gives them the illusion of being spindly, even though the legs are actually thicker than those of even the largest ordinary ox.

These shaggy-haired creatures have twisted horns that curve gracefully in an hourglass shape over the head, much more like goat horns than cow horns. The creatures are not aggressive, although they can use their horns to defend themselves; their only natural enemies are the very large flying predators such as dragons, manticores, and rocs.

Yak-beasts are commonly used throughout the provinces to pull plows and wagons, or to carry large packs. They can be used as riding beasts, but they are not suitable as battle-mounts due to their temperaments: They are inherently non-aggressive, and usually respond to stress by planting themselves in a defensive posture and refusing to move.

Appendix G: Legendary Relics and Artifacts

The Borderland Provinces have long been the battleground of distant powers: a disputed territory, both in the battles of divine and demonic beings, and also in the affairs of foreign empires. Heroes, villains, saints, and demons have died here, leaving their mark in legend. Moreover, they have, in some cases, left behind relics of themselves; or items of great power they carried in life, and lost in death.

Other than a couple of exceptions, the items described in this **Appendix** are truly lost; they are not specifically placed, and it is up to the GM to determine their location.

Staff of Zaroun the Quintessential ("Copperhead")

Legendary Staff (requires attunement by a sorcerer, warlock, or wizard)

History

Zaroun the Quintessential was one of the previous inhabitants of Tatterdemalion's Manse in the Gaelon River Valley. An archmage of legend, Zaroun had become weak with age and the loss of his magical staff weakened him further in the years before his death. Since it was a year or more before anyone knew of Zaroun's death in the tower, no one knows where the staff went. It was not found with the archmage's skeleton.

According to various commentaries, the staff is a six-foot length of blue-tinged wood topped by a copper ball and painted with a small number of runes at the top. Originally, the staff was called "*Copperhead*," and a shaman of the lizardfolk apparently first enchanted it with magic perhaps two hundred years ago in the Gaelon River Valley along one of the river's many tributaries. A group of dwarves subsequently destroyed the lair of these lizard men in the year 3374, but did not keep the staff, selling it to a trader in the free city of Mirquinoc. The trader in turn sold it to a warlock named Vendicar Goyne, at that time a resident of Troye in the Duchy of the Rampart. According to the tales, Goyne made a journey into the Yolbiac Vale with three other unknown individuals with whom he climbed to the top of one of the Cretian Mountain peaks and summoned an oni-spirit (an ogre mage) known as Azurbol. After a two-day conflict of wills in the high snow, Goyne managed to force the spirit's consciousness into the staff and bind it.

At some point in the year 3389, Goyne disappeared on a second expedition into the Yolbiac Vale, and *Copperhead* disappeared from history until Zaroun the Perennial (later to call himself Zaroun the Quintessential) purchased it from the warden of Endhome's prisons. Zaroun later established himself in his manse, now called the Manse of Tatterdemalion, and later died, at which point the staff was lost to all knowledge.

Nature

The staff contains and binds the spirit of Azurbol the oni-spirit (an ogre mage), lending the item a degree of malicious intelligence. It can hold a maximum of 10 charges, expended as the staff's powers are invoked. If the staff is ever reduced to zero charges, the imprisoned spirit is freed on 1 on a d20 and the staff becomes nothing more than an ordinary wooden staff. Its charge-expending powers may be used only by a wizard, although the staff's poisonous properties take effect if an assassin or one of the lizardfolk wields it. The staff regains 1d6+4 charges daily at dawn.

Powers
Constant

Copperhead's original enchantment by the lizardfolk shaman gives it the ability to poison an opponent with a successful hit. The poison takes effect if the target fails a DC 15 Con, but does not kill instantly. The victim holds on to life for a maximum period of 6 days. Each day the victim gains a level of exhaustion. During this time, the character is unable to manage serious physical exertion such as climbing a rope or carrying any particularly heavy weight. Rest will not remove the exhaustion. It can only be removed by a *greater restoration* but may require multiple castings. The staff's poisonous qualities require no charges to use.

The wielder can mentally communicate with the spirit Azurbol at any time. Azurbol's advice is usually poorly thought out and tends toward violent solutions, but the ogre mage shows occasional flashes of insight, especially in matters of tactics, believable lies, and avoiding fire. Occasionally the staff intrudes on the wielder's mind to offer such suggestions, but only if the spirit is concerned that its staff might be destroyed.

Expenditure of One Charge

Expending a single charge from the staff allows one of the following 3 uses:

Goblin Servitors: The staff summons forth two goblins from thin air, both of them utterly under the control of the staff's wielder. They remain in the staff's service until they die, or until the staff's wielder dismisses them.

Flight: The staff casts a *fly* spell upon any target (saving throw allowed if the target tries to resist). The spell remains in place for so long as the wielder concentrates upon maintaining it.

Spirit Link: The staff lends the wielder all the physical and magical powers of the oni spirit trapped within it, to the extent that they are superior or additional to the staff-wielder's own capabilities. Thus, the wielder would be able to fly, would have the maximum hit points of an ogre mage (if higher than the wielder's own), and would be able to use an ogre-mage's innate magical powers in addition to the wielder's own magic. The wielder also takes on the appearance and full size of an ogre mage while using this power. There is a risk involving the use of this power, however: The spirit of the staff has a cumulative 1% chance per round (e.g., 2% in the second round, 3% in the third, etc.) to possess the wielder, temporarily imprisoning the wielder's consciousness in the staff while the spirit is in control of the body. If this happens, the oni-spirit remains in possession of the body for 1d6+2 rounds before the wielder manages to cast out the spirit and regain control of the situation. Note: If the wielder is 4th level or higher, apply a –4 modifier to the spirit's percentage chance to gain control; if the wielder is 8th level or higher, apply a –6 modifier.

Expenditure of Two Charges

Expending 2 charges from the staff allows the use of one of the following 2 powers:

Cone of Cold: The staff casts *cone of cold* as per the spell.

Regeneration: The staff causes a lost limb or other permanent physical damage to *regenerate* for the next person touched by the copper ball at the top of the staff. A person may not be raised from the dead by the use of this power.

Mace of St. Jorb

Legendary Weapon (mace) (requires attunement)

History

The *Mace of St. Jorb* is an artifact last seen in the year 3507, when it was lost during the Wilderness Clan War in Keston Province. St. Jorb was a follower of Mithras, the Hyperborean god of soldiers. Jorb's date of birth is uncertain; he was enrolled as a warrior-acolyte in the Temple of Mithras at Kingston in the year 3318. In 3322, he departed the city as chaplain to a company of soldiers bound northward to guard the borders of the Duchy of the Rampart. Along the South Road where it runs close to the foothills of the Meridians, the soldiers came upon a huge dragon with a broken wing, its scales black as night and its jaws dripping with acid. Presumably, the dragon had somehow injured itself in flight and was making its way back to its mountain lair on foot, but the soldiers could see that it was headed toward a small hamlet near the road where a few peasants armed with pitchforks were huddled together in some futile attempt to protect their crops and livestock. The company of soldiers fell back in horror and fear as the dragon moved sinuously toward the anticipated slaughter, ignoring the lightly armed troop that clearly offered no serious threat to its progress.

As many of the soldiers fled before the dragon's evil gaze, Jorb stepped forward and invoked the name of Mithras, calling upon the god to grant him strength to protect the brave villagers defending their hearth and home. The terrified cleric advanced to do battle with the great wyrm, and it turned to face him, chuckling at the temerity of this feeble, lonely opponent. As Jorb drew near, the dragon opened its massive jaws and spewed forth a gout of acid, enveloping the cleric in a maelstrom of deadly corrosion. By all accounts submitted later to the Temple of Mithras in Reme, Jorb walked forward through the dragon's breath untouched, glowing with sudden light, to smash his mace against the dragon's head. On seeing this, the Kestoner soldiers rallied and swarmed forward to help their cleric, killing the dragon by force of numbers. Later legend simplified the event to recount that the dragon died at the single blow, but the account in the annals at Reme spell out the facts more clearly. It is still apparent that the final killing blow that laid the dragon low came from Jorb's mace.

After slaying the dragon, Jorb was assigned by his superiors to the command of a small, fortified chapel in the southern Wilderland Hills. There, the cleric performed numerous other miracles in defense of civilization, pushing back the barbarians and other fell creatures of these deadly highlands and keeping villagers safe from harm for many years (see, "Ruined Chapel of St. Jorb" in Exeter Province). Jorb died in the year 3372, and was canonized as a minor saint by the temple of Mithras in Reme shortly thereafter. His mace was brought to Kingston as a relic, and resided in the temple there until the beginning of the Wilderlands Clan War. In the desperation of that crisis, the clerics of Mithras removed the mace from its reliquary and ceremoniously assigned it to the hands of High Priest Kerinn Luadh, a fierce and famous cleric of Mithras. At the head of a column of Mithraic volunteers, Luadh set forth to the seething battlegrounds of the distant war. The column never arrived, and eventually their remains were discovered surrounding a ruined village that had been razed to the ground by hillfolk raiders, miles behind the shifting battle lines of the ruinous conflict. The heads and left hands of the soldiers had been removed, much as the Vanigoth tribes take trophies. Luadh's body was found at the center of the village, with skeletons piled around it, but the mace was gone along with most of the other weapons and armor of the soldiers.

It is worthy of note that the Vanigoths of Aen Vani take trophies from the dead, but they traditionally remove the right hand rather than the left, which throws any kind of search for the mace into a slight conundrum. Perhaps the historian recounting the discovery of the bodies recorded his facts incorrectly. Perhaps the Vanigoths altered their ordinary practices for some reason at this battle. Perhaps some other group of barbarians tried to implicate the Vanigoths. Perhaps a different Vanigothic tribe, one with trophy-taking traditions only slightly different from the Vanigoths of Aen Vani, fought the battle. Any characters seeking to recover the mace are confronted with all these possibilities.

The Mace

The mace can only be effectively wielded by a cleric or paladin of Good alignment, and if anyone of Evil alignment takes hold of it, the mace inflicts 3d6 radiant damage to such person.

When held in the wielder's hand, the mace grants magic resistance to the wielder against any spell (or similar supernatural ability) coming from an Evil creature. This mace when hitting a creature of Evil alignment does an extra 3d6 radiant damage. If the target has 50 hit points or fewer after taking this damage, it must succeed on a DC 20 Wis save or become frightened until the end of your next turn.

In addition to its other powers, the mace can cast *cure wounds* twice per day.

Ormoulande

Legendary Wondrous Item

History

The *Ormoulande* is a magic mirror supposedly used by the Count of Toullen and the Lord-Governor of Keston Province to coordinate their secession from the Kingdoms of Foere (see **Chapter 10: Toullen Province**). It allows two specific people to see and hear each other in particular mirrors across a great distance. The *Ormoulande* was originally crafted by the mage Aulndisc, a mysterious figure who served as advisor to Overking Graeltor in the years following the Overking's coronation in 3207. Aulndisc disappeared from the overking's court in 3216, and resurfaced, or at least someone claiming to be him arrived, in the city of Vermis in the year 3218. The mage departed from Vermis in 3221 in the company of three cloaked figures and was never seen again. At some unknown time, the Count of Toullen purchased the *Ormoulande* and it remained in the comital family until a thief known as Morwin stole it from the palace. As with Morwin's other thefts, the stolen mirror was replaced with a crescent of gold left behind in the empty space where the heavily guarded mirror had stood.

The mirror has not been seen or heard of since its theft from the Count's palace in Tertry.

Appearance

According to records dating back to the reign of Catrebrasse II, the last Count of Toullen to hold the mirror, it is a large oval of green stone, 5ft tall, carved with grotesque faces all around the edge. The mirror surface inside the oval is filled with what looks like shifting clouds until its owner speaks the command word to bring the mirror into a state of awareness.

Nature

The *Ormoulande* is an intelligent magic item, and can speak aloud when it chooses to do so. It is proud and haughty, and makes snide remarks to any owner that is not a member of the nobility. For various reasons, the spirit trapped within the *Ormoulande* will be plunged into hideous tortures in the Underworld if the mirror is ever broken, so it becomes extremely nervous if its physical housing is threatened.

Powers

The *Ormoulande* can "capture" a normal mirror if they are brought in contact and the owner of the *Ormoulande* speaks a word of command engraved at the bottom of the *Ormoulande's* shining surface. Once the other mirror is captured, the two mirrors can be used to communicate at great distances. It appears from legends and old records that the range of the *Ormoulande's* power is roughly 500 miles.

Appendix H: Heresies

The Nature of Heresy

As noted in the side box in the Introduction, the Borderland Provinces are plagued with heresies. There is no doubt this phenomenon is on the rise ever since the Kingdom of Foere began to withdraw from the region, since the empire's retreat has caused great instability and doubt even in the Provinces that still pay allegiance to the Overking.

Heresies seem to spring up from nowhere, and they are difficult to stamp out once they begin. These aberrant doctrines seem to take on a life of their own, spreading like wildfire through a peasant population that is hungry for stability and reassurance. Unfortunately, heretical beliefs and practices are actually badly damaging, seriously eroding the capabilities of Lawful and good temples to assist the very people who need help the most.

It is well known that the proper rituals of ordinary prayer, devotions, and sacrifices support a deity's power in some unfathomable way. This is why temples provide specific prayers, methods for sacred rituals, and educated leaders to conduct religious services, all of which support the deity (or deities) they venerate. By the same token, however, departing significantly from the proper rituals can render them completely ineffectual. Indeed, some apparently minor changes to important prayers or practices can actually divert the power of the rituals to another being such as a demon prince or a different god entirely.

Lesser Heresy

Even the most minor of heresies, doctrinal errors that do nothing other than divert people from offering meaningful support to the deity, can badly damage a faith. Such heresies can catch on and become popular misinterpretations, especially in the rural countryside where they may fester undiscovered for a long time before the clerics of the god learn of their existence. By diverting worshippers from the productive rituals of a god, and confusing others about which rituals are actually the proper ones, these minor heresies can be quite destructive to a religion. Rather than focusing on spiritual matters, the temples are forced to respond to a rapidly growing community of lost worshippers.

Innocent followers of a Lesser Heresy are generally considered to be retrievable if they recant their heretical beliefs. Most temples send reformed heretics on penitentiary pilgrimages, or put them through some sort of purification or punishment to cleanse the taint of heresy from them. The actual leaders and preachers of a Lesser Heresy can also be retrieved if they recant, but as a practical matter, they are usually firm in their beliefs and will not change them. These individuals are usually burned at the stake or executed in some other way. The penalty is harsh, but it is not merely to set an example: Most faiths, even the merciful ones, have execution rituals that remove the taint of heresy from a dying soul. In a world where the gods speak, demons exist, the Hells and Underworlds are demonstrably real, and souls are literally something that can be detected, religion is a deadly serious purpose with no room for error. The guardians of different faiths play hardball, by necessity.

Lesser heresies can range from subtle doctrinal difference all the way to outrageous and outlandish concepts believable only by the uneducated. In

some cases, only a cleric of the faith being corrupted can detect the heresy from casual conversation with a heretic, but the larger the error the easier it is for clerics of other faiths to recognize as heresy. Not all clerics bother responding to a heresy that corrupts a different faith, even if the two gods have the same alignment. However, they might pass the information along to the nearest representative of the other deity.

The Great Heresies

Even worse than the Lesser Heresies are the "Great Heresies," doctrines that literally divert the power of prayer to the wrong supernatural being. It was this sort of heresy, engineered by the demon prince Orcus, that eventually destroyed the priesthood of Thyr and Muir in the city of Tsar. These Great Heresies are ordinarily not the result of a simple mistake, for diverting divine power from one deity to another requires a complex understanding of supernatural powers and mystic channeling, possessed only by demon princes and deceptive gods.

The Canticalist Heresy

The Canticalist Heresy, also called the Heresy of the Discordian Hymnal, is perpetuated by followers of the demon prince Mathrigaunt. The center of the heresy is a book of hymns, called the *Pure Canticle* by those who distribute it, and the *Discordian Hymnal* by those who understand its true nature. The hymnal is not a magic item: It is an ordinary book of hymns and melodies. However, anyone who incorporates the hymns and melodies into prayer is actually feeding power to the demon prince Mathrigaunt rather than to the intended deity. Followers of Mathrigaunt distribute the hymnal into areas that are particularly vulnerable to heresy, masquerading as clerics of some other faith. They claim that using the hymnal in prayer offers "additional blessings" or some other attractive story. Then the demon-worshippers depart, hoping that use of the hymnal catches on. The hymns are beautiful and haunting, and unless the local clerics are quick to notice its use, it tends to become popular. The Canticalist Heresy crops up periodically everywhere in the Borderland Provinces as the followers of Mathrigaunt find new, vulnerable people to deceive. Even the leaders of Canticalist areas are unaware of the heretical nature of the book — part of the "fun," for the demon-worshippers, is that the heresy propagates itself.

The Eternal Life Heresy (also, the "Eternalist" Heresy)

The cult of Orcus fosters the Eternal Life Heresy. This demon prince plays a long-term, deep game, and the Eternal Life Heresy is thus slower and more labor-intensive than the Canticalist Heresy propagated by the followers of Mathrigaunt. It is also more reliable and becomes more deeply rooted than the Canticalist Heresy. In general, the Eternal Life Heresy is started in vulnerable areas by an Orcus cultist who insinuates himself into a community as a respectable farmer or other ordinary identity. Over the course of about a century, Orcus shields the cultist from dying of natural causes until the cultist's neighbors recognize his unnaturally long life. At this point, the cultist explains the particular rituals and practices that have supposedly prolonged his life, and most of them are quite pleasant debaucheries of some kind or another. The heresy is spread to only a few people at first, until it slowly catches on. Generally, the cultist remains on the scene to keep things moving, and deliberately tries to frustrate efforts by local clerics to contain the spread of the heresy.

Pockets of Eternalist heretics have seen what they consider proof-positive of the truth of their beliefs, and seldom recant the heresy.

The Idolist Heresy

The Idolist Heresy is particularly subtle, the product of efforts by followers of the demon-prince Fraz-Urb'luu. It involves the distribution of tiny idols, said to be the representations of saints who intercede with the gods on behalf of those who say prayers and make requests directly to the idol. The little figurines do not represent saints at all, of course. They divert prayer to the benefit of the demon-prince, rather than making an intercession with the intended deity. When they are found, the little idols are easily identifiable, for each one has a different face painted over the top of the original paint, like a mask. This heresy is somewhat labor intensive for the cult of Fraz-Urb'luu, since it requires distribution of the figurines, but it tends to spread undetected for a very long time.

The Inoculist Heresy

The Inoculist Heresy is one of the Great Heresies, fostered by followers of the goddess Hel, Mistress of Disease. It is simply a set of little prayers to be said when friends are ill, or during contagions such as plague or sweating sickness. These prayers actually go to the goddess Hel rather than to whatever god they were intended for, since they are worded with particular formulae that act somewhat like a diversionary code. To start the heresy, Hel usually really does protect the heretics from disease, and gives real effect to the prayers said over sick friends. Once the heresy has caught on due to its actual effectiveness, the goddess withdraws its protection and lets the heresy spread like the contagions she adores.

The Non-Substantiation Heresy

The Non-Substantiation Heresy is a Great Heresy that is equally vile to all religions and all deities, as it represents a threat to each equally. Originally espoused by the scholar Crasmus of Troye in his pamphlet "Limitations of the Divine," the heresy claims that the gods of the multiverse are essentially powerless in mortal affairs and have no ability act directly in the world beyond the granting of divine {clerical} spells and abilities. It argues that the gods are in fact beholden to mortals, rather than mortals beholden to their deities, and that through the propitiation acts by practitioners of the various religions the gods are essentially held hostage by their worshippers devotion and unwillingly leeched of their power. Its thesis states that the gods would gladly destroy the mortal world to be rid of what they see as swarms of parasitic insects if they could but that they have no power to do so and must, therefore, remain as the slaves of mankind and the other sentient races. Obviously the gods and their churches take a very dim view of this sort of heretical reductionism that threatens to stymy belief in them altogether. No demon lord surreptitiously stealing the devotion of worshippers here; if this heresy were to ever catch on universally it could possibly threaten the very existence of both the heavenly and fiendish realms. Needless to say, practice of this heresy is actively stamped out wherever it is found, and even owning a copy of Crasmus's writing can earn the death penalty in many realms if the heresy is not recanted.

The World's Pain Heresy (the "True Pentitents")

The World's Pain Heresy holds that physical pain cleanses the soul, and that those inflicting pain upon themselves are actually helping to bring divine peace and prosperity to the world. Cultists of the n'gathau propagate the heresy (see *The Tome of Horrors Complete* by **Frog God Games** for a description of the n'gathau). For some reason, something in human nature seems to accept this doctrine without much question when times are difficult and the world seems to be an unstable and frightening place. The World's Pain Heresy is easily started by the cultists, and spreads very quickly. However, it is also the most easily detected of all the Great Heresies: When people start walking down the road lashing themselves with small whips, it draws attention. Fighting the World's Pain Heresy tends to be a race by witch-hunters and inquisitors against the rapid word-of-mouth transmission of the heresy.

Even in casual religious conversation with a follower of one of the Great Heresies, most clerics of any god will recognize the poisonous patterns of the espoused heretical doctrines. Since the Great Heresies are a threat to all faiths except those of the perpetuators, clerics of different gods often work in concert to stamp out the growth of one of these cancerous heresies.

Heretical Clerics

As one of the Great Heresies spreads, it has the potential to spawn actual, spellcasting clerics who believe themselves to be worshipping the real deity but are actually receiving their spells, and directing their devotions, to the demon-prince or god who benefits from the heretical practices. It is strongly recommended that the Game Master does not play this trick on a player character: It is very poor form. Heretical clerics should only be NPCs.

Appendix I: Major Deities of the Borderland Provinces

Archeillus
God of Rightful Rule; Protector of the Nobility

Lesser God
Alignment: LG
Domain: Life
Symbol: A lion's head or mask, usually crowned
Garb: Nobles' finery, formal robes of office, royal vestments and regalia including crown, scepter, signet ring, coat-of-arms, chalice, royal seal, and sovereign orb
Favored Weapon: Longsword
Form of Worship and Holidays: Lavish ceremonies held on High Holy Days. Regional and local festivals held according to the traditions and customs of individual noble families.
Typical Worshippers: Many nobles, Foerdewaith traditionalists, some magistrates and judges in remote provincial areas of the Kingdoms of Foere

Archeillus once stood below only Thyr himself in the pantheon of the ancient Kingdoms of Foere. Though the first overking, Macobert, claimed familial descent from the sea god Quell, it was by virtue of the laws and customs of Archeillus that he claimed rightful rule over all the kingdoms and their client states. Despite these once heady heights of influence across the whole of Akados, with the decline of Foere, so too has the worship of Archeillus seen its decline. This has arguably been furthered by the slow increase of support for the foreign deity Mitra as the divine patron of the Foerdewaith sovereignty, a trend whose beginnings can be traced back to the time of the great, great, grandson of Macobert, Osbert II, some seven centuries ago.

Still an important god of the Foerdewaith, his religion is now often seen as old-fashioned or outdated, though he remains revered among many of the old noble families, especially in the more backwater areas. This devotion often even includes noble families that are not of Foerdewaith descent or rulers of lands outside Foere's sphere of influence. This is in large part because veneration of Archeillus is traditionally seen as a support of the current ruling class and serves to justify maintenance of the status quo of power among adherents. As a result of this common understanding, despite the fact that Archeillus is inherently a god of law and good, his religion is used by many a less-benign tyrant as means to consolidate and hold power with a veneer of legitimacy. The established church of Archeillus officially finds this practice repellant but also finds it prudent to not try and identify those who should or should not rule because of the inherent risk of opposing a true believer who has merely been mischaracterized by his subjects or, even worse, finding themselves forced to choose sides and ending up on the losing end of a political power struggle.

With its loss in influence over the last few centuries and the inevitable reduction in the number of followers, the clergy of Archeillus has learned to step carefully and walk a fine line between clearly upholding the morality and rule of just law represented by Archeillus and stepping cautiously to avoid upsetting the apple cart of local politics that could result in them being completely removed from the halls of power and spheres of influence altogether. Many priests of Archeillus take comfort in the oft-quoted axiom, "he that rules does so but by the will of Archeillus," allowing responsibility for the issue of rightful rulership to fall squarely upon the shoulders of the god himself. They trust that Archeillus's wisdom will sort out the details rather than muddying the waters by the machinations and inevitable disasters wrought by imperfect mortals, which is perhaps what the god has intended all along.

Archeillus first appeared in *K3: The Doom of Listonshire* by **Necromancer Games**.

Belon the Wise
God of Travel; Wanderer in White

Lesser God
Alignment: NG
Domain: Knowledge
Symbol: Clear quartz crystal or flawless diamond
Garb: Travelers clothes and long white traveling cloaks
Favored Weapon: Quarterstaff
Form of Worship and Holidays: Offerings of silver given at the beginning and end of long journeys.
Typical Worshippers: Rangers, bards, wandering wizards, those who make their living traveling

Belon appears to his worshippers as an elderly man wearing flowing white robes and carrying a walking staff. Belon is the embodiment of things learned upon the road, be they magical or mundane knowledge. Priests of Belon often serve as guides, educating themselves in local customs in order to afford better traveling conditions for those in their care. As such, Belon is patron of both journeys and knowledge, exemplified in the wisdom that can be gained by being well traveled. An emphasis on common sense ensures that he finds adherents among the stolid common folk of the world rather than only the scholars and learned.

Belon the Wise was not originally a god of the Hyperborean or Foerdewaith pantheons. He seems to have been an Eastern god of some as yet unidentified Libynosi pantheon. Some scholars speculate that he was a lesser god of the Gohtra of Far Jaati. Other evidence seems to suggest that he was perhaps once an apprentice to Thasizier, the Libynosi Master of Good Magic and ancient enemy of the witch-goddess Hecate. Whatever his origin, it seems likely that Belon became introduced to the folk of Akados after having been carried back home by Foerdewaith crusaders sojourning in eastern realms.

Belon's earliest influence in Akados seems to have been in and around the city of Bard's Gate where he enjoyed some popularity as a god of travel among a burgeoning city of merchants and travelers. Over time, however, his worship waned in favor of other gods that hold mercantilism and commerce among their areas of interest, deities such as Sefagreth and Tykee. Recently, however, the church of Belon has been on the rise again as interest in him as a god of arcane knowledge who can perhaps provide secrets of the ancient magic of the East. Less a travelers' god, it is now more in vogue for wizards who consider themselves to be sophisticated and well-traveled to venerate the White Wanderer. This upsurge has been noticed by the clergy of the traditional god of magic Jamboor, and discussions about what to do among that god's scholars have been going on for years now as more and more practitioners of the arcane arts turn to Belon as their patron.

Belon the Wise first appeared in *Bard's Gate* by **Necromancer Games**.

Ceres
The Revered Mother; Goddess of the Home and Midwives; Goddess of Healing, Mercy, and Patience; Goddess of the Millstone

Greater God
Alignment: LG
Domains: Life, Nature
Symbol: A millstone
Garb: Simple robes of white
Favored Weapons: Flail
Form of Worship and Holidays: Simple services are held each week on Ardsdag followed by a family or communal meal where freshly baked loaves of bread are broken in her honor. Half of each loaf is donated to orphans or others in need.

Typical Worshipers: Human matrons and mothers, midwives, bakers, millers, orphans, the poor, farmers, some civic leaders, halflings

Ceres is an old goddess of the Hyperborean pantheon who has protected home and hearth since the earliest recorded histories. She is seen as a motherly figure who protects her followers and their communities through gentle guidance and nurturing. It is also she who the common folk turn to in prayer to avoid famine from a bad harvest or natural calamities. Though not really a goddess of crops and weather like the god Telophus, her holy writings and liturgy do universally speak of a bountiful harvest to fill the bellies of the community and the needy.

More concerned with the benign use of the harvest from the standpoint of community well-being and stability rather than being seen as a matron of plant growth in general, Ceres is one of the few deities whose worship involves active benevolence in the form of feeding and sheltering the needy. She is revered by many who are not truly her worshippers (hence her title of "Revered Mother") because she is seen as the divine caretaker and overseer of healthy births, though she shares this role with the goddess Freya. So even those who venerate other gods or are even diametrically opposed to her through alignment or creed are not above uttering short prayer in her name at the birth of their own offspring. In her hands lies the well-being of the next generation, which all humans recognize and generally respect. That her followers are not crusaders or violent radicals seeking to bring judgment in her name makes this veneration by others more palatable.

For all of these qualities and that of providing succor to the sick, Ceres is often seen as the glue that holds families and communities together. The few hospices that exist for the indigent or those unable to afford the services of a personal physician are almost always established by her worshippers. Despite her recognized benevolence, Ceres is seen as somewhat rustic, and has been in decline in some urban centers. She retains her popularity and influence in the countryside among the simple folk, however. The halfling matron goddess Hester serves as her handmaiden, and many rural halflings revere Ceres as well as a result.

The Revered Mother first appeared in *K2: Diamond Fortress* by **Necromancer Games**. Her millstone symbol first appeared in *Bard's Gate* by **Necromancer Games**.

Darach-Albith
High God of the Elves; Firstborn; Father of the Elves

Greater God
Alignment: CG
Domains: Nature, War
Symbol: A bow and sword hanging from the Eternal Oak
Garb: Garments in shades of gray, green, hazel, chestnut, and sable
Favored Weapons: Longbow, longsword
Form of Worship and Holidays: Major religious services are held on the solstices and equinoxes, while special night festivals are held on the eve of every mid-month (Ides) during the summer.
Typical Worshipers: High and wood elves, elven warriors, wizards, and rangers

The father of all elves and firstborn of the race, Darach-Albith is portrayed as a handsome elven male draped in a cloak of forest green leaves. His skin varies at different times between the gleaming white of birch bark and any shades of brown or green found in primeval woodlands. Darach has keen golden eyes like those of an owl. His sword *Tian Tu Lan* and his bow *Fayar Nocht* are said to never miss a target and to slay those of evil intent instantly.

The ruler of the elven pantheon, almost all elves at least pay Darach-Albith lip service if not outright veneration. Though his religion is very ancient and steeped in many-layered tradition and ritual, to most non-elves he is known primarily for his legendary search for his wife Rialae-Aibaru (known as the Lost Queen of the Elves) who abandoned him and her duties in the elven pantheon to seek out her missing daughter Karelis sometime back in the mists of time. There are entire sects of elves who venerate the Lost Queen and her search through the rare appearances of the blue comet Rialae, though Darach-Albith for his part seems to remain stoic in the face of his unending grief.

Darach-Albith first appeared in *Bard's Gate* by **Necromancer Games**.

Dre'uain the Lame
God of Craft and Smiths;
God of Industry and Hard Work

Greater God
Alignment: LN
Domains: Light, Knowledge
Symbol: Three interlocked cogwheels
Garb: Crafter's outfit (different outfits for different crafts)
Favored Weapons: Warhammer
Form of Worship and Holidays: Worshippers sacrifice one high-quality item per year (if they can afford it). Worshippers without the means to create or purchase high-quality items for sacrifice can purchase small tin replicas at local temples for use in sacrifices. Late summer craft festivals, earthquakes, and volcanic eruptions are also occasions when sacrifices are made to Dre'uain.
Typical Worshipers: Human, gnome, dwarven, and halfling craftsmen, inventors, laborers, union organizers, maimed workers, wounded veterans, beggars

Dre'uain appears as a clubfooted gnome with strong but fine-fingered hands. His flame-red hair and beard always appear singed from his labors over the forge. He has a long nose and piercingly curious eyes and wears a soot-covered apron. Hammer Mittelschmerz claims to have learned all he knows of crafting and invention from Dre'uain.

Considered by many to be one of the oldest deities, Dre'uain embodies the creative mind and its ability to fashion objects and devices. Dre'uain is honored by creators, inventors, smiths, architects, and other craftsfolk of all races. His connection to earthquakes, volcanoes, and other seismic events seem to be a holdover from his earliest days as a mighty giant and earth deity. In that capacity early myths say that he battled the primordial earth spirit Demogorgon for supremacy. The result of the battle was the crippling of Dre'uain and the reduction to his current stature as well as his loss of mastery over the earth, turning instead to mastery of its resources in invention and crafting. Demogorgon faired perhaps worse, losing his mastery over the earth in exchange for knowledge of its deepest secrets instead but at the cost of having his psyche split into two competing halves and being cast into the Ginnungagap.

Since then Dre'uain has succeeded in one of the most difficult tasks in all the multiverse; he was a gnome god who ascended to a position of respect and major worship among humans, with many adherents among dwarves and halflings as well. While dwarven crafters and inventors are more likely to venerate Dwerfater or Crugas and Dre'uain has not been adopted into the Dwarven Pantheon as a result, there are still a fair number of dwarven craftsmen and smiths who prefer to follow his faith than the more magically oriented tenants of Crugas or the distinctly racial patronage of Dwerfater, especially among the hill dwarves who work more closely with other races.

Among humans, Dre'uain not only receives veneration among inventors, craftsmen, and smiths, but his propensity for hard work and virtue of honest labors has endeared him to all manner of manual laborers. Many such laborers follow Stryme, seeing the work of the god of strength in their labors, but for those whose work is less reliant upon physical prowess and more reliant on dogged determination or dedication to tedious or repetitive tasks, Dre'uain strikes a chord. The laborers or many manufactories turn to Dre'uain for their common beliefs and has resulted in the formation of labor unions in some locales.

The presence of Dre'uain's own clubbed foot as a model, and the tendency of some of his followers to unionize has created a following of maimed workers among his followers. This has likewise contributed to a growing number of wounded veteran soldiers among those who follow him, turning away from their former soldier gods in their disability and looking instead to Dre'uain to sustain them. An unexpected side effect of this is that an ever-growing number of beggars — crippled and healthy alike — are beginning to flock to faith. This latest development has created a great deal of discomfort and growing resentment among his clergy because many of these beggars are seen as individuals who eschew hard work in favor of the charity of others, which flies in the face of the very tenants of Dre'uain. Despite many temples openly preaching against the sin of sloth to discourage this or any affiliation with those they see as ne'er-do-wells, any number of almshouses and soup kitchens continue to pop up in Dre'uian's name, though not formally associated with actual members of the clergy. The church hierarchy has yet to come up with a good solution to this situation and are divided as to whether a solution is even necessary.

Dre'uain is frequently associated with the elven deity known as Wayland the Smith (Weland the Smith among the Tuatha De Pantheon). Many assume they are the same god by different names and in different aspects. The dwarves vehemently deny any suggestion of this, and the churches of Dre'uain and Wayland maintain themselves as entirely separate entities. If there is a connection between Dre'uain and Wayland, neither deity has deigned to comment.

Dre'uain's temples always contain an altar composed of large metal gears intended to represent the eternal mechanisms of the cosmos, which Dre'uain is said to understand and perhaps even serve as caretaker over. True members of Dre'uain's clergy can be identified by their ability to disassemble the interlocking cogs of Dre'uain's holy symbols or connect them back together. This secret, known as the "Blessing of Dre'uain", is given to them directly from the god. Others who attempt to do so must make a successful DC 45 Disable Device check.

Dre'uain the Lame first appeared in *Bard's Gate* by **Necromancer Games**.

The Father
Primeval God of Violence, Strength, and Warfare (Lost)

Greater God
Alignment: NE
Domains: Tempest, War
Symbol: A triangle
Garb: Skins of hunted animals or enemies
Favored Weapon: Stone greataxe
Form of Worship and Holidays: Blood sacrifices at solstices and equinoxes, before and after battles, and upon the birth or death of a chieftain
Typical Worshippers: Neolithic tribes (mostly extinct), Vanigoths of the Wilderland Hills, some Wildmen of the Mistwood, possibly others

The Father has existed as long as there has been life on the world now known as Lloegyr and has often been associated as an embodiment of the world itself or its primordial oceans. He has been known by many names through the ages, The Father simply being the most universal and enduring. To the ancient Phoromyceans who knew of him only through their own ancient legends, he was known as the Demiurge. To the Hyperboreans, who came along an age later, he was known as Boros and represented the planet upon which they lived as well as their home continent to the north. To the ancient peoples of the North before the coming of the Northlanders he was Buri, the grandfather of Wotan. To the Khemitite priest-kings of old he was Nun. The even more ancient Ashurians called him Engur or Abzu. The most ancient writings of Far Jaati refer to him as Dyaus Pitra, and to the Ancient Folk of Akados he was Lir.

Worship of The Father predated the formation of pantheons and culturally defined religions; in fact, the existence of The Father seems to predate the concept of worship or even the existence of humanoid life on Lloegyr. To these early cultures, The Father was known as patron of tribal warfare, competition for scarce resources, survival, dominance, and rulership by might, and he was seen as a primal creator of the world, life, and the gods themselves. The Father was typically not so much revered as feared, for the savage world was harsh and unforgiving with an equally harsh and unforgiving god for the strong to cling to and the weak to perish before. Ritual bloodshed marked the holy times and sites of The Father, and human sacrifice became a standard practice under his stern gaze.

Despite this near hegemony of devotion in the earliest ages of the world, worship for and even memory of The Father eventually died out, supplanted by belief in younger, gentler gods, many of whom are believed to be his children or even their offspring. Only in the most ancient records and esoteric circles is mention of The Father even found and usually then only disjointed and incomplete references. To those few with the depth of scholarship or requisite age (a few of the oldest elves and assorted dragons and undead beings) to even know of The Father, it is believed his eventual decline and erasure from the consciousness of humanity was in large part to the heroic and selfless actions of an equally primeval creator deity known only as The Goddess, mother of many of the oldest gods and both mate and mortal enemy of The Father. Thanks to her efforts, knowledge of The Father was forgotten from the world to the point that he is now considered a "lost" deity. None in this day and age revere The Father, nor is there liturgy available to revive his worship, except among a very few small and scattered tribal societies that exist as holdovers from those most ancient of times. Even in these cultures worship of The Father is corrupted and inexact due to lack of any written record, and such peoples themselves are in decline is well so that it is only a matter of time until The Father ceases to exist as a deific entity upon Lloegyr.

Freya
Goddess of Love and Fertility; Freyja

Lesser God
Alignment: NG
Domains: Life, War
Symbol: Falcon
Garb: Robes and cloaks of white, trimmed with white fur
Favored Weapons: Longsword, longbow, spear
Form of Worship and Holidays: Harvest moon feast and before large hunts. Feast of Freya at spring equinox. Secret rites at the new moon. The Calends of the third month is devoted to Freya and serve as a special holiday in her honor.
Typical Worshipers: Human females, farmers, midwives, hunters, druids

Freya is a lesser goddess of love and fertility. Freya is also the leader of a great band of women warriors — known as valkyries. Freya represents fertility in all its forms. In the Southlands, Freya represents the cycle of death and rebirth. She is a goddess of the coming harvest, as well as of sexuality and procreation. Her beast is the falcon, though she is fond of the winter wolf and the hind. She appears most frequently to her worshipers as a beautiful human woman dressed in robes and a cloak of winter wolf fur, though she occasionally appears as a hunter in leather armor with spear and bow or as a warrior in shining mail with a glowing sword. She can take the form of a falcon — or any other bird — at will, as well as that of a huge winter wolf.

Freya is a transplant to the Foerdewaith pantheon from the Vanir of the Northlands, where she is called Freyja. Despite this foreign origin, Freya is one of the single-most popular deities worshipped by the peoples of Akados. She is slowly but surely replacing the Hyperborean goddess Zadastha as the goddess of love. As a goddess of the harvest, there is natural friction between her followers and those of Telophus, though this rarely comes to open conflict. She and Ceres likewise share dominion over midwives and the birthing process, though Freya approaches it more from the procreation aspect and Ceres from the aspect of a healthy family and community. As such, there is little conflict between the followers of these faiths, and small villages tend to lean towards one or the other as a whole rather than having shrines of both in the same community.

Though not an inherently violent faith (at least not outside the Northlands), Freya despises any kind of arachnid, and her battles against the drow goddess known as the Queen of Spiders are legendary. Her followers also frequently conflict with those of the arachnid deity called The Spider, though that deity is too bestial and unsophisticated to truly carry a grudge against the goddess.

Freya first appeared in *W1: The Crucible of Freya* by **Necromancer Games**.

Jamboor
God of Knowledge, Magic, and Death; He Who Hears the Secrets of the Dead

Greater God
Alignment: N
Domains: Death, Knowledge
Symbol: An eclipsed sun
Garb: White robes trimmed in green and black
Favored Weapons: Quarterstaff, dart
Form of Worship and Holidays: Regular worship on the last day of the week, holidays at the end of each month, and the major holiday of Reckoning at the end of the year, funerary rites, and solemn observances of the dates of death of significant historical figures
Typical Worshipers: Arcane spellcasters, sages, seers, mediums, spies

Jamboor is a god of death, but only in the regard that death is a part of life and should be revered as such. It is not unusual for the clerics of Jamboor to multi-class with one or more arcane classes. Kings and noblemen consider it a true feather in their cap to have a priest of Jamboor as an advisor.

Jamboor is an ancient god of Hyperborea who has clung to his influence tenaciously since the earliest of days. This mysterious deity is seen as a benign or malignant entity depending on the standpoint of the viewer. To some folk, a god of death must be evil and, therefore, to be feared, while to others he merely maintains the proper order of things in the cycle of life and death. And still to others he is simply a god of magic and arcane knowledge which can be the faith of benevolent local wizard or a power-mad necromancer. Regardless, all rulers and leaders value his faith because his priests are known to possess a great many secrets and are willing to offer wise counsel to any ruler without regard to political or religious affiliation.

Many local superstitions find their roots in the practices of the followers of Jamboor, and entire sects of his priesthood are tasked with sussing out the secrets of existence through listening to the whispers of the dead. The dates and times for the High Holy Days of the continent of Akados are determined and published each year by the priests of Jamboor and are recognized by those of all faiths. While the Wheels of Inquiry used by his followers to determine local omens and auguries can be found in almost any community for use by any who know the secrets of their interpretation.

Despite his long and ongoing influence, Jamboor's age-old mastery of those who study the magical arts is now being challenged as the traveler deity Belon the Wise gains more and more followers among arcane practitioners. This situation has caused no small amount of consternation among the normally staid Jamboorites not only because of the encroachment upon their traditional sphere of influence but even more so because they did not foresee its coming.

Jamboor first appeared in *The Lost City of Barakus* by **Necromancer Games**.

Kamien
Goddess of Rivers, Streams, and Springs; The Sparkling Maiden; Old Widemouth; The Water Lady

Lesser God
Alignment: N

Domain: Nature
Symbol: A fish riding upon three wavy lines upon a green copper amulet
Garb: Robes of turquoise, brown, and azure with bracelets and anklets of blue
Favored Weapons: Javelin, spear
Form of Worship and Holidays: Spring and fall floods bring sacrifices to Kamien to ensure that rivers do not rise too high. At midsummer Rising, followers gather at rivers to appeal to the goddess to keep them flowing.
Typical Worshipers: Women, nymphs, sprites, nereids, other water creatures and fey, prostitutes, boatmen, bargemen, fishermen, river giants

Kamien is the embodiment of springs, streams, and rivers, appearing as a woman with skin like silvery rippling water — earning her name as the Sparkling Maiden — or as a great silvery scaled fish — usually called Old Widemouth for resembling a massive bass. Bargemen and fishermen who ply her waterways toss coins into streams, fountains, and brooks to ensure safe passage and plentiful catches.

Kamien is one of the earliest Hyperborean deities, even predating that civilization, representing the springs and streams that provided plentiful water sources that allowed early humanoid settlements to be established and thrive. As such she became a community deity and was seen as protector of the town well, spring, or other water source required for their continued survival. As societies advanced and maintenance of water sources and the ability to find them became more sophisticated and reliable, her role as the protector of the community transformed somewhat into that of protector of travel and trade upon the waters of her streams and rivers. It is this aspect that is most frequently seen in her worship today, though settlements that greatly rely upon yearly flooding or preservation from such floods still revere her in the older incarnations through semi-annual flood festivals and the yearly Rising ceremony at midsummer to beseech her to keep the waters flowing throughout the dry season.

Already considered an ancient deity among humans, Kamien's reach extends even farther back into the mists of time beyond even human civilization. In her earliest incarnation she is considered to be the mother of the nymphs and sprites and is a member of the Court of the Fey as a protector of fertility. Knowledge of this aspect is largely lost among human cultures today, though some prostitutes (usually in riverside communities) venerate the Sparkling Maiden for her seductive qualities, probably related to her relation to fey such as nymphs and nereids that are known for their beauty and allure. Her ancient background is further recalled vaguely in old wives' tales about the dangers of visiting the local spring or well at night because the Water Lady might come and steal the foolish visitor. That this could be a reference to Kamien and the sometimes predatory fey among her followers is a possibility, though it could just as easily be nothing more than a parental admonition to children to avoid drownings and other water accidents while unsupervised.

Kamien first appeared in **Bard's Gate** by **Necromancer Games**.

Mick O'Delving
God of Halflings; The Little Miner; Mickey Two-Cups

Greater God
Alignment: CG
Domain: Trickery
Symbol: A candle in a cave
Garb: Breeches, shirts, and waistcoats of browns, yellows, oranges, and other earth tones but always barefoot. For underground ceremonies a miner's helmet is worn.
Favored Weapons: War pick
Form of Worship and Holidays: Few formal worship services, followers of Mick O'Delving tend to offer up short personal prayers for luck when needed or spill a bit of libation in his honor before feasts. Most festivals honoring Pekko include some nods to Mick O'Delving as well. On one High Holy Day a year, a formal ceremony is held in a mine, basement, or other underground setting to praise the halfling patron, celebrate his tumultuous marriage to Mother Hester, toast his relationship with Vergrimm Earthsblood, and memorialize his late wife Suzanne.
Typical Worshipers: Halflings, some burrowing creatures, drunks, Barefeet assassins

The plucky and puckish God of Halflings, Mick O'Delving is the consummate prankster and ne'er-do-well. However, whereas the gnomish god Hammer Mittelschmerz represents the gnomes' propensity for elaborate jokes and tricks, Mick is much more about finding the advantage in any situation by hook or crook and making his way with a smile on his face, a twinkle in his eye, and always one eye on the authorities. His ability to get into trouble is surpassed only by his ability to get out again. He exemplifies the halflings' ability to survive under almost any circumstances while maintaining a certain humorous and affable outlook on life.

According to fables, Mick's first appearance occurred when some of the dwarven miners serving in the mines of the god Vergrimm Earthsblood complained to him about one miner who refused to wear his boots. Vergrimm descended into the depths to investigate where he found the unusually short, barefoot miner hammering away at a workface with his pickaxe while humming a jaunty tune, much to the annoyance of the dwarves laboring around him. When Vergrimm lifted the brim of his too-large helmet he met the eyes of the grimy-faced halfling good smiling merrily. Why Mick was laboring away in the dwarven mines is a question that the fables fail to answer beyond the fact that he thought it would be a grand joke upon the dwarves. Regardless, his propensity for delving and interminable sense of humor served as a perfect counterpoint to the dour dwarven god such that the two became fast friends and known drinking companions. The fact that Pekko often attends their late-night drinking bouts only adds to the legendarium of Mick and is probably the source of his nickname in many a drunken toast as Mickey Two-Cups, for the ale jack that he holds in each hand. His peculiar origins cause many dwarves to refer to him as the Little Miner, an appellation to which halflings usually take umbrage, though if it bothers Mick himself he has never said so.

Despite his merry, even happy-go-lucky reputation, all of the mythology of Mick is not so jolly. The god's first wife was the goddess Sotheryn, known as Lady Suzanne among the halflings. A goddess of community, fertility, and the life-death cycle, there's was a marriage of balance and happiness with her calming, quiet demeanor serving to offset and soothe his over-enthusiastic, almost manic nature. Yet eternal happiness was not to be even among the gods, for one of Mick O'Delving's many pranks mortally offended the Queen of Spiders, vindictive goddess of the drow, and she plotted to murder him. Lady Suzanne managed to learn of the plot at the last second and drank the poison intended for him, saving him but at the cost of her own life. Perhaps the most famous composition by any halfling bard is the Lay of Sotheryn, penned in honor of the Lady Suzanne.

This incident is also what has spawned own of the most peculiar organizations in the history of halflings, a secret society of halfling assassins known as the Barefeet. These folk lead seemingly normal halfling lives as farmers, brewers, bakers, or any other mundane and otherwise humble trade typically found among halflings, but all the way they wage a clandestine war against the drow and the clergy of the Queen of Spiders in particular. Spying, gathering information, and training in secret, these seemingly ordinary folk carefully plan and orchestrate deadly attacks against their hated foes at opportune moments. The local tailor might close up his shop one day to "go visit his cousin in the next town over." Meanwhile in the next town over a halfling barber closes up shop to "attend his aunt's funeral in the city," with the pattern repeating itself again and again across multiple communities. Then a week or so later, they return to reopen shops and resume business and life as if nothing out of the ordinary had occurred, while in some other location not far away a drow caravan or delegation of drow clerics is found completely slaughtered by unknown assailants.

After the death of his first wife, Mick O'Delving later married the halfling goddess Hester, Handmaiden of Ceres and Mother of the Hearthfire.

Theirs is a relationship less ideal than that of his first marriage, with the calm and dignified Hester providing counterpoint to Mick's often wild ways, but lacking the serenity enjoyed by her predecessor. Legends speak of the arguments that have occurred in the household of Mick O'Delving, and halfling children say that the thunder is another pot or pan flung by Hester at her wayward husband. Despite these high-spirited bouts their love is genuine, though some quiet whispers speak of Hester finding love with a mortal halfling causing clerics of both faiths to offer up prayers seeking shelter from any coming turmoil.

Mick O'Delving first appeared in *F1: Vindication* by **Necromancer Games**.

Mitra
God of Law, Justice, and the Sun;
Sun Father; The Truth-Speaker

Greater God
Alignment: LG
Domains: Life, Light
Symbol: A golden sunburst surrounded by the trifoliate leaves and thorns of a myrrh tree
Garb: A seamless linen tunic and hood of pure white without ornament or footwear
Favored Weapons: Longsword
Form of Worship and Holidays: Worship services are held on the first day of every week with congregational singing and prayer followed by acts of service among the community. The Calends of the eighth month is devoted to Mitra and are when a sacrificial collection of material wealth is made among the faithful for the purpose of establishing and funding hospitals and almshouses.
Typical Worshipers: Common folk, Foerdewaith knights and rulers, magistrates and judges, healers, the sick and disabled

Mitra has become one of the most commonly worshipped gods in Akados, despite being a transplant from eastern lands. Part of Mitra's appeal is his emphasis on humility among his worshippers while at the same time championing justice and rule of law. Thus while the powers-that-be worship Mitra to uphold their rightful rule and the laws of the land, he is appealing to the common folk for his insistence on the principles of mercy and fairness among the high and low alike. Another god that probably found its way into Akados through the crusading knights of the Foerdewaith, Mitra's true rise to prominence in the West undoubtedly stems from a single incident some 700 years ago when he allegedly appeared to the Foerdewaith overking, Osbert II, before the pivotal battle of Oescreheit Downs promising victory for the beleaguered Foerdewaith against the vastly superior numbers of the Heldring horde. When the Heldring were defeated and their threat finally broken once and for all, many took Mitra's appearance to mean that he favored the rightful rule of the Foerdewaith overkings and adopted him as the patron of Macobert's dynasty.

The shift as a result of this changing attitude was gradual and took place only in small incremental steps, but its progress has been inexorable. The adoption of Mitra as a specifically Macobertian sponsor largely pushed the traditional recognition of Quell in that role to the side until recent centuries when the most devout loyalty to the Sea King has largely shifted to the maritime Empire of Oceanus. Other gods that have felt the greatest decline as a result of Mitra's rise are the sun goddess Solanus (to such an extent that many folk of Akados have begun to refer to the sun as Mitra in the Eastern fashion rather than as Sol or Solanus as has been traditionally done in the West), Muir as a Lawful war goddess, and Thyr in his role of Lawgiver and god of justice. At point in time, virtually every judge and court in Akados looked to Thyr as its patron, but now Mitra predominates in that role by a narrow margin, and his influence in the areas of the sun and healing ensures that his adherents' growth continues even as Thyr's declines.

Mitra first appeared in *Rappan Athuk* by **Frog God Games**.

Muir
Goddess of Virtue and Paladins; Eostre

Greater God
Alignment: LG
Domains: Light, War
Symbol: Blood-red upraised sword on a white background
Garb: White wool robes with an upraised sword and hand in red
Favored Weapons: Longsword or greatsword
Form of Worship and Holidays: Regular worship and fasting on the eve before known battle or before confirmation or promotion of the ranks of the faithful. The Calends of the fourth month is devoted to Muir.
Typical Worshipers: Humans paladins, Heldring soldiers, Alcaldrich knights, Justicars

Muir is the twin sister of Thyr and one of the fabled Three Gods of old. While he represents law and peace, she represents the martial valor necessary to make that peace a reality. As such, she is the goddess of paladins and the principle martial deity of the Heldring. She is often depicted as a dark-tressed maiden warrior in shining mail with an upraised (often bloodstained) sword. She is noble and single-minded of purpose. The tenets of her worship include honor, truth, and courage. A great order of Hyperborean paladins known as the Justicars were sworn to her service but are believed to have died off at the time of the Battle of Tsar and the fall of Tircople some three centuries ago. She and Thyr serve as the combined state religion of the Empire of Alcaldar in Libynos and is seen as the matron of the martial Church Militans of its Holy Ecclesia Inquisitorial. The knights of the Church Militans see themselves as the modern incarnation of the Holy Order of Justicars, though followers of Muir outside Alcaldar do not support this claim.

Like her brother-deity Thyr, Muir has lost some of the predominance that she once enjoyed in Akados and throughout the Hyperborean Empire. Her High Altar was moved to the vicinity of Bard's Gate after the fall of Tircople and has since fallen into decline there as well. However, like Thyr she has enjoyed a resurgence of popularity among the now-devout Heldring of the Helcynngae Peninsula, where she is known as Eostre, and within the Empire of Alcaldar in Libynos. Both the Heldring hledwalda and the Alcaldrich empress press for relocation of the High Altar of Muir to their respective domains, but the goddess has yet to make a pronouncement on the matter so for now it remains in its diminished state in the city of Bard's Gate.

Muir expects self-sacrifice, humility, and charity as well as unswerving loyalty, and her worshipers must be lawful good. Her standards are extreme and she quickly turns her back on any who fail to live up to them. Those who maintain her standards, however, may strive to become Justicars, an order of paladins imbued with even greater holiness if the means to reviving that order can be discovered somewhere in the ruins of lost Tircople.

Her symbol is a blood-red uplifted sword on a white background, symbolizing her endless fight against evil, and the falcon is a sacred animal to her for its noble bearing and relentless pursuit of its prey. She is the tireless foe of all evil creatures, and undead, demons, and devils in particular are her sworn enemy.

Muir was first detailed in *D1: The Tomb of Abysthor* by **Necromancer Games**.

Narrah
The Lady of the Moon;
The Pale Sister; Luna

Greater God
Alignment: N
Domains: Nature
Symbol: The Sickle (a crescent moon)
Garb: Dark hooded robes, midnight blue cloaks

Favored Weapons: Sickle
Form of Worship and Holidays: Prayer services held weekly on the night of Sistersdag. Regular worship and fasting on nights of the full moon. Lunar eclipses and other astronomical events such as the new moon and the double moon (when Narrah and Sybil are both full), are sacred to Narrah. Each month on Moonless Night, the followers of Narrah hold a short prayer vigil at sundown and then go forth in numbers, armed and armored, to battle the followers of Cybele and defend against raids by the Nocturnals.
Typical Worshipers: Druids, stargazers, lycanthropes, oracles, bards, some fey

An ancient and oft-forgotten goddess, Narrah has looked down upon the face of the lands as the greater moon known as the Pale Sister, since the beginning of the world. Worshipped by star-gazers, lycanthropes, and lovers alike, the Lady of the Moon is neither good nor evil, light nor dark. She represents neutrality is its most natural form. She is the moonlight in the dark, the push and pull of the tides, and the navigation point when one is lost. Actively worshipped by druids who remember the ancient traditions of the Old Way, she imparts the secrets of the universe under the cover of night. Though most folk refer to her only as the Pale Sister or, perhaps, Luna and think of her only as the larger and brighter of the two moons rather than as an actual goddess.

Alongside her twin moon, Sybil the Dark Sister, Narrah has hovered over the world since the beginning. Her earliest followers were the fey and primitive humanoids, and since that time she has warred with the smaller moon for the dominance of the night. Narrah does not seek power, but Cybele the deity associated with the other moon has long sought the means to destroy Narrah and assume total dominion over the night sky. To this end she has allied with her idiot twin Shupnikkurat to seek away to devour Narrah whole and remove her from the sky forever.

Narrah first appeared in ***The Lost Lands: Stoneheart Valley*** by **Frog God Games**.

Solanus
Goddess of the Sun and Healing

Greater God
Alignment: NG
Domains: Life, Light
Symbol: A blazing sun inscribed with an open palm
Garb: Pale robes bearing the symbol of Solanus. The color of robes changes as adherents progress through the hierarchy of the church. Initiates wear robes of red which are then changed to those of orange, then yellow, and then white for the high priest. There are even multiple subtle shades between these main colors to denote gradations within their ranks.
Favored Weapons: Mace, quarterstaff
Form of Worship and Holidays: Regular worship on the first day of the week (Solsdag), special observances for the clergy at each dawn, major holidays on the summer and winter solstices (High Sol and Low Sol, respectively), and the Ides of the eighth month is devoted to Solanus as well.
Typical Worshipers: Rangers, bards, healers, soldiers, undead slayers

Solanus is the benevolent goddess of the sun, Sol as it has traditionally been named in Akados. She is a goddess of ancient Hyperborea who, as a founding deity of that culture, has known great popularity in Akados across the breadth of the empire. Her priests have often served as field medics in armies and once comprised an entire Legion of ancient Hyperborea. They have also commonly been the local healers in villages and small towns. Some hospitals were established in Solanus's name in certain imperial centers (namely Remenos and Curgantium), but the practice never caught on in more remote settings where sufficient funds from the imperial coffers were frequently unavailable. As a result, her rural clergy remained principally scattered as individual practitioners while her central high church maintained a rigid hierarchy that often looked with disdain upon the rural church as disorganized or even bumpkins. Perhaps the church's greatest claim to notoriety over the centuries, however, has been the propensity for members of her rural clergy to join adventuring bands. At one time in the empire's history, it is likely that as many as 8 out of 10 adventuring parties, mercenary companies, or freelance knights was accompanied by a cleric of Solanus, bringing great acceptance and goodwill among the common folk far beyond what could have been managed by the central offices of the church tucked away in the great cities of the empire. Many of the older bardic hero tales composed in the classical style of those times include a warrior of Thyr, a wizard of Jamboor, a paladin of Muir, and a cleric of Solanus as heroic archetypes. (They also typically include a scoundrel character devoted to Moccavallo, though this is less likely to be acknowledged in polite company.)

In recent centuries the church of Solanus has seen a steady, and in some cases precipitous, decline. This can be directly attributed to the equally steady rise in the encroaching faith of Mitra from the far reaches of the East after being embraced by the Foerdewaith overkings several centuries ago. In general her worship becomes more common the farther west one travels across Akados, as the faith of Mitra has not yet spread that far. Solanus is one of the three matron/patron deities of the great city of Reme (alongside Dame Torren and Mithras) and still enjoys a great degree of popularity and worship there. Her High Altar remains in that city at the venerable Hospital of St. Jethra the Martyred which still maintains 1,220 beds and accepts the sick and infirm from all over Akados who make their way to its doors.

Solanus first appeared in ***The Lost City of Barakus*** by **Necromancer Games**.

Telophus
Lord of Crops and the Seasons

Lesser God
Alignment: LN
Domains: Light, Nature
Symbol: Raining cloud partially obscuring a radiant sun
Garb: Green and earth tone woolen robes and vestments
Favored Weapons: Sickle or scythe
Form of Worship and Holidays: Harvest and planting celebrations as well as special devotions at the first frost and the first thaw.
Typical Worshipers: Farmers and halflings, some druids revering his natural cycle aspect

This Hyperborean god is the embodiment of the uncaring changing seasons. He is prayed to not so much to bring good crops, but to be convinced to hold off the early frost or bring the spring thaw. He requires appeasement and devoted following, being known to test his followers' faithfulness and resolve when it suits him. Telophus and Freya are natural antagonists to each other between his uncaring detachment and her personal interest in the well-being of her faithful. This translates into occasional confrontations and difficulties between the moribund priesthood of the Lord of Crops and Seasons and the fiery devotees of Freya.

Telophus has long been credited with bringing the orderly advance of the seasons for planting, growing, reaping, and storing. Farmers almost universally propitiate this god, though interestingly, as a primarily neutral diety; the bounty of this process is often accredited to Ceres or Freya, whereas Telophus seems simply to be more concerned that the natural processes continue as they should. The lawful aspect of his nature reflects this adherence to the strict natural cycles of day and night, sun and storm, and the endless revolution of the seasons. One result of this detached view of the process is that some strange druidic cults of Telophus have emerged over the centuries that take a distinctly anti-civilization view. Whether this more-malicious interpretation of his faith is bothersome to the deity is unclear, as he has never commented to his priesthood on it in one way or the other.

Telophus first appeared in ***Bard's Gate*** by **Necromancer Games**.

Thyr
God of Law and Justice;
The Lawgiver; Tyr; Tiwaz

Greater God
Alignment: LG
Domains: Life, Knowledge
Symbol: Silver cross on a white field
Garb: White robes trimmed with silver, purple or gold — the colors of kingship
Favored Weapons: Mace (bladed weapons are forbidden)
Form of Worship and Holidays: Worship services held on the last day of every month. Midwinter eve (called Commons) is set aside for the common folk to have their grievances heard before the highest courts of the land.
Typical Worshipers: Human royalty, ruling and legislative bodies, some magistrates and judges

Thyr is the god of wise and just rule. He is normally depicted as a wizened king seated on a great throne, holding the *Rod of Kingship* in one hand and the *Chalice of Peace* in the other. His principles are justice, order and peace. He represents proper and traditional rule and as such was once worshiped (at least in name) by all human royalty. He is the embodiment of the enlightened human caste system where each person has a fairly determined role in a lawful society intended to create the greatest good for the greatest number.

Thyr's symbol is a silver cross on a white field, symbolizing the upturned cross-haft of his sister's sword, which he thrust into the earth to end the Gods' War at the dawn of time. Upon seeing the blood of so many gods shed, Thyr foreswore the use of swords and his priests, for this reason, may not use bladed weapons. Many favor reinforced rods, similar to light maces, modeled after Thyr's own *Rod of Kingship*. The noble eagle and lion are his sacred creatures.

The Lawgiver, Thyr is a god that has transcended culture and appears in different aspects among different groups on the world of Lloegyr, spanning cultures from the Northlands to the Helcynngae Peninsula in the south. To Northlanders (and the Andøvan before them) he is known as Tiwaz and is depicted as having only one hand, the other having been bitten off by a powerful Godspawn of Chaos while Tiwaz distracted it and allowed it to be bound for the good of the world.

Thyr has actually been a part of the Hyperborean pantheon for thousands of years and for much of that empire's history was considered among its chief gods and most influential in its civilization alongside Muir and Arden (and later Solanus). Thyr is also one of the ancient trinity of deities known as the Three Gods that predates the Hyperboreans. The Heldring venerate him as Tyr in much the same aspect as Thyr, though they depict him as one handed like Tiwaz.

It is unknown whether Thyr is truly a Northlands transplant or if his worship in fact developed concurrently but separately in the two different cultures. Or for that matter if it didn't develop long prior to either of them existing only to diverge somewhere along the way. In fact, it is not entirely certain that he is truly aspects of the same god (though the belief of that is near universal). Regardless, Thyr does not seem to raise any objection to the correlation, and his Thyr identity has by far been his largest church historically. The modern Heldring have formed an almost-theocratic society devoted to Tyr and Eostre (their name for Muir), and their hledwalda petitions annually for the High Altar of Thyr to be moved from Bard's Gate to Kingsgardt in the Kingdom of the Helcynn, while the empress of the actual-theocracy of Alcaldar likewise presses for it to be established in the imperial capital of Mhaltra. To date Thyr's clergy have remained silent on the subject of relocation, though patience wears thin among the royalties of those respective nations.

Despite his millennia of success and the establishment of no less than two current monarchies largely based on his faith, Thyr has seen a near-continuous decline across the breadth of old Hyperborean lands, especially since the rise of the Eastern god Mitra. However, his high priest notes that this decline cannot be fully laid at the feet of the upstart Mitra, because it actually precedes his dramatic appearance to Overking Osbert II seven centuries ago. Rather, High Priest Bofred of Bard's Gate points out that the first hints of the decline had occurred even before the end of the Hyperborean Empire, much less the current decline of the Foerdewaith in recent centuries, pointing to a subtle but pervasive omnipresent diminishment in civilization over this time period. A diminishment that Bofred and others fear may be a harbinger of worse things to come.

Thyr was first detailed in *D1: The Tomb of Abysthor* by **Necromancer Games**.

Yenomesh
God of Glyphs and Writing

Lesser God
Alignment: N
Domain: Knowledge
Symbol: A gleaming silver scroll
Garb: Gray scribes' robes
Favored Weapons: Quarterstaff
Form of Worship and Holidays: Worship is through study, teaching, and learning. The last day of the week (Thingsdag) is given over to quiet contemplation. Monastic orders of Yenomesh set aside the High Holy Days of the Cusp of Freya (vernal equinox) and the Cusp of Mithras (autumnal equinox) for day-long ceremonies that take place in total silence.
Typical Worshipers: Loremasters, wizards, scribes, authors, historians

Yenomesh is the aged sage of the gods. He is said to have been the first to gain knowledge of the sacred runes of the Language Eternal which he taught to the gods and elevated them from the Original Chaos. Likewise it was he who created the written characters of the language known as Foundation, allowing the concepts of the Language Eternal to be grasped by mortal minds and brought the light of knowledge to the world. He is likewise credited with being the inventor of all written language since it is derived from the characters of Foundation, and his priests are often fluent in writing and speaking many different tongues. For his role in imparting knowledge upon the mortal races, libraries and archives are often dedicated to Yenomesh, and many have at least one small shrine in his honor.

Despite the universality of Yenomesh's contributions to the world in the form of writing, he was not always considered to be a part of the Hyperborean pantheon. Originally Yenomesh was found only in the ancient religions of the East. It was during the Hyperborean expansion into Libynos some three-and-a-half thousand years ago that the West encountered the monastics of Yenomesh. They later recognized the value and contributions of the Yenomeshi faith when Hyperborean scholarship realized that all known languages were derived from a script that the monastics used to write their own scrolls. As scholars practiced in the arcane arts discovered that this Foundation language also served as the basis for magical writings, western wizards began to show interest in the faith as well. Yenomesh has never had sufficient popularity among magical practitioners that it threatened the faith of Jamboor or later Belon the Wise, but he has also had a small and devoted following of these spellcasters who delve deeply into the mysteries of alternate forms of magical writing.

Yenomesh first appeared in *Bard's Gate* by **Necromancer Games**.

Alphabetical Index of Places and Pronunciations

ALPHABETICAL INDEX

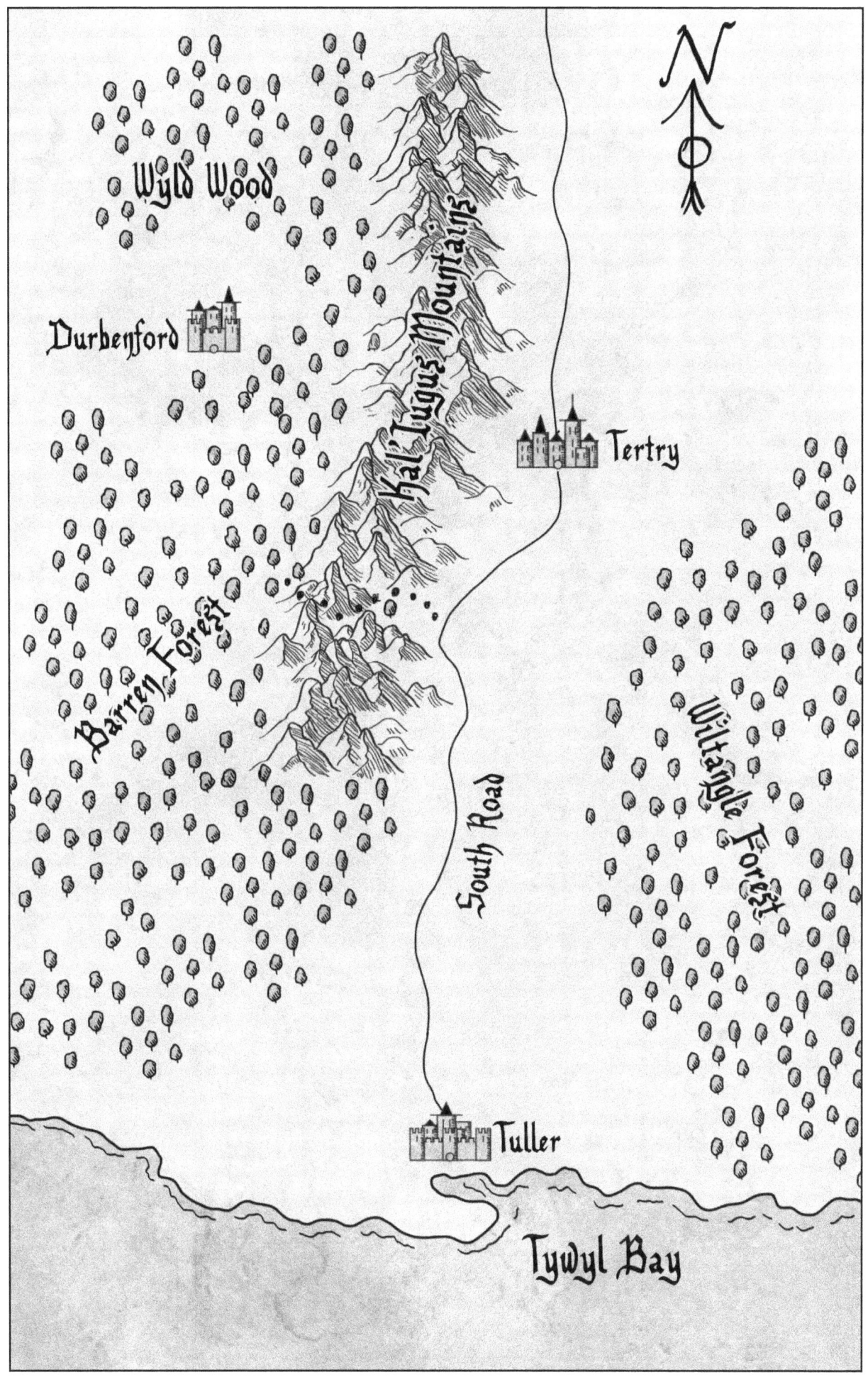

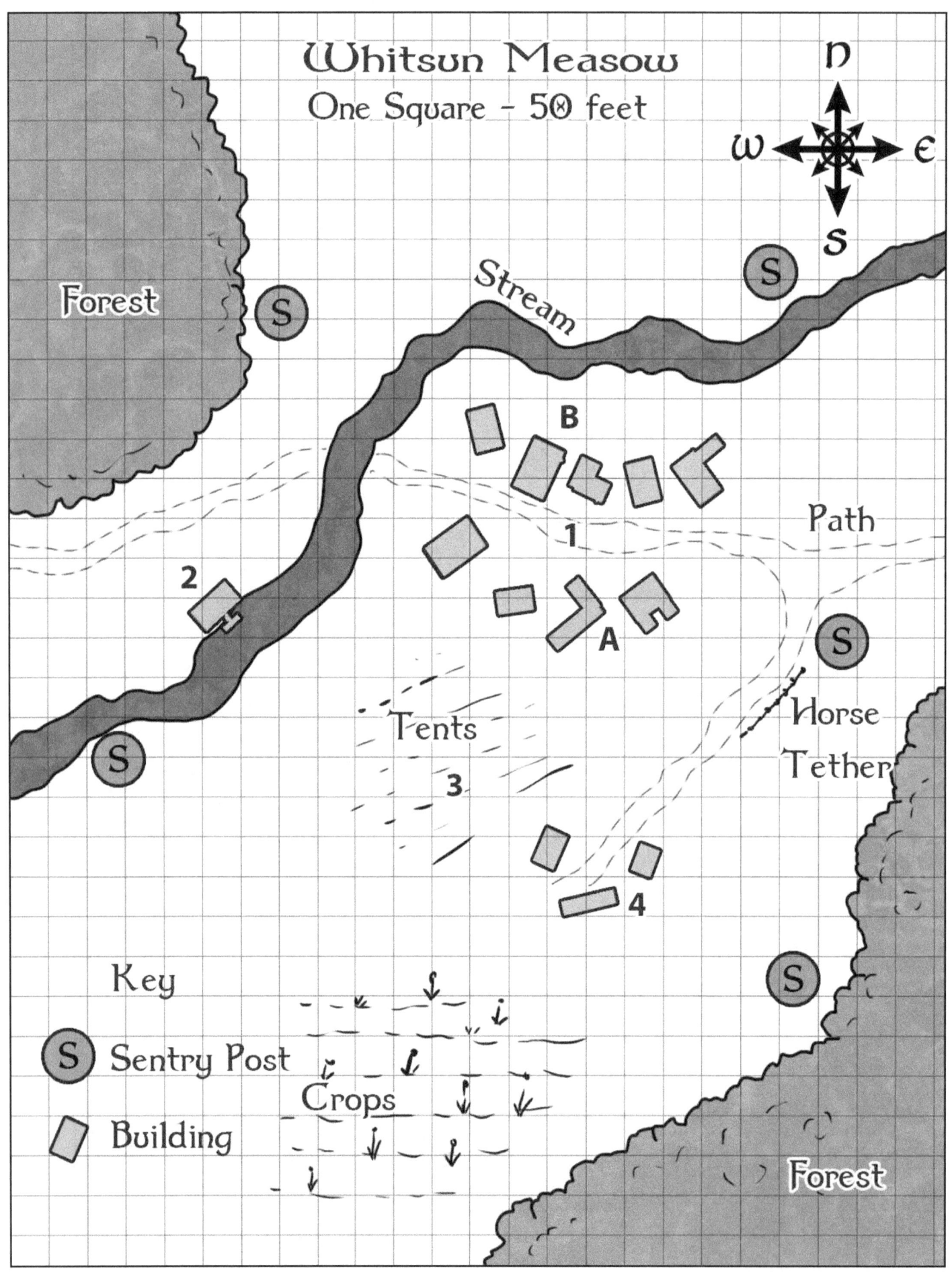

Whitsun Measow
One Square – 50 feet

Forest

Stream

Path

Horse
Tether

Tents

B

1

2

A

3

4

Key

S Sentry Post

Crops

Building

Forest

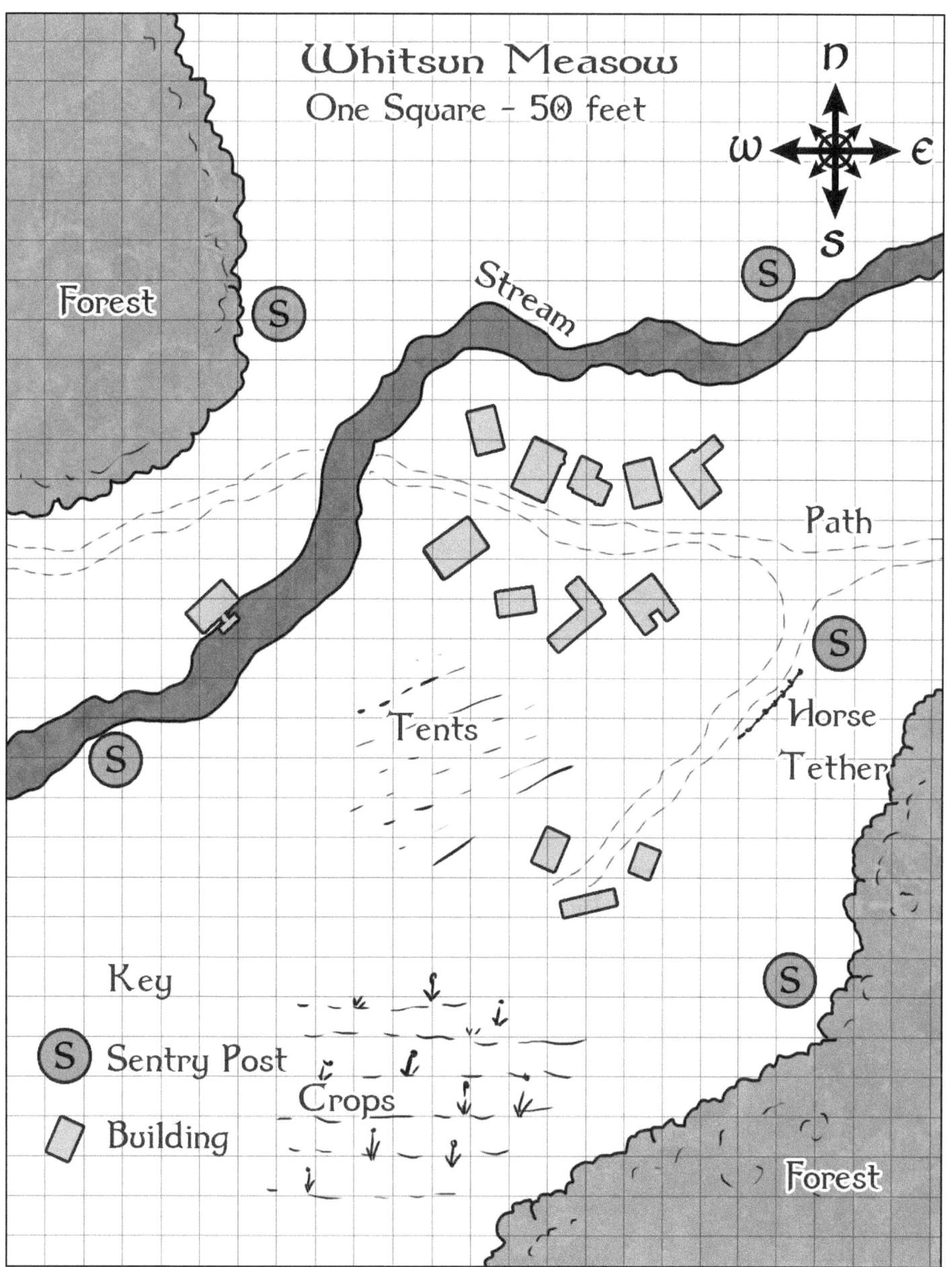

Whitsun Measow
One Square - 50 feet

Forest

Stream

Path

Tents

Horse
Tether

Key

S Sentry Post

Crops

Building

Forest

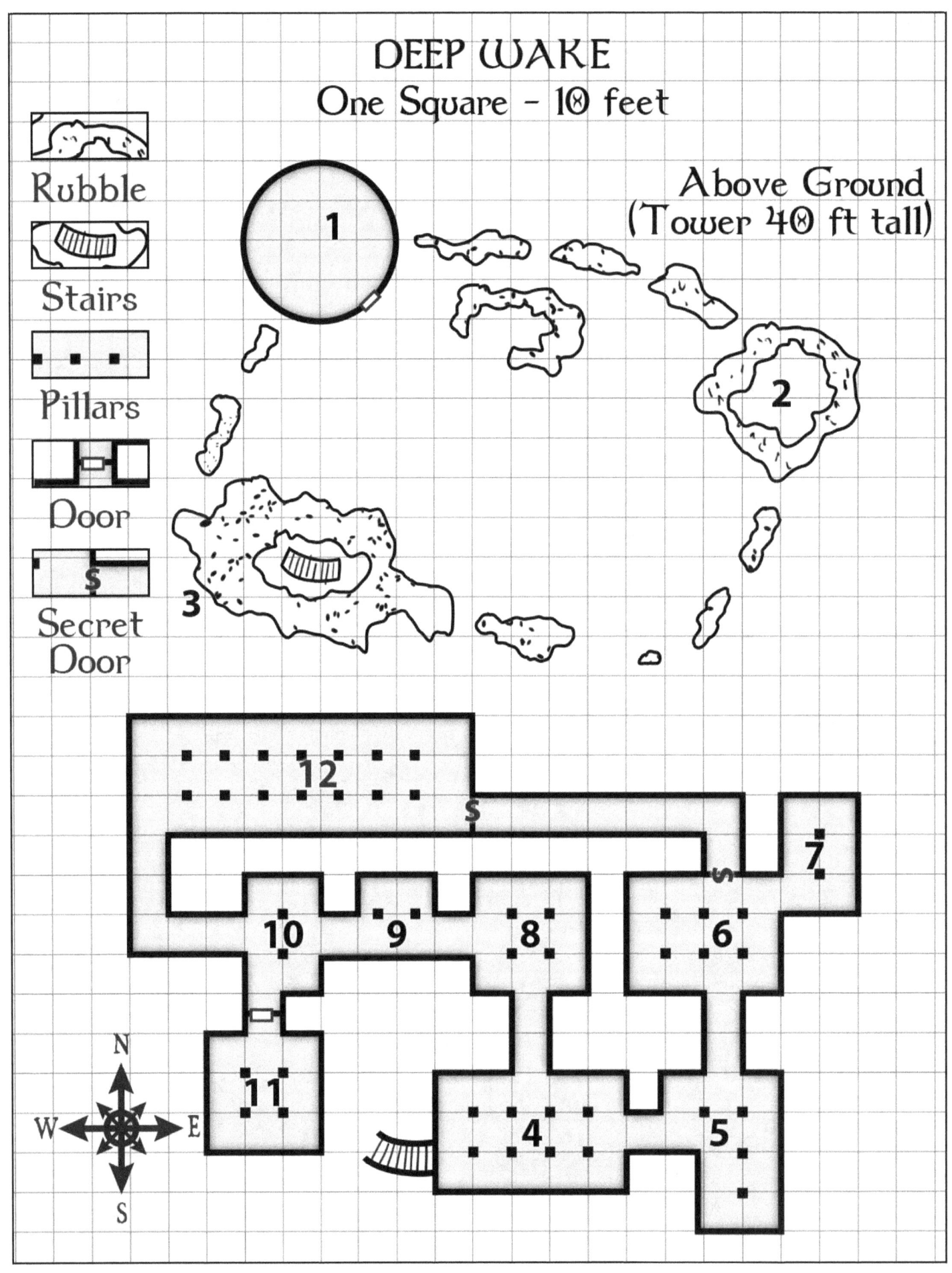

DEEP WAKE
One Square – 10 feet

Above Ground
(Tower 40 ft tall)

Rubble

Stairs

Pillars

Door

Secret
Door

DEEP WAKE
One Square - 10 feet

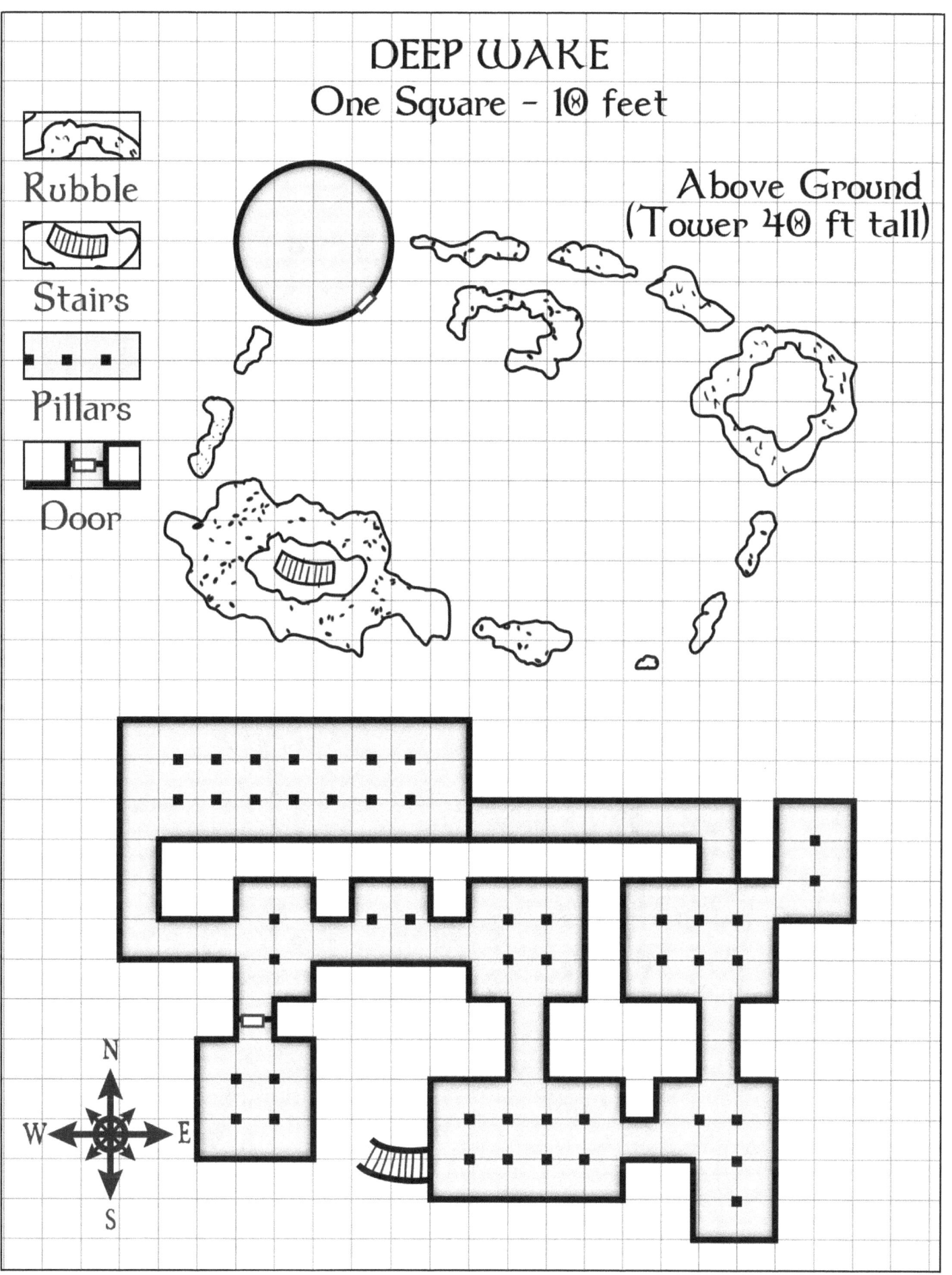

Rubble

Stairs

Pillars

Door

Above Ground
(Tower 40 ft tall)

FREE CITY OF MIRQUINOC

One Square - 100 feet

N E W S

Felony Lane

The Vialto

Market Lane

Processions Steep

Lantern St.

Trobadur St.

The Vialto

Nardah's Way

The Vialto

Fey Quarter

Pug St.

The Vialto

Street of Bells

Leech Lane

The Greentwine

Hob's Alley

King's Road

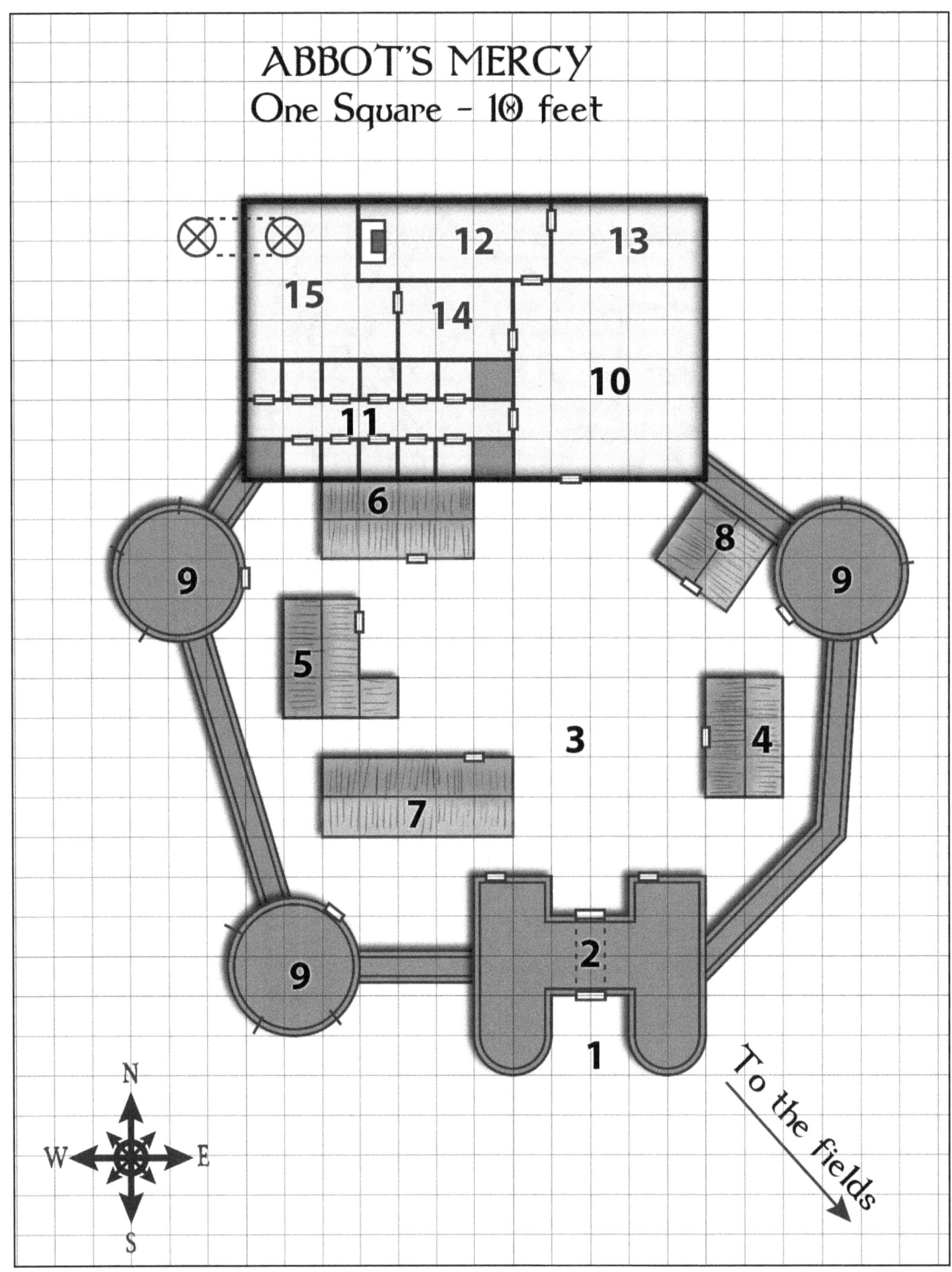

ABBOT'S MERCY
One Square – 10 feet

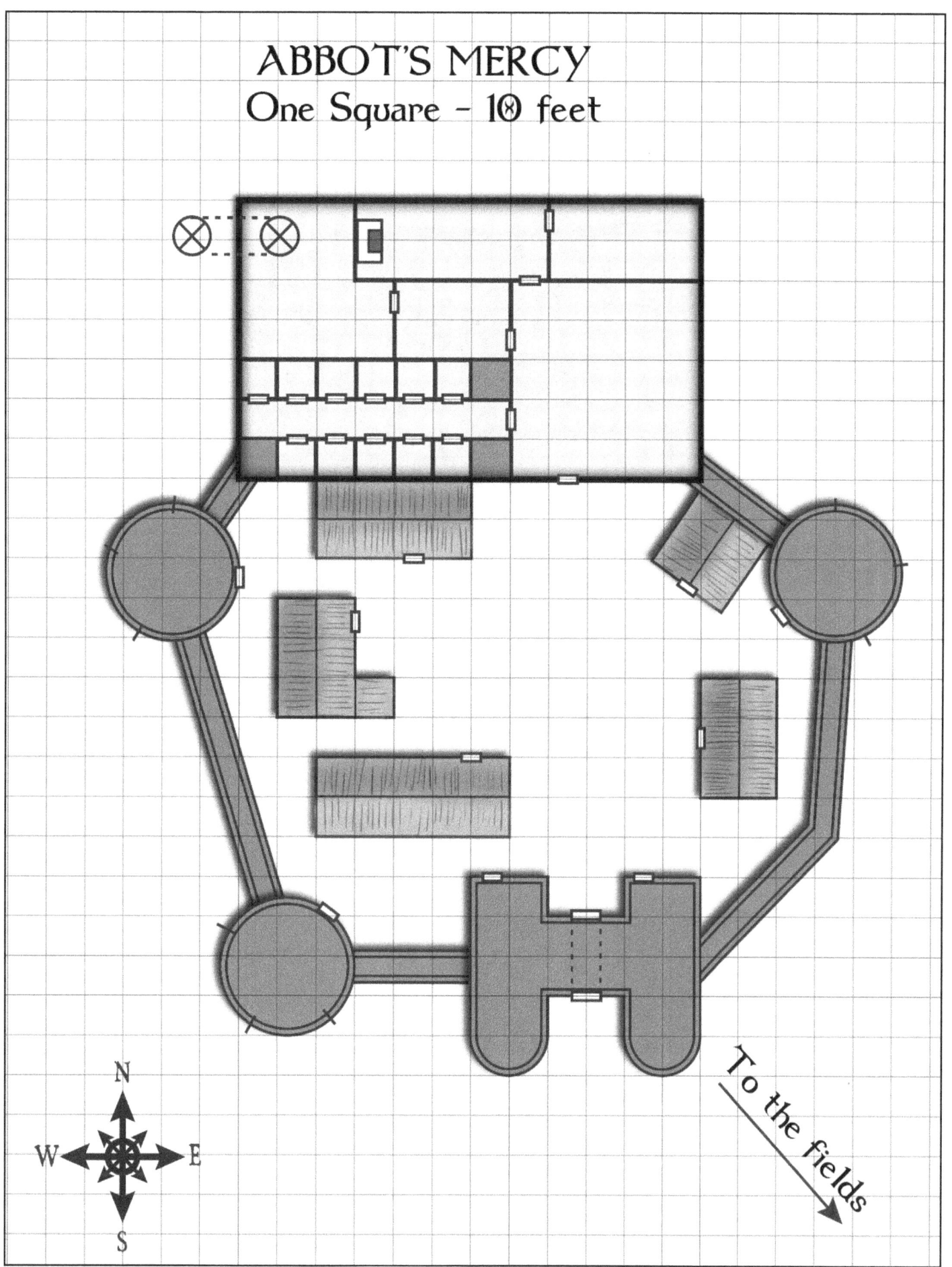

ABBOT'S MERCY
One Square – 10 feet

To the fields

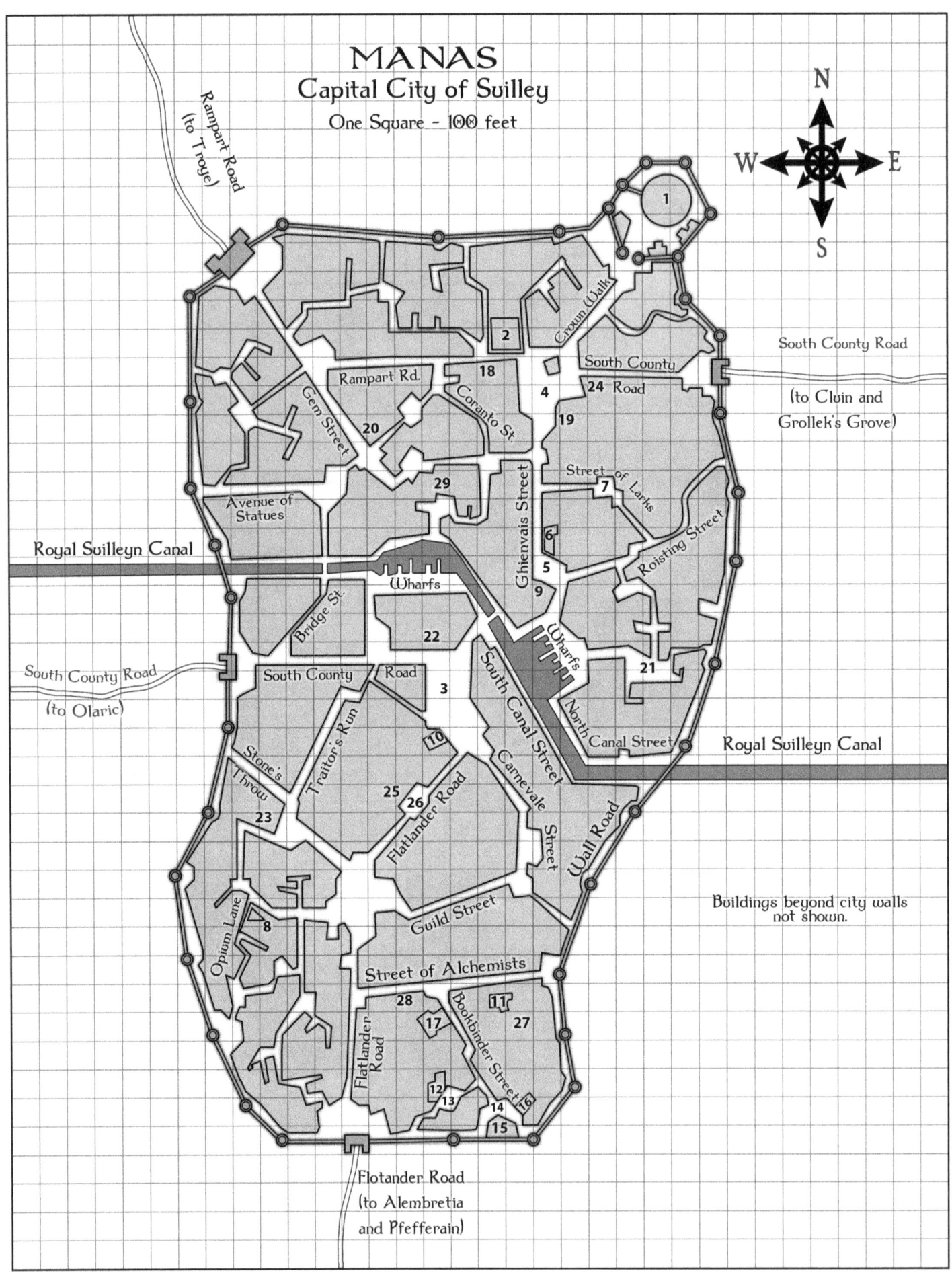

MANAS
Capital City of Svilley
One Square - 100 feet

Rampart Road
(to Troye)

South County Road

(to Cluin and
Grollek's Grove)

1

2

18

Rampart Rd.

Coranto St.

Crown Walk

South County

Road

4

24

19

Gem Street

20

Avenue of
Statues

29

Ghienvais Street

Street of Larks

7

6

5

9

Roisting Street

Royal Svilleyn Canal

Wharfs

Bridge St.

22

Wharfs

South Canal Street

North Canal Street

Royal Svilleyn Canal

21

South County Road

(to Olaric)

South County   Road

3

Traitor's Run

10

Stone's
Throw

25

26

Flatlander Road

Carnevale Street

Wall Road

Buildings beyond city walls
not shown.

23

Opium Lane

8

Guild Street

Street of Alchemists

28

17

Flatlander
Road

11

27

Bookbinder Street

12

13

14

16

15

Flotander Road

(to Alembretia
and Pfefferain)

232

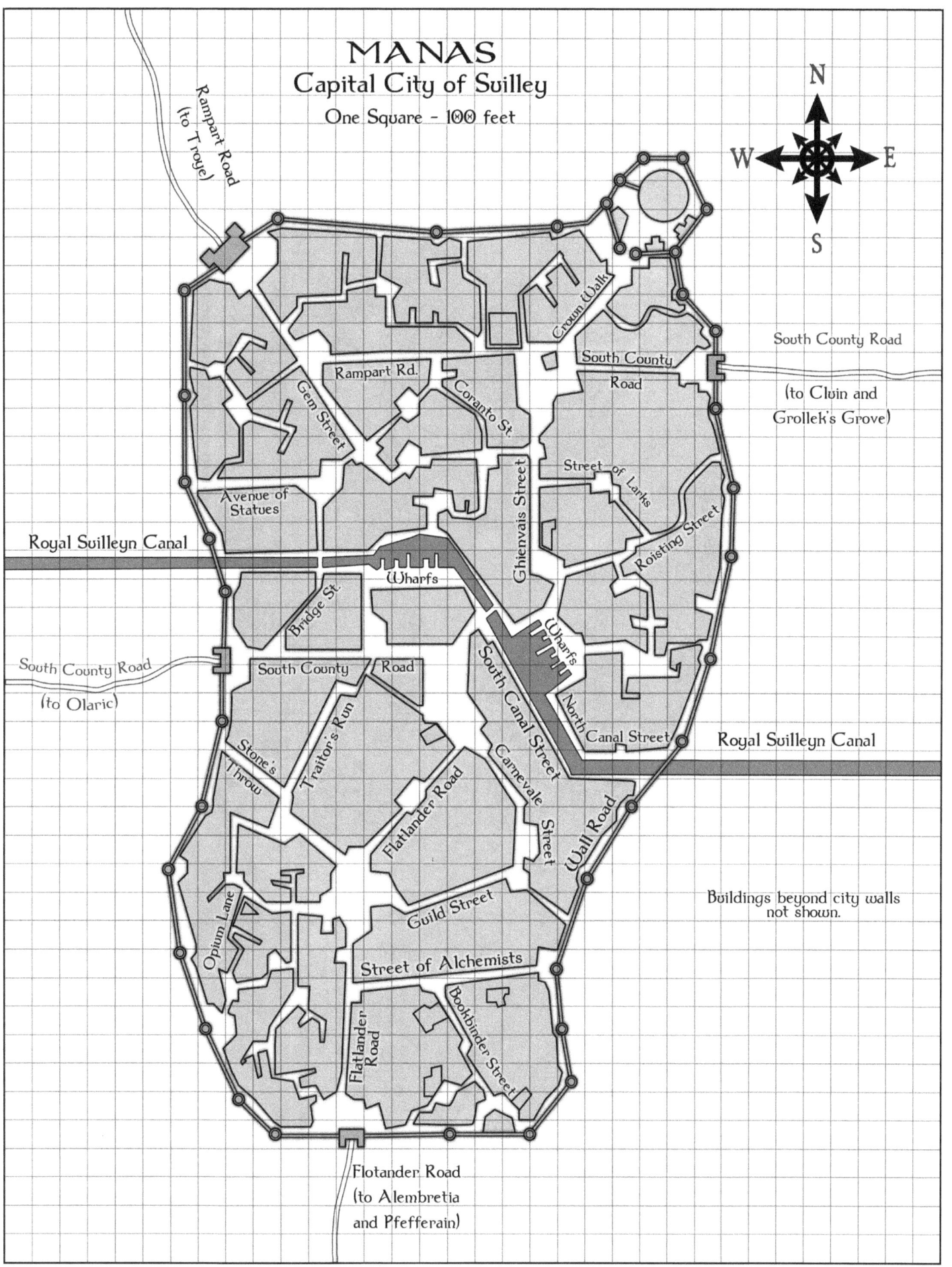

MANAS
Capital City of Suilley
One Square - 100 feet

Rampart Road (to Troye)

N
W E
S

Rampart Rd.

Gem Street

Coranto St

Crown Walk

South County Road

South County Road (to Cluin and Grollek's Grove)

Avenue of Statues

Ghienvais Street

Street of Larks

Roisting Street

Royal Suilleyn Canal

Wharfs

Bridge St.

Wharfs

South County Road

South Canal Street

North Canal Street

Royal Suilleyn Canal

South County Road (to Olaric)

Stone's Throw

Traitor's Run

Carnevale Street

Wall Road

Flatlander Road

Buildings beyond city walls not shown.

Opium Lane

Guild Street

Street of Alchemists

Bookbinder Street

Flatlander Road

Flotander Road (to Alembretia and Pfefferain)

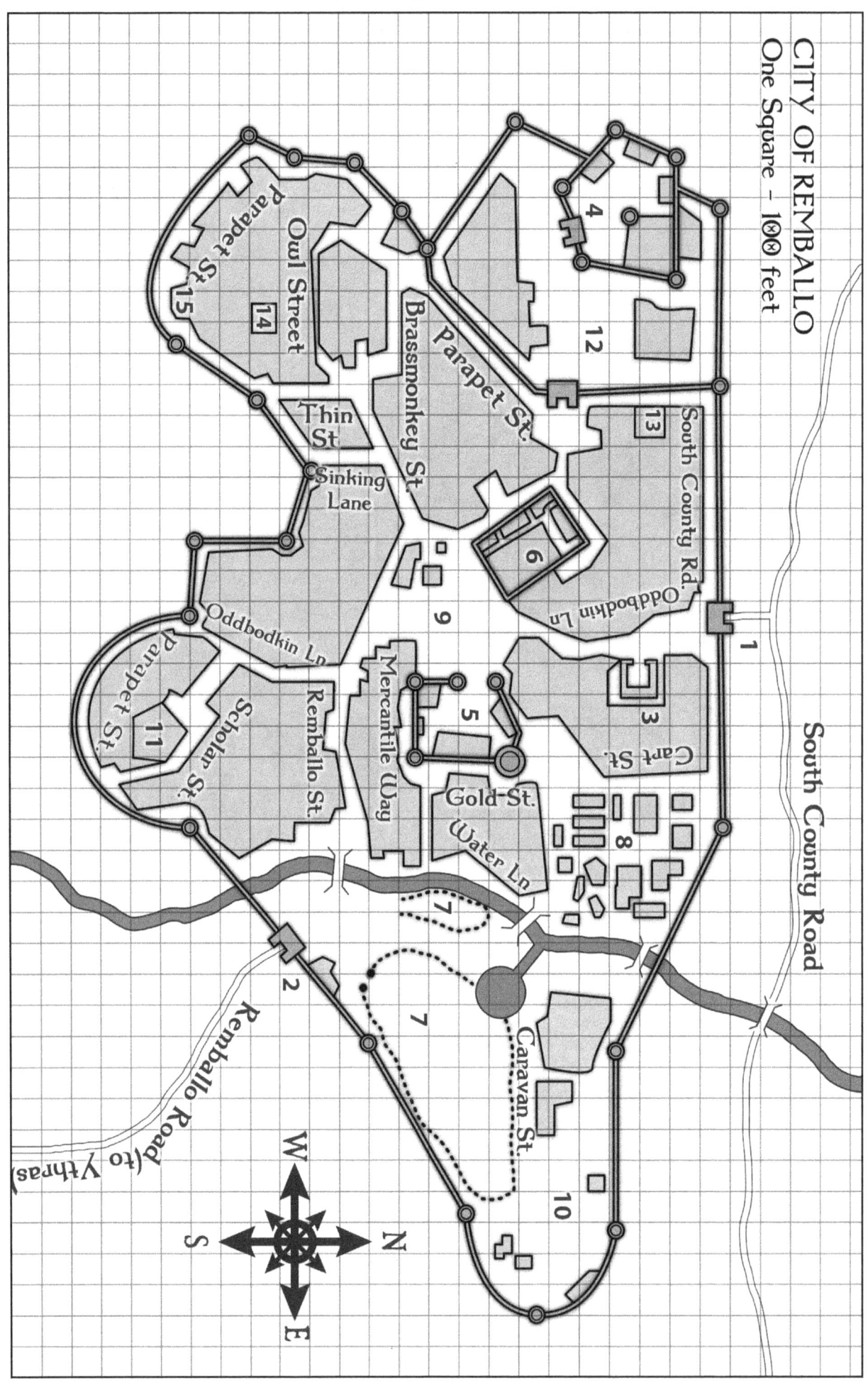

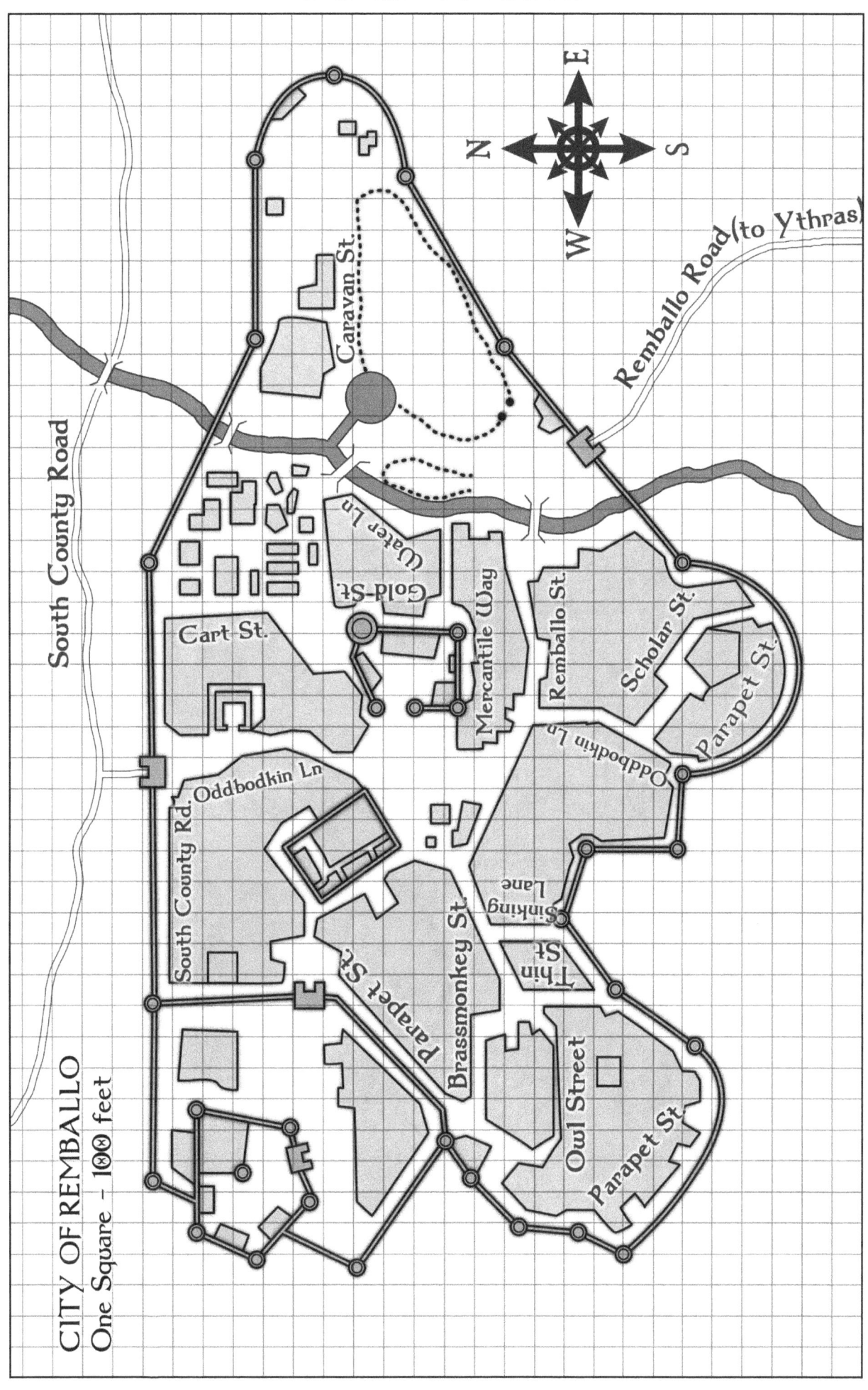

CITY OF REMBALLO
One Square - 100 feet

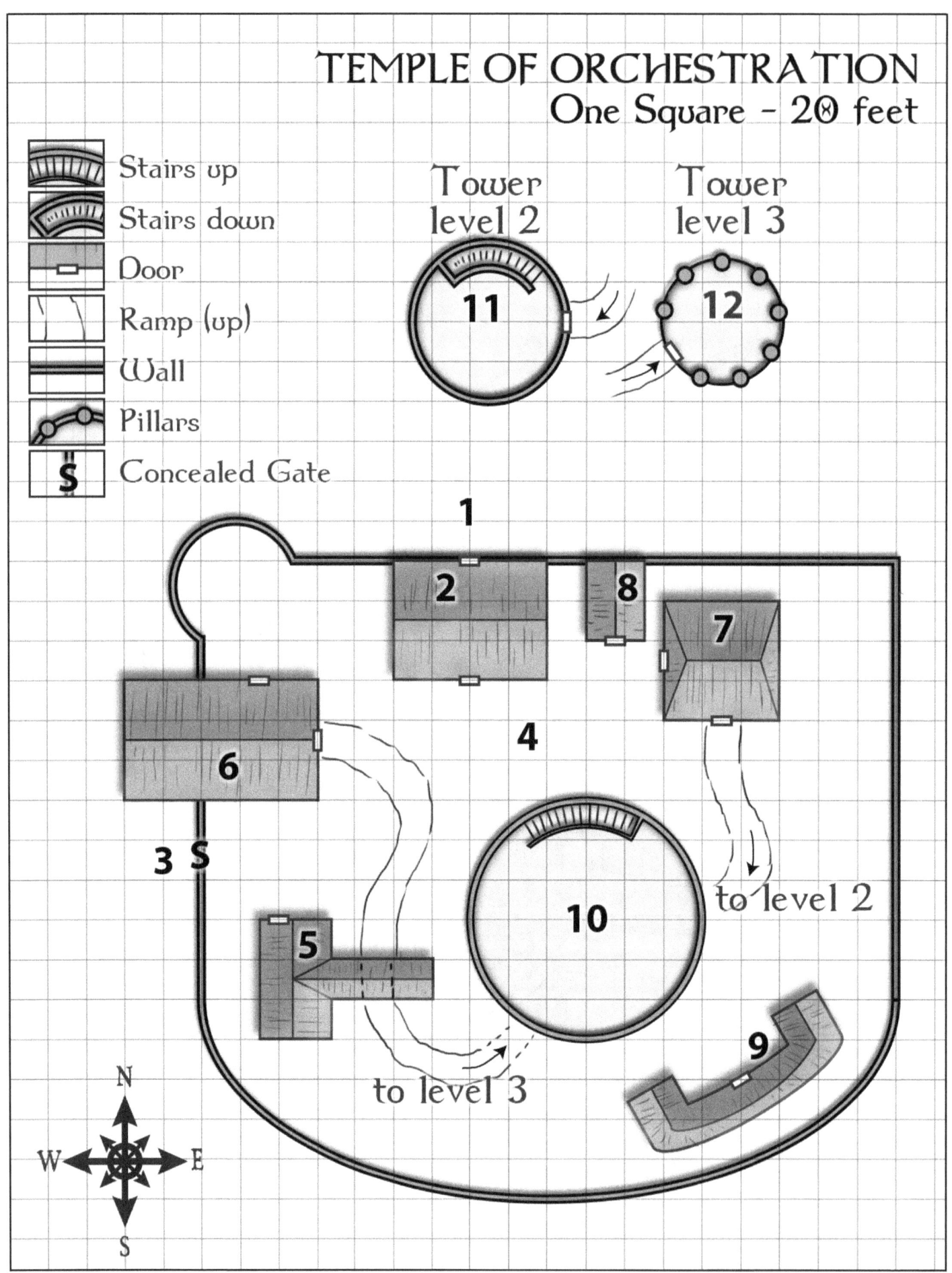

TEMPLE OF ORCHESTRATION
One Square – 20 feet

Stairs up
Stairs down
Door
Ramp (up)
Wall
Pillars
Concealed Gate

Tower level 2

Tower level 3

to level 2

to level 3

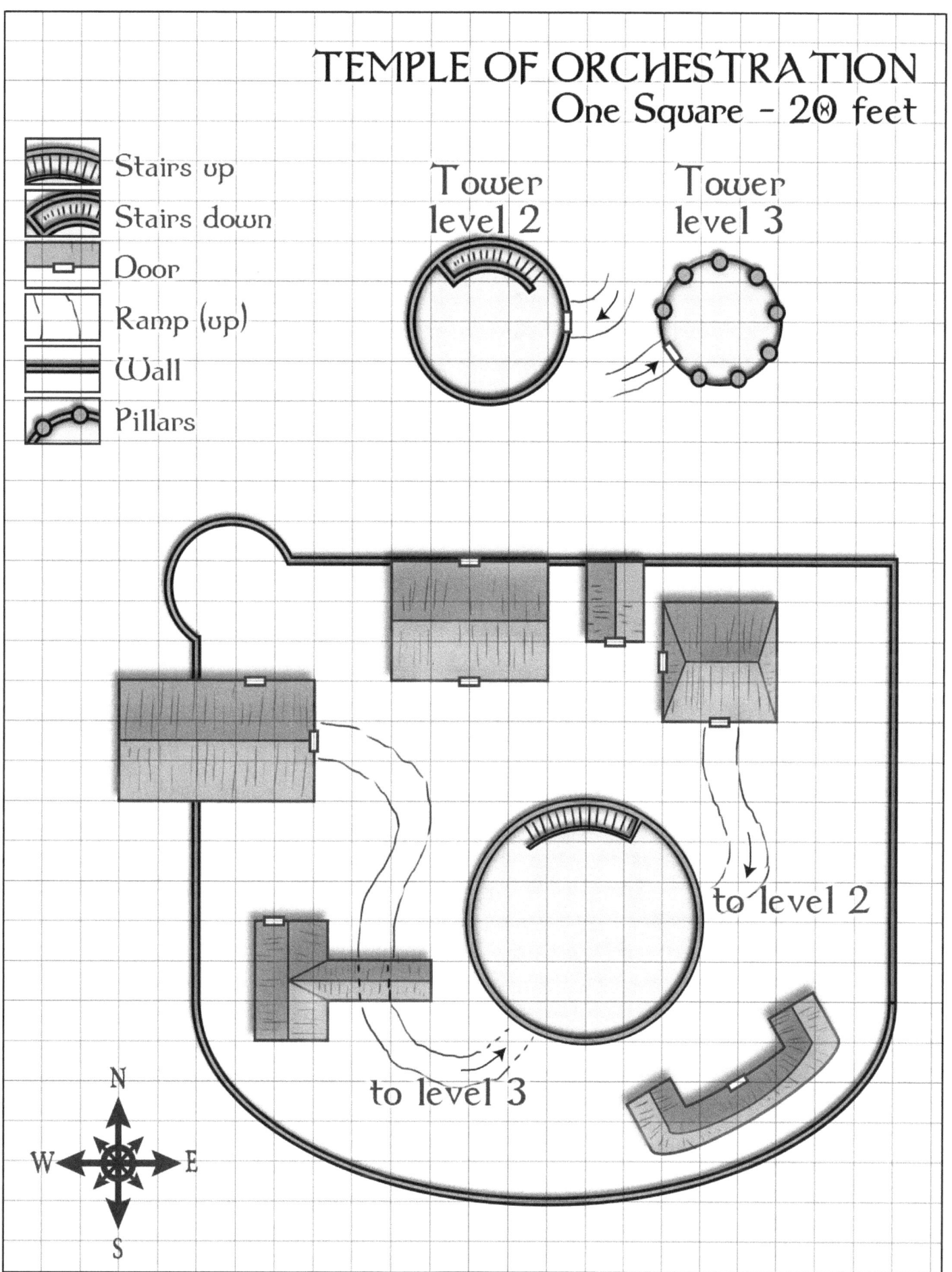

TEMPLE OF ORCHESTRATION
One Square – 20 feet

Stairs up

Stairs down

Door

Ramp (up)

Wall

Pillars

Tower level 2

Tower level 3

to level 2

to level 3

N
W   E
S

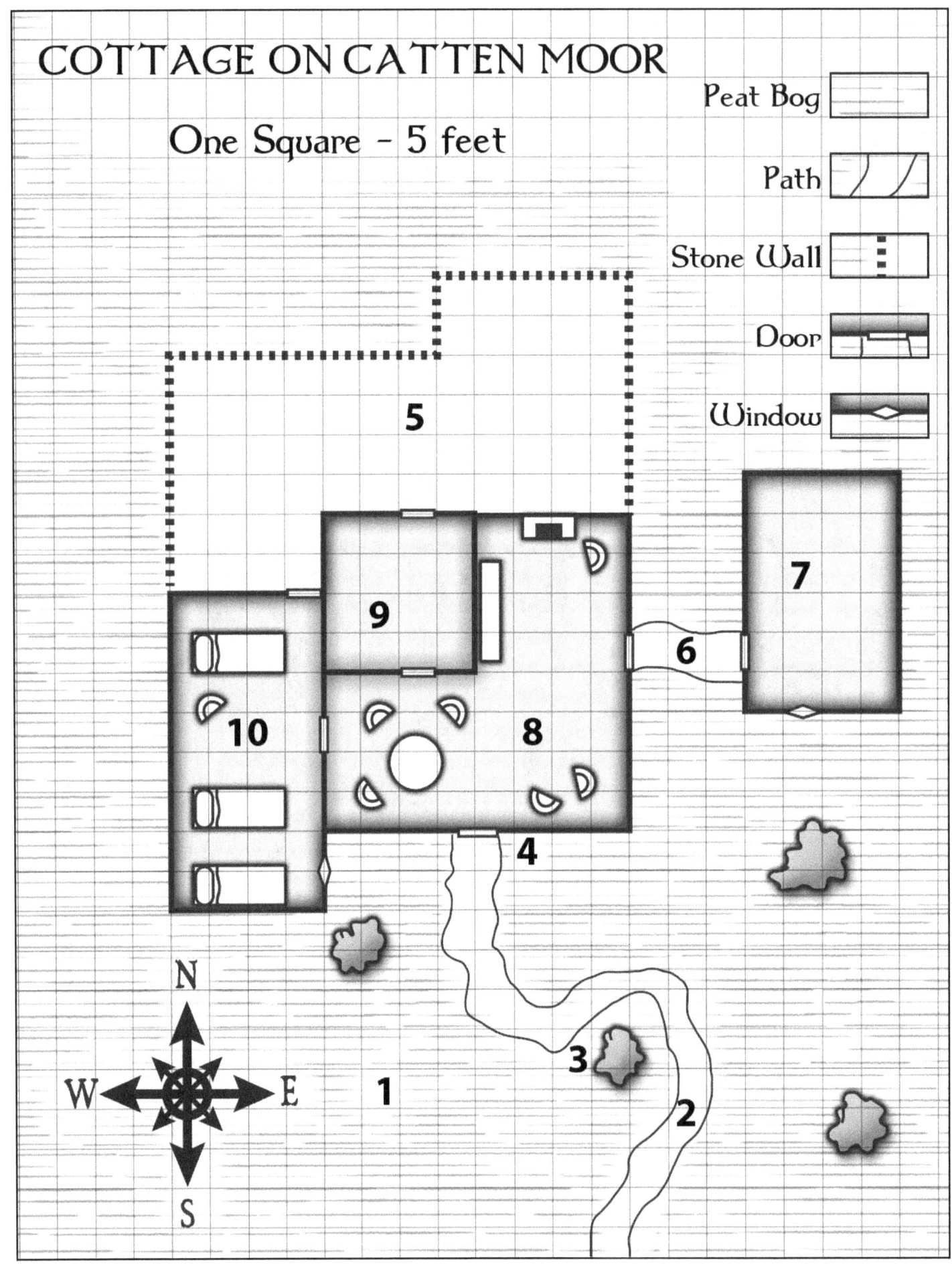

COTTAGE ON CATTEN MOOR

One Square – 5 feet

Peat Bog

Path

Stone Wall

Door

Window

5

9

10

8

7

6

4

N

W E

S

1

3

2

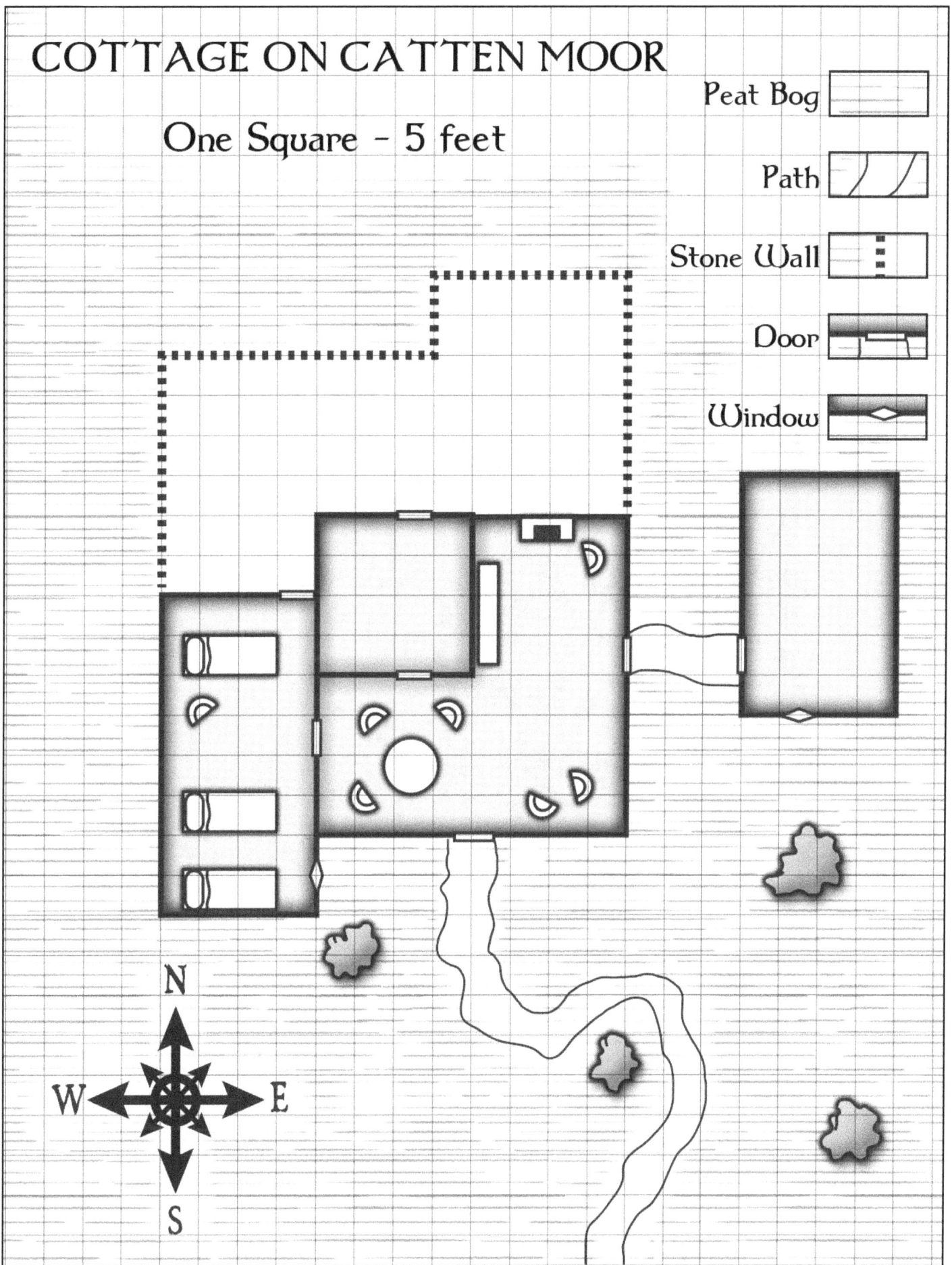

COTTAGE ON CATTEN MOOR

One Square – 5 feet

Peat Bog

Path

Stone Wall

Door

Window

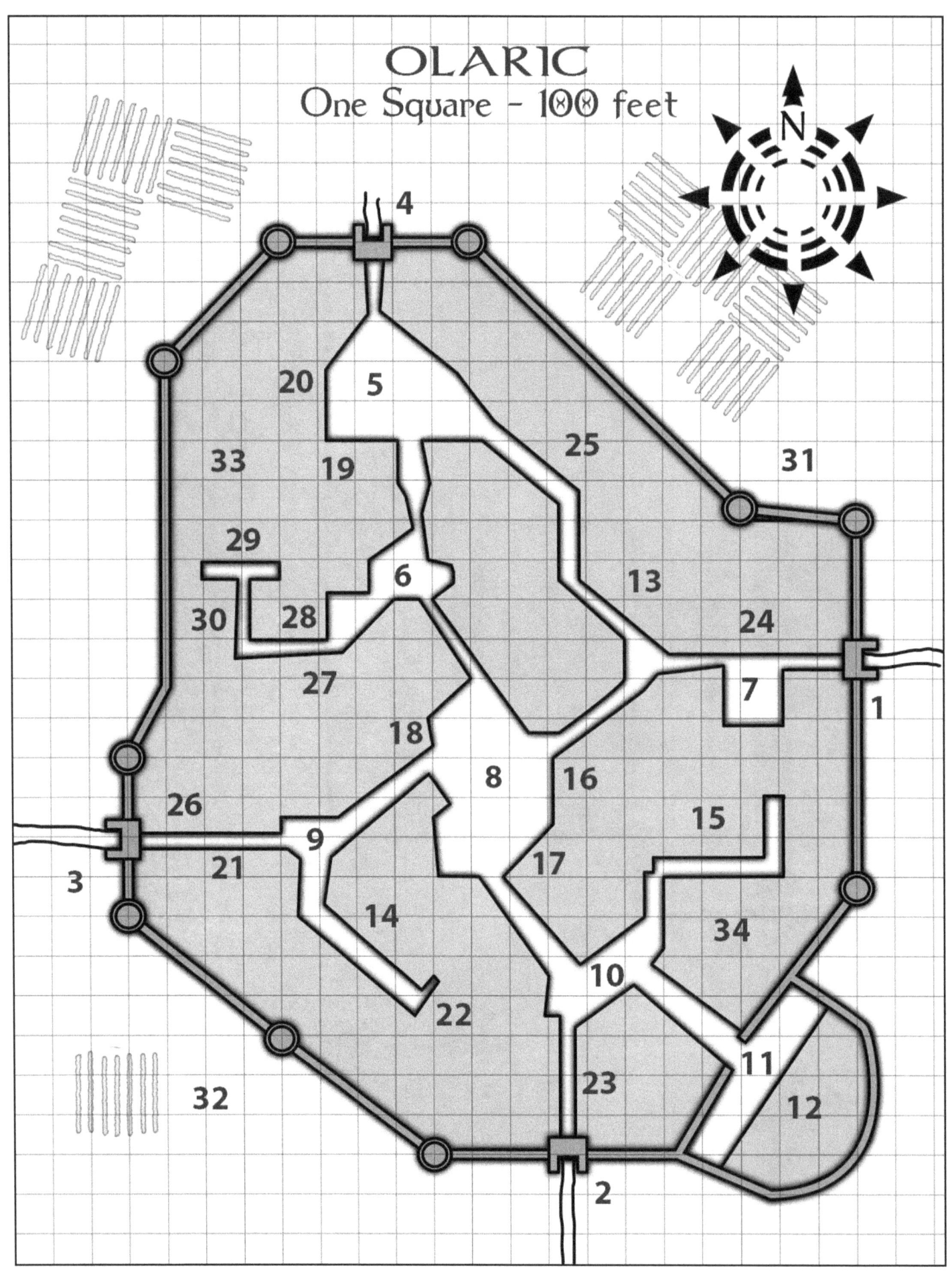

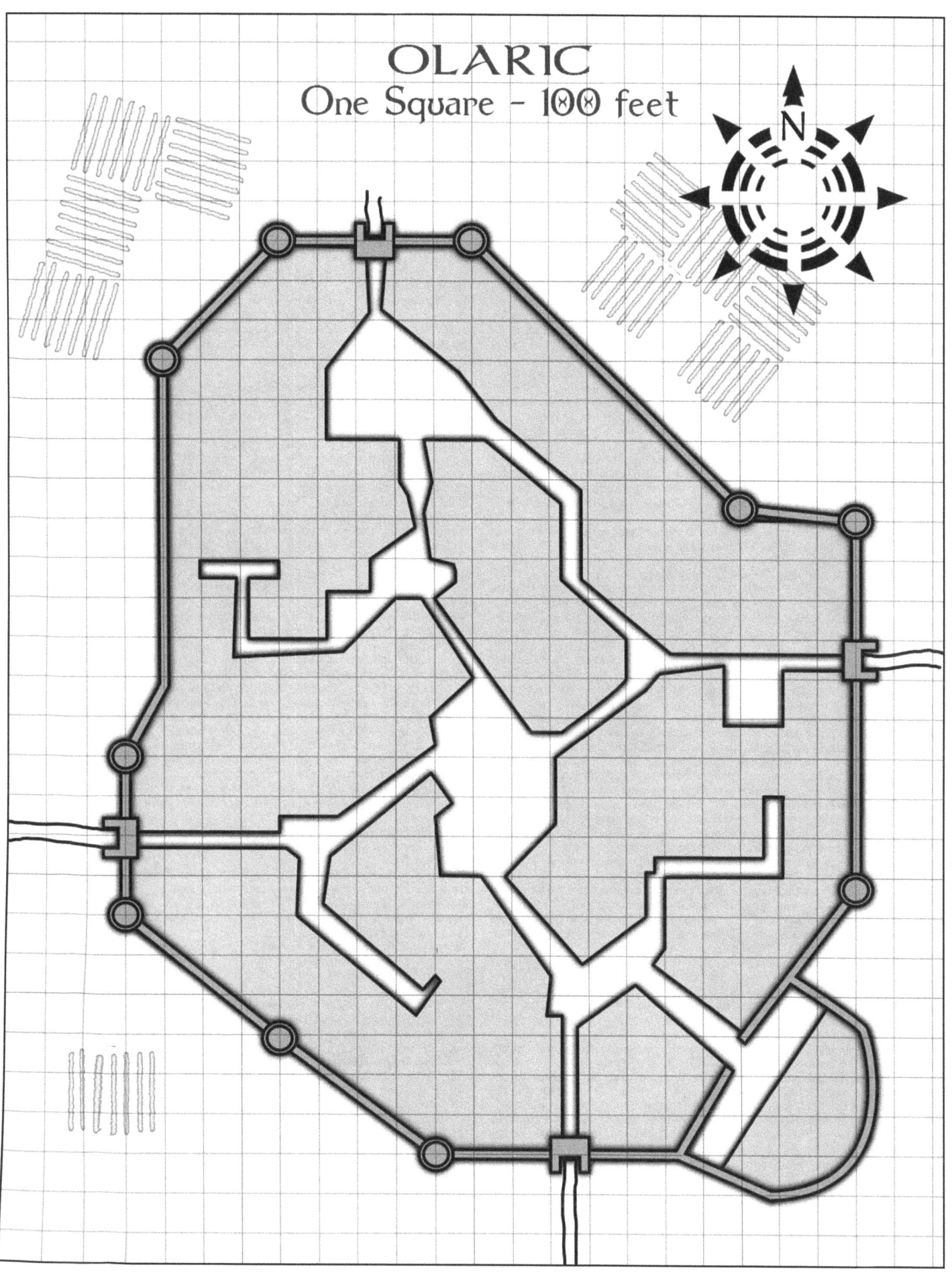

OLARIC
One Square – 100 feet

N